A FEAST FOR CROWS

George R.R. Martin is the author of fourteen novels, including five volumes of *A Song of Ice and Fire*, several collections of short stories and numerous screen plays for television drama and feature films. He lives in Santa Fe, New Mexico.

Praise for *A Song of Ice and Fire*:

'This is one of those rare and effortless reads.' ROBIN HOBB

'George R.R. Martin is one of our very best writers, and this is one of his very best books.' RAYMOND E. FEIST

'Such a splendid tale. I read my eyes out—I couldn't stop till I'd finished and it was dawn.' ANNE MCCAFFREY

'George R.R. Martin is assuredly a new master craftsman in the guild of heroic fantasy.' KATHARINE KERR

'Few created worlds are as imaginative and diverse.' JANNY WURTS

By George R.R. Martin

A FEAST FOR CROWS

BOOK FOUR OF
A Song of Ice and Fire

GEORGE R.R. MARTIN

HARPER
Voyager

HarperVoyager
An imprint of HarperCollins*Publishers*
77–85 Fulham Palace Road,
Hammersmith, London W6 8JB

www.harpercollins.co.uk

This paperback edition 2011
14

Previously published in paperback by Voyager in 2006

First published in Great Britain by Voyager in 2005

Copyright © George R.R. Martin 2005

George R.R. Martin asserts the moral right to
be identified as the author of this work

A catalogue record for this book
is available from the British Library

ISBN 978-0-00-648612-1

Set in Minion by Palimpsest Book Production Limited,
Falkirk, Stirlingshire

Printed and bound in Great Britain by
Clays Ltd, St Ives plc

MIX
Paper from
responsible sources

FSC
www.fsc.org

FSC® C007454

for Stephen Boucher
wizard of Windows, dragon of DOS
without whom this book would have
been written in crayon

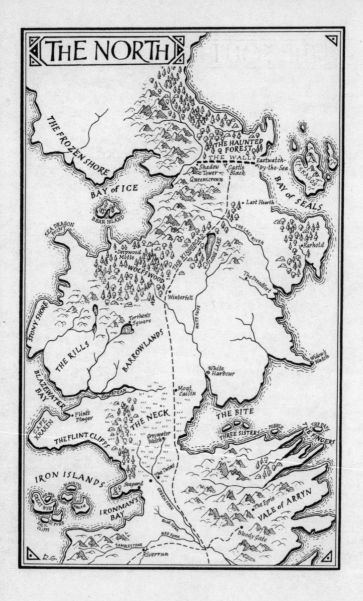

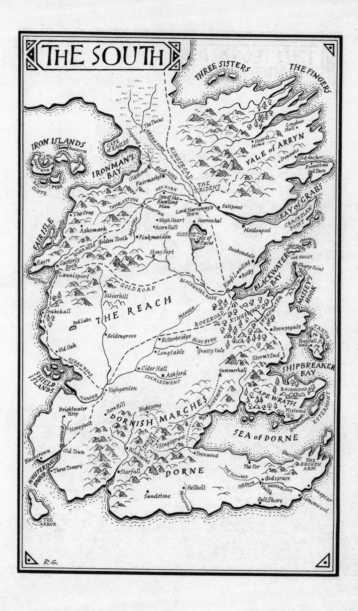

THE LAND BEYOND THE WALL

STRONGHOLDS of the NORTH

1 Westwatch-by-the-Bridge
2 **The Shadow Tower**
3 Sentinel Stand
4 Greyguard
5 Stonedoor
6 Hoarfrost Hill
7 Icemark
8 The Nightfort
9 Deep Lake
10 Queensgate
11 **Castle Black**
12 Oakenshield
13 Woodswatch-by-the-Pool
14 Sable Hall
15 Rimegate
16 The Long Barrow
17 The Torches
18 Greenguard
19 **Eastwatch-by-the-Sea**

THE LAND OF
ALWAYS WINTER
(UNMAPPED)

THE SHIVERING
SEA

THENN

THE FROSTFANGS

MILKWATER
THE SKIRLING PASS
Fist of the First Men
ANTLER RIVER
Hardhome
STFARROLD'S POINT

THE HAUNTED
FOREST

Craster's Keep
Whitetree

THE GORGE
THE WALL

BRANDON'S GIFT

Queenscrown

THE NEW GIFT

BAY of ICE

RINGSROAD

BAY of SEALS

SKAGOS

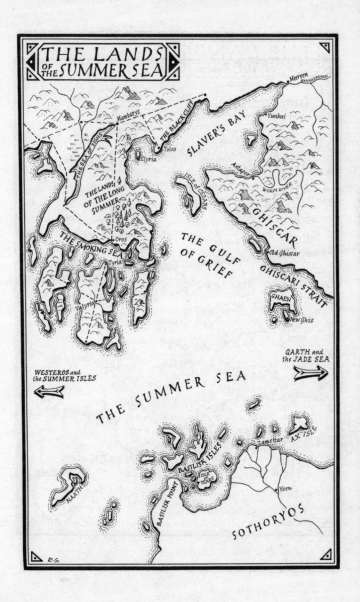

Iron Islands

Old Wyk
Blacktyde
Orkmont
Great Wyk
Ten Towers
Harlaw
Saltcliff
Pyke
Banefort
The Crag
Ashemark
Fair Isle
Faircastle
River Road
Golden Tooth
Sarsfield
Hornvale
Kayce
Casterly Rock
Deep Den
Feastfires
Lannisport
Silverhall
Cornfield
Crackhall
The Searoad
Red Lake
The Twins
Cape of Eagles
Seagard
Ironman's Bay
Oldstones
Fairmarket
Red Fork
Kneeling Man
Riverrun
High Heart
Acorn Hall
Pinkmaiden
Stoney Sept
Blackwater Rush
The Goldroad
Tumbleton
Mander
THE REACH
N
Green Fork
The Kingsroad
Blue Fork
Tumblestone

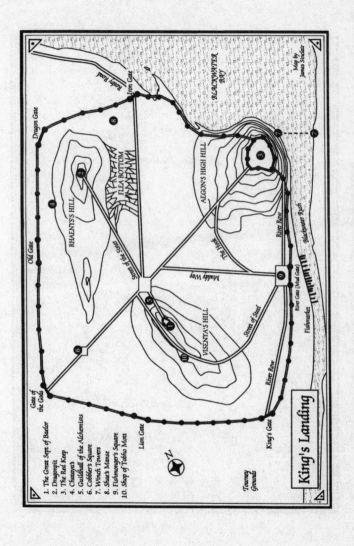

1. The Great Sept of Baelor
2. Dragonpit
3. The Red Keep
4. Chataya's
5. Guildhall of the Alchemists
6. Cobbler's Square
7. Winch Towers
8. Shae's Manse
9. Fishmonger's Square
10. Shop of Tobho Mott

King's Landing

Map by
James Sinclair

BLACKWATER BAY

AEGON'S HIGH HILL

RHAENYS'S HILL

VISENYA'S HILL

FLEA BOTTOM

Blackwater Rush

Rosby Road

Lion Gate

Dragon Gate

Old Gate

Gate of the Gods

Lion Gate

King's Gate

River Row

River Row

River Gate (Mud Gate)

Fishmarket

Muddy Way

Street of Steel

Street of the Sisters

Hill

Tourney Grounds

N

PROLOGUE

"D ragons," said Mollander. He snatched a withered apple off the ground and tossed it hand to hand.

"Throw the apple," urged Alleras the Sphinx. He slipped an arrow from his quiver and nocked it to his bowstring.

"I should like to see a dragon." Roone was the youngest of them, a chunky boy still two years shy of manhood. "I should like that very much."

And I should like to sleep with Rosey's arms around me, Pate thought. He shifted restlessly on the bench. By the morrow the girl could well be his. *I will take her far from Oldtown, across the narrow sea to one of the Free Cities.* There were no maesters there, no one to accuse him.

He could hear Emma's laughter coming through a shuttered window overhead, mingled with the deeper voice of the man she was entertaining. She was the oldest of the serving wenches at the Quill and Tankard, forty if she was a day, but still pretty in a fleshy sort of way. Rosey was her daughter, fifteen and freshly flowered. Emma had decreed that Rosey's maidenhead would cost a golden dragon. Pate had saved nine silver stags and a pot of copper stars and pennies, for all the good that would do him. He would have stood a better chance of hatching a real dragon than saving up enough coin to make a golden one.

"You were born too late for dragons, lad," Armen the Acolyte told

Roone. Armen wore a leather thong about his neck, strung with links of pewter, tin, lead, and copper, and like most acolytes he seemed to believe that novices had turnips growing from their shoulders in place of heads. "The last one perished during the reign of King Aegon the Third."

"The last dragon in *Westeros*," insisted Mollander.

"Throw the apple," Alleras urged again. He was a comely youth, their Sphinx. All the serving wenches doted on him. Even Rosey would sometimes touch him on the arm when she brought him wine, and Pate had to gnash his teeth and pretend not to see.

"The last dragon in Westeros *was* the last dragon," said Armen doggedly. "That is well known."

"The *apple*," Alleras said. "Unless you mean to eat it."

"Here." Dragging his clubfoot, Mollander took a short hop, whirled, and whipped the apple sidearm into the mists that hung above the Honeywine. If not for his foot, he would have been a knight like his father. He had the strength for it in those thick arms and broad shoulders. Far and fast the apple flew . . .

. . . but not as fast as the arrow that whistled after it, a yard-long shaft of golden wood fletched with scarlet feathers. Pate did not see the arrow catch the apple, but he heard it. A soft *chunk* echoed back across the river, followed by a splash.

Mollander whistled. "You cored it. Sweet."

Not half as sweet as Rosey. Pate loved her hazel eyes and budding breasts, and the way she smiled every time she saw him. He loved the dimples in her cheeks. Sometimes she went barefoot as she served, to feel the grass beneath her feet. He loved that too. He loved the clean fresh smell of her, the way her hair curled behind her ears. He even loved her toes. One night she'd let him rub her feet and play with them, and he'd made up a funny tale for every toe to keep her giggling.

Perhaps he would do better to remain on this side of the narrow sea. He could buy a donkey with the coin he'd saved, and he and Rosey could take turns riding it as they wandered Westeros. Ebrose might not think him worthy of the silver, but Pate knew how to set a bone and leech a fever. The smallfolk would be grateful for his help.

If he could learn to cut hair and shave beards, he might even be a barber. *That would be enough,* he told himself, *so long as I had Rosey.* Rosey was all that he wanted in the world.

That had not always been so. Once he had dreamed of being a maester in a castle, in service to some open-handed lord who would honor him for his wisdom and bestow a fine white horse on him to thank him for his service. How high he'd ride, how nobly, smiling down at the smallfolk when he passed them on the road . . .

One night in the Quill and Tankard's common room, after his second tankard of fearsomely strong cider, Pate had boasted that he would not always be a novice. "Too true," Lazy Leo had called out. "You'll be a former novice, herding swine."

He drained the dregs of his tankard. The torchlit terrace of the Quill and Tankard was an island of light in a sea of mist this morning. Downriver, the distant beacon of the Hightower floated in the damp of night like a hazy orange moon, but the light did little to lift his spirits.

The alchemist should have come by now. Had it all been some cruel jape, or had something happened to the man? It would not have been the first time that good fortune had turned sour on Pate. He had once counted himself lucky to be chosen to help old Archmaester Walgrave with the ravens, never dreaming that before long he would also be fetching the man's meals, sweeping out his chambers, and dressing him every morning. Everyone said that Walgrave had forgotten more of ravencraft than most maesters ever knew, so Pate assumed a black iron link was the least that he could hope for, only to find that Walgrave could not grant him one. The old man remained an archmaester only by courtesy. As great a maester as once he'd been, now his robes concealed soiled smallclothes oft as not, and half a year ago some acolytes found him weeping in the Library, unable to find his way back to his chambers. Maester Gormon sat below the iron mask in Walgrave's place, the same Gormon who had once accused Pate of theft.

In the apple tree beside the water, a nightingale began to sing. It was a sweet sound, a welcome respite from the harsh screams and endless *quork*ing of the ravens he had tended all day long. The white ravens knew his name, and would mutter it to each other whenever they caught sight of him, *"Pate, Pate, Pate,"* until he wanted to scream. The big white birds were Archmaester Walgrave's pride. He wanted them to eat him when he died, but Pate half suspected that they meant to eat him too.

Perhaps it was the fearsomely strong cider—he had not come here to drink, but Alleras had been buying to celebrate his copper link, and guilt had made him thirsty—but it almost sounded as if the nightingale were trilling *gold for iron, gold for iron, gold for iron.* Which was passing strange, because that was what the stranger had said the night Rosey brought the two of them together. "Who are you?" Pate had demanded of him, and the man had replied, "An alchemist. I can change iron into gold." And then the coin was in his hand, dancing across his knuckles, the soft yellow gold shining in the candlelight. On one side was a three-headed dragon, on the other the head of some dead king. *Gold for iron,* Pate remembered, *you won't do better. Do you want her? Do you love her?* "I am no thief," he had told the man who called himself the alchemist, "I am a novice of the Citadel." The alchemist had bowed his head, and said, "If you should reconsider, I shall return here three days hence, with my dragon."

Three days had passed. Pate had returned to the Quill and Tankard, still uncertain what he was, but instead of the alchemist he'd found Mollander and Armen and the Sphinx, with Roone in tow. It would have raised suspicions not to join them.

The Quill and Tankard never closed. For six hundred years it had been standing on its island in the Honeywine, and never once had its doors been shut to trade. Though the tall, timbered building leaned toward the south the way novices sometimes leaned after a tankard, Pate expected that the inn would go on standing for another six hundred years, selling wine and ale and fearsomely strong cider to rivermen and seamen, smiths and singers, priests and princes, and the novices and acolytes of the Citadel.

"Oldtown is not the world," declared Mollander, too loudly. He was a knight's son, and drunk as drunk could be. Since they brought him word of his father's death upon the Blackwater, he got drunk most every night. Even in Oldtown, far from the fighting and safe behind its walls, the War of the Five Kings had touched them all . . . although Archmaester Benedict insisted that there had never been a war of five kings, since Renly Baratheon had been slain before Balon Greyjoy had crowned himself.

"My father always said the world was bigger than any lord's castle," Mollander went on. "Dragons must be the least of the things a man might find in Qarth and Asshai and Yi Ti. These sailors' stories . . ."

". . . are stories told by sailors," Armen interrupted. "*Sailors,* my dear Mollander. Go back down to the docks, and I wager you'll find sailors who'll tell you of the mermaids that they bedded, or how they spent a year in the belly of a fish."

"How do you know they didn't?" Mollander thumped through the grass, looking for more apples. "You'd need to be down the belly yourself to swear they weren't. One sailor with a story, aye, a man might laugh at that, but when oarsmen off four different ships tell the same tale in four different tongues . . ."

"The tales are *not* the same," insisted Armen. "Dragons in Asshai, dragons in Qarth, dragons in Meereen, Dothraki dragons, dragons freeing slaves . . . each telling differs from the last."

"Only in details." Mollander grew more stubborn when he drank, and even when sober he was bullheaded. "All speak of *dragons,* and a beautiful young queen."

The only dragon Pate cared about was made of yellow gold. He wondered what had happened to the alchemist. *The third day. He said he'd be here.*

"There's another apple near your foot," Alleras called to Mollander, "and I still have two arrows in my quiver."

"Fuck your quiver." Mollander scooped up the windfall. "This one's wormy," he complained, but he threw it anyway. The arrow caught the apple as it began to fall and sliced it clean in two. One half landed on a turret roof, tumbled to a lower roof, bounced, and missed Armen by a foot. "If you cut a worm in two, you make two worms," the acolyte informed them.

"If only it worked that way with apples, no one would ever need go hungry," said Alleras with one of his soft smiles. The Sphinx was always smiling, as if he knew some secret jape. It gave him a wicked look that went well with his pointed chin, widow's peak, and dense mat of close-cropped jet-black curls.

Alleras would make a maester. He had only been at the Citadel for a year, yet already he had forged three links of his maester's chain. Armen might have more, but each of his had taken him a year to earn. Still, he would make a maester too. Roone and Mollander remained pink-necked novices, but Roone was very young and Mollander preferred drinking to reading.

Pate, though . . .

He had been five years at the Citadel, arriving when he was no more than three-and-ten, yet his neck remained as pink as it had been on the day he first arrived from the westerlands. Twice had he believed himself ready. The first time he had gone before Archmaester Vaellyn to demonstrate his knowledge of the heavens. Instead he learned how Vinegar Vaellyn had earned that name. It took Pate two years to summon up the courage to try again. This time he submitted himself to kindly old Archmaester Ebrose, renowned for his soft voice and gentle hands, but Ebrose's sighs had somehow proved just as painful as Vaellyn's barbs.

"One last apple," promised Alleras, "and I will tell you what I suspect about these dragons."

"What could you know that I don't?" grumbled Mollander. He spied an apple on a branch, jumped up, pulled it down, and threw. Alleras drew his bowstring back to his ear, turning gracefully to follow the target in flight. He loosed his shaft just as the apple began to fall.

"You always miss your last shot," said Roone.

The apple splashed down into the river, untouched.

"See?" said Roone.

"The day you make them all is the day you stop improving." Alleras unstrung his longbow and eased it into its leather case. The bow was carved from goldenheart, a rare and fabled wood from the Summer Isles. Pate had tried to bend it once, and failed. *The Sphinx looks slight, but there's strength in those slim arms,* he reflected, as Alleras threw a leg across the bench and reached for his wine cup. "The dragon has three heads," he announced in his soft Dornish drawl.

"Is this a riddle?" Roone wanted to know. "Sphinxes always speak in riddles in the tales."

"No riddle." Alleras sipped his wine. The rest of them were quaffing tankards of the fearsomely strong cider that the Quill and Tankard was renowned for, but he preferred the strange, sweet wines of his mother's country. Even in Oldtown such wines did not come cheap.

It had been Lazy Leo who dubbed Alleras "the Sphinx." A sphinx is a bit of this, a bit of that: a human face, the body of a lion, the wings of a hawk. Alleras was the same: his father was a Dornishman, his mother a black-skinned Summer Islander. His own skin was dark as teak. And like the green marble sphinxes that flanked the Citadel's main gate, Alleras had eyes of onyx.

"No dragon has ever had three heads except on shields and banners," Armen the Acolyte said firmly. "That was a heraldic charge, no more. Furthermore, the Targaryens are all dead."

"Not all," said Alleras. "The Beggar King had a sister."

"I thought her head was smashed against a wall," said Roone.

"No," said Alleras. "It was Prince Rhaegar's young son Aegon whose head was dashed against the wall by the Lion of Lannister's brave men. We speak of Rhaegar's sister, born on Dragonstone before its fall. The one they called Daenerys."

"The *Stormborn*. I recall her now." Mollander lifted his tankard high, sloshing the cider that remained. "Here's to her!" He gulped, slammed his empty tankard down, belched, and wiped his mouth with the back of his hand. "Where's Rosey? Our rightful queen deserves another round of cider, wouldn't you say?"

Armen the Acolyte looked alarmed. "Lower your voice, fool. You should not even jape about such things. You never know who could be listening. The Spider has ears everywhere."

"Ah, don't piss your breeches, Armen. I was proposing a drink, not a rebellion."

Pate heard a chuckle. A soft, sly voice called out from behind him. "I always knew you were a traitor, Hopfrog." Lazy Leo was slouching by the foot of the old plank bridge, draped in satin striped in green and gold, with a black silk half cape pinned to his shoulder by a rose of jade. The wine he'd dribbled down his front had been a robust red, judging from the color of the spots. A lock of his ash-blond hair fell down across one eye.

Mollander bristled at the sight of him. "Bugger that. Go away. You are not welcome here." Alleras laid a hand upon his arm to calm him, whilst Armen frowned. "Leo. My lord. I had understood that you were still confined to the Citadel for . . ."

". . . three more days." Lazy Leo shrugged. "Perestan says the world is forty thousand years old. Mollos says five hundred thousand. What are three days, I ask you?" Though there were a dozen empty tables on the terrace, Leo sat himself at theirs. "Buy me a cup of Arbor gold, Hopfrog, and perhaps I won't inform my father of your toast. The tiles turned against me at the Checkered Hazard, and I wasted my last stag on supper. Suckling pig in plum sauce, stuffed with chestnuts and white truffles. A man must eat. What did you lads have?"

"Mutton," muttered Mollander. He sounded none too pleased about it. "We shared a haunch of boiled mutton."

"I'm certain it was filling." Leo turned to Alleras. "A lord's son should be open-handed, Sphinx. I understand you won your copper link. I'll drink to that."

Alleras smiled back at him. "I only buy for friends. And I am no lord's son, I've told you that. My mother was a trader."

Leo's eyes were hazel, bright with wine and malice. "Your mother was a monkey from the Summer Isles. The Dornish will fuck anything with a hole between its legs. Meaning no offense. You may be brown as a nut, but at least you bathe. Unlike our spotted pig boy." He waved a hand toward Pate.

If I hit him in the mouth with my tankard, I could knock out half his teeth, Pate thought. Spotted Pate the pig boy was the hero of a thousand ribald stories: a good-hearted, empty-headed lout who always managed to best the fat lordlings, haughty knights, and pompous septons who beset him. Somehow his stupidity would turn out to have been a sort of uncouth cunning; the tales always ended with Spotted Pate sitting on a lord's high seat or bedding some knight's daughter. But those were stories. In the real world pig boys never fared so well. Pate sometimes thought his mother must have hated him to have named him as she did.

Alleras was no longer smiling. "You will apologize."

"Will I?" said Leo. "How can I, with my throat so dry . . ."

"You shame your House with every word you say," Alleras told him. "You shame the Citadel by being one of us."

"I know. So buy me some wine, that I might drown my shame."

Mollander said, "I would tear your tongue out by the roots."

"Truly? Then how would I tell you about the dragons?" Leo shrugged again. "The mongrel has the right of it. The Mad King's daughter is alive, and she's hatched herself three dragons."

"Three?" said Roone, astonished.

Leo patted his hand. "More than two and less than four. I would not try for my golden link just yet if I were you."

"You leave him be," warned Mollander.

"Such a chivalrous Hopfrog. As you wish. Every man off every ship that's sailed within a hundred leagues of Qarth is speaking of these dragons. A few will even tell you that they've seen them. The Mage is inclined to believe them."

Armen pursed his lips in disapproval. "Marwyn is unsound. Archmaester Perestan would be the first to tell you that."

"Archmaester Ryam says so too," said Roone.

Leo yawned. "The sea is wet, the sun is warm, and the menagerie hates the mastiff."

He has a mocking name for everyone, thought Pate, but he could not deny that Marwyn looked more a mastiff than a maester. *As if he wants to bite you.* The Mage was not like other maesters. People said that he kept company with whores and hedge wizards, talked with hairy Ibbenese and pitch-black Summer Islanders in their own tongues, and sacrificed to queer gods at the little sailors' temples down by the wharves. Men spoke of seeing him down in the undercity, in rat pits and black brothels, consorting with mummers, singers, sellswords, even beggars. Some even whispered that once he had killed a man with his fists.

When Marwyn had returned to Oldtown, after spending eight years in the east mapping distant lands, searching for lost books, and studying with warlocks and shadowbinders, Vinegar Vaellyn had dubbed him "Marwyn the Mage." The name was soon all over

Oldtown, to Vaellyn's vast annoyance. "Leave spells and prayers to priests and septons and bend your wits to learning truths a man can trust in," Archmaester Ryam had once counseled Pate, but Ryam's ring and rod and mask were yellow gold, and his maester's chain had no link of Valyrian steel.

Armen looked down his nose at Lazy Leo. He had the perfect nose for it, long and thin and pointed. "Archmaester Marwyn believes in many curious things," he said, "but he has no more proof of dragons than Mollander. Just more sailors' stories."

"You're wrong," said Leo. "There is a glass candle burning in the Mage's chambers."

A hush fell over the torchlit terrace. Armen sighed and shook his head. Mollander began to laugh. The Sphinx studied Leo with his big black eyes. Roone looked lost.

Pate knew about the glass candles, though he had never seen one burn. They were the worst-kept secret of the Citadel. It was said that they had been brought to Oldtown from Valyria a thousand years before the Doom. He had heard there were four; one was green and three were black, and all were tall and twisted.

"What are these glass candles?" asked Roone.

Armen the Acolyte cleared his throat. "The night before an acolyte says his vows, he must stand a vigil in the vault. No lantern is permitted him, no torch, no lamp, no taper . . . only a candle of obsidian. He must spend the night in darkness, unless he can light that candle. Some will try. The foolish and the stubborn, those who have made a study of these so-called higher mysteries. Often they cut their fingers, for the ridges on the candles are said to be as sharp as razors. Then, with bloody hands, they must wait upon the dawn, brooding on their failure. Wiser men simply go to sleep, or spend their night in prayer, but every year there are always a few who must try."

"Yes." Pate had heard the same stories. "But what's the *use* of a candle that casts no light?"

"It is a lesson," Armen said, "the last lesson we must learn before we don our maester's chains. The glass candle is meant to represent truth and learning, rare and beautiful and fragile things. It is made in the shape of a candle to remind us that a maester must cast light wherever he serves, and it is sharp to remind us that knowledge can be dangerous. Wise men may grow arrogant in their wisdom, but a maester must always remain humble. The glass candle reminds us of that as well. Even after he has said his vow and donned his chain and gone forth to serve, a maester will think back on the darkness of his vigil and remember how nothing that he did could make the candle burn . . . for even with knowledge, some things are not possible."

Lazy Leo burst out laughing. "Not possible for you, you mean. I saw the candle burning with my own eyes."

"You saw *some* candle burning, I don't doubt," said Armen. "A candle of black wax, perhaps."

"I know what I saw. The light was queer and bright, much brighter than any beeswax or tallow candle. It cast strange shadows and the flame never flickered, not even when a draft blew through the open door behind me."

Armen crossed his arms. "Obsidian does not burn."

"*Dragonglass,*" Pate said. "The smallfolk call it dragonglass." Somehow that seemed important.

"They do," mused Alleras, the Sphinx, "and if there are dragons in the world again . . ."

"Dragons and darker things," said Leo. "The grey sheep have closed their eyes, but the mastiff sees the truth. Old powers waken. Shadows stir. An age of wonder and terror will soon be upon us, an age for gods and heroes." He stretched, smiling his lazy smile. "That's worth a round, I'd say."

"We've drunk enough," said Armen. "Morn will be upon us sooner than we'd like, and Archmaester Ebrose will be speaking on the properties of urine. Those who mean to forge a silver link would do well not to miss his talk."

"Far be it from me to keep you from the piss tasting," said Leo. "Myself, I prefer the taste of Arbor gold."

"If the choice is piss or you, I'll drink piss." Mollander pushed back from the table. "Come, Roone."

The Sphinx reached for his bowcase. "It's bed for me as well. I expect I'll dream of dragons and glass candles."

"All of you?" Leo shrugged. "Well, Rosey will remain. Perhaps I'll wake our little sweetmeat and make a woman of her."

Alleras saw the look on Pate's face. "If he does not have a copper for a cup of wine, he cannot have a dragon for the girl."

"Aye," said Mollander. "Besides, it takes a man to make a woman. Come with us, Pate. Old Walgrave will wake when the sun comes up. He'll be needing you to help him to the privy."

If he remembers who I am today. Archmaester Walgrave had no trouble telling one raven from another, but he was not so good with people. Some days he seemed to think Pate was someone named Cressen. "Not just yet," he told his friends. "I'm going to stay awhile." Dawn had not broken, not quite. The alchemist might still be coming, and Pate meant to be here if he did.

"As you wish," said Armen. Alleras gave Pate a lingering look, then slung his bow over one slim shoulder and followed the others toward the bridge. Mollander was so drunk he had to walk with a hand on Roone's shoulder to keep from falling. The Citadel was no great distance as the raven flies, but none of them were ravens and Oldtown was a veritable labyrinth of a city, all wynds and crisscrossing alleys and narrow crookback streets. "Careful," Pate heard Armen say as the river mists swallowed up the four of them, "the night is damp, and the cobbles will be slippery."

When they were gone, Lazy Leo considered Pate sourly across the table. "How sad. The Sphinx has stolen off with all his silver, abandoning me to Spotted Pate the pig boy." He stretched, yawning. "How is our lovely little Rosey, pray?"

"She's sleeping," Pate said curtly.

"Naked, I don't doubt." Leo grinned. "Do you think she's truly worth a dragon? One day I suppose I must find out."

Pate knew better than to reply to that.

Leo needed no reply. "I expect that once I've broken in the wench, her price will fall to where even pig boys will be able to afford her. You ought to thank me."

I ought to kill you, Pate thought, but he was not near drunk enough to throw away his life. Leo had been trained to arms, and was known to be deadly with bravo's blade and dagger. And if Pate should somehow kill him, it would mean his own head too. Leo had two names where Pate had only one, and his second was *Tyrell*. Ser Moryn Tyrell, commander of the City Watch of Oldtown, was Leo's father. Mace Tyrell, Lord of Highgarden and Warden of the South, was Leo's cousin. And Oldtown's Old Man, Lord Leyton of the Hightower, who numbered "Protector of the Citadel" amongst his many titles, was a sworn bannerman of House Tyrell. *Let it go,* Pate told himself. *He says these things just to wound me.*

The mists were lightening to the east. *Dawn,* Pate realized. *Dawn has come, and the alchemist has not.* He did not know whether he should laugh or cry. *Am I still a thief if I put it all back and no one ever knows?* It was another question that he had no answer for, like those that Ebrose and Vaellyn had once asked him.

When he pushed back from the bench and got to his feet, the fearsomely strong cider all went to his head at once. He had to put a hand on the table to steady himself. "Leave Rosey be," he said, by way of parting. "Just leave her be, or I may kill you."

Leo Tyrell flicked the hair back from his eye. "I do not fight duels with pig boys. Go away."

Pate turned and crossed the terrace. His heels rang against the weathered planks of the old bridge. By the time he reached the other side, the eastern sky was turning pink. *The world is wide,* he told himself. *If I bought that donkey, I could still wander the roads and byways of the Seven Kingdoms, leeching the smallfolk and picking nits out of their hair. I could sign on to some ship, pull an oar, and sail to Qarth by the Jade Gates to see these bloody dragons for myself. I do not need to go back to old Walgrave and the ravens.*

Yet somehow his feet turned back toward the Citadel.

When the first shaft of sunlight broke through the clouds to the east, morning bells began to peal from the Sailor's Sept down by the harbor. The Lord's Sept joined in a moment later, then the Seven Shrines from their gardens across the Honeywine, and finally the Starry Sept that had been the seat of the High Septon for a thousand years before Aegon landed at King's Landing. They made a mighty music. *Though not so sweet as one small nightingale.*

He could hear singing too, beneath the pealing of the bells. Each

morning at first light the red priests gathered to welcome the sun
outside their modest wharfside temple. *For the night is dark and full
of terrors.* Pate had heard them cry those words a hundred times,
asking their god R'hllor to save them from the darkness. The Seven
were gods enough for him, but he had heard that Stannis Baratheon
worshiped at the nightfires now. He had even put the fiery heart of
R'hllor on his banners in place of the crowned stag. *If he should win
the Iron Throne, we'll all need to learn the words of the red priests' song,*
Pate thought, but that was not likely. Tywin Lannister had smashed
Stannis and R'hllor upon the Blackwater, and soon enough he would
finish them and mount the head of the Baratheon pretender on a
spike above the gates of King's Landing.

As the night's mists burned away, Oldtown took form around him,
emerging ghostlike from the predawn gloom. Pate had never seen
King's Landing, but he knew it was a daub-and-wattle city, a sprawl
of mud streets, thatched roofs, and wooden hovels. Oldtown was built
in stone, and all its streets were cobbled, down to the meanest alley.
The city was never more beautiful than at break of day. West of the
Honeywine, the Guildhalls lined the bank like a row of palaces.
Upriver, the domes and towers of the Citadel rose on both sides of
the river, connected by stone bridges crowded with halls and houses.
Downstream, below the black marble walls and arched windows
of the Starry Sept, the manses of the pious clustered like children
gathered round the feet of an old dowager.

And beyond, where the Honeywine widened into Whispering
Sound, rose the Hightower, its beacon fires bright against the dawn.
From where it stood atop the bluffs of Battle Island, its shadow cut
the city like a sword. Those born and raised in Oldtown could tell
the time of day by where that shadow fell. Some claimed a man could
see all the way to the Wall from the top. Perhaps that was why Lord
Leyton had not made the descent in more than a decade, preferring
to rule his city from the clouds.

A butcher's cart rumbled past Pate down the river road, five piglets
in the back squealing in distress. Dodging from its path, he just
avoided being spattered as a townswoman emptied a pail of night
soil from a window overhead. *When I am a maester in a castle I will*

have a horse to ride, he thought. Then he tripped upon a cobble and wondered who he was fooling. There would be no chain for him, no seat at a lord's high table, no tall white horse to ride. His days would be spent listening to ravens *quork* and scrubbing shit stains off Archmaester Walgrave's smallclothes.

He was on one knee, trying to wipe the mud off his robes, when a voice said, "Good morrow, Pate."

The alchemist was standing over him.

Pate rose. "The third day . . . you said you would be at the Quill and Tankard."

"You were with your friends. It was not my wish to intrude upon your fellowship." The alchemist wore a hooded traveler's cloak, brown and nondescript. The rising sun was peeking over the rooftops behind his shoulder, so it was hard to make out the face beneath his hood. "Have you decided what you are?"

Must he make me say it? "I suppose I am a thief."

"I thought you might be."

The hardest part had been getting down on his hands and knees to pull the strongbox from underneath Archmaester Walgrave's bed. Though the box was stoutly made and bound with iron, its lock was broken. Maester Gormon had suspected Pate of breaking it, but that wasn't true. Walgrave had broken the lock himself, after losing the key that opened it.

Inside, Pate had found a bag of silver stags, a lock of yellow hair tied up in a ribbon, a painted miniature of a woman who resembled Walgrave (even to her mustache), and a knight's gauntlet made of lobstered steel. The gauntlet had belonged to a prince, Walgrave claimed, though he could no longer seem to recall which one. When Pate shook it, the key fell out onto the floor.

If I pick that up, I am a thief, he remembered thinking. The key was old and heavy, made of black iron; supposedly it opened every door at the Citadel. Only the archmaesters had such keys. The others carried theirs upon their person or hid them away in some safe place, but if Walgrave had hidden his, no one would ever have seen it again. Pate snatched up the key and had been halfway to the door before turning back to take the silver too. A thief was a thief, whether he stole a little or a lot. *"Pate,"* one of the white ravens had called after him, *"Pate, Pate, Pate."*

"Do you have my dragon?" he asked the alchemist.

"If you have what I require."

"Give it here. I want to see." Pate did not intend to let himself be cheated.

"The river road is not the place. Come."

He had no time to think about it, to weigh his choices. The alchemist was walking away. Pate had to follow or lose Rosey and the dragon both, forever. He followed. As they walked, he slipped his hand up into his sleeve. He could feel the key, safe inside the hidden pocket he had sewn there. Maester's robes were full of pockets. He had known that since he was a boy.

He had to hurry to keep pace with the alchemist's longer strides. They went down an alley, around a corner, through the old Thieves Market, along Ragpicker's Wynd. Finally, the man turned into another alley, narrower than the first. "This is far enough," said Pate. "There's no one about. We'll do it here."

"As you wish."

"I want my dragon."

"To be sure." The coin appeared. The alchemist made it walk across his knuckles, the way he had when Rosey brought the two of them together. In the morning light the dragon glittered as it moved, and gave the alchemist's fingers a golden glow.

Pate grabbed it from his hand. The gold felt warm against his palm. He brought it to his mouth and bit down on it the way he'd seen men do. If truth be told, he wasn't sure what gold should taste like, but he did not want to look a fool.

"The key?" the alchemist inquired politely.

Something made Pate hesitate. "Is it some book you want?" Some of the old Valyrian scrolls down in the locked vaults were said to be the only surviving copies in the world.

"What I want is none of your concern."

"No." *It's done,* Pate told himself. *Go. Run back to the Quill and Tankard, wake Rosey with a kiss, and tell her she belongs to you.* Yet still he lingered. "Show me your face."

"As you wish." The alchemist pulled his hood down.

He was just a man, and his face was just a face. A young man's face, ordinary, with full cheeks and the shadow of a beard. A scar showed faintly on his right cheek. He had a hooked nose, and a mat of dense black hair that curled tightly around his ears. It was not a face Pate recognized. "I do not know you."

"Nor I you."

"Who are you?"

"A stranger. No one. Truly."

"Oh." Pate had run out of words. He drew out the key and put it in the stranger's hand, feeling light-headed, almost giddy. *Rosey,* he reminded himself. "We're done, then."

He was halfway down the alley when the cobblestones began to move beneath his feet. *The stones are slick and wet,* he thought, but that was not it. He could feel his heart hammering in his chest. "What's happening?" he said. His legs had turned to water. "I don't understand."

"And never will," a voice said sadly.

The cobblestones rushed up to kiss him. Pate tried to cry for help, but his voice was failing too.

His last thought was of Rosey.

THE PROPHET

The prophet was drowning men on Great Wyk when they came to tell him that the king was dead.

It was a bleak, cold morning, and the sea was as leaden as the sky. The first three men had offered their lives to the Drowned God fearlessly, but the fourth was weak in faith and began to struggle as his lungs cried out for air. Standing waist-deep in the surf, Aeron seized the naked boy by the shoulders and pushed his head back down as he tried to snatch a breath. "Have courage," he said. "We came from the sea, and to the sea we must return. Open your mouth and drink deep of god's blessing. Fill your lungs with water, that you may die and be reborn. It does no good to fight."

Either the boy could not hear him with his head beneath the waves, or else his faith had utterly deserted him. He began to kick and thrash so wildly that Aeron had to call for help. Four of his drowned men waded out to seize the wretch and hold him underwater. "Lord God who drowned for us," the priest prayed, in a voice as deep as the sea, "let Emmond your servant be reborn from the sea, as you were. Bless him with salt, bless him with stone, bless him with steel."

Finally, it was done. No more air was bubbling from his mouth, and all the strength had gone out of his limbs. Facedown in the shallow sea floated Emmond, pale and cold and peaceful.

That was when the Damphair realized that three horsemen had

joined his drowned men on the pebbled shore. Aeron knew the Sparr, a hatchet-faced old man with watery eyes whose quavery voice was law on this part of Great Wyk. His son Steffarion accompanied him, with another youth whose dark red fur-lined cloak was pinned at the shoulder with an ornate brooch that showed the black-and-gold warhorn of the Goodbrothers. *One of Gorold's sons,* the priest decided at a glance. Three tall sons had been born to Goodbrother's wife late in life, after a dozen daughters, and it was said that no man could tell one son from the others. Aeron Damphair did not deign to try. Whether this be Greydon or Gormond or Gran, the priest had no time for him.

He growled a brusque command, and his drowned men seized the dead boy by his arms and legs to carry him above the tideline. The priest followed, naked but for a sealskin clout that covered his private parts. Goosefleshed and dripping, he splashed back onto land, across cold wet sand and sea-scoured pebbles. One of his drowned men handed him a robe of heavy roughspun dyed in mottled greens and blues and greys, the colors of the sea and the Drowned God. Aeron donned the robe and pulled his hair free. Black and wet, that hair; no blade had touched it since the sea had raised him up. It draped his shoulders like a ragged, ropy cloak, and fell down past his waist. Aeron wove strands of seaweed through it, and through his tangled, uncut beard.

His drowned men formed a circle around the dead boy, praying. Norjen worked his arms whilst Rus knelt astride him, pumping on his chest, but all moved aside for Aeron. He pried apart the boy's cold lips with his fingers and gave Emmond the kiss of life, and again, and again, until the sea came gushing from his mouth. The boy began to cough and spit, and his eyes blinked open, full of fear.

Another one returned. It was a sign of the Drowned God's favor, men said. Every other priest lost a man from time to time, even Tarle the Thrice-Drowned, who had once been thought so holy that he was picked to crown a king. But never Aeron Greyjoy. He was the Damphair, who had seen the god's own watery halls and returned to tell of it. "Rise," he told the sputtering boy as he slapped him on his naked back. "You have drowned and been returned to us. What is dead can never die."

"But rises." The boy coughed violently, bringing up more water.

"Rises again." Every word was bought with pain, but that was the way of the world; a man must fight to live. "Rises again." Emmond staggered to his feet. "Harder. And stronger."

"You belong to the god now," Aeron told him. The other drowned men gathered round and each gave him a punch and a kiss to welcome him to the brotherhood. One helped him don a roughspun robe of mottled blue and green and grey. Another presented him with a driftwood cudgel. "You belong to the sea now, so the sea has armed you," Aeron said. "We pray that you shall wield your cudgel fiercely, against all the enemies of our god."

Only then did the priest turn to the three riders, watching from their saddles. "Have you come to be drowned, my lords?"

The Sparr coughed. "I was drowned as a boy," he said, "and my son upon his name day."

Aeron snorted. That Steffarion Sparr had been given to the Drowned God soon after birth he had no doubt. He knew the manner of it too, a quick dip into a tub of seawater that scarce wet the infant's head. Small wonder the ironborn had been conquered, they who once held sway everywhere the sound of waves was heard. "That is no true drowning," he told the riders. "He that does not die in truth cannot hope to rise from death. Why have you come, if not to prove your faith?"

"Lord Gorold's son came seeking you, with news." The Sparr indicated the youth in the red cloak.

The boy looked to be no more than six-and-ten. "Aye, and which are you?" Aeron demanded.

"Gormond. Gormond Goodbrother, if it please my lord."

"It is the Drowned God we must please. Have you been drowned, Gormond Goodbrother?"

"On my name day, Damphair. My father sent me to find you and bring you to him. He needs to see you."

"Here I stand. Let Lord Gorold come and feast his eyes." Aeron took a leather skin from Rus, freshly filled with water from the sea. The priest pulled out the cork and took a swallow.

"I am to bring you to the keep," insisted young Gormond, from atop his horse.

He is afraid to dismount, lest he get his boots wet. "I have the god's work to do." Aeron Greyjoy was a prophet. He did not suffer petty lords ordering him about like some thrall.

"Gorold's had a bird," said the Sparr.

"A maester's bird, from Pyke," Gormond confirmed.

Dark wings, dark words. "The ravens fly o'er salt and stone. If there are tidings that concern me, speak them now."

"Such tidings as we bear are for your ears alone, Damphair," the Sparr said. "These are not matters I would speak of here before these others."

"*These others* are my drowned men, god's servants, just as I am. I have no secrets from them, nor from our god, beside whose holy sea I stand."

The horsemen exchanged a look. "Tell him," said the Sparr, and the youth in the red cloak summoned up his courage. "The king is dead," he said, as plain as that. Four small words, yet the sea itself trembled when he uttered them.

Four kings there were in Westeros, yet Aeron did not need to ask which one was meant. Balon Greyjoy ruled the Iron Islands, and no other. *The king is dead. How can that be?* Aeron had seen his eldest brother not a moon's turn past, when he had returned to the Iron Islands from harrying the Stony Shore. Balon's grey hair had gone half-white whilst the priest had been away, and the stoop in his shoulders was more pronounced than when the longships sailed. Yet all in all the king had not seemed ill.

Aeron Greyjoy had built his life upon two mighty pillars. Those four small words had knocked one down. *Only the Drowned God remains to me. May he make me as strong and tireless as the sea.* "Tell me the manner of my brother's death."

"His Grace was crossing a bridge at Pyke when he fell and was dashed upon the rocks below."

The Greyjoy stronghold stood upon a broken headland, its keeps and towers built atop massive stone stacks that thrust up from the sea. Bridges knotted Pyke together; arched bridges of carved stone and swaying spans of hempen rope and wooden planks. "Was the storm raging when he fell?" Aeron demanded of them.

"Aye," the youth said, "it was."

"The Storm God cast him down," the priest announced. For a thousand thousand years sea and sky had been at war. From the sea had come the ironborn, and the fish that sustained them even in the depths of winter, but storms brought only woe and grief. "My brother Balon made us great again, which earned the Storm God's wrath. He feasts now in the Drowned God's watery halls, with mermaids to attend his every want. It shall be for us who remain behind in this dry and dismal vale to finish his great work." He pushed the cork back into his waterskin. "I shall speak with your lord father. How far from here to Hammerhorn?"

"Six leagues. You may ride pillion with me."

"One can ride faster than two. Give me your horse, and the Drowned God will bless you."

"Take my horse, Damphair," offered Steffarion Sparr.

"No. His mount is stronger. Your horse, boy."

The youth hesitated half a heartbeat, then dismounted and held the reins for the Damphair. Aeron shoved a bare black foot into a stirrup and swung himself onto the saddle. He was not fond of horses—they were creatures from the green lands and helped to make men weak—but necessity required that he ride. *Dark wings, dark words.* A storm was brewing, he could hear it in the waves, and storms brought naught but evil. "Meet with me at Pebbleton beneath Lord Merlyn's tower," he told his drowned men, as he turned the horse's head.

The way was rough, up hills and woods and stony defiles, along a narrow track that oft seemed to disappear beneath the horse's hooves. Great Wyk was the largest of the Iron Islands, so vast that some of its lords had holdings that did not front upon the holy sea. Gorold Goodbrother was one such. His keep was in the Hardstone Hills, as far from the Drowned God's realm as any place in the isles. Gorold's folk toiled down in Gorold's mines, in the stony dark beneath the earth. Some lived and died without setting eyes upon salt water. *Small wonder that such folk are crabbed and queer.*

As Aeron rode, his thoughts turned to his brothers.

Nine sons had been born from the loins of Quellon Greyjoy, the

Lord of the Iron Islands. Harlon, Quenton, and Donel had been born of Lord Quellon's first wife, a woman of the Stonetrees. Balon, Euron, Victarion, Urrigon, and Aeron were the sons of his second, a Sunderly of Saltcliffe. For a third wife, Quellon took a girl from the green lands, who gave him a sickly idiot boy named Robin, the brother best forgotten. The priest had no memory of Quenton or Donel, who had died as infants. Harlon he recalled but dimly, sitting grey-faced and still in a windowless tower room and speaking in whispers that grew fainter every day as the greyscale turned his tongue and lips to stone. *One day we shall feast on fish together in the Drowned God's watery halls, the four of us and Urri too.*

Nine sons had been born from the loins of Quellon Greyjoy, but only four had lived to manhood. That was the way of this cold world, where men fished the sea and dug in the ground and died, whilst women brought forth short-lived children from beds of blood and pain. Aeron had been the last and least of the four krakens, Balon the eldest and boldest, a fierce and fearless boy who lived only to restore the ironborn to their ancient glory. At ten he scaled the Flint Cliffs to the Blind Lord's haunted tower. At thirteen he could run a longship's oars and dance the finger dance as well as any man in the isles. At fifteen he had sailed with Dagmer Cleftjaw to the Stepstones and spent a summer reaving. He slew his first man there and took his first two salt wives. At seventeen Balon captained his own ship. He was all that an elder brother ought to be, though he had never shown Aeron aught but scorn. *I was weak and full of sin, and scorn was more than I deserved. Better to be scorned by Balon the Brave than beloved of Euron Crow's Eye.* And if age and grief had turned Balon bitter with the years, they had also made him more determined than any man alive. *He was born a lord's son and died a king, murdered by a jealous god,* Aeron thought, *and now the storm is coming, a storm such as these isles have never known.*

It was long after dark by the time the priest espied the spiky iron battlements of the Hammerhorn clawing at the crescent moon. Gorold's keep was hulking and blocky, its great stones quarried from the cliff that loomed behind it. Below its walls, the entrances of caves and ancient mines yawned like toothless black mouths. The

Hammerhorn's iron gates had been closed and barred for the night. Aeron beat on them with a rock until the clanging woke a guard.

The youth who admitted him was the image of Gormond, whose horse he'd taken. "Which one are you?" Aeron demanded.

"Gran. My father awaits you within."

The hall was dank and drafty, full of shadows. One of Gorold's daughters offered the priest a horn of ale. Another poked at a sullen fire that was giving off more smoke than heat. Gorold Goodbrother himself was talking quietly with a slim man in fine grey robes, who wore about his neck a chain of many metals that marked him for a maester of the Citadel.

"Where is Gormond?" Gorold asked when he saw Aeron.

"He returns afoot. Send your women away, my lord. And the maester as well." He had no love of maesters. Their ravens were creatures of the Storm God, and he did not trust their healing, not since Urri. *No proper man would choose a life of thralldom, nor forge a chain of servitude to wear about his throat.*

"Gysella, Gwin, leave us," Goodbrother said curtly. "You as well, Gran. Maester Murenmure will stay."

"He will go," insisted Aeron.

"This is my hall, Damphair. It is not for you to say who must go and who remains. The maester stays."

The man lives too far from the sea, Aeron told himself. "Then I shall go," he told Goodbrother. Dry rushes rustled underneath the cracked soles of his bare black feet as he turned and stalked away. It seemed he had ridden a long way for naught.

Aeron was almost at the door when the maester cleared his throat, and said, "Euron Crow's Eye sits the Seastone Chair."

The Damphair turned. The hall had suddenly grown colder. *The Crow's Eye is half a world away. Balon sent him off two years ago, and swore that it would be his life if he returned.* "Tell me," he said hoarsely.

"He sailed into Lordsport the day after the king's death, and claimed the castle and the crown as Balon's eldest brother," said Gorold Goodbrother. "Now he sends forth ravens, summoning the captains and the kings from every isle to Pyke, to bend their knees and do him homage as their king."

"No." Aeron Damphair did not weigh his words. "Only a godly man may sit the Seastone Chair. The Crow's Eye worships naught but his own pride."

"You were on Pyke not long ago, and saw the king," said Goodbrother. "Did Balon say aught to you of the succession?"

Aye. They had spoken in the Sea Tower, as the wind howled outside the windows and the waves crashed restlessly below. Balon had shaken his head in despair when he heard what Aeron had to tell him of his last remaining son. "The wolves have made a weakling of him, as I feared," the king had said. "I pray god that they killed him, so he cannot stand in Asha's way." That was Balon's blindness; he saw himself in his wild, headstrong daughter, and believed she could succeed him. He was wrong in that, and Aeron tried to tell him so. "No woman will ever rule the ironborn, not even a woman such as Asha," he insisted, but Balon could be deaf to things he did not wish to hear.

Before the priest could answer Gorold Goodbrother, the maester's mouth flapped open once again. "By rights the Seastone Chair belongs to Theon, or Asha if the prince is dead. That is the law."

"Green land law," said Aeron with contempt. "What is that to us? We are ironborn, the sons of the sea, chosen of the Drowned God. No woman may rule over us, nor any godless man."

"And Victarion?" asked Gorold Goodbrother. "He has the Iron Fleet. Will Victarion make a claim, Damphair?"

"Euron is the elder brother . . ." began the maester.

Aeron silenced him with a look. In little fishing towns and great stone keeps alike such a look from Damphair would make maids feel faint and send children shrieking to their mothers, and it was more than sufficient to quell the chain-neck thrall. "Euron is elder," the priest said, "but Victarion is more godly."

"Will it come to war between them?" asked the maester.

"Ironborn must not spill the blood of ironborn."

"A pious sentiment, Damphair," said Goodbrother, "but not one that your brother shares. He had Sawane Botley drowned for saying that the Seastone Chair by rights belonged to Theon."

"If he was drowned, no blood was shed," said Aeron.

The maester and the lord exchanged a look. "I must send word to

Pyke, and soon," said Gorold Goodbrother. "Damphair, I would have
your counsel. What shall it be, homage or defiance?"

Aeron tugged his beard, and thought. *I have seen the storm, and
its name is Euron Crow's Eye.* "For now, send only silence," he told
the lord. "I must pray on this."

"Pray all you wish," the maester said. "It does not change the law.
Theon is the rightful heir, and Asha next."

"*Silence!*" Aeron roared. "Too long have the ironborn listened to
you chain-neck maesters prating of the green lands and their laws. It
is time we listened to the sea again. It is time we listened to the voice
of god." His own voice rang in that smoky hall, so full of power that
neither Gorold Goodbrother nor his maester dared a reply. *The
Drowned God is with me,* Aeron thought. *He has shown me the way.*

Goodbrother offered him the comforts of the castle for the night,
but the priest declined. He seldom slept beneath a castle roof, and
never so far from the sea. "Comforts I shall know in the Drowned
God's watery halls beneath the waves. We are born to suffer, that our
sufferings might make us strong. All that I require is a fresh horse to
carry me to Pebbleton."

That Goodbrother was pleased to provide. He sent his son Greydon
as well, to show the priest the shortest way through the hills down
to the sea. Dawn was still an hour off when they set forth, but their
mounts were hardy and surefooted, and they made good time despite
the darkness. Aeron closed his eyes and said a silent prayer, and after
a while began to drowse in the saddle.

The sound came softly, the scream of a rusted hinge. "Urri," he
muttered, and woke, fearful. *There is no hinge here, no door, no Urri.*
A flying axe took off half of Urri's hand when he was ten-and-four,
playing at the finger dance whilst his father and his elder brothers
were away at war. Lord Quellon's third wife had been a Piper of
Pinkmaiden Castle, a girl with big soft breasts and brown doe's eyes.
Instead of healing Urri's hand the Old Way, with fire and seawater,
she gave him to her green land maester, who swore that he could sew
back the missing fingers. He did that, and later he used potions and
poltices and herbs, but the hand mortified and Urri took a fever. By
the time the maester sawed his arm off, it was too late.

Lord Quellon never returned from his last voyage; the Drowned God in his goodness granted him a death at sea. It was Lord Balon who came back, with his brothers Euron and Victarion. When Balon heard what had befallen Urri, he removed three of the maester's fingers with a cook's cleaver and sent his father's Piper wife to sew them back on. Poltices and potions worked as well for the maester as they had for Urrigon. He died raving, and Lord Quellon's third wife followed soon thereafter, as the midwife drew a stillborn daughter from her womb. Aeron had been glad. It had been his axe that sheared off Urri's hand, whilst they danced the finger dance together, as friends and brothers will.

It shamed him still to recall the years that followed Urri's death. At six-and-ten he called himself a man, but in truth he had been a sack of wine with legs. He would sing, he would dance (but not the finger dance, never again), he would jape and jabber and make mock. He played the pipes, he juggled, he rode horses, and could drink more than all the Wynches and the Botleys, and half the Harlaws too. The Drowned God gives every man a gift, even him; no man could piss longer or farther than Aeron Greyjoy, as he proved at every feast. Once he bet his new longship against a herd of goats that he could quench a hearthfire with no more than his cock. Aeron feasted on goat for a year, and named the longship *Golden Storm*, though Balon threatened to hang him from her mast when he heard what sort of ram his brother proposed to mount upon her prow.

In the end, the *Golden Storm* went down off Fair Isle during Balon's first rebellion, cut in half by a towering war galley called *Fury* when Stannis Baratheon caught Victarion in his trap and smashed the Iron Fleet. Yet the god was not done with Aeron, and carried him to shore. Some fishermen took him captive and marched him down to Lannisport in chains, and he spent the rest of the war in the bowels of Casterly Rock, proving that krakens can piss farther and longer than lions, boars, or chickens.

That man is dead. Aeron had drowned and been reborn from the sea, the god's own prophet. No mortal man could frighten him, no more than the darkness could . . . nor memories, the bones of the soul. *The sound of a door opening, the scream of a rusted iron hinge.*

Euron has come again. It did not matter. He was the Damphair priest, beloved of the god.

"Will it come to war?" asked Greydon Goodbrother as the sun was lightening the hills. "A war of brother against brother?"

"If the Drowned God wills it. No godless man may sit the Seastone Chair." *The Crow's Eye will fight, that is certain.* No woman could defeat him, not even Asha; women were made to fight their battles in the birthing bed. And Theon, if he lived, was just as hopeless, a boy of sulks and smiles. At Winterfell he proved his worth, such that it was, but the Crow's Eye was no crippled boy. The decks of Euron's ship were painted red, to better hide the blood that soaked them. *Victarion. The king must be Victarion, or the storm will slay us all.*

Greydon left him when the sun was up, to take the news of Balon's death to his cousins in their towers at Downdelving, Crow Spike Keep, and Corpse Lake. Aeron continued on alone, up hills and down vales along a stony track that drew wider and more traveled as he neared the sea. In every village he paused to preach, and in the yards of petty lords as well. "We were born from the sea, and to the sea we all return," he told them. His voice was as deep as the ocean, and thundered like the waves. "The Storm God in his wrath plucked Balon from his castle and cast him down, and now he feasts beneath the waves in the Drowned God's watery halls." He raised his hands. "*Balon is dead! The king is dead!* Yet a king will come again! For what is dead may never die, but rises again, harder and stronger! *A king will rise!*"

Some of those who heard him threw down their hoes and picks to follow, so by the time he heard the crash of waves a dozen men walked behind his horse, touched by god and desirous of drowning.

Pebbleton was home to several thousand fisherfolk, whose hovels huddled round the base of a square towerhouse with a turret at each corner. Twoscore of Aeron's drowned men there awaited him, camped along a grey sand beach in sealskin tents and shelters built of driftwood. Their hands were roughened by brine, scarred by nets and lines, callused from oars and picks and axes, but now those hands gripped driftwood cudgels hard as iron, for the god had armed them from his arsenal beneath the sea.

They had built a shelter for the priest just above the tideline. Gladly, he crawled into it, after he had drowned his newest followers. *My god,* he prayed, *speak to me in the rumble of the waves, and tell me what to do. The captains and the kings await your word. Who shall be our king in Balon's place? Sing to me in the language of leviathan, that I may know his name. Tell me, O Lord beneath the waves, who has the strength to fight the storm on Pyke?*

Though his ride to Hammerhorn had left him weary, Aeron Damphair was restless in his driftwood shelter, roofed over with black weeds from the sea. The clouds rolled in to cloak the moon and stars, and the darkness lay as thick upon the sea as it did upon his soul. *Balon favored Asha, the child of his body, but a woman cannot rule the ironborn. It must be Victarion.* Nine sons had been born from the loins of Quellon Greyjoy, and Victarion was the strongest of them, a bull of a man, fearless and dutiful. *And therein lies our danger.* A younger brother owes obedience to an elder, and Victarion was not a man to sail against tradition. *He has no love for Euron, though. Not since the woman died.*

Outside, beneath the snoring of his drowned men and the keening of the wind, he could hear the pounding of the waves, the hammer of his god calling him to battle. Aeron crept from his little shelter into the chill of the night. Naked he stood, pale and gaunt and tall, and naked he walked into the black salt sea. The water was icy cold, yet he did not flinch from his god's caress. A wave smashed against his chest, staggering him. The next broke over his head. He could taste the salt on his lips and feel the god around him, and his ears rang with the glory of his song. *Nine sons were born from the loins of Quellon Greyjoy, and I was the least of them, as weak and frightened as a girl. But no longer. That man is drowned, and the god has made me strong.* The cold salt sea surrounded him, embraced him, reached down through his weak man's flesh and touched his bones. *Bones,* he thought. *The bones of the soul. Balon's bones, and Urri's. The truth is in our bones, for flesh decays and bone endures. And on the hill of Nagga, the bones of the Grey King's Hall . . .*

And gaunt and pale and shivering, Aeron Damphair struggled back to the shore, a wiser man than he had been when he stepped into the sea. For he had found the answer in his bones, and the way was plain before him. The night was so cold that his body seemed to steam as he stalked back toward his shelter, but there was a fire burning in his heart, and sleep came easily for once, unbroken by the scream of iron hinges.

When he woke the day was bright and windy. Aeron broke his fast on a broth of clams and seaweed cooked above a driftwood fire. No sooner had he finished than the Merlyn descended from his tower-house with half a dozen guards to seek him out. "The king is dead," the Damphair told him.

"Aye. I had a bird. And now another." The Merlyn was a bald round fleshy man who styled himself "Lord" in the manner of the green lands, and dressed in furs and velvets. "One raven summons me to Pyke, another to Ten Towers. You krakens have too many arms, you pull a man to pieces. What say you, priest? Where should I send my longships?"

Aeron scowled. "Ten Towers, do you say? What kraken calls you there?" Ten Towers was the seat of the Lord of Harlaw.

"The Princess Asha. She has set her sails for home. The Reader sends out ravens, summoning all her friends to Harlaw. He says that Balon meant for her to sit the Seastone Chair."

"The Drowned God shall decide who sits the Seastone Chair," the priest said. "Kneel, that I might bless you." Lord Merlyn sank to his knees, and Aeron uncorked his skin and poured a stream of seawater on his bald pate. "Lord God who drowned for us, let Meldred your servant be born again from the sea. Bless him with salt, bless him with stone, bless him with steel." Water ran down Merlyn's fat cheeks to soak his beard and fox-fur mantle. "What is dead may never die," Aeron finished, "but rises again, harder and stronger." But when Merlyn rose, he told him, "Stay and listen, that you may spread god's word."

Three feet from the water's edge the waves broke around a rounded granite boulder. It was there that Aeron Damphair stood, so all his school might see him, and hear the words he had to say.

"We were born from the sea, and to the sea we all return," he began, as he had a hundred times before. "The Storm God in his wrath plucked Balon from his castle and cast him down, and now he feasts beneath the waves." He raised his hands. "*The iron king is dead! Yet a king will come again! For what is dead may never die, but rises again, harder and stronger!*"

"*A king shall rise!*" the drowned men cried.

"He shall. He must. But who?" The Damphair listened a moment, but only the waves gave answer. "*Who shall be our king?*"

The drowned men began to slam their driftwood cudgels one against the other. "*Damphair!*" they cried. "*Damphair King! Aeron King! Give us Damphair!*"

Aeron shook his head. "If a father has two sons and gives to one an axe and to the other a net, which does he intend should be the warrior?"

"The axe is for the warrior," Rus shouted back, "the net for a fisher of the seas."

"Aye," said Aeron. "The god took me deep beneath the waves and drowned the worthless thing I was. When he cast me forth again he gave me eyes to see, ears to hear, and a voice to spread his word, that I might be his prophet and teach his truth to those who have forgotten. I was not made to sit upon the Seastone Chair . . . no more than Euron Crow's Eye. For I have heard the god, who says, *No godless man may sit my Seastone Chair!*"

The Merlyn crossed his arms against his chest. "Is it Asha, then? Or Victarion? Tell us, priest!"

"The Drowned God will tell you, but not here." Aeron pointed at the Merlyn's fat white face. "Look not to me, nor to the laws of men, but to the sea. Raise your sails and unship your oars, my lord, and take yourself to Old Wyk. You, and all the captains and the kings. Go not to Pyke, to bow before the godless, nor to Harlaw, to consort with scheming women. Point your prow toward Old Wyk, where stood the Grey King's Hall. In the name of the Drowned God I summon you. *I summon all of you!* Leave your halls and hovels, your castles and your keeps, and return to Nagga's hill to make a kingsmoot!"

The Merlyn gaped at him. "A kingsmoot? There has not been a true kingsmoot in . . ."

". . . *too long a time!*" Aeron cried in anguish. "Yet in the dawn of days the ironborn chose their own kings, raising up the worthiest amongst them. It is time we returned to the Old Way, for only that shall make us great again. It was a kingsmoot that chose Urras Ironfoot for High King, and placed a driftwood crown upon his brows. Sylas Flatnose, Harrag Hoare, the Old Kraken, the kingsmoot raised them all. And from *this* kingsmoot shall emerge a man to finish the work King Balon has begun and win us back our freedoms. Go *not* to Pyke, nor to the Ten Towers of Harlaw, but to Old Wyk, I say again. Seek the hill of Nagga and the bones of the Grey King's Hall, for in that holy place when the moon has drowned and come again we shall make ourselves a worthy king, a *godly* king." He raised his bony hands on high again. "*Listen!* Listen to the waves! Listen to the god! He is speaking to us, and he says, *We shall have no king but from the kingsmoot!*"

A roar went up at that, and the drowned men beat their cudgels one against the other. "A *kingsmoot!*" they shouted. "*A kingsmoot, a kingsmoot. No king but from the kingsmoot!*" And the clamor that they made was so thunderous that surely the Crow's Eye heard the shouts on Pyke, and the vile Storm God in his cloudy hall. And Aeron Damphair knew he had done well.

THE CAPTAIN OF GUARDS

"The blood oranges are well past ripe," the prince observed in a weary voice, when the captain rolled him onto the terrace. After that he did not speak again for hours.

It was true about the oranges. A few had fallen to burst open on the pale pink marble. The sharp sweet smell of them filled Hotah's nostrils each time he took a breath. No doubt the prince could smell them too, as he sat beneath the trees in the rolling chair Maester Caleotte had made for him, with its goose-down cushions and rumbling wheels of ebony and iron.

For a long while the only sounds were the children splashing in the pools and fountains, and once a soft *plop* as another orange dropped onto the terrace to burst. Then, from the far side of the palace, the captain heard the faint drumbeat of boots on marble.

Obara. He knew her stride; long-legged, hasty, angry. In the stables by the gates, her horse would be lathered, and bloody from her spurs. She always rode stallions, and had been heard to boast that she could master any horse in Dorne . . . and any man as well. The captain could hear other footsteps as well, the quick soft scuffing of Maester Caleotte hurrying to keep up.

Obara Sand always walked too fast. *She is chasing after something she can never catch,* the prince had told his daughter once, in the captain's hearing.

When she appeared beneath the triple arch, Areo Hotah swung his longaxe sideways to block the way. The head was on a shaft of mountain ash six feet long, so she could not go around. "My lady, no farther." His voice was a bass grumble thick with the accents of Norvos. "The prince does not wish to be disturbed."

Her face had been stone before he spoke; then it hardened. "You are in my way, Hotah." Obara was the eldest Sand Snake, a big-boned woman near to thirty, with the close-set eyes and rat-brown hair of the Oldtown whore who'd birthed her. Beneath a mottled sandsilk cloak of dun and gold, her riding clothes were old brown leather, worn and supple. They were the softest things about her. On one hip she wore a coiled whip, across her back a round shield of steel and copper. She had left her spear outside. For that, Areo Hotah gave thanks. Quick and strong as she was, the woman was no match for him, he knew . . . but *she* did not, and he had no wish to see her blood upon the pale pink marble.

Maester Caleotte shifted his weight from foot to foot. "Lady Obara, I tried to tell you . . ."

"Does he know that my father is dead?" Obara asked the captain, paying the maester no more mind than she would a fly, if any fly had been foolish enough to buzz about her head.

"He does," the captain said. "He had a bird."

Death had come to Dorne on raven wings, writ small and sealed with a blob of hard red wax. Caleotte must have sensed what was in that letter, for he'd given it Hotah to deliver. The prince thanked him, but for the longest time he would not break the seal. All afternoon he'd sat with the parchment in his lap, watching the children at their play. He watched until the sun went down and the evening air grew cool enough to drive them inside; then he watched the starlight on the water. It was moonrise before he sent Hotah to fetch a candle, so he might read his letter beneath the orange trees in the dark of night.

Obara touched her whip. "Thousands are crossing the sands afoot to climb the Boneway, so they may help Ellaria bring my father home. The septs are packed to bursting, and the red priests have lit their temple fires. In the pillow houses women are coupling with every man who comes to them, and refusing any coin. In Sunspear, on the Broken

Arm, along the Greenblood, in the mountains, out in the deep sand, everywhere, *everywhere*, women tear their hair and men cry out in rage. The same question is heard on every tongue—what will Doran do? *What will his brother do to avenge our murdered prince?*" She moved closer to the captain. "And you say, *he does not wish to be disturbed!*"

"He does not wish to be disturbed," Areo Hotah said again.

The captain of guards knew the prince he guarded. Once, long ago, a callow youth had come from Norvos, a big broad-shouldered boy with a mop of dark hair. That hair was white now, and his body bore the scars of many battles . . . but his strength remained, and he kept his longaxe sharp, as the bearded priests had taught him. *She shall not pass,* he told himself, and said, "The prince is watching the children at their play. He is *never* to be disturbed when he is watching the children at their play."

"Hotah," said Obara Sand, "you will remove yourself from my path, else I shall take that longaxe and—"

"Captain," came the command, from behind. "Let her pass. I will speak with her." The prince's voice was hoarse.

Areo Hotah jerked his longaxe upright and stepped to one side. Obara gave him a lingering last look and strode past, the maester hurrying at her heels. Caleotte was no more than five feet tall and bald as an egg. His face was so smooth and fat that it was hard to tell his age, but he had been here before the captain, had even served the prince's mother. Despite his age and girth, he was still nimble enough, and clever as they came, but meek. *He is no match for any Sand Snake,* the captain thought.

In the shade of the orange trees, the prince sat in his chair with his gouty legs propped up before him, and heavy bags beneath his eyes . . . though whether it was grief or gout that kept him sleepless, Hotah could not say. Below, in the fountains and the pools, the children were still at their play. The youngest were no more than five, the oldest nine and ten. Half were girls and half were boys. Hotah could hear them splashing and shouting at each other in high, shrill voices. "It was not so long ago that you were one of the children in those pools, Obara," the prince said, when she took one knee before his rolling chair.

She snorted. "It has been twenty years, or near enough to make no matter. And I was not here long. I am the whore's whelp, or had you forgotten?" When he did not answer, she rose again and put her hands upon her hips. "My father has been murdered."

"He was slain in single combat during a trial by battle," Prince Doran said. "By law, that is no murder."

"He was your *brother*."

"He was."

"What do you mean to do about his death?"

The prince turned his chair laboriously to face her. Though he was but two-and-fifty, Doran Martell seemed much older. His body was soft and shapeless beneath his linen robes, and his legs were hard to look upon. The gout had swollen and reddened his joints grotesquely; his left knee was an apple, his right a melon, and his toes had turned to dark red grapes, so ripe it seemed as though a touch would burst them. Even the weight of a coverlet could make him shudder, though he bore the pain without complaint. *Silence is a prince's friend,* the captain had heard him tell his daughter once. *Words are like arrows, Arianne. Once loosed, you cannot call them back.* "I have written to Lord Tywin—"

"*Written?* If you were half the man my father was—"

"I am not your father."

"That I knew." Obara's voice was thick with contempt.

"You would have me go to war."

"I know better. You need not even leave your chair. Let *me* avenge my father. You have a host in the Prince's Pass. Lord Yronwood has another in the Boneway. Grant me the one and Nym the other. Let her ride the kingsroad, whilst I turn the marcher lords out of their castles and hook round to march on Oldtown."

"And how could you hope to hold Oldtown?"

"It will be enough to sack it. The wealth of Hightower—"

"Is it gold you want?"

"It is blood I want."

"Lord Tywin shall deliver us the Mountain's head."

"And who will deliver us Lord Tywin's head? The Mountain has always been his pet."

The prince gestured toward the pools. "Obara, look at the children, if it please you."

"It does not please me. I'd get more pleasure from driving my spear into Lord Tywin's belly. I'll make him sing 'The Rains of Castamere' as I pull his bowels out and look for gold."

"*Look*," the prince repeated. "I command you."

A few of the older children lay facedown upon the smooth pink marble, browning in the sun. Others paddled in the sea beyond. Three were building a sand castle with a great spike that resembled the Spear Tower of the Old Palace. A score or more had gathered in the big pool, to watch the battles as smaller children rode through the waist-deep shallows on the shoulders of the larger and tried to shove each other into the water. Every time a pair went down, the splash was followed by a roar of laughter. They watched a nut-brown girl yank a towheaded boy off his brother's shoulders to tumble him headfirst into the pool.

"Your father played that same game once, as I did before him," said the prince. "We had ten years between us, so I had left the pools by the time he was old enough to play, but I would watch him when I came to visit Mother. He was so fierce, even as a boy. Quick as a water snake. I oft saw him topple boys much bigger than himself. He reminded me of the day he left for King's Landing. He swore that he would do it one more time, else I would never have let him go."

"*Let* him go?" Obara laughed. "As if you could have stopped him. The Red Viper of Dorne went where he would."

"He did. I wish I had some word of comfort to—"

"I did not come to you for *comfort*." Her voice was full of scorn. "The day my father came to claim me, my mother did not wish for me to go. 'She is a girl,' she said, 'and I do not think that she is yours. I had a thousand other men.' He tossed his spear at my feet and gave my mother the back of his hand across the face, so she began to weep. 'Girl or boy, we fight our battles,' he said, 'but the gods let us choose our weapons.' He pointed to the spear, then to my mother's tears, and I picked up the spear. 'I told you she was mine,' my father said, and took me. My mother drank herself to death within the year. They say that she was weeping as she died." Obara edged closer to the prince in his chair. "Let me use the spear; I ask no more."

"It is a deal to ask, Obara. I shall sleep on it."

"You have slept too long already."

"You may be right. I will send word to you at Sunspear."

"So long as the word is war." Obara turned upon her heel and strode off as angrily as she had come, back to the stables for a fresh horse and another headlong gallop down the road.

Maester Caleotte remained behind. "My prince?" the little round man asked. "Do your legs hurt?"

The prince smiled faintly. "Is the sun hot?"

"Shall I fetch a draught for the pain?"

"No. I need my wits about me."

The maester hesitated. "My prince, is it . . . is it prudent to allow Lady Obara to return to Sunspear? She is certain to inflame the common people. They loved your brother well."

"So did we all." He pressed his fingers to his temples. "No. You are right. I must return to Sunspear as well."

The little round man hesitated. "Is that wise?"

"Not wise, but necessary. Best send a rider to Ricasso, and have him open my apartments in the Tower of the Sun. Inform my daughter Arianne that I will be there on the morrow."

My little princess. The captain had missed her sorely.

"You will be seen," the maester warned.

The captain understood. Two years ago, when they had left Sunspear for the peace and isolation of the Water Gardens, Prince Doran's gout had not been half so bad. In those days he had still walked, albeit slowly, leaning on a stick and grimacing with every step. The prince did not wish his enemies to know how feeble he had grown, and the Old Palace and its shadow city were full of eyes. *Eyes,* the captain thought, *and steps he cannot climb. He would need to fly to sit atop the Tower of the Sun.*

"I *must* be seen. Someone must pour oil on the waters. Dorne must be reminded that it still has a prince." He smiled wanly. "Old and gouty though he is."

"If you return to Sunspear, you will need to give audience to Princess Myrcella," Caleotte said. "Her white knight will be with her . . . and you *know* he sends letters to his queen."

"I suppose he does."

The white knight. The captain frowned. Ser Arys had come to Dorne to attend his own princess, as Areo Hotah had once come with his. Even their names sounded oddly alike: Areo and Arys. Yet there the likeness ended. The captain had left Norvos and its bearded priests, but Ser Arys Oakheart still served the Iron Throne. Hotah had felt a certain sadness whenever he saw the man in the long snowy cloak, the times the prince had sent him down to Sunspear. One day, he sensed, the two of them would fight; on that day Oakheart would die, with the captain's longaxe crashing through his skull. He slid his hand along the smooth ashen shaft of his axe and wondered if that day was drawing nigh.

"The afternoon is almost done," the prince was saying. "We will wait for morn. See that my litter is ready by first light."

"As you command." Caleotte bobbed a bow. The captain stood aside to let him pass, and listened to his footsteps dwindle.

"Captain?" The prince's voice was soft.

Hotah strode forward, one hand wrapped about his longaxe. The ash felt as smooth as a woman's skin against his palm. When he reached the rolling chair he thumped its butt down hard to announce his presence, but the prince had eyes only for the children. "Did you have brothers, captain?" he asked. "Back in Norvos, when you were young? Sisters?"

"Both," Hotah said. "Two brothers, three sisters. I was the youngest." *The youngest, and unwanted. Another mouth to feed, a big boy who ate too much and soon outgrew his clothes.* Small wonder they had sold him to the bearded priests.

"I was the oldest," the prince said, "and yet I am the last. After Mors and Olyvar died in their cradles, I gave up hope of brothers. I was nine when Elia came, a squire in service at Salt Shore. When the raven arrived with word that my mother had been brought to bed a month too soon, I was old enough to understand that meant the child would not live. Even when Lord Gargalen told me that I had a sister, I assured him that she must shortly die. Yet she lived, by the Mother's mercy. And a year later Oberyn arrived, squalling and kicking. I was a man grown when they were playing in these pools. Yet here I sit, and they are gone."

Areo Hotah did not know what to say to that. He was only a captain of guards, and still a stranger to this land and its seven-faced god, even after all these years. *Serve. Obey. Protect.* He had sworn those vows at six-and-ten, the day he wed his axe. *Simple vows for simple men,* the bearded priests had said. He had not been trained to counsel grieving princes.

He was still groping for some words to say when another orange fell with a heavy splat, no more than a foot from where the prince was seated. Doran winced at the sound, as if somehow it had hurt him. "Enough," he sighed, "it is enough. Leave me, Areo. Let me watch the children for a few more hours."

When the sun set the air grew cool and the children went inside in search of supper, still the prince remained beneath his orange trees, looking out over the still pools and the sea beyond. A serving man brought him a bowl of purple olives, with flatbread, cheese, and chickpea paste. He ate a bit of it, and drank a cup of the sweet, heavy strongwine that he loved. When it was empty, he filled it once again. Sometimes in the deep black hours of the morning sleep found him in his chair. Only then did the captain roll him down the moonlit gallery, past a row of fluted pillars and through a graceful archway, to a great bed with crisp cool linen sheets in a chamber by the sea. Doran groaned as the captain moved him, but the gods were good and he did not wake.

The captain's sleeping cell adjoined his prince's. He sat upon the narrow bed and found his whetstone and oilcloth in their niche, and set to work. *Keep your longaxe sharp,* the bearded priests had told him, the day they branded him. He always did.

As he honed the axe, Hotah thought of Norvos, the high city on the hill and the low beside the river. He could still recall the sounds of the three bells, the way that Noom's deep peals set his very bones to shuddering, the proud strong voice of Narrah, sweet Nyel's silvery laughter. The taste of wintercake filled his mouth again, rich with ginger and pine nuts and bits of cherry, with *nahsa* to wash it down, fermented goat's milk served in an iron cup and laced with honey. He saw his mother in her dress with the squirrel collar, the one she wore but once each year, when they went to see the bears dance down the Sinner's Steps. And he smelled the stench of burning hair as the bearded priest touched the brand to the center of his chest. The pain had been so fierce that he thought his heart might stop, yet Areo Hotah had not flinched. The hair had never grown back over the axe.

Only when both edges were sharp enough to shave with did the captain lay his ash-and-iron wife down on the bed. Yawning, he pulled off his soiled clothes, tossed them on the floor, and stretched out on his straw-stuffed mattress. Thinking of the brand had made it itch, so he had to scratch himself before he closed his eyes. *I should have gathered up the oranges that fell,* he thought, and went to sleep dreaming of the tart sweet taste of them, and the sticky feel of the red juice on his fingers.

Dawn came too soon. Outside the stables the smallest of the three horse litters stood ready, the cedarwood litter with the red silk draperies. The captain chose twenty spears to accompany it, out of the thirty who were posted at the Water Gardens; the rest would stay to guard the grounds and children, some of whom were the sons and daughters of great lords and wealthy merchants.

Although the prince had spoken of departing at first light, Areo Hotah knew that he would dawdle. Whilst the maester helped Doran Martell to bathe and bandaged up his swollen joints in linen wraps soaked with soothing lotions, the captain donned a shirt of copper scales as befit his rank, and a billowing cloak of dun-and-yellow sandsilk to keep the sun off the copper. The day promised to be hot, and the captain had long ago discarded the heavy horsehair cape and studded leather tunic he had worn in Norvos, which were like to cook a man in Dorne. He had kept his iron halfhelm, with its crest of sharpened spikes, but now he wore it wrapped in orange silk, weaving the cloth in and around the spikes. Elsewise the sun beating down on the metal would have his head pounding before they saw the palace.

The prince was still not ready to depart. He had decided to break his fast before he went, with a blood orange and a plate of gull's eggs diced with bits of ham and fiery peppers. Then nought would do but he must say farewell to several of the children who had become especial favorites: the Dalt boy and Lady Blackmont's brood and the round-faced orphan girl whose father had sold cloth and spices up and down the Greenblood. Doran kept a splendid Myrish blanket over his legs as he spoke with them, to spare the young ones the sight of his swollen, bandaged joints.

It was midday before they got under way; the prince in his litter, Maester Caleotte riding on a donkey, the rest afoot. Five spearmen walked ahead and five behind, with five more flanking the litter to either side. Areo Hotah himself took his familiar place at the left hand of the prince, resting his longaxe on a shoulder as he walked. The road from Sunspear to the Water Gardens ran beside the sea, so they had a cool fresh breeze to soothe them as they made their way across a sparse red-brown land of stone and sand and twisted stunted trees.

Halfway there, the second Sand Snake caught them.

She appeared suddenly upon a dune, mounted on a golden sand steed with a mane like fine white silk. Even ahorse, the Lady Nym looked graceful, dressed all in shimmering lilac robes and a great silk cape of cream and copper that lifted at every gust of wind, and made her look as if she might take flight. Nymeria Sand was five-and-twenty, and slender as a willow. Her straight black hair, worn in a long braid bound up with red-gold wire, made a widow's peak above her dark eyes, just as her father's had. With her high cheekbones, full lips, and milk-pale skin, she had all the beauty that her elder sister lacked . . . but Obara's mother had been an Oldtown whore, whilst Nym was born from the noblest blood of old Volantis. A dozen mounted spearmen tailed her, their round shields gleaming in the sun. They followed her down the dune.

The prince had tied back the curtains on his litter, the better to enjoy the breeze blowing off the sea. Lady Nym fell in beside him, slowing her pretty golden mare to match the litter's pace. "Well met, Uncle," she sang out, as if it had been chance that brought her here. "May I ride with you to Sunspear?" The captain was on the opposite side of the litter from Lady Nym, yet he could hear every word she said.

"I would be glad of it," Prince Doran replied, though he did not *sound* glad to the captain's ears. "Gout and grief make poor companions on the road." By which the captain knew him to mean that every pebble drove a spike through his swollen joints.

"The gout I cannot help," she said, "but my father had no use for grief. Vengeance was more to his taste. Is it true that Gregor Clegane admitted slaying Elia and her children?"

"He roared out his guilt for all the court to hear," the prince admitted. "Lord Tywin has promised us his head."

"And a Lannister always pays his debts," said Lady Nym, "yet it seems to me that Lord Tywin means to pay us with our own coin. I had a bird from our sweet Ser Daemon, who swears my father tickled that monster more than once as they fought. If so, Ser Gregor is as good as dead, and no thanks to Tywin Lannister."

The prince grimaced. Whether it was from the pain of gout or his niece's words, the captain could not say. "It may be so."

"May be? I say 'tis."

"Obara would have me go to war."

Nym laughed. "Yes, she wants to set the torch to Oldtown. She hates that city as much as our little sister loves it."

"And you?"

Nym glanced over a shoulder, to where her companions rode a dozen lengths behind. "I was abed with the Fowler twins when the word reached me," the captain heard her say. "You know the Fowler words? *Let Me Soar!* That is all I ask of you. Let me soar, Uncle. I need no mighty host, only one sweet sister."

"Obara?"

"Tyene. Obara is too loud. Tyene is so sweet and gentle that no man will suspect her. Obara would make Oldtown our father's funeral pyre, but I am not so greedy. Four lives will suffice for me. Lord Tywin's golden twins, as payment for Elia's children. The old lion, for Elia herself. And last of all the little king, for my father."

"The boy has never wronged us."

"The boy is a bastard born of treason, incest, and adultery, if Lord Stannis can be believed." The playful tone had vanished from her voice, and the captain found himself watching her through narrowed eyes. Her sister Obara wore her whip upon her hip and carried a spear where any man could see it. Lady Nym was no less deadly, though she kept her knives well hidden. "Only royal blood can wash out my father's murder."

"Oberyn died during single combat, fighting in a matter that was none of his concern. I do not call that murder."

"Call it what you will. We sent them the finest man in Dorne, and they are sending back a bag of bones."

"He went beyond anything I asked of him. 'Take the measure of this boy king and his council, and make note of their strengths and weaknesses,' I told him, on the terrace. We were eating oranges. 'Find us friends, if there are any to be found. Learn what you can of Elia's end, but see that you do not provoke Lord Tywin unduly,' those were my words to him. Oberyn laughed, and said, 'When have I provoked any man ... *unduly*? You would do better to warn the Lannisters against provoking me.' He wanted justice for Elia, but he would not wait—"

"He waited ten-and-seven years," the Lady Nym broke in. "Were it you they'd killed, my father would have led his banners north before your corpse was cold. Were it you, the spears would be falling thick as rain upon the marches now."

"I do not doubt it."

"No more should you doubt this, my prince—my sisters and I shall not wait ten-and-seven years for *our* vengeance." She put her spurs into the mare and she was off, galloping toward Sunspear with her tail in hot pursuit.

The prince leaned back against his pillows and closed his eyes, but Hotah knew he did not sleep. *He is in pain.* For a moment he considered calling Maester Caleotte up to the litter, but if Prince Doran had wanted him, he would have called himself.

The shadows of the afternoon were long and dark and the sun was as red and swollen as the prince's joints before they glimpsed the towers of Sunspear to the east. First, the slender Spear Tower, a hundred-and-a-half feet tall and crowned with a spear of gilded steel that added another thirty feet to its height; then the mighty Tower of the Sun, with its dome of gold and leaded glass; last the dun-colored Sandship, looking like some monstrous dromond that had washed ashore and turned to stone.

Only three leagues of coast road divided Sunspear from the Water Gardens, yet they were two different worlds. There children frolicked naked in the sun, music played in tiled courtyards, and the air was sharp with the smell of lemons and blood oranges. Here the air smelled of dust, sweat, and smoke, and the nights were alive with the babble of voices. In place of the pink marble of the Water Gardens, Sunspear was built from mud and straw, and colored brown and dun. The ancient stronghold of House Martell stood at the easternmost end of a little jut of stone and sand, surrounded on three sides by the sea. To the west, in the shadows of Sunspear's massive walls, mud-brick shops and windowless hovels clung to the castle like barnacles to a galley's hull. Stables and inns and winesinks and pillow houses had grown up west of those, many enclosed by walls of their own, and yet more hovels had risen beneath *those* walls. *And so and so and so, as the bearded priests would say.* Compared to Tyrosh or Myr or Great Norvos, the shadow city was no more than a town, yet it was the nearest thing to a true city that these Dornish had.

Lady Nym's arrival had preceded theirs by some hours, and no doubt she had warned the guards of their coming, for the Threefold Gate was open when they reached it. Only here were the gates lined up one behind the other to allow visitors to pass beneath all three of the Winding Walls directly to the Old Palace, without first making their way through miles of narrow alleys, hidden courts, and noisy bazaars.

Prince Doran had closed the draperies of his litter as soon as the Spear Tower came in sight, yet still the smallfolk shouted out to him as the litter passed. *The Sand Snakes have stirred them to a boil,* the captain thought uneasily. They crossed the squalor of the outer crescent and went through the second gate. Beyond, the wind stank of tar and salt water and rotting seaweed, and the crowd grew thicker with every step. "*Make way for Prince Doran!*" Areo Hotah boomed out, thumping the butt of his longaxe on the bricks. "*Make way for the Prince of Dorne!*"

"The prince is dead!" a woman shrilled behind him.

"To spears!" a man bellowed from a balcony.

"*Doran!*" called some highborn voice. "To the spears!"

Hotah gave up looking for the speakers; the press was too thick, and a third of them were shouting. "*To spears! Vengeance for the*

Viper!" By the time they reached the third gate, the guards were shoving people aside to clear a path for the prince's litter, and the crowd was throwing things. One ragged boy darted past the spearmen with a half-rotten pomegranate in one hand, but when he saw Areo Hotah in his path, with longaxe at the ready, he let the fruit fall unthrown and beat a quick retreat. Others farther back let fly with lemons, limes, and oranges, crying "*War! War! To the spears!*" One of the guards was hit in the eye with a lemon, and the captain himself had an orange splatter off his foot.

No answer came from within the litter. Doran Martell stayed cloaked within his silken walls until the thicker walls of the castle swallowed all of them, and the portcullis came down behind them with a rattling crunch. The sounds of shouting dwindled away slowly. Princess Arianne was waiting in the outer ward to greet her father, with half the court about her: the old blind seneschal Ricasso, Ser Manfrey Martell the castellan, young Maester Myles with his grey robes and silky perfumed beard, twoscore of Dornish knights in flowing linen of half a hundred hues. Little Myrcella Baratheon stood with her septa and Ser Arys of the Kingsguard, sweltering in his white-enameled scales.

Princess Arianne strode to the litter on snakeskin sandals laced up to her thighs. Her hair was a mane of jet-black ringlets that fell to the small of her back, and around her brow was a band of copper suns. *She is still a little thing,* the captain thought. Where the Sand Snakes were tall, Arianne took after her mother, who stood but five foot two. Yet beneath her jeweled girdle and loose layers of flowing purple silk and yellow samite she had a woman's body, lush and roundly curved. "Father," she announced as the curtains opened, "Sunspear rejoices at your return."

"Yes, I heard the joy." The prince smiled wanly and cupped his daughter's cheek with a reddened, swollen hand. "You look well. Captain, be so good as to help me down from here."

Hotah slid his longaxe into its sling across his back and gathered the prince into his arms, tenderly so as not to jar his swollen joints. Even so, Doran Martell bit back a gasp of pain.

"I have commanded the cooks to prepare a feast for this evening," Arianne said, "with all your favorite dishes."

"I fear I could not do them justice." The prince glanced slowly around the yard. "I do not see Tyene."

"She begs a private word. I sent her to the throne room to await your coming."

The prince sighed. "Very well. Captain? The sooner I am done with this, the sooner I may rest."

Hotah bore him up the long stone steps of the Tower of the Sun, to the great round chamber beneath the dome, where the last light of the afternoon was slanting down through thick windows of many-colored glass to dapple the pale marble with diamonds of half a hundred colors. There the third Sand Snake awaited them.

She was sitting cross-legged on a pillow beneath the raised dais where the high seats stood, but she rose as they entered, dressed in a clinging gown of pale blue samite with sleeves of Myrish lace that made her look as innocent as the Maid herself. In one hand was a piece of embroidery she had been working on, in the other a pair of golden needles. Her hair was gold as well, and her eyes were deep blue pools . . . and yet somehow they reminded the captain of her father's eyes, though Oberyn's had been as black as night. *All of Prince Oberyn's daughters have his viper eyes,* Hotah realized suddenly. *The color does not matter.*

"Uncle," said Tyene Sand, "I have been waiting for you."

"Captain, help me to the high seat."

There were two seats on the dais, near twin to one another, save that one had the Martell spear inlaid in gold upon its back, whilst the other bore the blazing Rhoynish sun that had flown from the masts of Nymeria's ships when first they came to Dorne. The captain placed the prince beneath the spear and stepped away.

"Does it hurt so much?" Lady Tyene's voice was gentle, and she looked as sweet as summer strawberries. Her mother had been a septa, and Tyene had an air of almost otherworldy innocence about her. "Is there aught that I might do to ease your pain?"

"Say what you would and let me rest. I am weary, Tyene."

"I made this for you, Uncle." Tyene unfolded the piece she'd been embroidering. It showed her father, Prince Oberyn, mounted on a sand steed and armored all in red, smiling. "When I finish, it is yours, to help you remember him."

"I am not like to forget your father."

"That is good to know. Many have wondered."

"Lord Tywin has promised us the Mountain's head."

"He is *so* kind . . . but a headsman's sword is no fit end for brave Ser Gregor. We have prayed so long for his death, it is only fair that he pray for it as well. I know the poison that my father used, and there is none slower or more agonizing. Soon we may hear the Mountain screaming, even here in Sunspear."

Prince Doran sighed. "Obara cries to me for war. Nym will be content with murder. And you?"

"War," said Tyene, "though not my sister's war. Dornishmen fight best at home, so I say let us hone our spears and wait. When the Lannisters and the Tyrells come down on us, we shall bleed them in the passes and bury them beneath the blowing sands, as we have a hundred times before."

"*If* they should come down on us."

"Oh, but they must, or see the realm riven once more, as it was before we wed the dragons. Father told me so. He said we had the Imp to thank, for sending us Princess Myrcella. She is so pretty, don't you think? I wish that I had curls like hers. She was made to be a queen, just like her mother." Dimples bloomed in Tyene's cheeks. "I would be honored to arrange the wedding, and to see to the making of the crowns as well. Trystane and Myrcella are so innocent, I thought perhaps white gold . . . with emeralds, to match Myrcella's eyes. Oh, diamonds and pearls would serve as well, so long as the children are wed and crowned. Then we need only hail Myrcella as the First of Her Name, Queen of the Andals, the Rhoynar, and the First Men, and lawful heir to the Seven Kingdoms of Westeros, and wait for the lions to come."

"The *lawful* heir?" The prince snorted.

"She is older than her brother," explained Tyene, as if he were some fool. "By law the Iron Throne should pass to her."

"By *Dornish* law."

"When good King Daeron wed Princess Myriah and brought us into his kingdom, it was agreed that Dornish law would always rule in Dorne. And *Myrcella* is in Dorne, as it happens."

"So she is." His tone was grudging. "Let me think on it."

Tyene grew cross. "You think too much, Uncle."

"Do I?"

"Father said so."

"Oberyn thought too little."

"Some men *think* because they are afraid to *do*."

"There is a difference between fear and caution."

"Oh, I must pray that I never see you *frightened*, Uncle. You might forget to breathe." She raised a hand . . .

The captain brought the butt of his longaxe down upon the marble with a thump. "My lady, you presume. Step from the dais, if it please you."

"I meant no harm, Captain. I love my uncle, as I know he loved my father." Tyene went to one knee before the prince. "I have said all I came to say, Uncle. Forgive me if I gave offense; my heart is broken all to pieces. Do I still have your love?"

"Always."

"Give me your blessing, then, and I shall go."

Doran hesitated half a heartbeat before placing his hand on his niece's head. "Be brave, child."

"Oh, how not? I am *his* daughter."

No sooner had she taken her leave than Maester Caleotte hurried to the dais. "My prince, she did not . . . here, let me see your hand." He examined the palm first, then gently turned it upside down to sniff at the back of the prince's fingers. "No, good. That is good. There are no scratches, so . . ."

The prince withdrew his hand. "Maester, could I trouble you for some milk of the poppy? A thimble cup will suffice."

"The poppy. Yes, to be sure."

"Now, I think," Doran Martell urged gently, and Caleotte scurried to the stairs.

Outside the sun had set. The light within the dome was the blue of dusk, and all the diamonds on the floor were dying. The prince sat in his high seat beneath the Martell spear, his face pale with pain. After a long silence he turned to Areo Hotah. "Captain," he said, "how loyal are my guards?"

"Loyal." The captain did not know what else to say.

"All of them? Or some?"

"They are good men. Good *Dornishmen*. They will do as I command." He thumped his longaxe on the floor. "I will bring the head of any man who would betray you."

"I want no heads. I want obedience."

"You have it." *Serve. Obey. Protect. Simple vows for a simple man.* "How many men are needed?"

"I will leave that for you to decide. It may be that a few good men will serve us better than a score. I want this done as quickly and as quietly as possible, with no blood spilled."

"Quick and quiet and bloodless, aye. What is your command?"

"You will find my brother's daughters, take them into custody, and confine them in the cells atop the Spear Tower."

"The Sand Snakes?" The captain's throat was dry. "All . . . all eight, my prince? The little ones, also?"

The prince considered. "Ellaria's girls are too young to be a danger, but there are those who might seek to use them against me. It would be best to keep them safe in hand. Yes, the little ones as well . . . but first secure Tyene, Nymeria, and Obara."

"As my prince commands." His heart was troubled. *My little princess will mislike this.* "What of Sarella? She is a woman grown, almost twenty."

"Unless she returns to Dorne, there's naught I can do about Sarella save pray that she shows more sense than her sisters. Leave her to her . . . game. Gather up the others. I shall not sleep until I know that they are safe and under guard."

"It will be done." The captain hesitated. "When this is known in the streets, the common folk will howl."

"All Dorne will howl," said Doran Martell in a tired voice. "I only pray Lord Tywin hears them in King's Landing, so he might know what a loyal friend he has in Sunspear."

CERSEI

She dreamt she sat the Iron Throne, high above them all.

The courtiers were brightly colored mice below. Great lords and proud ladies knelt before her. Bold young knights laid their swords at her feet and pleaded for her favors, and the queen smiled down at them. Until the dwarf appeared as if from nowhere, pointing at her and howling with laughter. The lords and ladies began to chuckle too, hiding their smiles behind their hands. Only then did the queen realize she was naked.

Horrified, she tried to cover herself with her hands. The barbs and blades of the Iron Throne bit into her flesh as she crouched to hide her shame. Blood ran red down her legs, as steel teeth gnawed at her buttocks. When she tried to stand, her foot slipped through a gap in the twisted metal. The more she struggled the more the throne engulfed her, tearing chunks of flesh from her breasts and belly, slicing at her arms and legs until they were slick and red, glistening.

And all the while her brother capered below, laughing.

His merriment still echoed in her ears when she felt a light touch on her shoulder, and woke suddenly. For half a heartbeat the hand seemed part of the nightmare, and Cersei cried out, but it was only Senelle. The maid's face was white and frightened.

We are not alone, the queen realized. Shadows loomed around her bed, tall shapes with chainmail glimmering beneath their cloaks. Armed men had no business here. *Where are my guards?* Her bedchamber was dark, but for the lantern one of the intruders held on high. *I must show no fear.* Cersei pushed back sleep-tousled hair, and said, "What do you want of me?" A man stepped into the lantern light, and she saw his cloak was white. "Jaime?" *I dreamt of one brother, but the other has come to wake me.*

"Your Grace." The voice was not her brother's. "The Lord Commander said come get you." His hair curled, as Jaime's did, but her brother's hair was beaten gold, like hers, where this man's was black and oily. She stared at him, confused, as he muttered about a privy and a crossbow, and said her father's name. *I am dreaming still,* Cersei thought. *I have not woken, nor has my nightmare ended. Tyrion will creep out from under the bed soon and begin to laugh at me.*

But that was folly. Her dwarf brother was down in the black cells, condemned to die this very day. She looked down at her hands, turning them over to make certain all her fingers were still there. When she ran a hand down her arm the skin was covered with gooseprickles, but unbroken. There were no cuts on her legs, no gashes on the soles of her feet. *A dream, that's all it was, a dream. I drank too much last night, these fears are only humors born of wine. I will be the one laughing, come dusk. My children will be safe, Tommen's throne will be secure, and my twisted little* valonqar *will be short a head and rotting.*

Jocelyn Swyft was at her elbow, pressing a cup on her. Cersei took a sip: water, mixed with lemon squeezings, so tart she spit it out. She could hear the night wind rattling the shutters, and she saw with a strange sharp clarity. Jocelyn was trembling like a leaf, as frightened as Senelle. Ser Osmund Kettleblack loomed over her. Behind him stood Ser Boros Blount, with a lantern. At the door were Lannister guardsmen with gilded lions shining on the crests of their helmets. They looked afraid as well. *Can it be?* the queen wondered. *Can it be true?*

She rose, and let Senelle slip a bedrobe over her shoulders to hide her nakedness. Cersei belted it herself, her fingers stiff and clumsy. "My lord father keeps guards about him, night and day," she said. Her tongue felt thick. She took another swallow of lemon water and sloshed it round her mouth to freshen her breath. A moth had gotten into the lantern Ser Boros was holding; she could hear it buzzing and see the shadow of its wings as it beat against the glass.

"The guards were at their posts, Your Grace," said Osmund Kettleblack. "We found a hidden door behind the hearth. A secret passage. The Lord Commander's gone down to see where it goes."

"Jaime?" Terror seized her, sudden as a storm. "Jaime should be with the *king*..."

"The lad's not been harmed. Ser Jaime sent a dozen men to look in on him. His Grace is sleeping peaceful."

Let him have a sweeter dream than mine, and a kinder waking. "Who is with the king?"

"Ser Loras has that honor, if it please you."

It did not please her. The Tyrells were only stewards that the dragon-kings had upjumped far above their station. Their vanity was exceeded only by their ambition. Ser Loras might be as pretty as a maiden's dream, but underneath his white cloak he was Tyrell to the bone. For all she knew, this night's foul fruit had been planted and nurtured in Highgarden.

But that was a suspicion she dare not speak aloud. "Allow me a moment to dress. Ser Osmund, you shall accompany me to the Tower of the Hand. Ser Boros, roust the gaolers and make certain the dwarf is still in his cell." She would not say his name. *He would never have found the courage to lift a hand against Father,* she told herself, but she had to be certain.

"As Your Grace commands." Blount surrendered the lantern to Ser Osmund. Cersei was not displeased to see the back of him. *Father should never have restored him to the white.* The man had proved himself a craven.

By the time they left Maegor's Holdfast, the sky had turned a deep cobalt blue, though the stars still shone. *All but one,* Cersei thought. *The bright star of the west has fallen, and the nights will be darker now.* She paused upon the drawbridge that spanned the dry moat, gazing down at the spikes below. *They would not dare lie to me about such a thing.* "Who found him?"

"One of his guards," said Ser Osmund. "Lum. He felt a call of nature, and found his lordship in the privy."

No, that cannot be. That is not the way a lion dies. The queen felt strangely calm. She remembered the first time she had lost a tooth, when she was just a little girl. It hadn't hurt, but the hole in her mouth felt so odd she could not stop touching it with her tongue. *Now there is a hole in the world where Father stood, and holes want filling.*

If Tywin Lannister was truly dead, no one was safe ... least of all her son upon his throne. When the lion falls the lesser beasts move in: the jackals and the vultures and the feral dogs. They would try to push her aside, as they always had. She would need to move quickly, as she had when Robert died. This might be the work of Stannis Baratheon, through some catspaw. It could well be the prelude to another attack upon the city. She hoped it was. *Let him come. I will smash him, just as Father did, and this time he will die.* Stannis did not frighten her, no more than Mace Tyrell did. No one frightened her. She was a daughter of the Rock, a lion. *There will be no more talk of forcing me to wed again.* Casterly Rock was hers now, and all the power of House Lannister. No one would ever disregard her again. Even when Tommen had no further need of a regent, the Lady of Casterly Rock would remain a power in the land.

The rising sun had painted the tower tops a vivid red, but beneath the walls the night still huddled. The outer castle was so hushed that she could have believed all its people dead. *They should be. It is not fitting for Tywin Lannister to die alone. Such a man deserves a retinue to attend his needs in hell.*

Four spearmen in red cloaks and lion-crested helms were posted at the door of the Tower of the Hand. "No one is to enter or leave without my permission," she told them. The command came easily to her. *My father had steel in his voice as well.*

Within the tower, the smoke from the torches irritated her eyes, but Cersei did not weep, no more than her father would have. *I am the only true son he ever had.* Her heels scraped against the stone as she climbed, and she could still hear the moth fluttering wildly inside Ser Osmund's lantern. *Die,* the queen thought at it, in irritation, *fly into the flame and be done with it.*

Two more red-cloaked guardsmen stood atop the steps. Red Lester muttered a condolence as she passed. The queen's breath was coming fast and short, and she could feel her heart fluttering in her chest.

The steps, she told herself, *this cursed tower has too many steps.* She had half a mind to tear it down.

The hall was full of fools speaking in whispers, as if Lord Tywin were asleep and they were afraid to wake him. Guards and servants alike shrank back before her, mouths flapping. She saw their pink gums and waggling tongues, but their words made no more sense than the buzzing of the moth. *What are they doing here? How did they know?* By rights they should have called her first. She was the Queen Regent, had they forgotten that?

Before the Hand's bedchamber stood Ser Meryn Trant in his white armor and cloak. The visor of his helm was open, and the bags beneath his eyes made him look still half-asleep. "Clear these people away," Cersei told him. "Is my father in the privy?"

"They carried him back to his bed, m'lady." Ser Meryn pushed the door open for her to enter.

Morning light slashed through the shutters to paint golden bars upon the rushes strewn across the floor of the bedchamber. Her uncle Kevan was on his knees beside the bed, trying to pray, but he could scarcely get the words out. Guardsmen clustered near the hearth. The secret door that Ser Osmund had spoken of gaped open behind the ashes, no bigger than an oven. A man would need to crawl. *But Tyrion is only half a man.* The thought made her angry. *No, the dwarf is locked in a black cell.* This could not be his work. *Stannis,* she told herself, *Stannis was behind it. He still has adherents in the city. Him, or the Tyrells . . .*

There had always been talk of secret passages within the Red Keep. Maegor the Cruel was supposed to have killed the men who built the castle to keep the knowledge of them secret. *How many other bedchambers have hidden doors?* Cersei had a sudden vision of the dwarf crawling out from behind a tapestry in Tommen's bedchamber with blade in hand. *Tommen is well guarded,* she told herself. But Lord Tywin had been well guarded too.

For a moment, she did not recognize the dead man. He had hair like her father, yes, but this was some other man, surely, a smaller man, and much older. His bedrobe was hiked up around his chest, leaving him naked below the waist. The quarrel had taken him in his groin between his navel and his manhood, and was sunk so deep that only the fletching showed. His pubic hair was stiff with dried blood. More was congealing in his navel.

The smell of him made her wrinkle her nose. "Take the quarrel out of him," she commanded. "This is the King's Hand!" *And my father. My lord father. Should I scream and tear my hair?* They said Catelyn Stark had clawed her own face to bloody ribbons when the Freys slew her precious Robb. *Would you like that, Father?* she wanted to ask him. *Or would you want me to be strong? Did you weep for your own father?* Her grandfather had died when she was only a year old, but she knew the story. Lord Tytos had grown very fat, and his heart burst one day when he was climbing the steps to his mistress. Her father was off in King's Landing when it happened, serving as the Mad King's Hand. Lord Tywin was often away in King's Landing when she and Jaime were young. If he wept when they brought him word of his father's death, he did it where no one could see the tears.

The queen could feel her nails digging into her palms. "How could you leave him like this? My father was Hand to three kings, as great a man as ever strode the Seven Kingdoms. The bells must ring for him, as they rang for Robert. He must be bathed and dressed as befits his stature, in ermine and cloth-of-gold and crimson silk. Where is Pycelle? *Where is Pycelle?*" She turned to the guardsmen. "Puckens, bring Grand Maester Pycelle. He must see to Lord Tywin."

"He's seen him, Your Grace," said Puckens. "He came and saw and went, to summon the silent sisters."

They sent for me last. The realization made her almost too angry for words. *And Pycelle runs off to send a message rather than soil his soft, wrinkled hands. The man is useless.* "Find Maester Ballabar," she commanded. "Find Maester Frenken. Any of them." Puckens and Shortear ran to obey. "Where is my brother?"

"Down the tunnel. There's a shaft, with iron rungs set in the stone. Ser Jaime went to see how deep it goes."

He has only one hand, she wanted to shout at them. *One of you should have gone. He has no business climbing ladders. The men who murdered Father might be down there, waiting for him.* Her twin had always been too rash, and it would seem that even losing a hand had not taught him caution. She was about to command the guards to go down after him and bring him back when Puckens and Shortear returned with a grey-haired man between them. "Your Grace," said Shortear, "this here claims he was a maester."

The man bowed low. "How may I serve Your Grace?"

His face was vaguely familiar, though Cersei could not place him. *Old, but not so old as Pycelle. This one has some strength in him still.* He was tall, though slightly stooped, with crinkles around his bold blue eyes. *His throat is naked.* "You wear no maester's chain."

"It was taken from me. My name is Qyburn, if it please Your Grace. I treated your brother's hand."

"His stump, you mean." She remembered him now. He had come with Jaime from Harrenhal.

"I could not save Ser Jaime's hand, it is true. My arts saved his arm, however, mayhaps his very life. The Citadel took my chain, but they could not take my knowledge."

"You may suffice," she decided. "If you fail me you will lose more than a chain, I promise you. Remove the quarrel from my father's belly and make him ready for the silent sisters."

"As my queen commands." Qyburn went to the bedside, paused, looked back. "And how shall I deal with the girl, Your Grace?"

"Girl?" Cersei had overlooked the second body. She strode to the bed, flung aside the heap of bloody coverlets, and there she was, naked, cold, and pink . . . save for her face, which had turned as black as Joff's had at his wedding feast. A chain of linked golden hands was half-buried in the flesh of her throat, twisted so tight that it had broken the skin. Cersei hissed like an angry cat. "What is *she* doing here?"

"We found her there, Your Grace," said Shortear. "It's the Imp's whore." As if that explained why she was here.

My lord father had no use for whores, she thought. *After our mother died he never touched a woman.* She gave the guardsman a chilly look. "This is not . . . when Lord Tywin's father died he returned to Casterly Rock to find a . . . a woman of this sort . . . bedecked in his lady mother's jewels, wearing one of her gowns. He stripped them off her, and all else as well. For a fortnight she was paraded naked through the streets of Lannisport, to confess to every man she met that she was a thief and a harlot. That was how Lord Tywin Lannister dealt with whores. He never ... this woman was here for some other purpose, not for ..."

"Perhaps his lordship was questioning the girl about her mistress," Qyburn suggested. "Sansa Stark vanished the night the king was murdered, I have heard."

"That's so." Cersei seized on the suggestion eagerly. "He was questioning her, to be sure. There can be no doubt." She could see Tyrion leering, his mouth twisted into a monkey's grin beneath the ruin of his nose. *And what better way to question her than naked, with her legs well spread?* the dwarf whispered. *That's how I like to question her too.*

The queen turned away. *I will not look at her.* Suddenly it was too much even to be in the same room as the dead woman. She pushed past Qyburn, out into the hall.

Ser Osmund had been joined by his brothers Osney and Osfryd. "There is a dead woman in the Hand's bedchamber," Cersei told the three Kettleblacks. "No one is ever to know that she was here."

"Aye, m'lady." Ser Osney had faint scratches on his cheek where another of Tyrion's whores had clawed him. "And what shall we do with her?"

"Feed her to your dogs. Keep her for a bedmate. What do I care? *She was never here.* I'll have the tongue of any man who dares to say she was. Do you understand me?"

Osney and Osfryd exchanged a look. "Aye, Your Grace."

She followed them back inside and watched as they bundled the girl up in her father's bloody blankets. *Shae, her name was Shae.* They had last spoken the night before the dwarf's trial by combat, after that smiling Dornish snake offered to champion him. Shae had been asking about some jewels Tyrion had given her, and certain promises Cersei might have made, a manse in the city and a knight to marry her. The queen made it plain that the whore would have nothing of her until she told them where Sansa Stark had gone. "You were her maid. Do you expect me to believe that you knew nothing of her plans?" she had said. Shae left in tears.

Ser Osfryd slung the bundled corpse up over his shoulder. "I want that chain," Cersei said. "See that you do not scratch the gold." Osfryd nodded and started toward the door. "No, not through the yard." She gestured toward the secret passage. "There's a shaft down to the dungeons. That way."

As Ser Osfryd went down on one knee before the hearth, the light brightened within, and the queen heard noises. Jaime emerged bent over like an old woman, his boots kicking up puffs of soot from Lord Tywin's last fire. "Get out of my way," he told the Kettleblacks.

Cersei rushed toward him. "Did you find them? Did you find the killers? How many were there?" Surely there had been more than one. One man alone could not have killed her father.

Her twin's face had a haggard look. "The shaft goes down to a chamber where half a dozen tunnels meet. They're closed off by iron gates, chained and locked. I need to find keys." He glanced around the bedchamber. "Whoever did this might still be lurking in the walls. It's a maze back there, and dark."

She imagined Tyrion creeping between the walls like some monstrous rat. *No. You are being silly. The dwarf is in his cell.* "Take hammers to the walls. Knock this tower down, if you must. I want them found. Whoever did this. I want them killed."

Jaime hugged her, his good hand pressing against the small of her back. He smelled of ash, but the morning sun was in his hair, giving it a golden glow. She wanted to draw his face to hers for a kiss. *Later,* she told herself, *later he will come to me, for comfort.* "We are his heirs, Jaime," she whispered. "It will be up to us to finish his work. You must take Father's place as Hand. You see that now, surely. Tommen will need you . . ."

He pushed away from her and raised his arm, forcing his stump into her face. "A Hand without a hand? A bad jape, sister. Don't ask me to rule."

Their uncle heard the rebuff. Qyburn as well, and the Kettleblacks, wrestling their bundle through the ashes. Even the guardsmen heard, Puckens and Hoke the Horseleg and Shortear. *It will be all over the castle by nightfall.* Cersei felt the heat rising up her cheeks. "Rule? I said naught of ruling. I shall rule until my son comes of age."

"I don't know who I pity more," her brother said. "Tommen, or the Seven Kingdoms."

She slapped him. Jaime's arm rose to catch the blow, cat-quick . . . but this cat had a cripple's stump in place of a right hand. Her fingers left red marks on his cheek.

The sound brought their uncle to his feet. "Your father lies here *dead*. Have the decency to take your quarrel outside."

Jaime inclined his head in apology. "Forgive us, Uncle. My sister is sick with grief. She forgets herself."

She wanted to slap him again for that. *I must have been mad to think he could be Hand.* She would sooner abolish the office. When had a Hand ever brought her anything but grief? Jon Arryn put Robert Baratheon in her bed, and before he died he'd begun sniffing about her and Jaime as well. Eddard Stark took up right where Arryn had left off; his meddling had forced her to rid herself of Robert sooner than she would have liked, before she could deal with his pestilential brothers. Tyrion sold Myrcella to the Dornishmen, made one of her sons his hostage, and murdered the other. And when Lord Tywin returned to King's Landing . . .

The next Hand will know his place, she promised herself. It would have to be Ser Kevan. Her uncle was tireless, prudent, unfailingly obedient. She could rely on him, as her father had. *The hand does not argue with the head.* She had a realm to rule, but she would need new men to help her rule it. Pycelle was a doddering lickspittle, Jaime had lost his courage with his sword hand, and Mace Tyrell and his cronies Redwyne and Rowan could not be trusted. For all she knew they might have had a part in this. Lord Tyrell had to know that he would never rule the Seven Kingdoms so long as Tywin Lannister lived.

I will need to move carefully with that one. The city was full of his men, and he'd even managed to plant one of his sons in the Kingsguard, and meant to plant his daughter in Tommen's bed. It still made her furious to think that Father had agreed to betroth Tommen to Margaery Tyrell. *The girl is twice his age and twice widowed.* Mace Tyrell claimed his daughter was still virgin, but Cersei had her doubts. Joffrey had been murdered before he could bed the girl, but she had been wed to Renly first . . . *A man may prefer the taste of hippocras, yet if you set a tankard of ale before him, he will quaff it quick enough.* She must command Lord Varys to find out what he could.

That stopped her where she stood. She had forgotten about Varys. *He should be here. He is always here.* Whenever anything of import happened in the Red Keep, the eunuch appeared as if from nowhere. *Jaime is here, and Uncle Kevan, and Pycelle has come and gone, but not Varys.* A cold finger touched her spine. *He was part of this. He must have feared that Father meant to have his head, so he struck first.* Lord Tywin had never had any love for the simpering master of whisperers. And if any man knew the Red Keep's secrets, it was surely the master of whisperers. *He must have made common cause with Lord Stannis. They served together on Robert's council, after all . . .*

Cersei strode to the door of the bedchamber, to Ser Meryn Trant. "Trant, bring me Lord Varys. Squealing and squirming if need be, but unharmed."

"As Your Grace commands."

But no sooner had one Kingsguard departed than another one returned. Ser Boros Blount was red-faced and puffing from his headlong rush up the steps. "Gone," he panted, when he saw the queen. He sank to one knee. "The Imp . . . his cell's open, Your Grace . . . no sign of him anywhere . . ."

The dream was true. "I gave orders," she said. "He was to be kept under guard, night and day . . ."

Blount's chest was heaving. "One of the gaolers has gone missing too. Rugen, his name was. Two other men we found asleep."

It was all she could do not to scream. "I hope you did not wake them, Ser Boros. Let them sleep."

"Sleep?" He looked up, jowly and confused. "Aye, Your Grace. How long shall—"

"Forever. See that they sleep forever, ser. I will not suffer guards to sleep on watch." *He is in the walls. He killed Father as he killed Mother, as he killed Joff.* The dwarf would come for her as well, the queen knew, just as the old woman had promised her in the dimness of that tent. *I laughed in her face, but she had powers. I saw my future in a drop of blood. My doom.* Her legs were weak as water. Ser Boros tried to take her by the arm, but the queen recoiled from his touch. For all she knew he might be one of Tyrion's creatures. "Get away from me," she said. *"Get away!"* She staggered to a settle.

"Your Grace?" said Blount. "Shall I fetch a cup of water?"

It is blood I need, not water. Tyrion's blood, the blood of the valonqar. The torches spun around her. Cersei closed her eyes, and saw the dwarf grinning at her. *No,* she thought, *no, I was almost rid of you.* But his fingers had closed around her neck, and she could feel them beginning to tighten.

BRIENNE

"Iam looking for a maid of three-and-ten," she told the grey-haired goodwife beside the village well. "A highborn maid and very beautiful, with blue eyes and auburn hair. She may have been traveling with a portly knight of forty years, or perhaps with a fool. Have you seen her?"

"Not as I recall, ser," the goodwife said, knuckling her forehead. "But I'll keep my eye out, that I will."

The blacksmith had not seen her either, nor the septon in the village sept, the swineherd with his pigs, the girl pulling up onions from her garden, nor any of the other simple folk that the Maid of Tarth found amongst the daub-and-wattle huts of Rosby. Still, she persisted. *This is the shortest road to Duskendale,* Brienne told herself. *If Sansa came this way, someone must have seen her.* At the castle gates she posed her question to two spearmen whose badges showed three red chevronels on ermine, the arms of House Rosby. "If she's on the roads these days she won't be no maid for long," said the older man. The younger wanted to know if the girl had that auburn hair between her legs as well.

I will find no help here. As Brienne mounted up again, she glimpsed a skinny boy atop a piebald horse at the far end of the village. *I have not talked with that one,* she thought, but he vanished behind the sept before she could seek him out. She did not trouble to chase after him. Most like he knew no more than the others had. Rosby was scarce more than a wide place in the road; Sansa would have had no reason to linger here. Returning to the road, Brienne headed north and east past apple orchards and fields of barley, and soon left the village and its castle well behind. It was at Duskendale that she would find her quarry, she told herself. *If she came this way at all.*

"I will find the girl and keep her safe," Brienne had promised Ser Jaime, back at King's Landing. "For her lady mother's sake. And for yours." Noble words, but words were easy. Deeds were hard. She had lingered too long and learned too little in the city. *I should have set out earlier . . . but to where?* Sansa Stark had vanished on the night King Joffrey died, and if anyone had seen her since, or had any inkling where she might have gone, they were not talking. *Not to me, at least.*

Brienne believed the girl had left the city. If she were still in King's Landing, the gold cloaks would have turned her up. She had to have gone elsewhere . . . but elsewhere is a big place. *If I were a maiden newly flowered, alone and afraid, in desperate danger, what would I do?* she had asked herself. *Where would I go?* For her, the answer came easy. She would make her way back to Tarth, to her father. Sansa's father had been beheaded whilst she watched, however. Her lady mother was dead too, murdered at the Twins, and Winterfell, the great Stark stronghold, had been sacked and burned, its people put to the sword. *She has no home to run to, no father, no mother, no brothers.* She might be in the next town, or on a ship to Asshai; one seemed as likely as the other.

Even if Sansa Stark had wanted to go home, how would she get there? The kingsroad was not safe; even a child would know that. The ironborn held Moat Cailin athwart the Neck, and at the Twins sat the Freys, who had murdered Sansa's brother and lady mother. The girl could go by sea if she had the coin, but the harbor at King's Landing was still in ruins, the river a jumble of broken quays and burned and sunken galleys. Brienne had asked along the docks, but no one could remember a ship leaving on the night King Joffrey died. A few trading ships were anchoring in the bay and off-loading by boat, one man told her, but more were continuing up the coast to Duskendale, where the port was busier than ever.

Brienne's mare was sweet to look upon and kept a pretty pace.

There were more travelers than she would have thought. Begging brothers trundled by with their bowls dangling on thongs about their necks. A young septon galloped past upon a palfrey as fine as any lord's, and later she met a band of silent sisters who shook their heads when Brienne put her question to them. A train of oxcarts lumbered south with grain and sacks of wool, and later she passed a swineherd driving pigs, and an old woman in a horse litter with an escort of mounted guards. She asked all of them if they had seen a highborn girl of three-and-ten years with blue eyes and auburn hair. None had. She asked about the road ahead as well. "'Twixt here and Duskendale is safe enough," one man told her, "but past Duskendale there's outlaws, and broken men in the woods."

Only the soldier pines and sentinels still showed green; the broad-leaf trees had donned mantles of russet and gold, or else uncloaked themselves to scratch against the sky with branches brown and bare. Every gust of wind drove swirling clouds of dead leaves across the rutted road. They made a rustling sound as they scuttled past the hooves of the big bay mare that Jaime Lannister had bestowed on her. *As easy to find one leaf in the wind as one girl lost in Westeros.* She found herself wondering whether Jaime had given her this task as some cruel jape. Perhaps Sansa Stark was dead, beheaded for her part in King Joffrey's death, buried in some unmarked grave. How better to conceal her murder than by sending some big stupid wench from Tarth to find her?

Jaime would not do that. He was sincere. He gave me the sword, and called it Oathkeeper. Anyway, it made no matter. She had promised Lady Catelyn that she would bring back her daughters, and no promise was as solemn as one sworn to the dead. The younger girl was long dead, Jaime claimed; the Arya the Lannisters sent north to marry Roose Bolton's bastard was a fraud. That left only Sansa. Brienne had to find her.

Near dusk she saw a campfire burning by a brook. Two men sat beside it grilling trout, their arms and armor stacked beneath a tree. One was old and one was somewhat younger, though far from young. The younger rose to greet her. He had a big belly straining at the laces of his spotted doeskin jerkin. A shaggy untrimmed beard covered his cheeks and chin, the color of old gold. "We have trout enough for three, ser," he called out.

It was not the first time Brienne had been mistaken for a man. She pulled off her greathelm, letting her hair spill free. It was yellow, the color of dirty straw, and near as brittle. Long and thin, it blew about her shoulders. "I thank you, ser."

The hedge knight squinted at her so earnestly that she realized he must be nearsighted. "A lady, is it? Armed and armored? Illy, gods be good, the *size* of her."

"I took her for a knight as well," the older knight said, turning the trout.

Had Brienne been a man, she would have been called big; for a woman, she was huge. *Freakish* was the word she had heard all her life. She was broad in the shoulder and broader in the hips. Her legs were long, her arms thick. Her chest was more muscle than bosom. Her hands were big, her feet enormous. And she was ugly besides, with a freckled, horsey face and teeth that seemed almost too big for her mouth. She did not need to be reminded of any of that. "Sers," she said, "have you seen a maid of three-and-ten upon the road? She has blue eyes and auburn hair, and may have been in company with a portly red-faced man of forty years."

The nearsighted hedge knight scratched his head. "I recall no such maid. What sort of hair is auburn?"

"Browny red," said the older man. "No, we saw her not."

"We saw her not, m'lady," the younger told her. "Come, dismount, the fish is almost done. Are you hungry?"

She was, as it happened, but she was wary as well. Hedge knights had an unsavory reputation. "A hedge knight and a robber knight are two sides of the same sword," it was said. *These two do not look too dangerous.* "Might I know your names, sers?"

"I have the honor to be Ser Creighton Longbough, of whom the singers sing," said the big-bellied one. "You will have heard of my deeds on the Blackwater, mayhaps. My companion is Ser Illifer the Penniless."

If there was a song about Creighton Longbough, it was not one Brienne had heard. Their names meant no more to her than did their arms. Ser Creighton's green shield showed only a brown chief, and a deep gouge made by some battle-axe. Ser Illifer bore gold and ermine gyronny, though everything about him suggested that painted gold and painted ermine were the only sorts he'd ever known. He was sixty if he was a day, his face pinched and narrow beneath the hood of a patched roughspun mantle. Mail-clad he went, but flecks of rust spotted the iron like freckles. Brienne stood a head taller than either of them, and was better mounted and better armed in the bargain. *If I fear the likes of these, I had as well swap my longsword for a pair of knitting needles.*

"I thank you, good sers," she said. "I will gladly share your trout." Swinging down, Brienne unsaddled her mare and watered her before hobbling her to graze. She stacked her arms and shield and saddle-bags beneath an elm. By then the trout was crisply done. Ser Creighton brought her a fish, and she sat cross-legged on the ground to eat it.

"We are bound for Duskendale, m'lady," Longbough told her, as he pulled apart his own trout with his fingers. "You would do well to ride with us. The roads are perilous."

Brienne could have told him more about the perils of the roads than he might have cared to know. "I thank you, ser, but I have no need of your protection."

"I insist. A true knight must defend the gentler sex."

She touched her sword hilt. "This will defend me, ser."

"A sword is only as good as the man who wields it."

"I wield it well enough."

"As you will. It would not be courteous to argue with a lady. We will see you safe to Duskendale. Three together may ride more safely than one alone."

We were three when we set out from Riverrun, yet Jaime lost his hand and Cleos Frey his life. "Your mounts could not keep up with mine." Ser Creighton's brown gelding was an old swaybacked creature with rheumy eyes, and Ser Illifer's horse looked weedy and half-starved.

"My steed served me well enough on the Blackwater," Ser Creighton insisted. "Why, I did great carnage there and won a dozen ransoms. Was m'lady familiar with Ser Herbert Bolling? You shall never meet him now. I slew him where he stood. When swords clash, you shall ne'er find Ser Creighton Longbough to the rear."

His companion gave a dry chuckle. "Creigh, leave off. The likes o' her has no need for the likes o' us."

"The likes of me?" Brienne was uncertain what he meant.

Ser Illifer crooked a bony finger at her shield. Though its paint was cracked and peeling, the device it bore showed plain: a black bat on a field divided bendwise, silver and gold. "You bear a liar's shield, to which you have no right. My grandfather's grandfather helped kill the last o' Lothston. None since has dared to show that bat, black as the deeds of them that bore it."

The shield was the one Ser Jaime had taken from the armory at Harrenhal. Brienne had found it in the stables with her mare, along with much else; saddle and bridle, chainmail hauberk and visored greathelm, purses of gold and silver and a parchment more valuable than either. "I lost mine own shield," she explained.

"A true knight is the only shield a maiden needs," declared Ser Creighton stoutly.

Ser Illifer paid him no mind. "A barefoot man looks for a boot, a chilly man a cloak. But who would cloak themselves in shame? Lord Lucas bore that bat, the Pander, and Manfryd o' the Black Hood, his son. Why wear such arms, I ask myself, unless your own sin is fouler still . . . and *fresher*." He unsheathed his dagger, an ugly piece of cheap iron. "A woman freakish big and freakish strong who hides her own true colors. Creigh, behold the Maid o' Tarth, who opened Renly's royal throat for him."

"That is a lie." Renly Baratheon had been more than a king to her. She had loved him since first he came to Tarth on his leisurely lord's progress, to mark his coming of age. Her father welcomed him with a feast and commanded her to attend; elsewise she would have hidden in her room like some wounded beast. She had been no older than Sansa, more afraid of sniggers than of swords. *They will know about the rose,* she told Lord Selwyn, *they will laugh at me.* But the Evenstar would not relent.

And Renly Baratheon had shown her every courtesy, as if she were a proper maid, and pretty. He even danced with her, and in his arms she'd felt graceful, and her feet had floated across the floor. Later others begged a dance of her, because of his example. From that day forth, she wanted only to be close to Lord Renly, to serve him and protect him. But in the end she failed him. *Renly died in my arms, but I did not kill him*, she thought, but these hedge knights would never understand. "I would have given my life for King Renly, and died happy," she said. "I did no harm to him. I swear it by my sword."

"A knight swears by his sword," Ser Creighton said.

"Swear it by the Seven," urged Ser Illifer the Penniless.

"By the Seven, then. I did no harm to King Renly. I swear it by the Mother. May I never know her mercy if I lie. I swear it by the Father, and ask that he might judge me justly. I swear it by the Maiden and Crone, by the Smith and the Warrior. And I swear it by the Stranger, may he take me now if I am false."

"She swears well, for a maid," Ser Creighton allowed.

"Aye." Ser Illifer the Penniless gave a shrug. "Well, if she's lied, the gods will sort her out." He slipped his dagger back away. "The first watch is yours."

As the hedge knights slept, Brienne paced restlessly around the little camp, listening to the crackle of the fire. *I should ride on whilst I can.* She did not know these men, yet she could not bring herself to leave them undefended. Even in the black of night, there were riders on the road, and noises in the woods that might or might not have been owls and prowling foxes. So Brienne paced, and kept her blade loose in its scabbard.

Her watch was easy, all in all. It was *after* that was hard, when Ser Illifer woke and said he would relieve her. Brienne spread a blanket on the ground, and curled up to close her eyes. *I will not sleep,* she told herself, bone weary though she was. She had never slept easily in the presence of men. Even in Lord Renly's camps, the risk of rape was always there. It was a lesson she had learned beneath the walls of Highgarden, and again when she and Jaime had fallen into the hands of the Brave Companions.

The cold in the earth seeped through Brienne's blankets to soak into her bones. Before long every muscle felt clenched and cramped, from her jaw down to her toes. She wondered whether Sansa Stark was cold as well, wherever she might be. Lady Catelyn had said that Sansa was a gentle soul who loved lemon cakes, silken gowns, and songs of chivalry, yet the girl had seen her father's head lopped off and been forced to marry one of his killers afterward. If half the tales were true, the dwarf was the cruelest Lannister of all. *If she did poison King Joffrey, the Imp surely forced her hand. She was alone and friendless at that court.* In King's Landing, Brienne had hunted down a certain Brella, who had been one of Sansa's maids. The woman told her that there was little warmth between Sansa and the dwarf. Perhaps she had been fleeing him as well as Joffrey's murder.

Whatever dreams Brienne dreamed were gone when dawn awoke her. Her legs were stiff as wood from the cold ground, but no one had molested her, and her goods remained untouched. The hedge knights were up and about. Ser Illifer was cutting up a squirrel for breakfast, while Ser Creighton stood facing a tree, having himself a good long piss. *Hedge knights,* she thought, *old and vain and plump and nearsighted, yet decent men for all that.* It cheered her to know that there were still decent men in the world.

They broke their fast on roast squirrel, acorn paste, and pickles, whilst Ser Creighton regaled her with his exploits on the Blackwater, where he had slain a dozen fearsome knights that she had never heard of. "Oh, it was a rare fight, m'lady," he said, "a rare and bloody fray." He allowed that Ser Illifer had fought nobly in the battle as well. Illifer himself said little.

When time came to resume their journey, the knights fell in on either side of her, like guards protecting some great lady . . . though this lady dwarfed both of her protectors and was better armed and armored in the nonce. "Did anyone pass by during your watches?" Brienne asked them.

"Such as a maid of three-and-ten, with auburn hair?" said Ser Illifer the Penniless. "No, my lady. No one."

"I had a few," Ser Creighton put in. "Some farm boy on a piebald horse went by, and an hour later half a dozen men afoot with staves and scythes. They caught sight of our fire, and stopped for a long look at our horses, but I showed them a glimpse of my steel and told them to be along their way. Rough fellows, by the look o' them, and desperate too, but ne'er so desperate as to trifle with Ser Creighton Longbough."

No, Brienne thought, *not so desperate as that.* She turned away to hide her smile. Thankfully, Ser Creighton was too intent on the tale of his epic battle with the Knight of the Red Chicken to make note of the maiden's mirth. It felt good to have companions on the road, even such companions as these two.

It was midday when Brienne heard chanting drifting through the bare brown trees. "What is that sound?" Ser Creighton asked.

"Voices, raised in prayer." Brienne knew the chant. *They are beseeching the Warrior for protection, asking the Crone to light their way.*

Ser Illifer the Penniless bared his battered blade and reined in his horse to wait their coming. "They are close now."

The chanting filled the woods like pious thunder. And suddenly the source of the sound appeared in the road ahead. A group of begging brothers led the way, scruffy bearded men in roughspun robes, some barefoot and some in sandals. Behind them marched threescore ragged men, women, and children, a spotted sow, and several sheep. Several of the men had axes, and more had crude wooden clubs and cudgels. In their midst there rolled a two-wheeled wayn of grey and splintered wood, piled high with skulls and broken bits of bone. When they saw the hedge knights, the begging brothers halted, and the chanting died away. "Good knights," one said, "the Mother loves you."

"And you, brother," said Ser Illifer. "Who are you?"

"Poor fellows," said a big man with an axe. Despite the chill of the autumnal wood, he was shirtless, and on his breast was carved a seven-pointed star. Andal warriors had carved such stars in their flesh when first they crossed the narrow sea to overwhelm the kingdoms of the First Men.

"We are marching to the city," said a tall woman in the traces of the wayn, "to bring these holy bones to Blessed Baelor, and seek succor and protection from the king."

"Join us, friends," urged a spare small man in a threadbare septon's robe, who wore a crystal on a thong about his neck. "Westeros has need of every sword."

"We were bound for Duskendale," declared Ser Creighton, "but mayhaps we could see you safely to King's Landing."

"If you have the coin to pay us for this escort," added Ser Illifer, who seemed practical as well as penniless.

"Sparrows need no gold," the septon said.

Ser Creighton was lost. "Sparrows?"

"The sparrow is the humblest and most common of birds, as we are the humblest and most common of men." The septon had a lean sharp face and a short beard, grizzled grey and brown. His thin hair was pulled back and knotted behind his head, and his feet were bare and black, gnarled and hard as tree roots. "These are the bones of holy men, murdered for their faith. They served the Seven even unto death. Some starved, some were tortured. Septs have been despoiled, maidens and mothers raped by godless men and demon worshipers. Even silent sisters have been molested. Our Mother Above cries out in her anguish. It is time for all anointed knights to forsake their worldly masters and defend our Holy Faith. Come with us to the city, if you love the Seven."

"I love them well enough," said Illifer, "yet I must eat."

"So must all the Mother's children."

"We are bound for Duskendale," Ser Illifer said flatly.

One of the begging brothers spat, and a woman gave a moan. "You are false knights," said the big man with the star carved on his chest. Several others brandished their cudgels.

The barefoot septon calmed them with a word. "Judge not, for judgment is the Father's. Let them pass in peace. They are poor fellows too, lost upon the earth."

Brienne edged her mare forward. "My sister is lost as well. A girl of three-and-ten with auburn hair, fair to look upon."

"All the Mother's children are fair to look upon. May the Maiden watch over this poor girl . . . and you as well, I think." The septon lifted one of the traces of the wayn upon his shoulder, and began to pull. The begging brothers took up the chant once more. Brienne and the hedge knights sat upon their horses as the procession moved slowly past, following the rutted road toward Rosby. The sound of their chanting slowly dwindled away and died.

Ser Creighton lifted one cheek off the saddle to scratch his arse. "What sort of man would slay a holy septon?"

Brienne knew what sort. Near Maidenpool, she recalled, the Brave Companions had strung a septon up by his heels from the limb of a tree and used his corpse for archery practice. She wondered if his bones were piled in that wayn with all the rest.

"A man would need to be a fool to rape a silent sister," Ser Creighton was saying. "Even to lay hands upon one . . . it's said they are the Stranger's wives, and their female parts are cold and wet as ice." He glanced at Brienne. "Uh . . . beg pardon."

Brienne spurred her mare toward Duskendale. After a moment, Ser Illifer followed, and Ser Creighton came bringing up the rear.

Three hours later, they came up upon another party struggling toward Duskendale; a merchant and his serving men, accompanied by yet another hedge knight. The merchant rode a dappled grey mare, whilst his servants took turns pulling his wagon. Four labored in the traces as the other two walked beside the wheels, but when they heard the sound of horses they formed up around the wagon with quarterstaffs of ash at the ready. The merchant produced a crossbow, the knight a blade. "You will forgive me if I am suspicious," called the merchant, "but the times are troubled, and I have only good Ser Shadrich to defend me. Who are you?"

"Why," Ser Creighton said, affronted, "I am the famous Ser Creighton Longbough, fresh from battle on the Blackwater, and this is my companion, Ser Illifer the Penniless."

"We mean you no harm," said Brienne.

The merchant considered her doubtfully. "My lady, you should be safe at home. Why do you wear such unnatural garb?"

"I am searching for my sister." She dared not mention Sansa's name, with her accused of regicide. "She is a highborn maid and beautiful, with blue eyes and auburn hair. Perhaps you saw her with a portly knight of forty years, or a drunken fool."

"The roads are full of drunken fools and despoiled maidens. As to portly knights, it is hard for any honest man to keep his belly

round when so many lack for food . . . though your Ser Creighton
has not hungered, it would seem."

"I have big bones," Ser Creighton insisted. "Shall we ride together
for a time? I do not doubt Ser Shadrich's valor, but he seems small,
and three blades are better than one."

Four blades, thought Brienne, but she held her tongue.

The merchant looked to his escort. "What say you, ser?"

"Oh, these three are nought to fear." Ser Shadrich was a wiry, fox-
faced man with a sharp nose and a shock of orange hair, mounted
on a rangy chestnut courser. Though he could not have been more
than five foot two, he had a cocksure manner. "The one is old, t'other
fat, and the big one is a woman. Let them come."

"As you say." The merchant lowered his crossbow.

As they resumed their journey, the hired knight dropped back and
looked her up and down as if she were a side of good salt pork.
"You're a strapping healthy wench, I'd say."

Ser Jaime's mockery had cut her deep; the little man's words hardly
touched her. "A giant, compared to some."

He laughed. "I am big enough where it counts, wench."

"The merchant called you Shadrich."

"Ser Shadrich of the Shady Glen. Some call me the Mad Mouse."
He turned his shield to show her his sigil, a large white mouse with
fierce red eyes, on bendy brown and blue. "The brown is for the lands
I've roamed, the blue for the rivers that I've crossed. The mouse is me."

"And are you mad?"

"Oh, quite. Your common mouse will run from blood and battle.
The mad mouse seeks them out."

"It would seem he seldom finds them."

"I find enough. 'Tis true, I am no tourney knight. I save my valor
for the battlefield, woman."

Woman was marginally better than *wench,* she supposed. "You and
good Ser Creighton have much in common, then."

Ser Shadrich laughed. "Oh, I doubt that, but it may be that you
and I share a quest. A little lost sister, is it? With blue eyes and auburn
hair?" He laughed again. "You are not the only hunter in the woods.
I seek for Sansa Stark as well."

Brienne kept her face a mask, to hide her dismay. "Who is this Sansa Stark, and why do you seek her?"

"For love, why else?"

She furrowed her brow. "Love?"

"Aye, love of gold. Unlike your good Ser Creighton, I did fight upon the Blackwater, but on the losing side. My ransom ruined me. You know who Varys is, I trust? The eunuch has offered a plump bag of gold for this girl you've never heard of. I am not a greedy man. If some oversized wench would help me find this naughty child, I would split the Spider's coin with her."

"I thought you were in this merchant's hire."

"Only so far as Duskendale. Hibald is as niggardly as he is fearful. And he is *very* fearful. What say you, wench?"

"I know no Sansa Stark," she insisted. "I am searching for my sister, a highborn girl . . ."

". . . with blue eyes and auburn hair, aye. Pray, who is this knight who travels with your sister? Or did you name him fool?" Ser Shadrich did not wait for her answer, which was good, since she had none. "A certain fool vanished from King's Landing the night King Joffrey died, a stout fellow with a nose full of broken veins, one Ser Dontos the Red, formerly of Duskendale. I pray your sister and *her* drunken fool are not mistaken for the Stark girl and Ser Dontos. That could be most unfortunate." He put his heels into his courser and trotted on ahead.

Even Jaime Lannister had seldom made Brienne feel such a fool. *You are not the only hunter in the woods.* The woman Brella had told her how Joffrey had stripped Ser Dontos of his spurs, how Lady Sansa begged Joffrey for his life. *He helped her flee,* Brienne had decided, when she heard the tale. *Find Ser Dontos, and I will find Sansa.* She should have known there would be others who would see it too. *Some may even be less savory than Ser Shadrich.* She could only hope that Ser Dontos had hidden Sansa well. *But if so, how will I ever find her?*

She hunched her shoulders down and rode on, frowning.

Night was gathering by the time their party came upon the inn, a tall, timbered building that stood beside a river junction, astride an old stone bridge. That was the inn's name, Ser Creighton told them: the Old Stone Bridge. The innkeep was a friend of his. "Not a bad cook, and the rooms have no more fleas than most," he vouched. "Who's for a warm bed tonight?"

"Not us, unless your friend is giving them away," said Ser Illifer the Penniless. "We have no coin for rooms."

"I can pay for the three of us." Brienne did not lack for coin; Jaime had seen to that. In her saddlebags she'd found a purse fat with silver stags and copper stars, a smaller one stuffed with golden dragons, and a parchment commanding all loyal subjects of the king to assist the bearer, Brienne of House Tarth, who was about His Grace's business. It was signed in a childish hand by Tommen, the First of His Name, King of the Andals, the Rhoynar, and the First Men, and Lord of the Seven Kingdoms.

Hibald was for stopping too, and bid his men to leave the wagon near the stables. Warm yellow light shone through the diamond-shaped panes of the inn's windows, and Brienne heard a stallion trumpet at the scent of her mare. She was loosening the saddle when a boy came out the stable door, and said, "Let me do that, ser."

"I am no *ser*," she told him, "but you may take the horse. See that she is fed and brushed and watered."

The boy reddened. "Beg pardons, m'lady. I thought . . ."

"It is a common mistake." Brienne gave him the reins and followed the others into the inn, with her saddlebags across a shoulder and her bedroll tucked up beneath one arm.

Sawdust covered the plank floor of the common room, and the air smelled of hops and smoke and meat. A roast was spitting and crackling over the fire, unattended for the moment. Six locals sat about a table, talking, but they broke off when the strangers entered. Brienne could feel their eyes. Despite chainmail, cloak, and jerkin, she felt naked. When one man said, "Have a look at that," she knew he was not speaking of Ser Shadrich.

The innkeep appeared, clutching three tankards in each hand and slopping ale at every step.

"Do you have rooms, good man?" the merchant asked him.

"I might," the innkeep said, "for them as has coin."

Ser Creighton Longbough looked offended. "Naggle, is that how you would greet an old friend? 'Tis me, Longbough."

"'Tis you indeed. You owe me seven stags. Show me some silver and I'll show you a bed." The innkeep set the tankards down one by one, slopping more ale on the table in the process.

"I will pay for one room for myself, and a second for my two companions." Brienne indicated Ser Creighton and Ser Illifer.

"I shall take a room as well," said the merchant, "for myself and good Ser Shadrich. My serving men will bed down in your stables, if it please you."

The innkeep looked them over. "It don't please me, but might be I'll allow it. Will you be wanting supper? That's good goat on the spit, that is."

"I shall judge its goodness for myself," Hibald announced. "My men will content themselves with bread and drippings."

And so they supped. Brienne tried the goat herself, after following the innkeep up the steps, pressing some coins into his hand, and stashing her goods in the second room he showed her. She ordered goat for Ser Creighton and Ser Illifer as well, since they had shared their trout with her. The hedge knights and the septon washed down the meat with ale, but Brienne drank a cup of goat's milk. She listened to the table talk, hoping against hope that she might hear something that would help her find Sansa.

"You come from King's Landing," one of the locals said to Hibald. "Is it true that the Kingslayer's been crippled?"

"True enough," Hibald said. "He's lost his sword hand."

"Aye," Ser Creighton said, "chewed off by a direwolf, I hear, one of them monsters come down from the north. Nought that's good ever come from the north. Even their gods are queer."

"It was not a wolf," Brienne heard herself say. "Ser Jaime lost his hand to a Qohorik sellsword."

"It is no easy thing to fight with your off hand," observed the Mad Mouse.

"Bah," said Ser Creighton Longbough. "As it happens, I fight as well with either hand."

"Oh, I have no doubt of that." Ser Shadrich lifted his tankard in salute.

Brienne remembered her fight with Jaime Lannister in the woods.

It had been all that she could do to keep his blade at bay. *He was weak from his imprisonment, and chained at the wrists. No knight in the Seven Kingdoms could have stood against him at his full strength, with no chains to hamper him.* Jaime had done many wicked things, but the man could *fight!* His maiming had been monstrously cruel. It was one thing to slay a lion, another to hack his paw off and leave him broken and bewildered.

Suddenly the common room was too loud to endure a moment longer. She muttered her good-nights and took herself up to bed. The ceiling in her room was low; entering with a taper in her hand, Brienne had to duck or crack her head. The only furnishings were a bed wide enough to sleep six, and the stub of a tallow candle on the sill. She lit it with the taper, barred the door, and hung her sword belt from a bedpost. Her scabbard was a plain thing, wood wrapped in cracked brown leather, and her sword was plainer still. She had bought it in King's Landing, to replace the blade the Brave Companions had stolen. *Renly's sword.* It still hurt, knowing she had lost it.

But she had another longsword hidden in her bedroll. She sat on the bed and took it out. Gold glimmered yellow in the candlelight and rubies smoldered red. When she slid Oathkeeper from the ornate scabbard, Brienne's breath caught in her throat. Black and red the ripples ran, deep within the steel. *Valyrian steel, spell-forged.* It was a sword fit for a hero. When she was small, her nurse had filled her ears with tales of valor, regaling her with the noble exploits of Ser Galladon of Morne, Florian the Fool, Prince Aemon the Dragonknight, and other champions. Each man bore a famous sword, and surely Oathkeeper belonged in their company, even if she herself did not. "You'll be defending Ned Stark's daughter with Ned Stark's own steel," Jaime had promised.

Kneeling between the bed and wall, she held the blade and said a silent prayer to the Crone, whose golden lamp showed men the way through life. *Lead me,* she prayed, *light the way before me, show me the path that leads to Sansa.* She had failed Renly, had failed Lady Catelyn. She must not fail Jaime. *He trusted me with his sword. He trusted me with his honor.*

Afterward she stretched out on the bed as best she could. For all its width it was not long enough, so Brienne lay across it sideways. She could hear the clatter of tankards from below, and voices drifting up the steps. The fleas that Longbough had spoken of put in their appearance. Scratching helped keep her awake.

She heard Hibald mount the stairs, and sometime later the knights as well. ". . . I never knew his name," Ser Creighton was saying as he went by, "but upon his shield he bore a blood-red chicken, and his blade was dripping gore . . ." His voice faded, and somewhere up above, a door opened and closed.

Her candle burned out. Darkness settled over the Old Stone Bridge, and the inn grew so still that she could hear the murmur of the river. Only then did Brienne rise to gather up her things. She eased the door open, listened, made her way barefoot down the steps. Outside she donned her boots and hurried to the stables to saddle her bay mare, asking a silent pardon of Ser Creighton and Ser Illifer as she mounted. One of Hibald's serving men woke when she rode past him, but made no move to stop her. Her mare's hooves rang upon the old stone bridge. Then the trees closed in around her, black as pitch and full of ghosts and memories. *I am coming for you, Lady Sansa,* she thought as she rode into the darkness. *Be not afraid. I shall not rest until I've found you.*

SAMWELL

S am was reading about the Others when he saw the mouse.

His eyes were red and raw. *I ought not rub them so much,* he always told himself as he rubbed them. The dust made them itch and water, and the dust was everywhere down here. Little puffs of it filled the air every time a page was turned, and it rose in grey clouds whenever he shifted a stack of books to see what might be hiding on the bottom.

Sam did not know how long it had been since last he'd slept, but scarce an inch remained of the fat tallow candle he'd lit when starting on the ragged bundle of loose pages that he'd found tied up in twine. He was beastly tired, but it was hard to stop. *One more book,* he had told himself, *then I'll stop. One more folio, just one more. One more page, then I'll go up and rest and get a bite to eat.* But there was always another page after that one, and another after that, and another book waiting underneath the pile. *I'll just take a quick peek to see what this one is about,* he'd think, and before he knew he would be halfway through it. He had not eaten since that bowl of bean-and-bacon soup with Pyp and Grenn. *Well, except for the bread and cheese, but that was only a nibble,* he thought. That was when he took a quick glance at the empty platter, and spied the mouse feasting on the bread crumbs.

The mouse was half as long as his pinky finger, with black eyes and soft grey fur. Sam knew he ought to kill it. Mice might prefer bread and cheese, but they ate paper too. He had found plenty of mouse droppings amongst the shelves and stacks, and some of the leather covers on the books showed signs of being gnawed.

It is such a little thing, though. And hungry. How could he begrudge it a few crumbs? *It's eating books, though . . .*

After hours in the chair Sam's back was stiff as a board, and his legs were half-asleep. He knew he was not quick enough to catch the mouse, but it might be he could squash it. By his elbow rested a massive leather-bound copy of *Annals of the Black Centaur,* Septon Jorquen's exhaustively detailed account of the nine years that Orbert Caswell had served as Lord Commander of the Night's Watch. There was a page for each day of his term, every one of which seemed to begin, "Lord Orbert rose at dawn and moved his bowels," except for the last, which said, "Lord Orbert was found to have died during the night."

No mouse is a match for Septon Jorquen. Very slowly, Sam took hold of the book with his left hand. It was thick and heavy, and when he tried to lift it one-handed, it slipped from his plump fingers and thumped back down. The mouse was gone in half a heartbeat, skittery-quick. Sam was relieved. Squishing the poor little thing would have given him nightmares. "You shouldn't eat the books, though," he said aloud. Maybe he should bring more cheese the next time he came down here.

He was surprised at how low the candle had burned. Had the bean-and-bacon soup been today or yesterday? *Yesterday. It must have been yesterday.* The realization made him yawn. Jon would be wondering what had become of him, though Maester Aemon would no doubt understand. Before he had lost his sight, the maester had loved books as much as Samwell Tarly did. He understood the way that you could sometimes fall right into them, as if each page was a hole into another world.

Pushing himself to his feet, Sam grimaced at the pins and needles in his calves. The chair was very hard and cut into the back of his thighs when he bent over a book. *I need to remember to bring a cushion.* It would be even better if he could sleep down here, in the cell he'd found half-hidden behind four chests full of loose pages that had gotten separated from the books they belonged to, but he did not want to leave Maester Aemon alone for so long. He had not been strong of late and required help, especially with the ravens. Aemon had Clydas, to be sure, but Sam was younger, and better with the birds.

With a stack of books and scrolls under his left arm and the candle in his right hand, Sam made his way through the tunnels the brothers called the wormways. A pale shaft of light illuminated the steep stone steps that led up to the surface, so he knew that day had come up top. He left the candle burning in a wall niche and began the climb. By the fifth step he was puffing. At the tenth he stopped to shift the books to his right arm.

He emerged beneath a sky the color of white lead. *A snow sky,* Sam thought, squinting up. The prospect made him uneasy. He remembered that night on the Fist of the First Men when the wights and the snows had come together. *Don't be so craven,* he thought. *You have your Sworn Brothers all around you, not to mention Stannis Baratheon and all his knights.* Castle Black's keeps and towers rose about him, dwarfed by the icy immensity of the Wall. A small army was crawling over the ice a quarter of the way up, where a new switchback stair was creeping upward to meet the remnants of the old one. The sounds of their saws and hammers echoed off the ice. Jon had the builders working night and day on the task. Sam had heard some of them complaining about it over supper, insisting that Lord Mormont never worked them half so hard. Without the great stair there was no way to reach the top of the Wall except by the chain winch, however. And as much as Samwell Tarly hated steps, he hated the winch cage more. He always closed his eyes when he was riding it, convinced that the chain was about to break. Every time the iron cage scraped against the ice his heart stopped beating for an instant.

There were dragons here two hundred years ago, Sam found himself thinking, as he watched the cage making a slow descent. *They would just have flown to the top of the Wall.* Queen Alysanne had visited Castle Black on her dragon, and Jaehaerys, her king, had come after her on his own. Could Silverwing have left an egg behind? Or had Stannis found one egg on Dragonstone? *Even if he has an egg, how can he hope to quicken it?* Baelor the Blessed had prayed over his eggs, and other Targaryens had sought to hatch theirs with sorcery. All they got for it was farce and tragedy.

"Samwell," said a glum voice, "I was coming to fetch you. I was told to bring you to the Lord Commander."

A snowflake landed on Sam's nose. "Jon wants to see me?"

"As to that, I could not say," said Dolorous Edd Tollett. "I never wanted to see half the things I've seen, and I've never seen half the things I wanted to. I don't think wanting comes into it. You'd best go all the same. Lord Snow wishes to speak with you as soon as he is done with Craster's wife."

"Gilly."

"That's the one. If my wet nurse had looked like her, I'd still be on the teat. Mine had whiskers."

"Most goats do," called Pyp, as he and Grenn emerged from around the corner, with longbows in hand and quivers of arrows on their backs. "Where have you been, Slayer? We missed you last night at supper. A whole roast ox went uneaten."

"Don't call me Slayer." Sam ignored the gibe about the ox. That was just Pyp. "I was reading. There was a mouse . . ."

"Don't mention mice to Grenn. He's terrified of mice."

"I am not," Grenn declared with indignation.

"You'd be too scared to eat one."

"I'd eat more mice than you would."

Dolorous Edd Tollett gave a sigh. "When I was a lad, we only ate mice on special feast days. I was the youngest, so I always got the tail. There's no meat on the tail."

"Where's your longbow, Sam?" asked Grenn. Ser Alliser used to call him *Aurochs,* and every day he seemed to grow into the name a little more. He had come to the Wall big but slow, thick of neck, thick of waist, red of face, and clumsy. Though his neck still reddened when Pyp twisted him around into some folly, hours of work with sword and shield had flattened his belly, hardened his arms, broadened his chest. He was *strong,* and shaggy as an aurochs too. "Ulmer was expecting you at the butts."

"Ulmer," Sam said, abashed. Almost the first thing Jon Snow had done as Lord Commander was institute daily archery drill for the entire garrison, even stewards and cooks. The Watch had been placing too much emphasis on the sword and too little on the bow, he had said, a relic of the days when one brother in every ten had been a knight, instead of one in every hundred. Sam saw the sense in the decree, but he hated longbow practice almost as much as he hated climbing steps. When he wore his gloves he could never hit anything, but when he took them off he got blisters on his fingers. Those bows were *dangerous*. Satin had torn off half his thumbnail on a bowstring. "I forgot."

"You broke the heart of the wildling princess, Slayer," said Pyp. Of late, Val had taken to watching them from the window of her chamber in the King's Tower. "She was looking for you."

"She was not! Don't say that!" Sam had only spoken to Val twice, when Maester Aemon called upon her to make sure the babes were healthy. The princess was so pretty that he oft found himself stammering and blushing in her presence.

"Why not?" asked Pyp. "She wants to have your children. Maybe we should call you Sam the Seducer."

Sam reddened. King Stannis had plans for Val, he knew; she was the mortar with which he meant to seal the peace between the northmen and the free folk. "I don't have time for archery today, I need to go see Jon."

"Jon? Jon? Do we know anyone named Jon, Grenn?"

"He means the Lord Commander."

"*Ohhh.* The Great Lord Snow. To be sure. Why do you want to see him? He can't even wiggle his ears." Pyp wiggled his, to show he could. They were large ears, and red from cold. "He's *Lord* Snow for true now, too bloody highborn for the likes of us."

"Jon has duties," Sam said in his defense. "The Wall is his, and all that goes with it."

"A man has duties to his friends as well. If not for us, Janos Slynt might be our lord commander. Lord Janos would have sent Snow ranging naked on a mule. 'Scamper on up to Craster's Keep,' he would have said, 'and fetch me back the Old Bear's cloak and boots.' We saved him from that, but now he has too many *duties* to drink a cup of mulled wine by the fire?"

Grenn agreed. "His duties don't keep him from the yard. More days than not, he's out there fighting someone."

That was true, Sam had to admit. Once, when Jon came to consult with Maester Aemon, Sam had asked him why he spent so much time at swordplay. "The Old Bear never trained much when he was Lord Commander," he had pointed out. In answer, Jon had pressed Longclaw into Sam's hand. He let him feel the lightness, the balance, had him turn the blade so that ripples gleamed in the smoke-dark metal. "Valyrian steel," he said, "spell-forged and razor-sharp, nigh on indestructible. A swordsman should be as good as his sword, Sam. Longclaw is Valyrian steel, but I'm not. The Halfhand could have killed me as easy as you swat a bug."

Sam handed back the sword. "When I try to swat a bug, it always flies away. All I do is slap my arm. It stings."

That made Jon laugh. "As you will. Qhorin could have killed me as easy as you eat a bowl of porridge." Sam was fond of porridge, especially when it was sweetened with honey.

"I don't have time for this." Sam left his friends and made his way toward the armory, clutching his books to his chest. *I am the shield that guards the realms of men,* he remembered. He wondered what those men would say if they realized their realms were being guarded by the likes of Grenn, Pyp, and Dolorous Edd.

The Lord Commander's Tower had been gutted by fire, and Stannis Baratheon had claimed the King's Tower for his own residence, so Jon Snow had established himself in Donal Noye's modest quarters behind the armory. Gilly was leaving as Sam arrived, wrapped up in the old cloak he'd given her when they were fleeing Craster's Keep. She almost rushed right past him, but Sam caught her arm, spilling two books as he did. "Gilly."

"Sam." Her voice sounded raw. Gilly was dark-haired and slim, with the big brown eyes of a doe. She was swallowed by the folds of Sam's old cloak, her face half-hidden by its hood, but shivering all the same. Her face looked wan and frightened.

"What's wrong?" Sam asked her. "How are the babes?"

Gilly pulled loose from him. "They're good, Sam. Good."

"Between the two of them it's a wonder you can sleep," Sam said pleasantly. "Which one was it that I heard crying last night? I thought he'd never stop."

"Dalla's boy. He cries when he wants the teat. Mine . . . mine hardly ever cries. Sometimes he gurgles, but . . ." Her eyes filled with tears. "I have to go. It's past time that I fed them. I'll be leaking all over myself if I don't go." She rushed across the yard, leaving Sam perplexed behind her.

He had to get down on his knees to gather up the books he'd dropped. *I should not have brought so many,* he told himself as he brushed the dirt off Colloquo Votar's *Jade Compendium,* a thick volume of tales and legends from the east that Maester Aemon had commanded him to find. The book appeared undamaged. Maester Thomax's *Dragonkin, Being a History of House Targaryen from Exile to Apotheosis, with a Consideration of the Life and Death of Dragons* had not been so fortunate. It had come open as it fell, and a few pages had gotten muddy, including one with a rather nice picture of Balerion the Black Dread done in colored inks. Sam cursed himself for a clumsy oaf as he smoothed the pages down and brushed them off. Gilly's presence always flustered him and gave rise to . . . well, *risings.* A Sworn Brother of the Night's Watch should not be feeling the sorts of things that Gilly made him feel, especially when she would talk about her breasts and . . .

"Lord Snow is waiting." Two guards in black cloaks and iron half-helms stood by the doors of the armory, leaning on their spears. Hairy Hal was the one who'd spoken. Mully helped Sam back to his feet. He blurted out thanks and hurried past them, clutching desperately at the stack of books as he made his way past the forge with its anvil and bellows. A shirt of ringmail rested on his workbench, half-completed. Ghost was stretched out beneath the anvil, gnawing on the bone of an ox to get at the marrow. The big white direwolf looked up when Sam went by, but made no sound.

Jon's solar was back beyond the racks of spears and shields. He was reading a parchment when Sam entered. Lord Commander Mormont's raven was on his shoulder, peering down as if it were reading too, but when the bird spied Sam it spread its wings and flapped toward him crying, *"Corn, corn!"*

Shifting the books, Sam thrust his arm into the sack beside the door and came out with a handful of kernels. The raven landed on his wrist and took one from his palm, pecking so hard that Sam yelped and snatched his hand back. The raven took to the air again, and yellow and red kernels went everywhere.

"Close the door, Sam." Faint scars still marked Jon's cheek, where an eagle had once tried to rip his eye out. "Did that wretch break the skin?"

Sam eased the books down and peeled off his glove. "He did." He felt faint. "I'm *bleeding*."

"We all shed our blood for the Watch. Wear thicker gloves." Jon shoved a chair toward him with a foot. "Sit, and have a look at this." He handed him the parchment.

"What is it?" asked Sam. The raven began to hunt out corn kernels amongst the rushes.

"A paper shield."

Sam sucked at the blood on his palm as he read. He knew Maester Aemon's hand on sight. His writing was small and precise, but the old man could not see where the ink had blotted, and sometimes he left unsightly smears. "A letter to King Tommen?"

"At Winterfell, Tommen fought my brother Bran with wooden swords. He wore so much padding he looked like a stuffed goose. Bran knocked him to the ground." Jon went to the window. "Yet Bran's dead, and pudgy pink-faced Tommen is sitting on the Iron Throne, with a crown nestled amongst his golden curls."

Bran's not dead, Sam wanted to say. *He's gone beyond the Wall with Coldhands.* The words caught in his throat. *I swore I would not tell.* "You haven't signed the letter."

"The Old Bear begged the Iron Throne for help a hundred times. They sent him Janos Slynt. No letter will make the Lannisters love us better. Not once they hear that we've been helping Stannis."

"Only to defend the Wall, not in his rebellion." Sam read the letter quickly once again. "That's what it *says* here."

"The distinction may escape Lord Tywin." Jon took the letter back. "Why would he help us now? He never did before."

"Well," said Sam, "he will not want it said that Stannis rode to the defense of the realm whilst King Tommen was playing with his toys. That would bring scorn down upon House Lannister."

"It's death and destruction I want to bring down upon House Lannister, not scorn." Jon lifted up the letter. "*The Night's Watch takes no part in the wars of the Seven Kingdoms,*" he read. "*Our oaths are sworn to the realm, and the realm now stands in dire peril. Stannis Baratheon aids us against our foes from beyond the Wall, though we are not his men . . .*"

"Well," said Sam, squirming, "we're *not*. Are we?"

"I gave Stannis food, shelter, and the Nightfort, plus leave to settle some free folk in the Gift. That's all."

"Lord Tywin will say it was too much."

"Stannis says it's not enough. The more you give a king the more he wants. We are walking on a bridge of ice with an abyss on either side. Pleasing one king is difficult enough. Pleasing two is hardly possible."

"Yes, but . . . if the Lannisters should prevail and Lord Tywin decides that we betrayed the king by aiding Stannis, it could mean the end of the Night's Watch. He has the Tyrells behind him, with all the strength of Highgarden. And he did defeat Lord Stannis on the Blackwater." The sight of blood might make Sam faint, but he knew how wars were won. His own father had seen to that.

"The Blackwater was one battle. Robb won all his battles and still lost his head. If Stannis can raise the north . . ."

He's trying to convince himself, Sam realized, *but he can't.* The ravens had gone forth from Castle Black in a storm of black wings, summoning the lords of the north to declare for Stannis Baratheon and join their strength to his. Sam had sent out most of them himself. Thusfar only one bird had returned, the one they'd sent to Karhold. Elsewise the silence had been thunderous.

Even if he should somehow win the northmen to his side, Sam did not see how Stannis could hope to match the combined powers of Casterly Rock, Highgarden, and the Twins. Yet without the north, his cause was surely doomed. *As doomed as the Night's Watch, if Lord Tywin marks us down as traitors.* "The Lannisters have northmen of their own. Lord Bolton and his bastard."

"Stannis has the Karstarks. If he can win White Harbor . . ."

"If," Sam stressed. "If not . . . my lord, even a paper shield is better than none."

Jon rattled the letter. "I suppose so." He sighed, then took up a quill and scrawled a signature across the bottom of the letter. "Get the sealing wax." Sam heated a stick of black wax over a candle and dribbled some onto the parchment, then watched as Jon pressed the Lord Commander's seal down firmly on the puddle. "Take this to Maester Aemon when you leave," he commanded, "and tell him to dispatch a bird to King's Landing."

"I will." Sam hesitated. "My lord, if I might ask . . . I saw Gilly leaving. She was almost crying."

"Val sent her to plead for Mance again."

"Oh." Val was the sister of the woman the King-beyond-the-Wall had taken for his queen. *The wildling princess* was what Stannis and his men were calling her. Her sister Dalla had died during the battle, though no blade had ever touched her; she had perished giving birth to Mance Rayder's son. Rayder himself would soon follow her to the grave, if the whispers Sam had heard had any truth to them. "What did you tell her?"

"That I would speak to Stannis, though I doubt my words will sway him. A king's first duty is to defend the realm, and Mance attacked it. His Grace is not like to forget that. My father used to say that Stannis Baratheon was a just man. No one has ever said he was forgiving." Jon paused, frowning. "I would sooner take off Mance's head myself. He was a man of the Night's Watch, once. By rights, his life belongs to us."

"Pyp says that Lady Melisandre means to give him to the flames, to work some sorcery."

"Pyp should learn to hold his tongue. I have heard the same from others. King's blood, to wake a dragon. Where Melisandre thinks to find a sleeping dragon, no one is quite sure. It's nonsense. Mance's blood is no more royal than mine own. He has never worn a crown nor sat a throne. He's a brigand, nothing more. There's no power in brigand's blood."

The raven looked up from the floor. *"Blood,"* it screamed.

Jon paid no mind. "I am sending Gilly away."

"Oh." Sam bobbed his head. "Well, that's . . . that's good, my lord." It would be the best thing for her, to go somewhere warm and safe, well away from the Wall and the fighting.

"Her and the boy. We will need to find another wet nurse for his milk brother."

"Goat's milk might serve, until you do. It's better for a babe than cow's milk." Sam had read that somewhere. He shifted in his seat. "My lord, when I was looking through the annals I came on another boy commander. Four hundred years before the Conquest. Osric Stark was ten when he was chosen, but he served for sixty years. That's four, my lord. You're not even close to being the youngest ever chosen. You're fifth youngest, so far."

"The younger four all being sons, brothers, or bastards of the King in the North. Tell me something useful. Tell me of our enemy."

"The Others." Sam licked his lips. "They are mentioned in the annals, though not as often as I would have thought. The annals I've found and looked at, that is. There's more I haven't found, I know. Some of the older books are falling to pieces. The pages crumble when I try and turn them. And the *really* old books . . . either they have crumbled all away or they are buried somewhere that I haven't looked yet or . . . well, it could be that there are no such books, and never were. The oldest histories we have were written after the Andals came to Westeros. The First Men only left us runes on rocks, so everything we think we know about the Age of Heroes and the Dawn Age and the Long Night comes from accounts set down by septons thousands of years later. There are archmaesters at the Citadel who question all of it. Those old histories are full of kings who reigned for hundreds of years, and knights riding around a thousand years before there *were* knights. You know the tales, Brandon the Builder, Symeon Star-Eyes, Night's King . . . we say that you're the nine hundred and ninety-eighth Lord Commander of the Night's Watch, but the oldest list I've found shows six hundred seventy-four commanders, which suggests that it was written during . . ."

"Long ago," Jon broke in. "What about the Others?"

"I found mention of dragonglass. The children of the forest used to give the Night's Watch a hundred obsidian daggers every year, during the Age of Heroes. The Others come when it is cold, most of the tales agree. Or else it gets cold when they come. Sometimes they appear during snowstorms and melt away when the skies clear. They hide from the light of the sun and emerge by night . . . or else night falls when they emerge. Some stories speak of them riding the corpses of dead animals. Bears, direwolves, mammoths, horses, it makes no matter, so long as the beast is dead. The one that killed Small Paul was riding a dead horse, so that part's plainly true. Some accounts speak of giant ice spiders too. I don't know what those are. Men who fall in battle against the Others must be burned, or else the dead will rise again as their thralls."

"We knew all this. The question is, how do we fight them?"

"The armor of the Others is proof against most ordinary blades, if the tales can be believed," said Sam, "and their own swords are so cold they shatter steel. Fire will dismay them, though, and they are vulnerable to obsidian." He remembered the one he had faced in the haunted forest, and how it had seemed to melt away when he stabbed it with the dragonglass dagger Jon had made for him. "I found one account of the Long Night that spoke of the last hero slaying Others with a blade of dragonsteel. Supposedly they could not stand against it."

"Dragonsteel?" Jon frowned. "*Valyrian* steel?"

"That was my first thought as well."

"So if I can just convince the lords of the Seven Kingdoms to give us their Valyrian blades, all is saved? That won't be hard." His laugh had no mirth in it. "Did you find who the Others are, where they come from, what they want?"

"Not yet, my lord, but it may be that I've just been reading the wrong books. There are hundreds I have not looked at yet. Give me more time and I will find whatever there is to be found."

"There is no more time." Jon sounded sad. "You need to get your things together, Sam. You're going with Gilly."

"Going?" For a moment, Sam did not understand. "I'm going? To Eastwatch, my lord? Or . . . where am I . . ."

"Oldtown."

"*Oldtown?*" It came out in a squeak. Horn Hill was close to Oldtown. *Home.* The notion made him light-headed. *My father.*

"Aemon as well."

"Aemon? *Maester* Aemon? But . . . he's one hundred and two years old, my lord, he can't . . . you're sending him *and* me? Who will tend the ravens? If they're sick or wounded, who . . ."

"Clydas. He's been with Aemon for years."

"Clydas is only a steward, and his eyes are going bad. You need a *maester.* Maester Aemon is so frail, a sea voyage . . ." He thought of the Arbor and the *Arbor Queen,* and almost choked on his tongue. "It might . . . he's old, and . . ."

"His life will be at risk. I am aware of that, Sam, but the risk is greater here. Stannis knows who Aemon is. If the red woman requires king's blood for her spells . . ."

"Oh." Sam paled.

"Dareon will join you at Eastwatch. My hope is that his songs will win some men for us in the south. The *Blackbird* will deliver you to Braavos. From there you'll arrange your own passage to Oldtown. If you still mean to claim Gilly's babe as your bastard, send her and the child on to Horn Hill. Elsewise, Aemon will find a servant's place for her at the Citadel."

"My b-b-bastard." He had said that, yes, but . . . *All that water. I could drown. Ships sink all the time, and autumn is a stormy season.* Gilly would be with him, though, and the babe would grow up safe. "Yes, I . . . my mother and my sisters will help Gilly with the child." *I can send a letter, I won't need to go to Horn Hill myself.* "Dareon could see her to Oldtown just as well as me. I'm . . . I've been working at my archery every afternoon with Ulmer, as you commanded . . . well, except when I'm in the vaults, but you told me to find out about the Others. The longbow makes my shoulders ache and raises blisters on my fingers." He showed Jon where one had burst. "I still do it, though. I can hit the target more often than not now, but I'm still the worst archer who ever bent a bow. I like Ulmer's stories, though. Someone needs to write them down and put them in a book."

"You do it. They have parchment and ink at the Citadel, as well as longbows. I will expect you to continue with your practice. Sam, the Night's Watch has hundreds of men who can loose an arrow, but only a handful who can read or write. I need you to become my new maester."

The word made him flinch. *No, Father, please, I won't speak of it again, I swear it by the Seven. Let me out, please let me out.* "My lord, I . . . my work is here, the books . . ."

". . . will be here when you return to us."

Sam put a hand to his throat. He could almost feel the chain there, choking him. "My lord, the Citadel . . . they make you cut up corpses there." *They make you wear a chain about your neck. If it is chains you want, come with me.* For three days and three nights Sam had sobbed himself to sleep, manacled hand and foot to a wall. The chain around his throat was so tight it broke the skin, and whenever he rolled the wrong way in his sleep it would cut off his breath. "I cannot wear a chain."

"You can. You will. Maester Aemon is old and blind. His strength is leaving him. Who will take his place when he dies? Maester Mullin at the Shadow Tower is more fighter than scholar, and Maester Harmune of Eastwatch is drunk more than he's sober."

"If you ask the Citadel for more maesters . . ."

"I mean to. We'll have need of every one. Aemon Targaryen is not so easily replaced, however." Jon seemed puzzled. "I was certain this would please you. There are so many books at the Citadel that no man can hope to read them all. You would do well there, Sam. I know you would."

"No. I could read the books, but . . . a m-maester must be a healer and b-b-blood makes me faint." He held out a shaky hand for Jon to see. "I'm Sam the Scared, not Sam the Slayer."

"Scared? Of what? The chidings of old men? Sam, you saw the wights come swarming up the Fist, a tide of living dead men with black hands and bright blue eyes. You slew an Other."

"It was the d-d-d-dragonglass, not me."

"Be quiet. You lied and schemed and plotted to make me Lord Commander. You *will* obey me. You'll go to the Citadel and forge a chain, and if you have to cut up corpses, so be it. At least in Oldtown the corpses won't object."

He doesn't understand. "My lord," Sam said, "my f-f-f-father, Lord Randyll, he, he, he, he, he . . . the life of a maester is a life of *servitude*." He was babbling, he knew. "No son of House Tarly will ever wear a chain. The men of Horn Hill do not bow and scrape to petty lords." *If it is chains you want, come with me.* "Jon, I cannot disobey my father."

Jon, he'd said, but Jon was gone. It was Lord Snow who faced him now, grey eyes as hard as ice. "You have no father," said Lord Snow. "Only brothers. Only us. Your life belongs to the Night's Watch, so go and stuff your smallclothes into a sack, along with anything else you care to take to Oldtown. You leave an hour before sunrise. And here's another order. From this day forth, you will *not* call yourself a craven. You've faced more things this past year than most men face in a lifetime. You can face the Citadel, but you'll face it as a Sworn Brother of the Night's Watch. I can't command you to be brave, but I *can* command you to hide your fears. You said the words, Sam. Remember?"

I am the sword in the darkness. But he was wretched with a sword, and the darkness scared him. "I . . . I'll try."

"You won't try. You will obey."

"Obey." Mormont's raven flapped its great black wings.

"As my lord commands. Does . . . does Maester Aemon know?"

"It was as much his idea as mine." Jon opened the door for him. "No farewells. The fewer folk who know of this, the better. An hour before first light, by the lichyard."

Sam did not recall leaving the armory. The next thing he knew he was stumbling through mud and patches of old snow, toward Maester Aemon's chambers. *I could hide,* he told himself. *I could hide in the vaults amongst the books. I could live down there with the mouse and sneak up at night to steal food.* Crazed thoughts, he knew, as futile as they were desperate. The vaults were the first place they would look for him. The *last* place they would look for him was beyond the Wall, but that was even madder. *The wildlings would catch me and kill me slowly. They might burn me alive, the way the red woman means to burn Mance Rayder.*

When he found Maester Aemon in the rookery, he gave him Jon's letter and blurted out his fears in a great green gush of words. "He does not *understand*." Sam felt as if he might throw up. "If I don a chain, my lord f-f-f-father . . . he, he, he . . ."

"My own father raised the same objections when I chose a life of service," the old man said. "It was *his* father who sent me to the Citadel. King Daeron had sired four sons, and three had sons of their own. *Too many dragons are as dangerous as too few*, I heard His Grace tell my lord father, the day they sent me off." Aemon raised a spotted hand to the chain of many metals that dangled loose about his thin neck. "The chain is heavy, Sam, but my grandsire had the right of it. So does your Lord Snow."

"*Snow*," a raven muttered. "*Snow*," another echoed. All of them picked it up then. "*Snow, snow, snow, snow, snow*." Sam had taught them that word. There was no help here, he saw. Maester Aemon was as trapped as he was. *He will die at sea*, he thought, despairing. *He is too old to survive such a voyage. Gilly's little son may die as well, he's not as large and strong as Dalla's boy. Does Jon mean to kill us all?*

The next morning, Sam found himself saddling the mare he'd ridden from Horn Hill and leading her toward the lichyard beside the eastern road. Her saddlebags bulged with cheese and sausages and hard-cooked eggs, and half a salted ham that Three-Finger Hobb had given him on his name day. "You're a man who *appreciates* cooking, Slayer," the cook had said. "We need more o' your sort." The ham would help, no doubt. Eastwatch was a long cold ride away, and there were no towns nor inns in the shadow of the Wall.

The hour before dawn was dark and still. Castle Black seemed strangely hushed. At the lichyard, a pair of two-wheeled wayns awaited him, along with Black Jack Bulwer and a dozen seasoned rangers, tough as the garrons they rode. Kedge Whiteye cursed loudly when his one good eye spied Sam. "Don't mind him, Slayer," said Black Jack. "He lost a wager, said we'd need to drag you out squealing from beneath some bed."

Maester Aemon was too frail to ride a horse, so a wayn had been made ready for him, its bed heaped high with furs, and a leather awning fastened overhead to keep off the rain and snow. Gilly and her child would ride with him. The second wayn would carry their clothing and possessions, along with a chest of rare old books that Aemon thought the Citadel might lack. Sam had spent half the night searching for them, though he'd found only one in four. *And a good thing, or we'd need another wayn.*

When the maester appeared, he was bundled up in a bearskin three times his size. As Clydas led him toward the wayn, a gust of wind came up, and the old man staggered. Sam hurried to his side and put an arm about him. *Another gust like that could blow him over the Wall.* "Keep hold of my arm, maester. It's not far."

The blind man nodded as the wind pushed back their hoods. "It is always warm in Oldtown. There is an inn on an island in the Honeywine where I used to go when I was a young novice. It will be pleasant to sit there once again, sipping cider."

By the time they got the maester into the wayn, Gilly had appeared, the child bundled in her arms. Beneath her hood her eyes were red from crying. Jon turned up at the same time, with Dolorous Edd. "Lord Snow," Maester Aemon called, "I left a book for you in my chambers. The *Jade Compendium.* It was written by the Volantene adventurer Colloquo Votar, who traveled to the east and visited all the lands of the Jade Sea. There is a passage you may find of interest. I've told Clydas to mark it for you."

"I'll be sure to read it," Jon Snow replied.

A line of pale snot ran from Maester Aemon's nose. He wiped it away with the back of his glove. "Knowledge is a weapon, Jon. Arm yourself well before you ride forth to battle."

"I will." A light snow had begun to fall, the big soft flakes drifting down lazily from the sky. Jon turned to Black Jack Bulwer. "Make as good a time as you can, but take no foolish risks. You have an old man and a suckling babe with you. See that you keep them warm and well fed."

"You do the same, m'lord," said Gilly. "You do the same for t'other. Find another wet nurse, like you said. You promised me you would. The boy . . . Dalla's boy . . . the little prince, I mean . . . you find him some good woman, so he grows up big and strong."

"You have my word," Jon Snow said solemnly.

"Don't you name him. Don't you do that till he's past two years.

It's ill luck to name them when they're still on the breast. You crows may not know that, but it's true."

"As you command, my lady."

A spasm of anger flashed across Gilly's face. "Don't you call me that. I'm a mother, not a lady. I'm Craster's wife and Craster's daughter, and a *mother*."

Dolorous Edd took the babe as Gilly climbed into the wayn and covered her legs with some musty pelts. By then the eastern sky was more grey than black. Left Hand Lew was anxious to be off. Edd handed the infant up and Gilly put him to her breast. *This may be the last I ever see of Castle Black,* thought Sam as he hoisted himself atop his mare. As much as he had once hated Castle Black, it was tearing him apart to leave it.

"*Let's do this,*" Bulwer commanded. A whip snapped, and the wayns began to rumble slowly down the rutted road as the snow came down around them. Sam lingered beside Clydas and Dolorous Edd and Jon Snow. "Well," he said, "farewell."

"And to you, Sam," said Dolorous Edd. "Your boat's not like to sink, I don't think. Boats only sink when I'm aboard."

Jon was watching the wayns. "The first time I saw Gilly," he said, "she was pressed back against the wall of Craster's Keep, this skinny dark-haired girl with her big belly, cringing away from Ghost. He had gotten in among her rabbits, and I think she was frightened that he would tear her open and devour the babe . . . but it was not the wolf she should have been afraid of, was it?"

No, Sam thought. *Craster was the danger, her own father.*

"She has more courage than she knows."

"So do you, Sam. Have a swift, safe voyage, and take care of her and Aemon and the child." Jon smiled a strange, sad smile. "And pull your hood up. The snowflakes are melting in your hair."

ARYA

Faint and far away the light burned, low on the horizon, shining through the sea mists.

"It looks like a star," said Arya.

"The star of home," said Denyo.

His father was shouting orders. Sailors scrambled up and down the three tall masts and moved along the rigging, reefing the heavy purple sails. Below, oarsmen heaved and strained over two great banks of oars. The decks tilted, creaking, as the galleas *Titan's Daughter* heeled to starboard and began to come about.

The star of home. Arya stood at the prow, one hand resting on the gilded figurehead, a maiden with a bowl of fruit. For half a heartbeat she let herself pretend that it *was* her home ahead.

But that was *stupid.* Her home was gone, her parents dead, and all her brothers slain but Jon Snow on the Wall. That was where she had wanted to go. She *told* the captain as much, but even the iron coin did not sway him. Arya never seemed to find the places she set out to reach. Yoren had sworn to deliver her to Winterfell, only she had ended up in Harrenhal and Yoren in his grave. When she escaped Harrenhal for Riverrun, Lem and Anguy and Tom o' Sevens took her captive and dragged her to the hollow hill instead. Then the Hound had stolen her and dragged her to the Twins. Arya had left him dying by the river and gone ahead to Saltpans, hoping to take passage for Eastwatch-by-the-Sea, only . . .

Braavos might not be so bad. Syrio was from Braavos, and Jaqen might be there as well. It was Jaqen who had given her the iron coin. He hadn't truly been her friend, the way that Syrio had, but what good had friends ever done her? *I don't need any friends, so long as I have Needle.* She brushed the ball of her thumb across the sword's smooth pommel, wishing, wishing . . .

If truth be told, Arya did not know what to wish for, any more than she knew what awaited her beneath that distant light. The captain had given her passage but he had no time to speak with her. Some of the crew shunned her, but others gave her gifts—a silver fork, fingerless gloves, a floppy woolen hat patched with leather. One man showed her how to tie sailor's knots. Another poured her thimble cups of fire wine. The friendly ones would tap their chests, repeating their names over and over until Arya said them back, though none ever thought to ask *her* name. They called her Salty, since she'd come aboard at Saltpans, near the mouth of the Trident. It was as good a name as any, she supposed.

The last of the night's stars had vanished . . . all but the pair dead ahead. "It's *two* stars now."

"Two eyes," said Denyo. "The Titan sees us."

The Titan of Braavos. Old Nan had told them stories of the Titan back in Winterfell. He was a giant as tall as a mountain, and whenever Braavos stood in danger he would wake with fire in his eyes, his rocky limbs grinding and groaning as he waded out into the sea to smash the enemies. "The Braavosi feed him on the juicy pink flesh of little highborn girls," Nan would end, and Sansa would give a stupid squeak. But Maester Luwin said the Titan was only a statue, and Old Nan's stories were only stories.

Winterfell is burned and fallen, Arya reminded herself. Old Nan and Maester Luwin were both dead, most like, and Sansa too. It did no good to think of them. *All men must die.* That was what the words meant, the words that Jaqen H'ghar had taught her when he gave her the worn iron coin. She had learned more Braavosi words since they left Saltpans, the words for *please* and *thank you* and *sea* and *star* and *fire wine,* but she came to them knowing that *all men must die.* Most of the *Daughter's* crew had a smattering of the Common Tongue from nights ashore in Oldtown and King's Landing and Maidenpool, though only the captain and his sons spoke it well enough to talk to her. Denyo was the youngest of those sons, a plump, cheerful boy of twelve who kept his father's cabin and helped his eldest brother do his sums.

"I hope your Titan isn't hungry," Arya told him.

"Hungry?" Denyo said, confused.

"It takes no matter." Even if the Titan *did* eat juicy pink girl flesh, Arya would not fear him. She was a scrawny thing, no proper meal for a giant, and almost eleven, practically a woman grown. *And Salty isn't highborn, either.* "Is the Titan the god of Braavos?" she asked. "Or do you have the Seven?"

"All gods are honored in Braavos." The captain's son loved to talk about his city almost as much as he loved to talk about his father's ship. "Your Seven have a sept here, the Sept-Beyond-the-Sea, but only Westerosi sailors worship there."

They are not my Seven. They were my mother's gods, and they let the Freys murder her at the Twins. She wondered whether she would find a godswood in Braavos, with a weirwood at its heart. Denyo might know, but she could not ask him. Salty was from Saltpans, and what would a girl from Saltpans know about the old gods of the north? *The old gods are dead,* she told herself, *with Mother and Father and Robb and Bran and Rickon, all dead.* A long time ago, she remembered her father saying that when the cold winds blow the lone wolf dies and the pack survives. *He had it all backwards.* Arya, the lone wolf, still lived, but the wolves of the pack had been taken and slain and skinned.

"The Moonsingers led us to this place of refuge, where the dragons of Valyria could not find us," Denyo said. "Theirs is the greatest temple. We esteem the Father of Waters as well, but his house is built anew whenever he takes his bride. The rest of the gods dwell together on an isle in the center of the city. That is where you will find the . . . the Many-Faced God."

The Titan's eyes seemed brighter now, and farther apart. Arya did not know any Many-Faced God, but if he answered prayers, he might be the god she sought. *Ser Gregor,* she thought, *Dunsen, Raff the*

Sweetling, Ser Ilyn, Ser Meryn, Queen Cersei. Only six now. Joffrey was dead, the Hound had slain Polliver, and she'd stabbed the Tickler herself, and that stupid squire with the pimple. *I wouldn't have killed him if he hadn't grabbed me.* The Hound had been dying when she left him on the banks of the Trident, burning up with fever from his wound. *I should have given him the gift of mercy and put a knife into his heart.*

"Salty, look!" Denyo took her by the arm and turned her. "Can you see? *There.*" He pointed.

The mists gave way before them, ragged grey curtains parted by their prow. The *Titan's Daughter* cleaved through the grey-green waters on billowing purple wings. Arya could hear the cries of seabirds overhead. There, where Denyo pointed, a line of stony ridges rose sudden from the sea, their steep slopes covered with soldier pines and black spruce. But dead ahead the sea had broken through, and there above the open water the Titan towered, with his eyes blazing and his long green hair blowing in the wind.

His legs bestrode the gap, one foot planted on each mountain, his shoulders looming tall above the jagged crests. His legs were carved of solid stone, the same black granite as the sea monts on which he stood, though around his hips he wore an armored skirt of greenish bronze. His breastplate was bronze as well, and his head in his crested halfhelm. His blowing hair was made of hempen ropes dyed green, and huge fires burned in the caves that were his eyes. One hand rested atop the ridge to his left, bronze fingers coiled about a knob of stone; the other thrust up into the air, clasping the hilt of a broken sword.

He is only a little bigger than King Baelor's statue in King's Landing, she told herself when they were still well off to sea. As the galleas drove closer to where the breakers smashed against the ridgeline, however, the Titan grew larger still. She could hear Denyo's father bellowing commands in his deep voice, and up in the rigging men were bringing in the sails. *We are going to row beneath the Titan's legs.* Arya could see the arrow slits in the great bronze breastplate, and stains and speckles on the Titan's arms and shoulders where the seabirds nested. Her neck craned upward. *Baelor the Blessed would not reach his knee. He could step right over the walls of Winterfell.*

Then the Titan gave a mighty roar.

The sound was as huge as he was, a terrible groaning and grinding, so loud it drowned out even the captain's voice and the crash of the waves against those pine-clad ridges. A thousand seabirds took to the air at once, and Arya flinched until she saw that Denyo was laughing. "He warns the Arsenal of our coming, that is all," he shouted. "You must not be afraid."

"I never *was*," Arya shouted back. "It was loud, is all."

Wind and wave had the *Titan's Daughter* hard in hand now, driving her swiftly toward the channel. Her double bank of oars stroked smoothly, lashing the sea to white foam as the Titan's shadow fell upon them. For a moment it seemed as though they must surely smash up against the stones beneath his legs. Huddled by Denyo at the prow, Arya could taste salt where the spray had touched her face. She had to look straight up to see the Titan's head. "The Braavosi feed him on the juicy pink flesh of little highborn girls," she heard Old Nan say again, but she was *not* a little girl, and she would not be frightened of a stupid *statue*.

Even so, she kept one hand on Needle as they slipped between his legs. More arrow slits dotted the insides of those great stone thighs, and when Arya craned her neck around to watch the crow's nest slip through with a good ten yards to spare, she spied murder holes beneath the Titan's armored skirts, and pale faces staring down at them from behind the iron bars.

And then they were past.

The shadow lifted, the pine-clad ridges fell away to either side, the winds dwindled, and they found themselves moving through a great lagoon. Ahead rose another sea mont, a knob of rock that pushed up from the water like a spiked fist, its stony battlements bristling with scorpions, spitfires, and trebuchets. "The Arsenal of Braavos," Denyo named it, as proud as if he'd built it. "They can build a war galley there in a day." Arya could see dozens of galleys tied up at quays and perched on launching slips. The painted prows of others poked from innumerable wooden sheds along the stony shores, like hounds in a kennel, lean and mean and hungry, waiting for a hunter's horn to call them forth. She tried to count them, but there were too many, and more docks and sheds and quays where the shoreline curved away.

Two galleys had come out to meet them. They seemed to skim upon the water like dragonflies, their pale oars flashing. Arya heard the captain shouting to them and their own captains shouting back, but she did not understand the words. A great horn sounded. The galleys passed to either side of them, so close that she could hear the muffled sound of drums from within their purple hulls, *bom bom bom bom bom bom bom bom,* like the beat of living hearts.

Then the galleys were behind them, and the Arsenal as well. Ahead stretched a broad expanse of pea-green water rippled like a sheet of colored glass. From its wet heart arose the city proper, a great sprawl of domes and towers and bridges, grey and gold and red. *The hundred isles of Braavos in the sea.*

Maester Luwin had taught them about Braavos, but Arya had forgotten much of what he'd said. It was a flat city, she could see that even from afar, not like King's Landing on its three high hills. The only hills here were the ones that men had raised of brick and granite, bronze and marble. Something else was missing as well, though it took her a few moments to realize what it was. *The city has no walls.* But when she said as much to Denyo, he laughed at her. "Our walls are made of wood and painted purple," he told her. "Our *galleys* are our walls. We need no other."

The deck creaked behind them. Arya turned to find Denyo's father looming over them in his long captain's coat of purple wool. Tradesman-Captain Ternesio Terys wore no whiskers and kept his grey hair cut short and neat, framing his square, windburnt face. On the crossing she had oft seen him jesting with his crew, but when he frowned men ran from him as if before a storm. He was frowning now. "Our voyage is at an end," he told Arya. "We make for the Chequy Port, where the Sealord's customs officers will come aboard to inspect our holds. They will be half a day at it, they always are, but there is no need for you to wait upon their pleasure. Gather your belongings. I shall lower a boat, and Yorko will put you ashore."

Ashore. Arya bit her lip. She had crossed the narrow sea to get here, but if the captain had asked she would have told him she wanted to

stay aboard the *Titan's Daughter*. Salty was too small to man an oar,
she knew that now, but she could learn to splice ropes and reef the
sails and steer a course across the great salt seas. Denyo had taken
her up to the crow's nest once, and she hadn't been afraid at all,
though the deck had seemed a tiny thing below her. *I can do sums
too, and keep a cabin neat.*

But the galleas had no need of a second boy. Besides, she had only
to look at the captain's face to know how anxious he was to be rid
of her. So Arya only nodded. "Ashore," she said, though ashore meant
only strangers.

"*Valar dohaeris.*" He touched two fingers to his brow. "I beg you
remember Ternesio Terys and the service he has done you."

"I will," Arya said in a small voice. The wind tugged at her cloak,
insistent as a ghost. It was time she was away.

Gather your belongings, the captain had said, but there were few
enough of those. Only the clothes she was wearing, her little pouch
of coins, the gifts the crew had given her, the dagger on her left hip
and Needle on her right.

The boat was ready before she was, and Yorko was at the oars. He
was the captain's son as well, but older than Denyo and less friendly.
I never said farewell to Denyo, she thought as she clambered down to
join him. She wondered if she would ever see the boy again. *I should
have said farewell.*

The *Titan's Daughter* dwindled in their wake, while the city grew
larger with every stroke of Yorko's oars. A harbor was visible off to
her right, a tangle of piers and quays crowded with big-bellied whalers
out of Ibben, swan ships from the Summer Isles, and more galleys
than a girl could count. Another harbor, more distant, was off to her
left, beyond a sinking point of land where the tops of half-drowned
buildings thrust themselves above the water. Arya had never seen so
many big buildings all together in one place. King's Landing had the
Red Keep and the Great Sept of Baelor and the Dragonpit, but Braavos
seemed to boast a score of temples and towers and palaces that were
as large or even larger. *I will be a mouse again,* she thought glumly,
the way I was in Harrenhal before I ran away.

The city had seemed like one big island from where the Titan stood, but as Yorko rowed them closer she saw that it was many small islands close together, linked by arched stone bridges that spanned innumerable canals. Beyond the harbor she glimpsed streets of grey stone houses, built so close they leaned one upon the other. To Arya's eyes they were queer-looking, four and five stories tall and very skinny, with sharp-peaked tile roofs like pointed hats. She saw no thatch, and only a few timbered houses of the sort she knew in Westeros. *They have no trees,* she realized. *Braavos is all stone, a grey city in a green sea.*

Yorko swung them north of the docks and down the gullet of a great canal, a broad green waterway that ran straight into the heart of the city. They passed under the arches of a carved stone bridge, decorated with half a hundred kinds of fish and crabs and squids. A second bridge appeared ahead, this one carved in lacy leafy vines, and beyond that a third, gazing down on them from a thousand painted eyes. The mouths of lesser canals opened to either side, and others still smaller off of those. Some of the houses were built *above* the waterways, she saw, turning the canals into a sort of tunnel. Slender boats slid in and out among them, wrought in the shapes of water serpents with painted heads and upraised tails. Those were not rowed but poled, she saw, by men who stood at their sterns in cloaks of grey and brown and deep moss green. She saw huge flat-bottomed barges too, heaped high with crates and barrels and pushed along by twenty polemen to a side, and fancy floating houses with lanterns of colored glass, velvet drapes, and brazen figureheads. Off in the far distance, looming above canals and houses both, was a massive grey stone roadway of some kind, supported by three tiers of mighty arches marching away south into the haze. "What's that?" Arya asked Yorko, pointing. "The sweetwater river," he told her. "It brings fresh water from the mainland, across the mudflats and the briny shallows. Good sweet water for the fountains."

When she looked behind her, the harbor and lagoon were lost to sight. Ahead, a row of mighty statues stood along both sides of the channel, solemn stone men in long bronze robes, spattered with the droppings of the seabirds. Some held books, some daggers, some hammers. One clutched a golden star in his upraised hand. Another was upending a stone flagon to send an endless stream of water splashing down into the canal. "Are they gods?" asked Arya.

"Sealords," said Yorko. "The Isle of the Gods is farther on. See? Six bridges down, on the right bank. That is the Temple of the Moonsingers."

It was one of those that Arya had spied from the lagoon, a mighty mass of snow-white marble topped by a huge silvered dome whose milk glass windows showed all the phases of the moon. A pair of marble maidens flanked its gates, tall as the Sealords, supporting a crescent-shaped lintel.

Beyond it stood another temple, a red stone edifice as stern as any fortress. Atop its great square tower a fire blazed in an iron brazier twenty feet across, whilst smaller fires flanked its brazen doors. "The red priests love their fires," Yorko told her. "The Lord of Light is their god, red R'hllor."

I know. Arya remembered Thoros of Myr in his bits of old armor, worn over robes so faded that he had seemed more a pink priest than a red one. Yet his kiss had brought Lord Beric back from death. She watched the red god's house drift by, wondering whether these Braavosi priests of his could do the same.

Next came a huge brick structure festooned with lichen. Arya might have taken it for a storehouse had not Yorko said, "That is the Holy Refuge, where we honor the small gods the world has forgotten. You will hear it called the Warren too." A small canal ran between the Warren's looming lichen-covered walls, and there he swung them right. They passed through a tunnel and out again into the light. More shrines loomed up to either side.

"I never knew there were so many gods," Arya said.

Yorko grunted. They went around a bend and beneath another bridge. On their left appeared a rocky knoll with a windowless temple of dark grey stone at its top. A flight of stone steps led from its doors down to a covered dock.

Yorko backed the oars, and the boat bumped gently against stone pilings. He grasped an iron ring set to hold them for a moment. "Here I leave you."

The dock was shadowed, the steps steep. The temple's black tile roof came to a sharp peak, like the houses along the canals. Arya chewed her lip. *Syrio came from Braavos. He might have visited this temple. He might have climbed those steps.* She grabbed a ring and pulled herself up onto the dock.

"You know my name," said Yorko from the boat.

"Yorko Terys."

"*Valar dohaeris.*" He pushed off with his oar and drifted back off into the deeper water. Arya watched him row back the way they'd come, until he vanished in the shadows of the bridge. As the swish of oars faded, she could almost hear the beating of her heart. Suddenly she was somewhere else . . . back in Harrenhal with Gendry, maybe, or with the Hound in the woods along the Trident. *Salty is a stupid child,* she told herself. *I am a wolf, and will not be afraid.* She patted Needle's hilt for luck and plunged into the shadows, taking the steps two at a time so no one could ever say she'd been afraid.

At the top she found a set of carved wooden doors twelve feet high. The left-hand door was made of weirwood pale as bone, the right of gleaming ebony. In their center was a carved moon face; ebony on the weirwood side, weirwood on the ebony. The look of it reminded her somehow of the heart tree in the godswood at Winterfell. *The doors are watching me,* she thought. She pushed upon both doors at once with the flat of her gloved hands, but neither one would budge. *Locked and barred.* "Let me in, you stupid," she said. "I crossed the narrow sea." She made a fist and pounded. "Jaqen told me to come. I have the iron coin." She pulled it from her pouch and held it up. "See? *Valar morghulis.*"

The doors made no reply, except to open.

They opened inward all in silence, with no human hand to move them. Arya took a step forward, and another. The doors closed behind her, and for a moment she was blind. Needle was in her hand, though she did not remember drawing it.

A few candles burned along the walls, but gave so little light that Arya could not see her own feet. Someone was whispering, too softly for her to make out words. Someone else was weeping. She heard light footfalls, leather sliding over stone, a door opening and closing. *Water, I hear water too.*

Slowly, her eyes adjusted. The temple seemed much larger within than it had without. The septs of Westeros were seven-sided, with seven altars for the seven gods, but here there were more gods than seven. Statues of them stood along the walls, massive and threatening. Around their feet red candles flickered, as dim as distant stars. The nearest was a marble woman twelve feet tall. Real tears were trickling from her eyes, to fill the bowl she cradled in her arms. Beyond her was a man with a lion's head seated on a throne, carved of ebony. On the other side of the doors, a huge horse of bronze and iron reared up on two great legs. Farther on she could make out a great stone face, a pale infant with a sword, a shaggy black goat the size of an aurochs, a hooded man leaning on a staff. The rest were only looming shapes to her, half-seen through the gloom. Between the gods were hidden alcoves thick with shadows, with here and there a candle burning.

Silent as a shadow, Arya moved between rows of long stone benches, her sword in hand. The floor was made of stone, her feet told her; not polished marble like the floor of the Great Sept of Baelor, but something rougher. She passed some women whispering together. The air was warm and heavy, so heavy that she yawned. She could smell the candles. The scent was unfamiliar, and she put it down to some queer incense, but as she got deeper into the temple, they seemed to smell of snow and pine needles and hot stew. *Good smells,* Arya told herself, and felt a little braver. Brave enough to slip Needle back into its sheath.

In the center of the temple she found the water she had heard; a pool ten feet across, black as ink and lit by dim red candles. Beside it sat a young man in a silvery cloak, weeping softly. She watched him dip a hand in the water, sending scarlet ripples racing across the pool. When he drew his fingers back he sucked them, one by one. *He must be thirsty.* There were stone cups along the rim of the pool. Arya filled one and brought it to him, so he could drink. The young man stared at her for a long moment when she offered it to him. "*Valar morghulis,*" he said.

"*Valar dohaeris,*" she replied.

He drank deep, and dropped the cup into the pool with a soft *plop.* Then he pushed himself to his feet, swaying, holding his belly. For a moment, Arya thought he was going to fall. It was only then that she saw the dark stain below his belt, spreading as she watched. "You're stabbed," she blurted, but the man paid her no mind. He lurched unsteadily toward the wall and crawled into an alcove onto a hard stone bed. When Arya peered around, she saw other alcoves too. On some there were old people sleeping.

No, a half-remembered voice seemed to whisper in her head. *They are dead, or dying. Look with your eyes.*

A hand touched her arm.

Arya spun away, but it was only a little girl: a pale little girl in a cowled robe that seemed to engulf her, black on the right side and white on the left. Beneath the cowl was a gaunt and bony face, hollow cheeks, and dark eyes that looked as big as saucers. "Don't grab me," Arya warned the waif. "I killed the boy who grabbed me last."

The girl said some words that Arya did not know.

She shook her head. "Don't you know the Common Tongue?"

A voice behind her said, "I do."

Arya did not like the way they kept surprising her. The hooded man was tall, enveloped in a larger version of the black-and-white robe the girl was wearing. Beneath his cowl all she could see was the faint red glitter of candlelight reflecting off his eyes. "What place is this?" she asked him.

"A place of peace." His voice was gentle. "You are safe here. This is the House of Black and White, my child. Though you are young to seek the favor of the Many-Faced God."

"Is he like the southron god, the one with seven faces?"

"Seven? No. He has faces beyond count, little one, as many faces as there are stars in the sky. In Braavos, men worship as they will . . . but at the end of every road stands Him of Many Faces, waiting. He will be there for you one day, do not fear. You need not rush to his embrace."

"I only came to find Jaqen H'ghar."

"I do not know this name."

Her heart sank. "He was from Lorath. His hair was white on one side and red on the other. He said he'd teach me secrets, and gave me this." The iron coin was clutched in her fist. When she opened her fingers, it clung to her sweaty palm.

The priest studied the coin, though he made no move to touch it. The waif with the big eyes was looking at it too. Finally, the cowled man said, "Tell me your name, child."

"Salty. I come from Saltpans, by the Trident."

Though she could not see his face, somehow she could feel him smiling. "No," he said. "Tell me your name."

"Squab," she answered this time.

"Your true name, child."

"My mother named me Nan, but they call me Weasel—"

"Your name."

She swallowed. "Arry. I'm *Arry*."

"Closer. And now the truth?"

Fear cuts deeper than swords, she told herself. "Arya." She whispered the word the first time. The second time she threw it at him. "I am *Arya,* of House Stark."

"You are," he said, "but the House of Black and White is no place for Arya, of House Stark."

"Please," she said. "I have no place to go."

"Do you fear death?"

She bit her lip. "No."

"Let us see." The priest lowered his cowl. Beneath he had no face; only a yellowed skull with a few scraps of skin still clinging to the cheeks, and a white worm wriggling from one empty eye socket. "Kiss me, child," he croaked, in a voice as dry and husky as a death rattle.

Does he think to scare me? Arya kissed him where his nose should be and plucked the grave worm from his eye to eat it, but it melted like a shadow in her hand.

The yellow skull was melting too, and the kindliest old man that she had ever seen was smiling down at her. "No one has ever tried to eat my worm before," he said. "Are you hungry, child?"

Yes, she thought, *but not for food.*

CERSEI

cold rain was falling, turning the walls and ramparts of the Red Keep dark as blood. The queen held the king's hand and led him firmly across the muddy yard to where her litter waited with its escort. "Uncle Jaime said I could ride my horse and throw pennies to the smallfolk," the boy objected.

"Do you want to catch a chill?" She would not risk it; Tommen had never been as robust as Joffrey. "Your grandfather would want you to look a proper king at his wake. We will not appear at the Great Sept wet and bedraggled." *Bad enough I must wear mourning again.* Black had never been a happy color on her. With her fair skin, it made her look half a corpse herself. Cersei had risen an hour before dawn to bathe and fix her hair, and she did not intend to let the rain destroy her efforts.

Inside the litter, Tommen settled back against his pillows and peered out at the falling rain. "The gods are weeping for grandfather. Lady Jocelyn says the raindrops are their tears."

"Jocelyn Swyft is a fool. If the gods could weep, they would have wept for your brother. Rain is rain. Close the curtain before you let any more in. That mantle is sable, would you have it soaked?"

Tommen did as he was bid. His meekness troubled her. A king had to be strong. *Joffrey would have argued. He was never easy to cow.* "Don't slump so," she told Tommen. "Sit like a king. Put your shoulders back and straighten your crown. Do you want it to tumble off your head in front of all your lords?"

"No, Mother." The boy sat straight and reached up to fix the crown. Joff's crown was too big for him. Tommen had always inclined to plumpness, but his face seemed thinner now. *Is he eating well?* She must remember to ask the steward. She could not risk Tommen growing ill, not with Myrcella in the hands of the Dornishmen. *He will grow into Joff's crown in time.* Until he did, a smaller one might be needed, one that did not threaten to swallow his head. She would take it up with the goldsmiths.

The litter made its slow way down Aegon's High Hill. Two Kingsguard rode before them, white knights on white horses with white cloaks hanging sodden from their shoulders. Behind came fifty Lannister guardsmen in gold and crimson.

Tommen peered through the drapes at the empty streets. "I thought there would be more people. When Father died, all the people came out to watch us go by."

"This rain has driven them inside." King's Landing had never loved Lord Tywin. *He never wanted love, though. "You cannot eat love, nor buy a horse with it, nor warm your halls on a cold night,"* she heard him tell Jaime once, when her brother had been no older than Tommen.

At the Great Sept of Baelor, that magnificence in marble atop Visenya's Hill, the little knot of mourners were outnumbered by the gold cloaks that Ser Addam Marbrand had drawn up across the plaza. *More will turn out later,* the queen told herself as Ser Meryn Trant helped her from the litter. Only the highborn and their retinues were to be admitted to the morning service; there would be another in the afternoon for the commons, and the evening prayers were open to all. Cersei would need to return for that, so that the smallfolk might see her mourn. *The mob must have its show.* It was a nuisance. She had offices to fill, a war to win, a realm to rule. Her father would have understood that.

The High Septon met them at the top of the steps. A bent old man with a wispy grey beard, he was so stooped by the weight of his ornate embroidered robes that his eyes were on a level with the queen's breasts ... though his crown, an airy confection of cut crystal and spun gold, added a good foot and a half to his height.

Lord Tywin had given him that crown to replace the one that was lost when the mob killed the previous High Septon. They had pulled the fat fool from his litter and torn him apart, the day Myrcella sailed for Dorne. *That one was a great glutton, and biddable. This one ...* This High Septon was of Tyrion's making, Cersei recalled suddenly. It was a disquieting thought.

The old man's spotted hand looked like a chicken claw as it poked from a sleeve encrusted with golden scrollwork and small crystals. Cersei knelt on the wet marble and kissed his fingers, and bid Tommen to do the same. *What does he know of me? How much did the dwarf tell him?* The High Septon smiled as he escorted her into the sept. But was it a threatening smile full of unspoken knowledge, or just some vacuous twitch of an old man's wrinkled lips? The queen could not be certain.

They made their way through the Hall of Lamps beneath colored globes of leaded glass, Tommen's hand in hers. Trant and Kettleblack flanked them, water dripping from their wet cloaks to puddle on the floor. The High Septon walked slowly, leaning on a weirwood staff topped by a crystal orb. Seven of the Most Devout attended him, shimmering in cloth-of-silver. Tommen wore cloth-of-gold beneath his sable mantle, the queen an old gown of black velvet lined with ermine. There'd been no time to have a new one made, and she could not wear the same dress she had worn for Joffrey, nor the one she'd buried Robert in.

At least I will not be expected to don mourning for Tyrion. I shall dress in crimson silk and cloth-of-gold for that, and wear rubies in my hair. The man who brought her the dwarf's head would be raised to lordship, she had proclaimed, no matter how mean and low his birth or station. Ravens were carrying her promise to every part of the Seven Kingdoms, and soon enough word would cross the narrow sea to the Nine Free Cities and the lands beyond. *Let the Imp run to the ends of the earth, he will not escape me.*

The royal procession passed through the inner doors into the cavernous heart of the Great Sept, and down a wide aisle, one of seven that met beneath the dome. To right and left, highborn mourners sank to their knees as the king and queen went by. Many of her father's bannermen were here, and knights who had fought beside Lord Tywin in half a hundred battles. The sight of them made her feel more confident. *I am not without friends.*

Under the Great Sept's lofty dome of glass and gold and crystal, Lord Tywin Lannister's body rested upon a stepped marble bier. At its head Jaime stood at vigil, his one good hand curled about the hilt of a tall golden greatsword whose point rested on the floor. The hooded cloak he wore was as white as freshly fallen snow, and the scales of his long hauberk were mother-of-pearl chased with gold. *Lord Tywin would have wanted him in Lannister gold and crimson,* she thought. *It always angered him to see Jaime all in white.* Her brother was growing his beard again as well. The stubble covered his jaw and cheeks, and gave his face a rough, uncouth look. *He might at least have waited till Father's bones were interred beneath the Rock.*

Cersei led the king up three short steps, to kneel beside the body. Tommen's eyes were filled with tears. "Weep quietly," she told him, leaning close. "You are a king, not a squalling child. Your lords are watching you." The boy swiped the tears away with the back of his hand. He had her eyes, emerald green, as large and bright as Jaime's eyes had been when he was Tommen's age. Her brother had been such a *pretty* boy . . . but fierce as well, as fierce as Joffrey, a true lion cub. The queen put her arm around Tommen and kissed his golden curls. *He will need me to teach him how to rule and keep him safe from his enemies.* Some of them stood around them even now, pretending to be friends.

The silent sisters had armored Lord Tywin as if to fight some final battle. He wore his finest plate, heavy steel enameled a deep, dark crimson, with gold inlay on his gauntlets, greaves, and breastplate. His rondels were golden sunbursts; a golden lioness crouched upon each shoulder; a maned lion crested the greathelm beside his head. Upon his chest lay a longsword in a gilded scabbard studded with rubies, his hands folded about its hilt in gloves of gilded mail. *Even in death his face is noble,* she thought, *although the mouth . . .* The corners of her father's lips curved upward ever so slightly, giving him a look of vague bemusement. *That should not be.* She blamed Pycelle; he should have told the silent sisters that Lord Tywin Lannister never smiled. *The man is as useless as nipples on a breastplate.* That half-smile made Lord Tywin seem less fearful, somehow. That, and the fact that his eyes were closed. Her father's eyes had always been unsettling; pale green, almost luminous, flecked with gold. His eyes could see inside you, could see how weak and worthless and ugly you were down deep. *When he looked at you, you knew.*

Unbidden, a memory came to her, of the feast King Aerys had thrown when Cersei first came to court, a girl as green as summer grass. Old Merryweather had been nattering about raising the duty on wine when Lord Rykker said, "If we need gold, His Grace should sit Lord Tywin on his chamber pot." Aerys and his lickspittles laughed loudly, whilst Father stared at Rykker over his wine cup. Long after the merriment had died that gaze had lingered. Rykker turned away, turned back, met Father's eyes, then ignored them, drank a tankard of ale, and stalked off red-faced, defeated by a pair of unflinching eyes.

Lord Tywin's eyes are closed forever now, Cersei thought. *It is my look they will flinch from now, my frown that they must fear. I am a lion too.*

It was gloomy within the sept with the sky so grey outside. If the rain ever stopped, the sun would slant down through the hanging crystals to drape the corpse in rainbows. The Lord of Casterly Rock deserved rainbows. He had been a great man. *I shall be greater, though. A thousand years from now, when the maesters write about this time, you shall be remembered only as Queen Cersei's sire.*

"Mother." Tommen tugged her sleeve. "What smells so bad?"

My lord father. "Death." She could smell it too; a faint whisper of decay that made her want to wrinkle her nose. Cersei paid it no mind. The seven septons in the silver robes stood behind the bier, beseeching the Father Above to judge Lord Tywin justly. When they were done, seventy-seven septas gathered before the altar of the Mother and began to sing to her for mercy. Tommen was fidgeting by then, and even the queen's knees had begun to ache. She glanced at Jaime. Her twin stood as if he had been carved from stone, and would not meet her eyes.

On the benches, their uncle Kevan knelt with his shoulders

slumped, his son beside him. *Lancel looks worse than Father.* Though
only seventeen, he might have passed for seventy; grey-faced, gaunt,
with hollow cheeks, sunken eyes, and hair as white and brittle as
chalk. *How can Lancel be among the living when Tywin Lannister is
dead? Have the gods taken leave of their wits?*

Lord Gyles was coughing more than usual and covering his nose
with a square of red silk. *He can smell it too.* Grand Maester Pycelle
had his eyes closed. *If he has fallen asleep, I swear I will have him
whipped.* To the right of the bier knelt the Tyrells: the Lord of
Highgarden, his hideous mother and vapid wife, his son Garlan and
his daughter Margaery. *Queen Margaery,* she reminded herself; Joff's
widow and Tommen's wife-to-be. Margaery looked very like her
brother, the Knight of Flowers. The queen wondered if they had other
things in common. *Our little rose has a good many ladies waiting
attendance on her, night and day.* They were with her now, almost a
dozen of them. Cersei studied their faces, wondering. *Who is the most
fearful, the most wanton, the hungriest for favor? Who has the loosest
tongue?* She would need to make a point of finding out.

It was a relief when the singing finally ended. The smell coming
off her father's corpse seemed to have grown stronger. Most of the
mourners had the decency to pretend that nothing was amiss, but
Cersei saw two of Lady Margaery's cousins wrinkling their little Tyrell
noses. As she and Tommen were walking back down the aisle the
queen thought she heard someone mutter "privy" and chortle, but
when she turned her head to see who had spoken a sea of solemn
faces gazed at her blankly. *They would never have dared make japes
about him when he was still alive. He would have turned their bowels
to water with a look.*

Back out in the Hall of Lamps, the mourners buzzed about them
thick as flies, eager to shower her with useless condolences. The
Redwyne twins both kissed her hand, their father her cheeks. Hallyne
the Pyromancer promised her that a flaming hand would burn in the
sky above the city on the day her father's bones went west. Between
coughs, Lord Gyles told her that he had hired a master stonecarver
to make a statue of Lord Tywin, to stand eternal vigil beside the Lion
Gate. Ser Lambert Turnberry appeared with a patch over his right

eye, swearing that he would wear it until he could bring her the head of her dwarf brother.

No sooner had the queen escaped the clutches of that fool than she found herself cornered by Lady Falyse of Stokeworth and her husband, Ser Balman Byrch. "My lady mother sends her regrets, Your Grace," Falyse burbled at her. "Lollys has been taken to bed with the child and she felt the need to stay with her. She begs that you forgive her, and said I should ask you . . . my mother admired your late father above all other men. Should my sister have a little boy, it is her wish that we might name him Tywin, if . . . if it please you."

Cersei stared at her, aghast. "Your lackwit sister gets herself raped by half of King's Landing, and Tanda thinks to honor the bastard with my lord father's name? I think not."

Falyse flinched back as if she'd been slapped, but her husband only stroked his thick blond mustache with a thumb. "I told Lady Tanda as much. We shall find a more, ah . . . a more fitting name for Lollys's bastard, you have my word."

"See that you do." Cersei showed them a shoulder and moved away. Tommen had fallen into the clutches of Margaery Tyrell and her grandmother, she saw. The Queen of Thorns was so short that for an instant Cersei took her for another child. Before she could rescue her son from the roses, the press brought her face-to-face with her uncle. When the queen reminded him of their meeting later, Ser Kevan gave a weary nod and begged leave to withdraw. But Lancel lingered, the very picture of a man with one foot in the grave. *But is he climbing in or climbing out?*

Cersei forced herself to smile. "Lancel, I am happy to see you looking so much stronger. Maester Ballabar brought us such dire reports, we feared for your life. But I would have thought you on your way to Darry by now, to take up your lordship." Her father had made Lancel a lord after the Battle of the Blackwater, as a sop to his brother Kevan.

"Not as yet. There are outlaws in my castle." Her cousin's voice was as wispy as the mustache on his upper lip. Though his hair had gone white, his mustache fuzz remained a sandy color. Cersei had often gazed up at it while the boy was inside her, pumping dutifully away. *It looks like a smudge of dirt on his lip.* She used to threaten to scrub it off with a little spit. "The riverlands have need of a strong hand, my father says."

A pity that they're getting yours, she wanted to say. Instead she smiled. "And you are to be wed as well."

A gloomy look passed across the young knight's ravaged face. "A Frey girl, and not of my choosing. She is not even maiden. A widow, of Darry blood. My father says that will help me with the peasants, but the peasants are all dead." He reached for her hand. "It is cruel, Cersei. Your Grace knows that I love—"

"—House Lannister," she finished for him. "No one can doubt that, Lancel. May your wife give you strong sons." *Best not let her lord grandfather host the wedding, though.* "I know you will do many noble deeds in Darry."

Lancel nodded, plainly miserable. "When it seemed that I might die, my father brought the High Septon to pray for me. He is a good man." Her cousin's eyes were wet and shiny, a child's eyes in an old man's face. "He says the Mother spared me for some holy purpose, so I might atone for my sins."

Cersei wondered how he intended to atone for her. *Knighting him was a mistake, and bedding him a bigger one.* Lancel was a weak reed, and she liked his newfound piety not at all; he had been much more amusing when he was trying to be Jaime. *What has this mewling fool told the High Septon? And what will he tell his little Frey when they lie together in the dark?* If he confessed to bedding Cersei, well, she could weather that. Men were always lying about women; she would put it down as the braggadocio of a callow boy smitten by her beauty. *If he sings of Robert and the strongwine, though . . .* "Atonement is best achieved through prayer," Cersei told him. "*Silent* prayer." She left him to think about that and girded herself to face the Tyrell host.

Margaery embraced her like a sister, which the queen found presumptuous, but this was not the place to reproach her. Lady Alerie and the cousins contented themselves with kissing fingers. Lady Graceford, who was large with child, asked the queen's leave to name it Tywin if it were a boy, or Lanna if it were a girl. *Another one?* she almost groaned. *The realm will drown in Tywins.* She gave consent as graciously as she could, feigning delight.

It was Lady Merryweather who truly pleased her. "Your Grace," that one said, in her sultry Myrish tones, "I have sent word to my friends across the narrow sea, asking them to seize the Imp at once should he show his ugly face in the Free Cities."

"Do you have many friends across the water?"

"In Myr, many. In Lys as well, and Tyrosh. Men of power."

Cersei could well believe it. The Myrish woman was too beautiful by half; long-legged and full-breasted, with smooth olive skin, ripe lips, huge dark eyes, and thick black hair that always looked as if she'd just come from bed. *She even smells of sin, like some exotic lotus.* "Lord Merryweather and I wish only to serve Your Grace and the little king," the woman purred, with a look that was as pregnant as Lady Graceford.

This one is ambitious, and her lord is proud but poor. "We must speak again, my lady. Taena, is it? You are most kind. I know that we shall be great friends."

Then the Lord of Highgarden descended on her.

Mace Tyrell was no more than ten years older than Cersei, yet she thought of him as her father's age, not her own. He was not quite so tall as Lord Tywin had been, but elsewise he was bigger, with a thick chest and a gut grown even thicker. His hair was chestnut-colored, but there were specks of white and grey in his beard. His face was often red. "Lord Tywin was a great man, an *extraordinary* man," he declared ponderously after he had kissed both her cheeks. "We shall never see his like again, I fear."

You are looking at his like, fool, Cersei thought. *It is his daughter standing here before you.* But she needed Tyrell and the strength of Highgarden to keep Tommen on his throne, so all she said was, "He will be greatly missed."

Tyrell put a hand upon her shoulder. "No man alive is fit to don Lord Tywin's armor, that is plain. Still, the realm goes on, and must be ruled. If there is aught that I might do to serve in this dark hour, Your Grace need only ask."

If you want to be the King's Hand, my lord, have the courage to say it plainly. The queen smiled. *Let him read into that as much as he likes.* "Surely my lord is needed in the Reach?"

"My son Willas is an able lad," the man replied, refusing to take her perfectly good hint. "His leg may be twisted but he has no want of wits. And Garlan will soon take Brightwater. Between them the Reach will be in good hands, if it happens that I am needed elsewhere. The governance of the realm must come first, Lord Tywin often said. And I am pleased to bring Your Grace good tidings in that regard. My uncle Garth has agreed to serve as master of coin, as your lord father wished. He is making his way to Oldtown to take ship. His sons will accompany him. Lord Tywin mentioned something about finding places for the two of them as well. Perhaps in the City Watch."

The queen's smile had frozen so hard she feared her teeth might crack. *Garth the Gross on the small council and his two bastards in the gold cloaks . . . do the Tyrells think I will just serve the realm up to them on a gilded platter?* The arrogance of it took her breath away.

"Garth has served me well as Lord Seneschal, as he served my father before me," Tyrell was going on. "Littlefinger had a nose for gold, I grant you, but Garth—"

"My lord," Cersei broke in, "I fear there has been some misunderstanding. I have asked Lord Gyles Rosby to serve as our new master of coin, and he has done me the honor of accepting."

Mace gaped at her. "Rosby? That . . . *cougher?* But . . . the matter was agreed, Your Grace. Garth is on his way to Oldtown."

"Best send a raven to Lord Hightower and ask him to make certain your uncle does not take ship. We would hate for Garth to brave an autumn sea for nought." She smiled pleasantly.

A flush crept up Tyrell's thick neck. "This . . . your lord father assured me . . ." He began to sputter.

Then his mother appeared and slid her arm through his own. "It would seem that Lord Tywin did not share his plans with our regent, I can't *imagine* why. Still, there 'tis, no use hectoring Her Grace. She is quite right, you must write Lord Leyton before Garth boards a ship. You know the sea will sicken him and make his farting worse." Lady Olenna gave Cersei a toothless smile. "Your council chambers will smell sweeter with Lord Gyles, though I daresay that coughing would drive me to distraction. We all adore dear old uncle Garth, but the man is flatulent, that cannot be gainsaid. I do abhor foul smells." Her wrinkled face wrinkled up even more. "I caught a whiff of something unpleasant in the holy sept, in truth. Mayhaps you smelled it too?"

"No," Cersei said coldly. "A scent, you say?"

"More like a stink."

"Perhaps you miss your autumn roses. We have kept you here too long." The sooner she rid the court of Lady Olenna the better. Lord Tyrell would doubtless dispatch a goodly number of knights to see his mother safely home, and the fewer Tyrell swords in the city, the more soundly the queen would sleep.

"I do long for the fragrances of Highgarden, I confess it," said the old lady, "but of course I cannot leave until I have seen my sweet Margaery wed to your precious little Tommen."

"I await that day eagerly as well," Tyrell put in. "Lord Tywin and I were on the point of setting a date, as it happens. Perhaps you and I might take up that discussion, Your Grace."

"Soon."

"Soon will serve," said Lady Olenna with a sniff. "Now come along, Mace, let Her Grace get on with her . . . grief."

I will see you dead, old woman, Cersei promised herself as the Queen of Thorns tottered off between her towering guardsmen, a pair of seven-footers that it amused her to call Left and Right. *We'll see how sweet a corpse you make.* The old woman was twice as clever as her lord son, that was plain.

The queen rescued her son from Margaery and her cousins, and made for the doors. Outside, the rain had finally stopped. The autumn air smelled sweet and fresh. Tommen took his crown off. "Put that back on," Cersei commanded him.

"It makes my neck hurt," the boy said, but he did as he was bid. "Will I be married soon? Margaery says that as soon as we're wed we can go to Highgarden."

"You are not going to Highgarden, but you can ride back to the castle." Cersei beckoned to Ser Meryn Trant. "Bring His Grace a mount, and ask Lord Gyles if he would do me the honor of sharing my litter."

Things were moving more quickly than she had anticipated; there was no time to be squandered.

Tommen was happy at the prospect of a ride, and of course Lord Gyles was honored by her invitation . . . though when she asked him to be her master of coin, he began coughing so violently that she feared he might die right then and there. But the Mother was merciful, and Gyles eventually recovered sufficiently to accept, and even began coughing out the names of men he wanted to replace, customs officers and wool factors appointed by Littlefinger, even one of the keepers of the keys.

"Name the cow what you will, so long as the milk flows. And should the question arise, you joined the council yesterday."

"Yester—" A fit of coughing bent him over. "Yesterday. To be sure." Lord Gyles coughed into a square of red silk, as if to hide the blood in his spittle. Cersei pretended not to notice.

When he dies I will find someone else. Perhaps she would recall Littlefinger. The queen could not imagine that Petyr Baelish would be allowed to remain Lord Protector of the Vale for very long, with Lysa Arryn dead. The Vale lords were already stirring, if what Pycelle said was true. *Once they take that wretched boy away from him, Lord Petyr will come crawling back.*

"Your Grace?" Lord Gyles coughed, and dabbed his mouth. "Might I . . ." He coughed again. ". . . ask who . . ." Another series of coughs racked him. ". . . who will be the King's Hand?"

"My uncle," she replied absently.

It was a relief to see the gates of the Red Keep looming large before her. She gave Tommen over to the charge of his squires and retired gratefully to her own chambers to rest.

No sooner had she eased off her shoes than Jocelyn entered timidly to say that Qyburn was without and craved audience. "Send him in," the queen commanded. *A ruler gets no rest.*

Qyburn was old, but his hair still had more ash than snow in it, and the laugh lines around his mouth made him look like some little girl's favorite grandfather. *A rather shabby grandfather, though.* The collar of his robe was frayed, and one sleeve had been torn and badly sewn. "I must beg Your Grace's pardon for my appearance," he said.

"I have been down in the dungeons making inquiries into the Imp's escape, as you commanded."

"And what have you discovered?"

"The night that Lord Varys and your brother disappeared, a third man also vanished."

"Yes, the gaoler. What of him?"

"Rugen was the man's name. An undergaoler who had charge of the black cells. The chief undergaoler describes him as portly, unshaven, gruff of speech. He held his appointment of the old king, Aerys, and came and went as he pleased. The black cells have not oft been occupied in recent years. The other turnkeys were afraid of him, it seems, but none knew much about him. He had no friends, no kin. Nor did he drink or frequent brothels. His sleeping cell was damp and dreary, and the straw he slept upon was mildewed. His chamber pot was overflowing."

"I know all this." Jaime had examined Rugen's cell, and Ser Addam's gold cloaks had examined it again.

"Aye, Your Grace," said Qyburn, "but did you know that under that stinking chamber pot was a loose stone, which opened on a small hollow? The sort of place where a man might hide valuables that he did not wish to be discovered?"

"Valuables?" This was new. "Coin, you mean?" She had suspected all along that Tyrion had somehow bought this gaoler.

"Beyond a doubt. To be sure, the hole was empty when I found it. No doubt Rugen took his ill-gotten treasure with him when he fled. But as I crouched over the hole with my torch, I saw something glitter, so I scratched in the dirt until I dug it out." Qyburn opened his palm. "A gold coin."

Gold, yes, but the moment Cersei took it she could tell that it was wrong. *Too small*, she thought, *too thin*. The coin was old and worn. On one side was a king's face in profile, on the other side the imprint of a hand. "This is no dragon," she said.

"No," Qyburn agreed. "It dates from before the Conquest, Your Grace. The king is Garth the Twelfth, and the hand is the sigil of House Gardener."

Of Highgarden. Cersei closed her hand around the coin. *What treachery is this?* Mace Tyrell had been one of Tyrion's judges, and had called loudly for his death. *Was that some ploy? Could he have been plotting with the Imp all the while, conspiring at Father's death?* With Tywin Lannister in his grave, Lord Tyrell was an obvious choice to be King's Hand, but even so ... "You will not speak of this with anyone," she commanded.

"Your Grace may trust in my discretion. Any man who rides with a sellsword company learns to hold his tongue, else he does not keep it long."

"In my company as well." The queen put the coin away. She would think about it later. "What of the other matter?"

"Ser Gregor." Qyburn shrugged. "I have examined him, as you commanded. The poison on the Viper's spear was manticore venom from the east, I would stake my life on that."

"Pycelle says no. He told my lord father that manticore venom kills the instant it reaches the heart."

"And so it does. But this venom has been *thickened* somehow, so as to draw out the Mountain's dying."

"Thickened? Thickened *how?* With some other substance?"

"It may be as Your Grace suggests, though in most cases adulterating a poison only lessens its potency. It may be that the cause is ... less natural, let us say. A spell, I think."

Is this one as big a fool as Pycelle? "So are you telling me that the Mountain is dying of some black *sorcery?*"

Qyburn ignored the mockery in her voice. "He is dying of the venom, but slowly, and in exquisite agony. My efforts to ease his pain have proved as fruitless as Pycelle's. Ser Gregor is overly accustomed to the poppy, I fear. His squire tells me that he is plagued by blinding headaches and oft quaffs the milk of the poppy as lesser men quaff ale. Be that as it may, his veins have turned black from head to heel, his water is clouded with pus, and the venom has eaten a hole in his side as large as my fist. It is a wonder that the man is still alive, if truth be told."

"His size," the queen suggested, frowning. "Gregor is a very large man. Also a very stupid one. Too stupid to know when he should die, it seems." She held out her cup, and Senelle filled it once again. "His screaming frightens Tommen. It has even been known to wake me of a night. I would say it is past time we summoned Ilyn Payne."

"Your Grace," said Qyburn, "mayhaps I might move Ser Gregor to the dungeons? His screams will not disturb you there, and I will be able to tend to him more freely."

"Tend to him?" She laughed. "Let Ser Ilyn tend to him."

"If that is Your Grace's wish," Qyburn said, "but this poison . . . it would be useful to know more about it, would it not? Send a knight to slay a knight and an archer to kill an archer, the smallfolk often say. To combat the black arts . . ." He did not finish the thought, but only smiled at her.

He is not Pycelle, that much is plain. The queen weighed him, wondering. "Why did the Citadel take your chain?"

"The archmaesters are all craven at heart. The grey sheep, Marwyn calls them. I was as skilled a healer as Ebrose, but aspired to surpass him. For hundreds of years the men of the Citadel have opened the bodies of the dead, to study the nature of life. I wished to understand the nature of death, so I opened the bodies of the living. For that crime the grey sheep shamed me and forced me into exile . . . but I understand the nature of life and death better than any man in Oldtown."

"Do you?" That intrigued her. "Very well. The Mountain is yours. Do what you will with him, but confine your studies to the black cells. When he dies, bring me his head. My father promised it to Dorne. Prince Doran would no doubt prefer to kill Gregor himself, but we all must suffer disappointments in this life."

"Very good, Your Grace." Qyburn cleared his throat. "I am not so well provided as Pycelle, however. I must needs equip myself with certain . . ."

"I shall instruct Lord Gyles to provide you with gold sufficient for your needs. Buy yourself some new robes as well. You look as though you've wandered up from Flea Bottom." She studied his eyes, wondering how far she dared trust this one. "Need I say that it will go ill for you if any word of your . . . labors . . . should pass beyond these walls?"

"No, Your Grace." Qyburn gave her a reassuring smile. "Your secrets are safe with me."

When he was gone, Cersei poured herself a cup of strongwine and drank it by the window, watching the shadows lengthen across the yard and thinking about the coin. *Gold from the Reach. Why would an undergaoler in King's Landing have gold from the Reach, unless he were paid to help bring about Father's death?*

Try as she might, she could not seem to bring Lord Tywin's face to mind without seeing that silly little half smile and remembering the foul smell coming off his corpse. She wondered whether Tyrion was somehow behind that as well. *It is small and cruel, like him.* Could Tyrion have made Pycelle his catspaw? *He sent the old man to the black cells, and this Rugen had charge of those cells,* she remembered. All the strings were tangled up together in ways she did not like. *This High Septon is Tyrion's creature too,* Cersei recalled suddenly, *and Father's poor body was in his care from dark till dawn.*

Her uncle arrived promptly at sunset, wearing a quilted doublet of charcoal-colored wool as somber as his face. Like all the Lannisters, Ser Kevan was fair-skinned and blond, though at five-and-fifty he had lost most of his hair. No one would ever call him comely. Thick of waist, round of shoulder, with a square jutting chin that his close-cropped yellow beard did little to conceal, he reminded her of some old mastiff . . . but a faithful old mastiff was the very thing that she required.

They ate a simple supper of beets and bread and bloody beef with a flagon of Dornish red to wash it all down. Ser Kevan said little and scarce touched his wine cup. *He broods too much,* she decided. *He needs to be put to work to get beyond his grief.*

She said as much, when the last of the food had been cleared away and the servants had departed. "I know how much my father relied on you, Uncle. Now I must do the same."

"You need a Hand," he said, "and Jaime has refused you."

He is blunt. Very well. "Jaime . . . I felt so lost with Father dead, I scarce knew what I was saying. Jaime is gallant, but a bit of a fool, let us be frank. Tommen needs a more seasoned man. Someone older . . ."

"Mace Tyrell is older."

Her nostrils flared. "Never." Cersei pushed a lock of hair off her brow. "The Tyrells overreach themselves."

"You would be a fool to make Mace Tyrell your Hand," Ser Kevan admitted, "but a bigger fool to make him your foe. I've heard what happened in the Hall of Lamps. Mace should have known better than to broach such matters in public, but even so, you were unwise to shame him in front of half the court."

"Better that than suffer another Tyrell on the council." His reproach annoyed her. "Rosby will make an adequate master of coin. You've seen that litter of his, with its carvings and silk draperies. His horses are better dressed than most knights. A man that rich should have no problem finding gold. As for Handship . . . who better to finish my father's work than the brother who shared all his counsels?"

"Every man needs someone he can trust. Tywin had me, and once your mother."

"He loved her very much." Cersei refused to think about the dead whore in his bed. "I know they are together now."

"So I pray." Ser Kevan studied her face for a long moment before he replied. "You ask much of me, Cersei."

"No more than my father did."

"I am tired." Her uncle reached for his wine cup and took a swallow. "I have a wife I have not seen in two years, a dead son to mourn, another son about to marry and assume a lordship. Castle Darry must be made strong again, its lands protected, its burned fields plowed and planted anew. Lancel needs my help."

"As does Tommen." Cersei had not expected Kevan to require coaxing. *He never played coy with Father.* "The realm needs you."

"The realm. Aye. And House Lannister." He sipped his wine again. "Very well. I will remain and serve His Grace . . ."

"Very good," she started to say, but Ser Kevan raised his voice and bulled right over her.

". . . so long as you name me regent as well as Hand and take yourself back to Casterly Rock."

For half a heartbeat Cersei could only stare at him. "*I* am the regent," she reminded him.

"You were. Tywin did not intend that you continue in that role. He told me of his plans to send you back to the Rock and find a new husband for you."

Cersei could feel her anger rising. "He spoke of such, yes. And I told him it was not my wish to wed again."

Her uncle was unmoved. "If you are resolved against another marriage, I will not force it on you. As to the other, though . . . you are the Lady of Casterly Rock now. Your place is there."

How dare you? she wanted to scream. Instead, she said, "I am also the Queen Regent. My place is with my son."

"Your father thought not."

"My father is dead."

"To my grief, and the woe of all the realm. Open your eyes and look about you, Cersei. The kingdom is in ruins. Tywin might have been able to set matters aright, but . . ."

"*I* shall set matters aright!" Cersei softened her tone. "With your help, Uncle. If you will serve me as faithfully as you served my father—"

"You are not your father. And Tywin always regarded Jaime as his rightful heir."

"*Jaime* . . . Jaime has taken vows. Jaime never thinks, he laughs at everything and everyone and says whatever comes into his head. Jaime is a handsome fool."

"And yet he was your first choice to be the King's Hand. What does that make you, Cersei?"

"I told you, I was sick with grief, I did not think—"

"No," Ser Kevan agreed. "Which is why you should return to Casterly Rock and leave the king with those who do."

"*The king is my son!*" Cersei rose to her feet.

"Aye," her uncle said, "and from what I saw of Joffrey, you are as unfit a mother as you are a ruler."

She threw the contents of her wine cup full in his face.

Ser Kevan rose with a ponderous dignity. "Your Grace." Wine trickled down his cheeks and dripped from his close-cropped beard. "With your leave, might I withdraw?"

"By what right do you presume to give *me* terms? You are no more than one of my father's household knights."

"I hold no lands, that is true. But I have certain incomes, and chests of coin set aside. My own father forgot none of his children when he died, and Tywin knew how to reward good service. I feed two hundred knights and can double that number if need be. There are freeriders who will follow my banner, and I have the gold to hire sellswords. You would be wise not to take me lightly, Your Grace . . . and wiser still not to make of me a foe."

"Are you *threatening* me?"

"I am counseling you. If you will not yield the regency to me, name me your castellan for Casterly Rock and make either Mathis Rowan or Randyll Tarly the Hand of the King."

Tyrell bannermen, both of them. The suggestion left her speechless. *Is he bought?* she wondered. *Has he taken Tyrell gold to betray House Lannister?*

"Mathis Rowan is sensible, prudent, well liked," her uncle went on, oblivious. "Randyll Tarly is the finest soldier in the realm. A poor Hand for peacetime, but with Tywin dead there's no better man to finish this war. Lord Tyrell cannot take offense if you choose one of his own bannermen as Hand. Both Tarly and Rowan are able men . . . and *loyal.* Name either one, and you make him yours. You strengthen yourself and weaken Highgarden, yet Mace will likely thank you for it." He gave a shrug. "That is my counsel, take it or no. You may make Moon Boy your Hand for all I care. My brother is dead, woman. I am going to take him home."

Traitor, she thought. *Turncloak.* She wondered how much Mace Tyrell had given him. "You would abandon your king when he needs you most," she told him. "You would abandon Tommen."

"Tommen has his mother." Ser Kevan's green eyes met her own, unblinking. A last drop of wine trembled wet and red beneath his chin, and finally fell. "Aye," he added softly, after a pause, "and his father too, I think."

JAIME

S er Jaime Lannister, all in white, stood beside his father's bier,
five fingers curled about the hilt of a golden greatsword.

At dusk, the interior of the Great Sept of Baelor turned dim
and eerie. The last light of day slanted down through the high windows,
washing the towering likenesses of the Seven in a red gloom. Around
their altars, scented candles flickered whilst deep shadows gathered in
the transepts and crept silently across the marble floors. The echoes of
the evensongs died away as the last mourners were departing.

Balon Swann and Loras Tyrell remained when the rest had gone.
"No man can stand a vigil for seven days and seven nights," Ser Balon
said. "When did you last sleep, my lord?"

"When my lord father was alive," said Jaime.

"Allow me to stand tonight in your stead," Ser Loras offered.

"He was not your father." *You did not kill him. I did. Tyrion may have
loosed the crossbow bolt that slew him, but I loosed Tyrion.* "Leave me."

"As my lord commands," said Swann. Ser Loras looked as if he
might have argued further, but Ser Balon took his arm and drew him
off. Jaime listened to the echoes of their footfalls die away. And then
he was alone again with his lord father, amongst the candles and the
crystals and the sickly sweet smell of death. His back ached from
the weight of his armor, and his legs felt almost numb. He shifted his
stance a bit and tightened his fingers around the golden greatsword.

He could not wield a sword, but he could hold one. His missing hand was throbbing. That was almost funny. He had more feeling in the hand he'd lost than in the rest of the body that remained to him.

My hand is hungry for a sword. I need to kill someone. Varys, for a start, but first I'd need to find the rock he's hiding under. "I commanded the eunuch to take him to a ship, not to your bedchamber," he told the corpse. "The blood is on his hands as much as . . . as Tyrion's." *The blood is on his hands as much as mine,* he meant to say, but the words stuck in his throat. *Whatever Varys did, I made him do.*

He had waited in the eunuch's chambers that night, when at last he had decided not to let his little brother die. As he waited, he had sharpened his dagger with one hand, taking a queer comfort from the *scrape-scrape-scrape* of steel on stone. At the sound of footsteps he stood beside the door. Varys entered in a wash of powder and lavender. Jaime stepped out behind him, kicked him in the back of the knee, knelt on his chest, and shoved the knife up under his soft white chin, forcing his head up. "Why, Lord Varys," he'd said pleasantly, "fancy meeting you here."

"Ser Jaime?" Varys panted. "You frightened me."

"I meant to." When he twisted the dagger, a trickle of blood ran down the blade. "I was thinking you might help me pluck my brother from his cell before Ser Ilyn lops his head off. It is an ugly head, I grant you, but he only has the one."

"Yes . . . well . . . if you would . . . remove the blade . . . yes, gently, as it please my lord, gently, oh, I'm pricked . . ." The eunuch touched his neck and gaped at the blood on his fingers. "I have always abhorred the sight of my own blood."

"You'll have more to abhor shortly, unless you help me."

Varys struggled to a sitting position. "Your brother . . . if the Imp should vanish unaccountably from his cell, q-questions would be asked. I would f-fear for my life . . ."

"Your life is mine. I do not care what secrets you know. If Tyrion dies, you will not long outlive him, I promise you."

"Ah." The eunuch sucked the blood off his fingers. "You ask a dreadful thing . . . to loose the Imp who slew our lovely king. Or is it that you believe him innocent?"

"Innocent or guilty," Jaime had said, like the fool he was, "a Lannister pays his debts." The words had come so easy.

He had not slept since. He could see his brother now, the way the dwarf had grinned beneath the stub of his nose as the torchlight licked his face. "You poor stupid blind crippled fool," he'd snarled, in a voice thick with malice. "Cersei is a lying whore, she's been fucking Lancel and Osmund Kettleblack and probably Moon Boy, for all I know. And I am the monster they all say I am. Yes, I killed your vile son."

He never said he meant to kill our father. If he had, I would have stopped him. Then I would be the kinslayer, not him.

Jaime wondered where Varys was hiding. Wisely, the master of whisperers had not returned to his own chambers, nor had a search of the Red Keep turned him up. It might be that the eunuch had taken ship with Tyrion, rather than remain to answer awkward questions. If so, the two of them were well out to sea by now, sharing a flagon of Arbor gold in the cabin of a galley.

Unless my brother murdered Varys too, and left his corpse to rot beneath the castle. Down there, it might be years before his bones were found. Jaime had led a dozen guards below, with torches and ropes and lanterns. For hours they had groped through twisting passages, narrow crawl spaces, hidden doors, secret steps, and shafts that plunged down into utter blackness. Seldom had he felt so utterly a cripple. A man takes much for granted when he has two hands. Ladders, for an instance. Even crawling did not come easy; not for nought do they speak of *hands* and knees. Nor could he hold a torch and climb, as others could.

And all for naught. They found only darkness, dust, and rats. *And dragons, lurking down below.* He remembered the sullen orange glow of the coals in the iron dragon's mouth. The brazier warmed a chamber at the bottom of a shaft where half a dozen tunnels met. On the floor he'd found a scuffed mosaic of the three-headed dragon of House Targaryen done in tiles of black and red. *I know you, Kingslayer,* the beast seemed to be saying. *I have been here all the time, waiting for you to come to me.* And it seemed to Jaime that he knew that voice, the iron tones that had once belonged to Rhaegar, Prince of Dragonstone.

The day had been windy when he said farewell to Rhaegar, in the yard of the Red Keep. The prince had donned his night-black armor, with the three-headed dragon picked out in rubies on his breastplate. "Your Grace," Jaime had pleaded, "let Darry stay to guard the king this once, or Ser Barristan. Their cloaks are as white as mine."

Prince Rhaegar shook his head. "My royal sire fears your father more than he does our cousin Robert. He wants you close, so Lord Tywin cannot harm him. I dare not take that crutch away from him at such an hour."

Jaime's anger had risen up in his throat. "I am not a crutch. I am a knight of the Kingsguard."

"Then guard the king," Ser Jon Darry snapped at him. "When you donned that cloak, you promised to obey."

Rhaegar had put his hand on Jaime's shoulder. "When this battle's done I mean to call a council. Changes will be made. I meant to do it long ago, but . . . well, it does no good to speak of roads not taken. We shall talk when I return."

Those were the last words Rhaegar Targaryen ever spoke to him. Outside the gates an army had assembled, whilst another descended on the Trident. So the Prince of Dragonstone mounted up and donned his tall black helm, and rode forth to his doom.

He was more right than he knew. When the battle was done, there were changes made. "Aerys thought no harm could come to him if he kept me near," he told his father's corpse. "Isn't that amusing?" Lord Tywin seemed to think so; his smile was wider than before. *He seems to enjoy being dead.*

It was queer, but he felt no grief. *Where are my tears? Where is my rage?* Jaime Lannister had never lacked for rage. "Father," he told the corpse, "it was you who told me that tears were a mark of weakness in a man, so you cannot expect that I should cry for you."

A thousand lords and ladies had come that morning to file past the bier, and several thousand smallfolk after noon. They wore somber clothes and solemn faces, but Jaime suspected that many and more were secretly delighted to see the great man brought low. Even in the west, Lord Tywin had been more respected than beloved, and King's Landing still remembered the Sack.

Of all the mourners, Grand Maester Pycelle had seemed the most distraught. "I have served six kings," he told Jaime after the second service, whilst sniffing doubtfully about the corpse, "but here before us lies the greatest man I ever knew. Lord Tywin wore no crown, yet he was all a king should be."

Without his beard, Pycelle looked not only old, but feeble. *Shaving him was the cruelest thing Tyrion could have done,* thought Jaime, who knew what it was to lose a part of yourself, the part that made you who you were. Pycelle's beard had been magnificent, white as snow and soft as lambswool, a luxuriant growth that covered cheeks and chin and flowed down almost to his belt. The Grand Maester had been wont to stroke it when he pontificated. It had given him an air of wisdom, and concealed all manner of unsavory things: the loose skin dangling beneath the old man's jaw, the small querulous mouth and missing teeth, warts and wrinkles and age spots too numerous to count. Though Pycelle was trying to regrow what he had lost, he was failing. Only wisps and tufts sprouted from his wrinkled cheeks and weak chin, so thin that Jaime could see the splotchy pink skin beneath.

"Ser Jaime, I have seen terrible things in my time," the old man said. "Wars, battles, murders most foul . . . I was a boy in Oldtown when the grey plague took half the city and three-quarters of the Citadel. Lord Hightower burned every ship in port, closed the gates, and commanded his guards to slay all those who tried to flee, be they men, women, or babes in arms. They killed him when the plague had run its course. On the very day he reopened the port, they dragged him from his horse and slit his throat, and his young son's as well. To this day the ignorant in Oldtown will spit at the sound of his name, but Quenton Hightower did what was needed. Your father was that sort of man as well. A man who did what was needed."

"Is that why he looks so pleased with himself?"

The vapors rising from the corpse were making Pycelle's eyes water. "The flesh . . . as the flesh dries, the muscles grow taut and pull his lips upward. That is no smile, only a . . . a *drying,* that is all." He blinked back tears. "You must excuse me. I am so very tired." Leaning heavily on his cane, Pycelle tottered slowly from the sept. *That one is dying too,* Jaime realized. Small wonder Cersei called him useless.

To be sure, his sweet sister seemed to think half the court was either useless or treasonous; Pycelle, the Kingsguard, the Tyrells, Jaime himself . . . even Ser Ilyn Payne, the silent knight who served as headsman. As King's Justice, the dungeons were his responsibility. Since he lacked a tongue, Payne had largely left the running of those dungeons to his underlings, but Cersei held him to blame for Tyrion's escape all the same. *It was my work, not his,* Jaime almost told her. Instead he had promised to find what answers he could from the chief undergaoler, a bentback old man named Rennifer Longwaters.

"I see you wonder, what sort of name is that?" the man had cackled when Jaime went to question him. "It is an old name, 'tis true. I am not one to boast, but there is royal blood in my veins. I am descended from a princess. My father told me the tale when I was a tad of a lad." Longwaters had not been a tad of a lad for many a year, to judge from his spotted head and the white hairs growing from his chin. "She was the fairest treasure of the Maidenvault. Lord Oakenfist the great admiral lost his heart to her, though he was married to another. She gave their son the bastard name of 'Waters' in honor of his father, and he grew to be a great knight, as did his own son, who put the 'Long' before the 'Waters' so men might know that he was not basely born himself. So I have a little dragon in me."

"Yes, I almost mistook you for Aegon the Conqueror," Jaime had answered. "Waters" was a common bastard name about Blackwater Bay; old Longwaters was more like to be descended from some minor household knight than from a princess. "As it matters, though, I have more pressing concerns than your lineage."

Longwaters inclined his head. "The lost prisoner."

"And the missing gaoler."

"Rugen," the old man supplied. "An undergaoler. He had charge of the third level, the black cells."

"Tell me of him," Jaime had to say. *A bloody farce.* He knew who Rugen was, even if Longwaters did not.

"Unkempt, unshaven, coarse of speech. I misliked the man, 'tis true, I do confess it. Rugen was here when I first came, twelve years past. He held his appointment from King Aerys. The man was seldom here, it must be said. I made note of it in my reports, my lord. I most suredly did, I give you my word upon it, the word of a man with royal blood."

Mention that royal blood once more and I may spill some of it, thought Jaime. "Who saw these reports?"

"Certain of them went to the master of coin, others to the master of whisperers. All to the chief gaoler and the King's Justice. It has always been so in the dungeons." Longwaters scratched his nose. "Rugen was here when need be, my lord. That must be said. The black cells are little used. Before your lordship's little brother was sent down, we had Grand Maester Pycelle for a time, and before him Lord Stark the traitor. There were three others, common men, but Lord Stark gave them to the Night's Watch. I did not think it good to free those three, but the papers were in proper order. I made note of that in a report as well, you may be certain of it."

"Tell me of the two gaolers who went to sleep."

"Gaolers?" Longwaters sniffed. "Those were no gaolers. They were merely *turnkeys*. The crown pays wages for twenty turnkeys, my lord, a full score, but during my time we have never had more than twelve. We are supposed to have six undergaolers as well, two on each level, but there are only the three."

"You and two others?"

Longwaters sniffed again. "I am the *chief* undergaoler, my lord. I am *above* the undergaolers. I am charged with keeping the counts. If my lord would like to look over my books, he will see that all the figures are exact." Longwaters had consulted the great leather-bound book spread out before him. "At present, we have four prisoners on the first level and one on the second, in addition to your lordship's brother." The old man frowned. "Who is fled, to be sure. 'Tis true. I will strike him out." He took up a quill and began to sharpen it.

Six prisoners, Jaime thought sourly, *while we pay wages for twenty turnkeys, six undergaolers, a chief undergaoler, a gaoler, and a King's Justice.* "I want to question these two turnkeys."

Rennifer Longwaters let up sharpening his quill and peered doubtfully up at Jaime. "Question them, my lord?"

"You heard me."

"I did, my lord, I surely did, and yet . . . my lord may question who he pleases, 'tis true, it is not my place to say that he may not. But, ser, if I may be so bold, I do not think them like to answer. They are dead, my lord."

"*Dead?* By whose command?"

"Your own, I thought, or . . . the king's, mayhaps? I did not ask. It . . . it is not my place to question the Kingsguard."

That was salt for his wound; Cersei had used his own men to do her bloody work, them and her precious Kettleblacks.

"You witless fools," Jaime had snarled at Boros Blount and Osmund Kettleblack later, in a dungeon that stank of blood and death. "What did you imagine you were doing?"

"No more'n we was told, my lord." Ser Boros was shorter than Jaime, but heavier. "Her Grace commanded it. Your sister."

Ser Osmund hooked a thumb through his swordbelt. "She said they were to sleep forever. So my brothers and me, we saw to it."

That you did. One corpse sprawled facedown upon the table, like a man passed out at a feast, but it was a puddle of blood beneath his head, not a puddle of wine. The second turnkey had managed to push back from the bench and draw his dagger before someone shoved a longsword through his ribs. His had been the longer, messier end. *I told Varys no one was to be harmed in this escape,* Jaime thought, *but I should have told my brother and my sister.* "This was ill done, ser."

Ser Osmund shrugged. "They won't be missed. I'll wager they was part of it, along with the one who's gone missing."

No, Jaime could have told him. *Varys dosed their wine to make them sleep.* "If so, we might have coaxed the truth from them." . . . *she's been fucking Lancel and Osmund Kettleblack and Moon Boy, for all I know* . . . "If I had a suspicious nature I might wonder why you were in such haste to make certain these two were never put to the question. Did you need to silence them to conceal your own part in this?"

"Us?" Kettleblack choked on that. "All we done was what the queen commanded. On my word as your Sworn Brother."

Jaime's phantom fingers twitched as he said, "Get Osney and Osfryd down here and clean up this mess you've made. And the next time my sweet sister commands you to kill a man, come to me first. Elsewise, stay out of my sight, ser."

The words echoed in his head in the dimness of Baelor's Sept. Above him, all the windows had gone black, and he could see the faint light of distant stars. The sun had set for good and all. The stench of death was growing stronger, despite the scented candles. The smell reminded Jaime Lannister of the pass below the Golden Tooth, where he had won a glorious victory in the first days of the war. On the morning after the battle, the crows had feasted on victors and vanquished alike, as once they had feasted on Rhaegar Targaryen after the Trident. *How much can a crown be worth, when a crow can dine upon a king?*

There were crows circling the seven towers and great dome of Baelor's Sept even now, Jaime suspected, their black wings beating against the night air as they searched for a way inside. *Every crow in the Seven Kingdoms should pay homage to you, Father. From Castamere to the Blackwater, you fed them well.* That notion pleased Lord Tywin; his smile widened further. *Bloody hell, he's grinning like a bridegroom at his bedding.*

That was so grotesque it made Jaime laugh aloud.

The sound echoed through the transepts and crypts and chapels, as if the dead interred within the walls were laughing too. *Why not? This is more absurd than a mummer's farce, me standing vigil for a father I helped to slay, sending men forth to capture the brother I helped to free* ... He had commanded Ser Addam Marbrand to search the Street of Silk. "Look under every bed, you know how fond my brother is of brothels." The gold cloaks would find more of interest beneath the whores' skirts than beneath their beds. He wondered how many bastard children would be born of the pointless search.

Unbidden, his thoughts went to Brienne of Tarth. *Stupid stubborn ugly wench.* He wondered where she was. *Father, give her strength.* Almost a prayer ... but was it the god he was invoking, the Father Above whose towering gilded likeness glimmered in the candlelight across the sept? Or was he praying to the corpse that lay before him? *Does it matter? They never listened, either one.* The Warrior had been Jaime's god since he was old enough to hold a sword. Other men might be fathers, sons, husbands, but never Jaime Lannister, whose sword was as golden as his hair. He was a warrior, and that was all he would ever be.

I should tell Cersei the truth, admit that it was me who freed our little brother from his cell. The truth had worked so splendidly with Tyrion, after all. *I killed your vile son, and now I'm off to kill your father too.* Jaime could hear the Imp laughing in the gloom. He turned his head to look, but the sound was only his own laughter coming back at him. He closed his eyes, and just as quickly snapped them open. *I must not sleep.* If he slept, he might dream. Oh, how Tyrion was sniggering. . . . *a lying whore . . . fucking Lancel and Osmund Kettleblack . . .*

At midnight, the hinges on the Father's Doors gave a groan as several hundred septons filed in for their devotions. Some were clad in the cloth-of-silver vestments and crystal coronals that marked the Most Devout; their humbler brethren wore their crystals on thongs about their necks and cinched white robes with seven-stranded belts, each plait a different color. Through the Mother's Doors marched white septas from their cloister, seven abreast and singing softly, while the silent sisters came single file down the Stranger's Steps. Death's handmaidens were garbed in soft grey, their faces hooded and shawled so only their eyes could be seen. A host of brothers appeared as well, in robes of brown and butternut and dun and even undyed roughspun, belted with lengths of hempen rope. Some hung the iron hammer of the Smith about their necks, whilst others carried begging bowls.

None of the devout paid Jaime any mind. They made a circuit of the sept, worshiping at each of the seven altars to honor the seven aspects of the deity. To each god they made sacrifice, to each they sang a hymn. Sweet and solemn rose their voices. Jaime closed his eyes to listen, but opened them again when he began to sway. *I am more weary than I knew.*

It had been years since his last vigil. *And I was younger then, a boy of fifteen years.* He had worn no armor then, only a plain white tunic. The sept where he'd spent the night was not a third as large as any of the Great Sept's seven transepts. Jaime had laid his sword across the Warrior's knees, piled his armor at his feet, and knelt upon the rough stone floor before the altar. When dawn came his knees were raw and bloody. "All knights must bleed, Jaime," Ser Arthur Dayne had said, when he saw. "Blood is the seal of our devotion." With dawn he tapped him on the shoulder; the pale blade was so sharp that even that light touch cut through Jaime's tunic, so he bled anew. He never felt it. A boy knelt; a knight rose. *The Young Lion, not the Kingslayer.*

But that was long ago, and the boy was dead.

He could not have said when the devotions ended. Perhaps he slept, still standing. When the devout had filed out, the Great Sept grew still once more. The candles were a wall of stars burning in the darkness, though the air was rank with death. Jaime shifted his grip upon the golden greatsword. Perhaps he should have let Ser Loras relieve him after all. *Cersei would have hated that.* The Knight of Flowers was still half a boy, arrogant and vain, but he had it in him to be great, to perform deeds worthy of the White Book.

The White Book would be waiting when this vigil was done, his page open in dumb reproach. *I'll hack the bloody book to pieces before I'll fill it full of lies.* Yet if he would not lie, what could he write but truth?

A woman stood before him.

It is raining again, he thought when he saw how wet she was. The water was trickling down her cloak to puddle round her feet. *How did she get here? I never heard her enter.* She was dressed like a tavern wench in a heavy roughspun cloak, badly dyed in mottled browns and fraying at the hem. A hood concealed her face, but he could see the candles dancing in the green pools of her eyes, and when she moved he knew her.

"Cersei." He spoke slowly, like a man waking from a dream, still wondering where he was. "What hour is it?"

"The hour of the wolf." His sister lowered her hood, and made a face. "The drowned wolf, perhaps." She smiled for him, so sweetly. "Do you remember the first time I came to you like this? It was some dismal inn off Weasel Alley, and I put on servant's garb to get past Father's guards."

"I remember. It was Eel Alley." *She wants something of me.* "Why are you here, at this hour? What would you have of me?" His last word echoed up and down the sept, *mememememememememememe,* fading to a whisper. For a moment he dared to hope that all she wanted was the comfort of his arms.

"Speak softly." Her voice sounded strange . . . breathless, almost frightened. "Jaime, Kevan has refused me. He will not serve as Hand, he . . . he knows about us. He said as much."

"Refused?" That surprised him. "How could he know? He will have read what Stannis wrote, but there is no . . ."

"*Tyrion* knew," she reminded him. "Who can say what tales that vile dwarf may have told, or to whom? Uncle Kevan is the least of it. The High Septon . . . Tyrion raised him to the crown, when the fat one died. He may know as well." She moved closer. "You *must* be Tommen's Hand. I do not trust Mace Tyrell. What if he had a hand in Father's death? He may have been conspiring with Tyrion. The Imp could be on his way to Highgarden . . ."

"He's not."

"Be my Hand," she pleaded, "and we'll rule the Seven Kingdoms together, like a king and his queen."

"You were Robert's queen. And yet you won't be mine."

"I would, if I dared. But our son—"

"Tommen is no son of mine, no more than Joffrey was." His voice was hard. "You made them Robert's too."

His sister flinched. "You swore that you would always love me. It is not loving to make me beg."

Jaime could smell the fear on her, even through the rank stench of the corpse. He wanted to take her in his arms and kiss her, to bury his face in her golden curls and promise her that no one would ever hurt her . . . *not here*, he thought, *not here in front of the gods, and Father*. "No," he said. "I cannot. Will not."

"I *need* you. I need my other half." He could hear the rain pattering against the windows high above. "You are me, I am you. I need you with me. *In* me. Please, Jaime. *Please*."

Jaime looked to make certain Lord Tywin was not rising from his bier in wrath, but his father lay still and cold, rotting. "I was made for a battlefield, not a council chamber. And now it may be that I am unfit even for that."

Cersei wiped her tears away on a ragged brown sleeve. "Very well. If it is battlefields you want, battlefields I shall give you." She jerked her hood up angrily. "I was a fool to come. I was a fool ever to love you." Her footsteps echoed loudly in the quiet, and left damp splotches on the marble floor.

Dawn caught Jaime almost unawares. As the glass in the dome began to lighten, suddenly there were rainbows shimmering off the walls and floors and pillars, bathing Lord Tywin's corpse in a haze of many-colored light. The King's Hand was rotting visibly. His face had taken on a greenish tinge, and his eyes were deeply sunken, two black pits. Fissures had opened in his cheeks, and a foul white fluid was seeping through the joints of his splendid gold-and-crimson armor to pool beneath his body.

The septons were the first to see, when they returned for their dawn devotions. They sang their songs and prayed their prayers and wrinkled up their noses, and one of the Most Devout grew so faint he had to be helped from the sept. Shortly after, a flock of novices came swinging censers, and the air grew so thick with incense that the bier seemed cloaked in smoke. All the rainbows vanished in that perfumed mist, yet the stench persisted, a sweet rotten smell that made Jaime want to gag.

When the doors were opened the Tyrells were amongst the first to enter, as befit their rank. Margaery had brought a great bouquet of golden roses. She placed them ostentatiously at the foot of Lord Tywin's bier but kept one back and held it beneath her nose as she took her seat. *So the girl is as clever as she is pretty. Tommen could do a deal worse for a queen. Others have.* Margaery's ladies followed her example.

Cersei waited until the rest were in their places to make her entrance, with Tommen at her side. Ser Osmund Kettleblack paced beside them in his white enamel plate and white wool cloak.

"... *she's been fucking Lancel and Osmund Kettleblack and Moon Boy, for all I know* ..."

Jaime had seen Kettleblack naked in the bathhouse, had seen the black hair on his chest, and the coarser thatch between his legs. He pictured that chest pressed against his sister's, that hair scratching the soft skin of her breasts. *She would not do that. The Imp lied.* Spun gold and black wire tangled, sweaty. Kettleblack's narrow cheeks clenching each time he thrust. Jaime could hear his sister moan. *No. A lie.*

Red-eyed and pale, Cersei climbed the steps to kneel above their father, drawing Tommen down beside her. The boy recoiled at the sight, but his mother seized his wrist before he could pull away. *"Pray,"* she whispered, and Tommen tried. But he was only eight and Lord Tywin was a horror. One desperate breath of air, then the king began to sob. *"Stop that!"* Cersei said. Tommen turned his head and doubled over, retching. His crown fell off and rolled across the marble floor. His mother pulled back in disgust, and all at once the king was running for the doors, as fast as his eight-year-old legs could carry him.

"Ser Osmund, relieve me," Jaime said sharply, as Kettleblack turned to chase the crown. He handed the man the golden sword and went after his king. In the Hall of Lamps he caught him, beneath the eyes of two dozen startled septas. "I'm sorry," Tommen wept. "I will do better on the morrow. Mother says a king must show the way, but the smell made me sick."

This will not do. Too many eager ears and watching eyes. "Best we go outside, Your Grace." Jaime led the boy out to where the air was as fresh and clean as King's Landing ever got. Twoscore gold cloaks had been posted around the plaza to guard the horses and the litters. He took the king off to the side, well away from everyone, and sat him down upon the marble steps. "I wasn't scared," the boy insisted. "The smell made me sick. Didn't it make you sick? How could you bear it, Uncle, ser?"

I have smelled my own hand rotting, when Vargo Hoat made me wear it for a pendant. "A man can bear most anything, if he must," Jaime told his son. *I have smelled a man roasting, as King Aerys cooked him in his own armor.* "The world is full of horrors, Tommen. You can fight them, or laugh at them, or look without seeing . . . go away inside."

Tommen considered that. "I . . . I used to go away inside sometimes," he confessed, "when Joffy . . ."

"Joffrey." Cersei stood over them, the wind whipping her skirts around her legs. "Your brother's name was *Joffrey.* He would never have shamed me so."

"I never meant to. I wasn't frightened, Mother. It was only that your lord father smelled so bad . . ."

"Do you think he smelled any sweeter to me? I have a nose too."
She caught his ear and pulled him to his feet. "Lord Tyrell has a nose.
Did you see him retching in the holy sept? Did you see Lady Margaery
bawling like a baby?"

Jaime got to his feet. "Cersei, enough."

Her nostrils flared. "Ser? Why are you here? You swore to stand
vigil over Father until the wake was done, as I recall."

"It *is* done. Go look at him."

"No. Seven days and seven nights, you said. Surely the Lord
Commander remembers how to count to seven. Take the number of
your fingers, then add two."

Others had begun to stream out onto the plaza, fleeing the noxious
odors in the sept. "Cersei, keep your voice down," Jaime warned. "Lord
Tyrell is approaching."

That reached her. The queen drew Tommen to her side. Mace
Tyrell bowed before them. "His Grace is not unwell, I hope?"

"The king was overwhelmed by grief," said Cersei.

"As are we all. If there is aught that I can do . . ."

High above, a crow screamed loudly. He was perched on the statue
of King Baelor, shitting on his holy head. "There is much and more
you can do for Tommen, my lord," Jaime said. "Perhaps you would
do Her Grace the honor of supping with her, after the evening
services?"

Cersei threw him a withering look, but for once she had the sense
to bite her tongue.

"Sup?" Tyrell seemed taken aback. "I suppose . . . of course, we
should be honored. My lady wife and I."

The queen forced a smile and made pleasant noises. But when
Tyrell had taken his leave and Tommen had been sent off with Ser
Addam Marbrand, she turned on Jaime angrily. "Are you drunk or
dreaming, ser? Pray tell, why am I having supper with that grasping
fool and his puerile wife?" A gust of wind stirred her golden hair. "I
will *not* name him Hand, if that's what—"

"You need Tyrell," Jaime broke in, "but not *here*. Ask him to capture
Storm's End for Tommen. Flatter him, and tell him you need him in
the field, to replace Father. Mace fancies himself a mighty warrior.

Either he will deliver Storm's End to you, or he will muck it up and look a fool. Either way, you win."

"Storm's End?" Cersei looked thoughtful. "Yes, but . . . Lord Tyrell has made it tediously plain that he will not leave King's Landing till Tommen marries Margaery."

Jaime sighed. "Then let them wed. It will be years before Tommen is old enough to consummate the marriage. And until he does, the union can always be set aside. Give Tyrell his wedding and send him off to play at war."

A wary smile crept across his sister's face. "Even sieges have their dangers," she murmured. "Why, our Lord of Highgarden might even lose his life in such a venture."

"There is that risk," conceded Jaime. "Especially if his patience runs thin this time, and he elects to storm the gate."

Cersei gave him a lingering look. "You know," she said, "for a moment, you sounded quite like Father."

BRIENNE

The gates of Duskendale were closed and barred. Through the predawn gloom the town walls shimmered palely. On their ramparts, wisps of fog moved like ghostly sentinels. A dozen wayns and oxcarts had drawn up outside the gates, waiting for the sun to rise. Brienne took her place behind some turnips. Her calves ached, and it felt good to dismount and stretch her legs. Before long another wayn came rumbling from the woods. By the time the sky began to lighten, the queue stretched back a quarter mile.

The farm folk gave her curious glances, but no one spoke to her. *It is for me to talk to them,* Brienne told herself, but she had always found it hard to speak with strangers. Even as a girl she had been shy. Long years of scorn had only made her shyer. *I must ask after Sansa. How else will I find her?* She cleared her throat. "Goodwife," she said to the woman on the turnip cart, "perhaps you saw my sister on the road? A young maid, three-and-ten and fair of face, with blue eyes and auburn hair. She may be riding with a drunken knight."

The woman shook her head, but her husband said, "Then she's no maid, I'll wager. Does the poor girl have a name?"

Brienne's head was empty. *I should have made up some name for her.* Any name would do, but none came to her.

"No name? Well, the roads are full of nameless girls."

"The lichyard's even fuller," said his wife.

As dawn broke, guardsmen appeared on the parapets. The farmers climbed onto their wagons and shook the reins. Brienne mounted as well and took a glance behind her. Most of the queue waiting to enter Duskendale were farm folk with loads of fruits and vegetables to sell. A pair of wealthy townsmen sat on well-bred palfreys a dozen places behind her, and farther back she spied a skinny boy on a piebald rounsey. There was no sign of the two knights, nor Ser Shadrich the Mad Mouse.

The guards were waving through the wayns with scarce a look, but when Brienne reached the gate she gave them pause. "Halt, you!" the captain cried. A pair of men in chainmail hauberks crossed their spears to bar her way. "State your purpose here."

"I seek the Lord of Duskendale, or his maester."

The captain's eyes lingered on her shield. "The black bat of Lothston. Those are arms of ill repute."

"They are not mine. I mean to have the shield repainted."

"Aye?" The captain rubbed his stubbled chin. "My sister does such work, as it happens. You'll find her at the house with the painted doors, across from the Seven Swords." He gestured to the guards. "Let her pass, lads. It's a wench."

The gatehouse opened on a market square, where those who had entered before her were unloading to hawk their turnips, yellow onions, and sacks of barleycorn. Others were selling arms and armor, and very cheaply to judge from the prices they shouted out as she rode by. *The looters come with the carrion crows after every battle.* Brienne walked her horse past mail shirts still caked with brown blood, dinted helms, notched longswords. There was clothing to be had as well: leather boots, fur cloaks, stained surcoats with suspicious rents. She knew many of the badges. The mailed fist, the moose, the white sun, the double-bladed axe, all those were northern sigils. Tarly men had perished here as well, though, and many from the stormlands. She saw red and green apples, a shield that bore the three thunderbolts of Leygood, horse trappings patterned with the ants of Ambrose. Lord Tarly's own striding huntsman appeared on many a badge and brooch and doublet. *Friend or foe, the crows care not.*

There were pine and linden shields to be had for pennies, but Brienne rode past them. She meant to keep the heavy oaken shield

Jaime had given her, the one he'd borne himself from Harrenhal to King's Landing. A pine shield had its advantages. It was lighter, and therefore easier to bear, and the soft wood was more like to trap a foeman's axe or sword. But oak gave more protection, if you were strong enough to bear its weight.

Duskendale was built around its harbor. North of town the chalk cliffs rose; to the south a rocky headland shielded the ships at anchor from storms coming up the narrow sea. The castle overlooked the port, its square keep and big drum towers visible from every part of town. In the crowded cobbled streets, it was easier to walk than ride, so Brienne put her mare up in a stable and continued on afoot, with her shield slung across her back and her bedroll tucked up beneath one arm.

The captain's sister was not hard to find. The Seven Swords was the largest inn in town, a four-story structure that towered over its neighbors, and the double doors on the house across the way were painted gorgeously. They showed a castle in an autumn wood, the trees done up in shades of gold and russet. Ivy crawled up the trunks of ancient oaks, and even the acorns had been done with loving care. When Brienne peered more closely, she saw creatures in the foliage: a sly red fox, two sparrows on a branch, and behind those leaves the shadow of a boar.

"Your door is very pretty," she told the dark-haired woman who answered when she knocked. "What castle is that meant to be?"

"All castles," said the captain's sister. "The only one I know is the Dun Fort by the harbor. I made t'other in my head, what a castle ought to look like. I never seen a dragon neither, nor a griffin, nor a unicorn." She had a cheerful manner, but when Brienne showed her the shield her face went dark. "My old ma used to say that giant bats flew out from Harrenhal on moonless nights, to carry bad children to Mad Danelle for her cookpots. Sometimes I'd hear them scrabbling at the shutters." She sucked her teeth a moment, thoughtful. "What goes in its place?"

The arms of Tarth were quartered rose and azure, and bore a yellow sun and crescent moon. But so long as men believed her to be a murderess, Brienne dare not carry them. "Your door reminded me of an old shield I once saw in my father's armory." She described the arms as best she could recall them.

The woman nodded. "I can paint it straightaway, but the paint will need to dry. Take a room at the Seven Swords, if it please you. I'll bring the shield to you by morning."

Brienne had not meant to overnight in Duskendale, but it might be for the best. She did not know if the lord of the castle was in residence, or whether he would consent to see her. She thanked the painter and crossed the cobblestones to the inn. Above its door, seven wooden swords swung beneath an iron spike. The whitewash that covered them was cracked and peeling, but Brienne knew their meaning. They stood for the seven sons of Darklyn who had worn the white cloaks of the Kingsguard. No other house in all the realm could claim as many. *They were the glory of their House. And now they are a sign above an inn.* She pushed into the common room and asked the innkeep for a room and a bath.

He put her on the second floor, and a woman with a liver-colored birthmark on her face brought up a wooden tub, and then the water, pail by pail. "Do any Darklyns remain in Duskendale?" Brienne asked as she climbed into the tub.

"Well, there's Darkes, I'm one myself. My husband says I was Darke before we wed, and darker afterward." She laughed. "Can't throw a stone in Duskendale without you hit some Darke or Darkwood or Dargood, but the lordly Darklyns are all gone. Lord Denys was the last o' them, the sweet young fool. Did you know the Darklyns were kings in Duskendale before the Andals come? You'd never know t'look at me, but I got me royal blood. Can you see it? 'Your Grace, another cup of ale,' I ought to make them say. 'Your Grace, the chamber pot needs emptying, and fetch in some fresh faggots, Your Bloody Grace, the fire's going out.'" She laughed again and shook the last drops from the pail. "Well, there you are. Is that water hot enough for you?"

"It will serve." The water was lukewarm.

"I'd bring up more, but it'd just slop over. A girl the size o' you, you fill a tub."

Only a cramped small tub like this one. At Harrenhal the tubs had been huge, and made of stone. The bathhouse had been thick with the steam rising off the water, and Jaime had come walking through that mist naked as his name day, looking half a corpse and half a god.

He climbed into the tub with me, she remembered, blushing. She seized a chunk of hard lye soap and scrubbed under her arms, trying to call up Renly's face again.

By the time the water had gone cold, Brienne was as clean as she was like to get. She put on the same clothes she had taken off and girded her swordbelt tight around her hips, but her mail and helm she left behind, so as not to seem so threatening at the Dun Fort. It felt good to stretch her legs. The guards at the castle gates wore leather jacks with a badge that showed crossed warhammers upon a white saltire. "I would speak with your lord," Brienne told them.

One laughed. "Best shout out loud, then."

"Lord Rykker rode to Maidenpool with Randyll Tarly," the other said. "He left Ser Rufus Leek as castellan, to look after Lady Rykker and the young ones."

It was to Leek that they escorted her. Ser Rufus was a short, stout greybeard whose left leg ended in a stump. "You will forgive me if I do not rise," he said. Brienne offered him her letter, but Leek could not read, so he sent her to the maester, a bald man with a freckled scalp and a stiff red mustache.

When he heard the name Hollard, the maester frowned with irritation. "How often must I sing this song?" Her face must have given her away. "Did you think you were the first to come seeking after Dontos? More like the twenty-first. The gold cloaks were here within days of the king's murder, with Lord Tywin's warrant. And what do you have, pray?"

Brienne showed him the letter, with Tommen's seal and childish signature. The maester *hmmmm*ed and *hrrrr*ed, picked at the wax, and finally gave it back. "It seems in order." He climbed onto a stool and gestured Brienne to another. "I never knew Ser Dontos. He was a boy when he left Duskendale. The Hollards were a noble House once, 'tis true. You know their arms? Barry red and pink, with three golden crowns upon a blue chief. The Darklyns were petty kings during the Age of Heroes, and three took Hollard wives. Later their little realm was swallowed up by larger kingdoms, yet the Darklyns endured and the Hollards served them . . . aye, even in defiance. You know of that?"

"A little." Her own maester used to say that it was the Defiance of Duskendale that had driven King Aerys mad.

"In Duskendale they love Lord Denys still, despite the woe he brought them. 'Tis Lady Serala that they blame, his Myrish wife. The Lace Serpent, she is called. If Lord Darklyn had only wed a Staunton or a Stokeworth . . . well, you know how smallfolk will go on. The Lace Serpent filled her husband's ear with Myrish poison, they say, until Lord Denys rose against his king and took him captive. In the taking, his master-at-arms Ser Symon Hollard cut down Ser Gwayne Gaunt of the Kingsguard. For half a year, Aerys was held within these very walls, whilst the King's Hand sat outside Duskendale with a mighty host. Lord Tywin had sufficient strength to storm the town any time he wished, but Lord Denys sent word that at the first sign of assault he'd kill the king."

Brienne remembered what came next. "The king was rescued," she said. "Barristan the Bold brought him out."

"He did," the maester said. "Once Lord Denys lost his hostage, he opened his gates and ended his defiance rather than let Lord Tywin take the town. He bent the knee and begged for mercy, but the king was not of a forgiving mind. Lord Denys lost his head, as did his brothers and his sister, uncles, cousins, all the lordly Darklyns. The Lace Serpent was burned alive, poor woman, though her tongue was torn out first, and her female parts, with which it was said that she had enslaved her lord. Half of Duskendale will still tell you that Aerys was too kind to her."

"And the Hollards?"

"Attainted and destroyed," said the maester. "I was forging my chain at the Citadel when this happened, but I have read the accounts of their trials and punishments. Ser Jon Hollard the Steward was wed to Lord Denys's sister and died with his wife, as did their young son, who was half-Darklyn. Robin Hollard was a squire, and when the king was seized he danced around him and pulled his beard. He died upon the rack. Ser Symon Hollard was slain by Ser Barristan during the king's escape. The Hollard lands were taken, their castle torn down, their villages put to the torch. As with the Darklyns, House Hollard was extinguished."

"Save for Dontos."

"True enough. Young Dontos was the son of Ser Steffon Hollard, the twin brother of Ser Symon, who had died of a fever some years before and had no part in the Defiance. Aerys would have taken the boy's head off nonetheless, but Ser Barristan asked that his life be spared. The king could not refuse the man who'd saved him, so Dontos was taken to King's Landing as a squire. To my knowledge he never returned to Duskendale, and why should he? He held no lands here, had neither kin nor castle. If Dontos and this northern girl helped murder our sweet king, it seems to me that they would want to put as many leagues as they could betwixt themselves and justice. Look for them in Oldtown, if you must, or across the narrow sea. Look for them in Dorne, or on the Wall. Look *elsewhere*." He rose. "I hear my ravens calling. You will forgive me if I bid you good morrow."

The walk back to the inn seemed longer than the walk to the Dun Fort, though perhaps that was only her mood. She would not find Sansa Stark in Duskendale, that seemed plain. If Ser Dontos had taken her to Oldtown or across the narrow sea, as the maester seemed to think, Brienne's quest was hopeless. *What was there for her in Oldtown?* she asked herself. *The maester never knew her, no more than he knew Hollard. She would not have gone to strangers.*

In King's Landing, Brienne had found one of Sansa's former maids doing washing in a brothel. "I served with Lord Renly before m'lady Sansa, and both turned traitor," the woman Brella complained bitterly. "No lord will touch me now, so I have to wash for whores." But when Brienne asked about Sansa, she said, "I'll tell you what I told Lord Tywin. That girl was always praying. She'd go to sept and light her candles like a proper lady, but near every night she went off to the godswood. She's gone back north, she has. That's where her *gods* are."

The north was huge, though, and Brienne had no notion which of her father's bannermen Sansa might have been most inclined to trust. *Or would she seek her own blood instead?* Though all of her siblings had been slain, Brienne knew that Sansa still had an uncle and a bastard half brother on the Wall, serving in the Night's Watch. Another uncle, Edmure Tully, was a captive at the Twins, but *his* uncle Ser Brynden still held Riverrun. And Lady Catelyn's younger sister ruled the Vale. *Blood calls to blood.* Sansa might well have run to one of them. Which one, though?

The Wall was too far, surely, and a bleak and bitter place besides. And to reach Riverrun the girl would need to cross the war-torn riverlands and pass through the Lannister siege lines. The Eyrie would be simpler, and Lady Lysa would surely welcome her sister's daughter . . .

Ahead, the alley bent. Somehow Brienne had taken a wrong turn. She found herself in a dead end, a small muddy yard where three pigs were rooting round a low stone well. One squealed at the sight of her, and an old woman drawing water looked her up and down suspiciously. "What would you be wanting?"

"I was looking for the Seven Swords."

"Back the way you come. Left at the sept."

"I thank you." Brienne turned to retrace her steps, and walked headfirst into someone hurrying round the bend. The collision knocked him off his feet, and he landed on his arse in the mud. "Pardons," she murmured. He was only a boy; a scrawny lad with straight, thin hair and a sty beneath one eye. "Are you hurt?" She offered a hand to help him up, but the boy squirmed back away from her on heels and elbows. He could not have been more than ten or twelve, though he wore a chainmail byrnie and had a longsword in a leather sheath slung across his back. "Do I know you?" Brienne asked. His face seemed vaguely familiar, though she could not think from where.

"No. You don't. You never . . ." He scrambled to his feet. "F-f-forgive me. My lady. I wasn't looking. I mean, I was, but down. I was looking down. At my feet." The boy took to his heels, plunging headlong back the way he'd come.

Something about him roused all of Brienne's suspicions, but she was not about to chase him through the streets of Duskendale. *Outside the gates this morning, that was where I saw him,* she realized. *He was riding a piebald rounsey.* And it seemed as if she had seen him somewhere else as well, but where?

By the time Brienne found the Seven Swords again, the common room was crowded. Four septas sat closest to the fire, in robes stained and dusty from the road. Elsewhere locals filled the benches, sopping up bowls of hot crab stew with chunks of bread. The smell made her stomach rumble, but she saw no empty seats. Then a voice behind her said, "M'lady, here, have my place." Not until he hopped off the bench did Brienne realize that the speaker was a dwarf. The little man was not quite five feet tall. His nose was veined and bulbous, his teeth red from sourleaf, and he was dressed in the brown roughspun robes of a holy brother, with the iron hammer of the Smith dangling down about his thick neck.

"Keep your seat," she said. "I can stand as well as you."

"Aye, but my head is not so apt to knock upon the ceiling." The dwarf's speech was coarse but courteous. Brienne could see the crown of his scalp where he had shaved it. Many holy brothers wore such tonsures. Septa Roelle once told her that it was meant to show that they had nothing to hide from the Father. "Can't the Father see through hair?" Brienne had asked. *A stupid thing to say.* She had been a slow child; Septa Roelle often told her so. She felt near as stupid now, so she took the little man's place at the end of the bench, signaled for stew, and turned to thank the dwarf. "Do you serve some holy house in Duskendale, brother?"

"'Twas nearer Maidenpool, m'lady, but the wolves burned us out," the man replied, gnawing on a heel of bread. "We rebuilt as best we could, until some sellswords come. I could not say whose men they were, but they took our pigs and killed the brothers. I squeezed inside a hollow log and hid, but t'others were too big. It took me a long time to bury them all, but the Smith, he gave me strength. When that was done I dug up a few coins the elder brother had hid by and set off by myself."

"I met some other brothers going to King's Landing."

"Aye, there's hundreds on the roads. Not only brothers. Septons too, and smallfolk. Sparrows all. Might be I'm a sparrow too. The Smith, he made me small enough." He chuckled. "And what's your sad tale, m'lady?"

"I am looking for my sister. She's highborn, only three-and-ten, a pretty maid with blue eyes and auburn hair. You may have seen her traveling with a man. A knight, perhaps a fool. There's gold for the man who helps me find her."

"Gold?" The brother gave her a red smile. "A bowl of that crab stew would be enough reward for me, but I fear I cannot help you. Fools I've met, and plenty, but not so many pretty maids." He cocked his head and thought a moment. "There was a fool at Maidenpool, now that I think of it. He was clad in rags and dirt, as near as I could tell, but under the dirt was motley."

Did Dontos Hollard wear motley? No one had told Brienne that he did . . . but no one had ever said he didn't, either. Why would the man be in rags, though? Had some misfortune overtaken him and Sansa after they fled King's Landing? That could well be, with the roads so dangerous. *It might not have been him at all.* "Did this fool have a red nose, full of broken veins?"

"I could not swear to that. I confess, I paid him little heed. I'd gone to Maidenpool after burying my brothers, thinking that I might find a ship to take me to King's Landing. I first glimpsed the fool down by the docks. He had a furtive air to him and took care to avoid Lord Tarly's soldiers. Later, I encountered him again, at the Stinking Goose."

"The Stinking Goose?" she said, uncertain.

"An unsavory place," the dwarf admitted. "Lord Tarly's men patrol the port at Maidenpool, but the Goose is always full of sailors, and sailors have been known to smuggle men aboard their ships, if the price is right. This fool was seeking passage for three across the narrow sea. I oft saw him there, talking with oarsmen off the galleys. Sometimes he would sing a funny song."

"Seeking passage for *three*? Not two?"

"Three, m'lady. That I'd swear to, by the Seven." *Three,* she thought. *Sansa, Ser Dontos . . . but who would be the third? The Imp?* "Did the fool find his ship?"

"That I could not say," the dwarf told her, "but one night some of Lord Tarly's soldiers visited the Goose looking for him, and a few days later I heard another man boasting that he'd fooled a fool and had the gold to prove it. He was drunk, and buying ale for everyone."

"'Fooled a fool,'" she said. "What did he mean by that?"

"I could not tell you. His name was Nimble Dick, though, that I do recall." The dwarf spread his hands. "I fear that's all that I can offer you, aside from a small man's prayers."

True to her word, Brienne bought him his bowl of hot crab

stew . . . and some hot fresh bread and a cup of wine as well. As he ate it, standing by her side, she mulled what he had told her. *Could the Imp have joined them?* If Tyrion Lannister were behind Sansa's disappearance, and not Dontos Hollard, it stood to reason that they would need to flee across the narrow sea.

When the little man was done with his bowl of stew, he finished what was left of hers as well. "You should eat more," he said. "A woman big as you needs t' keep her strength up. It is not far to Maidenpool, but the road is perilous these days."

I know. It was on that very road that Ser Cleos Frey had died, and she and Ser Jaime had been taken by the Bloody Mummers. *Jaime tried to kill me,* she remembered, *though he was gaunt and weak, and his wrists were chained.* It had been a close thing, even so, but that was before Zollo hacked his hand off. Zollo and Rorge and Shagwell would have raped her half a hundred times if Ser Jaime had not told them she was worth her weight in sapphires.

"M'lady? You look sad. Are you thinking of your sister?" The dwarf patted her on the hand. "The Crone will light your way to her, never fear. The Maiden will keep her safe."

"I pray that you are right."

"I am." He bowed. "But now I must be on my way. I've a long way yet to go to reach King's Landing."

"Do you have a horse? A mule?"

"Two mules." The little man laughed. "There they are, at the bottom of my legs. They get me where I want t' go." He bowed, and waddled to the door, swaying with each step.

She remained at the table after he had gone, lingering over a cup of watered wine. Brienne did not oft drink wine, but once in a great while she found it helped to settle her belly. *And where do I want to go?* she asked herself. *To Maidenpool, to look for a man named Nimble Dick in a place called the Stinking Goose?*

When last she had seen Maidenpool, the town had been a desolation, its lord shut up inside his castle, its smallfolk dead or fled or hiding. She remembered burned houses and empty streets, smashed and broken gates. Feral dogs had skulked along behind their horses, whilst swollen corpses floated like huge pale water lilies atop the spring-fed pool that gave the town its name. *Jaime sang "Six Maids in a Pool," and laughed when I begged him to be quiet.* And Randyll Tarly was at Maidenpool as well, another reason for her to avoid the town. She might do better to take ship for Gulltown or White Harbor. *I could do both, though. Pay a call on the Stinking Goose and talk to this Nimble Dick, then find a ship at Maidenpool to take me farther north.*

The common room had begun to empty. Brienne tore a chunk of bread in half, listening to the talk at the other tables. Most of it concerned the death of Lord Tywin Lannister. "Murdered by his own son, they say," a local man was saying, a cobbler by the look of him, "that vile little dwarf."

"And the king is just a boy," said the oldest of the four septas. "Who is to rule us till he comes of age?"

"Lord Tywin's brother," said a guardsman. "Or that Lord Tyrell, might be. Or the Kingslayer."

"Not him," declared the innkeep. "Not that oathbreaker." He spat into the fire. Brienne let the bread fall from her hands and wiped the crumbs off on her breeches. She'd heard enough.

That night she dreamed herself in Renly's tent again. All the candles were guttering out, and the cold was thick around her. Something was moving through green darkness, something foul and horrible was hurtling toward her king. She wanted to protect him, but her limbs felt stiff and frozen, and it took more strength than she had just to lift her hand. And when the shadow sword sliced through the green steel gorget and the blood began to flow, she saw that the dying king was not Renly after all but Jaime Lannister, and she had failed him.

The captain's sister found her in the common room, drinking a cup of milk and honey with three raw eggs mixed in. "You did beautifully," she said, when the woman showed her the freshly painted shield. It was more a picture than a proper coat of arms, and the sight of it took her back through the long years, to the cool dark of her father's armory. She remembered how she'd run her fingertips across the cracked and fading paint, over the green leaves of the tree, and along the path of the falling star.

Brienne paid the captain's sister half again the sum they had agreed, and slung the shield across one shoulder when she left the inn, after buying some hardbread, cheese, and flour from the cook. She left the town by the north gate, riding slowly through the fields and farms where the worst of the fighting had been, when the wolves came down on Duskendale.

Lord Randyll Tarly had commanded Joffrey's army, made up of westermen and stormlanders and knights from the Reach. Those men of his who had died here had been carried back inside the walls, to rest in heroes' tombs beneath the septs of Duskendale. The northern dead, far more numerous, were buried in a common grave beside the sea. Above the cairn that marked their resting place, the victors had raised a rough-hewn wooden marker. HERE LIE THE WOLVES was all it said. Brienne stopped beside it and said a silent prayer for them, and for Catelyn Stark and her son Robb and all the men who'd died with them as well.

She remembered the night that Lady Catelyn had learned her sons were dead, the two young boys she'd left at Winterfell to keep them safe. Brienne had known that something was terribly amiss. She had asked her if there had been news of her sons. "I have no sons but Robb," Lady Catelyn had replied. She had sounded as if a knife were twisting her belly. Brienne had reached across the table to give her comfort, but she stopped before her fingers brushed the older woman's, for fear that she would flinch away. Lady Catelyn had turned over her hands, to show Brienne the scars on her palms and fingers where a knife once bit deep into her flesh. Then she had begun to talk about her daughters. "Sansa was a little lady," she had said, "always courteous and eager to please. She loved tales of knightly valor. She will grow into a woman far more beautiful than I, you can see that. I would often brush her hair myself. She had auburn hair, thick and soft . . . the red in it would shine like copper in the light of the torches."

She had spoken of Arya too, her younger daughter, but Arya was lost, most likely dead by now. Sansa, though . . . *I will find her, my lady,* Brienne swore to Lady Catelyn's restless shade. *I will never stop looking. I will give up my life if need be, give up my honor, give up all my dreams, but I will find her.*

Beyond the battleground the road ran beside the shore, between the surging grey-green sea and a line of low limestone hills. Brienne was not the only traveler on the road. There were fishing villages up along the coast for many leagues, and the fisherfolk used this road to take their fish to market. She rode past a fishwife and her daughters, walking home with empty baskets on their shoulders. In her armor, they took her for a knight until they saw her face. Then the girls whispered to one another and gave her looks. "Have you seen a maid of three-and-ten along the road?" she asked them. "A highborn maid with blue eyes and auburn hair?" Ser Shadrich had made her wary, but she had to keep on trying. "She may have been traveling with a fool." But they only shook their heads and giggled at her behind their hands.

In the first village she came to, barefoot boys ran along beside her horse. She had donned her helm, stung by the giggles of the fisherfolk, so they took her for a man. One boy offered to sell her clams, one offered crabs, and one offered her his sister.

Brienne bought three crabs from the second boy. By the time she left the village it had begun to rain, and the wind was rising. *Storm coming,* she thought, glancing out to sea. The raindrops pinged against the steel of her helm, making her ears ring as she rode, but it was better than being out there in a boat.

An hour farther north, the road divided at a pile of tumbled stones that marked the ruins of a small castle. The right-hand fork followed the coast, meandering up along the shore toward Crackclaw Point, a dismal land of bogs and pine barrens; the left-hand ran through hills and fields and woods to Maidenpool. The rain was falling more heavily by then. Brienne dismounted and led her mare off the road to take shelter amongst the ruins. The course of the castle walls could still be discerned amongst the brambles, weeds, and wild elms, but the stones that had made them up were strewn like a child's blocks between the roads. Part of the main keep still stood, however. Its triple towers were grey granite, like the broken walls, but their merlons were yellow sandstone. *Three crowns,* she realized, as she gazed at them through the rain. *Three golden crowns.* This had been a Hollard castle. Ser Dontos had been born here, like as not.

She led her mare through the rubble to the keep's main entrance. Of the door only rusted iron hinges remained, but the roof was still sound, and it was dry within. Brienne tied her mare to a wall sconce, took off her helm, and shook out her hair. She was searching for some dry wood to light a fire when she heard the sound of another horse, coming closer. Some instinct made her step back into the shadows, where she could not be seen from the road. This was the very road where she and Ser Jaime had been captured. She did not intend to suffer that again.

The rider was a small man. *The Mad Mouse,* she thought, at her first sight of him. *Somehow he's followed me.* Her hand went to her sword hilt, and she found herself wondering if Ser Shadrich would think her easy prey just because she was a woman. Lord Grandison's castellan had once made that error. Humfrey Wagstaff was his name; a proud old man of five-and-sixty, with a nose like a hawk and a spotted head. The day they were betrothed, he warned Brienne that he would expect her to be a proper woman once they'd wed. "I will not have my lady wife cavorting about in man's mail. On this you shall obey me, lest I be forced to chastise you."

She was sixteen and no stranger to a sword, but still shy despite her prowess in the yard. Yet somehow she had found the courage to tell Ser Humfrey that she would accept chastisement only from a man who could outfight her. The old knight purpled, but agreed to don his own armor to teach her a woman's proper place. They fought with blunted tourney weapons, so Brienne's mace had no spikes. She broke Ser Humfrey's collarbone, two ribs, and their betrothal. He was her third prospective husband, and her last. Her father did not insist again.

If it *was* Ser Shadrich dogging her heels, she might well have a fight on her hands. She did not intend to partner with the man or let him follow her to Sansa. *He had the sort of easy arrogance that comes with skill at arms,* she thought, *but he was small. I'll have the reach on him, and I should be stronger too.*

Brienne was as strong as most knights, and her old master-at-arms used to say that she was quicker than any woman her size had any right to be. The gods had given her stamina too, which Ser Goodwin deemed a noble gift. Fighting with sword and shield was a wearisome business, and victory oft went to the man with most endurance. Ser Goodwin had taught her to fight cautiously, to conserve her strength while letting her foes spend theirs in furious attacks. "Men will always underestimate you," he said, "and their pride will make them want to vanquish you quickly, lest it be said that a woman tried them sorely." She had learned the truth of that once she went into the world. Even Jaime Lannister had come at her that way, in the woods by Maidenpool. If the gods were good, the Mad Mouse would make the same mistake. *He may be a seasoned knight,* she thought, *but he is no Jaime Lannister.* She slid her sword out of its scabbard.

But it was not Ser Shadrich's chestnut courser that drew up where the road forked, but a broken-down old piebald rounsey with a skinny boy upon his back. When Brienne saw the horse she drew back in confusion. *Only some boy,* she thought, until she glimpsed the face beneath his hood. *The boy in Duskendale, the one who bumped into me. It's him.*

The boy never gave the ruined castle a glance, but looked down one road, then the other. After a moment's hesitation, he turned the rounsey toward the hills and plodded on. Brienne watched him vanish through the falling rain, and suddenly it came to her that she had seen this same boy in Rosby. *He is stalking me,* she realized, *but that's a game that two can play.* She untied her mare, climbed back into the saddle, and went after him.

The boy was staring at the ground as he rode, watching the ruts in the road fill up with water. The rain muffled the sound of her approach, and no doubt his hood played a part as well. He never looked back once, until Brienne trotted up behind him and gave the rounsey a whack across the rump with the flat of her longsword.

The horse reared, and the skinny boy went flying, his cloak flapping like a pair of wings. He landed in the mud and came up with dirt and dead brown grass between his teeth to find Brienne standing over him. It was the same boy, beyond a doubt. She recognized the sty. "Who are you?" she demanded.

The boy's mouth worked soundlessly. His eyes were big as eggs. "Puh," was all he could manage. "Puh." His chainmail byrnie made a rattling sound when he shivered. "Puh. Puh."

"Please?" said Brienne. "Are you saying *please?*" She laid the point of her sword on the apple of his throat. "Please tell me who you are, and why you're following me."

"Not puh-puh-*please*." He stuck a finger in his mouth, and flicked away a clump of mud, spitting. "Puh-puh-*Pod*. My name. Puh-puh-*Podrick*. Puh-Payne."

Brienne lowered her sword. She felt a rush of sympathy for the boy. She remembered a day at Evenfall, and a young knight with a rose in his hand. *He brought the rose to give to me.* Or so her septa told her. All she had to do was welcome him to her father's castle. He was eighteen, with long red hair that tumbled to his shoulders. She was twelve, tightly laced into a stiff new gown, its bodice bright with garnets. The two of them were of a height, but she could not look him in the eye, nor say the simple words her septa had taught her. *Ser Ronnet. I welcome you to my lord father's hall. It is good to look upon your face at last.*

"Why are you following me?" she demanded of the boy. "Were you told to spy upon me? Do you belong to Varys, or the queen?"

"No. Not neither. No one."

Brienne put his age at ten, but she was terrible at judging how old a child was. She always thought they were younger than they were, perhaps because she had always been big for her age. *Freakish big,* Septa Roelle used to say, *and mannish.* "This road is too dangerous for a boy alone."

"Not for a *squire*. I'm his squire. The Hand's squire."

"Lord Tywin?" Brienne sheathed her blade.

"No. Not that Hand. The one before. His son. I fought with him in the battle. I shouted, '*Halfman! Halfman!*'"

The Imp's squire. Brienne had not even known he had one. Tyrion Lannister was no knight. He might have been expected to have a serving boy or two to attend him, she supposed, a page and a cupbearer, someone to help dress him. But a *squire?* "Why are you stalking after me?" she said. "What do you want?"

"To find her." The boy got to his feet. "His lady. You're looking for her. Brella told me. She's his wife. Not Brella, Lady Sansa. So I thought, if you found her . . ." His face twisted in sudden anguish. "I'm his *squire*," he repeated, as the rain ran down his face, "but he *left* me."

SANSA

Once, when she was just a little girl, a wandering singer had stayed with them at Winterfell for half a year. An old man he was, with white hair and windburnt cheeks, but he sang of knights and quests and ladies fair, and Sansa had cried bitter tears when he left them, and begged her father not to let him go. "The man has played us every song he knows thrice over," Lord Eddard told her gently. "I cannot keep him here against his will. You need not weep, though. I promise you, other singers will come."

They hadn't, though, not for a year or more. Sansa had prayed to the Seven in their sept and old gods of the heart tree, asking them to bring the old man back, or better still to send another singer, young and handsome. But the gods never answered, and the halls of Winterfell stayed silent.

But that was when she was a little girl, and foolish. She was a maiden now, three-and-ten and flowered. All her nights were full of song, and by day she prayed for silence.

If the Eyrie had been made like other castles, only rats and gaolers would have heard the dead man singing. Dungeon walls were thick enough to swallow songs and screams alike. But the sky cells had a wall of empty air, so every chord the dead man played flew free to echo off the stony shoulders of the Giant's Lance. And the songs he chose . . . He sang of the Dance of the Dragons, of fair Jonquil and her fool, of Jenny of Oldstones and the Prince of Dragonflies. He sang of betrayals, and murders most foul, of hanged men and bloody vengeance. He sang of grief and sadness.

No matter where she went in the castle, Sansa could not escape the music. It floated up the winding tower steps, found her naked in her bath, supped with her at dusk, and stole into her bedchamber even when she latched the shutters tight. It came in on the cold thin air, and like the air, it chilled her. Though it had not snowed upon the Eyrie since the day that Lady Lysa fell, the nights had all been bitter cold.

The singer's voice was strong and sweet. Sansa thought he sounded better than he ever had before, his voice richer somehow, full of pain and fear and longing. She did not understand why the gods would have given such a voice to such a wicked man. *He would have taken me by force on the Fingers if Petyr had not set Ser Lothor to watch over me*, she had to remind herself. *And he played to drown out my cries when Aunt Lysa tried to kill me.*

That did not make the songs any easier to hear. "Please," she begged Lord Petyr, "can't you make him stop?"

"I gave the man my word, sweetling." Petyr Baelish, Lord of Harrenhal, Lord Paramount of the Trident, and Lord Protector of the Eyrie and the Vale of Arryn, looked up from the letter he was writing. He had written a hundred letters since Lady Lysa's fall. Sansa had seen the ravens coming and going from the rookery. "I'd sooner suffer his singing than listen to his sobbing."

It is better that he sings, yes, but . . . "Must he play all night, my lord? Lord Robert cannot sleep. He cries . . ."

". . . for his mother. That cannot be helped, the wench is dead." Petyr shrugged. "It will not be much longer. Lord Nestor is making his ascent on the morrow."

Sansa had met Lord Nestor Royce once before, after Petyr's wedding to her aunt. Royce was the Keeper of the Gates of the Moon, the great castle that stood at the base of the mountain and guarded the steps up to the Eyrie. The wedding party had guested with him overnight before beginning their ascent. Lord Nestor had scarce looked at her twice, but the prospect of him coming here terrified her. He was High Steward of the Vale as well, Jon Arryn's trusted liege man, and

Lady Lysa's. "He won't . . . you won't let Lord Nestor see Marillion, will you?"

Her horror must have shown on her face, since Petyr put down his quill. "On the contrary. I shall insist on it." He beckoned her to take the seat beside him. "We have come to an agreement, Marillion and I. Mord can be most persuasive. And if our singer disappoints us and sings a song we do not care to hear, why, you and I need only say he lies. Whom do you imagine Lord Nestor will believe?"

"Us?" Sansa wished she could be certain.

"Of course. Our lies will profit him."

The solar was warm, the fire crackling merrily, but Sansa shivered all the same. "Yes, but . . . but what if . . ."

"What if Lord Nestor values honor more than profit?" Petyr put his arm around her. "What if it is truth he wants, and justice for his murdered lady?" He smiled. "I know Lord Nestor, sweetling. Do you imagine I'd ever let him harm my daughter?"

I am not your daughter, she thought. *I am Sansa Stark, Lord Eddard's daughter and Lady Catelyn's, the blood of Winterfell.* She did not say it, though. If not for Petyr Baelish it would have been *Sansa* who went spinning through a cold blue sky to stony death six hundred feet below, instead of Lysa Arryn. *He is so bold.* Sansa wished she had his courage. She wanted to crawl back into bed and hide beneath her blanket, to sleep and sleep. She had not slept a whole night through since Lysa Arryn's death. "Couldn't you tell Lord Nestor that I am . . . indisposed, or . . ."

"He will want to hear your account of Lysa's death."

"My lord, if . . . if Marillion tells what truly . . ."

"If he lies, you mean?"

"Lies? Yes . . . if he lies, if it is my tale against his, and Lord Nestor looks in my eyes and sees how scared I am . . ."

"A touch of fear will not be out of place, Alayne. You've seen a fearful thing. Nestor will be moved." Petyr studied her eyes, as if seeing them for the first time. "You have your mother's eyes. Honest eyes, and innocent. Blue as a sunlit sea. When you are a little older, many a man will drown in those eyes."

Sansa did not know what to say to that.

"All you need do is tell Lord Nestor the same tale that you told Lord Robert," Petyr went on.

Robert is only a sick little boy, she thought, *Lord Nestor is a man grown, stern and suspicious.* Robert was not strong and had to be protected, even from the truth. "Some lies are love," Petyr had assured her. She reminded him of that. "When we lied to Lord Robert, that was just to spare him," she said.

"And this lie may spare *us.* Else you and I must leave the Eyrie by the same door Lysa used." Petyr picked up his quill again. "We shall serve him lies and Arbor gold, and he'll drink them down and ask for more, I promise you."

He is serving me lies as well, Sansa realized. They were comforting lies, though, and she thought them kindly meant. *A lie is not so bad if it is kindly meant.* If only she believed them . . .

The things her aunt had said just before she fell still troubled Sansa greatly. "Ravings," Petyr called them. "My wife was mad, you saw that for yourself." And so she had. *All I did was build a snow castle, and she meant to push me out the Moon Door. Petyr saved me. He loved my mother well, and . . .*

And her? How could she doubt it? He had saved her.

He saved Alayne, his daughter, a voice within her whispered. But she was Sansa too . . . and sometimes it seemed to her that the Lord Protector was two people as well. He was Petyr, her protector, warm and funny and gentle . . . but he was also Littlefinger, the lord she'd known at King's Landing, smiling slyly and stroking his beard as he whispered in Queen Cersei's ear. And Littlefinger was no friend of hers. When Joff had her beaten, the Imp defended her, not Littlefinger. When the mob sought to rape her, the Hound carried her to safety, not Littlefinger. When the Lannisters wed her to Tyrion against her will, Ser Garlan the Gallant gave her comfort, not Littlefinger. Littlefinger never lifted so much as his little finger for her.

Except to get me out. He did that for me. I thought it was Ser Dontos, my poor old drunken Florian, but it was Petyr all the while. Littlefinger was only a mask he had to wear. Only sometimes Sansa found it hard to tell where the man ended and the mask began. Littlefinger and Lord Petyr looked so very much alike. She would have fled them both, perhaps, but there was nowhere for her to go. Winterfell was burned and desolate, Bran and Rickon dead and cold. Robb had been betrayed and murdered at the Twins, along with their lady mother. Tyrion had been put to death for killing Joffrey, and if she ever returned to King's Landing the queen would have her head as well. The aunt she'd hoped would keep her safe had tried to murder her instead. Her uncle Edmure was a captive of the Freys, while her great-uncle the Blackfish was under siege at Riverrun. *I have no place but here,* Sansa thought miserably, *and no true friend but Petyr.*

That night the dead man sang "The Day They Hanged Black Robin," "The Mother's Tears," and "The Rains of Castamere." Then he stopped for a while, but just as Sansa began to drift off he started to play again. He sang "Six Sorrows," "Fallen Leaves," and "Alysanne." *Such sad songs,* she thought. When she closed her eyes she could see him in his sky cell, huddled in a corner away from the cold black sky, crouched beneath a fur with his woodharp cradled against his chest. *I must not pity him,* she told herself. *He was vain and cruel, and soon he will be dead.* She could not save him. And why should she want to? Marillion tried to rape her, and Petyr had saved her life not once but twice. *Some lies you have to tell.* Lies had been all that kept her alive in King's Landing. If she had not lied to Joffrey, his Kingsguard would have beat her bloody.

After "Alysanne," the singer stopped again, long enough for Sansa to snatch an hour's rest. But as the first light of dawn was prying at her shutters, she heard the soft strains of "On a Misty Morn," drifting up from below, and woke at once. That was more properly a woman's song, a lament sung by a mother on the dawn after some terrible battle, as she searches amongst the dead for the body of her only son. *The mother sings her grief for her dead son,* Sansa thought, *but Marillion grieves for his fingers, for his eyes.* The words rose like arrows and pierced her in the darkness.

> *Oh, have you seen my boy, good ser?*
> *His hair is chestnut brown*
> *He promised he'd come back to me*
> *Our home's in Wendish Town.*

Sansa covered her ears with a goose down pillow to shut out the rest of it, but it was no good. Day had come and she had woken, and Lord Nestor Royce was coming up the mountain.

The High Steward and his party reached the Eyrie in the late afternoon, with the valley gold and red beneath them and the wind rising. He brought his son Ser Albar, along with a dozen knights and a score of men-at-arms. *So many strangers.* Sansa looked at their faces anxiously, wondering if they were friends or foes.

Petyr welcomed his visitors in a black velvet doublet with grey sleeves that matched his woolen breeches and lent a certain darkness to his grey-green eyes. Maester Colemon stood beside him, his chain of many metals hanging loose about his long, skinny neck. Although the maester was much the taller of the two men, it was the Lord Protector who drew the eye. He had put away his smiles for the day, it seemed. He listened solemnly as Royce introduced the knights who had accompanied him, then said, "My lords are welcome here. You know our Maester Colemon, of course. Lord Nestor, you will recall Alayne, my natural daughter?"

"To be sure." Lord Nestor Royce was a bullnecked, barrel-chested, balding man with a grey-shot beard and a stern look. He inclined his head a whole half inch in greeting.

Sansa curtsied, too frightened to speak for fear she might misspeak. Petyr drew her to her feet. "Sweetling, be a good girl and bring Lord Robert to the High Hall to receive his guests."

"Yes, Father." Her voice sounded thin and strained. *A liar's voice,* she thought as she hurried up the steps and across the gallery to the Moon Tower. *A guilty voice.*

Gretchel and Maddy were helping Robert Arryn squirm into his breeches when Sansa stepped into his bedchamber. The Lord of the Eyrie had been crying again. His eyes were red and raw, his lashes crusty, his nose swollen and runny. A trail of snot glistened underneath one nostril, and his lower lip was bloody where he'd bitten it. *Lord Nestor must not see him like this,* Sansa thought, despairing. "Gretchel, fetch me the washbasin." She took the boy by the hand and drew him to the bed. "Did my Sweetrobin sleep well last night?"

"No." He sniffed. "I never slept one bit, Alayne. He was *singing* again, and my *door* was locked. I called for them to let me out, but no one ever came. Someone locked me in my room."

"That was wicked of them." Dipping a soft cloth into the warm water, she began to clean his face . . . gently, oh so gently. If you scrubbed Robert too briskly, he might begin to shake. The boy was frail, and terribly small for his age. He was eight, but Sansa had known bigger five-year-olds.

Robert's lip quivered. "I was going to come sleep with you."

I know you were. Sweetrobin had been accustomed to crawling in beside his mother, until she wed Lord Petyr. Since Lady Lysa's death he had taken to wandering the Eyrie in quest of other beds. The one he liked best was Sansa's . . . which was why she had asked Ser Lothor Brune to lock his door last night. She would not have minded if he only slept, but he was always trying to nuzzle at her breasts, and when he had his shaking spells he often wet the bed.

"Lord Nestor Royce has come up from the Gates to see you." Sansa wiped beneath his nose.

"I don't want to see *him*," he said. "I want a story. A story of the Winged Knight."

"After," Sansa said. "First you must see Lord Nestor."

"Lord Nestor has a mole," he said, squirming. Robert was afraid of men with moles. "Mommy said he was *dreadful.*"

"My poor Sweetrobin." Sansa smoothed his hair back. "You miss her, I know. Lord Petyr misses her too. He loved her just as you do." That was a lie, though kindly meant. The only woman Petyr ever loved was Sansa's murdered mother. He had confessed as much to Lady Lysa just before he pushed her out the Moon Door. *She was mad and dangerous. She murdered her own lord husband, and would have murdered me if Petyr had not come along to save me.*

Robert did not need to know that, though. He was only a sick little boy who'd loved his mother. "There," Sansa said, "you look a proper lord now. Maddy, fetch his cloak." It was lambswool, soft and warm, a handsome sky-blue that set off the cream color of his tunic. She fastened it about his shoulders with a silver brooch in the shape of a crescent moon, and took him by the hand. Robert came meekly for once.

The High Hall had been closed since Lady Lysa's fall, and it gave

Sansa a chill to enter it again. The hall was long and grand and beautiful, she supposed, but she did not like it here. It was a pale cold place at the best of times. The slender pillars looked like fingerbones, and the blue veins in the white marble brought to mind the veins in an old crone's legs. Though fifty silver sconces lined the walls, less than a dozen torches had been lit, so shadows danced upon the floors and pooled in every corner. Their footsteps echoed off the marble, and Sansa could hear the wind rattling at the Moon Door. *I must not look at it,* she told herself, *else I'll start to shake as badly as Robert.*

With Maddy's help, she got Robert seated on his weirwood throne with a stack of pillows underneath him and sent word that his lordship would receive his guests. Two guards in sky-blue cloaks opened the doors at the lower end of the hall, and Petyr ushered them in and down the long blue carpet that ran between the rows of bone-white pillars.

The boy greeted Lord Nestor with squeaky courtesy and made no mention of his mole. When the High Steward asked about his lady mother, Robert's hands began to tremble ever so slightly. "Marillion hurt my mother. He threw her out the Moon Door."

"Did your lordship see this happen?" asked Ser Marwyn Belmore, a lanky ginger-headed knight who had been Lysa's captain of guards till Petyr had put Ser Lothor Brune in his place.

"Alayne saw it," the boy said. "And my lord stepfather."

Lord Nestor looked at her. Ser Albar, Ser Marwyn, Maester Colemon, all of them were looking. *She was my aunt but she wanted to kill me,* Sansa thought. *She dragged me to the Moon Door and tried to push me out. I never wanted a kiss, I was building a castle in the snow.* She hugged herself to keep from shaking.

"Forgive her, my lords," Petyr Baelish said softly. "She still has nightmares of that day. Small wonder if she cannot bear to speak of it." He came up behind her and put his hands gently on her shoulders. "I know how hard this is for you, Alayne, but our friends must hear the truth."

"Yes." Her throat felt so dry and tight it almost hurt to speak. "I saw . . . I was with the Lady Lysa when . . ." A tear rolled down her cheek. *That's good, a tear is good.* ". . . when Marillion . . . pushed her."

And she told the tale again, hardly hearing the words as they spilled out of her.

Before she was half-done Robert began to cry, the pillows shifting perilously beneath him. "He killed my *mother*. I want him to fly!" The trembling in his hands had grown worse, and his arms were shaking too. The boy's head jerked and his teeth began to chatter. "*Fly!*" he shrieked. "*Fly, fly.*" His arms and legs flailed wildly. Lothor Brune strode to the dais in time to catch the boy as he slipped from his throne. Maester Colemon was just a step behind, though there was naught that he could do.

Helpless as the rest, Sansa could only stand and watch as the shaking spell ran its course. One of Robert's legs kicked Ser Lothor in the face. Brune cursed, but still held on as the boy twitched and flailed and wet himself. Their visitors said not a word; Lord Nestor at least had seen these fits before. It was long moments before Robert's spasms began to subside, and seemed even longer. By the end, the little lordling was so weak he could not stand. "Best take his lordship back to bed and bleed him," Lord Petyr said. Brune lifted the boy in his arms and carried him from the hall. Maester Colemon followed, grim-faced.

When their footsteps died away there was no sound in the High Hall of the Eyrie. Sansa could hear the night wind moaning outside and scratching at the Moon Door. She was very cold and very tired. *Must I tell the tale again?* she wondered.

But she must have told it well enough. Lord Nestor cleared his throat. "I misliked that singer from the first," he grumbled. "I urged Lady Lysa to send him away. Many a time I urged her."

"You always gave her good counsel, my lord," Petyr said.

"She took no heed of it," Royce complained. "She heard me grudgingly and took no heed."

"My lady was too trusting for this world." Petyr spoke so tenderly that Sansa would have believed he'd loved his wife. "Lysa could not see the evil in men, only the good. Marillion sang sweet songs, and she mistook that for his nature."

"He called us pigs," Ser Albar Royce said. A blunt broad-shouldered knight who shaved his chin but cultivated thick black side-whiskers that framed his homely face like hedgerows, Ser Albar was a younger version of his father. "He made a song about two pigs snuffling round a mountain, eating a falcon's leavings. That was meant to be us, but when I said so he laughed at me. 'Why, ser, 'tis a song about some pigs,' he said."

"He made mock of me as well," Ser Marwyn Belmore said. "Ser Ding-Dong, he named me. When I vowed I'd cut his tongue out, he ran to Lady Lysa and hid behind her skirts."

"As oft he did," Lord Nestor said. "The man was craven, but the favor Lady Lysa showed him made him insolent. She dressed him like a lord, gave him gold rings and a moonstone belt."

"Even Lord Jon's favorite falcon." The knight's doublet showed the six white candles of Waxley. "His lordship loved that bird. King Robert gave it to him."

Petyr Baelish sighed. "It was unseemly," he agreed, "and I put an end to it. Lysa agreed to send him away. That was why she met him here, that day. I should have been with her, but I never dreamt . . . if I had not insisted . . . it was I who killed her."

No, Sansa thought, *you mustn't say that, you mustn't tell them, you mustn't.* But Albar Royce was shaking his head. "No, my lord, you must not blame yourself," he said.

"This was the singer's work," his father agreed. "Bring him up, Lord Petyr. Let us write an end to this sorry business."

Petyr Baelish composed himself, and said, "As you wish, my lord." He turned to his guardsmen and spoke a command, and the singer was fetched up from the dungeons. The gaoler Mord came with him, a monstrous man with small black eyes and a lopsided, scarred face. One ear and part of his cheek had been cleaved off in some battle, but twenty stone of pallid white flesh remained. His clothes fit poorly and had a rank, ripe smell.

Marillion by contrast looked almost elegant. Someone had bathed him and dressed him in a pair of sky-blue breeches and a loose-fitting white tunic with puffed sleeves, belted with a silvery sash that had been a gift from Lady Lysa. White silk gloves covered his hands, while a white silk bandage spared the lords the sight of his eyes.

Mord stood behind him with a lash. When the gaoler prodded him in the ribs, the singer went to one knee. "Good lords, I beg your forgiveness."

Lord Nestor scowled. "You confess your crime?"

"If I had eyes I should weep." The singer's voice, so strong and sure by night, was cracked and whispery now. "I loved her so, I could not bear to see her in another's arms, to know she shared his bed. I meant no harm to my sweet lady, I swear it. I barred the door so no one could disturb us whilst I declared my passion, but Lady Lysa was so cold . . . when she told that she was carrying Lord Petyr's child, a . . . a madness seized me . . ."

Sansa stared at his hands while he spoke. Fat Maddy claimed that Mord had taken off three of his fingers, both pinkies and a ring finger. His little fingers did appear somewhat stiffer than the others, but with those gloves it was hard to be certain. *It might have been no more than a story. How would Maddy know?*

"Lord Petyr has been kind enough to let me keep my harp," the blind singer said. "My harp and . . . my tongue . . . so I may sing my songs. Lady Lysa dearly loved my singing . . ."

"Take this creature away, or I'm like to kill him myself," Lord Nestor growled. "It sickens me to look at him."

"Mord, take him back to his sky cell," said Petyr.

"Yes, m'lord." Mord grabbed Marillion roughly by the collar. "No more mouth." When he spoke, Sansa saw to her astonishment that the gaoler's teeth were made of gold. They watched as he half dragged half shoved the singer toward the doors.

"The man must die," Ser Marywn Belmore declared when they were gone. "He should have followed Lady Lysa out the Moon Door."

"Without his tongue," Ser Albar Royce added. "Without that lying, mocking tongue."

"I have been too gentle with him, I know," Petyr Baelish said in an apologetic tone. "If truth be told, I pity him. He killed for love."

"For love or hate," said Belmore, "he must die."

"Soon enough," Lord Nestor said gruffly. "No man lingers long in the sky cells. The blue will call to him."

"It may," said Petyr Baelish, "but whether Marillion will answer, only he can say." He gestured, and his guardsmen opened the doors at the far end of the hall. "Sers, I know you must be weary after your ascent. Rooms have been prepared for all of you to spend the night, and food and wine await you in the Lower Hall. Oswell, show them the way, and see that they have all they need." He turned to Nestor Royce. "My lord, will you join me in the solar for a cup of wine? Alayne, sweetling, come pour for us."

A low fire burned in the solar, where a flagon of wine awaited them. *Arbor gold.* Sansa filled Lord Nestor's cup whilst Petyr prodded at the logs with an iron poker.

Lord Nestor seated himself beside the fire. "This will not be the end of it," he said to Petyr, as if Sansa were not there. "My cousin means to question the singer himself."

"Bronze Yohn mistrusts me." Petyr pushed a log aside.

"He means to come in force. Symond Templeton will join him, do not doubt it. And Lady Waynwood too, I fear."

"And Lord Belmore, Young Lord Hunter, Horton Redfort. They will bring Strong Sam Stone, the Tolletts, the Shetts, the Coldwaters, some Corbrays."

"You are well-informed. Which Corbrays? Not Lord Lyonel?"

"No, his brother. Ser Lyn mislikes me, for some reason."

"Lyn Corbray is a dangerous man," Lord Nestor said doggedly. "What do you intend to do?"

"What *can* I do but make them welcome if they come?" Petyr gave the flames another stir and set the poker down.

"My cousin means to remove you as Lord Protector."

"If so, I cannot stop him. I keep a garrison of twenty men. Lord Royce and his friends can raise twenty thousand." Petyr went to the oaken chest that sat beneath the window. "Bronze Yohn will do what he will do," he said, kneeling. He opened the chest, drew out a roll of parchment, and brought it to Lord Nestor. "My lord. This is a token of the love my lady bore you."

Sansa watched Royce unroll the parchment. "This . . . this is unexpected, my lord." She was startled to see tears in his eyes.

"Unexpected, but not undeserved. My lady valued you above all her other bannermen. You were her rock, she told me."

"Her rock." Lord Nestor reddened. "She said that?"

"Often. And this"—Petyr gestured at the parchment—"is the proof of it."

"That . . . that is good to know. Jon Arryn valued my service, I know, but Lady Lysa . . . she scorned me when I came to court her, and I feared . . ." Lord Nestor furrowed his brow. "It bears the Arryn seal, I see, but the signature . . ."

"Lysa was murdered before the document could be presented for her signature, so I signed as Lord Protector. I knew that would have been her wish."

"I see." Lord Nestor rolled the parchment. "You are . . . dutiful, my lord. Aye, and not without courage. Some will call this grant unseemly, and fault you for making it. The Keeper's post has never been hereditary. The Arryns raised the Gates, in the days when they still wore the Falcon Crown and ruled the Vale as kings. The Eyrie was their summer seat, but when the snows began to fall the court would make its descent. Some would say the Gates were as royal as the Eyrie."

"There has been no king in the Vale for three hundred years," Petyr Baelish pointed out.

"The dragons came," Lord Nestor agreed. "But even after, the Gates remained an Arryn castle. Jon Arryn himself was Keeper of the Gates whilst his father lived. After his ascent, he named his brother Ronnel to the honor, and later his cousin Denys."

"Lord Robert has no brothers, and only distant cousins."

"True." Lord Nestor clutched the parchment tightly. "I will not say I had not hoped for this. Whilst Lord Jon ruled the realm as Hand, it fell to me to rule the Vale for him. I did all that he required of me and asked nothing for myself. But by the gods, I earned this!"

"You did," said Petyr, "and Lord Robert sleeps more easily knowing that you are always there, a staunch friend at the foot of his mountain." He raised a cup. "So . . . a toast, my lord. To House Royce, Keepers of the Gates of the Moon . . . now and forever."

"Now and forever, aye!" The silver cups crashed together.

Later, much later, after the flagon of Arbor gold was dry, Lord Nestor took his leave to rejoin his company of knights. Sansa was asleep on her feet by then, wanting only to crawl off to her bed, but Petyr caught her by the wrist. "You see the wonders that can be worked with lies and Arbor gold?"

Why did she feel like weeping? It was good that Nestor Royce was with them. "Were they all lies?"

"Not *all*. Lysa often called Lord Nestor a rock, though I do not think she meant it as a compliment. She called his son a clod. She knew Lord Nestor dreamed of holding the Gates in his own right, a lord in truth as well as name, but Lysa dreamed of other sons and meant the castle to go to Robert's little brother." He stood. "Do you understand what happened here, Alayne?"

Sansa hesitated a moment. "You gave Lord Nestor the Gates of the Moon to be certain of his support."

"I did," Petyr admitted, "but our rock is a Royce, which is to say he is overproud and prickly. Had I asked him his price, he would have swelled up like an angry toad at the slight upon his honor. But this way ... the man is not *utterly* stupid, but the lies I served him were sweeter than the truth. He *wants* to believe that Lysa valued him above her other bannermen. One of those others is Bronze Yohn, after all, and Nestor is very much aware that he was born of the *lesser* branch of House Royce. He wants more for his son. Men of honor will do things for their children that they would never consider doing for themselves."

She nodded. "The signature ... you might have had Lord Robert put his hand and seal to it, but instead ..."

"... I signed myself, as Lord Protector. Why?"

"So ... if you are removed, or ... or killed ..."

"... Lord Nestor's claim to the Gates will suddenly be called into question. I promise you, that is not lost on him. It was clever of you to see it. Though no more than I'd expect of mine own daughter."

"Thank you." She felt absurdly proud for puzzling it out, but confused as well. "I'm not, though. Your daughter. Not truly. I mean, I pretend to be Alayne, but *you* know ..."

Littlefinger put a finger to her lips. "I know what I know, and so do you. Some things are best left unsaid, sweetling."

"Even when we are alone?"

"*Especially* when we are alone. Elsewise a day will come when a servant walks into a room unannounced, or a guardsman at the door chances to hear something he should not. Do you want more blood on your pretty little hands, my darling?"

Marillion's face seemed to float before her, the bandage pale across his eyes. Behind him she could see Ser Dontos, the crossbow bolts still in him. "No," Sansa said. "Please."

"I am tempted to say this is no game we play, daughter, but of course it is. The game of thrones."

I never asked to play. The game was too dangerous. *One slip and I am dead.* "Oswell . . . my lord, Oswell rowed me from King's Landing the night that I escaped. He must know who I am."

"If he's half as clever as a sheep pellet, you would think so. Ser Lothor knows as well. But Oswell has been in my service a long time, and Brune is close-mouthed by nature. Kettleblack watches Brune for me, and Brune watches Kettleblack. *Trust no one,* I once told Eddard Stark, but he would not listen. You are Alayne, and you must be Alayne *all the time.*" He put two fingers on her left breast. "Even here. In your heart. Can you do that? Can you be my daughter in your heart?"

"I . . ." *I do not know, my lord,* she almost said, but that was not what he wanted to hear. *Lies and Arbor gold,* she thought. "I am Alayne, Father. Who else would I be?"

Lord Littlefinger kissed her cheek. "With my wits and Cat's beauty, the world will be yours, sweetling. Now off to bed."

Gretchel had laid a fire in her hearth and plumped her featherbed. Sansa undressed and slipped beneath the blankets. *He will not sing tonight,* she prayed, *not with Lord Nestor and the others in the castle. He would not dare.* She closed her eyes.

Sometime during the night she woke, as little Robert climbed up into her bed. *I forgot to tell Lothor to lock him in again,* she realized. There was nothing to be done for it, so she put her arm around him. "Sweetrobin? You can stay, but try not to squirm around. Just close your eyes and sleep, little one."

"I will." He cuddled close and laid his head between her breasts. "Alayne? Are you my mother now?"

"I suppose I am," she said. If a lie was kindly meant, there was no harm in it.

THE KRAKEN'S DAUGHTER

The hall was loud with drunken Harlaws, distant cousins all. Each lord had hung his banner behind the benches where his men were seated. *Too few,* thought Asha Greyjoy, looking down from the gallery, *too few by far.* The benches were three-quarters empty.

Qarl the Maid had said as much, when the *Black Wind* was approaching from the sea. He had counted the longships moored beneath her uncle's castle, and his mouth had tightened. "They have not come," he observed, "or not enough of them." He was not wrong, but Asha could not agree with him, out where her crew might hear. She did not doubt their devotion, but even ironborn will hesitate to give their lives for a cause that's plainly lost.

Do I have so few friends as this? Amongst the banners, she saw the silver fish of Botley, the stone tree of the Stonetrees, the black leviathan of Volmark, the nooses of the Myres. The rest were Harlaw scythes. Boremund placed his upon a pale blue field, Hotho's was girdled within an embattled border, and the Knight had quartered his with the gaudy peacock of his mother's House. Even Sigfryd Silverhair showed two scythes counterchanged on a field divided bendwise. Only *the* Lord Harlaw displayed the silver scythe plain upon a night-black field, as it had flown in the dawn of days: Rodrik, called the Reader, Lord of the Ten Towers, Lord of Harlaw, Harlaw of Harlaw . . . her favorite uncle.

Lord Rodrik's high seat was vacant. Two scythes of beaten silver crossed above it, so huge that even a giant would have difficulty wielding them, but beneath were only empty cushions. Asha was not surprised. The feast was long concluded. Only bones and greasy platters remained upon the trestle tables. The rest was drinking, and her uncle Rodrik had never been partial to the company of quarrelsome drunks.

She turned to Three-Tooth, an old woman of fearful age who had been her uncle's steward since she was known as Twelve-Tooth. "My uncle is with his books?"

"Aye, where else?" The woman was so old that a septon had once said she must have nursed the Crone. That was when the Faith was still tolerated on the isles. Lord Rodrik had kept septons at Ten Towers, not for his soul's sake but for his books. "With the books, and Botley. He was with him too."

Botley's standard hung in the hall, a shoal of silver fish upon a pale green field, though Asha had not seen his *Swiftfin* amongst the other longships. "I had heard my nuncle Crow's Eye had old Sawane Botley drowned."

"Lord *Tristifer* Botley, this one is."

Tris. She wondered what had happened to Sawane's elder son, Harren. *I will find out soon enough, no doubt. This should be awkward.* She had not seen Tris Botley since . . . no, she ought not dwell on it. "And my lady mother?"

"Abed," said Three-Tooth, "in the Widow's Tower."

Aye, where else? The widow the tower was named after was her aunt. Lady Gwynesse had come home to mourn after her husband had died off Fair Isle during Balon Greyjoy's first rebellion. "I will only stay until my grief has passed," she had told her brother, famously, "though by rights Ten Towers should be mine, for I am seven years your elder." Long years had passed since then, but still the widow lingered, grieving, and muttering from time to time that the castle should be hers. *And now Lord Rodrik has a second half-mad widowed sister beneath his roof,* Asha reflected. *Small wonder if he seeks solace in his books.*

Even now, it was hard to credit that frail, sickly Lady Alannys had outlived her husband Lord Balon, who had seemed so hard and strong. When Asha had sailed away to war, she had done so with a heavy heart, fearing that her mother might well die before she could return. Not once had she thought that her father might perish instead. *The Drowned God plays savage japes upon us all, but men are crueler still.* A sudden storm and a broken rope had sent Balon Greyjoy to his death. *Or so they claim.*

Asha had last seen her mother when she stopped at Ten Towers to take on fresh water, on her way north to strike at Deepwood Motte. Alannys Harlaw never had the sort of beauty the singers cherished, but her daughter had loved her fierce strong face and the laughter in her eyes. On that last visit, though, she had found Lady Alannys in a window seat huddled beneath a pile of furs, staring out across the sea. *Is this my mother, or her ghost?* she remembered thinking as she'd kissed her cheek.

Her mother's skin had been parchment thin, her long hair white. Some pride remained in the way she held her head, but her eyes were dim and cloudy, and her mouth had trembled when she asked after Theon. "Did you bring my baby boy?" she had asked. Theon had been ten years old when he was carried off to Winterfell a hostage, and so far as Lady Alannys was concerned he would always be ten years old, it seemed. "Theon could not come," Asha had to tell her. "Father sent him reaving along the Stony Shore." Lady Alannys had naught to say to that. She only nodded slowly, yet it was plain to see how deep her daughter's words had cut her.

And now I must tell her that Theon is dead, and drive yet another dagger through her heart. There were two knives buried there already. On the blades were writ the words *Rodrik* and *Maron,* and many a time they twisted cruelly in the night. *I will see her on the morrow,* Asha vowed to herself. Her journey had been long and wearisome, she could not face her mother now.

"I must speak with Lord Rodrik," she told Three-Tooth. "See to my crew, once they're done unloading *Black Wind.* They'll bring captives. I want them to have warm beds and a hot meal."

"There's cold beef in the kitchens. And mustard in a big stone jar, from Oldtown." The thought of that mustard made the old woman smile. A single long brown tooth poked from her gums.

"That will not serve. We had a rough crossing. I want something hot in their bellies." Asha hooked a thumb through the studded belt about her hips. "Lady Glover and the children should not want for wood nor warmth. Put them in some tower, not the dungeons. The babe is sick."

"Babes are often sick. Most die, and folks are sorry. I shall ask my lord where to put these wolf folk."

She caught the woman's nose between thumb and forefinger and pinched. "You will do as I say. And if *this* babe dies, no one will be sorrier than you." Three-Tooth squealed and promised to obey, till Asha let her loose and went to find her uncle.

It was good to walk these halls again. Ten Towers had always felt like home to Asha, more so than Pyke. *Not one castle, ten castles squashed together,* she had thought, the first time she had seen it. She remembered breathless races up and down the steps and along wall-walks and covered bridges, fishing off the Long Stone Quay, days and nights lost amongst her uncle's wealth of books. His grandfather's grandfather had raised the castle, the newest on the isles. Lord Theomore Harlaw had lost three sons in the cradle and laid the blame upon the flooded cellars, damp stones, and festering nitre of ancient Harlaw Hall. Ten Towers was airier, more comfortable, better sited . . . but Lord Theomore was a changeable man, as any of his wives might have testified. He'd had six of those, as dissimilar as his ten towers.

The Book Tower was the fattest of the ten, octagonal in shape and made with great blocks of hewn stone. The stair was built within the thickness of the walls. Asha climbed quickly, to the fifth story and the room where her uncle read. *Not that there are any rooms where he does not read.* Lord Rodrik was seldom seen without a book in hand, be it in the privy, on the deck of his *Sea Song,* or whilst holding audience. Asha had oft seen him reading on his high seat beneath the silver scythes. He would listen to each case as it was laid before him, pronounce his judgment . . . and read a bit whilst his captain-of-guards went to bring in the next supplicant.

She found him hunched over a table by a window, surrounded by parchment scrolls that might have come from Valyria before its Doom, and heavy leather-bound books with bronze-and-iron hasps. Beeswax candles as thick and tall as a man's arm burned on either side of where he sat, on ornate iron holders. Lord Rodrik Harlaw was neither fat nor slim; neither tall nor short; neither ugly nor handsome. His hair was brown, as were his eyes, though the short, neat beard he favored had gone grey. All in all, he was an ordinary man, distinguished only by his love of written words, which so many ironborn found unmanly and perverse.

"Nuncle." She closed the door behind her. "What reading was so urgent that you leave your guests without a host?"

"Archmaester Marwyn's *Book of Lost Books*." He lifted his gaze from the page to study her. "Hotho brought me a copy from Oldtown. He has a daughter he would have me wed." Lord Rodrik tapped the book with a long nail. "See here? Marwyn claims to have found three pages of *Signs and Portents*, visions written down by the maiden daughter of Aenar Targaryen before the Doom came to Valyria. Does Lanny know that you are here?"

"Not as yet." *Lanny* was his pet name for her mother; only the Reader called her that. "Let her rest." Asha moved a stack of books off a stool and seated herself. "Three-Tooth seems to have lost two more of her teeth. Do you call her One-Tooth now?"

"I seldom call her at all. The woman frightens me. What hour is it?" Lord Rodrik glanced out the window, at the moonlit sea. "Dark, so soon? I had not noticed. You come late. We looked for you some days ago."

"The winds were against us, and I had captives to concern me. Robett Glover's wife and children. The youngest is still at the breast, and Lady Glover's milk dried up during our crossing. I had no choice but to beach *Black Wind* upon the Stony Shore and send my men out to find a wet nurse. They found a goat instead. The girl does not thrive. Is there a nursing mother in the village? Deepwood is important to my plans."

"Your plans must change. You come too late."

"Late and hungry." She stretched her long legs out beneath the table and turned the pages of the nearest book, a septon's discourse on Maegor the Cruel's war against the Poor Fellows. "Oh, and thirsty too. A horn of ale would go down well, Nuncle."

Lord Rodrik pursed his lips. "You know I do not permit food nor drink in my library. The books—"

"—might suffer harm." Asha laughed.

Her uncle frowned. "You do like to provoke me."

"Oh, don't look so aggrieved. I have never met a man I didn't provoke, you should know that well enough by now. But enough of me. You are well?"

He shrugged. "Well enough. My eyes grow weaker. I have sent to Myr for a lens to help me read."

"And how fares my aunt?"

Lord Rodrik sighed. "Still seven years my elder, and convinced Ten Towers should be hers. Gwynesse grows forgetful, but *that* she does not forget. She mourns for her dead husband as deeply as she did the day he died, though she cannot always recall his name."

"I am not certain she ever knew his name." Asha closed the septon's book with a *thump*. "Was my father murdered?"

"So your mother believes."

There were times when she would gladly have murdered him herself, she thought. "And what does my nuncle believe?"

"Balon fell to his death when a rope bridge broke beneath him. A storm was rising, and the bridge was swaying and twisting with each gust of wind." Rodrik shrugged. "Or so we are told. Your mother had a bird from Maester Wendamyr."

Asha slid her dirk out of its sheath and began to clean the dirt from beneath her fingernails. "Three years away, and the Crow's Eye returns the very day my father dies."

"The day after, we had heard. *Silence* was still out to sea when Balon died, or so it is claimed. Even so, I will agree that Euron's return was . . . timely, shall we say?"

"That is not how I would say it." Asha slammed the point of the dirk into the table. "*Where are my ships?* I counted twoscore longships moored below, not near enough to throw the Crow's Eye off my father's chair."

"I sent the summons. In your name, for the love I bear you and your mother. House Harlaw has gathered. Stonetree as well, and Volmark. Some Myres . . ."

"All from the isle of Harlaw . . . one isle out of seven. I saw one lonely Botley banner in the hall, from Pyke. Where are the ships from Saltcliffe, from Orkwood, from the Wyks?"

"Baelor Blacktyde came from Blacktyde to consult with me, and just as soon set sail again." Lord Rodrik closed *The Book of Lost Books.* "He is on Old Wyk by now."

"Old Wyk?" Asha had feared he was about to say that they all had gone to Pyke, to do homage to the Crow's Eye. "Why Old Wyk?"

"I thought you would have heard. Aeron Damphair has called a kingsmoot."

Asha threw back her head and laughed. "The Drowned God must have shoved a pricklefish up Uncle Aeron's arse. A *kingsmoot?* Is this some jape, or does he mean it truly?"

"The Damphair has not japed since he was drowned. And the other priests have taken up the call. Blind Beron Blacktyde, Tarle the Thrice-Drowned . . . even the Old Grey Gull has left that rock he lives on to preach this kingsmoot all across Harlaw. The captains are gathering on Old Wyk as we speak."

Asha was astonished. "Has the Crow's Eye agreed to attend this holy farce and abide by its decision?"

"The Crow's Eye does not confide in me. Since he summoned me to Pyke to do him homage, I have had no word from Euron."

A kingsmoot. This is something new . . . or rather, something very old. "And my uncle Victarion? What does he make of the Damphair's notion?"

"Victarion was sent word of your father's death. And of this kingsmoot too, I do not doubt. Beyond that, I cannot say."

Better a kingsmoot than a war. "I believe I'll kiss the Damphair's smelly feet and pluck the seaweed from out between his toes." Asha wrenched loose her dirk and sheathed it once again. "A bloody *kingsmoot!*"

"On Old Wyk," confirmed Lord Rodrik. "Though I pray it is not bloody. I have been consulting Haereg's *History of the Ironborn.* When last the salt kings and the rock kings met in kingsmoot, Urron of

Orkmont let his axemen loose among them, and Nagga's ribs turned red with gore. House Greyiron ruled unchosen for a thousand years from that dark day, until the Andals came."

"You must lend me Haereg's book, Nuncle." She would need to learn all she could of kingsmoots before she reached Old Wyk.

"You may read it here. It is old and fragile." He studied her, frowning. "Archmaester Rigney once wrote that history is a wheel, for the nature of man is fundamentally unchanging. What has happened before will perforce happen again, he said. I think of that whenever I contemplate the Crow's Eye. Euron Greyjoy sounds queerly like Urron Greyiron to these old ears. I shall not go to Old Wyk. Nor should you."

Asha smiled. "And miss the first kingsmoot called in . . . how long *has* it been, Nuncle?"

"Four thousand years, if Haereg can be believed. Half that, if you accept Maester Denestan's arguments in *Questions*. Going to Old Wyk serves no purpose. This dream of kingship is a madness in our blood. I told your father so the first time he rose, and it is more true now than it was then. It's land we need, not crowns. With Stannis Baratheon and Tywin Lannister contending for the Iron Throne, we have a rare chance to improve our lot. Let us take one side or the other, help them to victory with our fleets, and claim the lands we need from a grateful king."

"That might be worth some thought, once I sit the Seastone Chair," said Asha.

Her uncle sighed. "You will not want to hear this, Asha, but you will not be chosen. No woman has ever ruled the ironborn. Gwynesse *is* seven years my elder, but when our father died the Ten Towers came to me. It will be the same for you. You are Balon's daughter, not his son. And you have three uncles."

"Four."

"Three kraken uncles. I do not count."

"You do with me. So long as I have my nuncle of Ten Towers, I have Harlaw." Harlaw was not the largest of the Iron Islands, but it was the richest and most populous, and Lord Rodrik's power was not to be despised. On Harlaw, Harlaw had no rival. The Volmarks and

Stonetrees had large holdings on the isle and boasted famous captains and fierce warriors of their own, but even the fiercest bent beneath the scythe. The Kennings and the Myres, once bitter foes, had long ago been beaten down to vassals.

"My cousins do me fealty, and in war I should command their swords and sails. In kingsmoot, though . . ." Lord Rodrik shook his head. "Beneath the bones of Nagga every captain stands as equal. Some may shout your name, I do not doubt it. But not enough. And when the shouts ring out for Victarion or the Crow's Eye, some of those now drinking in my hall will join the rest. I say again, do not sail into this storm. Your fight is hopeless."

"No fight is hopeless till it has been fought. I have the best claim. I am the heir of Balon's body."

"You are still a willful child. Think of your poor mother. You are all that Lanny has left to her. I will put a torch to *Black Wind* if need be, to keep you here."

"What, and make me swim to Old Wyk?"

"A long cold swim, for a crown you cannot keep. Your father had more courage than sense. The Old Way served the isles well when we were one small kingdom amongst many, but Aegon's Conquest put an end to that. Balon refused to see what was plain before him. The Old Way died with Black Harren and his sons."

"I know that." Asha had loved her father, but she did not delude herself. Balon had been blind in some respects. *A brave man but a bad lord.* "Does that mean we must live and die as thralls to the Iron Throne? If there are rocks to starboard and a storm to port, a wise captain steers a third course."

"Show me this third course."

"I shall . . . at my queensmoot. Nuncle, how can you even think of not attending? This will be history, alive . . ."

"I prefer my history dead. Dead history is writ in ink, the living sort in blood."

"Do you want to die old and craven in your bed?"

"How else? Though not till I'm done reading." Lord Rodrik went to the window. "You have not asked about your lady mother."

I was afraid. "How is she?"

"Stronger. She may yet outlive us all. She will certainly outlive you, if you persist in this folly. She eats more than she did when she first came here, and oft sleeps through the night."

"Good." In her final years on Pyke, Lady Alannys could not sleep. She would wander the halls at night with a candle, looking for her sons. "*Maron?*" she would call shrilly. "*Rodrik, where are you? Theon, my baby, come to Mother.*" Many a time Asha had watched the maester draw splinters from her mother's heels of a morning, after she had crossed the swaying plank bridge to the Sea Tower on bare feet. "I will see her in the morning."

"She will ask for word of Theon."

The Prince of Winterfell. "What have you told her?"

"Little and less. There was naught to tell." He hesitated. "You are certain that he is dead?"

"I am certain of nothing."

"You found a body?"

"We found parts of many bodies. The wolves were there before us . . . the four-legged sort, but they showed scant reverence for their two-legged kin. The bones of the slain were scattered, cracked open for their marrow. I confess, it was hard to know what happened there. It seemed as though the northmen fought amongst themselves."

"Crows will fight over a dead man's flesh and kill each other for his eyes." Lord Rodrik stared across the sea, watching the play of moonlight on the waves. "We had one king, then five. Now all I see are crows, squabbling over the corpse of Westeros." He fastened the shutters. "Do not go to Old Wyk, Asha. Stay with your mother. We shall not have her long, I fear."

Asha shifted in her seat. "My mother raised me to be bold. If I do not go, I will spend the rest of my life wondering what might have happened if I had."

"If you do go, the rest of your life may be too short for wondering."

"Better that than fill the remainder of my days complaining that the Seastone Chair by rights was mine. I am no Gwynesse."

That made him wince. "Asha, my two tall sons fed the crabs of Fair Isle. I am not like to wed again. Stay, and I shall name you heir to the Ten Towers. Be content with that."

"Ten Towers?" *Would that I could.* "Your cousins will not like that. The Knight, old Sigfryd, Hotho Humpback . . ."

"They have lands and seats of their own."

True enough. Damp, decaying Harlaw Hall belonged to old Sigfryd Harlaw the Silverhair; humpbacked Hotho Harlaw had his seat at the Tower of Glimmering, on a crag above the western coast. The Knight, Ser Harras Harlaw, kept court at Grey Garden; Boremund the Blue ruled atop Harridan Hill. But each was subject to Lord Rodrik. "Boremund has three sons, Sigfryd Silverhair has grandsons, and Hotho has ambitions," Asha said. "They all mean to follow you, even Sigfryd. That one intends to live forever."

"The Knight will be the Lord of Harlaw after me," her uncle said, "but he can rule from Grey Garden as easily as from here. Do fealty to him for the castle and Ser Harras will protect you."

"I can protect myself. Nuncle, I am a kraken. Asha, of House *Greyjoy.*" She pushed to her feet. "It's my father's seat I want, not yours. Those scythes of yours look perilous. One could fall and slice my head off. No, I'll sit the Seastone Chair."

"Then you are just another crow, screaming for carrion." Rodrik sat again behind his table. "Go. I wish to return to Archmaester Marwyn and his search."

"Let me know if he should find another page." Her uncle was her uncle. He would never change. *But he will come to Old Wyk, no matter what he says.*

By now, her crew would be eating in the hall. Asha knew she ought to join them, to speak of this gathering on Old Wyk and what it meant for them. Her own men would be solidly behind her, but she would need the rest as well, her Harlaw cousins, the Volmarks, and the Stonetrees. *Those are the ones I must win.* Her victory at Deepwood Motte would serve her in good stead, once her men began to boast of it, as she knew they would. The crew of her *Black Wind* took a perverse pride in the deeds of their woman captain. Half of them loved her like a daughter, and other half wanted to spread her legs, but either sort would die for her. *And I for them,* she was thinking as she shouldered through the door at the bottom of the steps, into the moonlit yard.

"Asha?" A shadow stepped out from behind the well.

Her hand went to her dirk at once . . . until the moonlight transformed the dark shape into a man in a sealskin cloak. *Another ghost.* "Tris. I'd thought to find you in the hall."

"I wanted to see you."

"What part of me, I wonder?" She grinned. "Well, here I stand, all grown up. Look all you like."

"A woman." He moved closer. "And beautiful."

Tristifer Botley had filled out since last she'd seen him, but he had the same unruly hair that she remembered, and eyes as large and trusting as a seal's. *Sweet eyes, truly.* That was the trouble with poor Tristifer; he was too sweet for the Iron Islands. *His face has grown comely,* she thought. As a boy Tris had been much troubled by pimples. Asha had suffered the same affliction; perhaps that had been what drew them together.

"I was sorry to hear about your father," she told him.

"I grieve for yours."

Why? Asha almost asked. It was Balon who'd sent the boy away from Pyke, to be a ward of Baelor Blacktyde's. "Is it true you are Lord Botley now?"

"In name, at least. Harren died at Moat Cailin. One of the bog devils shot him with a poisoned arrow. But I am the lord of nothing. When my father denied his claim to the Seastone Chair, the Crow's Eye drowned him and made my uncles swear him fealty. Even after that he gave half my father's lands to Iron Holt. Lord Wynch was the first man to bend his knee and call him king."

House Wynch was strong on Pyke, but Asha took care not to let her dismay show. "Wynch never had your father's courage."

"Your uncle bought him," Tris said. "The *Silence* returned with holds full of treasure. Plate and pearls, emeralds and rubies, sapphires big as eggs, bags of coin so heavy that no man can lift them . . . the Crow's Eye has been buying friends at every hand. My uncle Germund calls himself Lord Botley now, and rules in Lordsport as your uncle's man."

"You are the rightful Lord Botley," she assured him. "Once I hold the Seastone Chair, your father's lands shall be restored."

"If you like. It's nought to me. You look so lovely in the moonlight, Asha. A woman grown now, but I remember when you were a skinny girl with a face all full of pimples."

Why must they always mention the pimples? "I remember that as well." *Though not as fondly as you do.* Of the five boys her mother had brought to Pyke to foster after Ned Stark had taken her last living son as hostage, Tris had been closest to Asha in age. He had not been the first boy she had ever kissed, but he was the first to undo the laces of her jerkin and slip a sweaty hand beneath to feel her budding breasts.

I would have let him feel more than that if he'd been bold enough. Her first flowering had come upon her during the war and wakened her desire, but even before that Asha had been curious. *He was there, he was mine own age, and he was willing, that was all it was . . . that, and the moon blood.* Even so, she'd called it love, till Tris began to go on about the children she would bear him; a dozen sons at least, and oh, some daughters too. "I don't want to have a dozen sons," she had told him, appalled. "I want to have *adventures*." Not long after, Maester Qalen found them at their play, and young Tristifer Botley was sent away to Blacktyde.

"I wrote you letters," he said, "but Maester Joseran would not send them. Once I gave a stag to an oarsman on a trader bound for Lordsport, who promised to put my letter in your hands."

"Your oarsman winkled you and threw your letter in the sea."

"I feared as much. They never gave me your letters either."

I wrote none. In truth, she had been relieved when Tris was sent away. By then his fumblings had begun to bore her. That was not something he would care to hear, however. "Aeron Damphair has called a kingsmoot. Will you come and speak for me?"

"I will go anywhere with you, but . . . Lord Blacktyde says this kingsmoot is a dangerous folly. He thinks your uncle will descend on them and kill them all, as Urron did."

He's mad enough. "He lacks the strength."

"You do not know his strength. He's been gathering men on Pyke. Orkwood of Orkmont brought him twenty longships, and Pinchface Jon Myre a dozen. Left-Hand Lucas Codd is with them. And Harren

Half-Hoare, the Red Oarsman, Kemmett Pyke the Bastard, Rodrik Freeborn, Torwold Browntooth . . ."

"Men of small account." Asha knew them, every one. "The sons of salt wives, the grandsons of thralls. The Codds . . . do you know their *words*?"

"*Though All Men Do Despise Us*," Tris said, "but if they catch you in those nets of theirs, you'll be as dead as if they had been dragon-lords. And there's worse. The Crow's Eye brought back monsters from the east . . . aye, and *wizards* too."

"Nuncle always had a fondness for freaks and fools," said Asha. "My father used to fight with him about it. Let the wizards call upon their gods. The Damphair will call on ours, and drown them. Will I have your voice at the queensmoot, Tris?"

"You shall have all of me. I am your man, forever. Asha, I would wed you. Your lady mother has given her consent."

She stifled a groan. *You might have asked me first . . . though you might not have liked the answer half so well.*

"I am no second son now," he went on. "I am the rightful Lord Botley, as you said yourself. And you are—"

"What I am will be settled on Old Wyk. Tris, we are no longer children fumbling at each other and trying to see what fits where. You think you want to wed me, but you don't."

"I do. All I dream about is you. Asha, I swear upon the bones of Nagga, I have never touched another woman."

"Go touch one . . . or two, or ten. I have touched more men than I can count. Some with my lips, more with my axe." She had surrendered her virtue at six-and-ten, to a beautiful blond-haired sailor on a trading galley up from Lys. He only knew six words of the Common Tongue, but "fuck" was one of them—the very word she'd hoped to hear. Afterward, Asha had the sense to find a woods witch, who showed her how to brew moon tea to keep her belly flat.

Botley blinked, as if he did not quite understand what she had said. "You . . . I thought you would wait. Why . . ." He rubbed his mouth. "Asha, were you *forced*?"

"So forced I tore his tunic. You do not want to wed me, take my word on that. You are a sweet boy and always were, but I am no sweet girl. If we wed, soon enough you'd come to hate me."

"Never. Asha, I have *ached* for you."

She had heard enough of this. A sickly mother, a murdered father, and a plague of uncles were enough for any woman to contend with; she did not require a lovesick puppy too. "Find a brothel, Tris. They'll cure you of that ache."

"I could never . . ." Tristifer shook his head. "You and I were meant to be, Asha. I have always known you would be my wife, and the mother of my sons." He seized her upper arm.

In a blink her dirk was at his throat. "Take your hand away or you won't live long enough to breed a son. *Now.*" When he did, she lowered the blade. "You want a woman, well and good. I'll put one in your bed tonight. Pretend she's me, if that will give you pleasure, but do not presume to grab at me again. I am your queen, not your wife. Remember that." Asha sheathed her dirk and left him standing there, with a fat drop of blood slowly creeping down his neck, black in the pale light of the moon.

CERSEI

"Oh, I pray the Seven will not let it rain upon the king's wedding," Jocelyn Swyft said as she laced up the queen's gown.

"No one wants rain," said Cersei. For herself, she wanted sleet and ice, howling winds, thunder to shake the very stones of the Red Keep. She wanted a storm to match her rage. To Jocelyn she said, "Tighter. Cinch it *tighter*, you simpering little fool."

It was the wedding that enraged her, though the slow-witted Swyft girl made a safer target. Tommen's hold upon the Iron Throne was not secure enough for her to risk offending Highgarden. Not so long as Stannis Baratheon held Dragonstone and Storm's End, so long as Riverrun continued in defiance, so long as ironmen prowled the seas like wolves. So Jocelyn must needs eat the meal Cersei would sooner have served to Margaery Tyrell and her hideous wrinkled grandmother.

To break her fast the queen sent to the kitchens for two boiled eggs, a loaf of bread, and a pot of honey. But when she cracked the first egg and found a bloody half-formed chick inside, her stomach roiled. "Take this away and bring me hot spiced wine," she told Senelle. The chill in the air was settling in her bones, and she had a long nasty day ahead of her.

Nor did Jaime help her mood when he turned up all in white and still unshaven, to tell her how he meant to keep her son from being poisoned. "I will have men in the kitchens watching as each dish is prepared," he said. "Ser Addam's gold cloaks will escort the servants as they bring the food to table, to make certain no tampering takes place along the way. Ser Boros will be tasting every course before Tommen puts a bite into his mouth. And if all that should fail, Maester Ballabar will be seated in the back of the hall, with purges and antidotes for twenty common poisons on his person. Tommen will be safe, I promise you."

"Safe." The word tasted bitter on her tongue. Jaime did not understand. No one understood. Only Melara had been in the tent to hear the old hag's croaking threats, and Melara was long dead. "Tyrion will not kill the same way twice. He is too cunning for that. He could be under the floor even now, listening to every word we say and making plans to open Tommen's throat."

"Suppose he was," said Jaime. "Whatever plans he makes, he will still be small and stunted. Tommen will be surrounded by the finest knights in Westeros. The Kingsguard will protect him."

Cersei glanced at where the sleeve of her brother's white silk tunic had been pinned up over his stump. "I remember how well they guarded Joffrey, these splendid knights of yours. I want you to remain with Tommen all night, is that understood?"

"I will have a guardsman outside his door."

She seized his arm. "Not a guardsman. You. And *inside* his bedchamber."

"In case Tyrion crawls out of the hearth? He won't."

"So you say. Will you tell me that you found all the hidden tunnels in these walls?" They both knew better. "I will *not* have Tommen alone with Margaery, not for so much as half a heartbeat."

"They will not be alone. Her cousins will be with them."

"As will you. I command it, in the king's name." Cersei had not wanted Tommen and his wife to share a bed at all, but the Tyrells had insisted. "Husband and wife should sleep together," the Queen of Thorns had said, "even if they do no more than sleep. His Grace's bed is big enough for two, surely." Lady Alerie had echoed her good-mother. "Let the children warm each other in the night. It will bring them closer. Margaery oft shares her blankets with her cousins. They sing and play games and whisper secrets to each other when the candles are snuffed out."

"How delightful," Cersei had said. "Let them continue, by all means. In the Maidenvault."

"I am sure Her Grace knows best," Lady Olenna had said to Lady Alerie. "She is the boy's own mother, after all, of *that* we are all sure. And surely we can agree about the wedding night? A man should not sleep apart from his wife on the night of their wedding. It is ill luck for their marriage if they do."

Someday, I will teach you the meaning of "ill luck," the queen had vowed. "Margaery may share Tommen's bedchamber for that one night," she had been forced to say. "No longer."

"Your Grace is so gracious," the Queen of Thorns had replied, and everyone had exchanged smiles.

Cersei's fingers were digging into Jaime's arm hard enough to leave bruises. "I need *eyes* inside that room," she said.

"To see *what*?" he said. "There can be no danger of a consummation. Tommen is much too young."

"And Ossifer Plumm was much too dead, but that did not stop him fathering a child, did it?"

Her brother looked lost. "Who was Ossifer Plumm? Was he Lord Philip's father, or . . . who?"

He is near as ignorant as Robert. All his wits were in his sword hand. "Forget Plumm, just remember what I told you. Swear to me that you will stay by Tommen's side until the sun comes up."

"As you command," he said, as if her fears were groundless. "Do you still mean to go ahead and burn the Tower of the Hand?"

"After the feast." It was the only part of the day's festivities that Cersei thought she might enjoy. "Our lord father was murdered in that tower. I cannot bear to look at it. If the gods are good, the fire may smoke a few rats from the rubble."

Jaime rolled his eyes. "Tyrion, you mean."

"Him, and Lord Varys, and this gaoler."

"If any of them were hiding in the tower, we would have found them. I've had a small army going at it with picks and hammers.

We've knocked through walls and ripped up floors and uncovered half a hundred secret passages."

"And for all you know there may be half a hundred more." Some of the secret crawlways had turned out to be so small that Jaime had needed pages and stableboys to explore them. A passage to the black cells had been found, and a stone well that seemed to have no bottom. They had found a chamber full of skulls and yellowed bones, and four sacks of tarnished silver coins from the reign of the first King Viserys. They had found a thousand rats as well . . . but neither Tyrion nor Varys had been amongst them, and Jaime had finally insisted on putting an end to the search. One boy had gotten stuck in a narrow passage and had to be pulled out by his feet, shrieking. Another fell down a shaft and broke his legs. And two guardsmen vanished exploring a side tunnel. Some of the other guards swore they could hear them calling faintly through the stone, but when Jaime's men tore down the wall they found only earth and rubble on the far side. "The Imp is small and cunning. He may still be in the walls. If he is, the fire will smoke him out."

"Even if Tyrion were still hiding in the castle, he won't be in the Tower of the Hand. We've reduced it to a shell."

"Would that we could do the same to the rest of this foul castle," said Cersei. "After the war I mean to build a new palace beyond the river." She had dreamed of it the night before last, a magnificent white castle surrounded by woods and gardens, long leagues from the stinks and noise of King's Landing. "This city is a cesspit. For half a groat I would move the court to Lannisport and rule the realm from Casterly Rock."

"That would be an even greater folly than burning the Tower of the Hand. So long as Tommen sits the Iron Throne, the realm sees him as the true king. Hide him under the Rock and he becomes just another claimant to the throne, no different than Stannis."

"I am aware of that," the queen said sharply. "I said that I *wanted* to move the court to Lannisport, not that I would. Were you always this slow, or did losing a hand make you stupid?"

Jaime ignored that. "If these flames spread beyond the tower, you may end up burning down the castle whether you mean to or not. Wildfire is treacherous."

"Lord Hallyne has assured me that his pyromancers can control the fire." The Guild of Alchemists had been brewing fresh wildfire for a fortnight. "Let all of King's Landing see the flames. It will be a lesson to our enemies."

"Now you sound like Aerys."

Her nostrils flared. "Guard your tongue, ser."

"I love you too, sweet sister."

How could I ever have loved that wretched creature? she wondered after he had gone. *He was your twin, your shadow, your other half,* another voice whispered. *Once, perhaps,* she thought. *No longer. He has become a stranger to me.*

Compared to the magnificence of Joffrey's nuptials, the wedding of King Tommen was a modest affair, and small. No one wanted another lavish ceremony, least of all the queen, and no one wanted to pay for one, least of all the Tyrells. So the young king took Margaery Tyrell to wife in the Red Keep's royal sept, with fewer than a hundred guests looking on in place of the thousands who had seen his brother joined to the same woman.

The bride was fair and gay and beautiful, the groom still baby-faced and plump. He recited his vows in a high, childish voice, promising his love and devotion to Mace Tyrell's twice-widowed daughter. Margaery wore the same gown she had worn to marry Joffrey, an airy confection of sheer ivory silk, Myrish lace, and seed pearls. Cersei herself was still in black, as a sign of mourning for her murdered firstborn. His widow might be pleased to laugh and drink and dance and put all memory of Joff aside, but his mother would not forget him so easily.

This is wrong, she thought. *It is too soon. A year, two years, that would have been time enough. Highgarden should have been content with a betrothal.* Cersei stared back to where Mace Tyrell stood between his wife and mother. *You forced me into this travesty of a wedding, my lord, and I shall not soon forget it.*

When it was time for the changing of the cloaks, the bride sank gracefully to her knees and Tommen covered her with the heavy cloth-of-gold monstrosity that Robert had cloaked Cersei in on their own wedding day, with the crowned stag of Baratheon worked upon its back in beads of onyx. Cersei had wanted to use the fine red silk cloak Joffrey had used. "It was the cloak my lord father used when he wed my lady mother," she explained to the Tyrells, but the Queen of Thorns had balked her in that as well. "That old thing?" the crone had said. "It looks a bit threadbare to me . . . and dare I say, unlucky? And wouldn't a *stag* be more fitting for King Robert's trueborn son? In my day, a bride donned her *husband*'s colors, not his lady mother's."

Thanks to Stannis and his filthy letter, there were already too many rumors concerning Tommen's parentage. Cersei dared not fan the fires by insisting that he drape his bride in Lannister crimson, so she yielded as gracefully as she could. But the sight of all that gold and onyx still filled her with resentment. *The more we give these Tyrells, the more they demand of us.*

When all the vows were spoken, the king and his new queen stepped outside the sept to accept congratulations. "Westeros has two queens now, and the young one is as beautiful as the old one," boomed Lyle Crakehall, an oaf of a knight who oft reminded Cersei of her late and unlamented husband. She could have slapped him. Gyles Rosby made to kiss her hand, and only succeeded in coughing on her fingers. Lord Redwyne kissed her on one cheek and Mace Tyrell on both. Grand Maester Pycelle told Cersei that she had not lost a son, but rather gained a daughter. At least she was spared Lady Tanda's tearful embraces. None of the Stokeworth women had appeared, and for that much the queen was grateful.

Amongst the last was Kevan Lannister. "I understand you mean to leave us for another wedding," the queen said to him.

"Hardstone has cleared the broken men from Darry castle," he replied. "Lancel's bride awaits us there."

"Will your lady wife be joining you for the nuptials?"

"The riverlands are still too dangerous. Vargo Hoat's scum remain abroad, and Beric Dondarrion has been hanging Freys. Is it true that Sandor Clegane has joined him?"

How does he know that? "Some say. Reports are confused." The bird had come last night, from a septry on an island hard by the mouth of the Trident. The nearby town of Saltpans had been savagely raided by a band of outlaws, and some of the survivors claimed a roaring brute in a hound's head helm was amongst the raiders. Supposedly, he'd killed a dozen men and raped a girl of twelve. "No doubt Lancel will be eager to hunt down Clegane and Lord Beric both, to restore the king's peace to the riverlands."

Ser Kevan stared into her eyes for a moment. "My son is not the man to deal with Sandor Clegane."

We agree on that much, at least. "His father might be."

Her uncle's mouth grew hard. "If my service is not required at the Rock . . ."

Your service was required here. Cersei had named her cousin Damion Lannister her castellan for the Rock, and another cousin, Ser Daven Lannister, the Warden of the West. *Insolence has its price, Uncle.* "Bring us Sandor's head, and I know His Grace will be most grateful. Joff may have liked the man, but Tommen was always afraid of him . . . with good reason, it would seem."

"When a dog goes bad, the fault lies with his master," Ser Kevan said. Then he turned and walked away.

Jaime escorted her to the Small Hall, where the feast was being readied. "I blame you for all this," she whispered as they walked. "*Let them wed,* you said. Margaery should be mourning Joffrey, not marrying his brother. She should be as sick with grief as I am. I do not believe she is a maid. Renly had a cock, didn't he? He was Robert's brother, he *surely* had a cock. If that disgusting old crone thinks that I will allow my son to—"

"You will be rid of Lady Olenna soon enough," Jaime broke in quietly. "She's returning to Highgarden on the morrow."

"So she says." Cersei did not trust any Tyrell promise.

"She's leaving," he insisted. "Mace is taking half the Tyrell strength to Storm's End, and the other half will be going back to the Reach with Ser Garlan to make good his claim on Brightwater. A few more days, and the only roses left in King's Landing will be Margaery and her ladies and a few guardsmen."

"And Ser Loras. Or have you forgotten your *Sworn Brother?*"

"Ser Loras is a knight of the Kingsguard."

"Ser Loras is so Tyrell he pisses rosewater. He should never have been given a white cloak."

"He would not have been my choice, I'll grant you. No one troubled to consult me. Loras will do well enough, I think. Once a man puts on that cloak, it changes him."

"It certainly changed *you*, and not for the better."

"I love you too, sweet sister." He held the door for her, and walked her to the high table and her seat beside the king. Margaery was on the other side of Tommen, in the place of honor. When she entered, arm in arm with the little king, she made a point of stopping to kiss Cersei on the cheeks and throw her arms around her. "Your Grace," the girl said, bold as polished brass, "I feel as though I have a second mother now. I pray that we shall be very close, united by our love for your sweet son."

"I loved both my sons."

"Joffrey is in my prayers as well," said Margaery. "I loved him dearly, though I never had the chance to know him."

Liar, the queen thought. *If you had loved him even for an instant, you would not have been in such unseemly haste to wed his brother. His crown was all you ever wanted.* For half a groat, she would have slapped the blushing bride right there upon the dais, in view of half the court.

Like the service, the wedding feast was modest. Lady Alerie had made all the arrangements; Cersei had not had the stomach to face that daunting task again, after the way Joffrey's wedding had ended. Only seven courses were served. Butterbumps and Moon Boy entertained the guests between dishes, and musicians played as they ate. They listened to pipers and fiddlers, a lute and a flute, a high harp. The only singer was some favorite of Lady Margaery's, a dashing young cock-a-whoop clad all in shades of azure who called himself the Blue Bard. He sang a few love songs and retired. "What a disappointment," Lady Olenna complained loudly. "I was hoping for 'The Rains of Castamere.'"

Whenever Cersei looked at the old crone, the face of Maggy the Frog seemed to float before her eyes, wrinkled and terrible and wise. *All old women look alike*, she tried to tell herself, *that's all it is.* In truth, the bent-back sorceress had looked nothing like the Queen of Thorns, yet somehow the sight of Lady Olenna's nasty little smile was enough to put her back in Maggy's tent again. She could still remember the smell of it, redolent with queer eastern spices, and the softness of Maggy's gums as she sucked the blood from Cersei's finger. *Queen you shall be,* the old woman had promised, with her lips still wet and red and glistening, *until there comes another, younger and more beautiful, to cast you down and take all that you hold dear.*

Cersei glanced past Tommen, to where Margaery sat laughing with her father. *She is pretty enough,* she had to admit, *but most of that is youth. Even peasant girls are pretty at a certain age, when they are still fresh and innocent and unspoiled, and most of them have the same brown hair and brown eyes as she does. Only a fool would ever claim she was more beautiful than I.* The world was full of fools, however. So was her son's court.

Her mood was not improved when Mace Tyrell arose to lead the toasts. He raised a golden goblet high, smiling at his pretty little daughter, and in a booming voice said, "To the king and queen!" The other sheep all *baaaaaa*ed along with him. "*The king and queen!*" they cried, smashing their cups together. "*The king and queen!*" She had no choice but to drink along with them, all the time wishing that the guests had but a single face, so she could throw her wine into their eyes and remind them that *she* was the true queen. The only one of Tyrell's lickspittles who seemed to remember her at all was Paxter Redwyne, who rose to make his own toast, swaying slightly. "*To both our queens!*" he chirruped. "*To the young queen and the old!*"

Cersei drank several cups of wine and pushed her food around a golden plate. Jaime ate even less, and seldom deigned to occupy his seat upon the dais. *He is as anxious as I am,* the queen realized as she watched him prowl the hall, twitching aside the tapestries with his good hand to assure himself that no one was hiding behind them. There were Lannister spearmen posted around the building, she knew. Ser Osmund Kettleblack guarded one door, Ser Meryn Trant the other. Balon Swann stood behind the king's chair, Loras Tyrell behind the queen's. No swords had been allowed inside the feast save for those the white knights bore.

My son is safe, Cersei told herself. *No harm can come to him, not here, not now.* Yet every time she looked at Tommen, she saw Joffrey clawing at his throat. And when the boy began to cough the queen's heart stopped beating for a moment. She knocked aside a serving girl in her haste to reach him.

"Only a little wine that went down the wrong way," Margaery Tyrell assured her, smiling. She took Tommen's hand in her own and kissed his fingers. "My little love needs to take smaller sips. See, you scared your lady mother half to death."

"I'm sorry, Mother," Tommen said, abashed.

It was more than Cersei could stand. *I cannot let them see me cry,* she thought, when she felt the tears welling in her eyes. She walked past Ser Meryn Trant and out into the back passage. Alone beneath a tallow candle, she allowed herself a shuddering sob, then another. *A woman may weep, but not a queen.*

"Your Grace?" said a voice behind her. "Do I intrude?"

It was a woman's voice, flavored with the accents of the east. For an instant she feared that Maggy the Frog was speaking to her from the grave. But it was only Merryweather's wife, the sloe-eyed beauty Lord Orton had wed during his exile and fetched home with him to Longtable. "The Small Hall is so stuffy," Cersei heard herself say. "The smoke was making my eyes water."

"And mine, Your Grace." Lady Merryweather was as tall as the queen, but dark instead of fair, raven-haired and olive-skinned and younger by a decade. She offered the queen a pale blue handkerchief of silk and lace. "I have a son as well. I know that I shall weep rivers on the day he weds."

Cersei wiped her cheeks, furious that she had let her tears be seen. "My thanks," she said stiffly.

"Your Grace, I . . ." The Myrish woman lowered her voice. "There is something you must know. Your maid is bought and paid for. She tells Lady Margaery everything you do."

"Senelle?" Sudden fury twisted in the queen's belly. Was there no one she could trust? "You are certain of this?"

"Have her followed. Margaery never meets with her directly. Her cousins are her ravens, they bring her messages. Sometimes Elinor, sometimes Alla, sometimes Megga. All of them are as close to Margaery as sisters. They meet in the sept and pretend to pray. Put your own man in the gallery on the morrow, and he will see Senelle whispering to Megga beneath the altar of the Maiden."

"If this is true, why tell me? You are one of Margaery's companions. Why would you betray her?" Cersei had learned suspicion at her father's knee; this could well be some trap, a lie meant to sow discord between the lion and the rose.

"Longtable may be sworn to Highgarden," the woman replied, with a toss of her black hair, "but I am of Myr, and my loyalty is to my husband and my son. I want all that is best for them."

"I see." In the closeness of the passage, the queen could smell the other woman's perfume, a musky scent that spoke of moss and earth and wildflowers. Under it, she smelled ambition. *She gave testimony at Tyrion's trial,* Cersei recalled suddenly. *She saw the Imp put the poison in Joff's cup and was not afraid to say so.* "I shall look into this," she promised. "If what you say is true, you will be rewarded." *And if you've lied to me, I'll have your tongue, and your lord husband's lands and gold as well.*

"Your Grace is kind. And beautiful." Lady Merryweather smiled. Her teeth were white, her lips full and dark.

When the queen returned to the Small Hall, she found her brother pacing restlessly. "It was only a gulp of wine that went down the wrong way. Though it startled me as well."

"My belly is such a knot that I cannot eat," she growled at him. "The wine tastes of bile. This wedding was a mistake."

"This wedding was necessary. The boy is safe."

"Fool. No one who wears a crown is ever safe." She looked about the hall. Mace Tyrell laughed amongst his knights. Lords Redwyne and Rowan were talking furtively. Ser Kevan sat brooding over his wine at the back of the hall, whilst Lancel whispered something to a septon. Senelle was moving down the table, filling the cups of the bride's cousins with wine as red as blood. Grand Maester Pycelle had fallen asleep. *There is no one I can rely upon, not even Jaime,* she realized grimly. *I will need to sweep them all away and surround the king with mine own people.*

Later, after sweets and nuts and cheese had been served and cleared away, Margaery and Tommen began the dancing, looking more than a bit ridiculous as they whirled about the floor. The Tyrell girl stood a good foot and a half taller than her little husband, and Tommen was a clumsy dancer at best, with none of Joffrey's easy grace. He did his earnest best, though, and seemed oblivious to the spectacle he was making of himself. And no sooner was Maid Margaery done with him than her cousins swooped in, one after the other, insisting that His Grace must dance with them as well. *They will have him stumbling and shuffling like a fool by the time they're done,* Cersei thought resentfully as she watched. *Half the court will be laughing at him behind his back.*

Whilst Alla, Elinor, and Megga took their turns with Tommen, Margaery took a turn around the floor with her father, then another with her brother Loras. The Knight of Flowers was in white silk, with a belt of golden roses about his waist and a jade rose fastening his cloak. *They could be twins,* Cersei thought as she watched them. Ser Loras was a year older than his sister, but they had the same big brown eyes, the same thick brown hair falling in lazy ringlets to their shoulders, the same smooth unblemished skin. *A ripe crop of pimples would teach them some humility.* Loras was taller and had a few wisps of soft brown fuzz on his face, and Margaery had a woman's shape, but elsewise they were more alike than she and Jaime. That annoyed her too.

Her own twin interrupted her musings. "Would Your Grace honor her white knight with a dance?"

She gave him a withering look. "And have you fumbling at me with that stump? No. I will let you fill my wine cup for me, though. If you think you can manage it without spilling."

"A cripple like me? Not likely." He moved away and made another circuit of the hall. She had to fill her own cup.

Cersei refused Mace Tyrell as well, and later Lancel. The others took the hint, and no one else approached her. *Our fast friends and loyal lords.* She could not even trust the westermen, her father's sworn swords and bannermen. Not if her own uncle was conspiring with her enemies . . .

Margaery was dancing with her cousin Alla, Megga with Ser Tallad the Tall. The other cousin, Elinor, was sharing a cup of wine with the handsome young Bastard of Driftmark, Aurane Waters. It was not the first time the queen had made note of Waters, a lean young man with grey-green eyes and long silver-gold hair. The first time she had seen him, for half a heartbeat she had almost thought Rhaegar Targaryen had returned from the ashes. *It is his hair,* she told herself. *He is not half as comely as Rhaegar was. His face is too narrow, and he has that cleft in his chin.* The Velaryons came from old Valyrian stock, however, and some had the same silvery hair as the dragonkings of old.

Tommen returned to his seat to nibble at an applecake. Her uncle's place was empty. The queen finally found him in a corner, talking intently with Mace Tyrell's son Garlan. *What do they have to talk about?* The Reach might call Ser Garlan gallant, but she trusted him no more than Margaery or Loras. She had not forgotten the gold coin that Qyburn had discovered beneath the gaoler's chamber pot. *A golden hand from Highgarden. And Margaery is spying on me.* When Senelle appeared to fill her wine cup, the queen had to resist an urge to take her by the throat and throttle her. *Do not presume to smile at me, you treacherous little bitch. You will be begging me for mercy before I'm done with you.*

"I think Her Grace has had enough wine for one night," she heard her brother Jaime say.

No, the queen thought. *All the wine in the world would not be enough to see me through this wedding.* She rose so fast she almost fell. Jaime caught her by the arm and steadied her. She wrenched free and clapped her hands together. The music died, the voices stilled. *"Lords and ladies,"* Cersei called out loudly, "if you will be so good as to come outside with me, we shall light a candle to celebrate the union of Highgarden and Casterly Rock, and a new age of peace and plenty for our Seven Kingdoms."

Dark and forlorn stood the Tower of the Hand, with only gaping holes where oaken doors and shuttered windows had once been. Yet even ruined and slighted, it loomed above the outer ward. As the wedding guests filed out of the Small Hall, they passed beneath its shadow. When Cersei looked up she saw the tower's crenellated battlements gnawing at a hunter's moon, and wondered for a moment how many Hands of how many kings had made their home there over the past three centuries.

A hundred yards from the tower, she took a breath to stop her head from spinning. "Lord Hallyne! You may commence."

Hallyne the pyromancer said *"Hmmmmmm"* and waved the torch he was holding, and the archers on the walls bent their bows and sent a dozen flaming arrows through the gaping windows.

The tower went up with a *whoosh*. In half a heartbeat its interior was alive with light, red, yellow, orange . . . and green, an ominous dark green, the color of bile and jade and pyromancer's piss. "The substance," the alchemists named it, but common folk called it *wildfire*. Fifty pots had been placed inside the Tower of the Hand, along with logs and casks of pitch and the greater part of the worldly possessions of a dwarf named Tyrion Lannister.

The queen could feel the heat of those green flames. The pyromancers said that only three things burned hotter than their substance: dragonflame, the fires beneath the earth, and the summer sun. Some of the ladies gasped when the first flames appeared in the windows, licking up the outer walls like long green tongues. Others cheered, and made toasts.

It is beautiful, she thought, *as beautiful as Joffrey, when they laid him in my arms.* No man had ever made her feel as good as she had felt when he took her nipple in his mouth to nurse.

Tommen stared wide-eyed at the fires, as fascinated as he was frightened, until Margaery whispered something in his ear that made him laugh. Some of the knights began to make wagers on how long it would be before the tower collapsed. Lord Hallyne stood humming to himself and rocking on his heels.

Cersei thought of all the King's Hands that she had known through the years: Owen Merryweather, Jon Connington, Qarlton Chelsted, Jon Arryn, Eddard Stark, her brother Tyrion. And her father, Lord Tywin Lannister, her father most of all. *All of them are burning now,* she told herself, savoring the thought. *They are dead and burning, every one, with all their plots and schemes and betrayals. It is my day now. It is my castle and my kingdom.*

The Tower of the Hand gave out a sudden groan, so loud that all the conversation stopped abruptly. Stone cracked and split, and part of the upper battlements fell away and landed with a crash that shook the hill, sending up a cloud of dust and smoke. As fresh air rushed in through the broken masonry, the fire surged upward. Green flames leapt into the sky and whirled around each other. Tommen shied away, till Margaery took his hand and said, "Look, the flames are dancing. Just as we did, my love."

"They are." His voice was filled with wonder. "Mother, look, they're dancing."

"I see them. Lord Hallyne, how long will the fires burn?"

"All night, Your Grace."

"It makes a pretty candle, I grant you," said Lady Olenna Tyrell, leaning on her cane between Left and Right. "Bright enough to see us safe to sleep, I think. Old bones grow weary, and these young ones have had enough excitement for one night. It is time the king and queen were put to bed."

"Yes." Cersei beckoned to Jaime. "Lord Commander, escort His Grace and his little queen to their pillows, if you would."

"As you command. And you as well?"

"No need." Cersei felt too alive for sleep. The wildfire was cleansing her, burning away all her rage and fear, filling her with resolve. "The flames are so pretty. I want to watch them for a while."

Jaime hesitated. "You should not stay alone."

"I will not be alone. Ser Osmund can remain with me and keep me safe. Your Sworn Brother."

"If it please Your Grace," said Kettleblack.

"It does." Cersei slid her arm through his, and side by side they watched the fire rage.

THE SOILED KNIGHT

The night was unseasonably cool, even for autumn. A brisk wet wind was swirling down the alleys, stirring up the day's dust. *A north wind, and full of chill.* Ser Arys Oakheart pulled up his hood to cover his face. It would not do for him to be recognized. A fortnight past, a trader had been butchered in the shadow city, a harmless man who'd come to Dorne for fruit and found death instead of dates. His only crime was being from King's Landing.

The mob would find a sterner foe in me. He would almost have welcomed an attack. His hand drifted down to brush lightly over the hilt on the longsword that hung half-hidden amongst the folds of his layered linen robes, the outer with its turquoise stripes and rows of golden suns, and the lighter orange one beneath. The Dornish garb was comfortable, but his father would have been aghast had he lived to see his son so dressed. He was a man of the Reach, and the Dornish were his ancient foes, as the tapestries at Old Oak bore witness. Arys only had to close his eyes to see them still. Lord Edgerran the Open-Handed, seated in splendor with the heads of a hundred Dornishmen piled round his feet. The Three Leaves in the Prince's Pass, pierced by Dornish spears, Alester sounding his warhorn with his last breath. Ser Olyvar the Green Oak all in white, dying at the side of the Young Dragon. *Dorne is no fit place for any Oakheart.*

Even before Prince Oberyn had died, the knight had been ill at ease whenever he left the grounds of Sunspear to walk the alleys of the shadow city. He could feel eyes upon him everywhere he went, small black Dornish eyes regarding him with thinly veiled hostility. The shop-keepers did their best to cheat him at every turn, and sometimes he wondered whether the taverners were spitting in his drinks. Once a group of ragged boys began pelting him with stones, until he drew his sword and ran them off. The Red Viper's death had inflamed the Dornish even more, though the streets had quieted a bit since Prince Doran had confined the Sand Snakes to a tower. Even so, to wear his white cloak openly in the shadow city would be asking for attack. He had brought three with him: two of wool, one light and one heavy, the third of fine white silk. He felt naked without one hanging from his shoulders.

Better naked than dead, he told himself. *I am a Kingsguard still, even uncloaked. She must respect that. I must make her understand.* He should never have let himself be drawn into this, but the singer said that love can make a fool of any man.

Sunspear's shadow city oft seemed deserted in the heat of the day, when only buzzing flies moved down the dusty streets, but once evening fell the same streets came to life. Ser Arys heard faint music drifting through louvered windows as he passed below, and somewhere finger drums were beating out the quick rhythm of a spear dance, giving the night a pulse. Where three alleys met beneath the second of the Winding Walls, a pillow girl called down from a balcony. She was dressed in jewels and oil. He took a look at her, hunched his shoulders, and pushed on, into the teeth of the wind. *We men are so weak. Our bodies betray even the noblest of us.* He thought of King Baelor the Blessed, who would fast to the point of fainting to tame the lusts that shamed him. Must he do the same?

A short man stood in an arched doorway grilling chunks of snake over a brazier, turning them with wooden tongs as they crisped. The pungent smell of his sauces brought tears to the knight's eyes. The best snake sauce had a drop of venom in it, he had heard, along with mustard seeds and dragon peppers. Myrcella had taken to Dornish food as quick as she had to her Dornish prince, and from time to time Ser Arys would try a dish or two to please her. The food seared his mouth and made him gasp for wine, and burned even worse coming out than it did going in. His little princess loved it, though.

He had left her in her chambers, bent over a gaming table opposite Prince Trystane, pushing ornate pieces across squares of jade and carnelian and lapis lazuli. Myrcella's full lips had been slightly parted, her green eyes narrowed with concentration. *Cyvasse,* the game was called. It had come to the Planky Town on a trading galley from Volantis, and the orphans had spread it up and down the Greenblood. The Dornish court was mad for it.

Ser Arys just found it maddening. There were ten different pieces, each with its own attributes and powers, and the board would change from game to game, depending on how the players arrayed their home squares. Prince Trystane had taken to the game at once, and Myrcella had learned it so she could play with him. She was not quite one-and-ten, her betrothed three-and-ten; even so, she had been winning more oft than not of late. Trystane did not seem to mind. The two children could not have looked more different, him with his olive skin and straight black hair, her pale as milk with a mop of golden curls; light and dark, like Queen Cersei and King Robert. He prayed Myrcella would find more joy in her Dornish boy than her mother had found with her storm lord.

It made him feel uneasy to leave her, though she should be safe enough within the castle. There were only two doors that gave access to Myrcella's chambers in the Tower of the Sun, and Ser Arys kept two men on each; Lannister household guards, men who had come with them from King's Landing, battle-tested, tough, and loyal to the bone. Myrcella had her maids and Septa Eglantine as well, and Prince Trystane was attended by his sworn shield, Ser Gascoyne of the Greenblood. *No one will trouble her,* he told himself, *and in a fortnight we shall be safely away.*

Prince Doran had promised as much. Though Arys had been shocked to see how aged and infirm the Dornish prince appeared, he did not doubt the prince's word. "I am sorry I could not see you until now, or meet Princess Myrcella," Martell had said when Arys was admitted to his solar, "but I trust that my daughter Arianne has made you welcome here in Dorne, ser."

"She has, my prince," he'd answered, and prayed that no blush would dare betray him.

"Ours is a harsh land, and poor, yet not without its beauties. It grieves us that you have seen no more of Dorne than Sunspear, but I fear that neither you nor your princess would be safe beyond these walls. We Dornish are a hot-blooded people, quick to anger and slow to forgive. It would gladden my heart if I could assure you that the Sand Snakes were alone in wanting war, but I will not tell you lies, ser. You have heard my smallfolk in the streets, crying out for me to call my spears. Half my lords agree with them, I fear."

"And you, my prince?" the knight had dared to ask.

"My mother taught me long ago that only madmen fight wars they cannot win." If the bluntness of the question had offended him, Prince Doran hid it well. "Yet this peace is fragile . . . as fragile as your princess."

"Only a beast would harm a little girl."

"My sister Elia had a little girl as well. Her name was Rhaenys. She was a princess too." The prince sighed. "Those who would plunge a knife into Princess Myrcella do not bear her any malice, no more than Ser Amory Lorch did when he killed Rhaenys, if indeed he did. They seek only to force my hand. For if Myrcella should be slain in Dorne whilst under my protection, who would believe my denials?"

"No one shall ever harm Myrcella whilst I live."

"A noble vow," said Doran Martell with a faint smile, "but you are only one man, ser. I had hoped that imprisoning my headstrong nieces would help to calm the waters, but all we've done is drive the roaches back beneath the rushes. Every night I hear them whispering and sharpening their knives."

He is afraid, Ser Arys realized then. *Look, his hand is shaking. The Prince of Dorne is terrified.* Words failed him.

"My apologies, ser," Prince Doran said. "I am frail and failing, and sometimes . . . Sunspear wearies me, with its noise and dirt and smells. As soon as my duty allows, I mean to return to the Water Gardens. When I do I shall take Princess Myrcella with me." Before the knight could protest, the prince raised a hand, its knuckles red and swollen. "You shall go as well. And her septa, her maids, her guards. Sunspear's

walls are strong, but beneath them is the shadow city. Even within
the castle hundreds come and go each day. The Gardens are my haven.
Prince Maron raised them as a gift for his Targaryen bride, to mark
Dorne's marriage to the Iron Throne. Autumn is a lovely season
there . . . hot days, cool nights, the salt breeze off the sea, the fountains
and the pools. And there are other children, boys and girls of high
and gentle birth. Myrcella will have friends of her own age to play
with. She will not be lonely."

"As you say." The prince's words pounded in his head. *She will be
safe there.* Only why had Doran Martell urged him not to write King's
Landing about the move? *Myrcella will be safest if no one knows just
where she is.* Ser Arys had agreed, but what choice did he have? He
was a knight of the Kingsguard, but only one man for all that, just
as the prince had said.

The alley opened suddenly onto a moonlit courtyard. *Past the
candlemaker's shop,* she wrote, *a gate and a short flight of exterior steps.*
He pushed through the gate and climbed the worn steps to an
unmarked door. *Should I knock?* He pushed the door open instead,
and found himself in a large, dim room with a low ceiling, lit by a
pair of scented candles that flickered in niches cut from the thick
earthen walls. He saw patterned Myrish carpets underneath his
sandals, a tapestry upon one wall, a bed. "My lady?" he called. "Where
are you?"

"Here." She stepped out from the shadow behind the door.

An ornate snake coiled around her right forearm, its copper and
gold scales glimmering when she moved. It was all she wore.

No, he meant to tell her, *I only came to tell you I must go,* but when
he saw her shining in the candlelight he seemed to lose the power of
speech. His throat felt as dry as the Dornish sands. Silent he stood,
drinking in the glories of her body, the hollow of her throat, the
round ripe breasts with their huge dark nipples, the lush curves at
waist and hip. And then somehow he was holding her, and she was
pulling off his robes. When she reached his undertunic she seized it
by the shoulders and ripped the silk down to his navel, but Arys was
past caring. Her skin was smooth beneath his fingers, as warm to the
touch as sand baked by the Dornish sun. He raised her head and

found her lips. Her mouth opened under his, and her breasts filled his hands. He felt her nipples stiffen as his thumbs brushed over them. Her hair was black and thick and smelled of orchids, a dark and earthy smell that made him so hard it almost hurt.

"Touch me, ser," the woman whispered in his ear. His hand slipped down her rounded belly to find the sweet wet place beneath the thicket of black hair. "Yes, there," she murmured as he slipped a finger up inside her. She made a whimpering sound, drew him to the bed, and pushed him down. "More, oh more, yes, sweet, my knight, my knight, my sweet white knight, yes you, you, I want you." Her hands guided him inside her, then slipped around his back to pull him closer. "Deeper," she whispered. "Yes, oh." When she wrapped her legs around him, they felt as strong as steel. Her nails raked his back as he drove into her, again and again and again, until she screamed and arched her back beneath him. As she did, her fingers found his nipples, pinching till he spent his seed within her. *I could die now, happy,* the knight thought, and for a dozen heartbeats at least he was at peace.

He did not die.

His desire was as deep and boundless as the sea, but when the tide receded, the rocks of shame and guilt thrust up as sharp as ever. Sometimes the waves would cover them, but they remained beneath the waters, hard and black and slimy. *What am I doing?* he asked himself. *I am a knight of the Kingsguard.* He rolled off of her to sprawl staring at the ceiling. A great crack ran across it, from one wall to the other. He had not noticed that before, no more than he had noticed the picture on the tapestry, a scene of Nymeria and her ten thousand ships. *I see only her. A dragon might have been peering in the window, and I would never have seen anything but her breasts, her face, her smile.*

"There is wine," she murmured against his neck. She slid a hand across his chest. "Are you thirsty?"

"No." He rolled away, and sat on the edge of the bed. The room was hot, and yet he shivered.

"You bleed," she said. "I scratched too hard."

When she touched his back, he flinched as if her fingers were afire. "Don't." Naked, he stood. "No more."

"I have balm. For the scratches."

But none for my shame. "The scratches are nothing. Forgive me, my lady, I must go . . ."

"So soon?" She had a husky voice, a wide mouth made for whispers, full lips ripe for kissing. Her hair tumbled down across her bare shoulders to the tops of her full breasts, black and thick. It curled in big soft lazy ringlets. Even the hair upon her mound was soft and curly. "Stay with me tonight, ser. I still have much to teach you."

"I have learned too much from you already."

"You seemed glad enough for the lessons at the time, ser. Are you certain you are not off to some other bed, some other woman? Tell me who she is. I will fight her for you, bare-breasted, knife to knife." She smiled. "Unless she is a Sand Snake. If so, we can share you. I love my cousins well."

"You know I have no other woman. Only . . . duty."

She rolled onto one elbow to look up at him, her big black eyes shining in the candlelight. "That poxy bitch? I know her. Dry as dust between the legs, and her kisses leave you bleeding. Let duty sleep alone for once, and stay with me tonight."

"My place is at the palace."

She sighed. "With your other princess. You will make me jealous. I think you love her more than me. The maid is much too young for you. You need a woman, not a little girl, but I can play the innocent if that excites you."

"You should not say such things." *Remember, she is Dornish.* In the Reach men said it was the food that made Dornishmen so hot-tempered and their women so wild and wanton. *Fiery peppers and strange spices heat the blood, she cannot help herself.* "I love Myrcella as a daughter." He could never have a daughter of his own, no more than he could have a wife. He had a fine white cloak instead. "We are going to the Water Gardens."

"Eventually," she agreed, "though with my father, everything takes four times as long as it should. If he says he means to leave upon the morrow, you will certainly set out within a fortnight. You will be lonely in the Gardens, I promise you. And where is the brave young gallant who said he wished to spend the rest of his life in my arms?"

"I was drunk when I said that."

"You'd had three cups of watered wine."

"I was drunk on you. It had been ten years since . . . I never touched a woman until you, not since I took the white. I never knew what love could be, yet now . . . I am afraid."

"What would frighten my white knight?"

"I fear for my honor," he said, "and for yours."

"I can tend to my own honor." She touched a finger to her breast, drawing it slowly round her nipple. "And to my own pleasures, if need be. I am a woman grown."

She was that, beyond a doubt. Seeing her there upon the featherbed, smiling that wicked smile, toying with her breast . . . was there ever a woman with nipples so large or so responsive? He could hardly look at them without wanting to grab them, to suckle them until they were hard and wet and shiny . . .

He looked away. His smallclothes were strewn on the carpets. The knight bent to pick them up.

"Your hands are shaking," she pointed out. "They would sooner be caressing me, I think. Must you be in such haste to don your clothes, ser? I prefer you as you are. Abed, unclad, we are our truest selves, a man and a woman, lovers, one flesh, as close as two can be. Our clothes make us different people. I would sooner be flesh and blood than silks and jewels, and you . . . you are not your white cloak, ser."

"I am," Ser Arys said. "I *am* my cloak. And this must end, for your sake as well as mine. If we should be discovered . . ."

"Men will think you fortunate."

"Men will think me an oathbreaker. What if someone were to go to your father and tell him how I'd dishonored you?"

"My father is many things, but no one has ever said he was a fool. The Bastard of Godsgrace had my maidenhead when we were both fourteen. Do you know what my father did when he learned of it?" She gathered the bedclothes in her fist and pulled them up under her chin, to hide her nakedness. "Nothing. My father is very good at doing nothing. He calls it *thinking*. Tell me true, ser, is it my dishonor that concerns you, or your own?"

"Both." Her accusation stung. "That is why this must be our last time."

"So you have said before."

I did, and meant it too. But I am weak, else I would not be here now. He could not tell her that; she was the sort of woman who despised weakness, he could sense that. *She has more of her uncle in her than her father.* He turned away and found his striped silk undertunic on a chair. She had ripped the fabric to the navel when she pulled it down over his arms. "This is ruined," he complained. "How can I wear it now?"

"Backwards," she suggested. "Once you don your robes, no one will see the tear. Perhaps your little princess will sew it up for you. Or shall I send a new one to the Water Gardens?"

"Send me no gifts." That would only draw attention. He shook out the undertunic and pulled it over his head, backwards. The silk felt cool against his skin, though it clung to his back where she'd scratched him. It would serve to get him back to the palace, at the least. "All I want is to end this . . . this . . ."

"Is that gallant, ser? You hurt me. I begin to think that all your words of love were lies."

I could never lie to you. Ser Arys felt as if she'd slapped him. "Why else would I have forsaken all my honor, but for love? When I am with you I . . . I can scarcely think, you are all I ever dreamt of, but . . ."

"Words are wind. If you love me, do not leave me."

"I swore a *vow* . . ."

". . . not to wed or father children. Well, I have drunk my moon tea, and you know I cannot marry you." She smiled. "Though I might be persuaded to keep you for my paramour."

"Now you mock me."

"Perhaps a little. Do you think you are the only Kingsguard who ever loved a woman?"

"There have always been men who found it easier to speak vows than to keep them," he admitted. Ser Boros Blount was no stranger to the Street of Silk, and Ser Preston Greenfield used to call at a certain draper's house whenever the draper was away, but Arys would not shame his Sworn Brothers by speaking of their failings. "Ser

Terrence Toyne was found abed with his king's mistress," he said instead. "'Twas love, he swore, but it cost his life and hers, and brought about the downfall of his House and the death of the noblest knight who ever lived."

"Yes, and what of Lucamore the Lusty, with his three wives and sixteen children? The song always makes me laugh."

"The truth is not so funny. He was never called Lucamore the Lusty whilst he lived. His name was Ser Lucamore Strong, and his whole life was a lie. When his deceit was discovered, his own Sworn Brothers gelded him, and the Old King sent him to the Wall. Those sixteen children were left weeping. He was no true knight, no more than Terrence Toyne . . ."

"And the Dragonknight?" She flung the bedclothes aside and swung her legs to the floor. "The noblest knight who ever lived, you said, and he took his queen to bed and got her with child."

"I will not believe that," he said, offended. "The tale of Prince Aemon's treason with Queen Naerys was only that, a tale, a lie his brother told when he wished to set his trueborn son aside in favor of his bastard. Aegon was not called the Unworthy without cause." He found his swordbelt and buckled it around his waist. Though it looked queer against the silken Dornish undertunic, the familiar weight of longsword and dagger reminded him of who and what he was. "I will not be remembered as Ser Arys the Unworthy," he declared. "I will not soil my cloak."

"Yes," she said, "that fine white cloak. You forget, my great-uncle wore the same cloak. He died when I was little, yet I still remember him. He was as tall as a tower and used to tickle me until I could not breathe for laughing."

"I never had the honor to know Prince Lewyn," Ser Arys said, "but all agree that he was a great knight."

"A great knight with a paramour. She is an old woman now, but she was a rare beauty in her youth, men say."

Prince Lewyn? That tale Ser Arys had not heard. It shocked him. Terrence Toyne's treason and the deceits of Lucamore the Lusty were recorded in the White Book, but there was no hint of a woman on Prince Lewyn's page.

"My uncle always said that it was the sword in a man's hand that determined his worth, not the one between his legs," she went on, "so spare me all your pious talk of soiled cloaks. It is not our love that has dishonored you, it is the monsters you have served and the brutes you've called your brothers."

That cut too close to the bone. "Robert was no monster."

"He climbed onto his throne over the corpses of children," she said, "though I will grant you he was no Joffrey."

Joffrey. He had been a handsome lad, tall and strong for his age, but that was all the good that could be said of him. It still shamed Ser Arys to remember all the times he'd struck that poor Stark girl at the boy's command. When Tyrion had chosen him to go with Myrcella to Dorne, he lit a candle to the Warrior in thanks. "Joffrey is dead, poisoned by the Imp." He would never have thought the dwarf capable of such enormity. "Tommen is king now, and he is not his brother."

"Nor is he his sister."

It was true. Tommen was a good-hearted little man who always tried his best, but the last time Ser Arys saw him he had been weeping on the quay. Myrcella never shed a tear, though it was she who was leaving hearth and home to seal an alliance with her maidenhood. The truth was, the princess was braver than her brother, and brighter and more confident as well. Her wits were quicker, her courtesies more polished. Nothing ever daunted her, not even Joffrey. *The women are the strong ones, truly.* He was thinking not only of Myrcella, but of her mother and his own, of the Queen of Thorns, of the Red Viper's pretty, deadly Sand Snakes. And of Princess Arianne Martell, her most of all. "I will not say that you are wrong." His voice was hoarse.

"Will not? *Cannot!* Myrcella is more fit for rule . . ."

"A son comes before a daughter."

"*Why?* What god has made it so? I am my father's heir. Should I give up my rights to my brothers?"

"You twist my words. I never said . . . Dorne is different. The Seven Kingdoms have never had a ruling queen."

"The first Viserys intended his daughter Rhaenyra to follow him, do you deny it? But as the king lay dying the Lord Commander of his Kingsguard decided that it should be otherwise."

Ser Criston Cole. Criston the Kingmaker had set brother against sister and divided the Kingsguard against itself, bringing on the terrible war the singers named the Dance of the Dragons. Some claimed he acted from ambition, for Prince Aegon was more tractable than his willful older sister. Others allowed him nobler motives, and argued that he was defending ancient Andal custom. A few whispered that Ser Criston had been Princess Rhaenyra's lover before he took the white and wanted vengeance on the woman who had spurned him. "The Kingmaker wrought grave harm," Ser Arys said, "and gravely did he pay for it, but . . ."

". . . but perhaps the Seven sent you here so that one white knight might make right what another set awry. You do know that when my father returns to the Water Gardens he plans to take Myrcella with him?"

"To keep her safe from those who would do her harm."

"No. To keep her away from those who'd seek to *crown* her. Prince Oberyn Viper would have placed the crown upon her head himself if he had lived, but my father lacks the courage." She got to her feet. "You say you love the girl as you would a daughter of your own blood. Would you let your daughter be despoiled of her rights and locked away in prison?"

"The Water Gardens are no prison," he protested feebly.

"A prison does not have fountains and fig trees, is that what you think? Yet once the girl is there, she will not be allowed to leave. No more than you will. Hotah will see to that. You do not know him as I do. He is terrible when aroused."

Ser Arys frowned. The big Norvoshi captain with the scarred face had always made him feel profoundly uneasy. *They say he sleeps with that great axe beside him.* "What would you have me do?"

"No more than you have sworn. Protect Myrcella with your life. Defend her . . . *and* her rights. Set a crown upon her head."

"I swore an *oath!*"

"To Joffrey, not to Tommen."

"Aye, but Tommen is a good-hearted boy. He will be a better king than Joffrey."

"But not better than Myrcella. She loves the boy as well. I know she will not let him come to any harm. Storm's End is his by rights, since Lord Renly left no heir and Lord Stannis is attainted. In time, Casterly Rock will pass to the boy as well, through his lady mother. He will be as great a lord as any in the realm . . . but Myrcella by rights should sit the Iron Throne."

"The law . . . I do not know . . ."

"I do." When she stood, the long black tangle of her hair fell down to the small of her back. "Aegon the Dragon made the Kingsguard and its vows, but what one king does another can undo, or change. Formerly the Kingsguard served for life, yet Joffrey dismissed Ser Barristan so his dog could have a cloak. Myrcella would want you to be happy, and she is fond of me as well. She will give us leave to marry if we ask." Arianne put her arms around him and laid her face against his chest. The top of her head came to just beneath his chin. "You can have me and your white cloak both, if that is what you want."

She is tearing me apart. "You know I do, but . . ."

"I am a princess of Dorne," she said in her husky voice, "and it is not meet that you should make me beg."

Ser Arys could smell the perfume in her hair and feel her heart beating as she pressed against him. His body was responding to her closeness, and he did not doubt that she could feel it too. When he put his arms upon her shoulders, he realized she was trembling. "Arianne? My princess? What is it, my love?"

"Must I say it, ser? I am afraid. You call me *love,* yet you refuse me, when I have most desperate need of you. Is it so wrong of me to want a knight to keep me safe?"

He had never heard her sound so vulnerable. "No," he said, "but you have your father's guards to keep you safe, why—"

"It is my father's guards I fear." For a moment she sounded younger than Myrcella. "It was my father's guards who dragged my sweet cousins off in chains."

"Not in chains. I have heard that they have every comfort."

She gave a bitter laugh. "Have you seen them? He will not permit me to see them, did you know that?"

"They were speaking treason, fomenting war . . ."

"Loreza is six, Dorea eight. What wars could they foment? Yet my father has imprisoned them with their sisters. You have seen him. Fear makes even strong men do things they might never do otherwise, and my father was never strong. Arys, my heart, hear me for the love you say you bear me. I have never been as fearless as my cousins, for I was made with weaker seed, but Tyene and I are of an age and have been close as sisters since we were little girls. We have no secrets between us. If she can be imprisoned, so can I, and for the same cause . . . this of Myrcella."

"Your father would never do that."

"You do not know my father. I have been disappointing him since I first arrived in this world without a cock. Half a dozen times he has tried to marry me to toothless greybeards, each more contemptible than the last. He never *commanded* me to wed them, I grant you, but the offers alone prove how little he regards me."

"Even so, you are his heir."

"Am I?"

"He left you to rule in Sunspear when he took himself off to his Water Gardens, did he not?"

"To *rule*? No. He left his cousin Ser Manfrey as castellan, old blind Ricasso as seneschal, his bailiffs to collect duties and taxes for his treasurer Alyse Ladybright to count, his shariffs to police the shadow city, his justiciars to sit in judgment, and Maester Myles to deal with any letters not requiring the prince's own attention. Above them all he placed the Red Viper. My charge was feasts and frolics, and the entertainment of distinguished guests. Oberyn would visit the Water Gardens twice a fortnight. Me, he summoned twice a year. I am not the heir my father wants, he has made that plain. Our laws constrain him, but he would sooner have my brother follow him, I know it."

"Your brother?" Ser Arys put his hand beneath her chin and raised her head, the better to look her in the eyes. "You cannot mean Trystane, he is just a boy."

"Not Trys. Quentyn." Her eyes were bold and black as sin, unflinching. "I have known the truth since I was four-and-ten, since the day that I went to my father's solar to give him a good night kiss, and found him gone. My mother had sent for him, I learned later.

He'd left a candle burning. When I went to blow it out, I found a letter lying incomplete beside it, a letter to my brother Quentyn, off at Yronwood. My father told Quentyn that he must do all that his maester and his master-at-arms required of him, because '*one day you will sit where I sit and rule all Dorne, and a ruler must be strong of mind and body.*'" A tear crept down Arianne's soft cheek. "My father's words, written in his own hand. They burned themselves into my memory. I cried myself to sleep that night, and many nights thereafter."

Ser Arys had yet to meet Quentyn Martell. The prince had been fostered by Lord Yronwood from a tender age, had served him as a page, then a squire, had even taken knighthood at his hands in preference to the Red Viper's. *If I were a father, I would want my son to follow me as well,* he thought, but he could hear the hurt in her voice, and he knew that if he said what he was thinking, he would lose her. "Perhaps you misunderstood," he said. "You were only a child. Perhaps the prince was only saying that to encourage your brother to be more diligent."

"You think so? Then tell me, where is Quentyn now?"

"The prince is with Lord Yronwood's host in the Boneway," Ser Arys said cautiously. That was what Sunspear's ancient castellan had told him, when first he came to Dorne. The maester with the silky beard said the same.

Arianne demurred. "So my father wishes us to believe, but I have friends who tell me otherwise. My brother has crossed the narrow sea in secret, posing as a common merchant. Why?"

"How would I know? There could be a hundred reasons."

"Or one. Are you aware that the Golden Company has broken its contract with Myr?"

"Sellswords break their contracts all the time."

"Not the Golden Company. *Our word is good as gold* has been their boast since the days of Bittersteel. Myr is on the point of war with Lys and Tyrosh. Why break a contract that offered them the prospect of good wages and good plunder?"

"Perhaps Lys offered them better wages. Or Tyrosh."

"No," she said. "I would believe it of any of the other free companies, yes. Most of them would change sides for half a groat. The Golden Company is different. A brotherhood of exiles and the sons of exiles, united by the dream of Bittersteel. It's home they want, as much as gold. Lord Yronwood knows that as well as I do. His forebears rode with Bittersteel during three of the Blackfyre Rebellions." She took Ser Arys by the hand, and wove her fingers through his own. "Have you ever seen the arms of House Toland of Ghost Hill?"

He had to think a moment. "A dragon eating its own tail?"

"The dragon is time. It has no beginning and no ending, so all things come round again. Anders Yronwood is Criston Cole reborn. He whispers in my brother's ear that *he* should rule after my father, that it is not right for men to kneel to women . . . that Arianne especially is unfit to rule, being the willful wanton that she is." She tossed her hair defiantly. "So your two princesses share a common cause, ser . . . and they share as well a knight who claims to love them both, but will not fight for them."

"I will." Ser Arys sank to one knee. "Myrcella *is* the elder, and better suited to the crown. Who will defend her rights if not her Kingsguard? My sword, my life, my honor, all belong to her . . . and to you, my heart's delight. I swear, no man will steal your birthright whilst I still have the strength to lift a sword. I am yours. What would you have of me?"

"All." She knelt to kiss his lips. "*All*, my love, my true love, my sweet love, and forever. But first . . ."

"Ask, and it is yours."

". . . Myrcella."

BRIENNE

The stone wall was old and crumbling, but the sight of it across the field made the hairs on Brienne's neck stand up.

That was where the archers hid and slew poor Cleos Frey, she thought . . . but half a mile farther on she passed another wall that looked much like the first and found herself uncertain. The rutted road turned and twisted, and the bare brown trees looked different from the green ones she remembered. Had she ridden past the place where Ser Jaime had snatched his cousin's sword from its scabbard? Where were the woods they'd fought in? The stream where they'd splashed and slashed at one another until they drew the Brave Companions down upon them?

"My lady? Ser?" Podrick never seemed certain what to call her. "What are you looking for?"

Ghosts. "A wall I rode by once. It does not matter." *It was when Ser Jaime still had both his hands. How I loathed him, with all his taunts and smiles.* "Stay quiet, Podrick. There may still be outlaws in these woods."

The boy looked at the bare brown trees, the wet leaves, the muddy road ahead. "I have a longsword. I can fight."

Not well enough. Brienne did not doubt the boy's courage, only his training. A squire he might be, in name at least, but the men he'd squired for had served him ill.

She had gotten his story out of him in fits and starts on the road from Duskendale. His was a lesser branch of House Payne, an impoverished offshoot sprouted from the loins of a younger son. His father had spent his life squiring for richer cousins and had sired Podrick upon a chandler's daughter he'd wed before going off to die in the Greyjoy Rebellion. His mother had abandoned him with one of those cousins when he was four, so she could run after a wandering singer who had put another baby in her belly. Podrick did not remember what she looked like. Ser Cedric Payne had been the nearest thing to a parent the boy had ever known, though from his stammered stories it seemed to Brienne that cousin Cedric had treated Podrick more like a servant than a son. When Casterly Rock called its banners, the knight had taken him along to tend his horse and clean his mail. Then Ser Cedric had been slain in the riverlands whilst fighting in Lord Tywin's host.

Far from home, alone, and penniless, the boy had attached himself to a fat hedge knight named Ser Lorimer the Belly, who was part of Lord Lefford's contingent, charged with protecting the baggage train. "The boys who guard the foodstuffs always eat the best," Ser Lorimer liked to say, until he was discovered with a salted ham he'd stolen from Lord Tywin's personal stores. Tywin Lannister chose to hang him as a lesson to other looters. Podrick had shared the ham and might have shared the rope as well, but his name had saved him. Ser Kevan Lannister took charge of him, and sometime later sent the boy to squire for his nephew Tyrion.

Ser Cedric had taught Podrick how to groom a horse and check his shoes for stones, and Ser Lorimer had taught him how to steal, but neither had given him much training with a sword. The Imp at least had dispatched him to the Red Keep's master-at-arms when they came to court. But during the bread riots Ser Aron Santagar had been amongst those slain, and that had been the end of Podrick's training.

Brienne cut two wooden swords from fallen branches to get a sense of Podrick's skills. The boy was slow of speech but not of hand, she was pleased to learn. Though fearless and attentive, he was also underfed and skinny, and not near strong enough. If he had survived the Battle of the Blackwater as he claimed, it could only be because no one thought him worth the killing. "You may call yourself a squire," she told him, "but I've seen pages half your age who could have beat you bloody. If you stay with me, you'll go to sleep with blisters on your hands and bruises on your arms most every night, and you'll be so stiff and sore you'll hardly sleep. You don't want that."

"I do," the boy insisted. "I want that. The bruises and the blisters. I mean, I don't, but I do. Ser. My lady."

So far he had been true to his word, and Brienne had been true to hers. Podrick had not complained. Every time he raised a new blister on his sword hand, he felt the need to show it to her proudly. He took good care of their horses too. *He is still no squire,* she reminded herself, *but I am no knight, no matter how many times he calls me "ser."* She would have sent him on his way, but he had nowhere to go. Besides, though Podrick said he did not know where Sansa Stark had gone, it might be that he knew more than he realized. Some chance remark, half-remembered, might hold the key to Brienne's quest.

"Ser? My lady?" Podrick pointed. "There's a cart ahead."

Brienne saw it: a wooden oxcart, two-wheeled and high-sided. A man and a woman were laboring in the traces, pulling the cart along the ruts toward Maidenpool. *Farm folk, by the look of them.* "Slowly now," she told the boy. "They may take us for outlaws. Say no more than you must and be courteous."

"I will, ser. Be courteous. My lady." The boy seemed almost pleased by the prospect of being taken for an outlaw.

The farm folk watched them warily as they came trotting up, but once Brienne made it plain that she meant them no harm, they let her ride beside them. "We used to have an ox," the old man told her as they made their way through the weed-choked fields, lakes of soft mud, and burnt and blackened trees, "but the wolves made off with him." His face was red from the effort of pulling the cart. "They took off our daughter too and had their way with her, but she come wandering back after the battle down at Duskendale. The ox never did. The wolves ate him, I expect."

The woman had little to add. She was younger than the man by twenty years, but never spoke a word, only looked at Brienne the same way she might have looked at a two-headed calf. The Maid of

Tarth had seen such eyes before. Lady Stark had been kind to her, but most women were just as cruel as men. She could not have said which she found most hurtful, the pretty girls with their waspish tongues and brittle laughter or the cold-eyed ladies who hid their disdain behind a mask of courtesy. And common women could be worse than either. "Maidenpool was all in ruins when last I saw it," she said. "The gates were broken and half the town was burned."

"They rebuilt it some. This Tarly, he's a hard man, but a braver lord than Mooton. There's still outlaws in the woods, but not so many as there was. Tarly hunted down the worst o' them and shortened them with that big sword o' his." He turned his head and spat. "You've seen no outlaws on the road?"

"None." *Not this time.* The farther they had come from Duskendale, the emptier the road had been. The only travelers they'd glimpsed had melted away into the woods before they reached them, save for a big, bearded septon they met walking south with twoscore footsore followers. Such inns as they passed had either been sacked and abandoned or turned into armed camps. Yesterday they had encountered one of Lord Randyll's patrols, bristling with longbows and lances. The horsemen had surrounded them while their captain questioned Brienne, but in the end he'd let them continue on their way. "Be wary, woman. The next men you meet may not be as honest as my lads. The Hound has crossed the Trident with a hundred outlaws, and it's said they're raping every wench they come upon and cutting off their teats for trophies."

Brienne felt obligated to pass along that warning to the farmer and his wife. The man nodded as she told him, but when she was done he spat again and said, "Dogs and wolves and lions, may the Others take them all. These outlaws won't dare come too near to Maidenpool. Not so long as Lord Tarly has the rule there."

Brienne knew Lord Randyll Tarly from her time with King Renly's host. Though she could not find it in herself to like the man, she could not forget the debt she owed him either. *If the gods are good, we will pass Maidenpool before he knows that I am there.* "The town will be restored to Lord Mooton once the fighting's done," she told the farmer. "His lordship has been pardoned by the king."

"Pardoned?" The old man laughed. "For what? Sitting on his arse in his bloody castle? He sent men off to Riverrun to fight but never went himself. Lions sacked his town, then wolves, then sellswords, and his lordship just sat safe behind his walls. His brother 'ud never have hid like that. Ser Myles was bold as brass till that Robert killed him."

More ghosts, Brienne thought. "I am looking for my sister, a fair maid of three-and-ten. Perhaps you've seen her?"

"I've not seen no maids, fair nor foul."

No one has. But she had to keep asking.

"Mooton's daughter, she's a maid," the man went on. "Till the bedding, anyways. These eggs, they're for her wedding. Her and Tarly's son. The cooks will need eggs for cakes."

"They will." *Lord Tarly's son. Young Dickon's to be wed.* She tried to recall how old he was; eight or ten, she thought. Brienne had been betrothed at seven, to a boy three years her senior, Lord Caron's younger son, a shy boy with a mole above his lip. They had only met the once, on the occasion of their betrothal. Two years later he was dead, carried off by the same chill that took Lord and Lady Caron and their daughters. Had he lived, they would have been wed within a year of her first flowering, and her whole life would have been different. She would not be here now, dressed in man's mail and carrying a sword, hunting for a dead woman's child. More like she'd be at Nightsong, swaddling a child of her own and nursing another. It was not a new thought for Brienne. It always made her feel a little sad, but a little relieved as well.

The sun was half-hidden behind a bank of clouds when they emerged from the blackened trees to find Maidenpool before them, with the deep waters of the bay beyond. The town's gates had been rebuilt and strengthened, Brienne saw at once, and crossbowmen walked its pink stone walls once more. Above the gatehouse floated King Tommen's royal banner, a black stag and golden lion combatant on a field divided gold and crimson. Other banners displayed the Tarly huntsman, but the red salmon of House Mooton flew only from their castle on its hill.

At the portcullis they came upon a dozen guards armed with

halberds. Their badges marked them for soldiers of Lord Tarly's host, though none was Tarly's own. She saw two centaurs, a thunderbolt, a blue beetle and a green arrow, but not the striding huntsman of Horn Hill. Their serjeant had a peacock on his breast, its bright tail faded by the sun. When the farmers drew their cart up he gave a whistle. "What's this now? Eggs?" He tossed one up, caught it, and grinned. "We'll take them."

The old man squawked. "Our eggs is for Lord Mooton. For the wedding cakes and such."

"Have your hens lay more. I haven't had an egg in half a year. Here, don't say you weren't paid." He flung a handful of pennies at the old man's feet.

The farmer's wife spoke up. "That's not enough," she said. "Not near enough."

"I say it is," said the serjeant. "For them eggs, and you as well. Bring her here, boys. She's too young for that old man." Two of the guards leaned their halberds against the wall and pulled the woman away from the cart, struggling. The farmer watched grey-faced, but dared not move.

Brienne spurred her mare forward. "Release her."

Her voice made the guards hesitate long enough for the farmer's wife to wrench free of their grasp. "This is none of your concern," one man said. "You mind your mouth, wench."

Brienne drew her sword instead.

"Well now," the serjeant said, "naked steel. Seems to me I smell an outlaw. You know what Lord Tarly does with outlaws?" He still held the egg he'd taken from the cart. His hand closed, and the yolk oozed through his fingers.

"I know what Lord Randyll does with outlaws," Brienne said. "I know what he does with rapers too."

She had hoped the name might cow them, but the serjeant only flicked egg off his fingers and signaled to his men to spread out. Brienne found herself surrounded by steel points. "What was it you was saying, wench? What is it that Lord Tarly does to . . ."

". . . rapers," a deeper voice finished. "He gelds them or sends them to the Wall. Sometimes both. And he cuts fingers off thieves." A languid young man stepped from the gatehouse, a swordbelt buckled at his waist. The surcoat he wore above his steel had once been white, and here and there still was, beneath the grass stains and dried blood. His sigil was displayed across his chest: a brown deer, dead and bound and slung beneath a pole.

Him. His voice was a punch in her stomach, his face a blade in her bowels. "Ser Hyle," she said stiffly.

"Best let her by, lads," warned Ser Hyle Hunt. "This is Brienne the Beauty, the Maid of Tarth, who slew King Renly and half his Rainbow Guard. She's as mean as she is ugly, and there's no one uglier . . . except perhaps for you, Pisspot, but your father was the rear end of an aurochs, so you have a good excuse. *Her* father is the Evenstar of Tarth."

The guards laughed, but the halberds parted. "Shouldn't we seize her, ser?" the serjeant asked. "For killing Renly?"

"Why? Renly was a rebel. So were we all, rebels to a man, but now we're Tommen's loyal lads." The knight waved the farm folk through the gate. "His lordship's steward will be pleased to see those eggs. You'll find him in the market."

The old man knuckled his forehead. "My thanks, m'lord. You're a true knight, it's plain to see. Come, wife." They put their shoulders to the cart again and rumbled through the gate.

Brienne trotted after them, with Podrick at her heels. *A true knight,* she thought, frowning. Inside the town she reined up. The ruins of a stable could be seen off to her left, fronting on a muddy alley. Across from it three half-dressed whores stood on the balcony of a brothel, whispering to one another. One looked a bit like a camp follower who had once come up to Brienne to ask if she had a cunt or a cock inside her breeches.

"That rounsey may be the most hideous horse I've ever seen," said Ser Hyle of Podrick's mount. "I am surprised that you're not riding it, my lady. Do you plan to thank me for my help?"

Brienne swung down off her mare. She stood a head taller than Ser Hyle. "One day, I'll thank you in a mêlée, ser."

"The way you thanked Red Ronnet?" Hunt laughed. He had a full, rich laugh, though his face was plain. An honest face, she'd thought once, before she learned better; shaggy brown hair, hazel eyes, a little scar by his left ear. His chin had a cleft and his nose was crooked, but he did laugh well, and often.

"Shouldn't you be watching your gate?"

He made a wry face at her. "My cousin Alyn is off hunting outlaws. Doubtless he'll return with the Hound's head, gloating and covered in glory. Meanwhile, I am condemned to guard this gate, thanks to you. I hope you're pleased, my beauty. What is it that you're looking for?"

"A stable."

"Over by the east gate. This one burned."

I can see that. "What you said to those men . . . I was with King Renly when he died, but it was some sorcery that slew him, ser. I swear it on my sword." She put her hand upon her hilt, ready to fight if Hunt named her a liar to her face.

"Aye, and it was the Knight of Flowers who carved up the Rainbow Guard. On a good day, you might have been able to defeat Ser Emmon. He was a rash fighter, and he tired easily. Royce, though? No. Ser Robar was twice the swordsman that you are . . . though you're *not* a swordsman, are you? Is there such a word as swordswench? What quest brings the Maid to Maidenpool, I wonder?"

Searching for my sister, a maid of three-and-ten, she almost said, but Ser Hyle would know she had no sisters. "There's a man I seek, at a place called the Stinking Goose."

"I thought Brienne the Beauty had no use for men." There was a cruel edge to his smile. "The Stinking Goose. An apt name, that . . . the stinking part, at least. It's by the harbor. First you will come with me to see his lordship."

Brienne did not fear Ser Hyle, but he was one of Randyll Tarly's captains. A whistle, and a hundred men would come running to defend him. "Am I to be arrested?"

"What, for Renly? Who was he? We've changed kings since then, some of us twice. No one cares, no one remembers." He laid a hand lightly on her arm. "This way, if you please."

She wrenched away. "I would thank you not to touch me."

"Thanks at last," he said, with a wry smile.

When last she had seen Maidenpool, the town had been a desolation, a grim place of empty streets and burned homes. Now the streets were full of pigs and children, and most of the burned buildings had been pulled down. Vegetables had been planted in the lots where some once stood; merchant's tents and knight's pavilions took the place of others. Brienne saw new houses going up, a stone inn rising where a wooden inn had burned, a new slate roof on the town sept. The cool autumn air rang to the sounds of saw and hammer. Men carried timber through the streets, and quarrymen drove their wagons down muddy lanes. Many wore the striding huntsman on their breasts. "The soldiers are rebuilding the town," she said, surprised.

"They would sooner be dicing, drinking, and fucking, I don't doubt, but Lord Randyll believes in putting idle men to work."

She had expected to be taken to the castle. Instead, Hunt led them toward the busy harbor. The traders had returned to Maidenpool, she was pleased to see. A galley, a galleas, and a big two-masted cog were in port, along with a score of little fishing boats. More fishermen were visible out on the bay. *If the Stinking Goose yields nothing, I will take passage on a ship,* she decided. Gulltown was only a short voyage away. From there she could make her way to the Eyrie easily enough.

They found Lord Tarly in the fishmarket, doing justice.

A platform had been thrown up beside the water, from which his lordship could look down upon the men accused of crimes. To his left stood a long gallows, with ropes enough for twenty men. Four corpses swung beneath it. One looked fresh, but the other three had plainly been there for some time. A crow was pulling strips of flesh from the ripe ruins of one of the dead men. The other crows had scattered, wary of the crowd of townsfolk who'd gathered in hopes of someone's being hanged.

Lord Randyll shared the platform with Lord Mooton, a pale, soft, fleshy man in a white doublet and red breeches, his ermine cloak pinned at the shoulder by a red-gold brooch in the shape of a salmon. Tarly wore mail and boiled leather, and a breastplate of grey steel. The hilt of a greatsword poked up above his left shoulder. *Heartsbane,* it was named, the pride of his House.

A stripling in a roughspun cloak and soiled jerkin was being heard

when they came up. "I never hurt no one, m'lord," Brienne heard him
say. "I only took what the septons left when they run off. If you got
to take my finger for that, do it."

"It is customary to take a finger from a thief," Lord Tarly replied
in a hard voice, "but a man who steals from a sept is stealing from
the gods." He turned to his captain of guards. "Seven fingers. Leave
his thumbs."

"*Seven?*" The thief paled. When the guards seized hold of him he
tried to fight, but feebly, as if he were already maimed. Watching him,
Brienne could not help think of Ser Jaime, and the way he'd screamed
when Zollo's *arakh* came flashing down.

The next man was a baker, accused of mixing sawdust in his flour.
Lord Randyll fined him fifty silver stags. When the baker swore he
did not have that much silver, his lordship declared that he could
have a lash for every stag that he was short. He was followed by a
haggard grey-faced whore, accused of giving the pox to four of Tarly's
soldiers. "Wash out her private parts with lye and throw her in a
dungeon," Tarly commanded. As the whore was dragged off sobbing,
his lordship saw Brienne on the edge of the crowd, standing between
Podrick and Ser Hyle. He frowned at her, but his eyes betrayed not
a flicker of recognition.

A sailor off the galleas came next. His accuser was an archer of
Lord Mooton's garrison, with a bandaged hand and a salmon on his
breast. "If it please m'lord, this bastid put his dagger through my
hand. He said I was cheating him at dice."

Lord Tarly took his gaze away from Brienne to consider the men
before him. "Were you?"

"No, m'lord. I never."

"For theft, I will take a finger. Lie to me and I will hang you. Shall
I ask to see these dice?"

"The dice?" The archer looked to Mooton, but his lordship was
gazing at the fishing boats. The bowman swallowed. "Might be
I . . . them dice, they're lucky for me, 's true, but I . . ."

Tarly had heard enough. "Take his little finger. He can choose which
hand. A nail through the palm for the other." He stood. "We're done.
March the rest of them back to the dungeon, I'll deal with them on

the morrow." He turned to beckon Ser Hyle forward. Brienne followed.
"My lord," she said, when she stood before him. She felt eight years
old again.

"My lady. To what do we owe this . . . honor?"

"I have been sent to look for . . . for . . ." She hesitated.

"How will you find him if you do not know his name? Did you
slay Lord Renly?"

"No."

Tarly weighed the word. *He is judging me, as he judged those others.*
"No," he said at last, "you only let him die."

He had died in her arms, his life's blood drenching her. Brienne
flinched. "It was sorcery. I never . . ."

"You *never?*" His voice became a whip. "Aye. You never should have
donned mail, nor buckled on a sword. You never should have left
your father's hall. This is a war, not a harvest ball. By all the gods, I
ought to ship you back to Tarth."

"Do that and answer to the throne." Her voice sounded high and
girlish, when she wanted to sound fearless. "Podrick. In my bag you'll
find a parchment. Bring it to his lordship."

Tarly took the letter and unrolled it, scowling. His lips moved as
he read. "The king's business. What sort of business?"

Lie to me and I will hang you. "S-Sansa Stark."

"If the Stark girl were here, I'd know it. She's run back north, I'll
wager. Hoping to find refuge with one of her father's bannermen. She
had best hope she chooses the right one."

"She might have gone to the Vale instead," Brienne heard herself
blurt out, "to her mother's sister."

Lord Randyll gave her a contemptuous look. "Lady Lysa is dead.
Some singer pushed her off a mountain. Littlefinger holds the Eyrie
now . . . though not for long. The lords of the Vale are not the sort
to bend their knees to some upjumped jackanapes whose only skill
is counting coppers." He handed her back her letter. "Go where you
want and do as you will . . . but when you're raped don't look to me
for justice. You will have earned it with your folly." He glanced at Ser
Hyle. "And you, ser, should be at your gate. I gave you the command
there, did I not?"

"You did, my lord," said Hyle Hunt, "but I thought—"

"You think too much." Lord Tarly strode away.

Lysa Tully is dead. Brienne stood beneath the gallows, the precious parchment in her hand. The crowd had dispersed, and the crows had returned to resume their feast. *A singer pushed her off a mountain.* Had the crows dined on Lady Catelyn's sister too?

"You spoke of the Stinking Goose, my lady," said Ser Hyle. "If you want me to show you—"

"Go back to your gate."

A look of annoyance flashed across his face. *A plain face, not an honest one.* "If that's your wish."

"It is."

"It was only a game to pass the time. We meant no harm." He hesitated. "Ben died, you know. Cut down on the Blackwater. Farrow too, and Will the Stork. And Mark Mullendore took a wound that cost him half his arm."

Good, Brienne wanted to say. *Good, he deserved it.* But she remembered Mullendore sitting outside his pavilion with his monkey on his shoulder in a little suit of chainmail, the two of them making faces at each other. What was it Catelyn Stark had called them, that night at Bitterbridge? *The knights of summer.* And now it was autumn and they were falling like leaves. . . .

She turned her back on Hyle Hunt. "Podrick, come."

The boy trotted after her, leading their horses. "Are we going to find the place? The Stinking Goose?"

"I am. You are going to the stables, by the east gate. Ask the stableman if there's an inn where we can spend the night."

"I will, ser. My lady." Podrick stared at the ground as they went, kicking stones from time to time. "Do you know where it is? The Goose? The Stinking Goose, I mean."

"No."

"He said he'd show us. That knight. Ser Kyle."

"Hyle."

"Hyle. What did he do to you, ser? I mean, my lady."

The boy may be a stumbletongue, but he's not stupid. "At Highgarden, when King Renly called his banners, some men played a game with me. Ser Hyle was one of them. It was a cruel game, hurtful and unchivalrous." She stopped. "The east gate is that way. Wait for me there."

"As you say, my lady. Ser."

No sign marked the Stinking Goose. It took her most of an hour to find it, down a flight of wooden steps beneath a knacker's barn. The cellar was dim and the ceiling low, and Brienne thumped her head on a beam as she entered. No geese were in evidence. A few stools were scattered about, and a bench had been shoved up against one earthen wall. The tables were old wine casks, grey and wormholed. The promised stink pervaded everything. Mostly it was wine and damp and mildew, her nose told her, but there was a little of the privy too, and something of the lichyard.

The only drinkers were three Tyroshi seamen in a corner, growling at each other through green and purple beards. They gave her a brief inspection, and one said something that made the others laugh. The proprietor stood behind a plank that had been placed across two barrels. She was a woman, round and pale and balding, with huge soft breasts swaying beneath a soiled smock. She looked as though the gods had made her out of uncooked dough.

Brienne did not dare to ask for water here. She bought a cup of wine and said, "I am looking for a man called Nimble Dick."

"Dick Crabb. Comes in most every night." The woman eyed Brienne's mail and sword. "If you're going to cut him, do it somewheres else. We don't want no trouble with Lord Tarly."

"I want to talk with him. Why would I do him harm?"

The woman shrugged.

"If you would nod when he comes in I'd be thankful."

"How thankful?"

Brienne put a copper star on the plank between them and found a place in the shadows with a good view of the steps.

She tried the wine. It was oily on the tongue and there was a hair floating in it. *A hair as slender as my hopes of finding Sansa,* she thought as she plucked it out. Chasing after Ser Dontos had been fruitless, and with Lady Lysa dead the Vale no longer seemed a likely refuge. *Where are you, Lady Sansa? Did you run home to Winterfell, or are you with your husband, as Podrick seems to think?* Brienne did not want to chase the girl across the narrow sea, where even the language would be strange to her. *I will be even more a freak there, grunting and gesturing to make myself understood. They will laugh at me, as they laughed at Highgarden.* A blush stole up her cheeks as she remembered.

When Renly donned his crown, the Maid of Tarth had ridden all the way across the Reach to join him. The king himself had greeted her courteously and welcomed her to his service. Not so his lords and knights. Brienne had not expected a warm welcome. She was prepared for coldness, for mockery, for hostility. She had supped upon such meat before. It was not the scorn of the many that left her confused and vulnerable, but the kindness of the few. The Maid of Tarth had been betrothed three times, but she had never been courted until she came to Highgarden.

Big Ben Bushy was the first, one of the few men in Renly's camp who overtopped her. He sent his squire to her to clean her mail, and made her a gift of a silver drinking horn. Ser Edmund Ambrose went him one better, bringing flowers and asking her to ride with him. Ser Hyle Hunt outdid them both. He gave her a book, beautifully illuminated and filled with a hundred tales of knightly valor. He brought apples and carrots for her horses, and a blue silk plume for her helm. He told her the gossip of the camp and said clever, cutting things that made her smile. He even trained with her one day, which meant more than all the rest.

She thought it was because of him that the others started being courteous. *More than courteous.* At table men fought for the place beside her, offering to fill her wine cup or fetch her sweetbreads. Ser Richard Farrow played love songs on his lute outside her pavilion. Ser Hugh Beesbury brought her a pot of honey "as sweet as the maids of Tarth." Ser Mark Mullendore made her laugh with the antics of his monkey, a curious little black-and-white creature from the Summer Islands. A hedge knight called Will the Stork offered to rub the knots from her shoulders.

Brienne refused him. She refused them all. When Ser Owen Inchfield seized her one night and pressed a kiss upon her, she knocked him arse-backwards into a cookfire. Afterward she looked at herself in a glass. Her face was as broad and bucktoothed and freckled as ever, big-lipped, thick of jaw, so ugly. All she wanted was to be a knight and serve King Renly, yet now . . .

It was not as if she were the only woman there. Even the camp followers were prettier than she was, and up in the castle Lord Tyrell feasted King Renly every night, whilst highborn maids and lovely ladies danced to the music of pipe and horn and harp. *Why are you being kind to me?* she wanted to scream, every time some strange knight paid her a compliment. *What do you want?*

Randyll Tarly solved the mystery the day he sent two of his men-at-arms to summon her to his pavilion. His young son Dickon had overheard four knights laughing as they saddled up their horses, and had told his lord father what they said.

They had a wager.

Three of the younger knights had started it, he told her: Ambrose, Bushy, and Hyle Hunt, of his own household. As word spread through the camp, however, others had joined the game. Each man was required to buy into the contest with a golden dragon, the whole sum to go to whoever claimed her maidenhead.

"I have put an end to their sport," Tarly told her. "Some of these . . . challengers . . . are less honorable than others, and the stakes were growing larger every day. It was only a matter of time before one of them decided to claim the prize by force."

"They were knights," she said, stunned, "anointed knights."

"And honorable men. The blame is yours."

The accusation made her flinch. "I would never . . . my lord, I did nought to encourage them."

"Your being here encouraged them. If a woman will behave like a camp follower, she cannot object to being treated like one. A war host is no place for a maiden. If you have any regard for your virtue or the honor of your House, you will take off that mail, return home, and beg your father to find a husband for you."

"I came to fight," she insisted. "To be a knight."

"The gods made men to fight, and women to bear children," said Randyll Tarly. "A woman's war is in the birthing bed."

Someone was coming down the cellar steps. Brienne pushed her wine aside as a ragged, scrawny, sharp-faced man with dirty brown hair stepped into the Goose. He gave the Tyroshi sailors a quick look and Brienne a longer one, then went up to the plank. "Wine," he said, "and none o' your horse piss in it, thank'e."

The woman gave Brienne a look and nodded.

"I'll buy your wine," she called out, "for a word."

The man looked her over, his eyes wary. "A word? I know a lot o' words." He sat down on the stool across from her. "Tell me which m'lady wants t' hear, and Nimble Dick will say it."

"I heard you fooled a fool."

The ragged man sipped his wine, thinking. "Mighten be I did. Or not." He wore a faded, torn doublet from which some lord's badge had been ripped. "Who is it wants t' know?"

"King Robert." She put a silver stag on the barrel between them. Robert's head was on one side, the stag on the other.

"Does he now?" The man took the coin and spun it, smiling. "I like to see a king dance, hey-nonny hey-nonny hey-nonny-ho. Mighten be I saw this fool of yours."

"Was there a girl with him?"

"Two girls," he said at once.

"*Two* girls?" *Could the other one be Arya?*

"Well," the man said, "I never seen the little sweets, mind you, but he was wanting passage for three."

"Passage where?"

"T'other side o' the sea, as I recall."

"Do you remember what he looked like?"

"A fool." He snatched the spinning coin off the table as it began to slow, and made it vanish. "A frightened fool."

"Frightened why?"

He shrugged. "He never said, but old Nimble Dick knows the smell o' fear. He come here most every night, buying drinks for sailors, making japes, singing little songs. Only one night some men come in with that hunter on their teats, and your fool went white as milk and got quiet till they left." He edged his stool closer to hers. "That Tarly's got soldiers crawling over the docks, watching every ship that comes or goes. Man wants a deer, he goes t' the woods. He wants a ship, he goes t' the docks. Your fool didn't dare. So I offered him some help."

"What sort of help?"

"The sort that costs more than one silver stag."

"Tell me, and you'll have another."

"Let's see it," he said. She put another stag on the barrel. He spun it, smiled, scooped it up. "A man who can't go t' the ships need for the ships t' come t' him. I told him I knew a place where that might happen. A hidden place, like."

Gooseprickles rose along Brienne's arms. "A smugglers' cove. You sent the fool to smugglers."

"Him and them two girls." He chuckled. "Only thing, well, the place I sent them, been no ships there for a while. Thirty years, say." He scratched his nose. "What's this fool to you?"

"Those two girls are my sisters."

"Are they, now? Poor little things. Had a sister once meself. Skinny girl with knobby knees, but then she grew a pair o' teats and a knight's son got between her legs. Last I saw her she was off for King's Landing t' make a living on her back."

"Where did you send them?"

Another shrug. "As t' that, I can't recall."

"*Where?*" Brienne slapped another silver stag down.

He flicked the coin back at her with his forefinger. "Someplace no stag ever found . . . though a dragon might."

Silver would not get the truth from him, she sensed. *Gold might, or it might not. Steel would be more certain.* Brienne touched her dagger, then reached into her purse instead. She found a golden dragon and put in on the barrel. "Where?"

The ragged man snatched up the coin and bit it. "Sweet. Puts me in mind o' Crackclaw Point. Up north o' here, 'tis a wild land o' hills and bogs, but it happens I was born and bred there. Dick Crabb, I'm named, though most call me Nimble Dick."

She did not offer her own name. "*Where* in Crackclaw Point?"

"The Whispers. You heard o' Clarence Crabb, o' course."

"No."

That seemed to surprise him. "*Ser* Clarence Crabb, I said. I got his blood in me. He was eight foot tall, and so strong he could uproot pine trees with one hand and chuck them half a mile. No horse could bear his weight, so he rode an aurochs."

"What does he have to do with this smugglers' cove?"

"His wife was a woods witch. Whenever Ser Clarence killed a man, he'd fetch his head back home and his wife would kiss it on the lips and bring it back t' life. Lords, they were, and wizards, and famous knights and pirates. One was king o' Duskendale. They gave old Crabb good counsel. Being they was just heads, they couldn't talk real loud, but they never shut up neither. When you're a head, talking's all you got to pass the day. So Crabb's keep got named the Whispers. Still is, though it's been a ruin for a thousand years. A lonely place, the Whispers." The man walked the coin deftly across his knuckles. "One dragon by hisself gets lonely. Ten, now . . ."

"Ten dragons are a fortune. Do you take me for a fool?"

"No, but I can take you to one." The coin danced one way, and back the other. "Take you to the Whispers, m'lady."

Brienne did not like the way his fingers played with that gold coin. Still . . . "Six dragons if we find my sister. Two if we only find the fool. Nothing if nothing is what we find."

Crabb shrugged. "Six is good. Six will serve."

Too quick. She caught his wrist before he could tuck the gold away. "Do not play me false. You'll not find me easy meat."

When she let go, Crabb rubbed his wrist. "Bloody piss," he muttered. "You hurt my hand."

"I am sorry for that. My sister is a girl of three-and-ten. I need to find her before—"

"—before some knight gets in her slit. Aye, I hear you. She's good as saved. Nimble Dick is with you now. Meet me by east gate at first light. I need t' see this man about a horse."

SAMWELL

The sea made Samwell Tarly greensick.

It was not all his fear of drowning, though that was surely some of it. It was the motion of the ship as well, the way the decks rolled beneath his feet. "I have a queasy belly," he confessed to Dareon the day they sailed from Eastwatch-by-the-Sea. The singer slapped him on the back and said, "With a belly big as yours, Slayer, that is a lot of quease."

Sam tried to keep a brave face on him, for Gilly's sake if little else. She had never seen the sea before. When they were struggling through the snows after fleeing Craster's Keep, they had come on several lakes, and even those had been a wonder to her. As *Blackbird* slipped away from shore the girl began to tremble, and big salt tears rolled down her cheeks. "Gods be good," Sam heard her whisper. Eastwatch vanished first, and the Wall grew smaller and smaller in the distance, until it finally disappeared. The wind was coming up by then. The sails were the faded grey of a black cloak that had been washed too often, and Gilly's face was white with fear. "This is a good ship," Sam tried to tell her. "You don't have to be afraid." But she only looked at him, held her baby tighter, and fled below.

Sam soon found himself clutching tightly to the gunwale and watching the sweep of the oars. The way they all moved together was somehow beautiful to behold, and better than looking at the water.

Looking at the water only made him think of drowning. When he was small his lord father had tried to teach him how to swim by throwing him into the pond beneath Horn Hill. The water had gotten in his nose and in his mouth and in his lungs, and he coughed and wheezed for hours after Ser Hyle pulled him out. After that he never dared go in any deeper than his waist.

The Bay of Seals was a *lot* deeper than his waist, and not so friendly as that little fishpond below his father's castle. Its waters were grey and green and choppy, and the wooded shore they followed was a snarl of rocks and whirlpools. Even if he could kick and crawl that far somehow, the waves were like to smash him up against some stone and break his head to pieces.

"Looking for mermaids, Slayer?" asked Dareon when he saw Sam staring off across the bay. Fair-haired and hazel-eyed, the handsome young singer out of Eastwatch looked more like some dark prince than a black brother.

"No." Sam did not know what he was looking for, or what he was doing on this boat. *Going to the Citadel to forge a chain and be a maester, to be of better service to the Watch,* he told himself, but the thought just made him weary. He did not want to be a maester, with a heavy chain wrapped around his neck, cold against his skin. He did not want to leave his brothers, the only friends he'd ever had. And he certainly did not want to face the father who had sent him to the Wall to die.

It was different for the others. For them, the voyage would have a happy ending. Gilly would be safe at Horn Hill, with all the width of Westeros between her and the horrors she had known in the haunted forest. As a serving maid in his father's castle, she would be warm and well fed, a small part of a great world she could never have dreamed of as Craster's wife. She would watch her son grow up big and strong, and become a huntsman or a stablehand or a smith. If the boy showed any aptitude for arms, some knight might even take him as a squire.

Maester Aemon was going to a better place as well. It was pleasant to think of him spending whatever time remained him bathed by the warm breezes of Oldtown, conversing with his fellow maesters and sharing his wisdom with acolytes and novices. He had earned his rest, a hundred times over.

Even Dareon would be happier. He had always claimed to be innocent of the rape that sent him to the Wall, insisting that he belonged at some lord's court, singing for his supper. Now he would have that chance. Jon had named him a recruiter, to take the place of a man named Yoren, who had vanished and was presumed dead. His task would be to travel the Seven Kingdoms, singing of the valor of the Night's Watch, and from time to time returning to the Wall with new recruits.

The voyage would be long and rough, no one could deny that, but for the others at least there would be a happy end. That was Sam's solace. *I am going for them,* he told himself, *for the Night's Watch, and for the happy ending.* The longer he looked at the sea, though, the colder and deeper it appeared.

But *not* looking at the water was even worse, Sam realized in the cramped cabin beneath the sterncastle that the passengers were sharing. He tried to take his mind off the roiling in his stomach by talking with Gilly as she nursed her son. "This ship will take us as far as Braavos," he said. "We'll find another ship to carry us to Oldtown. I read a book about Braavos when I was small. The whole city is built in a lagoon on a hundred little islands, and they have a titan there, a stone man hundreds of feet high. They have boats instead of horses, and their mummers play out written stories instead of just making up the usual stupid farces. The food is very good too, especially the fish. They have all kinds of clams and eels and oysters, fresh from their lagoon. We ought to have a few days between ships. If we do, we can go and see a mummer show, and have some oysters."

He thought that would excite her. He could not have been more wrong. Gilly peered at him with flat, dull eyes, looking through some strands of unwashed hair. "If you want, m'lord."

"What do *you* want?" Sam asked her.

"Nothing." She turned away from him and moved her son from one breast to the other.

The motion of the boat was stirring up the eggs and bacon and fried bread that Sam had eaten before the ship set out. All at once he could not stand the cabin one more instant. He pushed himself back to his feet and clambered up the ladder to give his breakfast to the sea. The sickness came on Sam so strongly that he did not stop to gauge which way the wind was blowing, so he retched from the wrong rail and ended up spattering himself. Even so, he felt much better afterward . . . though not for long.

The ship was *Blackbird*, the largest of the Watch's galleys. *Storm Crow* and *Talon* were faster, Cotter Pyke told Maester Aemon back at Eastwatch-by-the-Sea, but they were fighting ships, lean, swift birds of prey where the rowers sat on open decks. *Blackbird* was a better choice for the rough waters of the narrow sea beyond Skagos. "There have been storms," Pyke warned them. "Winter storms are worse, but autumn's are more frequent."

The first ten days were calm enough, as *Blackbird* crept across the Bay of Seals, never out of sight of land. It was cold when the wind was blowing, but there was something bracing about the salt smell in the air. Sam could hardly eat, and when he did force something down it did not stay down for long, but aside from that he did not do too badly. He tried to bolster Gilly's courage and give her what cheer he could, but that proved hard. She would not come up on deck, no matter what he said, and seemed to prefer to huddle in the dark with her son. The babe liked the ship no more than his mother did, it seemed. When he was not squalling, he was retching up his mother's milk. His bowels were loose and always moving, staining the furs that Gilly wrapped him in to keep him warm and filling the air with a brown stench. No matter how many tallow candles Sam lit, the smell of shit persisted.

It was more pleasant out in the open air, especially when Dareon was singing. The singer was known to *Blackbird*'s oarsmen, and would play for them as they rowed. He knew all their favorite songs: sad ones like "The Day They Hanged Black Robin," "The Mermaid's Lament," and "Autumn of My Day," rousing ones like "Iron Lances" and "Seven Swords for Seven Sons," bawdy ones like "Milady's Supper," "Her Little Flower," and "Meggett Was a Merry Maid, a Merry Maid Was She." When he sang "The Bear and the Maiden Fair," all the oarsmen joined in, and *Blackbird* seemed to fly across the water. Dareon had not been much of a swordsman, Sam knew from their days training under Alliser Thorne, but he had a beautiful voice. "Honey poured over thunder," Maester Aemon had once called it. He played woodharp and fiddle too, and even wrote his own songs . . . though Sam did not think them very good. Still, it was good to sit and listen, though the chest was so hard and splintery that Sam was almost grateful for his fleshy buttocks. *Fat men take a cushion with them wherever they go,* he thought.

Maester Aemon preferred to spend his days on deck as well, huddled beneath a pile of furs and gazing out across the water. "What is he looking at?" Dareon wondered one day. "For him it's as dark up here as it is down in the cabin."

The old man heard him. Though Aemon's eyes had dimmed and gone dark, there was nothing wrong with his ears. "I was not born blind," he reminded them. "When last I passed this way, I saw every rock and tree and whitecap, and watched the grey gulls flying in our wake. I was five-and-thirty and had been a maester of the chain for sixteen years. Egg wanted me to help him rule, but I knew my place was here. He sent me north aboard the *Golden Dragon,* and insisted that his friend Ser Duncan see me safe to Eastwatch. No recruit had arrived at the Wall with so much pomp since Nymeria sent the Watch six kings in golden fetters. Egg emptied out the dungeons too, so I would not need to say my vows alone. My honor guard, he called them. One was no less a man than Brynden Rivers. Later, he was chosen lord commander."

"Bloodraven?" said Dareon. "I know a song about him. 'A Thousand Eyes, and One,' it's called. But I thought he lived a hundred years ago."

"We all did. Once I was as young as you." That seemed to make him sad. He coughed, and closed his eyes, and went to sleep, swaying in his furs whenever some wave rocked the ship.

Beneath grey skies they sailed, east and south and east again, as the Bay of Seals widened about them. The captain, a grizzled brother with a belly like a keg of ale, wore blacks so stained and faded that the crew called him Old Tattersalt. He seldom said a word. His mate made up for him, blistering the salt air with curses whenever the wind died or the oarsmen seemed to flag. They ate oaten porridge in the mornings, pease porridge in the afternoons, and salt beef, salt cod, and salt mutton at night, and washed it down with ale. Dareon sang, Sam retched, Gilly cried and nursed her babe, Maester Aemon slept and shivered, and the winds grew colder and more blustery with every passing day.

Even so, it was a better voyage than the last one Sam had taken. He had been no more than ten when he set sail on Lord Redwyne's galleas, the *Arbor Queen*. Five times as large as *Blackbird* and magnificent to behold, she had three great burgundy sails and banks of oars that flashed gold and white in the sunlight. The way they rose and fell as the ship departed Oldtown had made Sam hold his breath . . . but that was the last good memory he had of the Redwyne Straits. Then as now the sea had made him sick, to his lord father's disgust.

And when they reached the Arbor, things had gone from bad to worse. Lord Redwyne's twin sons had despised Sam on first sight. Every morn they found some fresh way to shame him in the practice yard. On the third day Horas Redwyne made him squeal like a pig when he begged for quarter. On the fifth his brother Hobber clad a kitchen girl in his own armor and let her beat Sam with a wooden sword until he began to cry. When she revealed herself, all the squires and pages and stableboys howled with laughter.

"The boy needs a bit of seasoning, that's all," his father had told Lord Redwyne that night, but Redwyne's fool rattled his rattle and replied, "Aye, a pinch of pepper, a few nice cloves, and an apple in his mouth." Thereafter, Lord Randyll forbade Sam to eat apples so long as they remained beneath Paxter Redwyne's roof. He had been seasick on their voyage home as well, but so relieved to be going that he almost welcomed the taste of vomit at the back of his throat. It was not until they were back at Horn Hill that his mother told Sam that his father had never meant for him to return. "Horas was to come with us in your place, whilst you remained on the Arbor as Lord Paxter's page and cupbearer. If you had pleased him, you would have been betrothed to his daughter." Sam could still recall the soft touch of his mother's hand as she washed the tears off his face with a bit of lace, dampened with her spit. "My poor Sam," she murmured. "My poor poor Sam."

It will be good to see her again, he thought, as he clung to *Blackbird*'s rail and watched waves breaking on the stony shore. *If she saw me in my blacks, it might even make her proud.* "I am a man now, Mother," *I could tell her, "a steward, and a man of the Night's Watch. My brothers call me Sam the Slayer sometimes."* He would see his brother Dickon too, and his sisters. *"See,"* I could tell them, *"see, I was good for something after all."*

If he went to Horn Hill, though, his father might be there.

The thought made his belly heave again. Sam bent over the gunwale and retched, but not into the wind. He had gone to the right rail this time. He was getting good at retching.

Or so he thought, until *Blackbird* left the land behind and struck east across the bay for the shores of Skagos.

The island sat at the mouth of the Bay of Seals, massive and mountainous, a stark and forbidding land peopled by savages. They lived in caves and grim mountain fastnesses, Sam had read, and rode great shaggy unicorns to war. *Skagos* meant "stone" in the Old Tongue. The Skagosi named themselves the stoneborn, but their fellow northmen called them Skaggs and liked them little. Only a hundred years ago Skagos had risen in rebellion. Their revolt had taken years to quell and claimed the life of the Lord of Winterfell and hundreds of his sworn swords. Some songs said the Skaggs were cannibals; supposedly their warriors ate the hearts and livers of the men they slew. In ancient days, the Skagosi had sailed to the nearby isle of Skane, seized its women, slaughtered its men, and ate them on a pebbled beach in a feast that lasted for a fortnight. Skane remained unpeopled to this day.

Dareon knew the songs as well. When the bleak grey peaks of Skagos rose up from the sea, he joined Sam at *Blackbird's* prow, and said, "If the gods are good, we may catch a glimpse of a unicorn."

"If the captain is good, we won't come that close. The currents are treacherous around Skagos, and there are rocks that can crack a ship's hull like an egg. But don't you mention that to Gilly. She's scared enough."

"Her and that squalling whelp of hers. I don't know which of them is noisier. The only time he ever stops crying is when she shoves a nipple in his mouth, and then *she* starts to sob."

Sam had noticed that as well. "Maybe the babe is hurting her," he said, feebly. "If his teeth are coming in . . ."

Dareon plucked at his lute with one finger, sending up a derisive note. "I'd heard that wildlings were braver than that."

"She *is* brave," Sam insisted, though even he had to admit that he had never seen Gilly in such a wretched state. Though she hid her face more oft than not and kept the cabin dark, he could see that her eyes were always red, her cheeks wet with tears. When he asked her what was wrong, though, she only shook her head, leaving him to find answers of his own. "The sea scares her, that's all," he told Dareon. "Before she came to the Wall, all she knew was Craster's Keep and the woods around it. I don't know that she went more than half a league from the place that she was born. She knows streams and rivers, but she had never seen a lake until we came on one, and the sea . . . the sea is a scary thing."

"We've never been out of sight of land."

"We will be." Sam did not relish that part himself.

"Surely a little water does not frighten the Slayer."

"No," Sam lied, "not me. But Gilly . . . maybe if you played some lullabies for them, it would help the babe to sleep."

Dareon's mouth twisted in disgust. "Only if she shoves a plug up his arse. I cannot abide the smell."

The next day the rains began, and the seas grew rougher. "We had best go below, where it's dry," Sam said to Aemon, but the old maester only smiled, and said, "The rain feels good against my face, Sam. It feels like tears. Let me stay a while longer, I pray you. It has been a long time since last I wept."

If Maester Aemon meant to stay on deck, old and frail as he was, Sam had no choice but to do the same. He stayed beside the old man for nigh unto an hour, huddled in his cloak as a soft, steady rain soaked him to his skin. Aemon hardly seemed to feel it. He sighed and closed his eyes, and Sam moved closer to him, to shield him from the worst of the wind. *He will ask me to help him to the cabin soon,* he told himself. *He must.* But he never did, and finally thunder began to rumble in the distance, off to the east. "We *have* to get below," Sam said, shivering. Maester Aemon did not reply. It was only then that Sam realized the old man had gone to sleep. "Maester," he said, shaking him gently by one shoulder. "Maester Aemon, wake up."

Aemon's blind white eyes came open. "Egg?" he said, as the rain streamed down his cheeks. "Egg, I dreamed that I was old."

Sam did not know what to do. He knelt and scooped the old man up and carried him below. No one had ever called him strong, and the rain had soaked through Maester Aemon's blacks and made him twice as heavy, but even so, he weighed no more than a child.

When he shoved into the cabin with Aemon in his arms, he found that Gilly had let all the candles gutter out. The babe was asleep and she was curled up in a corner, sobbing softly in the folds of the big black cloak that Sam had given her. "Help me," he said urgently. "Help me dry him off and get him warm."

She rose at once, and together they got the old maester out of his wet clothes and buried him beneath a pile of furs. His skin was damp and cold, though, clammy to the touch. "You get in with him," Sam told Gilly. "Hold him. Warm him with your body. We have to warm him up." She did that too, never saying a word, all the while still sniffling. "Where's Dareon?" asked Sam. "We'd all be warmer if we were together. He needs to be here too." He was headed back up top to find the singer when the deck rose up beneath him, then fell away beneath his feet. Gilly wailed, Sam slammed down hard and lost his legs, and the babe woke screaming.

The next roll of the ship came as he was struggling back to his feet. It threw Gilly into his arms, and the wildling girl clung to him so fiercely that Sam could hardly breathe. "Don't you be frightened," he told her. "This is just an adventure. One day you'll tell your son this tale." That only made her dig her nails into his arm. She shuddered, her whole body shaking with the violence of her sobs. *Whatever I say just makes her worse.* He held her tightly, uncomfortably aware of her breasts pressing up against him. As frightened as he was, somehow that was enough to make him stiff. *She'll feel it,* he thought, ashamed, but if she did, she gave no sign, only clung to him the harder.

The days ran together after that. They never saw the sun. The days were grey and the nights black, except when lightning lit the sky above the peaks of Skagos. All of them were starved yet none could eat. The captain broached a cask of firewine to fortify the oarsmen. Sam tried a cup and sighed as hot snakes wriggled down his throat and through his chest. Dareon took a liking to the drink as well, and was seldom sober thereafter.

The sails went up, the sails came down, and one ripped free of the

mast and flew away like a great grey bird. As *Blackbird* rounded
the south coast of Skagos, they spotted the wreckage of a galley on the
rocks. Some of her crew had washed up on the shore, and the rooks
and crabs had gathered to pay them homage. "Too bloody close,"
grumbled Old Tattersalt when he saw. "One good blow, and we'll be
breaking up aside them." Exhausted as they were, his rowers bent to
their oars again, and the ship clawed south toward the narrow sea,
till Skagos dwindled to no more than a few dark shapes in the sky
that might have been thunderheads, or the tops of tall black mountains, or both. After that, they had eight days and seven nights of
clear, smooth sailing.

Then came more storms, worse than before.

Was it three storms, or only one, broken up by lulls? Sam never
knew, though he tried desperately to care. "*What does it matter?*"
Dareon screamed at him once, when all of them were huddled in the
cabin. *It doesn't,* Sam wanted to tell him, *but so long as I'm thinking
about that I'm not thinking about drowning or being sick or Maester
Aemon's shivering.* "It doesn't," he managed to squeak, but the thunder
drowned out all the rest of it, and the deck lurched and knocked him
sideways. Gilly was sobbing. The babe was shrieking. And up top he
could hear Old Tattersalt bellowing at his crew, the ragged captain
who never spoke at all.

I hate the sea, Sam thought, *I hate the sea, I hate the sea, I hate
the sea.* The next lightning flash was so bright it lit the cabin through
the seams in the planking overhead. *This is a good sound ship, a
good sound ship, a good ship,* he told himself. *It will not sink. I am
not afraid.*

During one of the lulls between the gales, as Sam clung white-
knuckled to the rail wanting desperately to retch, he heard some of
the crew muttering that this was what came of bringing a woman
aboard ship, and a wildling woman at that. "Fucked her own father,"
Sam heard one man say, as the wind was rising once again. "Worse
than whoring, that. Worse than *anything.* We'll all drown unless we
get rid of her, and that abomination that she whelped."

Sam dared not confront them. They were older men, hard and
sinewy, their arms and shoulders thickened by years at the oars. But

he made certain that his knife was sharp, and whenever Gilly left the cabin to make water, he went with her.

Even Dareon had no good to say about the wildling girl. Once, at Sam's urging, the singer played a lullaby to soothe the babe, but partway through the first verse Gilly began to sob inconsolably. "Seven bloody hells," Dareon snapped, "can't you even stop weeping long enough to hear a *song*?"

"Just play," Sam pleaded, "just sing the song for her."

"She doesn't need a song," said Dareon. "She needs a good spanking, or maybe a hard fuck. Get out of my way, Slayer." He shoved Sam aside and went from the cabin to find some solace in a cup of firewine and the rough brotherhood of the oars.

Sam was at his wit's end by then. He had almost gotten used to the smells, but between the storms and Gilly's sobbing he had not slept for days. "Isn't there something you can give her?" he asked Maester Aemon very softly, when he saw that the old man was awake. "Some herb or potion, so she won't be so afraid?"

"It is not fear you hear," the old man told him. "That is the sound of grief, and there is no potion for that. Let her tears run their course, Sam. You cannot stem the flow."

Sam had not understood. "She's going to a safe place. A *warm* place. Why should she be grieving?"

"Sam," the old man whispered, "you have two good eyes, and yet you do not see. She is a mother grieving for her child."

"He's greensick, that's all. We're all greensick. Once we make port in Braavos . . ."

". . . the babe will still be Dalla's son, and not the child of her body."

It took Sam a moment to grasp what Aemon was suggesting. "That couldn't . . . she wouldn't . . . of course he's hers. Gilly would never have left the Wall without her *son*. She loves him."

"She nursed them both and loved them both," said Aemon, "but not alike. No mother loves all her children the same, not even the Mother Above. Gilly did not leave the child willingly, I am certain. What threats the Lord Commander made, what promises, I can only guess . . . but threats and promises there surely were."

"No. No, that's wrong. Jon would never . . ."

"Jon would never. Lord Snow did. Sometimes there is no happy choice, Sam, only one less grievous than the others."

No happy choice. Sam thought of all the trials that he and Gilly suffered, Craster's Keep and the death of the Old Bear, snow and ice and freezing winds, days and days and days of walking, the wights at Whitetree, Coldhands and the tree of ravens, the Wall, the Wall, the Wall, the Black Gate beneath the earth. What had it all been for? *No happy choices and no happy endings.*

He wanted to scream. He wanted to howl and sob and shake and curl up in a little ball and whimper. *He switched the babes,* he told himself. *He switched the babes to protect the little prince, to keep him away from Lady Melisandre's fires, away from her red god. If she burns Gilly's boy, who will care? No one but Gilly. He was only Craster's whelp, an abomination born of incest, not the son of the King-beyond-the-Wall. He's no good for a hostage, no good for a sacrifice, no good for anything, he doesn't even have a name.*

Wordless, Sam staggered up onto the deck to retch, but there was nothing in his belly to bring up. Night had come upon them, a strange still night such as they had not seen for many days. The sea was black as glass. At the oars, the rowers rested. One or two were sleeping where they sat. The wind was in the sails, and to the north Sam could even see a scattering of stars, and the red wanderer the free folk called the Thief. *That ought to be my star,* Sam thought miserably. *I helped to make Jon Lord Commander, and I brought him Gilly and the babe. There are no happy endings.*

"Slayer." Dareon appeared beside him, oblivious to Sam's pain. "A sweet night, for once. Look, the stars are coming out. We might even get a bit of moon. Might be the worst is done."

"No." Sam wiped his nose, and pointed south with a fat finger, toward the gathering darkness. "There," he said. No sooner had he spoken than lightning flashed, sudden and silent and blinding bright. The distant clouds glowed for half a heartbeat, mountains heaped on mountains, purple and red and yellow, taller than the world. "The worst isn't done. The worst is just beginning, and there are no happy endings."

"Gods be good," said Dareon, laughing. "Slayer, you are *such* a craven."

JAIME

Lord Tywin Lannister had entered the city on a stallion, his enameled crimson armor polished and gleaming, bright with gems and goldwork. He left it in a tall wagon draped with crimson banners, with six silent sisters riding attendance on his bones.

The funeral procession departed King's Landing through the Gate of the Gods, wider and more splendid than the Lion Gate. The choice felt wrong to Jaime. His father had been a lion, that no one could deny, but even Lord Tywin never claimed to be a god.

An honor guard of fifty knights surrounded Lord Tywin's wagon, crimson pennons fluttering from their lances. The lords of the west followed close behind them. The winds snapped at their banners, making their charges dance and flutter. As he trotted up the column, Jaime passed boars, badgers, and beetles, a green arrow and a red ox, crossed halberds, crossed spears, a treecat, a strawberry, a maunch, four sunbursts counterchanged.

Lord Brax was wearing a pale grey doublet slashed with cloth-of-silver, an amethyst unicorn pinned above his heart. Lord Jast was armored in black steel, three gold lion's heads inlaid on his breastplate. The rumors of his death had not been far wrong, to look at him; wounds and imprisonment had left him a shadow of the man he'd been. Lord Banefort had weathered battle better, and looked ready to return to war at once. Plumm wore purple, Prester ermine, Moreland russet and green, but each had donned a cloak of crimson silk, in honor of the man they were escorting home.

Behind the lords came a hundred crossbowmen and three hundred men-at-arms, and crimson flowed from their shoulders as well. In his white cloak and white scale armor, Jaime felt out of place amongst that river of red.

Nor did his uncle make him more at ease. "Lord Commander," Ser Kevan said, when Jaime trotted up beside him at the head of the column. "Does Her Grace have some last command for me?"

"I am not here for Cersei." A drum began to beat behind them, slow, measured, funereal. *Dead,* it seemed to say, *dead, dead.* "I came to make my farewells. He was my father."

"And hers."

"I am not Cersei. I have a beard, and she has breasts. If you are still confused, nuncle, count our hands. Cersei has two."

"Both of you have a taste for mockery," his uncle said. "Spare me your japes, ser, I have no taste for them."

"As you will." *This is not going as well as I might have hoped.* "Cersei would have wanted to see you off, but she has many pressing duties."

Ser Kevan snorted. "So do we all. How fares your king?" His tone made the question a reproach.

"Well enough," Jaime said defensively. "Balon Swann is with him during the mornings. A good and valiant knight."

"Once that went without saying when men spoke of those who wore the white cloak."

No man can choose his brothers, Jaime thought. *Give me leave to pick my own men, and the Kingsguard will be great again.* Put that baldly, though, it sounded feeble; an empty boast from a man the realm called Kingslayer. *A man with shit for honor.* Jaime let it go. He had not come to argue with his uncle. "Ser," he said, "you need to make your peace with Cersei."

"Are we at war? No one told me."

Jaime ignored that. "Strife between Lannister and Lannister can only help the enemies of our House."

"If there is strife, it will not be my doing. Cersei wants to rule. Well and good. The realm is hers. All I ask is to be left in peace. My place is at Darry with my son. The castle must needs be restored, the lands planted and protected." He gave a bark of bitter laughter. "And your sister has left me little else to occupy my time. I had as well see Lancel wed. His bride has grown impatient waiting for us to make our way to Darry."

His widow from the Twins. His cousin Lancel was riding ten yards behind them. With his hollow eyes and dry white hair, he looked older than Lord Jast. Jaime could feel his phantom fingers itching at the sight of him. . . . *fucking Lancel and Osmund Kettleblack and Moon Boy, for all I know* . . . He had tried to speak with Lancel more times than he could count, but never found him alone. If his father was not with him, some septon was. *He may be Kevan's son, but he has milk in his veins. Tyrion was lying to me. His words were meant to wound.*

Jaime put his cousin from his thoughts and turned back to his uncle. "Will you remain at Darry after the wedding?"

"For a while, mayhaps. Sandor Clegane is raiding along the Trident, it would seem. Your sister wants his head. It may be that he has joined Dondarrion."

Jaime had heard about Saltpans. By now half the realm had heard. The raid had been exceptionally savage. Women raped and mutilated, children butchered in their mothers' arms, half the town put to the torch. "Randyll Tarly is at Maidenpool. Let him deal with the outlaws. I would sooner have you go to Riverrun."

"Ser Daven has command there. The Warden of the West. He has no need of me. Lancel does."

"As you say, uncle." Jaime's head was pounding to the same beat as the drum. *Dead, dead, dead.* "You would do well to keep your knights around you."

His uncle gave him a cool stare. "Is that a threat, ser?"

A threat? The suggestion took him aback. "A caution. I only meant . . . Sandor is dangerous."

"I was hanging outlaws and robber knights when you were still shitting in your swaddling clothes. I am not like to go off and face Clegane and Dondarrion by myself, if that is what you fear, ser. Not every Lannister is a fool for glory."

Why, nuncle, I believe you are talking about me. "Addam Marbrand could deal with these outlaws just as well as you. So could Brax, Banefort, Plumm, any of these others. But none would make a good King's Hand."

"Your sister knows my terms. They have not changed. Tell her that, the next time you are in her bedchamber." Ser Kevan put his heels into his courser and galloped ahead, putting an abrupt end to their conversation.

Jaime let him go, his missing sword hand twitching. He had hoped against hope that Cersei had somehow misunderstood, but plainly that was wrong. *He knows about the two of us. About Tommen and Myrcella. And Cersei knows he knows.* Ser Kevan was a Lannister of Casterly Rock. He could not believe that she would ever do him harm, but . . . *I was wrong about Tyrion, why not about Cersei?* When sons were killing fathers, what was there to stop a niece from ordering an uncle slain? *An inconvenient uncle, who knows too much.* Though perhaps Cersei was hoping that the Hound might do her work for her. If Sandor Clegane cut down Ser Kevan, she would not need to bloody her own hands. *And he will, if they should meet.* Kevan Lannister had once been a stout man with a sword, but he was no longer young, and the Hound . . .

The column had caught up to him. As his cousin rode past, flanked by his two septons, Jaime called out to him. "Lancel. Coz. I wanted to congratulate you upon your marriage. I only regret that my duties do not permit me to attend."

"His Grace must be protected."

"And will be. Still, I hate to miss your bedding. It is your first marriage and her second, I understand. I'm sure my lady will be pleased to show you what goes where."

The bawdy remark drew a laugh from several nearby lords and a disapproving look from Lancel's septons. His cousin squirmed uncomfortably in the saddle. "I know enough to do my duty as a husband, ser."

"That's just the thing a bride wants on her wedding night," said Jaime. "A husband who knows how to do his *duty.*"

A flush crept up Lancel's cheeks. "I pray for you, cousin. And for

Her Grace the queen. May the Crone lead her to her wisdom and the Warrior defend her."

"Why would Cersei need the Warrior? She has me." Jaime turned his horse about, his white cloak snapping in the wind. *The Imp was lying. Cersei would sooner have Robert's corpse between her legs than a pious fool like Lancel. Tyrion, you evil bastard, you should have lied about someone more likely.* He galloped past his lord father's funeral wayn toward the city in the distance.

The streets of King's Landing seemed almost deserted as Jaime Lannister made his way back to the Red Keep atop Aegon's High Hill. The soldiers who had crowded the city's gambling dens and pot shops were largely gone now. Garlan the Gallant had taken half the Tyrell strength back to Highgarden, and his lady mother and grandmother had gone with him. The other half had marched south with Mace Tyrell and Mathis Rowan to invest Storm's End.

As for the Lannister host, two thousand seasoned veterans remained encamped outside the city walls, awaiting the arrival of Paxter Redwyne's fleet to carry them across Blackwater Bay to Dragonstone. Lord Stannis appeared to have left only a small garrison behind him when he sailed north, so two thousand men would be more than sufficient, Cersei had judged.

The rest of the westermen had gone back to their wives and children, to rebuild their homes, plant their fields, and bring in one last harvest. Cersei had taken Tommen round their camps before they marched, to let them cheer their little king. She had never looked more beautiful than she did that day, with a smile on her lips and the autumn sunlight shining on her golden hair. Whatever else one might say about his sister, she did know how to make men love her when she cared enough to try.

As Jaime trotted through the castle gates, he came upon two dozen knights riding at a quintain in the outer yard. *Something else I can no longer do,* he thought. A lance was heavier and more cumbersome than a sword, and swords were proving trial enough. He supposed he might try holding the lance with his left hand, but that would mean shifting his shield to his right arm. In a tilt, a man's foe was always to the left. A shield on his right arm would prove about as useful as nipples on his breastplate. *No, my jousting days are done,* he thought as he dismounted . . . but all the same, he stopped to watch a while.

Ser Tallad the Tall lost his mount when the sandbag came around and thumped him in the head. Strongboar struck the shield so hard he cracked it. Kennos of Kayce finished the destruction. A new shield was hung for Ser Dermot of the Rainwood. Lambert Turnberry only struck a glancing blow, but Beardless Jon Bettley, Humfrey Swyft, and Alyn Stackspear all scored solid hits, and Red Ronnet Connington broke his lance clean. Then the Knight of Flowers mounted up and put the others all to shame.

Jousting was three-quarters horsemanship, Jaime had always believed. Ser Loras rode superbly, and handled a lance as if he'd been born holding one . . . which no doubt accounted for his mother's pinched expression. *He puts the point just where he means to put it, and seems to have the balance of a cat. Perhaps it was not such a fluke that he unhorsed me.* It was a shame that he would never have the chance to try the boy again. He left the whole men to their sport.

Cersei was in her solar in Maegor's Holdfast, with Tommen and Lord Merryweather's dark-haired Myrish wife. The three of them were laughing at Grand Maester Pycelle. "Did I miss some clever jape?" Jaime said, as he shoved through the door.

"Oh, look," purred Lady Merryweather, "your brave brother has returned, Your Grace."

"Most of him." The queen was in her cups, Jaime realized. Of late, Cersei always seemed to have a flagon of wine to hand, she who had once scorned Robert Baratheon for his drinking. He misliked that, but these days he seemed to mislike everything his sister did. "Grand Maester," she said, "share the tidings with the Lord Commander, if you would."

Pycelle looked desperately uncomfortable. "There has been a bird," he said. "From Stokeworth. Lady Tanda sends word that her daughter Lollys has been delivered of a strong, healthy son."

"And you will never guess what they have named the little bastard, brother."

"They wanted to name him Tywin, I recall."

"Yes, but I forbade it. I told Falyse that I would not have our father's noble name bestowed upon the ill-gotten spawn of some pig boy and a feeble-witted sow."

"Lady Stokeworth insists the child's name was not her doing," Grand Maester Pycelle put in. Perspiration dotted his wrinkled forehead. "Lollys's husband made the choice, she writes. This man Bronn, he . . . it would seem that he . . ."

"Tyrion," ventured Jaime. "He named the child *Tyrion*."

The old man gave a tremulous nod, mopping at his brow with the sleeve of his robe.

Jaime had to laugh. "There you are, sweet sister. You have been looking everywhere for Tyrion, and all the time he's been hiding in Lollys's womb."

"Droll. You and Bronn are both so droll. No doubt the bastard is sucking on one of Lollys Lackwit's dugs even as we speak, whilst this sellsword looks on, smirking at his little insolence."

"Perhaps this child bears some resemblance to your brother," suggested Lady Merryweather. "He might have been born deformed, or without a nose." She laughed a throaty laugh.

"We shall have to send the darling boy a gift," the queen declared. "Won't we, Tommen?"

"We could send him a kitten."

"A lion cub," said Lady Merryweather. *To rip his little throat out,* her smile suggested.

"I had a different sort of gift in mind," said Cersei.

A new stepfather, most like. Jaime knew the look in his sister's eyes. He had seen it before, most recently on the night of Tommen's wedding, when she burned the Tower of the Hand. The green light of the wildfire had bathed the face of the watchers, so they looked like nothing so much as rotting corpses, a pack of gleeful ghouls, but some of the corpses were prettier than others. Even in the baleful glow, Cersei had been beautiful to look upon. She'd stood with one hand on her breast, her lips parted, her green eyes shining. *She is crying,* Jaime had realized, but whether it was from grief or ecstasy he could not have said.

The sight had filled him with disquiet, reminding him of Aerys

Targaryen and the way a burning would arouse him. A king has no secrets from his Kingsguard. Relations between Aerys and his queen had been strained during the last years of his reign. They slept apart and did their best to avoid each other during the waking hours. But whenever Aerys gave a man to the flames, Queen Rhaella would have a visitor in the night. The day he burned his mace-and-dagger Hand, Jaime and Jon Darry had stood at guard outside her bedchamber whilst the king took his pleasure. "You're hurting me," they had heard Rhaella cry through the oaken door. "You're *hurting* me." In some queer way, that had been worse than Lord Chelsted's screaming. "We are sworn to protect her as well," Jaime had finally been driven to say. "We are," Darry allowed, "but not from him."

Jaime had only seen Rhaella once after that, the morning of the day she left for Dragonstone. The queen had been cloaked and hooded as she climbed inside the royal wheelhouse that would take her down Aegon's High Hill to the waiting ship, but he heard her maids whispering after she was gone. They said the queen looked as if some beast had savaged her, clawing at her thighs and chewing on her breasts. *A crowned beast,* Jaime knew.

By the end, the Mad King had become so fearful that he would allow no blade in his presence, save for the swords his Kingsguard wore. His beard was matted and unwashed, his hair a silver-gold tangle that reached his waist, his fingernails cracked yellow claws nine inches long. Yet still the blades tormented him, the ones he could never escape, the blades of the Iron Throne. His arms and legs were always covered with scabs and half-healed cuts.

Let him be king over charred bones and cooked meat, Jaime remembered, studying his sister's smile. *Let him be the king of ashes.* "Your Grace," he said, "might we have a private word?"

"As you wish. Tommen, it is past time you had your lesson for the day. Go with the Grand Maester."

"Yes, Mother. We are learning about Baelor the Blessed."

Lady Merryweather took her leave as well, kissing the queen on both cheeks. "Shall I return for supper, Your Grace?"

"I shall be very cross with you if you do not."

Jaime could not help but note the way the Myrish woman moved her hips as she walked. *Every step is a seduction.* When the door closed behind her, he cleared his throat and said, "First these Kettleblacks, then Qyburn, now her. It's a queer menagerie you are keeping these days, sweet sister."

"I am growing very fond of Lady Taena. She amuses me."

"She is one of Margaery Tyrell's companions," Jaime reminded her. "She's informing on you to the little queen."

"Of course she is." Cersei went to the sideboard to fill her cup anew. "Margaery was thrilled when I asked her leave to take Taena on as my companion. You should have heard her. '*She will be a sister to you, as she's been to me. Of course you must have her! I have my cousins and my other ladies.*' Our little queen does not want me to be lonely."

"If you know she is a spy, why take her on?"

"Margaery is not half so clever as she thinks. She has no notion what a sweet serpent she has in that Myrish slut. I use Taena to feed the little queen what I want her to know. Some of it is even true." Cersei's eyes were bright with mischief. "And Taena tells me everything Maid Margaery is doing."

"Does she? How much do you know about this woman?"

"I know she is a mother, with a young son that she wants to rise high in this world. She will do whatever is required to see that he does. Mothers are all the same. Lady Merryweather may be a serpent, but she is far from stupid. She knows I can do more for her than Margaery, so she makes herself useful to me. You would be surprised at all the interesting things she's told me."

"What sorts of things?"

Cersei sat beneath the window. "Did you know that the Queen of Thorns keeps a chest of coins in her wheelhouse? Old gold from before the Conquest. Should any tradesman be so unwise as to name a price in golden coins, she pays him with hands from Highgarden, each half the weight of one of our dragons. What merchant would dare complain of being cheated by Mace Tyrell's lady mother?" She sipped her wine, and said, "Did you enjoy your little ride?"

"Our uncle remarked upon your absence."

"Our uncle's remarks do not concern me."

"They should. You could make good use of him. If not at Riverrun or the Rock, then in the north against Lord Stannis. Father always relied upon Kevan when—"

"Roose Bolton is our Warden of the North. He will deal with Stannis."

"Lord Bolton is trapped below the Neck, cut off from the north by the ironmen at Moat Cailin."

"Not for long. Bolton's bastard son will soon remove that little obstacle. Lord Bolton will have two thousand Freys to augment his own strength, under Lord Walder's sons Hosteen and Aenys. That should be more than enough to deal with Stannis and a few thousand broken men."

"Ser Kevan—"

"—will have his hands full at Darry, teaching Lancel how to wipe his arse. Father's death has unmanned him. He is an old done man. Daven and Damion will serve us better."

"They'll suffice." Jaime had no quarrel with his cousins. "You still require a Hand, however. If not our uncle, who?"

His sister laughed. "Not you. Have no fear on that count. Perhaps Taena's husband. His grandfather was Hand under Aerys."

The horn-of-plenty Hand. Jaime remembered Owen Merryweather well enough; an amiable man, but ineffectual. "As I recall, he did so well that Aerys exiled him and seized his lands."

"Robert gave them back. Some, at least. Taena would be pleased if Orton could recover the rest."

"Is this about pleasing some Myrish whore? Here I thought it was about governing the realm."

"*I* govern the realm."

Seven save us all, you do. His sister liked to think of herself as Lord Tywin with teats, but she was wrong. Their father had been as relentless and implacable as a glacier, where Cersei was all wildfire, especially when thwarted. She had been giddy as a maiden when she learned that Stannis had abandoned Dragonstone, certain that he had finally given up the fight and sailed away to exile. When word came down from the north that he had turned up again at the Wall, her fury had been fearful to behold. *She does not lack for wits, but she has no judgment, and no patience.* "You need a strong Hand to help you."

"A *weak* ruler needs a strong Hand, as Aerys needed Father. A strong ruler requires only a diligent servant to carry out his orders." She swirled her wine. "Lord Hallyne might suit. He would not be the first pyromancer to serve as the King's Hand."

No. I killed the last one. "There is talk that you mean to make Aurane Waters the master of ships."

"Has someone been informing on me?" When he did not answer, Cersei tossed her hair back, and said, "Waters is well suited to the office. He has spent half his life on ships."

"Half his life? He cannot be more than twenty."

"Two-and-twenty, and what of it? Father was not even one-and-twenty when Aerys Targaryen named him Hand. It is past time Tommen had some young men about him in place of all these wrinkled greybeards. Aurane is strong and vigorous."

Strong and vigorous and handsome, Jaime thought. . . . *she's been fucking Lancel and Osmund Kettleblack and Moon Boy, for all I know . . .* "Paxter Redwyne would be a better choice. He commands the largest fleet in Westeros. Aurane Waters could command a skiff, but only if you bought him one."

"You are a child, Jaime. Redwyne is Tyrell's bannerman, and nephew to that hideous grandmother of his. I want none of Lord Tyrell's creatures on my council."

"Tommen's council, you mean."

"You know what I mean."

Too well. "I know that Aurane Waters is a bad idea, and Hallyne is a worse one. As for Qyburn . . . gods be good, Cersei, he rode with *Vargo Hoat.* The Citadel *stripped him of his chain!*"

"The grey sheep. Qyburn has made himself most useful to me. And he is loyal, which is more than I can say of mine own kin."

The crows will feast upon us all if you go on this way, sweet sister. "Cersei, listen to yourself. You are seeing dwarfs in every shadow and making foes of friends. Uncle Kevan is not your enemy. *I* am not your enemy."

Her face twisted in fury. "I begged you for your help. I went down on my knees to you, and *you refused me!*"

"My vows . . ."

". . . did not stop you slaying Aerys. Words are wind. You could have had me, but you chose a cloak instead. Get out."

"Sister . . ."

"*Get out,* I said. I am sick of looking at that ugly stump of yours. *Get out!*" To speed him on his way, she heaved her wine cup at his head. She missed, but Jaime took the hint.

Evenfall found him sitting alone in the common room of White Sword Tower, with a cup of Dornish red and the White Book. He was turning pages with the stump of his sword hand when the Knight of Flowers entered, removed his cloak and swordbelt and hung them on a wall peg next to Jaime's.

"I saw you in the yard today," said Jaime. "You rode well."

"Better than *well,* surely." Ser Loras poured himself a cup of wine, and took a seat across the half-moon table.

"A more modest man might have answered 'My lord is too kind,' or 'I had a good mount.'"

"The horse was adequate, and my lord is as kind as I am modest." Loras waved at the book. "Lord Renly always said that books were for maesters."

"This one is for us. The history of every man who has ever worn a white cloak is written here."

"I have glanced at it. The shields are pretty. I prefer books with more illuminations. Lord Renly owned a few with drawings that would turn a septon blind."

Jaime had to smile. "There's none of that here, ser, but the histories will open your eyes. You would do well to know about the lives of those who went before."

"I do. Prince Aemon the Dragonknight, Ser Ryam Redwyne, the Greatheart, Barristan the Bold . . ."

". . . Gwayne Corbray, Alyn Connington, the Demon of Darry, aye. You will have heard of Lucamore Strong as well."

"Ser Lucamore the Lusty?" Ser Loras seemed amused. "Three wives and thirty children, was it? They cut his cock off. Shall I sing the song for you, my lord?"

"And Ser Terrence Toyne?"

"Bedded the king's mistress and died screaming. The lesson is, men who wear white breeches need to keep them tightly laced."

"Gyles Greycloak? Orivel the Open-Handed?"

"Gyles was a traitor, Orivel a coward. Men who shamed the white cloak. What is my lord suggesting?"

"Little and less. Don't take offense where none was meant, ser. How about Long Tom Costayne?"

Ser Loras shook his head.

"He was a Kingsguard knight for sixty years."

"When was that? I've never—"

"Ser Donnel of Duskendale, then?"

"I may have heard the name, but—"

"Addison Hill? The White Owl, Michael Mertyns? Jeffory Norcross? They called him Neveryield. Red Robert Flowers? What can you tell me of them?"

"Flowers is a bastard name. So is Hill."

"Yet both men rose to command the Kingsguard. Their tales are in the book. Rolland Darklyn is in here too. The youngest man ever to serve in the Kingsguard, until me. He was given his cloak on a battlefield and died within an hour of donning it."

"He can't have been very good."

"Good enough. He died, but his king lived. A lot of brave men have worn the white cloak. Most have been forgotten."

"Most deserve to be forgotten. The heroes will always be remembered. The best."

"The best and the worst." *So one of us is like to live in song.* "And a few who were a bit of both. Like him." He tapped the page he had been reading.

"Who?" Ser Loras craned his head around to see. "Ten black pellets on a scarlet field. I do not know those arms."

"They belonged to Criston Cole, who served the first Viserys and the second Aegon." Jaime closed the White Book. "They called him Kingmaker."

CERSEI

Three *wretched fools with a leather sack,* the queen thought as they sank to their knees before her. The look of them did not encourage her. *I suppose there is always a chance.*

"Your Grace," said Qyburn quietly, "the small council . . ."

". . . will await my pleasure. It may be that we can bring them word of a traitor's death." Off across the city, the bells of Baelor's Sept sang their song of mourning. *No bells will ring for you, Tyrion,* Cersei thought. *I shall dip your head in tar and give your twisted body to the dogs.* "Off your knees," she told the would-be lords. "Show me what you've brought me."

They rose; three ugly men, and ragged. One had a boil on his neck, and none had washed in half a year. The prospect of raising such to lordship amused her. *I could seat them next to Margaery at feasts.* When the chief fool undid the drawstring on the sack and plunged his hand inside, the smell of decay filled her audience chamber like some rank rose. The head he pulled out was grey-green and crawling with maggots. *It smells like Father.* Dorcas gasped, and Jocelyn covered her mouth and retched.

The queen considered her prize, unflinching. "You've killed the wrong dwarf," she said at last, grudging every word.

"We never did," one of the fools dared to say. "This is got to be him, ser. A dwarf, see. He's rotted some, is all."

"He has also grown a new nose," Cersei observed. "A rather bulbous one, I'd say. Tyrion's nose was hacked off in a battle."

The three fools exchanged a look. "No one told us," said the one with head in hand. "This one come walking along as bold as you please, some ugly dwarf, so we thought . . ."

"He *said* he were a sparrow," the one with the boil added, "and *you* said he was lying." That was directed at the third man.

The queen was angry to think that she had kept her small council waiting for this mummer's farce. "You have wasted my time and slain an innocent man. I should have your own heads off." But if she did, the next man might hesitate and let the Imp slip the net. She would pile dead dwarfs ten feet high before she let that happen. "Remove yourselves from my sight."

"Aye, Your Grace," said the boil. "We beg your pardons."

"Do you want the head?" asked the man who held it.

"Give it to Ser Meryn. No, *in* the sack, you lackwit. Yes. Ser Osmund, see them out."

Trant removed the head and Kettleblack the headsmen, leaving only Lady Jocelyn's breakfast as evidence of their visit. "Clean that up at once," the queen commanded her. This was the third head that had been delivered to her. *At least this one was a dwarf.* The last had simply been an ugly child.

"Someone will find the dwarf, never fear," Ser Osmund assured her. "And when they do, we'll kill him good."

Will you? Last night, Cersei had dreamed of the old woman, with her pebbly jowls and croaking voice. Maggy the Frog, they had called her in Lannisport. *If Father had known what she said to me, he would have had her tongue out.* Cersei had never told anyone, though, not even Jaime. *Melara said that if we never spoke about her prophecies, we would forget them. She said that a forgotten prophecy couldn't come true.*

"I have informers sniffing after the Imp everywhere, Your Grace," said Qyburn. He had garbed himself in something very like maester's robes, but white instead of grey, immaculate as the cloaks of the Kingsguard. Whorls of gold decorated his hem, sleeves, and stiff high collar, and a golden sash was tied about his waist. "Oldtown,

Gulltown, Dorne, even the Free Cities. Wheresoever he might run, my whisperers will find him."

"You assume he left King's Landing. He could be hiding in Baelor's Sept for all we know, swinging on the bell ropes to make that awful din." Cersei made a sour face and let Dorcas help her to her feet. "Come, my lord. My council awaits." She took Qyburn by the arm as they made their way down the stairs. "Have you attended to that little task I set you?"

"I have, Your Grace. I am sorry that it took so long. Such a large head. It took the beetles many hours to clean the flesh. By way of pardon, I have lined a box of ebony and silver with felt, to make a fitting presentation for the skull."

"A cloth sack would serve as well. Prince Doran wants his head. He won't give a fig what sort of box it comes in."

The pealing of the bells was louder in the yard. *He was only a High Septon. How long must we endure this?* The ringing was more melodious than the Mountain's screams had been, but . . .

Qyburn seemed to sense what she was thinking. "The bells will stop at sunset, Your Grace."

"That will be a great relief. How can you know?"

"Knowing is the nature of my service."

Varys had all of us believing he was irreplaceable. What fools we were. Once the queen let it become known that Qyburn had taken the eunuch's place, the usual vermin had wasted no time in making themselves known to him, to trade their whispers for a few coins. *It was the silver all along, not the Spider. Qyburn will serve us just as well.* She was looking forward to the look on Pycelle's face when Qyburn took his seat.

A knight of the Kingsguard was always posted outside the doors of the council chambers when the small council was in session. Today it was Ser Boros Blount. "Ser Boros," the queen said pleasantly, "you look quite grey this morning. Something you ate, perchance?" Jaime had made him the king's food taster. *A tasty task, but shameful for a knight.* Blount hated it. His sagging jowls quivered as he held the door for them.

The councillors quieted as she entered. Lord Gyles coughed by way of greeting, loud enough to wake Pycelle. The others rose, mouthing pleasantries. Cersei allowed herself the faintest of smiles. "My lords, I know you will forgive my lateness."

"We are here to serve Your Grace," said Ser Harys Swyft. "It is our pleasure to anticipate your coming."

"You all know Lord Qyburn, I am sure."

Grand Maester Pycelle did not disappoint her. "*Lord* Qyburn?" he managed, purpling. "Your Grace, this . . . a maester swears sacred vows, to hold no lands or lordships . . ."

"Your Citadel took away his chain," Cersei reminded him. "If he is not a maester, he cannot be held to a maester's vows. We called the eunuch *lord* as well, you may recall."

Pycelle sputtered. "This man is . . . he is unfit . . ."

"Do not presume to speak to me of *fitness*. Not after the stinking mockery you made of my lord father's corpse."

"Your Grace cannot think . . ." He raised a spotted hand, as if to ward off a blow. "The silent sisters removed Lord Tywin's bowels and organs, drained his blood . . . every care was taken . . . his body was stuffed with salts and fragrant herbs . . ."

"Oh, spare me the disgusting details. I smelled the results of your *care*. Lord Qyburn's healing arts saved my brother's life, and I do not doubt that he will serve the king more ably than that simpering eunuch. My lord, you know your fellow councillors?"

"I would be a poor informer if I did not, Your Grace." Qyburn seated himself between Orton Merryweather and Gyles Rosby.

My councillors. Cersei had uprooted every rose, and all those beholden to her uncle and her brothers. In their places were men whose loyalty would be to her. She had even given them new styles, borrowed from the Free Cities; the queen would have no "masters" at court beside herself. Orton Merryweather was her justiciar, Gyles Rosby her lord treasurer. Aurane Waters, the dashing young Bastard of Driftmark, would be her grand admiral.

And for her Hand, Ser Harys Swyft.

Soft, bald, and obsequious, Swyft had an absurd little white puff of beard where most men had a chin. The blue bantam rooster of his House was worked across the front of his plush yellow doublet in beads of lapis. Over that he wore a mantle of blue velvet decorated with a hundred golden hands. Ser Harys had been thrilled by his appointment, too dim to realize that he was more hostage than Hand.

His daughter was her uncle's wife, and Kevan loved his chinless lady, flat-chested and chicken-legged as she was. So long as she had Ser Harys in hand, Kevan Lannister must needs think twice about opposing her. *To be sure, a good-father is not the ideal hostage, but better a flimsy shield than none.*

"Will the king be joining us?" asked Orton Merryweather.

"My son is playing with his little queen. For the moment, his idea of kingship is stamping papers with the royal seal. His Grace is still too young to comprehend affairs of state."

"And our valiant Lord Commander?"

"Ser Jaime is at his armorer's being fitted for a hand. I know we were all tired of that ugly stump. And I daresay he would find these proceedings as tiresome as Tommen." Aurane Waters chuckled at that. *Good,* Cersei thought, *the more they laugh, the less he is a threat. Let them laugh.* "Do we have wine?"

"We do, Your Grace." Orton Merryweather was not a comely man, with his big lumpish nose and shock of unruly reddish-orange hair, but he was never less than courteous. "We have Dornish red and Arbor gold, and a fine sweet hippocras from Highgarden."

"The gold, I think. I find Dornish wines as sour as the Dornish." As Merryweather filled her cup, Cersei said, "I suppose we had as well begin with them."

Grand Maester Pycelle's lips were still quivering, yet somehow he found his tongue. "As you command. Prince Doran has taken his brother's unruly bastards into custody, yet Sunspear still seethes. The prince writes that he cannot hope to calm the waters until he receives the justice that was promised him."

"To be sure." *A tiresome creature, this prince.* "His long wait is almost done. I am sending Balon Swann to Sunspear, to deliver him the head of Gregor Clegane." Ser Balon would have another task as well, but that part was best left unsaid.

"Ah." Ser Harys Swyft fumbled at his funny little beard with thumb and forefinger. "He is dead then? Ser Gregor?"

"I would think so, my lord," Aurane Waters said dryly. "I am told that removing the head from the body is often mortal."

Cersei favored him with a smile; she liked a bit of wit, so long as she was not its target. "Ser Gregor perished of his wounds, just as Grand Maester Pycelle foretold."

Pycelle *harrumph*ed and eyed Qyburn sourly. "The spear was poisoned. No man could have saved him."

"So you said. I recall it well." The queen turned to her Hand. "What were you speaking of when I arrived, Ser Harys?"

"Sparrows, Your Grace. Septon Raynard says there may be as many as two thousand in the city, and more arriving every day. Their leaders preach of doom and demon worship . . ."

Cersei took a taste of wine. *Very nice.* "And long past time, wouldn't you agree? What would you call this red god that Stannis worships, if not a demon? The Faith should oppose such evil." Qyburn had reminded her of that, the clever man. "Our late High Septon let too much pass, I fear. Age had dimmed his sight and sapped his strength."

"He was an old done man, Your Grace." Qyburn smiled at Pycelle. "His passing should not have surprised us. No man can ask for more than to die peacefully in his sleep, full of years."

"No," said Cersei, "but we must hope that his successor is more vigorous. My friends upon the other hill tell me that it will most like be Torbert or Raynard."

Grand Maester Pycelle cleared his throat. "I have friends among the Most Devout as well, and they speak of Septon Ollidor."

"Do not discount this man Luceon," Qyburn said. "Last night he feted thirty of the Most Devout on suckling pig and Arbor gold, and by day he hands out hardbread to the poor to prove his piety."

Aurane Waters seemed as bored as Cersei by all this prattle about septons. Seen up close, his hair was more silvery than gold, and his eyes were grey-green where Prince Rhaegar's had been purple. Even so, the resemblance . . . She wondered if Waters would shave his beard for her. Though he was ten years her junior, he wanted her; Cersei could see it in the way he looked at her. Men had been looking at her that way since her breasts began to bud. *Because I was so beautiful, they said, but Jaime was beautiful as well, and they never looked at him that way.* When she was small she would sometimes don her brother's clothing as a lark. She was always startled by how differently men treated her when they thought that she was Jaime. Even Lord Tywin himself . . .

Pycelle and Merryweather were still quibbling about who the new High Septon was like to be. "One will serve as well as another," the queen announced abruptly, "but whosoever dons the crystal crown must pronounce an anathema upon the Imp." This last High Septon had been conspicuously silent regarding Tyrion. "As for these pink sparrows, so long as they preach no treason they are the Faith's problem, not ours."

Lord Orton and Ser Harys murmured agreement. Gyles Rosby's attempt to do the same dissolved into a fit of coughing. Cersei turned away in distaste as he was hacking up a gob of bloody phlegm. "Maester, have you brought the letter from the Vale?"

"I have, Your Grace." Pycelle plucked it from his pile of papers and smoothed it out. "It is a declaration, rather than a letter. Signed at Runestone by Bronze Yohn Royce, Lady Waynwood, Lords Hunter, Redfort, and Belmore, and Symond Templeton, the Knight of Ninestars. All have affixed their seals. They write—"

A deal of rubbish. "My lords may read the letter if they wish. Royce and these others are massing men below the Eyrie. They mean to remove Littlefinger as Lord Protector of the Vale, forcibly if need be. The question is, ought we allow this?"

"Does Lord Baelish seek our help?" asked Harys Swyft.

"Not as yet. In truth, he seems quite unconcerned. His last letter mentions the rebels only briefly before beseeching me to ship him some old tapestries of Robert's."

Ser Harys fingered his chin beard. "And these lords of the declaration, do *they* appeal to the king to take a hand?"

"They do not."

"Then . . . mayhaps we need do nothing."

"A war in the Vale would be most tragic," said Pycelle.

"War?" Orton Merryweather laughed. "Lord Baelish is a most amusing man, but one does not fight a war with witticisms. I doubt there will be bloodshed. And does it matter who is regent for little Lord Robert, so long as the Vale remits its taxes?"

No, Cersei decided. If truth be told, Littlefinger had been more use at court. *He had a gift for finding gold, and never coughed.* "Lord Orton has convinced me. Maester Pycelle, instruct these Lords Declarant that no harm must come to Petyr. Elsewise, the crown is content with whatever dispositions they might make for the governance of the Vale during Robert Arryn's minority."

"Very good, Your Grace."

"Might we discuss the fleet?" asked Aurane Waters. "Fewer than a dozen of our ships survived the inferno on the Blackwater. We must needs restore our strength at sea."

Harys Swyft nodded. "Strength at sea is most essential."

"Could we make use of the ironmen?" asked Orton Merryweather. "The enemy of our enemy? What would the Seastone Chair want of us as the price of an alliance?"

"They want the north," Grand Maester Pycelle said, "which our queen's noble father promised to House Bolton."

"How inconvenient," said Merryweather. "Still, the north is large. The lands could be divided. It need not be a permanent arrangement. Bolton might consent, so long as we assure him that our strength will be his once Stannis is destroyed."

"Balon Greyjoy is dead, I had heard," said Ser Harys Swyft. "Do we know who rules the isles now? Did Lord Balon have a son?"

"Leo?" coughed Lord Gyles. "Theo?"

"Theon Greyjoy was raised at Winterfell, a ward of Eddard Stark," Qyburn said. "He is not like to be a friend of ours."

"I had heard he was slain," said Merryweather.

"Was there only one son?" Ser Harys Swyft tugged upon his chin beard. "Brothers. There were brothers. Were there not?"

Varys would have known, Cersei thought with irritation. "I do not propose to climb in bed with that sorry pack of squids. Their turn will come, once we have dealt with Stannis. What we require is our own fleet."

"I propose we build new dromonds," said Aurane Waters. "Ten, to start with."

"Where is the coin to come from?" asked Pycelle.

Lord Gyles took that as an invitation to begin coughing again. He brought up more pink spittle and dabbed it away with a square of red silk. "There is no ..." he managed, before the coughing ate his words. "... no ... we do not ..."

Ser Harys proved swift enough at least to grasp the meaning between the coughs. "The crown incomes have never been greater," he objected. "Ser Kevan told me so himself."

Lord Gyles coughed. ". . . expenses . . . gold cloaks . . ."

Cersei had heard his objections before. "Our lord treasurer is trying to say that we have too many gold cloaks and too little gold." Rosby's coughing had begun to vex her. *Perhaps Garth the Gross would not have been so ill.* "Though large, the crown incomes are not large enough to keep abreast of Robert's debts. Accordingly, I have decided to defer our repayment of the sums owed the Holy Faith and the Iron Bank of Braavos until war's end." The new High Septon would doubtless wring his holy hands, and the Braavosi would squeak and squawk at her, but what of it? "The monies saved will be used for the building of our new fleet."

"Your Grace is prudent," said Lord Merryweather. "This is a wise measure. And needed, until the war is done. I concur."

"And I," said Ser Harys.

"Your Grace," Pycelle said in a quavering voice, "this will cause more trouble than you know, I fear. The Iron Bank . . ."

". . . remains on Braavos, far across the sea. They shall have their gold, maester. A Lannister pays his debts."

"The Braavosi have a saying too." Pycelle's jeweled chain clinked softly. "*The Iron Bank will have its due,* they say."

"The Iron Bank will have its due when I say they will. Until such time, the Iron Bank will wait respectfully. Lord Waters, commence the building of your dromonds."

"Very good, Your Grace."

Ser Harys shuffled through some papers. "The next matter . . . we have had a letter from Lord Frey putting forth some claims . . ."

"How many lands and honors does that man want?" snapped the queen. "His mother must have had three teats."

"My lords may not know," said Qyburn, "but in the winesinks and pot shops of this city, there are those who suggest that the crown might have been somehow complicit in Lord Walder's crime."

The other councillors stared at him uncertainly. "Do you refer to the Red Wedding?" asked Aurane Waters. "Crime?" said Ser Harys. Pycelle cleared his throat noisily. Lord Gyles coughed.

"These sparrows are especially outspoken," warned Qyburn. "The Red Wedding was an affront to all the laws of gods and men, they say, and those who had a hand in it are damned."

Cersei was not slow to take his meaning. "Lord Walder must soon face the Father's judgment. He is very old. Let the sparrows spit upon his memory. It has nought to do with us."

"No," said Ser Harys. "No," said Lord Merryweather. "No one could think so," said Pycelle. Lord Gyles coughed.

"A little spittle on Lord Walder's tomb is not like to disturb the grave worms," Qyburn agreed, "but it would also be useful if someone were to be *punished* for the Red Wedding. A few Frey heads would do much to mollify the north."

"Lord Walder will never sacrifice his own," said Pycelle.

"No," mused Cersei, "but his heirs may be less squeamish. Lord Walder will soon do us the courtesy of dying, we can hope. What better way for the new Lord of the Crossing to rid himself of inconvenient half brothers, disagreeable cousins, and scheming sisters than by naming them the culprits?"

"Whilst we await Lord Walder's death, there is another matter," said Aurane Waters. "The Golden Company has broken its contract with Myr. Around the docks I've heard men say that Lord Stannis has hired them and is bringing them across the sea."

"What would he pay them with?" asked Merryweather. "Snow? They are called the *Golden* Company. How much gold does Stannis have?"

"Little enough," Cersei assured him. "Lord Qyburn has spoken to the crew of that Myrish galley in the bay. They claim the Golden Company is making for Volantis. If they mean to cross to Westeros, they are marching in the wrong direction."

"Perhaps they grew weary of fighting on the losing side," suggested Lord Merryweather.

"There is that as well," agreed the queen. "Only a blind man could fail to see our war is all but won. Lord Tyrell has Storm's End invested. Riverrun is besieged by the Freys and my cousin Daven, our new Warden of the West. Lord Redwyne's ships have passed through the Straits of Tarth and are moving swiftly up the coast. Only a few fishing boats remain on Dragonstone to oppose Redwyne's landing. The castle may hold for some time, but once we have the port we can cut the garrison off from the sea. Then only Stannis himself will remain to vex us."

"If Lord Janos can be believed, he is trying to make common cause with the wildlings," warned Grand Maester Pycelle.

"Savages in skins," declared Lord Merryweather. "Lord Stannis must be desperate indeed, to seek such allies."

"Desperate and foolish," the queen agreed. "The northmen hate the wildlings. Roose Bolton should have no trouble winning them to our cause. A few have already joined up with his bastard son to help him clear the wretched ironmen from Moat Cailin and clear the way for Lord Bolton to return. Umber, Ryswell . . . I forget the other names. Even White Harbor is on the point of joining us. Its lord has agreed to marry both his granddaughters to our friends of Frey and open his port to our ships."

"I thought we had no ships," Ser Harys said, confused.

"Wyman Manderly was a loyal bannerman to Eddard Stark," said Grand Maester Pycelle. "Can such a man be trusted?"

No one can be trusted. "He's a fat old man, and frightened. However, he is proving stubborn on one point. He insists that he will not bend the knee until his heir has been returned to him."

"Do we have this heir?" asked Ser Harys.

"He will be at Harrenhal, if he is still alive. Gregor Clegane took him captive." The Mountain had not always been gentle with his prisoners, even those worth a goodly ransom. "If he is dead, I suppose we will need to send Lord Manderly the heads of those who killed him, with our most sincere apologies." If one head was enough to appease a prince of Dorne, a bag of them should be more than adequate for a fat northman wrapped in sealskins.

"Will not Lord Stannis seek to win the allegiance of White Harbor as well?" asked Grand Maester Pycelle.

"Oh, he has tried. Lord Manderly has sent his letters on to us and replied with evasions. Stannis demands White Harbor's swords and silver, for which he offers . . . well, *nothing.*" One day she must light a candle to the Stranger for carrying Renly off and leaving

Stannis. If it had been the other way around, her life would have been harder. "Just this morning there was another bird. Stannis has sent his onion smuggler to treat with White Harbor on his behalf. Manderly has clapped the wretch inside a cell. He asks us what he should do with him."

"Send him here, that we might question him," suggested Lord Merryweather. "The man might know much of value."

"Let him die," said Qyburn. "His death will be a lesson to the north, to show them what becomes of traitors."

"I quite agree," the queen said. "I have instructed Lord Manderly to have his head off forthwith. That should put an end to any chance of White Harbor supporting Stannis."

"Stannis will need another Hand," observed Aurane Waters with a chuckle. "The turnip knight, perhaps?"

"A turnip knight?" said Ser Harys Swyft, confused. "Who is this man? I have not heard of him."

Waters did not reply, except to roll his eyes.

"What if Lord Manderly should refuse?" asked Merryweather.

"He dare not. The onion knight's head is the coin he'll need to buy his son's life." Cersei smiled. "The fat old fool may have been loyal to the Starks in his own way, but with the wolves of Winterfell extinguished—"

"Your Grace has forgotten the Lady Sansa," said Pycelle.

The queen bristled. "I most certainly have *not* forgotten that little she-wolf." She refused to say the girl's name. "I ought to have shown her to the black cells as the daughter of a traitor, but instead I made her part of mine own household. She shared my hearth and hall, played with my own children. I fed her, dressed her, tried to make her a little less ignorant about the world, and how did she repay me for my kindness? She helped murder my son. When we find the Imp, we will find the Lady Sansa too. She is not dead . . . but before I am done with her, I promise you, she will be singing to the Stranger, begging for his kiss."

An awkward silence followed. *Have they all swallowed their tongues?* Cersei thought, with irritation. It was enough to make her wonder why she bothered with a council.

"In any case," the queen went on, "Lord Eddard's *younger* daughter is with Lord Bolton, and will be wed to his son Ramsay as soon as Moat Cailin has fallen." So long as the girl played her role well enough to cement their claim to Winterfell, neither of the Boltons would much care that she was actually some steward's whelp tricked up by Littlefinger. "If the north must have a Stark, we'll give them one." She let Lord Merryweather fill her cup once again. "Another problem has arisen on the Wall, however. The brothers of the Night's Watch have taken leave of their wits and chosen Ned Stark's bastard son to be their Lord Commander."

"Snow, the boy is called," Pycelle said unhelpfully.

"I glimpsed him once at Winterfell," the queen said, "though the Starks did their best to hide him. He looks very like his father." Her husband's by-blows had his look as well, though at least Robert had the grace to keep them out of sight. Once, after that sorry business with the cat, he had made some noises about bringing some base-born daughter of his to court. "Do as you please," she'd told him, "but you may find that the city is not a healthy place for a growing girl." The bruise those words had won her had been hard to hide from Jaime, but they heard no more about the bastard girl. *Catelyn Tully was a mouse, or she would have smothered this Jon Snow in his cradle. Instead, she's left the filthy task to me.* "Snow shares Lord Eddard's taste for treason too," she said. "The father would have handed the realm to Stannis. The son has given him lands and castles."

"The Night's Watch is sworn to take no part in the wars of the Seven Kingdoms," Pycelle reminded them. "For thousands of years the black brothers have upheld that tradition."

"Until now," said Cersei. "The bastard boy has written us to avow that the Night's Watch takes no side, but his actions give the lie to his words. He has given Stannis food and shelter, yet has the insolence to plead with us for arms and men."

"An outrage," declared Lord Merryweather. "We cannot allow the Night's Watch to join its strength to that of Lord Stannis."

"We must declare this Snow a traitor and a rebel," agreed Ser Harys Swyft. "The black brothers must remove him."

Grand Maester Pycelle nodded ponderously. "I propose that we inform Castle Black that no more men will be sent to them until such time as Snow is gone."

"Our new dromonds will need oarsmen," said Aurane Waters. "Let us instruct the lords to send their poachers and thieves to me henceforth, instead of to the Wall."

Qyburn leaned forward with a smile. "The Night's Watch defends us all from snarks and grumkins. My lords, I say that we must *help* the brave black brothers."

Cersei gave him a sharp look. "What are you saying?"

"This," Qyburn said. "For years now, the Night's Watch has begged for men. Lord Stannis has answered their plea. Can King Tommen do less? His Grace should send the Wall a hundred men. To take the black, ostensibly, but in truth . . ."

". . . to remove Jon Snow from the command," Cersei finished, delighted. *I knew I was right to want him on my council.* "That is just what we shall do." She laughed. *If this bastard boy is truly his father's son, he will not suspect a thing. Perhaps he will even thank me, before the blade slides between his ribs.* "It will need to be done carefully, to be sure. Leave the rest to me, my lords." This was how an enemy should be dealt with: with a dagger, not a declaration. "We have done good work today, my lords. I thank you. Is there aught else?"

"One last thing, Your Grace," said Aurane Waters, in an apologetic tone. "I hesitate to take up the council's time with trifles, but there has been some queer talk heard along the docks of late. Sailors from the east. They speak of dragons . . ."

". . . and manticores, no doubt, and bearded snarks?" Cersei chuckled. "Come back to me when you hear talk of *dwarfs,* my lord." She stood, to signal that the meeting was at an end.

A blustery autumn wind was blowing when Cersei left the council chambers, and bells of Blessed Baelor still sang their song of mourning off across the city. In the yard twoscore knights were hammering each other with sword and shield, adding to the din. Ser Boros Blount escorted the queen back to her apartments, where she found Lady Merryweather chuckling with Jocelyn and Dorcas. "What is it you all find so amusing?"

"The Redwyne twins," said Taena. "Both of them have fallen in love with Lady Margaery. They used to fight over which would be the next Lord of the Arbor. Now both of them want to join the Kingsguard, just to be near the little queen."

"The Redwynes have always had more freckles than wits." It was a useful thing to know, though. *If Horror or Slobber were to be found abed with Margaery* . . . Cersei wondered if the little queen liked freckles. "Dorcas, fetch me Ser Osney Kettleblack."

Dorcas blushed. "As you command."

When the girl was gone, Taena Merryweather gave the queen a quizzical look. "Why did she turn so red?"

"Love." It was Cersei's turn to laugh. "She fancies our Ser Osney." He was the youngest Kettleblack, the clean-shaved one. Though he had the same black hair, hooked nose, and easy smile as his brother Osmund, one cheek bore three long scratches, courtesy of one of Tyrion's whores. "She likes his scars, I think."

Lady Merryweather's dark eyes shone with mischief. "Just so. Scars make a man look dangerous, and danger is exciting."

"You shock me, my lady," the queen said, teasing. "If danger excites you so, why wed Lord Orton? We all love him, it is true, but still . . ." Petyr had once remarked that the horn of plenty that adorned House Merryweather's arms suited Lord Orton admirably, since he had carrot-colored hair, a nose as bulbous as a beetroot, and pease porridge for wits.

Taena laughed. "My lord is more bountiful than dangerous, this is so. Yet . . . I hope Your Grace will not think the less of me, but I did not come a maid entire to Orton's bed."

You are all whores in the Free Cities, aren't you? That was good to know; one day, she might be able to make use of it. "And pray, who was this lover who was so . . . full of danger?"

Taena's olive skin turned even darker as she blushed. "Oh, I should not have spoken. Your Grace will keep my secret, yes?"

"Men have scars, women mysteries." Cersei kissed her cheek. *I will have his name out of you soon enough.*

When Dorcas returned with Ser Osney Kettleblack, the queen dismissed her ladies. "Come sit with me by the window, Ser Osney.

Will you take a cup of wine?" She poured for them herself. "Your cloak is threadbare. I have a mind to put you in a new one."

"What, a white one? Who's died?"

"No one, as yet," the queen said. "Is that your wish, to join your brother Osmund in our Kingsguard?"

"I'd rather be the *queen's* guard, if it please Your Grace." When Osney grinned, the scars on his cheek turned bright red.

Cersei's fingers traced their path across his cheek. "You have a bold tongue, ser. You will make me forget myself again."

"Good." Ser Osney caught her hand and kissed her fingers roughly. "My sweet queen."

"You are a wicked man," the queen whispered, "and no true knight, I think." She let him touch her breasts through the silk of her gown. "Enough."

"It isn't. I want you."

"You've had me."

"Only once." He grabbed her left breast again and gave it a clumsy squeeze that reminded her of Robert.

"One good night for one good knight. You did me valiant service, and you had your reward." Cersei walked her fingers up his laces. She could feel him stiffening through his breeches. "Was that a new horse you were riding in the yard yestermorn?"

"The black stallion? Aye. A gift from my brother Osfryd. Midnight, I call him."

How wonderfully original. "A fine mount for a battle. For pleasure, though, there is nothing to compare to a gallop on a spirited young filly." She gave him a smile and a squeeze. "Tell me true. Do you think our little queen is pretty?"

Ser Osney drew back, wary. "I suppose. For a girl. I'd sooner have a woman."

"Why not both?" she whispered. "Pluck the little rose for me, and you will not find me to be ungrateful."

"The little . . . Margaery, you mean?" Ser Osney's ardor was wilting in his breeches. "She's the king's wife. Wasn't there some Kingsguard who lost his head for bedding the king's wife?"

"Ages ago." *She was his king's mistress, not his wife, and his head was the only thing he did not lose. Aegon dismembered him piece by piece, and made the woman watch.* Cersei did not want Osney dwelling on that ancient unpleasantness, however. "Tommen is not Aegon the Unworthy. Have no fear, he will do as I bid him. I mean for Margaery to lose her head, not you."

That gave him pause. "Her maidenhead, you mean?"

"That too. Assuming she has still one." She traced his scars again. "Unless you think Margaery would prove unresponsive to your . . . charms?"

Osney gave her a wounded look. "She likes me well enough. Them cousins of hers are always teasing with me about my nose. How big it is, and all. The last time Megga did that, Margaery told them to stop and said I had a lovely face."

"There you are, then."

"There I am," the man agreed, in a doubtful tone, "but where am I going to be if she . . . if I . . . after we . . . ?"

". . . do the deed?" Cersei gave him a barbed smile. "Lying with a queen is treason. Tommen would have no choice but to send you to the Wall."

"The Wall?" he said with dismay.

It was all she could do not to laugh. *No, best not. Men hate being laughed at.* "A black cloak would go well with your eyes, and that black hair of yours."

"No one returns from the Wall."

"You will. All you need to do is kill a boy."

"What boy?"

"A bastard boy in league with Stannis. He's young and green, and you'll have a hundred men."

Kettleblack was afraid, she could smell it on him, but he was too proud to own up to that fear. *Men are all alike.* "I've killed more boys than I can count," he insisted. "Once this boy is dead, I'd get my pardon from the king?"

"That, and a lordship." *Unless Snow's brothers hang you first.* "A queen must have a consort. One who knows no fear."

"Lord Kettleblack?" A slow smile spread across his face, and his scars flamed red. "Aye, I like the sound o' that. A lordly lord . . ."

"... and fit to bed a queen."

He frowned. "The Wall is cold."

"And I am warm." Cersei put her arms about his neck. "Bed a girl and kill a boy and I am yours. Do you have the courage?"

Osney thought a moment before he nodded. "I am your man."

"You are, ser." She kissed him, and let him have a little taste of tongue before she broke away. "Enough for now. The rest must wait. Will you dream of me tonight?"

"Aye." His voice was hoarse.

"And when you're abed with our Maid Margaery?" she asked him, teasing. "When you're in her, will you dream of me then?"

"I will," swore Osney Kettleblack.

"Good."

After he was gone, Cersei summoned Jocelyn to brush her hair out whilst she slipped off her shoes and stretched like a cat. *I was made for this,* she told herself. It was the sheer elegance of it that pleased her most. Even Mace Tyrell would not dare defend his darling daughter if she was caught in the act with the likes of Osney Kettleblack, and neither Stannis Baratheon nor Jon Snow would have cause to wonder why Osney was being sent to the Wall. She would see to it that Ser Osmund was the one to discover his brother with the little queen; that way the loyalty of the other two Kettleblacks need not be impugned. *If Father could only see me now, he would not be so quick to speak of marrying me off again. A pity he's so dead. Him and Robert, Jon Arryn, Ned Stark, Renly Baratheon, all dead. Only Tyrion remains, and not for long.*

That night the queen summoned Lady Merryweather to her bedchamber. "Will you take a cup of wine?" she asked her.

"A small one." The Myrish woman laughed. "A big one."

"On the morrow, I want you to pay a call on my good-daughter," Cersei said as Dorcas was dressing her for bed.

"Lady Margaery is always happy to see me."

"I know." The queen did not fail to note the style that Taena used when referring to Tommen's little wife. "Tell her I've sent seven beeswax candles to the Baelor's Sept in memory of our dear High Septon."

Taena laughed. "If so, she will send seven-and-seventy candles of her own, so as not to be outmourned."

"I will be very cross if she does not," the queen said, smiling. "Tell her also that she has a secret admirer, a knight so smitten with her beauty that he cannot sleep at night."

"Might I ask Your Grace which knight?" Mischief sparkled in Taena's big dark eyes. "Could it be Ser Osney?"

"It could be," the queen said, "but do not offer up that name freely. Make her worm it out of you. Will you do that?"

"If it please you. That is all I wish, Your Grace."

Outside a cold wind was rising. They stayed up late into the morning, drinking Arbor gold and telling one another tales. Taena got quite drunk and Cersei pried the name of her secret lover from her. He was a Myrish sea captain, half a pirate, with black hair to the shoulders and a scar that ran across his face from chin to ear. "A hundred times I told him no, and he said yes," the other woman told her, "until finally I was saying yes as well. He was not the sort of man to be denied."

"I know the sort," the queen said with a wry smile.

"Has Your Grace ever known a man like that, I wonder?"

"Robert," she lied, thinking of Jaime.

Yet when she closed her eyes, it was the other brother that she dreamt of, and the three wretched fools with whom she had begun her day. In the dream it was Tyrion's head they brought her in their sack. She had it bronzed, and kept it in her chamber pot.

THE IRON CAPTAIN

The wind was blowing from the north as the *Iron Victory* came round the point and entered the holy bay called Nagga's Cradle. Victarion joined Nute the Barber at her prow. Ahead loomed the sacred shore of Old Wyk and the grassy hill above it, where the ribs of Nagga rose from the earth like the trunks of great white trees, as wide around as a dromond's mast and twice as tall.

The bones of the Grey King's Hall. Victarion could feel the magic of this place. "Balon stood beneath those bones, when first he named himself a king," he recalled. "He swore to win us back our freedoms, and Tarle the Thrice-Drowned placed a driftwood crown upon his head. *'BALON!'* they cried. *'BALON! BALON KING!'*"

"They will shout your name as loud," said Nute.

Victarion nodded, though he did not share the Barber's certainty. *Balon had three sons, and a daughter he loved well.*

He had said as much to his captains at Moat Cailin, when first they urged him to claim the Seastone Chair. "Balon's sons are dead," Red Ralf Stonehouse had argued, "and Asha is a woman. You were your brother's strong right arm, you must pick up the sword that he let fall." When Victarion reminded them that Balon had commanded him to hold the Moat against the northmen, Ralf Kenning said, "The wolves are broken, lord. What good to win this swamp and lose the isles?" And Ralf the Limper added, "The Crow's Eye has been too long away. He knows us not."

Euron Greyjoy, King of the Isles and the North. The thought woke an old rage in his heart, but still . . .

"Words are wind," Victarion told them, "and the only good wind is that which fills our sails. Would you have me fight the Crow's Eye? Brother against brother, ironborn against ironborn?" Euron was still his elder, no matter how much bad blood might be between them. *No man is as accursed as the kinslayer.*

But when the Damphair's summons came, the call to kingsmoot, then all was changed. *Aeron speaks with the Drowned God's voice,* Victarion reminded himself, *and if the Drowned God wills that I should sit the Seastone Chair* . . . The next day he gave command of Moat Cailin to Ralf Kenning and set off overland for the Fever River where the Iron Fleet lay amongst the reeds and willows. Rough seas and fickle winds had delayed him, but only one ship had been lost, and he was home.

Grief and *Iron Vengeance* were close behind as *Iron Victory* passed the headland. Behind came *Hardhand, Iron Wind, Grey Ghost, Lord Quellon, Lord Vickon, Lord Dagon,* and the rest, nine-tenths of the Iron Fleet, sailing on the evening tide in a ragged column that extended back long leagues. The sight of their sails filled Victarion Greyjoy with content. No man had ever loved his wives half so well as the Lord Captain loved his ships.

Along the sacred strand of Old Wyk, longships lined the shore as far as the eye could see, their masts thrust up like spears. In the deeper waters rode prizes: cogs, carracks, and dromonds won in raid or war, too big to run ashore. From prow and stern and mast flew familiar banners.

Nute the Barber squinted toward the strand. "Is that Lord Harlaw's *Sea Song*?" The Barber was a thickset man with bandy legs and long arms, but his eyes were not so keen as they had been when he was young. In those days he could throw an axe so well that men said he could shave you with it.

"*Sea Song,* aye." Rodrik the Reader had left his books, it would seem. "And there's old Drumm's *Thunderer,* with Blacktyde's *Nightflyer* beside her." Victarion's eyes were as sharp as they had ever been. Even with their sails furled and their banners hanging limp, he knew them, as befit the Lord Captain of the Iron Fleet. "*Silverfin* too. Some kin of Sawane Botley." The Crow's Eye had drowned Lord Botley, Victarion had heard, and his heir had died at Moat Cailin, but there had been brothers, and other sons as well. *How many? Four? No, five, and none with any cause to love the Crow's Eye.*

And then he saw her: a single-masted galley, lean and low, with a dark red hull. Her sails, now furled, were black as a starless sky. Even at anchor *Silence* looked both cruel and fast. On her prow was a black iron maiden with one arm outstretched. Her waist was slender, her breasts high and proud, her legs long and shapely. A windblown mane of black iron hair streamed from her head, and her eyes were mother-of-pearl, but she had no mouth.

Victarion's hands closed into fists. He had beaten four men to death with those hands, and one wife as well. Though his hair was flecked with hoarfrost, he was as strong as he had ever been, with a bull's broad chest and a boy's flat belly. *The kinslayer is accursed in the eyes of gods and men,* Balon had reminded him on the day he sent the Crow's Eye off to sea.

"He is here," Victarion told the Barber. "Drop sail. We proceed on oars alone. Command *Grief* and *Iron Vengeance* to stand between *Silence* and the sea. The rest of the fleet to seal the bay. None is to leave save at my command, neither man nor crow."

The men upon the shore had spied their sails. Shouts echoed across the bay as friends and kin called out greetings. But not from *Silence*. On her decks a motley crew of mutes and mongrels spoke no word as the *Iron Victory* drew nigh. Men black as tar stared out at him, and others squat and hairy as the apes of Sothoros. *Monsters,* Victarion thought.

They dropped anchor twenty yards from *Silence*. "Lower a boat. I would go ashore." He buckled on his swordbelt as the rowers took their places; his longsword rested on one hip, a dirk upon the other. Nute the Barber fastened the Lord Captain's cloak about his shoulders. It was made of nine layers of cloth-of-gold, sewn in the shape of the kraken of Greyjoy, arms dangling to his boots. Beneath he wore heavy grey chainmail over boiled black leather. In Moat Cailin he had taken to wearing mail day and night. Sore shoulders and an aching back were easier to bear than bloody bowels. The poisoned arrows of the bog devils need only scratch a man, and a few hours later he would be squirting and screaming as his life ran down his legs in gouts of red and brown. *Whoever wins the Seastone Chair, I shall deal with the bog devils.*

Victarion donned a tall black warhelm, wrought in the shape of an iron kraken, its arms coiled down around his cheeks to meet beneath his jaw. By then the boat was ready. "I put the chests into your charge," he told Nute as he climbed over the side. "See that they are strongly guarded." Much depended on the chests.

"As you command, Your Grace."

Victarion returned a sour scowl. "I am no king as yet." He clambered down into the boat.

Aeron Damphair was waiting for him in the surf with his waterskin slung beneath one arm. The priest was gaunt and tall, though shorter than Victarion. His nose rose like a shark's fin from a bony face, and his eyes were iron. His beard reached to his waist, and tangled ropes of hair slapped at the back of his legs when the wind blew. "Brother," he said as the waves broke white and cold around their ankles, "what is dead can never die."

"But rises again, harder and stronger." Victarion lifted off his helm and knelt. The bay filled his boots and soaked his breeches as Aeron poured a stream of salt water down upon his brow. And so they prayed.

"Where is our brother Crow's Eye?" the Lord Captain demanded of Aeron Damphair when the prayers were done.

"His is the great tent of cloth-of-gold, there where the din is loudest. He surrounds himself with godless men and monsters, worse than before. In him our father's blood went bad."

"Our mother's blood as well." Victarion would not speak of kinslaying, here in this godly place beneath the bones of Nagga and the Grey King's Hall, but many a night he dreamed of driving a mailed fist into Euron's smiling face, until the flesh split and his bad blood ran red and free. *I must not. I pledged my word to Balon.* "All have come?" he asked his priestly brother.

"All who matter. The captains and the kings." On the Iron Islands they were one and the same, for every captain was a king on his own deck, and every king must be a captain. "Do you mean to claim our father's crown?"

Victarion imagined himself seated on the Seastone Chair. "If the Drowned God wills it."

"The waves will speak," said Aeron Damphair as he turned away. "Listen to the waves, brother."

"Aye." He wondered how his name would sound whispered by waves and shouted by the captains and the kings. *If the cup should pass to me, I will not set it by.*

A crowd had gathered round to wish him well and seek his favor. Victarion saw men from every isle: Blacktydes, Tawneys, Orkwoods, Stonetrees, Wynches, and many more. The Goodbrothers of Old Wyk, the Goodbrothers of Great Wyk, and the Goodbrothers of Orkmont all had come. The Codds were there, though every decent man despised them. Humble Shepherds, Weavers, and Netleys rubbed shoulders with men from Houses ancient and proud; even humble Humbles, the blood of thralls and salt wives. A Volmark clapped Victarion on the back; two Sparrs pressed a wineskin into his hands. He drank deep, wiped his mouth, and let them bear him off to their cookfires, to listen to their talk of war and crowns and plunder, and the glory and the freedom of his reign.

That night the men of the Iron Fleet raised a huge sailcloth tent above the tideline, so Victarion might feast half a hundred famous captains on roast kid, salted cod, and lobster. Aeron came as well. He ate fish and drank water, whilst the captains quaffed enough ale to float the Iron Fleet. Many promised him their voices: Fralegg the Strong, clever Alvyn Sharp, humpbacked Hotho Harlaw. Hotho offered him a daughter for his queen. "I have no luck with wives," Victarion told him. His first wife died in childbed, giving him a stillborn daughter. His second had been stricken by a pox. And his third . . .

"A king must have an heir," Hotho insisted. "The Crow's Eye brings three sons to show before the kingsmoot."

"Bastards and mongrels. How old is this daughter?"

"Twelve," said Hotho. "Fair and fertile, newly flowered, with hair the color of honey. Her breasts are small as yet, but she has good hips. She takes after her mother, more than me."

Victarion knew that to mean the girl did not have a hump. Yet when he tried to picture her, he only saw the wife he'd killed. He had sobbed each time he struck her, and afterward carried her down to the rocks to give her to the crabs. "I will gladly look at the girl once I am crowned," he said. That was as much as Hotho dared hope for, and he shambled off, content.

Baelor Blacktyde was more difficult to please. He sat by Victarion's elbow in his lambswool tunic of black-and-green vairy, smooth-faced and comely. His cloak was sable, and pinned with a silver seven-pointed star. He had been eight years a hostage in Oldtown, and had returned a worshiper of the seven green land gods. "Balon was mad, Aeron is madder, and Euron is maddest of them all," Lord Baelor said. "What of you, Lord Captain? If I shout your name, will you make an end of this mad war?"

Victarion frowned. "Would you have me bend the knee?"

"If need be. We cannot stand alone against all Westeros. King Robert proved that, to our grief. Balon would pay the iron price for freedom, he said, but our women bought Balon's crowns with empty beds. My mother was one such. The Old Way is dead."

"What is dead can never die, but rises harder and stronger. In a hundred years men will sing of Balon the Bold."

"Balon the Widowmaker, call him. I will gladly trade his freedom for a father. Have you one to give me?" When Victarion did not answer, Blacktyde snorted and moved off.

The tent grew hot and smoky. Two of Gorold Goodbrother's sons knocked a table over fighting; Will Humble lost a wager and had to eat his boot; Little Lenwood Tawney fiddled whilst Romny Weaver sang "The Bloody Cup" and "Steel Rain" and other old reaving songs. Qarl the Maid and Eldred Codd danced the finger dance. A roar of laughter went up when one of Eldred's fingers landed in Ralf the Limper's wine cup.

A woman was amongst those laughing. Victarion rose and saw her by the tent flap, whispering something in the ear of Qarl the Maid that made him laugh as well. He had hoped she would not be fool enough to come here, yet the sight of her made him smile all the same. "*Asha*," he called in a commanding voice. "*Niece*."

She made her way to his side, lean and lithe in high boots of salt-stained leather, green woolen breeches, and brown quilted tunic, a sleeveless leather jerkin half-unlaced. "Nuncle." Asha Greyjoy was tall for a woman, yet she had to stand on her toes to kiss his cheek. "I am pleased to see you at my queensmoot."

"Queensmoot?" Victarion laughed. "Are you drunk, niece? Sit. I did not spy your *Black Wind* on the strand."

"I beached her beneath Norne Goodbrother's castle and rode across the island." She sat upon a stool and helped herself unasked to Nute the Barber's wine. Nute raised no objection; he had passed out drunk some time ago. "Who holds the Moat?"

"Ralf Kenning. With the Young Wolf dead, only the bog devils remain to plague us."

"The Starks were not the only northmen. The Iron Throne has named the Lord of the Dreadfort as Warden of the North."

"Would you lesson me in warfare? I was fighting battles when you were sucking mother's milk."

"And losing battles too." Asha took a drink of wine.

Victarion did not like to be reminded of Fair Isle. "Every man should lose a battle in his youth, so he does not lose a war when he is old. You have not come to make a claim, I hope."

She teased him with a smile. "And if I have?"

"There are men who remember when you were a little girl, swimming naked in the sea and playing with your doll."

"I played with axes too."

"You did," he had to grant, "but a woman wants a husband, not a crown. When I am king I'll give you one."

"My nuncle is so good to me. Shall I find a pretty wife for you, when I am queen?"

"I have no luck with wives. How long have you been here?"

"Long enough to see that Uncle Damphair has woken more than he intended. The Drumm means to make a claim, and Tarle the Thrice-Drowned was heard to say that Maron Volmark is the true heir of the black line."

"The king must be a kraken."

"The Crow's Eye is a kraken. The elder brother comes before the younger." Asha leaned close. "But I am the child of King Balon's body, so I come before you both. Hear me, nuncle . . ."

But then a sudden silence fell. The singing died, Little Lenwood Tawney lowered his fiddle, men turned their heads. Even the clatter of plates and knives was hushed.

A dozen newcomers had entered the feast tent. Victarion saw Pinchface Jon Myre, Torwold Browntooth, Left-Hand Lucas Codd. Germund Botley crossed his arms against the gilded breastplate he had taken off a Lannister captain during Balon's first rebellion. Orkwood of Orkmont stood beside him. Behind them were Stonehand, Quellon Humble, and the Red Oarsman with his fiery hair in braids. Ralf the Shepherd too, and Ralf of Lordsport, and Qarl the Thrall.

And the Crow's Eye, Euron Greyjoy.

He looks unchanged, Victarion thought. *He looks the same as he did the day he laughed at me and left.* Euron was the most comely of Lord Quellon's sons, and three years of exile had not changed that. His hair was still black as a midnight sea, with never a whitecap to be seen, and his face was still smooth and pale beneath his neat dark beard. A black leather patch covered Euron's left eye, but his right was blue as a summer sky.

His smiling eye, thought Victarion. "Crow's Eye," he said.

"*King* Crow's Eye, brother." Euron smiled. His lips looked very dark in the lamplight, bruised and blue.

"We shall have no king but from the kingsmoot." The Damphair stood. "No godless man—"

"—may sit the Seastone Chair, aye." Euron glanced about the tent. "As it happens as I have oft sat upon the Seastone Chair of late. It raises no objections." His smiling eye was glittering. "Who knows more of gods than I? Horse gods and fire gods, gods made of gold with gemstone eyes, gods carved of cedar wood, gods chiseled into mountains, gods of empty air . . . I know them all. I have seen their peoples garland them with flowers, and shed the blood of goats and bulls and children in their names. And I have heard the prayers, in half a hundred tongues. Cure my withered leg, make the maiden love me, grant me a healthy son. Save me, succor me, make me wealthy . . . *protect* me! Protect me from mine enemies, protect me from the darkness, protect me from the crabs inside my belly, from the horselords, from the slavers, from the sellswords at my door. Protect me from the *Silence*." He laughed. "*Godless?* Why, Aeron, I am the godliest man ever to raise sail! You serve one god, Damphair, but I have served ten thousand. From Ib to Asshai, when men see *my* sails, they pray."

The priest raised a bony finger. "They pray to trees and golden idols and goat-headed abominations. False gods . . ."

"Just so," said Euron, "and for that sin I kill them all. I spill their blood upon the sea and sow their screaming women with my seed. Their little gods cannot stop me, so plainly they are false gods. I am more devout than even you, Aeron. Perhaps it should be you who kneels to me for blessing."

The Red Oarsman laughed loudly at that, and the others took their lead from him.

"*Fools*," said the priest, "fools and thralls and blind men, that is what you are. Do you not see what stands before you?"

"A king," said Quellon Humble.

The Damphair spat, and strode out into the night.

When he was gone, the Crow's Eye turned his smiling eye upon Victarion. "Lord Captain, have you no greeting for a brother long away? Nor you, Asha? How fares your lady mother?"

"Poorly," Asha said. "Some man made her a widow."

Euron shrugged. "I had heard the Storm God swept Balon to his death. Who is this man who slew him? Tell me his name, niece, so I might revenge myself on him."

Asha got to her feet. "You know his name as well as I. Three years you were gone from us, and yet *Silence* returns within a day of my lord father's death."

"Do you accuse me?" Euron asked mildly.

"Should I?" The sharpness in Asha's voice made Victarion frown. It was dangerous to speak so to the Crow's Eye, even when his smiling eye was shining with amusement.

"Do I command the winds?" the Crow's Eye asked his pets.

"No, Your Grace," said Orkwood of Orkmont.

"No man commands the winds," said Germund Botley.

"Would that you did," the Red Oarsman said. "You would sail wherever you liked and never be becalmed."

"There you have it, from the mouths of three brave men," Euron said. "The *Silence* was at sea when Balon died. If you doubt an uncle's word, I give you leave to ask my crew."

"A crew of mutes? Aye, that would serve me well."

"A husband would serve you well." Euron turned to his followers again. "Torwold, I misremember, do you have a wife?"

"Only the one." Torwold Browntooth grinned, and showed how he had won his name.

"I am unwed," announced Left-Hand Lucas Codd.

"And for good reason," Asha said. "All *women* do despise the Codds as well. Don't look at me so mournful, Lucas. You still have your famous hand." She made a pumping motion with her fist.

Codd cursed, till the Crow's Eye put a hand upon his chest. "Was that courteous, Asha? You have wounded Lucas to the quick."

"Easier than wounding him in the prick. I throw an axe as well as any man, but when the target is so small . . ."

"This girl forgets herself," snarled Pinchface Jon Myre. "Balon let her believe she was a man."

"Your father made the same mistake with you," said Asha.

"Give her to me, Euron," suggested the Red Oarsman. "I'll spank her till her arse is as red as my hair."

"Come try," said Asha, "and hereafter we can call you the Red Eunuch." A throwing axe was in her hand. She tossed it in the air and caught it deftly. "Here is my husband, Nuncle. Any man who wants me should take it up with him."

Victarion slammed his fist upon the table. "I'll have no blood shed here. Euron, take your . . . pets . . . and go."

"I had looked for a warmer welcome from you, brother. I *am* your elder . . . and soon, your rightful king."

Victarion's face darkened. "When the kingsmoot speaks, we shall see who wears the driftwood crown."

"On that we can agree." Euron lifted two fingers to the patch that covered his left eye, and took his leave. The others followed at his heels like mongrel dogs. Silence lingered behind them, till Little

Lenwood Tawney took up his fiddle. The wine and ale began to flow again, but several guests had lost their thirst. Eldred Codd slipped out, cradling his bloody hand. Then Will Humble, Hotho Harlaw, a goodly lot of Goodbrothers.

"Nuncle." Asha put a hand upon his shoulder. "Walk with me, if you would."

Outside the tent the wind was rising. Clouds raced across the moon's pale face. They looked a bit like galleys, stroking hard to ram. The stars were few and faint. All along the strand the longships rested, tall masts rising like a forest from the surf. Victarion could hear their hulls creaking as they settled on the sand. He heard the keening of their lines, the sound of banners flapping. Beyond, in the deeper waters of the bay, larger ships bobbed at anchor, grim shadows wreathed in mist.

They walked along the strand together just above the surf, far from the camps and the cookfires. "Tell me true, nuncle," Asha said, "why did Euron go away so suddenly?"

"The Crow's Eye oft went reaving."

"Never for so long."

"He took the *Silence* east. A lengthy voyage."

"I asked *why* he went, not where." When he did not answer, Asha said, "I was away when *Silence* sailed. I had taken *Black Wind* around the Arbor to the Stepstones, to steal a few trinkets from the Lyseni pirates. When I came home, Euron was gone and your new wife was dead."

"She was only a salt wife." He had not touched another woman since he gave her to the crabs. *I will need to take a wife when I am king. A true wife, to be my queen and bear me sons. A king must have an heir.*

"My father refused to speak of her," said Asha.

"It does no good to speak of things no man can change." He was weary of the subject. "I saw the Reader's longship."

"It took all my charm to winkle him out of his Book Tower."

She has the Harlaws, then. Victarion's frown grew deeper. "You cannot hope to rule. You are a woman."

"Is that why I always lose the pissing contests?" Asha laughed. "Nuncle, it grieves me to say so, but you may be right. For four days and four nights, I have been drinking with the captains and the kings, listening to what they say . . . and what they will not say. Mine own are with me, and many Harlaws. I have Tris Botley too, and some few others. Not enough." She kicked a rock, and sent it splashing into the water between two longships. "I am of a mind to shout my nuncle's name."

"Which uncle?" he demanded. "You have three."

"Four. Nuncle, hear me. I will place the driftwood crown upon your brow myself . . . if you will agree to share the rule."

"*Share* the rule? How could that be?" The woman was not making sense. *Does she want to be my queen?* Victarion found himself looking at Asha in a way he had never looked at her before. He could feel his manhood beginning to stiffen. *She is Balon's daughter,* he reminded himself. He remembered her as a little girl, throwing axes at a door. He crossed his arms against his chest. "The Seastone Chair seats but one."

"Then let my nuncle sit," Asha said. "I will stand behind you, to guard your back and whisper in your ear. No king can rule alone. Even when the dragons sat the Iron Throne, they had men to help them. The King's Hands. Let me be your Hand, Nuncle."

No King of the Isles had ever needed a Hand, much less one who was a woman. *The captains and the kings would mock me in their cups.* "Why would you wish to be my Hand?"

"To end this war before this war ends us. We have won all that we are like to win . . . and stand to lose all just as quick, unless we make a peace. I have shown Lady Glover every courtesy, and she swears her lord will treat with me. If we hand back Deepwood Motte, Torrhen's Square, and Moat Cailin, she says, the northmen will cede us Sea Dragon Point and all the Stony Shore. Those lands are thinly peopled, yet ten times larger than all the isles put together. An exchange of hostages will seal the pact, and each side will agree to make common cause with the other should the Iron Throne—"

Victarion chuckled. "This Lady Glover plays you for a fool, niece. Sea Dragon Point and the Stony Shore are ours. Why hand back anything? Winterfell is burnt and broken, and the Young Wolf rots headless in the earth. We will have *all* the north, as your lord father dreamed."

"When longships learn to row through trees, perhaps. A fisherman may hook a grey leviathan, but it will drag him down to death unless he cuts it loose. The north is too large for us to hold, and too full of northmen."

"Go back to your dolls, niece. Leave the winning of wars to warriors." Victarion showed her his fists. "I have two hands. No man needs three."

"I know a man who needs House Harlaw, though."

"Hotho Humpback has offered me his daughter for my queen. If I take her, I will have the Harlaws."

That took the girl aback. "Lord Rodrik rules House Harlaw."

"Rodrik has no daughters, only books. Hotho will be his heir, and I will be the king." Once he had said the words aloud, they sounded true. "The Crow's Eye has been too long away."

"Some men look larger at a distance," Asha warned. "Walk amongst the cookfires if you dare, and listen. They are not telling tales of your strength, nor of my famous beauty. They talk only of the Crow's Eye; the far places he has seen, the women he has raped and the men he's killed, the cities he has sacked, the way he burnt Lord Tywin's fleet at Lannisport . . ."

"*I* burnt the lion's fleet," Victarion insisted. "With mine own hands I flung the first torch onto his flagship."

"The Crow's Eye hatched the scheme." Asha put her hand upon his arm. "And killed your wife as well . . . did he not?"

Balon had commanded them not to speak of it, but Balon was dead. "He put a baby in her belly and made me do the killing. I would have killed him too, but Balon would have no kinslaying in his hall. He sent Euron into exile, never to return . . ."

". . . so long as Balon lived?"

Victarion looked at his fists. "She gave me horns. I had no choice." *Had it been known, men would have laughed at me, as the Crow's Eye laughed when I confronted him. "She came to me wet and willing,"* he had boasted. *"It seems Victarion is big everywhere but where it matters."* But he could not tell her that.

"I am sorry for you," said Asha, "and sorrier for her . . . but you leave me small choice but to claim the Seastone Chair myself."

You cannot. "Your breath is yours to waste, woman."

"It is," she said, and left him.

THE DROWNED MAN

Only when his arms and legs were numb from the cold did Aeron Greyjoy struggle back to shore and don his robes again.

He had run before the Crow's Eye as if he were still the weak thing he had been, but when the waves broke over his head they reminded once more that that man was dead. *I was reborn from the sea, a harder man and stronger.* No mortal man could frighten him, no more than the darkness could, nor the bones of his soul, the grey and grisly bones of his soul. *The sound of a door opening, the scream of a rusted iron hinge.*

The priest's robes crackled as he pulled them down, still stiff with salt from their last washing a fortnight past. The wool clung to his wet chest, drinking the brine that ran down from his hair. He filled his waterskin and slung it over his shoulder.

As he strode across the strand, a drowned man returning from a call of nature stumbled into him in the darkness. "Damphair," he murmured. Aeron laid a hand upon his head, blessed him, and moved on. The ground rose beneath his feet, gently at first, then more steeply. When he felt scrub grass between his toes, he knew that he had left the strand behind. Slowly he climbed, listening to the waves. *The sea is never weary. I must be as tireless.*

On the crown of the hill four-and-forty monstrous stone ribs rose from the earth like the trunks of great pale trees. The sight made Aeron's heart beat faster. Nagga had been the first sea dragon, the mightiest ever to rise from the waves. She fed on krakens and leviathans and drowned whole islands in her wrath, yet the Grey King had slain her and the Drowned God had changed her bones to stone so that men might never cease to wonder at the courage of the first of kings. Nagga's ribs became the beams and pillars of his longhall, just as her jaws became his throne. *For a thousand years and seven he reigned here,* Aeron recalled. *Here he took his mermaid wife and planned his wars against the Storm God. From here he ruled both stone and salt, wearing robes of woven seaweed and a tall pale crown made from Nagga's teeth.*

But that was in the dawn of days, when mighty men still dwelt on earth and sea. The hall had been warmed by Nagga's living fire, which the Grey King had made his thrall. On its walls hung tapestries woven from silver seaweed most pleasing to the eyes. The Grey King's warriors had feasted on the bounty of the sea at a table in the shape of a great starfish, whilst seated upon thrones carved from mother-of-pearl. *Gone, all the glory gone.* Men were smaller now. Their lives had grown short. The Storm God drowned Nagga's fire after the Grey King's death, the chairs and tapestries had been stolen, the roof and walls had rotted away. Even the Grey King's great throne of fangs had been swallowed by the sea. Only Nagga's bones endured to remind the ironborn of all the wonder that had been.

It is enough, thought Aeron Greyjoy.

Nine wide steps had been hewn from the stony hilltop. Behind rose the howling hills of Old Wyk, with mountains in the distance black and cruel. Aeron paused where the doors once stood, pulled the cork from his waterskin, took a swallow of salt water, and turned to face the sea. *We were born from the sea, and to the sea we must return.* Even here he could hear the ceaseless rumble of the waves and feel the power of the god who lurked below the waters. Aeron went to his knees. *You have sent your people to me,* he prayed. *They have left their halls and hovels, their castles and their keeps, and come here to Nagga's bones, from every fishing village and every hidden vale. Now grant to them the wisdom to know the true king when he stands before them, and the strength to shun the false.* All night he prayed, for when the god was in him Aeron Greyjoy had no need of sleep, no more than the waves did, nor the fishes of the sea.

Dark clouds ran before the wind as the first light stole into the world. The black sky went grey as slate; the black sea turned grey-green; the black mountains of Great Wyk across the bay put on the blue-green hues of soldier pines. As color stole back into the world, a hundred banners lifted and began to flap. Aeron beheld the silver fish of Botley, the bloody moon of Wynch, the dark green trees of Orkwood. He saw warhorns and leviathans and scythes, and everywhere the krakens great and golden. Beneath them, thralls and salt wives begin to move about, stirring coals into new life and gutting fish for the captains and the kings to break their fasts. The dawnlight touched the stony strand, and he watched men wake from sleep, throwing aside their sealskin blankets as they called for their first horn of ale. *Drink deep,* he thought, *for we have god's work to do today.*

The sea was stirring too. The waves grew larger as the wind rose, sending plumes of spray to crash against the longships. *The Drowned God wakes,* thought Aeron. He could hear his voice welling from the depths of the sea. *I shall be with you here this day, my strong and faithful servant,* the voice said. *No godless man will sit my Seastone Chair.*

It was there beneath the arch of Nagga's ribs that his drowned men found him, standing tall and stern with his long black hair blowing in the wind. "Is it time?" Rus asked. Aeron gave a nod, and said, "It is. Go forth and sound the summons."

The drowned men took up their driftwood cudgels and began to beat them one against the other as they walked back down the hill. Others joined them, and the clangor spread along the strand. Such a fearful clacking and a clattering it made, as if a hundred trees were pummeling one another with their limbs. Kettledrums began to beat as well, *boom-boom-boom-boom-boom, boom-boom-boom-boom-boom.* A warhorn bellowed, then another. *AAAAAAooooooooooooooooooooooooo.*

Men left their fires to make their way toward the bones of the Grey King's Hall; oarsmen, steersmen, sailmakers, shipwrights, the warriors with their axes and the fishermen with their nets. Some had thralls to serve them; some had salt wives. Others, who had sailed too often to the green lands, were attended by maesters and singers and knights. The common men crowded together in a crescent around the base of the knoll, with the thralls, children, and women toward the rear. The captains and the kings made their way up the slopes. Aeron Damphair saw cheerful Sigfry Stonetree, Andrik the Unsmiling, the knight Ser Harras Harlaw. Lord Baelor Blacktyde in his sable cloak stood beside The Stonehouse in ragged sealskin. Victarion loomed above all of them save Andrik. His brother wore no helm, but elsewise he was all in armor, his kraken cloak hanging golden from his shoulders. *He shall be our king. What man could look on him and doubt it?*

When the Damphair raised his bony hands the kettledrums and the warhorns fell silent, the drowned men lowered their cudgels, and all the voices stilled. Only the sound of the waves pounding remained, a roar no man could still. "We were born from the sea, and to the sea we all return," Aeron began, softly at first, so men would strain to hear. "The Storm God in his wrath plucked Balon from his castle and cast him down, yet now he feasts beneath the waves in the Drowned God's watery halls." He lifted his eyes to the sky. *"Balon is dead! The iron king is dead!"*

"The king is dead!" his drowned men shouted.

"Yet what is dead may never die, but rises again, harder and stronger!" he reminded them. "Balon has fallen, Balon my brother, who honored the Old Way and paid the iron price. Balon the Brave, Balon the Blessed, Balon Twice-Crowned, who won us back our freedoms and our god. Balon is dead . . . but an iron king shall rise again, to sit upon the Seastone Chair and rule the isles."

"A king shall rise!" they answered. *"He shall rise!"*

"He shall. He must." Aeron's voice thundered like the waves. "But who? Who shall sit in Balon's place? Who shall rule these holy isles? Is he here among us now?" The priest spread his hands wide. *"Who shall be king over us?"*

A seagull screamed back at him. The crowd began to stir, like men waking from a dream. Each man looked at his neighbors, to see which of them might presume to claim a crown. *The Crow's Eye was never patient,* Aeron Damphair told himself. *Mayhaps he will speak first.* If so, it would be his undoing. The captains and the kings had come a long way to this feast and would not choose the first dish set before them. *They will want to taste and sample, a bite of him, a nibble of the other, until they find the one that suits them best.*

Euron must have known that as well. He stood with his arms crossed amongst his mutes and monsters. Only the wind and the waves answered Aeron's call.

"The ironborn must have a king," the priest insisted, after a long silence. "I ask again. *Who shall be king over us?*"

"I will," came the answer from below.

At once a ragged cry of "Gylbert! Gylbert King!" went up. The captains gave way to let the claimant and his champions ascend the hill to stand at Aeron's side beneath the ribs of Nagga.

This would-be king was a tall spare lord with a melancholy visage, his lantern jaw shaved clean. His three champions took up their position two steps below him, bearing his sword and shield and banner. They shared a certain look with the tall lord, and Aeron took them for his sons. One unfurled his banner, a great black longship against a setting sun. "I am Gylbert Farwynd, Lord of the Lonely Light," the lord told the kingsmoot.

Aeron knew some Farwynds, a queer folk who held lands on the westernmost shores of Great Wyk and the scattered isles beyond, rocks so small that most could support but a single household. Of those, the Lonely Light was the most distant, eight days' sail to the northwest amongst rookeries of seals and sea lions and the boundless grey oceans. The Farwynds there were even queerer than the rest. Some said they were skinchangers, unholy creatures who could take on the forms of sea lions, walruses, even spotted whales, the wolves of the wild sea.

Lord Gylbert began to speak. He told of a wondrous land beyond the Sunset Sea, a land without winter or want, where death had no dominion. "Make me your king, and I shall lead you there," he cried. "We will build ten thousand ships as Nymeria once did and take sail with all our people to the land beyond the sunset. There every man shall be a king and every wife a queen."

His eyes, Aeron saw, were now grey, now blue, as changeable as the seas. *Mad eyes,* he thought, *fool's eyes.* The vision he spoke of was doubtless a snare set by the Storm God to lure the ironborn to destruction. The offerings that his men spilled out before the kingsmoot included sealskins and walrus tusks, arm rings made of whalebone, warhorns banded in bronze. The captains looked and turned away, leaving lesser men to help themselves to the gifts. When the fool was done talking and his champions began to shout his name, only the Farwynds took up the cry, and not even all of them. Soon enough the cries of "Gylbert! Gylbert King!" faded away to silence. The gull screamed loudly above them, and landed atop one of Nagga's ribs as the Lord of the Lonely Light made his way back down the hill.

Aeron Damphair stepped forward once more. "I ask again. *Who shall be king over us?*"

"Me!" a deep voice boomed, and once more the crowd parted.

The speaker was borne up the hill in a carved driftwood chair carried on the shoulders of his grandsons. A great ruin of a man, twenty stones heavy and ninety years old, he was cloaked in a white bearskin. His own hair was snow white as well, and his huge beard covered him like a blanket from cheeks to thighs, so it was hard to tell where the beard ended and the pelt began. Though his grandsons were great strapping men, they struggled with his weight on the steep stone steps. Before the Grey King's Hall they set him down, and three remained below him as his champions.

Sixty years ago, this one might well have won the favor of the moot, Aeron thought, *but his hour is long past.*

"Aye, me!" the man roared from where he sat, in a voice as huge as he was. "Why not? Who better? I am Erik Ironmaker, for them who's blind. Erik the Just. Erik Anvil-Breaker. Show them my hammer, Thormor." One of his champions lifted it up for all to see; a monstrous thing it was, its haft wrapped in old leather, its head a brick of steel as large as a loaf of bread. "I can't count how many hands I've smashed to pulp with that hammer," Erik said, "but might be some thief could tell you. I can't say how many heads I've crushed against my anvil neither, but there's some widows could. I could tell you all the deeds I've done in battle, but I'm eight-and-eighty and won't live long enough to finish. If old is wise, no one is wiser than me. If big is strong, no one's stronger. You want a king with heirs? I've more'n I can count. King Erik, aye, I like the sound o' that. Come, say it with me. *ERIK! ERIK ANVIL-BREAKER! ERIK KING!*"

As his grandsons took up the cry, their own sons came forward with chests upon their shoulders. When they upended them at the base of the stone steps, a torrent of silver, bronze, and steel spilled forth; arm rings, collars, daggers, dirks, and throwing axes. A few captains snatched up the choicest items and added their voices to the swelling chant. But no sooner had the cry begun to build than a woman's voice cut through it. "*Erik!*" Men moved aside to let her through. With one foot on the lowest step, she said, "Erik, stand up."

A hush fell. The wind blew, waves broke against the shore, men murmured in each other's ears. Erik Ironmaker stared down at Asha Greyjoy. "Girl. Thrice-damned girl. What did you say?"

"Stand up, Erik," she called. "Stand up and I'll shout your name with all the rest. Stand up and I'll be the first to follow you. You want a crown, aye. Stand up and take it."

Elsewhere in the press, the Crow's Eye laughed. Erik glared at him. The big man's hands closed tight around the arms of his driftwood throne. His face went red, then purple. His arms trembled with effort. Aeron could see a thick blue vein pulsing in his neck as he struggled to rise. For a moment it seemed as though he might do it, but the breath went out of him all at once, and he groaned and sank back onto his cushion. Euron laughed all the louder. The big man hung his head and grew old, all in the blink of an eye. His grandsons carried him back down the hill.

"Who shall rule the ironborn?" Aeron Damphair called again. "Who shall be king over us?"

Men looked at one another. Some looked at Euron, some at Victarion, a few at Asha. Waves broke green and white against the longships. The gull cried once more, a raucous scream, forlorn. "Make your claim, Victarion," the Merlyn called. "Let us have done with this mummer's farce."

"When I am ready," Victarion shouted back.

Aeron was pleased. *It is better if he waits.*

The Drumm came next, another old man, though not so old as Erik. He climbed the hill on his own two legs, and on his hip rode Red Rain, his famous sword, forged of Valyrian steel in the days before the Doom. His champions were men of note: his sons Denys and Donnel, both stout fighters, and between them Andrik the Unsmiling, a giant of a man with arms as thick as trees. It spoke well of the Drumm that such a man would stand for him.

"Where is it written that our king must be a kraken?" Drumm began. "What right has Pyke to rule us? Great Wyk is the largest isle, Harlaw the richest, Old Wyk the most holy. When the black line was consumed by dragonfire, the ironborn gave the primacy to Vickon Greyjoy, aye . . . but as *lord*, not king."

It was a good beginning. Aeron heard shouts of approval, but they dwindled as the old man began to tell of the glory of the Drumms. He spoke of Dale the Dread, Roryn the Reaver, the hundred sons of Gormond Drumm the Oldfather. He drew Red Rain and told them how Hilmar Drumm the Cunning had taken the blade from an armored knight with wits and a wooden cudgel. He spoke of ships long lost and battles eight hundred years forgotten, and the crowd grew restive. He spoke and spoke, and then he spoke still more.

And when Drumm's chests were thrown open, the captains saw the niggard's gifts he'd brought them. *No throne was ever bought with bronze,* the Damphair thought. The truth of that was plain to hear, as the cries of *"Drumm! Drumm! Dunstan King!"* died away.

Aeron could feel a tightness in his belly, and it seemed to him that the waves were pounding louder than before. *It is time,* he thought. *It is time for Victarion to make his claim.* "Who shall be king over us?" the priest cried once more, but this time his fierce black eyes found his brother in the crowd. "Nine sons were born from the loins of Quellon Greyjoy. One was mightier than all the rest, and knew no fear."

Victarion met his eyes, and nodded. The captains parted before him as he climbed the steps. "Brother, give me blessing," he said when he reached the top. He knelt and bowed his head. Aeron uncorked his waterskin and poured a stream of seawater down upon his brow.

"*What is dead can never die,*" the priest said, and Victarion replied, "*but rises again, harder and stronger.*"

When Victarion rose, his champions arrayed themselves beneath him; Ralf the Limper, Red Ralf Stonehouse, and Nute the Barber, noted warriors all. Stonehouse bore the Greyjoy banner; the golden kraken on a field as black as the midnight sea. As soon as it unfurled, the captains and the kings began to shout out the Lord Captain's name. Victarion waited till they quieted, then said, "You all know me. If you want sweet words, look elsewhere. I have no singer's tongue. I have an axe, and I have these." He raised his huge mailed hands up to show them, and Nute the Barber displayed his axe, a fearsome piece of steel. "I was a loyal brother," Victarion went on. "When Balon was wed, it was me he sent to Harlaw to bring him back his bride. I led his longships into many a battle, and never lost but one. The first time Balon took a crown, it was me sailed into Lannisport to singe the lion's tail. The second time, it was me he sent to skin the Young Wolf should he come howling home. All you'll get from me is more of what you got from Balon. That's all I have to say."

With that his champions began to chant: "*VICTARION! VICTARION! VICTARION KING!*" Below, his men were spilling out his chests, a cascade of silver, gold, and gems, a wealth of plunder. Captains scrambled to seize the richest pieces, shouting as they did so. "*VICTARION! VICTARION! VICTARION KING!*" Aeron watched the Crow's Eye. *Will he speak now, or let the kingsmoot run its course?* Orkwood of Orkmont was whispering in Euron's ear.

But it was not Euron who put an end to the shouting, it was the *woman.* She put two fingers in her mouth and *whistled,* a sharp shrill sound that cut through the tumult like a knife through curds. "Nuncle! Nuncle!" Bending, she snatched up a twisted golden collar and bounded up the steps. Nute seized her by the arm, and for half a heartbeat Aeron was hopeful that his brother's champions would keep her silent, but Asha wrenched free of the Barber's hand and said something to Red Ralf that made him step aside. As she pushed past, the cheering died away. She was Balon Greyjoy's daughter, and the crowd was curious to hear her speak.

"It was good of you to bring such gifts to my queensmoot, Nuncle," she told Victarion, "but you need not have worn so much armor. I promise not to hurt you." Asha turned to face the captains. "There's no one braver than my nuncle, no one stronger, no one fiercer in a fight. And he counts to ten as quick as any man, I have seen him do it . . . though when he needs to go to twenty he does take off his boots." That made them laugh. "He has no sons, though. His wives keep dying. The Crow's Eye is his elder and has a better claim . . ."

"He does!" the Red Oarsman shouted from below.

"Ah, but my claim is better still." Asha set the collar on her head at a jaunty angle, so the gold gleamed against her dark hair. "Balon's brother cannot come before Balon's son!"

"Balon's sons are dead," cried Ralf the Limper. "All I see is Balon's little daughter!"

"Daughter?" Asha slipped a hand beneath her jerkin. "Oho! What's this? Shall I show you? Some of you have not seen one since they weaned you." They laughed again. "Teats on a king are a terrible thing, is that the song? Ralf, you have me, I *am* a woman . . . though not an *old* woman like you. Ralf the Limper . . . shouldn't that be Ralf the Limp?" Asha drew a dirk from between her breasts. "I'm a mother too, and here's my suckling babe!" She held it up. "And here, my champions." They pushed past Victarion's three to stand below her: Qarl the Maid, Tristifer Botley, and the knight Ser Harras Harlaw, whose sword Nightfall was as storied as Dunstan Drumm's Red Rain. "My nuncle said you know him. You know me too—"

"I want to know you better!" someone shouted.

"Go home and know your wife," Asha shot back. "Nuncle says he'll give you more of what my father gave you. Well, what was that? Gold and glory, some will say. *Freedom,* ever sweet. Aye, it's so, he gave us that . . . and widows too, as Lord Blacktyde will tell you. How many of you had your homes put to the torch when Robert came? How many had daughters raped and despoiled? Burnt towns and broken castles, my father gave you that. *Defeat* was what he gave you. Nuncle here will give you more. Not me."

"What will you give us?" asked Lucas Codd. "Knitting?"

"Aye, Lucas. I'll knit us all a kingdom." She tossed her dirk from hand to hand. "We need to take a lesson from the Young Wolf, who won every battle . . . and lost all."

"A wolf is not a kraken," Victarion objected. "What the kraken grasps it does not lose, be it longship or leviathan."

"And what *have* we grasped, Nuncle? The north? What is that, but leagues and leagues of leagues and leagues, far from the sound of the sea? We have taken Moat Cailin, Deepwood Motte, Torrhen's Square, even *Winterfell*. What do we have to show for it?" She beckoned, and her *Black Wind* men pushed forward, chests of oak and iron on their shoulders. "I give you the wealth of the Stony Shore," Asha said as the first was upended. An avalanche of pebbles clattered forth, cascading down the steps; pebbles grey and black and white, worn smooth by the sea. "I give you the riches of Deepwood," she said, as the second chest was opened. Pinecones came pouring out, to roll and bounce down into the crowd. "And last, the gold of Winterfell." From the third chest came yellow turnips, round and hard and big as a man's head. They landed amidst the pebbles and the pinecones. Asha stabbed one with her dirk. "Harmund Sharp," she shouted, "your son Harrag died at Winterfell, for this." She pulled the turnip off her blade and tossed it to him. "You have other sons, I think. If you'd trade their lives for turnips, shout my nuncle's name!"

"And if I shout *your* name?" Harmund demanded. "What then?"

"Peace," said Asha. "Land. Victory. I'll give you Sea Dragon Point and the Stony Shore, black earth and tall trees and stones enough for every younger son to build a hall. We'll have the northmen too . . . as friends, to stand with us against the Iron Throne. Your choice is simple. Crown me, for peace and victory. Or crown my nuncle, for more war and more defeat." She sheathed her dirk again. "What will you have, ironmen?"

"*VICTORY!*" shouted Rodrik the Reader, his hands cupped about his mouth. "*Victory, and Asha!*"

"*ASHA!*" Lord Baelor Blacktyde echoed. "*ASHA QUEEN!*"

Asha's own crew took up the cry. "*ASHA! ASHA! ASHA QUEEN!*" They stamped their feet and shook their fists and yelled, as the Damphair listened in disbelief. *She would leave her father's work undone!* Yet Tristifer Botley was shouting for her, with many Harlaws, some Goodbrothers, red-faced Lord Merlyn, more men than the priest would ever have believed . . . for a *woman!*

But others were holding their tongues, or muttering asides to their neighbors. *"No craven's peace!"* Ralf the Limper roared. Red Ralf Stonehouse swirled the Greyjoy banner and bellowed, *"Victarion! VICTARION! VICTARION!"* Men began to shove at one another. Someone flung a pinecone at Asha's head. When she ducked, her makeshift crown fell off. For a moment it seemed to the priest as if he stood atop a giant anthill, with a thousand ants in a boil at his feet. Shouts of *"Asha!"* and *"Victarion!"* surged back and forth, and it seemed as though some savage storm was about to engulf them all. *The Storm God is amongst us,* the priest thought, *sowing fury and discord.*

Sharp as a swordthrust, the sound of a horn split the air.

Bright and baneful was its voice, a shivering hot scream that made a man's bones seem to *thrum* within him. The cry lingered in the damp sea air: *aaaaRREEEEeeeeeeeeeeeeeeeeeeeeeeeeee.*

All eyes turned toward the sound. It was one of Euron's mongrels winding the call, a monstrous man with a shaved head. Rings of gold and jade and jet glistened on his arms, and on his broad chest was tattooed some bird of prey, talons dripping blood.

aaaaRRREEEEeeeeeeeeeeeeeeeeeeeeeeeeeeee.

The horn he blew was shiny black and twisted, and taller than a man as he held it with both hands. It was bound about with bands of red gold and dark steel, incised with ancient Valyrian glyphs that seemed to glow redly as the sound swelled.

aaaaaaaRRREEEEEEEEEEEEEEeeeeeeeeeeeeeeeeeeeeeeeeeeeeeeeeeeee.

It was a terrible sound, a wail of pain and fury that seemed to burn the ears. Aeron Damphair covered his, and prayed for the Drowned God to raise a mighty wave and smash the horn to silence, yet still the shriek went on and on. *It is the horn of hell,* he wanted to scream, though no man would have heard him. The cheeks of the tattooed man were so puffed out they looked about to burst, and the muscles in his chest twitched in a way that it made it seem as if the bird were about to rip free of his flesh and take wing. And now the glyphs were burning brightly, every line and letter shimmering with white fire. On and on and on the sound went, echoing amongst the howling hills behind them and across the waters of Nagga's Cradle to ring against the mountains of Great Wyk, on and on and on until it filled the whole wet world.

And when it seemed the sound would never end, it did.

The hornblower's breath failed at last. He staggered and almost fell. The priest saw Orkwood of Orkmont catch him by one arm to hold him up, whilst Left-Hand Lucas Codd took the twisted black horn from his hands. A thin wisp of smoke was rising from the horn, and the priest saw blood and blisters upon the lips of the man who'd sounded it. The bird on his chest was bleeding too.

Euron Greyjoy climbed the hill slowly, with every eye upon him. Above the gull screamed and screamed again. *No godless man may sit the Seastone Chair*, Aeron thought, but he knew that he must let his brother speak. His lips moved silently in prayer.

Asha's champions stepped aside, and Victarion's as well. The priest took a step backward and put one hand upon the cold rough stone of Nagga's ribs. The Crow's Eye stopped atop the steps, at the doors of the Grey King's Hall, and turned his smiling eye upon the captains and the kings, but Aeron could feel his other eye as well, the one that he kept hidden.

"IRONMEN," said Euron Greyjoy, "you have heard my horn. Now hear my words. I am Balon's brother, Quellon's eldest living son. Lord Vickon's blood is in my veins, and the blood of the Old Kraken. Yet I have sailed farther than any of them. Only one living kraken has never known defeat. Only one has never bent his knee. Only one has sailed to Asshai by the Shadow, and seen wonders and terrors beyond imagining . . ."

"If you liked the Shadow so well, go back there," called out pink-cheeked Qarl the Maid, one of Asha's champions.

The Crow's Eye ignored him. "My little brother would finish Balon's war, and claim the north. My sweet niece would give us peace and pinecones." His blue lips twisted in a smile. "Asha prefers victory to defeat. Victarion wants a kingdom, not a few scant yards of earth. From me, you shall have both.

"Crow's Eye, you call me. Well, who has a keener eye than the crow? After every battle the crows come in their hundreds and their thousands to feast upon the fallen. A crow can espy death from afar. And I say that all of Westeros is dying. Those who follow me will feast until the end of their days.

"We are the ironborn, and once we were conquerors. Our writ ran everywhere the sound of the waves was heard. My brother would have you be content with the cold and dismal north, my niece with even less . . . but I shall give you Lannisport. Highgarden. The Arbor. Oldtown. The riverlands and the Reach, the kingswood and the rainwood, Dorne and the marches, the Mountains of the Moon and the Vale of Arryn, Tarth and the Stepstones. I say we take it *all!* I say, we take *Westeros.*" He glanced at the priest. "All for the greater glory of our Drowned God, to be sure."

For half a heartbeat even Aeron was swept away by the boldness of his words. The priest had dreamed the same dream, when first he'd seen the red comet in the sky. *We shall sweep over the green lands with fire and sword, root out the seven gods of the septons and the white trees of the northmen . . .*

"Crow's Eye," Asha called, "did you leave your wits at Asshai? If we cannot hold the north—and we cannot—how can we win the whole of the Seven Kingdoms?"

"Why, it has been done before. Did Balon teach his girl so little of the ways of war? Victarion, our brother's daughter has never heard of Aegon the Conqueror, it would seem."

"Aegon?" Victarion crossed his arms against his armored chest. "What has the Conqueror to do with us?"

"I know as much of war as you do, Crow's Eye," Asha said. "Aegon Targaryen conquered Westeros with *dragons.*"

"And so shall we," Euron Greyjoy promised. "That horn you heard I found amongst the smoking ruins that were Valyria, where no man has dared to walk but me. You heard its call, and felt its power. It is a dragon horn, bound with bands of red gold and Valyrian steel graven with enchantments. The dragonlords of old sounded such horns, before the Doom devoured them. With this horn, ironmen, I can bind *dragons* to my will."

Asha laughed aloud. "A horn to bind goats to your will would be of more use, Crow's Eye. There are no more dragons."

"Again, girl, you are wrong. There are three, and I know where to find them. Surely that is worth a driftwood crown."

"*EURON!*" shouted Left-Hand Lucas Codd.

"*EURON! CROW'S EYE! EURON!*" cried the Red Oarsman.

The mutes and mongrels from the *Silence* threw open Euron's chests and spilled out his gifts before the captains and the kings. Then it was Hotho Harlaw the priest heard, as he filled his hands with gold. Gorold Goodbrother shouted out as well, and Erik Anvil-Breaker. "*EURON! EURON! EURON!*" The cry swelled, became a roar. "*EURON! EURON! CROW'S EYE! EURON KING!*" It rolled up Nagga's hill, like the Storm God rattling the clouds. "*EURON! EURON! EURON! EURON! EURON! EURON!*"

Even a priest may doubt. Even a prophet may know terror. Aeron Damphair reached within himself for his god and discovered only silence. As a thousand voices shouted out his brother's name, all he could hear was the scream of a rusted iron hinge.

BRIENNE

East of Maidenpool the hills rose wild, and the pines closed in about them like a host of silent grey-green soldiers.

Nimble Dick said the coast road was the shortest way, and the easiest, so they were seldom out of sight of the bay. The towns and villages along the shore grew smaller as they went, and less frequent. At nightfall they would seek an inn. Crabb would share the common bed with other travelers, whilst Brienne took a room for her and Podrick. "Cheaper if we all shared the same bed, m'lady," Nimble Dick would say. "You could lay your sword between us. Old Dick's a harmless fellow. Chivalrous as a knight, and honest as the day is long."

"The days are growing shorter," Brienne pointed out.

"Well, that may be. If you don't trust me in the bed, I could just curl up on the floor, m'lady."

"Not on my floor."

"A man might think you don't trust me none."

"Trust is earned. Like gold."

"As you say, m'lady," said Crabb, "but up north where the road gives out, you'll need t' trust Dick then. If I wanted t' take your gold at swordpoint, who's to stop me?"

"You don't own a sword. I do."

She shut the door between them and stood there listening until she was certain he had moved away. However nimble he might be,

Dick Crabb was no Jaime Lannister, no Mad Mouse, not even a Humfrey Wagstaff. He was scrawny and ill fed, his only armor a dinted halfhelm spotted with rust. In place of a sword, he carried an old, nicked dagger. So long as she was awake, he posed no danger to her. "Podrick," she said, "there will come a time when there are no more inns to shelter us. I do not trust our guide. When we make camp, can you watch over me as I sleep?"

"Stay awake, my lady? Ser." He thought. "I have a sword. If Crabb tries to hurt you, I could kill him."

"No," she said sternly. "You are not to try and fight him. All I ask is that you watch him as I sleep, and wake me if he does anything suspicious. I wake quickly, you will find."

Crabb showed his true colors the next day, when they stopped to water the horses. Brienne had to step behind some bushes to empty her bladder. As she was squatting, she heard Podrick say, "What are you doing? You get away from there." She finished her business, hiked up her breeches, and returned to the road to find Nimble Dick wiping flour off his fingers. "You won't find any dragons in your saddlebags," she told him. "I keep my gold upon my person." Some of it was in the pouch at her belt, the rest hidden in a pair of pockets sewn inside her clothing. The fat purse inside her saddlebag was filled with coppers large and small, pennies and halfpennies, groats and stars . . . and fine white flour, to make it fatter still. She had bought the flour from the cook at the Seven Swords the morning she rode out from Duskendale.

"Dick meant no harm, m'lady." He wriggled his flour-spotted fingers to show he held no weapon. "I was only looking to see if you had these dragons what you promised me. The world's full o' liars, ready to cheat an honest man. Not that *you're* one."

Brienne hoped he was a better guide than he was a thief. "We had best be going." She mounted up again.

Dick would oft sing as they rode along together; never a whole song, only a snatch of this and a verse of that. She suspected that he meant to charm her, to put her off her guard. Sometimes he would try to get her and Podrick to sing along with him, to no avail. The boy was too shy and tongue-tied, and Brienne did not sing. *Did you sing for your father?* Lady Stark had asked her once, at Riverrun. *Did you sing for Renly?* She had not, not ever, though she had wanted . . . she had wanted . . .

When he was not singing, Nimble Dick would talk, regaling them with tales of Crackclaw Point. Every gloomy valley had its lord, he said, the lot of them united only by their mistrust of outsiders. In their veins the blood of the First Men ran dark and strong. "The Andals tried t' take Crackclaw, but we bled them in the valleys and drowned them in the bogs. Only what their sons couldn't win with swords, their pretty daughters won with kisses. They married into the houses they couldn't conquer, aye."

The Darklyn kings of Duskendale had tried to impose their rule on Crackclaw Point; the Mootons of Maidenpool had tried as well, and later the haughty Celtigars of Crab Isle. But the Crackclaws knew their bogs and forests as no outsider could, and if hard pressed would vanish into the caverns that honeycombed their hills. When not fighting would-be conquerors, they fought each other. Their blood feuds were as deep and dark as the bogs between their hills. From time to time some champion would bring peace to the Point, but it never lasted longer than his lifetime. Lord Lucifer Hardy, he was a great one, and the Brothers Brune as well. Old Crackbones even more so, but the Crabbs were the mightiest of all. Dick still refused to believe that Brienne had never heard of Ser Clarence Crabb and his exploits.

"Why would I lie?" she asked him. "Every place has its local heroes. Where I come from, the singers sing of Ser Galladon of Morne, the Perfect Knight."

"Ser Gallawho of What?" He snorted. "Never heard o' him. Why was he so bloody perfect?"

"Ser Galladon was a champion of such valor that the Maiden herself lost her heart to him. She gave him an enchanted sword as a token of her love. The Just Maid, it was called. No common sword could check her, nor any shield withstand her kiss. Ser Galladon bore the Just Maid proudly, but only thrice did he unsheathe her. He would not use the Maid against a mortal man, for she was so potent as to make any fight unfair."

Crabb thought that was hilarious. "The Perfect Knight? The Perfect Fool, he sounds like. What's the point o' having some magic sword if you don't bloody well use it?"

"Honor," she said. "The point is honor."

That only made him laugh the louder. "Ser Clarence Crabb would have wiped his hairy arse with your Perfect Knight, m'lady. If they'd ever have met, there'd be one more bloody head sitting on the shelf at the Whispers, you ask me. 'I should have used the magic sword,' it'd be saying to all the other heads. 'I should have used the bloody sword.'"

Brienne could not help but smile. "Perhaps," she allowed, "but Ser Galladon was no fool. Against a foe eight feet tall mounted on an aurochs, he might well have unsheathed the Just Maid. He used her once to slay a dragon, they say."

Nimble Dick was unimpressed. "Crackbones fought a dragon too, but he didn't need no magic sword. He just tied its neck in a knot, so every time it breathed fire it roasted its own arse."

"And what did Crackbones do when Aegon and his sisters came?" Brienne asked him.

"He was dead. M'lady must know that." Crabb gave her a sideways look. "Aegon sent his sister up to Crackclaw, that Visenya. The lords had heard o' Harren's end. Being no fools, they laid their swords at her feet. The queen took them as her own men, and said they'd owe no fealty to Maidenpool, Crab Isle, or Duskendale. Don't stop them bloody Celtigars from sending men to t' eastern shore to collect his taxes. If he sends enough, a few come back to him . . . elsewise, we bow only to our own lords, and the king. The *true* king, not Robert and his ilk." He spat. "There was Crabbs and Brunes and Boggses with Prince Rhaegar on the Trident, and in the Kingsguard too. A Hardy, a Cave, a Pyne, and *three* Crabbs, Clement and Rupert and Clarence the Short. Six foot tall, he was, but short compared to the *real* Ser Clarence. We're all good dragon men, up Crackclaw way."

The traffic continued to dwindle as they moved north and east, until finally there were no inns to be found. By then the bayside road was more weeds than ruts. That night they took shelter in a fishing village. Brienne paid the villagers a few coppers to allow them to bed down in a hay barn. She claimed the loft for Podrick and herself, and pulled the ladder up after them.

"You leave me down here alone, I could bloody well steal your horses," Crabb called up from below. "Best you get them up the ladder too, m'lady." When she ignored him, he went on to say, "It's going to rain tonight. A cold hard rain. You and Pods will sleep all snug and warm, and poor old Dick will be shivering down here by myself." He shook his head, muttering, as he made a bed on a pile of hay. "I never knew such a mistrustful maid as you."

Brienne curled up beneath her cloak, with Podrick yawning at her side. *I was not always wary,* she might have shouted down at Crabb. *When I was a little girl I believed that all men were as noble as my father.* Even the men who told her what a pretty girl she was, how tall and bright and clever, how graceful when she danced. It was Septa Roelle who had lifted the scales from her eyes. "They only say those things to win your lord father's favor," the woman had said. "You'll find truth in your looking glass, not on the tongues of men." It was a harsh lesson, one that left her weeping, but it had stood her in good stead at Harrenhal when Ser Hyle and his friends had played their game. *A maid has to be mistrustful in this world, or she will not be a maid for long,* she was thinking, as the rain began to fall.

In the mêlée at Bitterbridge, she had sought out her suitors and battered them one by one, Farrow and Ambrose and Bushy, Mark Mullendore and Raymond Nayland and Will the Stork. She had ridden over Harry Sawyer and broken Robin Potter's helm, giving him a nasty scar. And when the last of them had fallen, the Mother had delivered Connington to her. This time Ser Ronnet held a sword and not a rose. Every blow she dealt him was sweeter than a kiss.

Loras Tyrell had been the last to face her wroth that day. He'd never courted her, had hardly looked at her at all, but he bore three golden roses on his shield that day, and Brienne hated roses. The sight of them had given her a furious strength. She went to sleep dreaming of the fight they'd had, and of Ser Jaime fastening a rainbow cloak about her shoulders.

It was still raining the next morning. As they broke their fast, Nimble Dick suggested that they wait for it to stop.

"When will that be? On the morrow? In a fortnight? When summer comes again? No. We have cloaks, and leagues to ride."

It rained all that day. The narrow track they followed soon turned to mud beneath them. What trees they saw were naked, and the steady rain had turned their fallen leaves into a sodden brown mat. Despite its squirrel-skin lining, Dick's cloak soaked through, and she could see him shivering. Brienne felt a moment's pity for the man. *He has not eaten well, that's plain.* She wondered if there truly was a smugglers' cove, or a ruined castle called the Whispers. Hungry men do desperate things. This all might be some ploy to cozen her. Suspicion soured her stomach.

For a time it seemed as though the steady wash of rain was the only sound in the world. Nimble Dick plowed on, heedless. She watched closely, noting how he bent his back, as if huddling low in the saddle would keep him dry. This time there was no village close at hand when darkness came upon them. Nor were there any trees to give them shelter. They were forced to camp amongst some rocks, fifty yards above the tideline. The rocks at least would keep the wind off. "Best we keep a watch tonight, m'lady," Crabb told her, as she was struggling to get a driftwood fire lit. "A place like this, there might be squishers."

"Squishers?" Brienne gave him a suspicious look.

"Monsters," Nimble Dick said, with relish. "They look like men till you get close, but their heads is too big, and they got scales where a proper man's got hair. Fish-belly white they are, with webs between their fingers. They're always damp and fishy-smelling, but behind these blubbery lips they got rows of green teeth sharp as needles. Some say the First Men killed them all, but don't you believe it. They come by night and steal bad little children, padding along on them webbed feet with a little *squish-squish* sound. The girls they keep to breed with, but the boys they eat, tearing at them with those sharp green teeth." He grinned at Podrick. "They'd eat you, boy. They'd eat you *raw*."

"If they try, I'll kill them." Podrick touched his sword.

"You try that. You just try. Squishers don't die easy." He winked at Brienne. "You a bad little girl, m'lady?"

"No." *Just a fool.* The wood was too damp to light, no matter how many sparks Brienne struck off her flint and steel. The kindling sent up some smoke, but that was all. Disgusted, she settled down with her back to a rock, pulled her cloak over herself, and resigned herself to a cold, wet night. Dreaming of a hot meal, she gnawed on a strip of hard salt beef whilst Nimble Dick talked about the time Ser Clarence Crabb had fought the squisher king. *He tells a lively tale,* she had to admit, *but Mark Mullendore was amusing too, with his little monkey.*

It was too wet to see the sun go down, too grey to see the moon come up. The night was black and starless. Crabb ran out of tales and went to sleep. Podrick was soon snoring too. Brienne sat with her back to the rock, listening to the waves. *Are you near the sea, Sansa?* she wondered. *Are you waiting at the Whispers for a ship that will never come? Who do you have with you? Passage for three, he said. Has the Imp joined you and Ser Dontos, or did you find your little sister?*

The day had been a long one, and Brienne was tired. Even sitting up against the rock, with rain pattering softly all around her, she found her eyelids growing heavy. Twice she dozed. The second time she woke all at once, heart pounding, convinced that someone was looming over her. Her limbs were stiff, and her cloak had gotten tangled round her ankles. She kicked free of it and stood. Nimble Dick was curled against a rock, half-buried in wet, heavy sand, asleep. *A dream. It was a dream.*

Perhaps she had made a mistake in abandoning Ser Creighton and Ser Illifer. They had seemed like honest men. *Would that Jaime had come with me,* she thought . . . but he was a knight of the Kingsguard, his rightful place was with his king. Besides, it was Renly that she wanted. *I swore I would protect him, and I failed. Then I swore I would avenge him, and I failed at that as well. I ran off with Lady Catelyn instead, and failed her too.* The wind had shifted, and the rain was running down her face.

The next day the road dwindled to a pebbled thread, and finally to a mere suggestion. Near midday, it came to an abrupt end at the foot of a wind-carved cliff. Above, a small castle stood frowning over the waves, its three crooked towers outlined against a leaden sky. "Is that the Whispers?" Podrick asked.

"That look a bloody ruin t' you?" Crabb spat. "That's the Dyre Den, where old Lord Brune keeps his seat. Road ends here, though. It's the pines for us from here on."

Brienne studied the cliff. "How do we get up there?"

"Easy." Nimble Dick turned his horse. "Stay close t' Dick. The squishers are apt t' take the laggards."

The way up proved to be a steep stony path hidden within a cleft in the rock. Most of it was natural, but here and there steps had been carved to ease the climb. Sheer walls of rock, eaten away by centuries of wind and spray, hemmed them in to either side. In some places they had assumed fantastic shapes. Nimble Dick pointed out a few as they climbed. "There's an ogre's head, see?" he said, and Brienne smiled when she saw it. "And that there's a stone dragon. T'other wing fell off when my father was a boy. Above it, that's the dugs drooping down, like some hag's teats." He glanced back at her own chest.

"Ser? My lady?" said Podrick. "There's a rider."

"Where?" None of the rocks suggested a rider to her.

"On the road. Not a rock rider. A real rider. Following us. Down there." He pointed.

Brienne twisted in her saddle. They had climbed high enough to see for leagues along the shore. The horse was coming up the same road they had taken, two or three miles behind them. *Again?* She glanced at Nimble Dick suspiciously.

"Don't squint at me," Crabb said. "He's naught t' do with old Nimble Dick, whoever he is. Some man o' Brune's, most like, come back from the wars. Or one o' them singers, wandering from place to place." He turned his head and spat. "He's no squisher, that's bloody certain. Their sort don't ride horses."

"No," said Brienne. On that, at least, they could agree.

The last hundred feet of the climb proved the steepest and most treacherous. Loose pebbles rolled beneath their horse's hooves and went rattling down the stony path behind them. When they emerged from the cleft in the rock, they found themselves under the castle walls. On a parapet above, a face peered down at them, then vanished. Brienne thought it might have been a woman, and said as much to Nimble Dick.

He agreed. "Brune's too old to go climbing wallwalks, and his sons and grandsons went off to the wars. No one left in there but wenches, and a snot-nosed babe or three."

It was on her lips to ask her guide which king Lord Brune had espoused, but it made no matter any longer. Brune's sons were gone; some might not be coming back. *We will have no hospitality here tonight.* A castle full of old men, women, and children was not like to open its doors to armed strangers. "You speak of Lord Brune as if you know him," she said to Nimble Dick.

"Might be I did, once."

She glanced at the breast of his doublet. Loose threads and a ragged patch of darker fabric showed where some badge had been torn away. Her guide was a deserter, she did not doubt. Could the rider behind them be one of his brothers-in-arms?

"We should ride on," he urged, "before Brune starts to wonder why we're here beneath his walls. Even a wench can wind a bloody crossbow." Dick gestured toward the limestone hills that rose beyond the castle, with their wooded slopes. "No more roads from here on, only streams and game trails, but m'lady need not fear. Nimble Dick knows these parts."

That was what Brienne was afraid of. The wind was gusting along the top of the cliff, but all she could smell was a trap. "What about that rider?" Unless his horse could walk on waves, he would soon be coming up the cliff.

"What about him? If he's some fool from Maidenpool, he might not even find the bloody path. And if he does, we'll lose him in the woods. He won't have no road to follow there."

Only our tracks. Brienne wondered if it wouldn't be better to meet the rider here, with her blade in hand. *I'll look an utter fool if it is a wandering singer or one of Lord Brune's sons.* Crabb had the right of it, she supposed. *If he is still behind us on the morrow, I can deal with him then.* "As you will," she said, turning her mare toward the trees.

Lord Brune's castle dwindled at their backs, and soon was lost to sight. Sentinels and soldier pines rose all around them, towering green-clad spears thrusting toward the sky. The forest floor was a bed of fallen needles as thick as a castle wall, littered with pinecones. The hooves of their horses seemed to make no sound. It rained a bit, stopped for a time, then started once again, but amongst the pines they scarce felt a drop.

The going was much slower in the woods. Brienne prodded her mare through the green gloom, weaving in and out amongst the trees. It would be very easy to get lost here, she realized. Every way she looked appeared the same. The very air seemed grey and green and still. Pine boughs scratched against her arms and scraped noisily against her newly painted shield. The eerie stillness grated on her more with every passing hour.

It bothered Nimble Dick as well. Late that day, as dusk was coming on, he tried to sing. *"A bear there was, a bear, a bear, all black and brown, and covered with hair,"* he sang, his voice as scratchy as a pair of woolen breeches. The pines drank his song, as they drank the wind and rain. After a little while he stopped.

"It's bad here," Podrick said. "This is a bad place."

Brienne felt the same, but it would not serve to admit it. "A pine wood is a gloomy place, but in the end it's just a wood. There's naught here that we need fear."

"What about the squishers? And the heads?"

"There's a clever lad," said Nimble Dick, laughing.

Brienne gave him a look of annoyance. "There are no squishers," she told Podrick, "and no heads."

The hills went up, the hills went down. Brienne found herself praying that Nimble Dick was honest, and knew where he was taking them. By herself, she was not even certain she could have found the sea again. Day or night, the sky was solid grey and overcast, with neither sun nor stars to help her find her way.

They made camp early that night, after they came down a hill and found themselves on the edge of a glistening green bog. In the grey-green light, the ground ahead looked solid enough, but when they'd ridden out it had swallowed their horses up to their withers. They had to turn and fight their way back onto more solid footing. "It's no matter," Crabb assured them. "We'll go back up the hill and come down another way."

The next day was the same. They rode through pines and bogs, under dark skies and intermittent rain, past sinkholes and caves and the ruins of ancient strongholds whose stones were blanketed in moss. Every heap of stones had a story, and Nimble Dick told them all. To hear him tell it, the men of Crackclaw Point had watered their pine trees with blood. Brienne's patience soon began to fray. "How much longer?" she demanded finally. "We must have seen every tree in Crackclaw Point by now."

"Not hardly," said Crabb. "We're close now. See, the woods is thinning out. We're near the narrow sea."

This fool he promised me is like to be my own reflection in a pond, Brienne thought, but it seemed pointless to turn back when she had come so far. She was weary, though, she could not deny that. Her thighs were hard as iron from the saddle, and of late she had been sleeping only four hours a night, whilst Podrick watched over her. If Nimble Dick meant to try and murder them, she was convinced it would happen here, on ground that he knew well. He could be taking them to some robbers' den where he had kin as treacherous as he was. Or perhaps he was just leading them in circles, waiting for that rider to catch up. They had not seen any sign of the man since leaving Lord Brune's castle, but that did not mean he had given up the hunt.

It may be that I will need to kill him, she told herself one night as she paced about the camp. The notion made her queasy. Her old master-at-arms had always questioned whether she was hard enough for battle. "You have a man's strength in your arms," Ser Goodwin had said to her, more than once, "but your heart is as soft as any maid's. It is one thing to train in the yard with a blunted sword in hand, and another to drive a foot of sharpened steel into a man's gut and see the light go out of his eyes." To toughen her, Ser Goodwin used to send her to her father's butcher to slaughter lambs and suckling pigs. The piglets squealed and the lambs screamed like frightened children. By the time the butchering was done Brienne had been blind with tears, her clothes so bloody that she had given them to her maid to burn. But Ser Goodwin still had doubts. "A piglet is a piglet. It is different with a man. When I was a squire young as you, I had a friend who was strong and quick and agile, a champion in the yard.

We all knew that one day he would be a splendid knight. Then war came to the Stepstones. I saw my friend drive his foeman to his knees and knock the axe from his hand, but when he might have finished he held back for half a heartbeat. In battle half a heartbeat is a lifetime. The man slipped out his dirk and found a chink in my friend's armor. His strength, his speed, his valor, all his hard-won skill . . . it was worth less than a mummer's fart, *because he flinched from killing*. Remember that, girl."

I will, she promised his shade, there in the piney wood. She sat down on a rock, took out her sword, and began to hone its edge. *I will remember, and I pray I will not flinch.*

The next day dawned bleak and cold and overcast. They never saw the sun come up, but when the blackness turned to grey Brienne knew it was time to saddle up again. With Nimble Dick leading the way, they rode back into the pines. Brienne followed close behind him, with Podrick bringing up the rear upon his rounsey.

The castle came upon them without warning. One moment they were in the depths of the forest, with nothing but pines to see for leagues and leagues. Then they rode around a boulder, and a gap appeared ahead. A mile farther on, the forest ended abruptly. Beyond was sky and sea . . . and an ancient, tumbledown castle, abandoned and overgrown on the edge of a cliff. "The Whispers," said Nimble Dick. "Have a listen. You can hear the heads."

Podrick's mouth gaped open. "I hear them."

Brienne heard them too. A faint, soft murmuring that seemed to be coming from the ground as much as from the castle. The sound grew louder as she neared the cliffs. It was the sea, she realized suddenly. The waves had eaten holes in the cliffs below and were rumbling through caves and tunnels beneath the earth. "There are no heads," she said. "It's the waves you hear whispering."

"Waves don't whisper. It's heads."

The castle was built of old, unmortared stones, no two the same. Moss grew thick in clefts between the rocks, and trees were growing up from the foundations. Most old castles had a godswood. By the look of it, the Whispers had little else. Brienne walked her mare to the cliff's edge, where the curtain wall had collapsed. Mounds of poisonous red ivy grew over the heap of broken stones. She tied the horse to a tree and edged as close to the precipice as she dared. Fifty feet below, the waves were swirling in and over the remnants of a shattered tower. Behind it, she glimpsed the mouth of a large cavern.

"That's the old beacon tower," said Nimble Dick as he came up behind her. "It fell when I was half as old as Pods here. Used to be steps down to the cove, but when the cliff collapsed they went too. The smugglers stopped landing here after that. Time was, they could row their boats into the cave, but no more. See?" He put one hand on her back, and pointed with the other.

Brienne's flesh prickled. *One shove, and I'll be down there with the tower.* She stepped back. "Keep your hands off me."

Crabb made a face. "I was only . . ."

"I don't care what you were *only.* Where's the gate?"

"Around t'other side." He hesitated. "This fool o' yours, he's not a man to hold a grudge, is he?" he said nervously. "I mean, last night I got to thinking that he might be angry at old Nimble Dick, on account o' that map I sold him, and how I left out that the smugglers don't land here no more."

"With the gold that you've got coming, you can give him back whatever he paid you for your *help.*" Brienne could not imagine Dontos Hollard posing a threat. "That is, if he's even here."

They made a circuit of the walls. The castle had been triangular, with square towers at each corner. Its gates were badly rotted. When Brienne tugged at one, the wood cracked and peeled away in long wet splinters, and half the gate came down on her. She could see more green gloom inside. The forest had breached the walls, and swallowed keep and bailey. But there was a portcullis behind the gate, its teeth sunk deep into the soft muddy ground. The iron was red with rust, but it held when Brienne rattled it. "No one's used this gate for a long time."

"I could climb over," offered Podrick. "By the cliff. Where the wall fell down."

"It's too dangerous. Those stones looked loose to me, and that red ivy's poisonous. There has to be a postern gate."

They found it on the north side of the castle, half-hidden behind a huge blackberry bramble. The berries had all been picked, and half the bush had been hacked down to cut a path to the door. The sight of the broken branches filled Brienne with disquiet. "Someone's been through here, and recently."

"Your fool and those girls," said Crabb. "I told you."

Sansa? Brienne could not believe it. Even a wine-soaked sot like Dontos Hollard would have better sense than to bring her to this bleak place. Something about the ruins filled her with unease. She would not find the Stark girl here . . . but she had to have a look. *Someone was here,* she thought. *Someone who needed to stay hidden.* "I'm going in," she said. "Crabb, you'll come with me. Podrick, I want you to watch the horses."

"I want to come too. I'm a squire. I can fight."

"That's why I want you to stay here. There may be outlaws in these woods. We dare not leave the horses unprotected."

Podrick scuffed at a rock with his boot. "As you say."

She shouldered through the blackberries and pulled at a rusted iron ring. The postern door resisted for a moment, then jerked open, its hinges screaming protest. The sound made the hairs on the back of Brienne's neck stand up. She drew her sword. Even in mail and boiled leather, she felt naked.

"Go on, m'lady," urged Nimble Dick, behind her. "What are you waiting for? Old Crabb's been dead a thousand years."

What *was* she waiting for? Brienne told herself that she was being foolish. The sound was just the sea, echoing endlessly through the caverns beneath the castle, rising and falling with each wave. It *did* sound like whispering, though, and for a moment she could almost see the heads, sitting on their shelves and muttering to one another. *"I should have used the sword"* one of them was saying. *"I should have used the magic sword."*

"Podrick," said Brienne. "There's a sword and scabbard wrapped up in my bedroll. Bring them here to me."

"Yes, ser. My lady. I will." The boy went running off.

"A sword?" Nimble Dick scratched behind his ear. "You got a sword in your hand. What do you need another for?"

"This one's for you." Brienne offered him the hilt.

"For true?" Crabb reached out hesitantly, as if the blade might bite him. "The mistrustful maid's giving old Dick a sword?"

"You do know how to use one?"

"I'm a Crabb." He snatched the longsword from her hand. "I got the same blood as old Ser Clarence." He slashed the air and grinned at her. "It's the sword that makes the lord, some say."

When Podrick Payne returned, he held Oathkeeper as gingerly as if it were a child. Nimble Dick gave a whistle at the sight of the ornate scabbard with its row of lion's heads, but grew quiet when she drew the blade and tried a cut. *Even the sound of it is sharper than an ordinary sword.* "With me," she told Crabb. She slipped sideways through the postern, ducking her head to pass beneath the doorway's arch.

The bailey opened up before her, overgrown. To her left was the main gate, and the collapsed shell of what might have been a stable. Saplings were poking out of half the stalls and growing up through the dry brown thatch of its roof. To her right she saw rotted wooden steps descending into the darkness of a dungeon or a root cellar. Where the keep had been was a pile of collapsed stones, overgrown with green and purple moss. The yard was all weeds and pine needles. Soldier pines were everywhere, drawn up in solemn ranks. In their midst was a pale stranger; a slender young weirwood with a trunk as white as a cloistered maid. Dark red leaves sprouted from its reaching branches. Beyond was the emptiness of sky and sea where the wall had collapsed . . .

. . . and the remnants of a fire.

The whispers nibbled at her ears, insistent. Brienne knelt beside the fire. She picked up a blackened stick, sniffed at it, stirred the ashes. *Someone was trying to keep warm last night. Or else they were trying to send a signal to a passing ship.*

"Halloooooo," called Nimble Dick. "Anyone here?"

"Be quiet," Brienne told him.

"Someone might be hiding. Wanting to get a look at us before they show themself." He walked to where the steps went down beneath the ground, and peered down into the darkness. "*Hallooooo,*" he called again. "Anyone down there?"

Brienne saw a sapling sway. From the bushes slid a man, so caked with dirt that he looked as if he had sprouted from the earth. A broken sword was in his hand, but it was his face that gave her pause, the small eyes and wide flat nostrils.

She knew that nose. She knew those eyes. *Pyg*, his friends had called him.

Everything seemed to happen in a heartbeat. A second man slipped over the lip of the well, making no more noise than a snake might make slithering across a pile of wet leaves. He wore an iron halfhelm wrapped in stained red silk, and had a short, thick throwing spear in hand. Brienne knew him too. From behind her came a rustling as a head poked down through the red leaves. Crabb was standing underneath the weirwood. He looked up and saw the face. "Here," he called to Brienne. "It's your fool."

"Dick," she called urgently, "to me."

Shagwell dropped from the weirwood, braying laughter. He was garbed in motley, but so faded and stained that it showed more brown than grey or pink. In place of a jester's flail he had a triple morningstar, three spiked balls chained to a wooden haft. He swung it hard and low, and one of Crabb's knees exploded in a spray of blood and bone. "*That's* funny," Shagwell crowed as Dick fell. The sword she'd given him went flying from his hand and vanished in the weeds. He writhed on the ground, screaming and clutching at the ruins of his knee. "Oh, look," said Shagwell, "it's Smuggler Dick, the one who made the map for us. Did you come all this way to give us back our gold?"

"*Please*," Dick whimpered, "please don't, my leg . . ."

"Does it hurt? I can make it stop."

"Leave him be," said Brienne.

"*DON'T!*" shrieked Dick, lifting bloody hands to shield his head. Shagwell whirled the spiked ball once around his head and brought it down in the middle of Crabb's face. There was a sickening crunch. In the silence that followed, Brienne could hear the sound of her own heart.

"Bad Shags," said the man who'd come creeping from the well. When he saw Brienne's face, he laughed. "You again, woman? What, come to hunt us down? Or did you miss our friendly faces?"

Shagwell danced from foot to foot and spun his flail. "It's me she come for. She dreams of me every night, when she sticks her fingers up her slit. She wants me, lads, the big horse missed her merry Shags! I'm going to fuck her up the arse and pump her full of motley seed, until she whelps a little me."

"You need to use a different hole for that, Shags," said Timeon, in his Dornish drawl.

"I best use all her holes, then. Just to make certain." He moved to her right as Pyg was circling around to her left, forcing her back toward the ragged edge of the cliff. *Passage for three*, Brienne remembered. "There are only three of you."

Timeon shrugged. "We all went our own ways, after we left Harrenhal. Urswyck and his lot rode south for Oldtown. Rorge thought he might slip out at Saltpans. Me and my lads made for Maidenpool, but we couldn't get near a ship." The Dornishman hefted his spear. "You did for Vargo with that bite, you know. His ear turned black and started leaking pus. Rorge and Urswyck were for leaving, but the Goat says we got to hold his castle. Lord of Harrenhal, he says he is, no one was going to take it off him. He said it slobbery, the way he always talked. We heard the Mountain killed him piece by piece. A hand one day, a foot the next, lopped off neat and clean. They bandaged up the stumps so Hoat didn't die. He was saving his cock for last, but some bird called him to King's Landing, so he finished it and rode off."

"I am not here for you. I am looking for my . . ." She almost said *my sister.* ". . . for a fool."

"*I'm* a fool," Shagwell announced happily.

"The wrong fool," blurted Brienne. "The one I want is with a highborn girl, the daughter of Lord Stark of Winterfell."

"Then it's the Hound you want," said Timeon. "He's not here neither, as it happens. Just us."

"Sandor Clegane?" said Brienne. "What do you mean?"

"He's the one that's got the Stark girl. The way I hear it, she was making for Riverrun, and he stole her. Damned dog."

Riverrun, thought Brienne. *She was making for Riverrun. For her uncles.* "How do you know?"

"Had it from one of Beric's bunch. The lightning lord is looking for her too. He's sent his men all up and down the Trident, sniffing after her. We chanced on three of them after Harrenhal, and winkled the tale from one before he died."

"He might have lied."

"He might have, but he didn't. Later on, we heard how the Hound slew three of his brother's men at an inn by the crossroads. The girl was with him there. The innkeep swore to it before Rorge killed him, and the whores said the same. An ugly bunch, they were. Not so ugly as you, mind you, but still . . ."

He is trying to distract me, Brienne realized, *to lull me with his voice.* Pyg was edging closer. Shagwell took a hop toward her. She backed away from them. *They will back me off the cliff if I let them.* "Stay away," she warned them.

"I think I'm going to fuck you up the nose, wench," Shagwell announced. "Won't that be amusing?"

"He has a very small cock," Timeon explained. "Drop that pretty sword and might be we'll go gentle on you, woman. We need gold to pay these smugglers, that's all."

"And if I give you gold, you'll let us go?"

"We will." Timeon smiled. "Once you've fucked the lot of us. We'll pay you like a proper whore. A silver for each fuck. Or else we'll take the gold and rape you anyway, and do you like the Mountain did Lord Vargo. What's your choice?"

"This." Brienne threw herself toward Pyg.

He jerked his broken blade up to protect his face, but as he went high she went low. Oathkeeper bit through leather, wool, skin, and muscle, into the sellsword's thigh. Pyg cut back wildly as his leg went out from under him. His broken sword scraped against her chainmail before he landed on his back. Brienne stabbed him through the throat, gave the blade a hard turn, and slid it out, whirling just as Timeon's spear came flashing past her face. *I did not flinch,* she thought, as blood ran red down her cheek. *Did you see, Ser Goodwin?* She hardly felt the cut.

"Your turn," she told Timeon, as the Dornishman pulled out a second spear, shorter and thicker than the first. "Throw it."

"So you can dance away and charge me? I'd end up dead as Pyg. No. Get her, Shags."

"You get her," Shagwell said. "Did you see what she did to Pyg? She's mad with moon blood." The fool was behind her, Timeon in front. No matter how she turned, one was at her back.

"Get her," urged Timeon, "and you can fuck her corpse."

"Oh, you *do* love me." The morningstar was whirling. *Choose one,* Brienne told herself. *Choose one and kill him quickly.* Then a stone came out of nowhere, and hit Shagwell in the head. Brienne did not hesitate. She flew at Timeon.

He was better than Pyg, but he had only a short throwing spear, and she had a Valyrian steel blade. Oathkeeper was alive in her hands. She had never been so quick. The blade became a grey blur. He wounded her in the shoulder as she came at him, but she slashed off his ear and half his cheek, hacked the head off his spear, and put a foot of rippled steel into his belly through the links of the chainmail byrnie he was wearing.

Timeon was still trying to fight as she pulled her blade from him, its fullers running red with blood. He clawed at his belt and came up with a dagger, so Brienne cut his hand off. *That one was for Jaime.* "Mother have mercy," the Dornishman gasped, the blood bubbling from his mouth and spurting from his wrist. "Finish it. Send me back to Dorne, you bloody bitch."

She did.

Shagwell was on his knees when she turned, looking dazed as he fumbled for the morningstar. As he staggered to his feet, another stone slammed him in the ear. Podrick had climbed the fallen wall and was standing amongst the ivy glowering, a fresh rock in his hand. "I *told* you I could fight!" he shouted down.

Shagwell tried to crawl away. "I yield," the fool cried, "I *yield*. You mustn't hurt sweet Shagwell, I'm too droll to die."

"You are no better than the rest of them. You have robbed and raped and murdered."

"Oh, I have, I have, I shan't deny it . . . but I'm *amusing*, with all my japes and capers. I make men laugh."

"And women weep."

"Is that my fault? Women have no sense of humor."

Brienne lowered Oathkeeper. "Dig a grave. There, beneath the weirwood." She pointed with her blade.

"I have no spade."

"You have two hands." *One more than you left Jaime.*

"Why bother? Leave them for the crows."

"Timeon and Pyg can feed the crows. Nimble Dick will have a grave. He was a Crabb. This is his place."

The ground was soft from rain, but even so it took the fool the rest of the day to dig down deep enough. Night was falling by the time he was done, and his hands were bloody and blistered. Brienne sheathed Oathkeeper, gathered up Dick Crabb, and carried him to the hole. His face was hard to look on. "I'm sorry that I never trusted you. I don't know how to do that anymore."

As she knelt to lay the body down, she thought, *The fool will make his try now, whilst my back is turned.*

She heard his ragged breathing half a heartbeat before Podrick cried out his warning. Shagwell had a jagged chunk of rock clutched in one hand. Brienne had her dagger up her sleeve.

A dagger will beat a rock almost every time.

She knocked aside his arm and punched the steel into his bowels. "Laugh," she snarled at him. He moaned instead. "Laugh," she repeated, grabbing his throat with one hand and stabbing at his belly with the other. *"Laugh!"* She kept saying it, over and over, until her hand was red up to the wrist and the stink of the fool's dying was like to choke her. But Shagwell never laughed. The sobs that Brienne heard were all her own. When she realized that, she threw down her knife and shuddered.

Podrick helped her lower Nimble Dick into his hole. By the time they were done the moon was rising. Brienne rubbed the dirt from her hands and tossed two dragons down into the grave.

"Why did you do that, my lady? Ser?" asked Pod.

"It was the reward I promised him for finding me the fool."

Laughter sounded from behind them. She ripped Oathkeeper from her sheath and whirled, expecting more Bloody Mummers . . . but it was only Hyle Hunt atop the crumbling wall, his legs crossed. "If there are brothels down in hell, the wretch will thank you," the knight called down. "Elsewise, that's a waste of good gold."

"I keep my promises. What are *you* doing here?"

"Lord Randyll bid me follow you. If by some freak's chance you stumbled onto Sansa Stark, he told me to bring her back to Maidenpool. Have no fear, I was commanded not to harm you."

Brienne snorted. "As if you could."

"What will you do now, my lady?"

"Cover him."

"About the girl, I meant. The Lady Sansa."

Brienne thought a moment. "She was making for Riverrun, if Timeon told it true. Somewhere along the way she was taken by the Hound. If I find him . . ."

". . . he'll kill you."

"Or I'll kill him," she said stubbornly. "Will you help me cover up poor Crabb, ser?"

"No true knight could refuse such beauty." Ser Hyle climbed down from the wall. Together, they shoved the dirt on top of Nimble Dick as the moon rose higher in the sky, and down below the ground the heads of forgotten kings whispered secrets.

THE QUEENMAKER

Beneath the burning sun of Dorne, wealth was measured as much in water as in gold, so every well was zealously guarded. The well at Shandystone had gone dry a hundred years before, however, and its guardians had departed for some wetter place, abandoning their modest holdfast with its fluted columns and triple arches. Afterward the sands had crept back in to reclaim their own.

Arianne Martell arrived with Drey and Sylva just as the sun was going down, with the west a tapestry of gold and purple and the clouds all glowing crimson. The ruins seemed aglow as well; the fallen columns glimmered pinkly, red shadows crept across the cracked stone floors, and the sands themselves turned from gold to orange to purple as the light faded. Garin had arrived a few hours earlier, and the knight called Darkstar the day before.

"It is lovely here," Drey observed as he was helping Garin water the horses. They had carried their own water with them. The sand steeds of Dorne were swift and tireless, and would keep going for long leagues after other horses had given out, but even such as they could not run dry. "How did you know of this place?"

"My uncle brought me here, with Tyene and Sarella." The memory made Arianne smile. "He caught some vipers and showed Tyene the safest way to milk them for their venom. Sarella turned over rocks, brushed sand off the mosaics, and wanted to know everything there was to know about the people who had lived here."

"And what did you do, princess?" asked Spotted Sylva.

I sat beside the well and pretended that some robber knight had brought me here to have his way with me, she thought, *a tall hard man with black eyes and a widow's peak.* The memory made her uneasy. "I dreamed," she said, "and when the sun went down I sat cross-legged at my uncle's feet and begged him for a story."

"Prince Oberyn was full of stories." Garin had been with them as well that day; he was Arianne's milk brother, and they had been inseparable since before they learned to walk. "He told about Prince Garin, I remember, the one that I was named for."

"Garin the Great," offered Drey, "the wonder of the Rhoyne."

"That's the one. He made Valyria tremble."

"They trembled," said Ser Gerold, "then they killed him. If I led a quarter of a million men to death, would they call me Gerold the Great?" He snorted. "I shall remain Darkstar, I think. At least it is mine own." He unsheathed his longsword, sat upon the lip of the dry well, and began to hone the blade with an oilstone.

Arianne watched him warily. *He is highborn enough to make a worthy consort,* she thought. *Father would question my good sense, but our children would be as beautiful as dragonlords.* If there was a handsomer man in Dorne, she did not know him. Ser Gerold Dayne had an aquiline nose, high cheekbones, a strong jaw. He kept his face clean-shaven, but his thick hair fell to his collar like a silver glacier, divided by a streak of midnight black. *He has a cruel mouth, though, and a crueler tongue.* His eyes seemed black as he sat outlined against the dying sun, sharpening his steel, but she had looked at them from a closer vantage and she knew that they were purple. *Dark purple. Dark and angry.*

He must have felt her gaze upon him, for he looked up from his sword, met her eyes, and smiled. Arianne felt heat rushing to her face. *I should never have brought him. If he gives me such a look when Arys is here, we will have blood on the sand.* Whose, she could not say. By tradition the Kingsguard were the finest knights in all the Seven Kingdoms . . . but Darkstar was Darkstar.

The Dornish nights grow cold out upon the sands. Garin gathered wood for them, bleached white branches from trees that had withered up and died a hundred years ago. Drey built a fire, whistling as he struck sparks off his flint.

Once the kindling caught, they sat around the flames and passed a skin of summerwine from hand to hand ... all but Darkstar, who preferred to drink unsweetened lemonwater. Garin was in a lively mood and entertained them with the latest tales from the Planky Town at the mouth of the Greenblood, where the orphans of the river came to trade with the carracks, cogs, and galleys from across the narrow sea. If the sailors could be believed, the east was seething with wonders and terrors: a slave revolt in Astapor, dragons in Qarth, grey plague in Yi Ti. A new corsair king had risen in the Basilisk Isles and raided Tall Trees Town, and in Qohor followers of the red priests had rioted and tried to burn down the Black Goat. "And the Golden Company broke its contract with Myr, just as the Myrmen were about to go to war with Lys."

"The Lyseni bought them off," suggested Sylva.

"Clever Lyseni," Drey said. "Clever, craven Lyseni."

Arianne knew better. *If Quentyn has the Golden Company behind him* ... "Beneath the gold the bitter steel," was their cry. *You will need bitter steel and more, brother, if you think to set me aside.* Arianne was loved in Dorne, Quentyn little known. No company of sellswords could change that.

Ser Gerold rose. "I believe I'll have a piss."

"Watch where you set your feet," Drey cautioned. "It has been a while since Prince Oberyn milked the local vipers."

"I was weaned on venom, Dalt. Any viper takes a bite of me will rue it." Ser Gerold vanished through a broken arch.

When he was gone, the others exchanged glances. "Forgive me, princess," said Garin softly, "but I do not like that man."

"A pity," Drey said. "I believe he's half in love with you."

"We need him," Arianne reminded them. "It may be that we will need his sword, and we will surely need his castle."

"High Hermitage is not the only castle in Dorne," Spotted Sylva pointed out, "and you have other knights who love you well. Drey is a knight."

"I am," he affirmed. "I have a wonderful horse and a very fine sword, and my valor is second to ... well, several, actually."

"More like several hundred, ser," said Garin.

Arianne left them to their banter. Drey and Spotted Sylva were her dearest friends, aside from her cousin Tyene, and Garin had been teasing her since both of them were drinking from his mother's teats, but just now she was in no mood for japery. The sun was gone, and the sky was full of stars. *So many.* She leaned her back against a fluted pillar and wondered if her brother was looking at the same stars tonight, wherever he might be. *Do you see the white one, Quentyn? That is Nymeria's star, burning bright, and that milky band behind her, those are ten thousand ships. She burned as bright as any man, and so shall I. You will not rob me of my birthright!*

Quentyn had been very young when he was sent to Yronwood; too young, according to their mother. Norvoshi did not foster out their children, and Lady Mellario had never forgiven Prince Doran for taking her son away from her. "I like it no more than you do," Arianne had overheard her father say, "but there is a blood debt, and Quentyn is the only coin Lord Ormond will accept."

"Coin?" her mother had screamed. "He is your *son.* What sort of father uses his own flesh and blood to pay his debts?"

"The princely sort," Doran Martell had answered.

Prince Doran was still pretending that her brother was with Lord Yronwood, but Garin's mother had seen him at the Planky Town, posing as a merchant. One of his companions had a lazy eye, the same as Cletus Yronwood, Lord Anders's randy son. A maester traveled with them too, a maester skilled in tongues. *My brother is not as clever as he thinks. A clever man would have left from Oldtown, even if it meant a longer voyage. In Oldtown he might have gone unrecognized.* Arianne had friends amongst the orphans of the Planky Town, and some had grown curious as to why a prince and a lord's son might be traveling under false names and seeking passage across the narrow sea. One of them had crept through a window of a night, tickled the lock on Quentyn's little strongbox, and found the scrolls within.

Arianne would have given much and more to know that this secret trip across the narrow sea was Quentyn's own doing, and his alone . . . but parchments he had carried had been sealed with the sun and spear of Dorne. Garin's cousin had not dared break the seal to read them, but . . .

"Princess." Ser Gerold Dayne stood behind her, half in starlight and half in shadow.

"How was your piss?" Arianne inquired archly.

"The sands were duly grateful." Dayne put a foot upon the head of a statue that might have been the Maiden till the sands had scoured her face away. "It occurred to me as I was pissing that this plan of yours may not yield you what you want."

"And what is it I want, ser?"

"The Sand Snakes freed. Vengeance for Oberyn and Elia. Do I know the song? You want a little taste of lion blood."

That, and my birthright. I want Sunspear, and my father's seat. I want Dorne. "I want justice."

"Call it what you will. Crowning the Lannister girl is a hollow gesture. She will never sit the Iron Throne. Nor will you get the war you want. The lion is not so easily provoked." Ser Gerold drew his sword. It glimmered in the starlight, sharp as lies. "This is how you start a war. Not with a crown of gold, but with a blade of steel."

I am no murderer of children. "Put that away. Myrcella is under my protection. And Ser Arys will permit no harm to come to his precious princess, you know that."

"No, my lady. What I know is that Daynes have been killing Oakhearts for several thousand years."

His arrogance took her breath away. "It seems to me that Oakhearts have been killing Daynes for just as long."

"We all have our family traditions." Darkstar sheathed his sword. "The moon is rising, and I see your paragon approaching."

His eyes were sharp. The horseman on the tall grey palfrey did indeed prove to be Ser Arys, white cloak fluttering bravely as he spurred across the sand. Princess Myrcella rode pillion behind him, swaddled in a cowled robe that hid her golden curls.

As Ser Arys helped her from the saddle, Drey went to one knee before her. "Your Grace."

"My lady liege." Spotted Sylva knelt beside him.

"My queen, I am your man." Garin dropped to both knees.

Confused, Myrcella clutched Arys Oakheart by the arm. "Why do they call me Grace?" she asked in a plaintive voice. "Ser Arys, what is this place, and who are they?"

Has he told her nought? Arianne moved forward in a swirl of silk, smiling to put the child at ease. "They are my true and loyal friends, Your Grace . . . and would be your friends as well."

"Princess Arianne?" The girl threw her arms around her. "Why do they call me queen? Did something bad happen to Tommen?"

"He fell in with evil men, Your Grace," Arianne said, "and I fear they have conspired with him to steal your throne."

"My throne? You mean, the *Iron* Throne?" The girl was more confused than ever. "He never stole that, Tommen is . . ."

". . . younger than you, surely?"

"I am older by a year."

"That means the Iron Throne by rights is yours," Arianne said. "Your brother is only a little boy, you must not blame him. He has bad counselors . . . but *you* have friends. May I have the honor of presenting them?" She took the child by the hand. "Your Grace, I give you Ser Andrey Dalt, the heir to Lemonwood."

"My friends call me Drey," he said, "and I should be greatly honored if Your Grace would do the same."

Though Drey had an open face and an easy smile, Myrcella regarded him warily. "Until I know you I must call you *ser*."

"Whatever name Your Grace prefers, I am her man."

Sylva cleared her throat, till Arianne said, "Might I present Lady Sylva Santagar, my queen? My dearest Spotted Sylva."

"Why do they call you that?" Myrcella asked.

"For my freckles, Your Grace," Sylva answered, "though they all pretend it is because I am the heir to Spottswood."

Garin was next, a loose-limbed, swarthy, long-nosed fellow with a jade stud in one ear. "Here is gay Garin of the orphans, who makes me laugh," said Arianne. "His mother was my wet nurse."

"I am sorry she is dead," Myrcella said.

"She's not, sweet queen." Garin flashed the golden tooth Arianne had bought him to replace the one she'd broken. "I'm of the orphans of the Greenblood, is what my lady means."

Myrcella would have time enough to learn the history of the orphans on her voyage up the river. Arianne led her queen-to-be to the final member of her little band. "Last, but first in valor, I give you Ser Gerold Dayne, a knight of Starfall."

Ser Gerold went to one knee. The moonlight shone in his dark eyes as he studied the child coolly.

"There was an Arthur Dayne," Myrcella said. "He was a knight of the Kingsguard in the days of Mad King Aerys."

"He was the Sword of the Morning. He is dead."

"Are you the Sword of the Morning now?"

"No. Men call me Darkstar, and I am of the night."

Arianne drew the child away. "You must be hungry. We have dates and cheese and olives, and lemonsweet to drink. You ought not eat or drink too much, though. After a little rest, we must ride. Out here on the sands it is always best to travel by night, before the sun ascends the sky. It is kinder to the horses."

"And the riders," Spotted Sylva said. "Come, Your Grace, warm yourself. I should be honored if you'd let me serve you."

As she led the princess to the fire, Arianne found Ser Gerold behind her. "My House goes back ten thousand years, unto the dawn of days," he complained. "Why is it that my cousin is the only Dayne that anyone remembers?"

"He was a great knight," Ser Arys Oakheart put in.

"He had a great sword," Darkstar said.

"And a great heart." Ser Arys took Arianne by the arm. "Princess, I beg a moment's word."

"Come." She led Ser Arys deeper into the ruins. Beneath his cloak, the knight wore a cloth-of-gold doublet embroidered with the three green oak leaves of his House. On his head was a light steel helm topped by a jagged spike, wound about with a yellow scarf in the Dornish fashion. He might have passed for any knight, but for the cloak. Of shimmering white silk it was, pale as moonlight and airy as a breeze. *A Kingsguard cloak beyond all doubt, the gallant fool.* "How much does the child know?"

"Little enough. Before we left King's Landing, her uncle reminded her that I was her protector and that any commands that I might give her were meant to keep her safe. She has heard them in the streets as well, shouting out for vengeance. She knew this was no game. The girl is brave, and wise beyond her years. She did all I asked of her, and never asked a question." The knight took her arm, glanced about, lowered his voice. "There are other tidings you should hear. Tywin Lannister is dead."

That was a shock. "Dead?"

"Murdered by the Imp. The queen has assumed the regency."

"Has she?" *A woman on the Iron Throne?* Arianne thought about that for a moment and decided it was all to the good. If the lords of the Seven Kingdoms grew accustomed to Queen Cersei's rule, it would be that much easier for them to bend their knees to Queen Myrcella. And Lord Tywin had been a dangerous foe; without him, Dorne's enemies would be much weaker. *Lannisters are killing Lannisters, how sweet.* "What became of the dwarf?"

"He's fled," Ser Arys said. "Cersei is offering a lordship to whosoever delivers her his head." In a tiled inner courtyard half-buried by the drifting sands, he pushed her back against a column to kiss her, and his hand went to her breast. He kissed her long and hard and would have pushed her skirts up, but Arianne broke free of him, laughing. "I see that queenmaking excites you, ser, but we have no time for this. Later, I promise you." She touched his cheek. "Did you meet with any problems?"

"Only Trystane. He wanted to sit beside Myrcella's bedside and play *cyvasse* with her."

"He had redspots when he was four, I told you. You can only get it once. You should have put out that Myrcella was suffering from greyscale, that would have kept him well away."

"The boy perhaps, but not your father's maester."

"Caleotte," she said. "Did he try to see her?"

"Not once I described the red spots on her face. He said that nothing could be done until the disease had run its course, and gave me a pot of salve to soothe her itching."

No one under ten ever died of redspots, but it could be mortal in adults, and Maester Caleotte had never suffered it as a child. Arianne learned that when she suffered her own spots, at eight. "Good," she said. "And the handmaid? Is she convincing?"

"From a distance. The Imp picked her for this purpose, over many girls of nobler birth. Myrcella helped her curl her hair, and painted the dots on her face herself. They are distant kin. Lannisport teems with Lannys, Lannetts, Lantells, and lesser Lannisters, and half of them have that yellow hair. Dressed in Myrcella's bedrobe with the maester's salve smeared across her face . . . she might even have fooled me, in a dim light. It was a deal harder to find a man to take my place. Dake is closest to my height, but he's too fat, so I put Rolder in my armor and told him to keep his visor down. The man is three inches shorter than I am, but perhaps no one will notice if I'm not there to stand beside him. He'll keep to Myrcella's chambers in any case."

"All we need is a few days. By that time the princess will be beyond my father's reach."

"Where?" He drew her close and nuzzled at her neck. "It's time you told me the rest of the plan, don't you think?"

She laughed, pushing him away. "No, it's time we rode."

The moon had crowned the Moonmaid as they set out from the dust-dry ruins of Shandystone, striking south and west. Arianne and Ser Arys took the lead, with Myrcella on a frisky mare between them. Garin followed close behind with Spotted Sylva, whilst her two Dornish knights took the rear. *We are seven,* Arianne realized as they rode. She had not thought of that before, but it seemed a good omen for their cause. *Seven riders on their way to glory. One day the singers will make all of us immortal.* Drey had wanted a larger party, but that might have attracted unwelcome attention, and every additional man doubled the risk of betrayal. *That much my father taught me, at the least.* Even when he was younger and stronger, Doran Martell had been a cautious man much given to silences and secrets. *It is time he put his burdens down, but I will suffer no slights to his honor or his person.* She would return him to his Water Gardens, to live out what years remained him surrounded by laughing children and the smell of limes and oranges. *Yes, and Quentyn can keep him company. Once I crown Myrcella and free the Sand Snakes, all Dorne will rally to my banners.* The Yronwoods might declare for Quentyn, but alone they were no threat. If they went over to Tommen and the Lannisters, she would have Darkstar destroy them root and branch.

"I am tired," Myrcella complained, after several hours in the saddle. "Is it much farther? Where are we going?"

"Princess Arianne is taking Your Grace to a place where you'll be safe," Ser Arys assured her.

"It is a long journey," Arianne said, "but it will go easier once we reach the Greenblood. Some of Garin's people will meet us there, the orphans of the river. They live on boats, and pole them up and down the Greenblood and its vassals, fishing and picking fruit and doing whatever work needs doing."

"Aye," Garin called out cheerfully, "and we sing and play and dance on water, and know much and more of healing. My mother is the best midwife in Westeros, and my father can cure warts."

"How can you be orphans if you have mothers and fathers?" the girl asked.

"They are the Rhoynar," Arianne explained, "and their Mother was the river Rhoyne."

Myrcella did not understand. "I thought *you* were the Rhoynar. You Dornishmen, I mean."

"We are in part, Your Grace. Nymeria's blood is in me, along with that of Mors Martell, the Dornish lord she married. On the day they wed, Nymeria fired her ships, so her people would understand that there could be no going back. Most were glad to see those flames, for their voyagings had been long and terrible before they came to Dorne, and many and more had been lost to storm, disease, and slavery. There were a few who mourned, however. They did not love this dry red land or its seven-faced god, so they clung to their old ways, hammered boats together from the hulks of the burned ships, and became the orphans of the Greenblood. The Mother in their songs is not *our* Mother, but Mother Rhoyne, whose waters nourished them from the dawn of days."

"I'd heard the Rhoynar had some turtle god," said Ser Arys.

"The Old Man of the River is a lesser god," said Garin. "He was born from Mother River too, and fought the Crab King to win dominion over all who dwell beneath the flowing waters."

"Oh," said Myrcella.

"I understand you've fought some mighty battles too, Your Grace," said Drey in his most cheerful voice. "It is said you show our brave Prince Trystane no mercy at the *cyvasse* table."

"He always sets his squares up the same way, with all the mountains in the front and his elephants in the passes," said Myrcella. "So I send my dragon through to eat his elephants."

"Does your handmaid play the game as well?" asked Drey.

"Rosamund?" asked Myrcella. "No. I tried to teach her, but she said the rules were too hard."

"She is a Lannister as well?" said Lady Sylva.

"A Lannister of *Lannisport,* not a Lannister of Casterly Rock. Her hair is the same color as mine, but straight instead of curly. Rosamund doesn't truly favor me, but when she dresses up in my clothes people who don't know us think she's me."

"You have done this before, then?"

"Oh, yes. We traded places on the *Seaswift,* on the way to Braavos. Septa Eglantine put brown dye in my hair. She said we were doing it as a game, but it was meant to keep me safe in case the ship was taken by my uncle Stannis."

The girl was plainly growing tired, so Arianne called a halt. They watered the horses once again, rested for a bit, and had some cheese and fruit. Myrcella split an orange with Spotted Sylva, whilst Garin ate olives and spit the stones at Drey.

Arianne had hoped to reach the river before the sun came up, but they had started much later than she'd planned, so they were still in the saddle when the eastern sky turned red. Darkstar cantered up beside her. "Princess," he said, "I'd set a faster pace, unless you mean to kill the child after all. We have no tents, and by day the sands are cruel."

"I know the sands as well as you do, ser," she told him. All the same, she did as he suggested. It was hard on their mounts, but better she should lose six horses than one princess.

Soon enough the wind came gusting from the west, hot and dry and full of grit. Arianne drew her veil across her face. It was made of shimmering silk, pale green above and yellow below, the colors blending into one another. Small green pearls gave it weight, and rattled softly against each other as she rode.

"I know why my princess wears a veil," Ser Arys said as she was fastening it to the temples of her copper helm. "Elsewise, her beauty would outshine the sun above."

She had to laugh. "No, your princess wears a veil to keep the glare out of her eyes and the sand out of her mouth. You should do the same, ser." She wondered how long her white knight had been polishing his ponderous gallantry. Ser Arys was pleasant company abed, but wit and he were strangers.

Her Dornishmen covered their faces as she did, and Spotted Sylva helped veil the little princess from the sun, but Ser Arys stayed stubborn. Before long the sweat was running down his face, and his cheeks had taken on a rosy blush. *Much longer and he will cook in those heavy clothes,* she reflected. He would not be the first. In centuries past, many a host had come down from the Prince's Pass with banners streaming, only to wither and broil on the hot red Dornish sands. "The arms of House Martell display the sun and spear, the Dornishman's two favored weapons," the Young Dragon had once written in his boastful *Conquest of Dorne*, "but of the two, the sun is the more deadly."

Thankfully, they did not need to cross the deep sands but only a sliver of the drylands. When Arianne spied a hawk wheeling high above them against a cloudless sky, she knew the worst was behind them. Soon they came upon a tree. It was a gnarled and twisted thing with as many thorns as leaves, of the sort called sandbeggars, but it meant that they were not far from water.

"We're almost there, Your Grace," Garin told Myrcella cheerfully when they spied more sandbeggars up ahead, a thicket of them growing all around the dry bed of a stream. The sun was beating down like a fiery hammer, but it did not matter with their journey at its end. They stopped to water the horses again, drank deep from their skins and wet their veils, then mounted for the last push. Within half a league they were riding over devilgrass and past olive groves. Beyond a line of stony hills the grass grew greener and more lush, and there were lemon orchards watered by a spider's web of old canals. Garin was the first to spy the river glimmering green. He gave a shout and raced ahead.

Arianne Martell had crossed the Mander once, when she had gone with three of the Sand Snakes to visit Tyene's mother. Compared to that mighty waterway, the Greenblood was scarce worthy of the name of river, yet it remained the life of Dorne. It took its name from the murky green of its sluggish waters; but as they approached, the sunlight seemed to turn those waters gold. She had seldom seen a sweeter sight. *The next part should be slow and simple,* she thought, *up the Greenblood and onto the Vaith, as far as a poleboat can go.* That would give her time enough to prepare Myrcella for all that was to come. Beyond Vaith the deep sands waited. They would need help from Sandstone and the Hellholt to make that crossing, but she did not doubt that it would be forthcoming. The Red Viper had been fostered at Sandstone, and Prince Oberyn's paramour Ellaria Sand was Lord Uller's natural daughter; four of the Sand Snakes were his granddaughters. *I will crown Myrcella at the Hellholt and raise my banners there.*

They found the boat half a league downstream, hidden beneath the drooping branches of a great green willow. Low of roof and wide abeam, the poleboats had hardly any draft to speak of; the Young Dragon had disparaged them as "hovels built on rafts," but that was hardly fair. All but the poorest orphan boats were wonderfully carved and painted. This one was done in shades of green, with a curved wooden tiller shaped like a mermaid, and fish faces peering through her rails. Poles and ropes and jars of olive oil cluttered her decks, and iron lanterns swung fore and aft. Arianne saw no orphans. *Where is her crew?* she wondered.

Garin reined up beneath the willow. "Wake up, you fish-eyed lagabeds," he called as he leapt down from the saddle. "Your *queen* is here, and wants her royal welcome. Come up, come out, we'll have some songs and sweetwine. My mouth is set for—"

The door on the poleboat slammed open. Out into the sunlight stepped Areo Hotah, longaxe in hand.

Garin jerked to a halt. Arianne felt as though an axe had caught her in the belly. *It was not supposed to end this way. This was not supposed to happen.* When she heard Drey say, "There's the last face I'd hoped to see," she knew she had to act. *"Away!"* she cried, vaulting back into the saddle. "Arys, protect the princess—"

Hotah thumped the butt of his longaxe upon the deck. Behind the ornate rails of the poleboat, a dozen guardsmen rose, armed with throwing spears or crossbows. Still more appeared atop the cabin. "Yield, my princess," the captain called, "else we must slay all but the child and yourself, by your father's word."

Princess Myrcella sat motionless upon her mount. Garin backed slowly from the poleboat, his hands in the air. Drey unbuckled his swordbelt. "Yielding seems the wisest course," he called to Arianne, as his sword thumped to the ground.

"*No!*" Ser Arys Oakheart put his horse between Arianne and the crossbows, his blade shining silver in his hand. He had unslung his shield and slipped his left arm through the straps. "You will not take her whilst I still draw breath."

You reckless fool, was all that Arianne had time to think, *what do you think you're doing?*

Darkstar's laughter rang out. "Are you blind or stupid, Oakheart? There are too many. Put up your sword."

"Do as he says, Ser Arys," Drey urged.

We are taken, ser, Arianne might have called out. *Your death will not free us. If you love your princess, yield.* But when she tried to speak, the words caught in her throat.

Ser Arys Oakheart gave her one last longing look, then put his golden spurs into his horse and charged.

He rode headlong for the poleboat, his white cloak streaming behind him. Arianne Martell had never seen anything half so gallant, or half so stupid. "*Noooo,*" she shrieked, but she had found her tongue too late. A crossbow *thrumm*ed, then another. Hotah bellowed a command. At such close range, the white knight's armor had as well been made of parchment. The first bolt punched right through his heavy oaken shield, pinning it to his shoulder. The second grazed his temple. A thrown spear took Ser Arys's mount in the flank, yet still the horse came on, staggering as he hit the gangplank. "*No,*" some girl was shouting, some foolish little girl, "*no, please, this was not supposed to happen.*" She could hear Myrcella shrieking too, her voice shrill with fear.

Ser Arys's longsword slashed right and left, and two spearmen went down. His horse reared, and kicked a crossbowman in the face as he was trying to reload, but the other crossbows were firing, feathering the big courser with their quarrels. The bolts hit home so hard they knocked the horse sideways. His legs went out from under him and sent him crashing down the deck. Somehow Arys Oakheart leapt free. He even managed to keep hold of his sword. He struggled to his knees beside his dying horse . . .

. . . and found Areo Hotah standing over him.

The white knight raised his blade, too slowly. Hotah's longaxe took his right arm off at the shoulder, spun away spraying blood, and came flashing back again in a terrible two-handed slash that removed the head of Arys Oakheart and sent it spinning through the air. It landed amongst the reeds, and the Greenblood swallowed the red with a soft splash.

Arianne did not remember climbing from her horse. Perhaps she'd fallen. She did not remember that either. Yet she found herself on her hands and feet in the sand, shaking and sobbing and retching up her supper. *No,* was all that she could think, *no, no one was to be hurt, it was all planned, I was so careful.* She heard Areo Hotah roar, "After him. He must not escape. *After him!*" Myrcella was on the ground, wailing, shaking, her pale face in her hands, blood streaming through her fingers. Arianne did not understand. Men were scrambling onto horses whilst others swarmed over her and her companions, but none of it made sense. She had fallen into a dream, some terrible red nightmare. *This cannot be real. I will wake soon, and laugh at my night terrors.*

When they sought to bind her hands behind her back, she did not resist. One of the guardsmen jerked her to her feet. He wore her father's colors. Another bent and seized the throwing knife inside her boot, a gift from her cousin Lady Nym.

Areo Hotah took it from the man and frowned at it. "The prince said I must bring you back to Sunspear," he announced. His cheeks and brow were freckled with the blood of Arys Oakheart. "I am sorry, little princess."

Arianne raised a tear-streaked face. "How could he know?" she asked the captain. "I was so careful. How could he know?"

"Someone told." Hotah shrugged. "Someone always tells."

ARYA

Each night before sleep, she murmured her prayer into her pillow. "Ser Gregor," it went. "Dunsen, Raff the Sweetling, Ser Ilyn, Ser Meryn, Queen Cersei." She would have whispered the names of the Freys of the Crossing too, if she had known them. *One day I'll know,* she told herself, *and then I'll kill them all.*

No whisper was too faint to be heard in the House of Black and White. "Child," said the kindly man one day, "what are those names you whisper of a night?"

"I don't whisper any names," she said.

"You lie," he said. "All men lie when they are afraid. Some tell many lies, some but a few. Some have only one great lie they tell so often that they almost come to believe it . . . though some small part of them will always know that it is still a lie, and that will show upon their faces. Tell me of these names."

She chewed her lip. "The names don't matter."

"They do," the kindly man insisted. "Tell me, child."

Tell me, or we will turn you out, she heard. "They're people I hate. I want them to die."

"We hear many such prayers in this House."

"I know," said Arya. Jaqen H'ghar had granted three of her prayers once. *All I had to do was whisper . . .*

"Is that why you have come to us?" the kindly man went on. "To learn our arts, so you may kill these men you hate?"

Arya did not know how to answer that. "Maybe."

"Then you have come to the wrong place. It is not for you to say who shall live and who shall die. That gift belongs to Him of Many Faces. We are but his servants, sworn to do his will."

"Oh." Arya glanced at the statues that stood along the walls, candles glimmering round their feet. "Which god is he?"

"Why, all of them," said the priest in black and white.

He never told her his name. Neither did the waif, the little girl with the big eyes and hollow face who reminded her of another little girl, named Weasel. Like Arya, the waif lived below the temple, along with three acolytes, two serving men, and a cook called Umma. Umma liked to talk as she worked, but Arya could not understand a word she said. The others had no names, or did not choose to share them. One serving man was very old, his back bent like a bow. The second was red-faced, with hair growing from his ears. She took them both for mutes until she heard them praying. The acolytes were younger. The eldest was her father's age; the other two could not have been much older than Sansa, who had been her sister. The acolytes wore black and white too, but their robes had no cowls, and were black on the left side and white on the right. With the kindly man and the waif, it was the opposite. Arya was given servant's garb: a tunic of undyed wool, baggy breeches, linen smallclothes, cloth slippers for her feet.

Only the kindly man knew the Common Tongue. "Who are you?" he would ask her every day.

"No one," she would answer, she who had been Arya of House Stark, Arya Underfoot, Arya Horseface. She had been Arry and Weasel too, and Squab and Salty, Nan the cupbearer, a grey mouse, a sheep, the ghost of Harrenhal . . . but not for true, not in her heart of hearts. In there she was Arya of Winterfell, the daughter of Lord Eddard Stark and Lady Catelyn, who had once had brothers named Robb and Bran and Rickon, a sister named Sansa, a direwolf called Nymeria, a half-brother named Jon Snow. In there she was someone . . . but that was not the answer that he wanted.

Without a common language, Arya had no way of talking to the others. She listened to them, though, and repeated the words she heard to herself as she went about her work. Though the youngest acolyte was blind, he had charge of the candles. He would walk the temple in soft slippers, surrounded by the murmurings of the old women who came each day to pray. Even without eyes, he always knew which candles had gone out. "He has the scent to guide him," the kindly man explained, "and the air is warmer where a candle burns." He told Arya to close her eyes and try it for herself.

They prayed at dawn before they broke their fast, kneeling around the still, black pool. Some days the kindly man led the prayer. Other days it was the waif. Arya only knew a few words of Braavosi, the ones that were the same in High Valyrian. So she prayed her own prayer to the Many-Faced God, the one that went, "Ser Gregor, Dunsen, Raff the Sweetling, Ser Ilyn, Ser Meryn, Queen Cersei." She prayed in silence. If the Many-Faced God was a proper god, he would hear her.

Worshipers came to the House of Black and White every day. Most came alone and sat alone; they lit candles at one altar or another, prayed beside the pool, and sometimes wept. A few drank from the black cup and went to sleep; more did not drink. There were no services, no songs, no paeans of praise to please the god. The temple was never full. From time to time, a worshiper would ask to see a priest, and the kindly man or the waif would take him down into the sanctum, but that did not happen often.

Thirty different gods stood along the walls, surrounded by their little lights. The Weeping Woman was the favorite of old women, Arya saw; rich men preferred the Lion of Night, poor men the Hooded Wayfarer. Soldiers lit candles to Bakkalon, the Pale Child, sailors to the Moon-Pale Maiden and the Merling King. The Stranger had his shrine as well, though hardly anyone ever came to him. Most of the time only a single candle stood flickering at his feet. The kindly man said it did not matter. "He has many faces, and many ears to hear."

The knoll on which the temple stood was honeycombed with passageways hewn from the rock. The priests and acolytes had their sleeping cells on the first level, Arya and the servants on the second. The lowest level was forbidden to all save the priests. That was where the holy sanctum lay.

When she was not working, Arya was free to wander as she would amongst the vaults and storerooms, so long as she did not leave the temple, nor descend to the third cellar. She found a room full of weapons and armor: ornate helms and curious old breastplates, long-swords, daggers, and dirks, crossbows and tall spears with leaf-shaped heads. Another vault was crammed with clothing, thick furs and splendid silks in half a hundred colors, next to piles of foul-smelling rags and threadbare roughspuns. *There must be treasure chambers too,* Arya decided. She pictured stacks of golden plates, bags of silver coins, sapphires blue as the sea, ropes of fat green pearls.

One day the kindly man came on her unexpectedly and asked what she was doing. She told him that she had gotten lost.

"You lie. Worse, you lie *poorly*. Who are you?"

"No one."

"Another lie." He sighed.

Weese would have beaten her bloody if he had caught her in a lie, but it was different in the House of Black and White. When she was helping in the kitchen, Umma would sometimes smack her with her spoon if she got in the way, but no one else ever raised a hand to her. *They only raise their hands to kill,* she thought.

She got along well enough with the cook. Umma would slap a knife into her hand and point at an onion, and Arya would chop it. Umma would shove her toward a mound of dough, and Arya would knead it until the cook said stop (*stop* was the first Braavosi word she learned). Umma would hand her a fish, and Arya would bone it and fillet it and roll it in the nuts the cook was crushing. The brackish waters that surrounded Braavos teemed with fish and shellfish of every sort, the kindly man explained. A slow brown river entered the lagoon from the south, wandering through a wide expanse of reeds, tidal pools, and mudflats. Clams and cockles abounded hereabouts; mussels and muskfish, frogs and turtles, mud crabs and leopard crabs and climber crabs, red eels, black eels, striped eels, lampreys, and oysters; all made frequent appearances on the carved wooden table where the servants of the Many-Faced God took their meals. Some nights Umma spiced the fish with sea salt and cracked peppercorns, or cooked the eels with chopped garlic. Once in a great while the cook would even use some saffron. *Hot Pie would have liked it here,* Arya thought.

Supper was her favorite time. It had been a long while since Arya had gone to sleep every night with a full belly. Some nights the kindly man would allow her to ask him questions. Once she asked him why the people who came to the temple always seemed so peaceful; back home, people were scared to die. She remembered how that pimply squire had wept when she stabbed him in the belly, and the way Ser Amory Lorch had begged when the Goat had him thrown in the bear pit. She remembered the village by the God's Eye, and the way the villagers shrieked and screamed and whimpered whenever the Tickler started asking after gold.

"Death is not the worst thing," the kindly man replied. "It is His gift to us, an end to want and pain. On the day that we are born the Many-Faced God sends each of us a dark angel to walk through life beside us. When our sins and our sufferings grow too great to be borne, the angel takes us by the hand to lead us to the nightlands, where the stars burn ever bright. Those who come to drink from the black cup are looking for their angels. If they are afraid, the candles soothe them. When you smell our candles burning, what does it make you think of, my child?"

Winterfell, she might have said. *I smell snow and smoke and pine needles. I smell the stables. I smell Hodor laughing, and Jon and Robb battling in the yard, and Sansa singing about some stupid lady fair. I smell the crypts where the stone kings sit, I smell hot bread baking, I smell the godswood. I smell my wolf, I smell her fur, almost as if she were still beside me.* "I don't smell anything," she said, to see what he would say.

"You lie," he said, "but you may keep your secrets if you wish, Arya of House Stark." He only called her that when she displeased him. "You know that you may leave this place. You are not one of us, not yet. You may go home anytime you wish."

"You told me that if I left, I couldn't come back."

"Just so."

Those words made her sad. *Syrio used to say that too,* Arya remembered. *He said it all the time.* Syrio Forel had taught her needle-work and died for her. "I don't want to leave."

"Then stay . . . but remember, the House of Black and White is not a home for orphans. All men must serve beneath this roof. *Valar dohaeris* is how we say it here. Remain if you will, but know that we shall require your obedience. At all times and in all things. If you cannot obey, you must depart."

"I can obey."

"We shall see."

She had other tasks besides helping Umma. She swept the temple floors; she served and poured at meals; she sorted piles of dead men's clothing, emptied their purses, and counted out stacks of queer coins. Every morning she walked beside the kindly man as he made his circuit of the temple to find the dead. *Silent as a shadow,* she would tell herself, remembering Syrio. She carried a lantern with thick iron shutters. At each alcove, she would open the shutter a crack, to look for corpses.

The dead were never hard to find. They came to the House of Black and White, prayed for an hour or a day or a year, drank sweet dark water from the pool, and stretched out on a stone bed behind one god or another. They closed their eyes, and slept, and never woke. "The gift of the Many-Faced God takes myriad forms," the kindly man told her, "but here it is always gentle." When they found a body he would say a prayer and make certain life had fled, and Arya would fetch the serving men, whose task it was to carry the dead down to the vaults. There acolytes would strip and wash the bodies. The dead men's clothes and coins and valuables went into a bin for sorting. Their cold flesh would be taken to the lower sanctum where only the priests could go; what happened in there Arya was not allowed to know. Once, as she was eating her supper, a terrible suspicion seized hold of her, and she put down her knife and stared suspiciously at a slice of pale white meat. The kindly man saw the horror on her face. "It is pork, child," he told her, "only pork."

Her bed was stone, and reminded her of Harrenhal and the bed she'd slept in when scrubbing steps for Weese. The mattress was stuffed with rags instead of straw, which made it lumpier than the one she'd had at Harrenhal, but less scratchy too. She was allowed as many blankets as she wished; thick woolen blankets, red and green and plaid. And her cell was hers alone. She kept her treasures there: the silver fork and floppy hat and fingerless gloves given her by the sailors on the *Titan's Daughter,* her dagger, boots, and belt, her small store of coins, the clothes she had been wearing . . .

And Needle.

Though her duties left her little time for needlework, she practiced when she could, dueling with her shadow by the light of a blue candle. One night the waif happened to be passing and saw Arya at her swordplay. The girl did not say a word, but the next day, the kindly man walked Arya back to her cell. "You need to rid yourself of all this," he said of her treasures.

Arya felt stricken. "They're mine."

"And who are you?"

"No one."

He picked up her silver fork. "This belongs to Arya of House Stark. All these things belong to her. There is no place for them here. There is no place for her. Hers is too proud a name, and we have no room for pride. We are servants here."

"I serve," she said, wounded. She liked the silver fork.

"You play at being a servant, but in your heart you are a lord's daughter. You have taken other names, but you wore them as lightly as you might wear a gown. Under them was always Arya."

"I don't wear *gowns*. You can't fight in a stupid *gown*."

"Why would you wish to fight? Are you some bravo, strutting through the alleys, spoiling for blood?" He sighed. "Before you drink from the cold cup, you must offer up all you are to Him of Many Faces. Your body. Your soul. *Yourself.* If you cannot bring yourself to do that, you must leave this place."

"The iron coin—"

"—has paid your passage here. From this point you must pay your own way, and the cost is dear."

"I don't have any gold."

"What we offer cannot be bought with gold. The cost is all of you. Men take many paths through this vale of tears and pain. Ours is the hardest. Few are made to walk it. It takes uncommon strength of body and spirit, and a heart both hard and strong."

I have a hole where my heart should be, she thought, *and nowhere else to go.* "I'm strong. As strong as you. I'm hard."

"You believe this is the only place for you." It was as if he'd heard her thoughts. "You are wrong in that. You would find softer service in the household of some merchant. Or would you sooner be a courtesan, and have songs sung of your beauty? Speak the word, and we will send you to the Black Pearl or the Daughter of the Dusk. You will sleep on rose petals and wear silken skirts that rustle when you walk, and great lords will beggar themselves for your maiden's blood. Or if it is marriage and children you desire, tell me, and we shall find a husband for you. Some honest apprentice boy, a rich old man, a seafarer, whatever you desire."

She wanted none of that. Wordless, she shook her head.

"Is it Westeros you dream of, child? Luco Prestayn's *Lady Bright* leaves upon the morrow, for Gulltown, Duskendale, King's Landing, and Tyrosh. Shall we find you passage on her?"

"I only just *came* from Westeros." Sometimes it seemed a thousand years since she had fled King's Landing, and sometimes it seemed like only yesterday, but she knew she could not go back. "I'll go if you don't want me, but I won't go *there.*"

"My wants do not matter," said the kindly man. "It may be that the Many-Faced God has led you here to be His instrument, but when I look at you I see a child . . . and worse, a girl child. Many have served Him of Many Faces through the centuries, but only a few of His servants have been women. Women bring life into the world. We bring the gift of death. No one can do both."

He is trying to scare me away, Arya thought, *the way he did with the worm.* "I don't care about that."

"You should. Stay, and the Many-Faced God will take your ears, your nose, your tongue. He will take your sad grey eyes that have seen so much. He will take your hands, your feet, your arms and legs, your private parts. He will take your hopes and dreams, your loves and hates. Those who enter His service must give up all that makes them who they are. Can you do that?" He cupped her chin and gazed deep into her eyes, so deep it made her shiver. "No," he said, "I do not think you can."

Arya knocked his hand away. "I could if I *wanted* to."

"So says Arya of House Stark, eater of grave worms."

"I can give up *anything* I want!"

He gestured at her treasures. "Then start with these."

That night after supper, Arya went back to her cell and took off her robe and whispered her names, but sleep refused to take her. She tossed on her mattress stuffed with rags, gnawing on her lip. She could feel the hole inside her where her heart had been.

In the black of night she rose again, donned the clothes she'd worn from Westeros, and buckled on her swordbelt. Needle hung from one hip, her dagger from the other. With her floppy hat on her head, her fingerless gloves tucked into her belt, and her silver fork in one hand, she went stealing up the steps. *There is no place here for Arya of House Stark,* she was thinking. Arya's place was Winterfell, only Winterfell was gone. *When the snows fall and the white winds blow, the lone wolf dies, but the pack survives.* She had no pack, though. They had killed her pack, Ser Ilyn and Ser Meryn and the queen, and when she tried to make a new one all of them ran off, Hot Pie and Gendry and Yoren and Lommy Greenhands, even Harwin, who had been her father's man. She shoved through the doors, out into the night.

It was the first time she had been outside since entering the temple. The sky was overcast, and fog covered the ground like a frayed grey blanket. Off to her right she heard paddling from the canal. *Braavos, the Secret City,* she thought. The name seemed very apt. She crept down the steep steps to the covered dock, the mists swirling round her feet. It was so foggy she could not see the water, but she heard it lapping softly at stone pilings. In the distance, a light glowed through the gloom: the nightfire at the temple of the red priests, she thought.

At the water's edge she stopped, the silver fork in hand. It was real silver, solid through and through. *It's not my fork. It was Salty that he gave it to.* She tossed it underhand, heard the soft *plop* as it sank below the water.

Her floppy hat went next, then the gloves. They were Salty's too. She emptied her pouch into her palm; five silver stags, nine copper stars, some pennies and halfpennies and groats. She scattered them across the water. Next her boots. They made the loudest splashes. Her dagger followed, the one she'd gotten off the archer who had begged the Hound for mercy. Her swordbelt went into the canal. Her cloak, tunic, breeches, smallclothes, all of it. All but Needle.

She stood on the end of the dock, pale and gooseprickled and shivering in the fog. In her hand, Needle seemed to whisper to her. *Stick them with the pointy end,* it said, and, *don't tell Sansa!* Mikken's mark was on the blade. *It's just a sword.* If she needed a sword, there were a hundred under the temple. Needle was too small to be a *proper* sword, it was hardly more than a toy. She'd been a stupid little girl when Jon had it made for her. "It's just a sword," she said, aloud this time . . .

. . . but it wasn't.

Needle was Robb and Bran and Rickon, her mother and her father, even Sansa. Needle was Winterfell's grey walls, and the laughter of its people. Needle was the summer snows, Old Nan's stories, the heart tree with its red leaves and scary face, the warm earthy smell of the glass gardens, the sound of the north wind rattling the shutters of her room. Needle was Jon Snow's smile. *He used to mess my hair and call me "little sister,"* she remembered, and suddenly there were tears in her eyes.

Polliver had stolen the sword from her when the Mountain's men took her captive, but when she and the Hound walked into the inn at the crossroads, there it was. *The gods wanted me to have it.* Not the Seven, nor Him of Many Faces, but her father's gods, the old gods of the north. *The Many-Faced God can have the rest,* she thought, *but he can't have this.*

She padded up the steps as naked as her name day, clutching Needle. Halfway up, one of the stones rocked beneath her feet. Arya knelt and dug around its edges with her fingers. It would not move at first, but she persisted, picking at the crumbling mortar with her nails. Finally, the stone shifted. She grunted and got both hands in and pulled. A crack opened before her.

"You'll be safe here," she told Needle. "No one will know where you are but me." She pushed the sword and sheath behind the step, then shoved the stone back into place, so it looked like all the other stones. As she climbed back to the temple, she counted steps, so she would know where to find the sword again. One day she might have need of it. "One day," she whispered to herself.

She never told the kindly man what she had done, yet he knew. The next night, he came to her cell after supper. "Child," he said, "come sit with me. I have a tale to tell you."

"What kind of tale?" she asked, wary.

"The tale of our beginnings. If you would be one of us, you had best know who we are and how we came to be. Men may whisper of the Faceless Men of Braavos, but we are older than the Secret City. Before the Titan rose, before the Unmasking of Uthero, before the Founding, we were. We have flowered in Braavos amongst these northern fogs, but we first took root in Valyria, amongst the wretched slaves who toiled in the deep mines beneath the Fourteen Flames that lit the Freehold's nights of old. Most mines are dank and chilly places, cut from cold dead stone, but the Fourteen Flames were living mountains with veins of molten rock and hearts of fire. So the mines of old Valyria were always hot, and they grew hotter as the shafts were driven deeper, ever deeper. The slaves toiled in an oven. The rocks around them were too hot to touch. The air stank of brimstone and would sear their lungs as they breathed it. The soles of their feet would burn and blister, even through the thickest sandals. Sometimes, when they broke through a wall in search of gold, they would find steam instead, or boiling water, or molten rock. Certain shafts were cut so low that the slaves could not stand upright, but had to crawl or bend. And there were wyrms in that red darkness too."

"Earthworms?" she asked, frowning.

"Firewyrms. Some say they are akin to dragons, for wyrms breathe fire too. Instead of soaring through the sky, they bore through stone and soil. If the old tales can be believed, there were wyrms amongst the Fourteen Flames even before the dragons came. The young ones are no larger than that skinny arm of yours, but they can grow to monstrous size and have no love for men."

"Did they kill the slaves?"

"Burnt and blackened corpses were oft found in shafts where the rocks were cracked or full of holes. Yet still the mines drove deeper. Slaves perished by the score, but their masters did not care. Red gold and yellow gold and silver were reckoned to be more precious than the lives of slaves, for slaves were cheap in the old Freehold. During war, the Valyrians took them by the thousands. In times of peace they bred them, though only the worst were sent down to die in the red darkness."

"Didn't the slaves rise up and fight?"

"Some did," he said. "Revolts were common in the mines, but few accomplished much. The dragonlords of the old Freehold were strong in sorcery, and lesser men defied them at their peril. The first Faceless Man was one who did."

"Who was he?" Arya blurted, before she stopped to think.

"No one," he answered. "Some say he was a slave himself. Others insist he was a freeholder's son, born of noble stock. Some will even tell you he was an overseer who took pity on his charges. The truth is, no one knows. Whoever he was, he moved amongst the slaves and would hear them at their prayers. Men of a hundred different nations labored in the mines, and each prayed to his own god in his own tongue, yet all were praying for the same thing. It was release they asked for, an end to pain. A small thing, and simple. Yet their gods made no answer, and their suffering went on. *Are their gods all deaf?* he wondered . . . until a realization came upon him, one night in the red darkness.

"All gods have their instruments, men and women who serve them and help to work their will on earth. The slaves were not crying out to a hundred different gods, as it seemed, but to one god with a hundred different faces . . . and *he* was that god's instrument. That very night he chose the most wretched of the slaves, the one who had prayed most earnestly for release, and freed him from his bondage. The first gift had been given."

Arya drew back from him. "He killed the *slave?*" That did not sound right. "He should have killed the *masters!*"

"He would bring the gift to them as well . . . but that is a tale for another day, one best shared with no one." He cocked his head. "And who are you, child?"

"No one."

"A lie."

"How do you *know?* Is it magic?"

"A man does not need to be a wizard to know truth from falsehood, not if he has eyes. You need only learn to read a face. Look at the eyes. The mouth. The muscles here, at the corners of the jaw, and here, where the neck joins the shoulders." He touched her lightly with two fingers. "Some liars blink. Some stare. Some look away. Some lick their lips. Many cover their mouths just before they tell a lie, as if to hide their deceit. Other signs may be more subtle, but they are always there. A false smile and a true one may look alike, but they are as different as dusk from dawn. Can you tell dusk from dawn?"

Arya nodded, though she was not certain that she could.

"Then you can learn to see a lie . . . and once you do, no secret will be safe from you."

"Teach me." She would be no one if that was what it took. No one had no holes inside her.

"*She* will teach you," said the kindly man as the waif appeared outside her door. "Starting with the tongue of Braavos. What use are you if you cannot speak or understand? And you shall teach her your own tongue. The two of you shall learn together, each from the other. Will you do this?"

"Yes," she said, and from that moment she was a novice in the House of Black and White. Her servant's garb was taken away, and she was given a robe to wear, a robe of black and white as buttery soft as the old red blanket she'd once had at Winterfell. Beneath it she wore smallclothes of fine white linen, and a black undertunic that hung down past her knees.

Thereafter, she and the waif spent their time together touching things and pointing, as each tried to teach the other a few words of her own tongue. Simple words at first, cup and candle and shoe; then harder words; then sentences. Once Syrio Forel used to make Arya stand on one leg until she was trembling. Later he sent her chasing after cats. She had danced the water dance on the limbs of trees, a stick sword in her hand. Those things had all been hard, but this was harder.

Even sewing was more fun than tongues, she told herself, after a night when she had forgotten half the words she thought she knew, and pronounced the other half so badly that the waif had laughed at her. *My sentences are as crooked as my stitches used to be.* If the girl had not been so small and starved, Arya would have smashed her stupid face. Instead she gnawed her lip. *Too stupid to learn and too stupid to give up.*

The Common Tongue came to the waif more quickly. One day at supper she turned to Arya, and asked, "Who are you?"

"No one," Arya answered, in Braavosi.

"You lie," said the waif. "You must lie gooder."

Arya laughed. "Gooder? You mean *better,* stupid."

"Better stupid. I will show you."

The next day they began the lying game, asking questions of one another, taking turns. Sometimes they would answer truly, sometimes they would lie. The questioner had to try and tell what was true and what was false. The waif always seemed to know. Arya had to guess. Most of the time she guessed wrong.

"How many years have you?" the waif asked her once, in the Common Tongue. "Ten," said Arya, and raised ten fingers. She *thought* she was still ten, though it was hard to know for certain. The Braavosi counted days differently than they did in Westeros. For all she knew her name day had come and gone.

The waif nodded. Arya nodded back, and in her best Braavosi said, "How many years have *you?*"

The waif showed ten fingers. Then ten again, and yet again. Then six. Her face remained as smooth as still water. *She can't be six-and-thirty,* Arya thought. *She's a little girl.* "You're lying," she said. The waif shook her head and showed her once again: ten and ten and ten and six. She said the words for six-and-thirty, and made Arya say them too.

The next day she told the kindly man what the waif had claimed. "She did not lie," the priest said, chuckling. "The one you call *waif* is a woman grown who has spent her life serving Him of Many Faces. She gave Him all she was, all she ever might have been, all the lives that were within her."

Arya bit her lip. "Will I be like her?"

"No," he said, "not unless you wish it. It is the poisons that have made her as you see her."

Poisons. She understood then. Every evening after prayer the waif emptied a stone flagon into the waters of the black pool.

The waif and kindly man were not the only servants of the Many-Faced God. From time to time others would visit the House of Black and White. The fat fellow had fierce black eyes, a hook nose, and a wide mouth full of yellow teeth. The stern face never smiled; his eyes were pale, his lips full and dark. The handsome man had a beard of a different color every time she saw him, and a different nose, but he was never less than comely. Those three came most often, but there were others: the squinter, the lordling, the starved man. One time the fat fellow and the squinter came together. Umma sent Arya to pour for them. "When you are not pouring, you must stand as still as if you had been carved of stone," the kindly man told her. "Can you do that?"

"Yes." *Before you can learn to move you must learn to be still,* Syrio Forel had taught her long ago at King's Landing, and she had. She had served as Roose Bolton's cupbearer at Harrenhal, and he would flay you if you spilled his wine.

"Good," the kindly man said. "It would be best if you were blind and deaf as well. You may hear things, but you must let them pass in one ear and out the other. Do not listen."

Arya heard much and more that night, but almost all of it was in the tongue of Braavos, and she hardly understood one word in ten. *Still as stone,* she told herself. The hardest part was struggling not to yawn. Before the night was done, her wits were wandering. Standing there with the flagon in her hands, she dreamed she was a wolf, running free through a moonlit forest with a great pack howling at her heels.

"Are the other men all priests?" she asked the kindly man the next morning. "Were those their real faces?"

"What do you think, child?"

She thought *no.* "Is Jaqen H'ghar a priest too? Do you know if Jaqen will be coming back to Braavos?"

"Who?" he said, all innocence.

"Jaqen *H'ghar.* He gave me the iron coin."

"I know no one by this name, child."

"I asked him how he changed his face, and he said it was no harder than taking a new name, if you knew the way."

"Did he?"

"Will you show me how to change my face?"

"If you wish." He cupped her chin in his hand and turned her head. "Puff up your cheeks and stick out your tongue."

Arya puffed up her cheeks and stuck out her tongue.

"There. Your face is changed."

"That's not how I meant. Jaqen used magic."

"All sorcery comes at a cost, child. Years of prayer and sacrifice and study are required to work a proper glamor."

"*Years?*" she said, dismayed.

"If it were easy all men would do it. You must walk before you run. Why use a spell, where mummer's tricks will serve?"

"I don't know any mummer's tricks either."

"Then practice making faces. Beneath your skin are muscles. Learn to use them. It is your face. Your cheeks, your lips, your ears. Smiles and scowls should not come upon you like sudden squalls. A smile should be a servant, and come only when you call it. Learn to *rule* your face."

"Show me how."

"Puff up your cheeks." She did. "Lift your eyebrows. No, higher." She did that too. "Good. See how long you can hold that. It will not be long. Try it again on the morrow. You will find a Myrish mirror in the vaults. Train before it for an hour every day. Eyes, nostrils, cheeks, ears, lips, learn to rule them all." He cupped her chin. "Who are you?"

"No one."

"A lie. A sad little lie, child."

She found the Myrish mirror the next day, and every morn and every night she sat before it with a candle on each side of her, making faces. *Rule your face,* she told herself, *and you can lie.*

Soon thereafter the kindly man commanded her to help the other acolytes prepare the corpses. The work was not near as hard as scrubbing steps for Weese. Sometimes if the corpse was big or fat she would struggle with the weight, but most of the dead were old dry bones in wrinkled skins. Arya would look at them as she washed them, wondering what brought them to the black pool. She remembered a tale she had heard from Old Nan, about how sometimes during a long winter men who'd lived beyond their years would announce that they were going hunting. *And their daughters would weep and their sons would turn their faces to the fire,* she could hear Old Nan saying, *but no one would stop them, or ask what game they meant to hunt, with the snows so deep and the cold wind howling.* She wondered what the old Braavosi told their sons and daughters, before they set off for the House of Black and White.

The moon turned and turned again, though Arya never saw it. She served, washed the dead, made faces at the mirrors, learned the Braavosi tongue, and tried to remember that she was no one.

One day the kindly man sent for her. "Your accent is a horror," he said, "but you have enough words to make your wants understood after a fashion. It is time that you left us for a while. The only way you will ever truly master our tongue is if you speak it every day from dawn to dusk. You must go."

"When?" she asked him. "Where?"

"Now," he answered. "Beyond these walls you will find the hundred isles of Braavos in the sea. You have been taught the words for mussels, cockles, and clams, have you not?"

"Yes." She repeated them, in her best Braavosi.

Her best Braavosi made him smile. "It will serve. Along the wharves below the Drowned Town you will find a fishmonger named Brusco, a good man with a bad back. He has need of a girl to push his barrow and sell his cockles, clams, and mussels to the sailors off the ships. You shall be that girl. Do you understand?"

"Yes."

"And when Brusco asks, who are you?"

"No one."

"No. That will not serve, outside this House."

She hesitated. "I could be Salty, from Saltpans."

"Salty is known to Ternesio Terys and the men of the *Titan's Daughter.* You are marked by the way you speak, so you must be some girl of Westeros . . . but a different girl, I think."

She bit her lip. "Could I be Cat?"

"Cat." He considered. "Yes. Braavos is full of cats. One more will not be noticed. You are Cat, an orphan of . . ."

"King's Landing." She had visited White Harbor with her father twice, but she knew King's Landing better.

"Just so. Your father was oarmaster on a galley. When your mother died, he took you off to sea with him. Then he died as well, and his captain had no use for you, so he put you off the ship in Braavos. And what was the name of the ship?"

"*Nymeria*," she said at once.

That night she left the House of Black and White. A long iron knife rode on her right hip, hidden by her cloak, a patched and faded thing of the sort an orphan might wear. Her shoes pinched her toes and her tunic was so threadbare that the wind cut right through it. But Braavos lay before her. The night air smelled of smoke and salt and fish. The canals were crooked, the alleys crookeder. Men gave her curious looks as she went past, and beggar children called out words she could not understand. Before long she was completely lost.

"Ser Gregor," she chanted, as she crossed a stone bridge supported by four arches. From the center of its span she could see the masts of ships in the Ragman's Harbor. "Dunsen, Raff the Sweetling, Ser Ilyn, Ser Meryn, Queen Cersei." Rain began to fall. Arya turned her face up to let the raindrops wash her cheeks, so happy she could dance. "*Valar morghulis,*" she said, "*valar morghulis, valar morghulis.*"

ALAYNE

As the rising sun came streaming through the windows, Alayne sat up in bed and stretched. Gretchel heard her stir and rose at once to fetch her bedrobe. The rooms had grown chilly during the night. *It will be worse when winter has us in its grip,* she thought. *Winter will make this place as cold as any tomb.* Alayne slipped into the robe and belted it about her waist. "The fire's almost out," she observed. "Put another log on, if you would."

"As my lady wishes," the old woman said.

Alayne's apartments in the Maiden's Tower were larger and more lavish than the little bedchamber where she'd been kept when Lady Lysa was alive. She had a dressing room and a privy of her own now, and a balcony of carved white stone that looked off across the Vale. While Gretchel was tending to the fire, Alayne padded barefoot across the room and slipped outside. The stone was cold beneath her feet, and the wind was blowing fiercely, as it always did up here, but the view made her forget all that for half a heartbeat. Maiden's was the easternmost of the Eyrie's seven slender towers, so she had the Vale before her, its forests and rivers and fields all hazy in the morning light. The way the sun was hitting the mountains made them look like solid gold.

So lovely. The snow-clad summit of the Giant's Lance loomed above her, an immensity of stone and ice that dwarfed the castle perched upon its shoulder. Icicles twenty feet long draped the lip of the precipice where Alyssa's Tears fell in summer. A falcon soared above the frozen waterfall, blue wings spread wide against the morning sky. *Would that I had wings as well.*

She rested her hands on the carved stone balustrade and made herself peer over the edge. She could see Sky six hundred feet below, and the stone steps carved into the mountain, the winding way that led past Snow and Stone all the way down to the valley floor. She could see the towers and keeps of the Gates of the Moon, as small as a child's toys. Around the walls the hosts of Lords Declarant were stirring, emerging from their tents like ants from an anthill. *If only they were truly ants,* she thought, *we could step on them and crush them.*

Young Lord Hunter and his levies had joined the others two days past. Nestor Royce had closed the Gates against them, but he had fewer than three hundred men in his garrison. Each of the Lords Declarant had brought a thousand, and there were six of them. Alayne knew their names as well as her own. Benedar Belmore, Lord of Strongsong. Symond Templeton, the Knight of Ninestars. Horton Redfort, Lord of Redfort. Anya Waynwood, Lady of Ironoaks. Gilwood Hunter, called Young Lord Hunter by all and sundry, Lord of Longbow Hall. And Yohn Royce, mightiest of them all, the redoubtable Bronze Yohn, Lord of Runestone, Nestor's cousin and the chief of the senior branch of House Royce. The six had gathered at Runestone after Lysa Arryn's fall, and there made a pact together, vowing to defend Lord Robert, the Vale, and one another. Their declaration made no mention of the Lord Protector, but spoke of "misrule" that must be ended, and of "false friends and evil counselors" as well.

A cold gust of wind blew up her legs. She went inside to choose a gown to break her fast in. Petyr had given her his late wife's wardrobe, a wealth of silks, satins, velvets, and furs far beyond anything she had ever dreamed, though the great bulk of it was far too large for her; Lady Lysa had grown very stout during her long succession of pregnancies, stillbirths, and miscarriages. A few of the oldest gowns had been made for young Lysa Tully of Riverrun, however, and others Gretchel had been able to alter to fit Alayne, who was almost as long of leg at three-and-ten as her aunt had been at twenty.

This morning her eye was caught by a parti-colored gown of Tully red and blue, lined with vair. Gretchel helped her slide her arms into the belled sleeves and laced her back, then brushed and pinned her hair. Alayne had darkened it again last night before she went to bed. The wash her aunt had given her changed her own rich auburn into Alayne's burnt brown, but it was seldom long before the red began creeping back at the roots. *And what must I do when the dye runs out?* The wash had come from Tyrosh, across the narrow sea.

As she went down to break her fast, Alayne was struck again by the stillness of the Eyrie. There was no quieter castle in all the Seven Kingdoms. The servants here were few and old and kept their voices down so as not to excite the young lord. There were no horses on the mountain, no hounds to bark and growl, no knights training in the yard. Even the footsteps of the guards seemed strangely muffled as they walked the pale stone halls. She could hear the wind moaning and sighing round the towers, but that was all. When she had first come to Eyrie, there had been the murmur of Alyssa's Tears as well, but the waterfall was frozen now. Gretchel said it would stay silent till the spring.

She found Lord Robert alone in the Morning Hall above the kitchens, pushing a wooden spoon listlessly through a big bowl of porridge and honey. "I wanted eggs," he complained when he saw her. "I wanted *three* eggs boiled soft, and some back bacon."

They had no eggs, no more than they had bacon. The Eyrie's granaries held sufficient oats and corn and barley to feed them for a year, but they depended on a bastard girl named Mya Stone to bring fresh foodstuffs up from the valley floor. With the Lords Declarant encamped at the foot of the mountain there was no way for Mya to get through. Lord Belmore, first of the six to reach the Gates, had sent a raven to tell Littlefinger that no more food would go up to the Eyrie until he sent Lord Robert down. It was not quite a siege, not as yet, but it was the next best thing.

"You can have eggs when Mya comes, as many as you like," Alayne promised the little lordling. "She'll bring eggs and butter and melons, all sorts of tasty things."

The boy was unappeased. "I wanted eggs *today*."

"Sweetrobin, there are no eggs, you know that. Please, eat your porridge, it's very nice." She ate a spoonful of her own.

Robert pushed his spoon across the bowl and back, but never brought it to his lips. "I am not hungry," he decided. "I want to go back to bed. I never slept last night. I heard *singing*. Maester Colemon gave me dreamwine but I could still hear it."

Alayne put down her spoon. "If there had been singing, I should have heard it too. You had a bad dream, that's all."

"No, it *wasn't* a dream." Tears filled his eyes. "Marillion was singing again. Your father says he's dead, but he *isn't*."

"He is." It frightened her to hear him talk like this. *Bad enough that he is small and sickly, what if he is mad as well?* "Sweetrobin, he *is*. Marillion loved your lady mother too much and could not live with what he'd done to her, so he walked into the sky." Alayne had not seen the body, no more than Robert had, but she did not doubt the fact of the singer's death. "He's gone, truly."

"But I hear him every night. Even when I close the shutters and put a *pillow* on my head. Your father should have cut his tongue out. I *told* him to, but he wouldn't."

He needed a tongue to confess. "Be a good boy and eat your porridge," Alayne pleaded. "Please? For me?"

"I don't want porridge." Robert flung his spoon across the hall. It bounced off a hanging tapestry, and left a smear of porridge upon a white silk moon. "The *lord* wants *eggs!*"

"The lord shall eat porridge and be thankful for it," said Petyr's voice, behind them.

Alayne turned, and saw him in the doorway arch with Maester Colemon at his side. "You should heed the Lord Protector, my lord," the maester said. "Your lord's bannermen are coming up the mountain to pay you homage, so you will need all your strength."

Robert rubbed at his left eye with a knuckle. "Send them away. I don't *want* them. If they come, I'll make them fly."

"You tempt me sorely, my lord, but I fear I promised them safe conduct," said Petyr. "In any case, it is too late to turn them back. By now they may have climbed as far as Stone."

"Why won't they leave us be?" wailed Alayne. "We never did them any harm. What do they *want* of us?"

"Just Lord Robert. Him, and the Vale." Petyr smiled. "There will be eight of them. Lord Nestor is showing them up, and they have Lyn Corbray with them. Ser Lyn is not the sort of man to stay away when blood is in the offing."

His words did little to soothe her fears. Lyn Corbray had slain almost as many men in duels as he had in battle. He had won his spurs during Robert's Rebellion, she knew, fighting first against Lord Jon Arryn at the gates of Gulltown, and later beneath his banners on the Trident, where he had cut down Prince Lewyn of Dorne, a white knight of the Kingsguard. Petyr said that Prince Lewyn had been sorely wounded by the time the tide of battle swept him to his final dance with Lady Forlorn, but added, "That's not a point you'll want to raise with Corbray, though. Those who do are soon given the chance to ask Martell himself the truth of it, down in the halls of hell." If even half of what she had heard from Lord Robert's guards was true, Lyn Corbray was more dangerous than all six of the Lords Declarant put together. "Why is *he* coming?" she asked. "I thought the Corbrays were for you."

"Lord Lyonel Corbray is well disposed toward my rule," said Petyr, "but his brother goes his own way. On the Trident, when their father fell wounded, it was Lyn who snatched up Lady Forlorn and slew the man who'd cut him down. Whilst Lyonel was carrying the old man back to the maesters in the rear, Lyn led his charge against the Dornishmen threatening Robert's left, broke their lines to pieces, and slew Lewyn Martell. So when old Lord Corbray died, he bestowed the Lady upon his younger son. Lyonel got his lands, his title, his castle, and all his coin, yet still feels he was cheated of his birthright, whilst Ser Lyn . . . well, he loves Lyonel as much as he loves me. He wanted Lysa's hand for himself."

"I don't like Ser Lyn," Robert insisted. "I won't have him here. You send him back down. I never said that he could come. Not *here*. The Eyrie is im*preg*nable, Mother said."

"Your mother is dead, my lord. Until your sixteenth name day, *I* rule the Eyrie." Petyr turned to the stoop-backed serving woman hovering near the kitchen steps. "Mela, fetch his lordship a new spoon. He wants to eat his porridge."

"I do *not*! Let my porridge *fly*!" This time Robert flung the bowl, porridge and honey and all. Petyr Baelish ducked aside nimbly, but

Maester Colemon was not so quick. The wooden bowl caught him square in the chest, and its contents exploded upward over his face and shoulders. He yelped in a most unmaesterlike fashion, while Alayne turned to soothe the little lordling, but too late. The fit was on him. A pitcher of milk went flying as his hand caught it, flailing. When he tried to rise he knocked his chair backwards and fell on top of it. One foot caught Alayne in the belly, so hard it knocked the wind from her. "Oh, gods be good," she heard Petyr say, disgusted.

Globs of porridge dotted Maester Colemon's face and hair as he knelt over his charge, murmuring soothing words. One gobbet crept slowly down his right cheek, like a lumpy grey-brown tear. *It is not so bad a spell as the last one,* Alayne thought, trying to be hopeful. By the time the shaking stopped, two guards in sky-blue cloaks and silvery mail shirts had come at Petyr's summons. "Take him back to bed and leech him," the Lord Protector said, and the taller guardsman scooped the boy up in his arms. *I could carry him myself,* Alayne thought. *He is no heavier than a doll.*

Colemon lingered a moment before following. "My lord, this parley might best be left for another day. His lordship's spells have grown worse since Lady Lysa's death. More frequent and more violent. I bleed the child as often as I dare, and mix him dreamwine and milk of the poppy to help him sleep, but . . ."

"He sleeps twelve hours a day," Petyr said. "I require him awake from time to time."

The maester combed his fingers through his hair, dribbling globs of porridge on the floor. "Lady Lysa would give his lordship her breast whenever he grew overwrought. Archmaester Ebrose claims that mother's milk has many heathful properties."

"Is that your counsel, maester? That we find a wet nurse for the Lord of the Eyrie and Defender of the Vale? When shall we wean him, on his wedding day? That way he can move directly from his nurse's nipples to his wife's." Lord Petyr's laugh made it plain what he thought of that. "No, I think not. I suggest you find another way. The boy is fond of sweets, is he not?"

"Sweets?" said Colemon.

"Sweets. Cakes and pies, jams and jellies, honey on the comb.

Perhaps a pinch of sweetsleep in his milk, have you tried that? Just a pinch, to calm him and stop his wretched shaking."

"A pinch?" The apple in the maester's throat moved up and down as he swallowed. "One small pinch . . . perhaps, perhaps. Not too much, and not too often, yes, I might try . . ."

"A pinch," Lord Petyr said, "before you bring him forth to meet the lords."

"As you command, my lord." The maester hurried out, his chain clinking softly with every step.

"Father," Alayne asked when he was gone, "will you have a bowl of porridge to break your fast?"

"I despise porridge." He looked at her with Littlefinger's eyes. "I'd sooner break my fast with a kiss."

A true daughter would not refuse her sire a kiss, so Alayne went to him and kissed him, a quick dry peck upon the cheek, and just as quickly stepped away.

"How . . . dutiful." Littlefinger smiled with his mouth, but not his eyes. "Well, I have other duties for you, as it happens. Tell the cook to mull some red wine with honey and raisins. Our guests will be cold and thirsty after their long climb. You are to meet them when they arrive, and offer them refreshment. Wine, bread, and cheese. What sort of cheese is left to us?"

"The sharp white and the stinky blue."

"The white. And you'd best change as well."

Alayne looked down at her dress, the deep blue and rich dark red of Riverrun. "Is it too—"

"It is too *Tully*. The Lords Declarant will not be pleased by the sight of my bastard daughter prancing about in my dead wife's clothes. Choose something else. Need I remind you to avoid sky blue and cream?"

"No." Sky blue and cream were the colors of House Arryn. "Eight, you said . . . Bronze Yohn is one of them?"

"The only one who matters."

"Bronze Yohn *knows* me," she reminded him. "He was a guest at Winterfell when his son rode north to take the black." She had fallen wildly in love with Ser Waymar, she remembered dimly, but that was a lifetime ago, when she was a stupid little girl. "And that was not the only time. Lord Royce saw ... he saw Sansa Stark again at King's Landing, during the Hand's tourney."

Petyr put a finger under her chin. "That Royce glimpsed this pretty face I do not doubt, but it was one face in a thousand. A man fighting in a tourney has more to concern him than some child in the crowd. And at Winterfell, Sansa was a little girl with auburn hair. My daughter is a maiden tall and fair, and her hair is chestnut. Men see what they expect to see, Alayne." He kissed her nose. "Have Maddy lay a fire in the solar. I shall receive our Lords Declarant there."

"Not the High Hall?"

"No. Gods forbid they glimpse me near the high seat of the Arryns, they might think that I mean to sit in it. Cheeks born so low as mine must never aspire to such lofty cushions."

"The solar." She should have stopped with that, but the words came tumbling out of her. "If you gave them Robert ..."

"... and the Vale?"

"They *have* the Vale."

"Oh, much of it, that's true. Not all, however. I am well loved in Gulltown, and have some lordly friends of mine own as well. Grafton, Lynderly, Lyonel Corbray ... though I'll grant you, they are no match for the Lords Declarant. Still, where would you have us go, Alayne? Back to my mighty stronghold on the Fingers?"

She had thought about that. "Joffrey gave you Harrenhal. You are lord in your own right there."

"By title. I needed a great seat to marry Lysa, and the Lannisters were not about to grant me Casterly Rock."

"Yes, but the castle is *yours*."

"Ah, and what a castle it is. Cavernous halls and ruined towers, ghosts and draughts, ruinous to heat, impossible to garrison ... and there's that small matter of a curse."

"Curses are only in songs and stories."

That seemed to amuse him. "Has someone made a song about Gregor Clegane dying of a poisoned spear thrust? Or about the sellsword before him, whose limbs Ser Gregor removed a joint at a time? That one took the castle from Ser Amory Lorch, who received it from

Lord Tywin. A bear killed one, your dwarf the other. Lady Whent's died as well, I hear. Lothstons, Strongs, Harroways, . . . Harrenhal has withered every hand to touch it."

"Then give it to Lord Frey."

Petyr laughed. "Perhaps I shall. Or better still, to our sweet Cersei. Though I should not speak harshly of her, she is sending me some splendid tapestries. Isn't that kind of her?"

The mention of the queen's name made her stiffen. "She's *not* kind. She scares me. If she should learn where I am—"

"—I might have to remove her from the game sooner than I'd planned. Provided she does not remove herself first." Petyr teased her with a little smile. "In the game of thrones, even the humblest pieces can have wills of their own. Sometimes they refuse to make the moves you've planned for them. Mark that well, Alayne. It's a lesson that Cersei Lannister still has yet to learn. Now, don't you have some duties to perform?"

She did indeed. She saw to the mulling of the wine first, found a suitable wheel of sharp white cheese, and commanded the cook to bake bread enough for twenty, in case the Lords Declarant brought more men than expected. *Once they eat our bread and salt they are our guests and cannot harm us.* The Freys had broken all the laws of hospitality when they'd murdered her lady mother and her brother at the Twins, but she could not believe that a lord as noble as Yohn Royce would ever stoop to do the same.

The solar next. Its floor was covered by a Myrish carpet, so there was no need to lay down rushes. Alayne asked two serving men to erect the trestle table and bring up eight of the heavy oak-and-leather chairs. For a feast she would have placed one at the head of the table, one at the foot, and three along each side, but this was no feast. She had the men arrange six chairs on one side of the table, two on the other. By now the Lords Declarant might have climbed as far as Snow. It took most of a day to make the climb, even on muleback. Afoot, most men took several days.

It might be that the lords would talk late into the night. They would need fresh candles. After Maddy laid the fire, she sent her down to find the scented beeswax candles Lord Waxley had given Lady Lysa when he sought to win her hand. Then she visited the kitchens once again, to make certain of the wine and bread. All seemed well in hand, and there was still time enough for her to bathe and wash her hair and change.

There was a gown of purple silk that gave her pause, and another of dark blue velvet slashed with silver that would have woken all the color in her eyes, but in the end she remembered that Alayne was after all a bastard, and must not presume to dress above her station. The dress she picked was lambswool, dark brown and simply cut, with leaves and vines embroidered around the bodice, sleeves, and hem in golden thread. It was modest and becoming, though scarce richer than something a serving girl might wear. Petyr had given her all of Lady Lysa's jewels as well, and she tried on several necklaces, but they all seemed ostentatious. In the end she chose a simple velvet ribbon in autumn gold. When Gretchel fetched her Lysa's silvered looking glass, the color seemed just perfect with Alayne's mass of dark brown hair. *Lord Royce will never know me*, she thought. *Why, I hardly know myself.*

Feeling near as bold as Petyr Baelish, Alayne Stone donned her smile and went down to meet their guests.

The Eyrie was the only castle in the Seven Kingdoms where the main entrance was underneath the dungeons. Steep stone steps crept up the mountainside past the waycastles Stone and Snow, but they came to an end at Sky. The final six hundred feet of the ascent were vertical, forcing would-be visitors to dismount their mules and make a choice. They could ride the swaying wooden basket that was used to lift supplies, or clamber up a rocky chimney using handholds carved into the rock.

Lord Redfort and Lady Waynwood, the most elderly of the Lords Declarant, chose to be drawn up by the winch, after which the basket was lowered once more for fat Lord Belmore. The other lords made the climb. Alayne met them in the Crescent Chamber beside a warming fire, where she welcomed them in Lord Robert's name and served them bread and cheese and cups of hot mulled wine in silver cups.

Petyr had given her a roll of arms to study, so she knew their heraldry if not their faces. The red castle was Redfort, plainly; a short man with a neat grey beard and mild eyes. Lady Anya was the only woman amongst the Lords Declarant, and wore a deep green mantle with the broken wheel of Waynwood picked out in beads of jet. Six silver bells on purple, that was Belmore, pear-bellied and round of shoulder. His beard was a ginger-grey horror sprouting from a multiplicity of chins. Symond Templeton's, by contrast, was black and sharply pointed. A beak of a nose and icy blue eyes made the Knight of Ninestars look like some elegant bird of prey. His doublet displayed nine black stars within a golden saltire. Young Lord Hunter's ermine cloak confused her till she spied the brooch that pinned it, five silver arrows fanned. Alayne would have put his age closer to fifty than to forty. His father had ruled at Longbow Hall for nigh on sixty years, only to die so abruptly that some whispered the new lord had hastened his inheritance. Hunter's cheeks and nose were red as apples, which bespoke a certain fondness for the grape. She made certain to fill his cup as often as he emptied it.

The youngest man in the party had three ravens on his chest, each clutching a blood-red heart in its talons. His brown hair was shoulder length; one stray lock curled down across his forehead. *Ser Lyn Corbray,* Alayne thought, with a wary glance at his hard mouth and restless eyes.

Last of all came the Royces, Lord Nestor and Bronze Yohn. The Lord of Runestone stood as tall as the Hound. Though his hair was grey and his face lined, Lord Yohn still looked as though he could break most younger men like twigs in those huge gnarled hands. His seamed and solemn face brought back all of Sansa's memories of his time at Winterfell. She remembered him at table, speaking quietly with her mother. She heard his voice booming off the walls when he rode back from a hunt with a buck behind his saddle. She could see him in the yard, a practice sword in hand, hammering her father to the ground and turning to defeat Ser Rodrik as well. *He will know me. How could he not?* She considered throwing herself at his feet to beg for his protection. *He never fought for Robb, why should he fight for me? The war is finished and Winterfell is fallen.* "Lord Royce," she asked timidly, "will you have a cup of wine, to take the chill off?"

Bronze Yohn had slate-grey eyes, half-hidden beneath the bushiest eyebrows she had ever seen. They crinkled when he looked down at her. "Do I know you, girl?"

Alayne felt as though she had swallowed her tongue, but Lord Nestor rescued her. "Alayne is the Lord Protector's natural daughter," he told his cousin gruffly.

"Littlefinger's little finger has been busy," said Lyn Corbray, with a wicked smile. Belmore laughed, and Alayne could feel the color rising in her cheeks.

"How old are you, child?" asked Lady Waynwood.

"Four-fourteen, my lady." For a moment she forgot how old Alayne should be. "And I am no child, but a maiden flowered."

"But not *de*flowered, one can hope." Young Lord Hunter's bushy mustache hid his mouth entirely.

"Yet," said Lyn Corbray, as if she were not there. "But ripe for plucking soon, I'd say."

"Is that what passes for courtesy at Heart's Home?" Anya Waynwood's hair was greying and she had crow's-feet around her eyes and loose skin beneath her chin, but there was no mistaking the air of nobility about her. "The girl is young and gently bred, and has suffered enough horrors. Mind your tongue, ser."

"My tongue is my concern," Corbray replied. "Your ladyship should take care to mind her own. I have never taken kindly to chastisement, as any number of dead men could tell you."

Lady Waynwood turned away from him. "Best take us to your father, Alayne. The sooner we are done with this, the better."

"The Lord Protector awaits you in the solar. If my lords would follow me." From the Crescent Chamber they climbed a steep flight of marble steps that bypassed both undercrofts and dungeons and passed beneath three murder holes, which the Lords Declarant pretended not to notice. Belmore was soon puffing like a bellows, and Redfort's face turned as grey as his hair. The guards atop the stairs raised the portcullis at their coming. "This way, if it please my lords." Alayne led them down the arcade past a dozen splendid tapestries. Ser Lothor Brune stood outside the solar. He opened the door for them and followed them inside.

Petyr was seated at the trestle table with a cup of wine to hand, looking over a crisp white parchment. He glanced up as the Lords Declarant filed in. "My lords, be welcome. And you as well, my lady.

The ascent is wearisome, I know. Please be seated. Alayne, my sweet, more wine for our noble guests."

"As you say, Father." The candles had been lighted, she was pleased to see; the solar smelled of nutmeg and other costly spices. She went to fetch the flagon whilst the visitors arranged themselves side by side . . . all save Nestor Royce, who hesitated before walking around the table to take the empty chair beside Lord Petyr, and Lyn Corbray, who went to stand beside the hearth instead. The heart-shaped ruby in the pommel of his sword shone redly as he warmed his hands. Alayne saw him smile at Ser Lothor Brune. *Ser Lyn is very handsome, for an older man,* she thought, *but I do not like the way he smiles.*

"I have been reading this remarkable declaration of yours," Petyr began. "Splendid. Whatever maester wrote this has a gift for words. I only wish you had invited me to sign as well."

That took them unawares. "You?" said Belmore. "Sign?"

"I wield a quill as well as any man, and no one loves Lord Robert more than I do. As for these false friends and evil counselors, by all means let us root them out. My lords, I am with you, heart and hand. Show me where to sign, I beg you."

Alayne, pouring, heard Lyn Corbray chuckle. The others seemed at a loss till Bronze Yohn Royce cracked his knuckles, and said, "We did not come for your signature. Nor do we mean to bandy words with you, Littlefinger."

"What a pity. I do so love a nicely bandied word." Petyr set the parchment to one side. "As you wish. Let us be blunt. What would you have of me, my lords and lady?"

"We will have naught of you." Symond Templeton fixed the Lord Protector with his cold blue stare. "We will have you gone."

"Gone?" Petyr feigned surprise. "Where would I go?"

"The crown has made you Lord of Harrenhal," Young Lord Hunter pointed out. "That should be enough for any man."

"The riverlands have need of a lord," old Horton Redfort said. "Riverrun stands besieged, Bracken and Blackwood are at open war, and outlaws roam freely on both sides of the Trident, stealing and killing as they will. Unburied corpses litter the landscape everywhere you go."

"You make it sound so wonderfully attractive, Lord Redfort," Petyr answered, "but as it happens I have pressing duties here. And there is Lord Robert to consider. Would you have me drag a sickly child into the midst of such carnage?"

"His lordship will remain in the Vale," declared Yohn Royce. "I mean to take the boy with me to Runestone, and raise him up to be a knight that Jon Arryn would be proud of."

"Why Runestone?" Petyr mused. "Why not Ironoaks or the Redfort? Why not Longbow Hall?"

"Any of these would serve as well," declared Lord Belmore, "and his lordship will visit each in turn, in due time."

"Will he?" Petyr's tone seemed to hint at doubts.

Lady Waynwood sighed. "Lord Petyr, if you think to set us one against the other, you may spare yourself the effort. We speak with one voice here. Runestone suits us all. Lord Yohn raised three fine sons of his own, there is no man more fit to foster his young lordship. Maester Helliweg is a good deal older and more experienced than your own Maester Colemon, and better suited to treat Lord Robert's frailties. In Runestone, the boy will learn the arts of war from Strong Sam Stone. No man could hope for a finer master-at-arms. Septon Lucos will instruct him in matters of the spirit. At Runestone he will also find other boys his own age, more suitable companions than the old women and sellswords that presently surround him."

Petyr Baelish fingered his beard. "His lordship needs companions, I do not disagree. Alayne is hardly an old woman, though. Lord Robert loves my daughter dearly, he will be glad to tell you so himself. And as it happens, I have asked Lord Grafton and Lord Lynderly to send me each a son to ward. Each of them has a boy of an age with Robert."

Lyn Corbray laughed. "Two pups from a pair of lapdogs."

"Robert should have an older boy about him too. A promising young squire, say. Someone he could admire and try to emulate." Petyr turned to Lady Waynwood. "You have such a boy at Ironoaks, my lady. Perhaps you might agree to send me Harrold Hardyng."

Anya Waynwood seemed amused. "Lord Petyr, you are as bold a thief as I'd ever care to meet."

"I do not wish to steal the boy," said Petyr, "but he and Lord Robert should be friends."

Bronze Yohn Royce leaned forward. "It is meet and proper that Lord Robert should befriend young Harry, and he shall . . . at Runestone, under my care, as my ward and squire."

"Give us the boy," said Lord Belmore, "and you may depart the Vale unmolested for your proper seat at Harrenhal."

Petyr gave him a look of mild reproach. "Are you suggesting that elsewise I might come to harm, my lord? I cannot think why. My late wife seemed to think *this* was my proper seat."

"Lord Baelish," Lady Waynwood said, "Lysa Tully was Jon Arryn's widow and the mother of his child, and ruled here as his regent. You . . . let us be frank, you are no Arryn, and Lord Robert is no blood of yours. By what right do you presume to rule us?"

"Lysa named me Lord Protector, I do seem to recall."

Young Lord Hunter said, "Lysa Tully was never truly of the Vale, nor had she the right to dispose of us."

"And Lord Robert?" Petyr asked. "Will your lordship also claim that Lady Lysa had no right to dispose of her own son?"

Nestor Royce had been silent all this while, but now he spoke up loudly. "I once hoped to wed Lady Lysa myself. As did Lord Hunter's father and Lady Anya's son. Corbray scarce left her side for half a year. Had she chosen any one of us, no man here would dispute his right to be the Lord Protector. It happens that she chose Lord Littlefinger, and entrusted her son to his care."

"He was Jon Arryn's son as well, cousin," Bronze Yohn said, frowning at the Keeper. "He belongs to the Vale."

Petyr feigned puzzlement. "The Eyrie is as much a part of the Vale as Runestone. Unless someone has moved it?"

"Jape all you like, Littlefinger," Lord Belmore blustered. "The boy shall come with us."

"I am loath to disappoint you, Lord Belmore, but my stepson will be remaining here with me. He is not a robust child, as all of you know well. The journey would tax him sorely. As his stepfather and Lord Protector, I cannot permit it."

Symond Templeton cleared his throat, and said, "Each of us has a thousand men at the foot of this mountain, Littlefinger."

"What a splendid place for them."

"If need be, we can summon many more."

"Are you threatening me with war, ser?" Petyr did not sound the least afraid.

Bronze Yohn said, "We *shall* have Lord Robert."

For a moment it seemed as though they had come to an impasse, until Lyn Corbray turned from the fire. "All this talk makes me ill. Littlefinger will talk you out of your smallclothes if you listen long enough. The only way to settle his sort is with steel." He drew his longsword.

Petyr spread his hands. "I wear no sword, ser."

"Easily remedied." Candlelight rippled along the smoke-grey steel of Corbray's blade, so dark that it put Sansa in mind of Ice, her father's greatsword. "Your apple-eater holds a blade. Tell him to give it to you, or draw that dagger."

She saw Lothor Brune reach for his own sword, but before the blades could meet Bronze Yohn rose in wrath. "*Put up your steel, ser!* Are you a Corbray or a *Frey?* We are guests here."

Lady Waynwood pursed her lips, and said, "This is unseemly."

"Sheathe your sword, Corbray," Young Lord Hunter echoed. "You shame us all with this."

"Come, Lyn," chided Redfort in a softer tone. "This will serve for nought. Put Lady Forlorn to bed."

"My lady has a thirst," Ser Lyn insisted. "Whenever she comes out to dance, she likes a drop of red."

"Your lady must go thirsty." Bronze Yohn put himself squarely in Corbray's path.

"The Lords Declarant." Lyn Corbray snorted. "You should have named yourselves the Six Old Women." He slid the dark sword back into its scabbard and left them, shouldering Brune aside as if he were not there. Alayne listened to his footsteps recede.

Anya Waynwood and Horton Redfort exchanged a look. Hunter drained his wine cup and held it out to be refilled. "Lord Baelish," Ser Symond said, "you must forgive us that display."

"Must I?" Littlefinger's voice had grown cold. "You brought him here, my lords."

Bronze Yohn said, "It was never our intent—"

"*You brought him here.* I would be well within my rights to call my guards and have all of you arrested."

Hunter lurched to his feet so wildly that he almost knocked the flagon out of Alayne's hands. "You gave us safe conduct!"

"Yes. Be grateful that I have more honor than some." Petyr sounded as angry as she had ever heard him. "I have read your *declaration* and heard your demands. Now hear mine. Remove your armies from this mountain. Go home and leave my son in peace. Misrule there has been, I will not deny it, but that was Lysa's work, not mine. Grant me but a year, and with Lord Nestor's help I promise that none of you shall have any cause for grievance."

"So you say," said Belmore. "Yet how shall we trust you?"

"You dare call *me* untrustworthy? It was not me who bared steel at a parley. You write of defending Lord Robert even as you deny him food. That must end. I am no warrior, but I *will* fight you if you do not lift this siege. There are other lords besides you in the Vale, and King's Landing will send men as well. If it is war you want, say so now and the Vale will bleed."

Alayne could see the doubt blooming in the eyes of the Lords Declarant. "A year is not so long a time," Lord Redfort said uncertainly. "Mayhaps . . . if you gave assurances . . ."

"None of us wants war," acknowledged Lady Waynwood. "Autumn wanes, and we must gird ourselves for winter."

Belmore cleared his throat. "At the end of this year . . ."

". . . if I have not set the Vale to rights, I shall willingly step down as Lord Protector," Petyr promised them.

"I call that more than fair," Lord Nestor Royce put in.

"There must be no reprisals," insisted Templeton. "No talk of treason or rebellion. You must swear to that as well."

"Gladly," said Petyr. "It is friends I want, not foes. I shall pardon all of you, in writing if you wish. Even Lyn Corbray. His brother is a good man, there is no need to bring down shame upon a noble House."

Lady Waynwood turned to her fellow Lords Declarant. "My lords, perhaps we might confer?"

"There is no need. It is plain that he has won." Bronze Yohn's grey eyes considered Petyr Baelish. "I like it not, but it would seem you have your year. Best use it well, my lord. Not all of us are fooled." He opened the door so forcefully that he all but wrenched it off its hinges.

Later there was a feast of sorts, though Petyr was forced to make apologies for the humble fare. Robert was trotted out in a doublet of cream and blue, and played the little lord quite graciously. Bronze Yohn was not there to see; he had already departed from the Eyrie to begin the long descent, as had Ser Lyn Corbray before him. The other lords remained with them till morn.

He bewitched them, Alayne thought as she lay abed that night listening to the wind howl outside her windows. She could not have said where the suspicion came from, but once it crossed her mind it would not let her sleep. She tossed and turned, worrying at it like a dog at some old bone. Finally, she rose and dressed herself, leaving Gretchel to her dreams.

Petyr was still awake, scratching out a letter. "Alayne," he said. "My sweet. What brings you here so late?"

"I had to know. What will happen in a year?"

He put down his quill. "Redfort and Waynwood are old. One or both of them may die. Gilwood Hunter will be murdered by his brothers. Most likely by young Harlan, who arranged Lord Eon's death. In for a penny, in for a stag, I always say. Belmore is corrupt and can be bought. Templeton I shall befriend. Bronze Yohn Royce will continue to be hostile, I fear, but so long as he stands alone he is not so much a threat."

"And Ser Lyn Corbray?"

The candlelight was dancing in his eyes. "Ser Lyn will remain my implacable enemy. He will speak of me with scorn and loathing to every man he meets, and lend his sword to every secret plot to bring me down."

That was when her suspicion turned to certainty. "And how shall you reward him for this service?"

Littlefinger laughed aloud. "With gold and boys and promises, of course. Ser Lyn is a man of simple tastes, my sweetling. All he likes is gold and boys and killing."

CERSEI

The king was pouting. "I want to sit on the Iron Throne," he told her. "You always let Joff sit up there."

"Joffrey was twelve."

"But I'm the *king*. The throne *belongs* to me."

"Who told you that?" Cersei took a deep breath, so Dorcas could lace her up more tightly. She was a big girl, much stronger than Senelle, though clumsier as well.

Tommen's face turned red. "No one told me."

"*No one?* Is that what you call your lady wife?" The queen could smell Margaery Tyrell all over this rebellion. "If you lie to me, I will have no choice but to send for Pate and have him beaten till he bleeds." Pate was Tommen's whipping boy, as he had been Joffrey's. "Is that what you want?"

"No," the king muttered sullenly.

"Who told you?"

He shuffled his feet. "Lady Margaery." He knew better than to call her *queen* in his mother's hearing.

"That is better. Tommen, I have grave matters to decide, matters that you are far too young to understand. I do not need a silly little boy fidgeting on the throne behind me and distracting me with childish questions. I suppose Margaery thinks you ought to be at my council meetings too?"

"Yes," he admitted. "She says I have to learn to be king."

"When you are older, you can attend as many councils as you wish," Cersei told him. "I promise you, you will soon grow sick of them. Robert used to doze through the sessions." *When he troubled to attend at all.* "He preferred to hunt and hawk, and leave the tedium to old Lord Arryn. Do you remember him?"

"He died of a bellyache."

"So he did, poor man. As you are so eager to learn, perhaps you should learn the names of all the kings of Westeros *and* the Hands who served them. You may recite them to me on the morrow."

"Yes, Mother," he said meekly.

"That's my good boy." The rule was hers; Cersei did not mean to give it up until Tommen came of age. *I waited, so can he. I waited half my life.* She had played the dutiful daughter, the blushing bride, the pliant wife. She had suffered Robert's drunken groping, Jaime's jealousy, Renly's mockery, Varys with his titters, Stannis endlessly grinding his teeth. She had contended with Jon Arryn, Ned Stark, and her vile, treacherous, murderous dwarf brother, all the while promising herself that one day it would be her turn. *If Margaery Tyrell thinks to cheat me of my hour in the sun, she had bloody well think again.*

Still, it was an ill way to break her fast, and Cersei's day did not soon improve. She spent the rest of the morning with Lord Gyles and his ledger books, listening to him cough about stars and stags and dragons. After him Lord Waters arrived, to report that the first three dromonds were nearing completion and beg for more gold to finish them in the splendor they deserved. The queen was pleased to grant him his request. Moon Boy capered as she took her midday meal with members of the merchant guilds and listened to them complain about sparrows wandering the streets and sleeping in the squares. *I may need to use the gold cloaks to chase these sparrows from the city,* she was thinking, when Pycelle intruded.

The Grand Maester had been especially querulous in council of late. At the last session he had complained bitterly about the men that Aurane Waters had chosen to captain her new dromonds. Waters meant to give the ships to younger men, whilst Pycelle argued for experience, insisting that the commands should go to those captains who had survived the fires of the Blackwater. "Seasoned men of proven loyalty," he called them. Cersei called them old, and sided with Lord Waters. "The only thing these captains proved was that they know how to swim," she'd said. "No mother should outlive her children, and no captain should outlive his ship." Pycelle had taken the rebuke with ill grace.

He seemed less choleric today, and even managed a sort of tremulous smile. "Your Grace, glad tidings," he announced. "Wyman Manderly has done as you commanded, and beheaded Lord Stannis's onion knight."

"We know this for a certainty?"

"The man's head and hands have been mounted above the walls of White Harbor. Lord Wyman avows this, and the Freys confirm. They have seen the head there, with an onion in its mouth. And the hands, one marked by his shortened fingers."

"Very good," said Cersei. "Send a bird to Manderly and inform him that his son will be returned forthwith, now that he has demonstrated his loyalty." White Harbor would soon return to the king's peace, and Roose Bolton and his bastard son were closing in on Moat Cailin from south and north. Once the Moat was theirs, they would join their strength and clear the ironmen out of Torrhen's Square and Deepwood Motte as well. That should win them the allegiance of Ned Stark's remaining bannermen when the time came to march against Lord Stannis.

To the south, meanwhile, Mace Tyrell had raised a city of tents outside Storm's End and had two dozen mangonels flinging stones against the castle's massive walls, thus far to small effect. *Lord Tyrell the warrior,* the queen mused. *His sigil ought to be a fat man sitting on his arse.*

That afternoon the dour Braavosi envoy turned up for his audience. Cersei had put him off for a fortnight and would have gladly put him off another year, but Lord Gyles claimed he could no longer deal with the man ... though the queen was starting to wonder if Gyles was capable of doing *anything* but coughing.

Noho Dimittis, the Braavosi named himself. *An irritating name for an irritating man.* His voice was irritating too. Cersei shifted in her seat as he went on, wondering how long she must endure his hectoring. Behind her loomed the Iron Throne, its barbs and blades throwing twisted shadows across the floor. Only the king or his Hand could sit upon the throne itself. Cersei sat by its foot, in a seat of gilded wood piled with crimson cushions.

When the Braavosi paused for breath, she saw her chance. "This is more properly a matter for our lord treasurer."

That answer did not please the noble Noho, it would seem. "I have spoken with Lord Gyles six times. He coughs at me and makes excuses, Your Grace, but the gold is not forthcoming."

"Speak to him a seventh time," Cersei suggested pleasantly. "The number seven is sacred to our gods."

"It pleases Your Grace to make a jest, I see."

"When I make a jest I smile. Do you see me smiling? Do you hear laughter? I assure you, when I make a jest, men laugh."

"King Robert—"

"—is dead," she said sharply. "The Iron Bank will have its gold when this rebellion has been put down."

He had the insolence to scowl at her. "Your Grace—"

"This audience is at an end." Cersei had suffered quite enough for one day. "Ser Meryn, show the noble Noho Dimittis to the door. Ser Osmund, you may escort me back to my apartments." Her guests would soon arrive, and she had to bathe and change. Supper promised to be a tedious affair as well. It was hard work to rule a kingdom, much less seven of them.

Ser Osmund Kettleblack fell in beside her on the steps, tall and lean in his Kingsguard whites. When Cersei was certain they were quite alone, she slid her arm through his. "How is your little brother faring, pray?"

Ser Osmund looked uneasy. "Ah . . . well enough, only . . ."

"*Only?*" The queen let a hint of anger edge her words. "I must confess, I am running short of patience with dear Osney. It is past time he broke in that little filly. I named him Tommen's sworn shield so he could spend part of every day in Margaery's company. He should have plucked the rose by now. Is the little queen blind to his charms?"

"His charms is fine. He's a Kettleblack, ain't he? Begging your pardon." Ser Osmund ran his fingers through his oily black hair. "It's her that's the trouble."

"And why is that?" The queen had begun to nurse doubts about Ser Osney. Perhaps another man would have been more to Margaery's liking. *Aurane Waters, with that silvery hair, or a big strapping fellow like Ser Tallad.* "Would the maid prefer someone else? Does your brother's face displease her?"

"She likes his face. She touched his scars two days ago, he told me. 'What woman gave you these?' she asked. Osney never said it was a woman, but she knew. Might be someone told her. She's always touching him when they talk, he says. Straightening the clasp on his cloak, brushing back his hair, and like that. One time at the archery butts she had him show her how to hold a longbow, so he had to put his arms around her. Osney tells her bawdy jests, and she laughs and comes back with ones that are even bawdier. No, she wants him, that's plain, but . . ."

"But?" Cersei prompted.

"They are never alone. The king's with them most all the time, and when he's not, there's someone else. Two of her ladies share her bed, different ones every night. Two others bring her breakfast and help her dress. She prays with her septa, reads with her cousin Elinor, sings with her cousin Alla, sews with her cousin Megga. When she's not off hawking with Janna Fossoway and Merry Crane, she's playing come-into-my-castle with that little Bulwer girl. She never goes riding but she takes a tail, four or five companions and a dozen guards at least. And there's always men about her, even in the Maidenvault."

"Men." That was something. That had possibilities. "What men are these, pray tell?"

Ser Osmund shrugged. "Singers. She's a fool for singers and jugglers and such. Knights, come round to moon over her cousins. Ser Tallad's the worst, Osney says. That big oaf don't seem to know if it's Elinor or Alla he wants, but he knows he wants her awful bad. The Redwyne twins come calling too. Slobber brings flowers and fruit, and Horror's taken up the lute. To hear Osney tell it, you could make a sweeter sound strangling a cat. The Summer Islander's always underfoot as well."

"Jalabhar Xho?" Cersei gave a derisive snort. "Begging her for gold and swords to win his homeland back, most like." Beneath his jewels and feathers, Xho was little more than a wellborn beggar. Robert could have put an end to his importuning for good with one firm "No," but the notion of conquering the Summer Isles had appealed to her drunken lout of a husband. No doubt he dreamt of brown-skinned wenches naked beneath feathered cloaks, with nipples black as coal. So instead of "No," Robert always told Xho, "Next year," though somehow next year never came.

"I couldn't say if he was begging, Your Grace," Ser Osmund answered. "Osney says he's teaching them the Summer Tongue. Not Osney, the quee—the filly and her cousins."

"A horse that speaks the Summer Tongue would make a great sensation," the queen said dryly. "Tell your brother to keep his spurs well honed. I shall find some way for him to mount his filly soon, you may rely on that."

"I'll tell him, Your Grace. He's eager for that ride, don't think he ain't. She's a pretty little thing, that filly."

It is me he's eager for, fool, the queen thought. *All he wants of Margaery is the lordship between her legs.* As fond as she was of Osmund, at times he seemed as slow as Robert. *I hope his sword is quicker than his wits. The day may come that Tommen has some need of it.*

They were crossing beneath the shadow of the broken Tower of the Hand when the sound of cheers swept over them. Across the yard, some squire had made a pass at the quintain and sent the crossarm spinning. The cheers were being led by Margaery Tyrell and her hens. *A lot of uproar for very little. You would think the boy had won a tourney.* Then she was startled to see that it was Tommen on the courser, clad all in gilded plate.

The queen had little choice but to don a smile and go to see her son. She reached him as the Knight of Flowers was helping him from his horse. The boy was breathless with excitement. "Did you see?" he was asking everyone. "I did it just the way Ser Loras said. Did you see, Ser Osney?"

"I did," said Osney Kettleblack. "A pretty sight."

"You have a better seat than me, sire," put in Ser Dermot.

"I broke the lance too. Ser Loras, did you hear it?"

"As loud as a crack of thunder." A rose of jade and gold clasped Ser Loras's white cloak at the shoulder, and the wind was riffling artfully through his brown locks. "You rode a splendid course, but once is not enough. You must do it again upon the morrow. You must ride every day, until every blow lands true and straight, and your lance is as much a part of you as your arm."

"I want to."

"You were glorious." Margaery went to one knee, kissed the king upon his cheek, and put an arm around him. "Brother, take care," she warned Loras. "My gallant husband will be unhorsing you in a few more years, I think." Her three cousins all agreed, and the wretched little Bulwer girl began to hop about, chanting, "Tommen will be the *champion*, the *champion*, the *champion*."

"When he is a man grown," said Cersei.

Their smiles withered like roses kissed by frost. The pock-faced old septa was the first to bend her knee. The rest followed, save for the little queen and her brother.

Tommen did not seem to notice the sudden chill in the air. "Mother, did you see me?" he burbled happily. "I broke my lance on the shield, and the bag never hit me!"

"I was watching from across the yard. You did very well, Tommen. I would expect no less of you. Jousting is in your blood. One day you shall rule the lists, as your father did."

"No man will stand before him." Margaery Tyrell gave the queen a coy smile. "But I never knew that King Robert was so accomplished at the joust. Pray tell us, Your Grace, what tourneys did he win? What great knights did he unseat? I know the king should like to hear about his father's victories."

A flush crept up Cersei's neck. The girl had caught her out. Robert Baratheon had been an indifferent jouster, in truth. During tourneys he had much preferred the mêlée, where he could beat men bloody with blunted axe or hammer. It had been Jaime she had been thinking of when she spoke. *It is not like me to forget myself.* "Robert won the tourney of the Trident," she had to say. "He overthrew Prince Rhaegar and named me his queen of love and beauty. I am surprised you do not know that story, good-daughter." She gave Margaery no time to frame a reply. "Ser Osmund, help my son from his armor, if you would be so good. Ser Loras, walk with me. I need a word with you."

The Knight of Flowers had no recourse but to follow at her heels like the puppy he was. Cersei waited until they were on the serpentine steps before she said, "Whose notion was that, pray?"

"My sister's," he admitted. "Ser Tallad, Ser Dermot, and Ser Portifer were riding at the quintain, and the queen suggested that His Grace might like to have a turn."

He calls her that to irk me. "And your part?"

"I helped His Grace to don his armor and showed him how to couch his lance," he answered.

"That horse was much too large for him. What if he had fallen off? What if the sandbag had smashed his head in?"

"Bruises and bloody lips are all part of being a knight."

"I begin to understand why your brother is a cripple." That wiped the smile off his pretty face, she was pleased to see. "Perhaps my brother failed to explain your duties to you, ser. You are here to protect my son from his enemies. Training him for knighthood is the province of the master-at-arms."

"The Red Keep has had no master-at-arms since Aron Santagar was slain," Ser Loras said, with a hint of reproach in his voice. "His Grace is almost nine, and eager to learn. At his age he should be a squire. Someone has to teach him."

Someone will, but it will not be you. "Pray, who did you squire for, ser?" she asked sweetly. "Lord Renly, was it not?"

"I had that honor."

"Yes, I thought as much." Cersei had seen how tight the bonds grew between squires and the knights they served. She did not want Tommen growing close to Loras Tyrell. The Knight of Flowers was no sort of man for any boy to emulate. "I have been remiss. With a realm to rule, a war to fight, and a father to mourn, somehow I overlooked the crucial matter of naming a new master-at-arms. I shall rectify that error at once."

Ser Loras pushed back a brown curl that had fallen across his forehead. "Your Grace will not find any man half so skilled with sword and lance as I."

Humble, aren't we? "Tommen is your king, not your squire. You are to fight for him and die for him, if need be. No more."

She left him on the drawbridge that spanned the dry moat with its bed of iron spikes and entered Maegor's Holdfast alone. *Where am I to find a master-at-arms?* she wondered as she climbed to her apartments. Having refused Ser Loras, she dare not turn to any of the Kingsguard knights; that would be salt in the wound, certain to anger Highgarden. *Ser Tallad? Ser Dermot? There must be someone.* Tommen was growing fond of his new sworn shield, but Osney was proving himself less capable than she had hoped in the matter of Maid Margaery, and she had a different office in mind for his brother Osfryd. It was rather a pity that the Hound had gone rabid. Tommen had always been frightened of Sandor Clegane's harsh voice and burned face, and Clegane's scorn would have been the perfect antidote to Loras Tyrell's simpering chivalry.

Aron Santagar was Dornish, Cersei recalled. *I could send to Dorne.* Centuries of blood and war lay between Sunspear and Highgarden. *Yes, a Dornishman might suit my needs admirably. There must be some good swords in Dorne.*

When she entered her solar, Cersei found Lord Qyburn reading in a window seat. "If it please Your Grace, I have reports."

"More plots and treasons?" Cersei asked. "I have had a long and tiring day. Tell me quickly."

He smiled sympathetically. "As you wish. There is talk that the Archon of Tyrosh has offered terms to Lys, to end their present trade war. It had been rumored that Myr was about to enter the war on the Tyroshi side, but without the Golden Company the Myrish did not believe they . . ."

"What the Myrish believe does not concern me." The Free Cities were always fighting one another. Their endless betrayals and alliances meant little and less to Westeros. "Do you have any news of more import?"

"The slave revolt in Astapor has spread to Meereen, it would seem. Sailors off a dozen ships speak of dragons . . ."

"Harpies. It is harpies in Meereen." She remembered that from somewhere. Meereen was at the far end of the world, out east beyond Valyria. "Let the slaves revolt. Why should I care? We keep no slaves in Westeros. Is that all you have for me?"

"There is some news from Dorne that Your Grace may find of more interest. Prince Doran has imprisoned Ser Daemon Sand, a bastard who once squired for the Red Viper."

"I recall him." Ser Daemon had been amongst the Dornish knights who had accompanied Prince Oberyn to King's Landing. "What did he do?"

"He demanded that Prince Oberyn's daughters be set free."

"More fool him."

"Also," Lord Qyburn said, "the daughter of the Knight of Spottswood was betrothed quite unexpectedly to Lord Estermont, our friends in Dorne inform us. She was sent to Greenstone that very night, and it is said she and Estermont have already wed."

"A bastard in the belly would explain that." Cersei toyed with a lock of her hair. "How old is the blushing bride?"

"Three-and-twenty, Your Grace. Whereas Lord Estermont—"

"—must be seventy. I am aware of that." The Estermonts were her good-kin through Robert, whose father had taken one of them to wife in what must have been a fit of lust or madness. By the time Cersei wed the king, Robert's lady mother was long dead, though both of her brothers had turned up for the wedding and stayed for half a year. Robert had later insisted on returning the courtesy with a visit to Estermont, a mountainous little island off Cape Wrath. The dank and dismal fortnight Cersei spent at Greenstone, the seat of House Estermont, was the longest of her young life. Jaime dubbed the castle *"Greenshit"* at first sight, and soon had Cersei doing it too. Elsewise she passed her days watching her royal husband hawk, hunt, and drink with his uncles, and bludgeon various male cousins sense-less in Greenshit's yard.

There had been a female cousin too, a chunky little widow with breasts as big as melons whose husband and father had both died at Storm's End during the siege. "Her father was good to me," Robert told her, "and she and I would play together when the two of us were small." It did not take him long to start playing with her again. As soon as Cersei closed her eyes, the king would steal off to console the poor lonely creature. One night she had Jaime follow him, to confirm her suspicions. When her brother returned he asked her if she wanted Robert dead. "No," she had replied, "I want him horned." She liked to think that was the night when Joffrey was conceived.

"Eldon Estermont has taken a wife fifty years his junior," she said to Qyburn. "Why should that concern me?"

He shrugged. "I do not say it should . . . but Daemon Sand and this Santagar girl were both close to Prince Doran's own daughter, Arianne, or so the Dornishmen would have us believe. Perhaps it means little or less, but I thought Your Grace should know."

"Now I do." She was losing patience. "Do you have more?"

"One more thing. A trifling matter." He gave her an apologetic smile and told her of a puppet show that had recently become popular amongst the city's smallfolk; a puppet show wherein the kingdom of the beasts was ruled by a pride of haughty lions. "The puppet lions grow greedy and arrogant as this treasonous tale proceeds, until they begin to devour their own subjects. When the noble stag makes objection, the lions devour him as well, and roar that it is their right as the mightiest of beasts."

"And is that the end of it?" Cersei asked, amused. Looked at in the right light, it could be seen as a salutary lesson.

"No, Your Grace. At the end a dragon hatches from an egg and devours all of the lions."

The ending took the puppet show from simple insolence to treason. "Witless fools. Only cretins would hazard their heads upon a wooden dragon." She considered a moment. "Send some of your whisperers to these shows and make note of who attends. If any of them should be men of note, I would know their names."

"What will be done with them, if I may be so bold?"

"Any men of substance shall be fined. Half their worth should be sufficient to teach them a sharp lesson and refill our coffers, without quite ruining them. Those too poor to pay can lose an eye, for watching treason. For the puppeteers, the axe."

"There are four. Perhaps Your Grace might allow me two of them for mine own purposes. A woman would be especially . . ."

"I gave you Senelle," the queen said sharply.

"Alas. The poor girl is quite . . . exhausted."

Cersei did not like to think about that. The girl had come with her unsuspecting, thinking she was along to serve and pour. Even when Qyburn clapped the chain around her wrist, she had not seemed to understand. The memory still made the queen queasy. *The cells were bitter cold. Even the torches shivered. And that foul thing screaming in the darkness . . .* "Yes, you may take a woman. Two, if it please you. But first I will have names."

"As you command." Qyburn withdrew.

Outside, the sun was setting. Dorcas had prepared a bath for her. The queen was soaking pleasantly in the warm water and contemplating what she would say to her supper guests when Jaime came bursting through the door and ordered Jocelyn and Dorcas from the room. Her brother looked rather less than immaculate and had a smell of horse about him. He had Tommen with him too. "Sweet sister," he said, "the king requires a word."

Cersei's golden tresses floated in the bathwater. The room was steamy. A drop of sweat trickled down her cheek. "Tommen?" she said, in a dangerously soft voice. "What is it now?"

The boy knew that tone. He shrank back.

"His Grace wants his white courser on the morrow," Jaime said. "For his jousting lesson."

She sat up in the tub. "There will be no jousting."

"Yes, there will." Tommen puffed out his lower lip. "I have to ride *every day.*"

"And you shall," the queen declared, "once we have a proper master-at-arms to supervise your training."

"I don't *want* a proper master-at-arms. I want Ser Loras."

"You make too much of that boy. Your little wife has filled your head with foolish notions of his prowess, I know, but Osmund Kettleblack is thrice the knight that Loras is."

Jaime laughed. "Not the Osmund Kettleblack I know."

She could have throttled him. *Perhaps I need to command Ser Loras to allow Ser Osmund to unhorse him.* That might chase the stars from Tommen's eyes. *Salt a slug and shame a hero, and they shrink right up.* "I am sending for a Dornishman to train you," she said. "The Dornish are the finest jousters in the realm."

"They are not," said Tommen. "Anyway, I don't want any stupid Dornishman, I want *Ser Loras.* I *command* it."

Jaime laughed. *He is no help at all. Does he think this is amusing?* The queen slapped the water angrily. "Must I send for Pate? You do *not* command me. I am your mother."

"Yes, but I'm the *king.* Margaery says that everyone has to do what the king says. I want my white courser saddled on the morrow so Ser Loras can teach me how to joust. I want a kitten too, and I don't want to eat beets." He crossed his arms.

Jaime was still laughing. The queen ignored him. "Tommen, come here." When he hung back, she sighed. "Are you afraid? A king should not show fear." The boy approached the tub, his eyes downcast. She reached out and stroked his golden curls. "King or no, you are a little boy. Until you come of age, the rule is mine. You *will* learn to joust, I promise you. But not from Loras. The knights of the Kingsguard have more important duties than playing with a child. Ask the Lord Commander. Isn't that so, ser?"

"Very important duties." Jaime smiled thinly. "Riding round the city walls, for an instance."

Tommen looked close to tears. "Can I still have a kitten?"

"Perhaps," the queen allowed. "So long as I hear no more nonsense about jousting. Can you promise me that?"

He shuffled his feet. "Yes."

"Good. Now run along. My guests will be here shortly."

Tommen ran along, but before he left he turned back to say, "When I'm king in my own right, I'm going to *outlaw* beets."

Her brother shoved the door shut with his stump. "Your Grace," he said, when he and Cersei were alone, "I was wondering. Are you drunk, or merely stupid?"

She slapped the water once again, sending up another splash to wash across his feet. "Guard your tongue, or—"

"—or what? Will you send me to inspect the city walls again?" He sat and crossed his legs. "Your bloody walls are fine. I've crawled over every inch of them and had a look at all seven of the gates. The hinges on the Iron Gate are rusted, and the King's Gate and Mud Gate need to be replaced after the pounding Stannis gave them with his rams. The walls are as strong as they have ever been . . . but perchance Your Grace has forgotten that our friends of Highgarden are *inside* the walls?"

"I forget nothing," she told him, thinking of a certain gold coin, with a hand on one face and the head of a forgotten king on the other. *How did some miserable wretch of a gaoler come to have such a coin hidden beneath his chamber pot? How does a man like Rugen come to have old gold from Highgarden?*

"This is the first I have heard of a new master-at-arms. You'll need to look long and hard to find a better jouster than Loras Tyrell. Ser Loras is—"

"I know what he is. I won't have him near my son. You had best remind him of his duties." Her bath was growing cool.

"He knows his duties, and there's no better lance—"

"*You* were better, before you lost your hand. Ser Barristan, when he was young. Arthur Dayne was better, and Prince Rhaegar was a match for even him. Do not prate at me about how fierce the Flower is. He's just a boy." She was tired of Jaime balking her. No one had ever balked her lord father. When Tywin Lannister spoke, men obeyed. When Cersei spoke, they felt free to counsel her, to contradict her, even *refuse* her. *It is all because I am a woman. Because I cannot fight them with a sword. They gave Robert more respect than they give me, and Robert was a witless sot.* She would not suffer it, especially not from Jaime. *I need to rid myself of him, and soon.* Once upon a time she had dreamt that the two of them might rule the Seven Kingdoms side by side, but Jaime had become more of a hindrance than a help.

Cersei rose from the bath. Water ran down her legs and trickled from her hair. "When I want your counsel I will ask for it. Leave me, ser. I must needs dress."

"Your supper guests, I know. What plot is this, now? There are so many I lose track." His glance fell to the water beading in the golden hair between her legs.

He still wants me. "Pining for what you've lost, brother?"

Jaime raised his eyes. "I love you too, sweet sister. But you're a fool. A beautiful golden fool."

The words stung. *You called me kinder words at Greenstone, the night you planted Joff inside me,* Cersei thought. "Get out." She turned her back to him and listened to him leave, fumbling at the door with his stump.

Whilst Jocelyn was making certain that all was in readiness for the supper, Dorcas helped the queen into her new gown. It had stripes of shiny green satin alternating with stripes of plush black velvet, and intricate black Myrish lace above the bodice. Myrish lace was costly, but it was necessary for a queen to look her best at all times, and her wretched washerwomen had shrunk several of her old gowns so they no longer fit. She would have whipped them for their carelessness, but Taena had urged her to be merciful. "The smallfolk will love you more if you are kind," she had said, so Cersei had ordered the value of the gowns deducted from the women's wages, a much more elegant solution.

Dorcas put a silver looking glass into her hand. *Very good,* the queen thought, smiling at her reflection. It was pleasant to be out of mourning. Black made her look too pale. *A pity I am not supping with Lady Merryweather,* the queen reflected. It had been a long day, and Taena's wit always cheered her. Cersei had not had a friend she so enjoyed since Melara Hetherspoon, and Melara had turned out to be a greedy little schemer with ideas above her station. *I should not think ill of her. She's dead and drowned, and she taught me never to trust anyone but Jaime.*

By the time she joined them in the solar, her guests had made a good start on the hippocras. *Lady Falyse not only looks like a fish, she drinks like one,* she reflected, when she made note of the half-empty flagon. "Sweet Falyse," she exclaimed, kissing the woman's cheek, "and brave Ser Balman. I was so distraught when I heard about your dear, dear mother. How fares our Lady Tanda?"

Lady Falyse looked as if she were about to cry. "Your Grace is good to ask. Mother's hip was shattered by the fall, Maester Frenken says. He did what he could. Now we pray, but . . ."

Pray all you like, she will still be dead before the moon turns. Women as old as Tanda Stokeworth did not survive a broken hip. "I shall add my prayers to your own," said Cersei. "Lord Qyburn tells me that Tanda was thrown from her horse."

"Her saddle girth burst whilst she was riding," said Ser Balman Byrch. "The stableboy should have seen the strap was worn. He has been chastised."

"Severely, I hope." The queen seated herself and indicated that her guests should sit as well. "Will you have another cup of hippocras, Falyse? You were always fond of it, I seem to recall."

"It is so good of you to remember, Your Grace."

How could I have forgotten? Cersei thought. *Jaime said it was a wonder you did not piss the stuff.* "How was your journey?"

"Uncomfortable," complained Falyse. "It rained most of the day. We thought to spend the night at Rosby, but that young ward of Lord Gyles refused us hospitality." She sniffed. "Mark my word, when Gyles dies that ill-born wretch will make off with his gold. He may even try and claim the lands and lordship, though by rights Rosby should come to us when Gyles passes. My lady mother was aunt to his second wife, third cousin to Gyles himself."

Is your sigil a lamb, my lady, or some sort of grasping monkey? Cersei thought. "Lord Gyles has been threatening to die for as long as I have known him, but he is still with us, and will be for many years, I do hope." She smiled pleasantly. "No doubt he will cough the whole lot of us into our graves."

"Like as not," Ser Balman agreed. "Rosby's ward was not the only one to vex us, Your Grace. We encountered ruffians on the road as well. Filthy, unkempt creatures, with leather shields and axes. Some had stars sewn on their jerkins, sacred stars of seven points, but they had an evil look about them all the same."

"They were lice-ridden, I am certain," added Falyse.

"They call themselves *sparrows*," said Cersei. "A plague upon the land. Our new High Septon will need to deal with them, once he is crowned. If not, I shall deal with them myself."

"Has His High Holiness been chosen yet?" asked Falyse.

"No," the queen had to confess. "Septon Ollidor was on the verge of being chosen, until some of these sparrows followed him to a brothel and dragged him naked out into the street. Luceon seems the likely choice now, though our friends on the other hill say that he is still a few votes short of the required number."

"May the Crone guide the deliberations with her golden lamp of wisdom," said Lady Falyse, most piously.

Ser Balman shifted in his seat. "Your Grace, an awkward matter, but . . . lest bad feeling fester between us, you should know that neither my good wife nor her mother had any hand in the naming of this bastard child. Lollys is a simple creature, and her husband is given to black humors. I told him to choose a more fitting name for the boy. He laughed."

The queen sipped her wine and studied him. Ser Balman had been a noted jouster once, and one of the handsomest knights in the Seven Kingdoms. He could still boast a handsome mustache; elsewise, he had not aged well. His wavy blond hair had retreated, whilst his belly advanced inexorably against his doublet. *As a catspaw he leaves much to be desired,* she reflected. *Still, he should serve.* "Tyrion was a king's name before the dragons came. The Imp has despoiled it, but perhaps this child can restore the name to honor." *If the bastard lives so long.* "I know you are not to blame. Lady Tanda is the sister that I never had, and you . . ." Her voice broke. "Forgive me. I live in fear."

Falyse opened and closed her mouth, which made her look like some especially stupid fish. "In . . . in fear, Your Grace?"

"I have not slept a whole night through since Joffrey died." Cersei filled the goblets with hippocras. "My friends . . . you *are* my friends, I hope? And King Tommen's?"

"That sweet lad," Ser Balman declared. "Your Grace, the very words of House Stokeworth are *Proud to Be Faithful.*"

"Would that there were more like you, good ser. I tell you truly, I have grave doubts about Ser Bronn of the Blackwater."

Husband and wife exchanged a look. "The man is insolent, Your Grace," Falyse said. "Uncouth and foul-mouthed."

"He is no true knight," Ser Balman said.

"No." Cersei smiled, all for him. "And you are a man who would know true knighthood. I remember watching you joust in . . . which tourney was it where you fought so brilliantly, ser?"

He smiled modestly. "That affair at Duskendale six years ago? No, you were not there, else you would surely have been crowned the queen of love and beauty. Was it the tourney at Lannisport after Greyjoy's Rebellion? I unhorsed many a good knight in that one . . ."

"That was the one." Her face grew somber. "The Imp vanished the night my father died, leaving two honest gaolers behind in pools of blood. Some claim he fled across the narrow sea, but I wonder. The dwarf is cunning. Perhaps he still lurks near, planning more murders. Perhaps some friend is hiding him."

"Bronn?" Ser Balman stroked his bushy mustache.

"He was ever the Imp's creature. Only the Stranger knows how many men he's sent to hell at Tyrion's behest."

"Your Grace, I think I should have noticed a dwarf skulking about our lands," said Ser Balman.

"My brother is small. He was made for skulking." Cersei let her hand shake. "A child's name is a small thing . . . but insolence unpunished breeds rebellion. And this man Bronn has been gathering sellswords to him, Qyburn has told me."

"He has taken four knights into his household," said Falyse.

Ser Balman snorted. "My good wife flatters them, to call them knights. They're upjumped sellswords, with not a thimble of chivalry to be found amongst the four of them."

"As I feared. Bronn is gathering swords for the dwarf. May the Seven save my little son. The Imp will kill him as he killed his brother." She sobbed. "My friends, I put my honor in your hands . . . but what is a queen's honor against a mother's fears?"

"Say on, Your Grace," Ser Balman assured her. "Your words shall ne'er leave this room."

Cersei reached across the table and gave his hand a squeeze. "I . . . I would sleep more easily of a night if I were to hear that Ser Bronn had suffered a . . . a mishap . . . whilst hunting, perhaps."

Ser Balman considered a moment. "A *mortal* mishap?"

No, I desire you to break his little toe. She had to bite her lip. *My enemies are everywhere and my friends are fools.* "I beg you, ser," she whispered, "do not make me say it . . ."

"I understand." Ser Balman raised a finger.

A turnip would have grasped it quicker. "You are a true knight indeed, ser. The answer to a frightened mother's prayers." Cersei kissed him. "Do it quickly, if you would. Bronn has only a few men about him now, but if we do not act, he will surely gather more." She kissed Falyse. "I shall never forget this, my friends. My *true* friends of Stokeworth. *Proud to Be Faithful.* You have my word, we shall find Lollys a better husband when this is done." *A Kettleblack, perhaps.* "We Lannisters pay our debts."

The rest was hippocras and buttered beets, hot-baked bread, herb-crusted pike, and ribs of wild boar. Cersei had become very fond of boar since Robert's death. She did not even mind the company, though Falyse simpered and Balman preened from soup to sweet. It was past midnight before she could rid herself of them. Ser Balman proved a great one for suggesting yet another flagon, and the queen did not think it prudent to refuse. *I could have hired a Faceless Man to kill Bronn for half of what I've spent on hippocras,* she reflected when they were gone at last.

At that hour, her son was fast asleep, but Cersei looked in upon him before seeking her own bed. She was surprised to find three black kittens cuddled up beside him. "Where did those come from?" she asked Ser Meryn Trant, outside the royal bedchamber.

"The little queen gave them to him. She only meant to give him one, but he couldn't decide which one he liked the best."

Better than cutting them out of their mother with a dagger, I suppose. Margaery's clumsy attempts at seduction were so obvious as to be laughable. *Tommen is too young for kisses, so she gives him kittens.* Cersei rather wished they were not black, though. Black cats brought ill luck, as Rhaegar's little girl had discovered in this very castle. *She would have been my daughter, if the Mad King had not played his cruel jape on Father.* It had to have been the madness that led Aerys to refuse Lord Tywin's daughter and take his son instead, whilst marrying his own son to a feeble Dornish princess with black eyes and a flat chest.

The memory of the rejection still rankled, even after all these years. Many a night she had watched Prince Rhaegar in the hall, playing his silver-stringed harp with those long, elegant fingers of his. Had any man ever been so beautiful? *He was more than a man, though. His blood was the blood of old Valyria, the blood of dragons and gods.* When she was just a little girl, her father had promised her that she would marry Rhaegar. She could not have been more than six or seven. "Never speak of it, child," he had told her, smiling his secret smile that only Cersei ever saw. "Not until His Grace agrees to the betrothal. It must remain our secret for now." And so it had, though once she had drawn a picture of herself flying behind Rhaegar on a dragon, her arms wrapped tight about his chest. When Jaime had discovered it she told him it was Queen Alysanne and King Jaehaerys.

She was ten when she finally saw her prince in the flesh, at the tourney her lord father had thrown to welcome King Aerys to the west. Viewing stands had been raised beneath the walls of Lannisport, and the cheers of the smallfolk had echoed off Casterly Rock like rolling thunder. *They cheered Father twice as loudly as they cheered the king,* the queen recalled, *but only half as loudly as they cheered Prince Rhaegar.*

Seventeen and new to knighthood, Rhaegar Targaryen had worn black plate over golden ringmail when he cantered onto the lists. Long streamers of red and gold and orange silk had floated behind his helm, like flames. Two of her uncles fell before his lance, along with a dozen of her father's finest jousters, the flower of the west. By night the prince played his silver harp and made her weep. When she had been presented to him, Cersei had almost drowned in the depths of his sad purple eyes. *He has been wounded,* she recalled thinking, *but I will mend his hurt when we are wed.* Next to Rhaegar, even her beautiful Jaime had seemed no more than a callow boy. *The prince is going to be my husband,* she had thought, giddy with excitement, *and when the old king dies I'll be the queen.* Her aunt had confided that truth to her before the tourney. "You must be especially beautiful," Lady Genna told her, fussing with her dress, "for at the final feast it shall be announced that you and Prince Rhaegar are betrothed."

Cersei had been so happy that day. Elsewise she would never have dared visit the tent of Maggy the Frog. She had only done it to show Jeyne and Melara that the lioness fears nothing. *I was going to be a queen. Why should a queen be afraid of some hideous old woman?* The memory of that foretelling still made her flesh crawl a lifetime later. *Jeyne ran shrieking from the tent in fear,* the queen remembered, *but Melara stayed and so did I. We let her taste our blood, and laughed at her stupid prophecies. None of them made the least bit of sense.* She was going to be Prince Rhaegar's wife, no matter what the woman said. Her *father* had promised it, and Tywin Lannister's word was gold.

Her laughter died at tourney's end. There had been no final feast, no toasts to celebrate her betrothal to Prince Rhaegar. Only cold silences and chilly looks between the king and her father. Later, when Aerys and his son and all his gallant knights had departed for King's Landing, the girl had gone to her aunt in tears, not understanding. "Your father proposed the match," Lady Genna told her, "but Aerys refused to hear of it. 'You are my most able servant, Tywin,' the king said, 'but a man does not marry his heir to his servant's daughter.' Dry those tears, little one. Have you ever seen a lion weep? Your father will find another man for you, a better man than Rhaegar."

Her aunt had lied, though, and her father had failed her, just as Jaime was failing her now. *Father found no better man. Instead he gave me Robert, and Maggy's curse bloomed like some poisonous flower.* If she had only married Rhaegar as the gods intended, he would never have looked twice at the wolf girl. *Rhaegar would be our king today and I would be his queen, the mother of his sons.*

She had never forgiven Robert for killing him.

But then, lions were not good at forgiving. As Ser Bronn of the Blackwater would shortly learn.

BRIENNE

It was Hyle Hunt who insisted that they take the heads. "Tarly will want them for the walls," he said.

"We have no tar," Brienne pointed out. "The flesh will rot. Leave them." She did not want to travel through the green gloom of the piney woods with the heads of the men she'd killed.

Hunt would not listen. He hacked through the dead men's necks himself, tied the three heads together by the hair, and slung them from his saddle. Brienne had no choice but to try and pretend they were not there, but sometimes, especially at night, she could feel their dead eyes on her back, and once she dreamed she heard them whispering to one another.

It was cold and wet on Crackclaw Point as they retraced their steps. Some days it rained and some days it threatened rain. They were never warm. Even when they made camp, it was hard to find enough dry wood for a fire.

By the time they reached the gates of Maidenpool, a host of flies attended them, a crow had eaten Shagwell's eyes, and Pyg and Timeon were crawling with maggots. Brienne and Podrick had long since taken to riding a hundred yards ahead, to keep the smell of rot well behind them. Ser Hyle claimed to have lost all sense of smell by then. "Bury them," she told him every time they made camp for a night, but Hunt was nothing if not stubborn. *He will most like tell Lord Randyll that he slew all three of them.*

To his honor, though, the knight did nothing of the sort.

"The stammering squire threw a rock," he said, when he and Brienne were ushered into Tarly's presence in the yard of Mooton's castle. The heads had been presented to a serjeant of the guard, who was told to have them cleaned and tarred and mounted above the gate. "The swordswench did the rest."

"All three?" Lord Randyll was incredulous.

"The way she fought, she could have killed three more."

"And did you find the Stark girl?" Tarly demanded of her.

"No, my lord."

"Instead you slew some rats. Did you enjoy it?"

"No, my lord."

"A pity. Well, you've had your taste of blood. Proved whatever it is you meant to prove. It's time you took off that mail and donned proper clothes again. There are ships in port. One's bound to stop at Tarth. I'll have you on it."

"Thank you, my lord, but no."

Lord Tarly's face suggested he would have liked nothing better than to stick her own head on a spike and mount it above the gates of Maidenpool with Timeon, Pyg, and Shagwell. "You mean to continue with this folly?"

"I mean to find the Lady Sansa."

"If it please my lord," Ser Hyle said, "I watched her fight the Mummers. She is stronger than most men, and quick—"

"The *sword* is quick," Tarly snapped. "That is the nature of Valyrian steel. Stronger than most men? Aye. She's a freak of nature, far be it from me to deny it."

His sort will never love me, Brienne thought, *no matter what I do.* "My lord, it may be that Sandor Clegane has some knowledge of the girl. If I could find him . . ."

"Clegane's turned outlaw. He rides with Beric Dondarrion now, it would seem. Or not, the tales vary. Show me where they're hiding, I will gladly slit their bellies open, pull their entrails out, and burn them. We've hanged dozens of outlaws, but the leaders still elude us. Clegane, Dondarrion, the red priest, and now this woman Stoneheart . . . how do *you* propose to find them, when I cannot?"

"My lord, I . . ." She had no good answer for him. "All I can do is try."

"Try, then. You have your letter, you do not need my leave, but I'll give it nonetheless. If you're fortunate, all you'll get for your trouble are saddle sores. If not, perhaps Clegane will let you live after he and his pack are done raping you. You can crawl back to Tarth with some dog's bastard in your belly."

Brienne ignored that. "If it please my lord, how many men ride with the Hound?"

"Six or sixty or six hundred. It would seem to depend on whom we ask." Randyll Tarly had plainly had enough of the conversation. He started to turn away.

"If my squire and I might beg your hospitality until—"

"Beg all you want. I will not suffer you beneath my roof."

Ser Hyle Hunt stepped forward. "If it please my lord, I had understood that it was still Lord Mooton's roof."

Tarly gave the knight a venomous look. "Mooton has the courage of a worm. You will not speak to me of Mooton. As for you, my lady, it is said that your father is a good man. If so, I pity him. Some men are blessed with sons, some with daughters. No man deserves to be cursed with such as you. Live or die, Lady Brienne, do not return to Maidenpool whilst I rule here."

Words are wind, Brienne told herself. *They cannot hurt you. Let them wash over you.* "As you command, my lord," she tried to say, but Tarly had gone before she got it out. She walked from the yard like one asleep, not knowing where she was going.

Ser Hyle fell in beside her. "There are inns."

She shook her head. She did not want words with Hyle Hunt.

"Do you recall the Stinking Goose?"

Her cloak still smelled of it. "Why?"

"Meet me there on the morrow, at midday. My cousin Alyn was one of those sent out to find the Hound. I'll speak with him."

"Why would you do that?"

"Why not? If you succeed where Alyn failed, I shall be able to taunt him with that for years."

There were still inns in Maidenpool; Ser Hyle had not been wrong. Some had burned during one sack or the other, however, and had yet to be rebuilt, and those that remained were full to bursting with men from Lord Tarly's host. She and Podrick visited all of them that afternoon, but there were no beds to be had anywhere.

"Ser? My lady?" Podrick said as the sun was going down. "There are ships. Ships have beds. Hammocks. Or bunks."

Lord Randyll's men still prowled the docks, as thick as the flies had been on the heads of the three Bloody Mummers, but their serjeant knew Brienne by sight and let her pass. The local fisherfolk were tying up for the night and crying the day's catch, but her interest was in the larger ships that plied the stormy waters of the narrow sea. Half a dozen were in port, though one, a galleas called the *Titan's Daughter,* was casting off her lines to ride out on the evening tide. She and Podrick Payne made the rounds of the ships that remained. The master of the *Gulltown Girl* took Brienne for a whore and told them that his ship was not a bawdy house, and a harpooner on the Ibbenese whaler offered to buy her boy, but they had better fortune elsewhere. She purchased Podrick an orange on the *Seastrider,* a cog just in from Oldtown by way of Tyrosh, Pentos, and Duskendale. "Gulltown next," her captain told her, "thence around the Fingers to Sisterton and White Harbor, if the storms allow. She's a clean ship, *'Strider,* not so many rats as most, and we'll have fresh eggs and new-churned butter aboard. Is m'lady seeking passage north?"

"No." *Not yet.* She was tempted, but . . .

As they were making their way to the next pier, Podrick shuffled his feet, and said, "Ser? My lady? What if my lady did go home? My other lady, I mean. Ser. Lady Sansa."

"They burned her home."

"Still. That's where her *gods* are. And gods can't die."

Gods cannot die, but girls can. "Timeon was a cruel man and a murderer, but I do not think he lied about the Hound. We cannot go north until we know for certain. There will be other ships."

At the east end of the harbor they finally found shelter for the

night, aboard a storm-wracked trading galley called the *Lady of Myr*.
She was listing badly, having lost her mast and half her crew in a
storm, but her master did not have the coin he needed to refit her,
so he was glad to take a few pennies from Brienne and allow her and
Pod to share an empty cabin.

They had a restless night. Thrice Brienne woke. Once when the rain
began, and once at a creak that made her think Nimble Dick was creeping
in to kill her. The second time, she woke with knife in hand, but it was
nothing. In the darkness of the cramped little cabin, it took her a moment
to remember that Nimble Dick was dead. When she finally drifted back
to sleep, she dreamed about the men she'd killed. They danced around
her, mocking her, pinching at her as she slashed at them with her sword.
She cut them all to bloody ribbons, yet still they swarmed around
her . . . Shagwell, Timeon, and Pyg, aye, but Randyll Tarly too, and Vargo
Hoat, and Red Ronnet Connington. Ronnet had a rose between his
fingers. When he held it out to her, she cut his hand off.

She woke sweating, and spent the rest of the night huddled under
her cloak, listening to rain pound against the deck over her head. It was
a wild night. From time to time she heard the sound of distant thunder,
and thought of the Braavosi ship that had sailed upon the evening tide.

The next morning, she found the Stinking Goose again, woke its
slatternly proprietor, and paid her for some greasy sausages, fried
bread, half a cup of wine, a flagon of boiled water, and two clean
cups. The woman squinted at Brienne as she was putting the water
on to boil. "You're the big one went off with Nimble Dick. I remember.
He cheat you?"

"No."

"Rape you?"

"No."

"Steal your horse?"

"No. He was slain by outlaws."

"Outlaws?" The woman seemed more curious than upset. "I always
figured Dick would hang, or get sent off to that Wall."

They ate the fried bread and half the sausages. Podrick Payne
washed his down with wine-flavored water whilst Brienne nursed a
cup of watered wine and wondered why she'd come. Hyle Hunt was

no true knight. His honest face was just a mummer's mask. *I do not need his help, I do not need his protection, and I do not need him,* she told herself. *He is probably not even coming. Telling me to meet him here was just another jape.*

She was getting up to go when Ser Hyle arrived. "My lady. Podrick." He glanced at the cups and plates and the half-eaten sausages cooling in a puddle of grease, and said, "Gods, I hope you did not eat the food here."

"What we ate is no concern of yours," Brienne said. "Did you find your cousin? What did he tell you?"

"Sandor Clegane was last seen in Saltpans, the day of the raid. Afterward he rode west, along the Trident."

She frowned. "The Trident is a long river."

"Aye, but I don't think our dog will have wandered too far from its mouth. Westeros has lost its charm for him, it would seem. At Saltpans he was looking for a *ship*." Ser Hyle drew a roll of sheepskin from his boot, pushed the sausages aside, and unrolled it. It proved to be a map. "The Hound butchered three of his brother's men at the old inn by the crossroads, here. He led the raid on Saltpans, here." He tapped Saltpans with his finger. "He may be trapped. The Freys are up here at the Twins, Darry and Harrenhal are south across the Trident, west he's got the Blackwoods and the Brackens fighting, and Lord Randyll's here at Maidenpool. The high road to the Vale is closed by snow, even if he could get past the mountain clans. Where's a dog to go?"

"If he is with Dondarrion . . .?"

"He's not. Alyn is certain of that. Dondarrion's men are looking for him too. They have put out word that they mean to hang him for what he did at Saltpans. They had no part of that. Lord Randyll is putting it about that they did in hopes of turning the commons against Beric and his brotherhood. He will never take the lightning lord so long as the smallfolk are protecting him. And there's this other band, led by this woman Stoneheart . . . Lord Beric's lover, according to one tale. Supposedly she was hanged by the Freys, but Dondarrion kissed her and brought her back to life, and now she cannot die, no more than he can." Brienne considered the map. "If Clegane was last seen at Saltpans, that would be the place to find his trail."

"There is no one left at Saltpans but an old knight hiding in his castle, Alyn said."

"Still, it would be a place to start."

"There's a man," Ser Hyle said. "A septon. He came in through my gate the day before you turned up. Meribald, his name is. River-born and river-bred and he's served here all his life. He's departing on the morrow to make his circuit, and he always calls at Saltpans. We should go with him."

Brienne looked up sharply. "*We?*"

"I am going with you."

"You're not."

"Well, I'm going with Septon Meribald to Saltpans. You and Podrick can go wherever you bloody well like."

"Did Lord Randyll command you to follow me again?"

"He commanded me to stay away from you. Lord Randyll is of the view that you might benefit from a good hard raping."

"Then why would you come with me?"

"It was that, or return to gate duty."

"If your lord commanded—"

"He is no longer my lord."

That took her aback. "You left his service?"

"His lordship informed me that he had no further need of my sword, or my insolence. It amounts to the same thing. Henceforth I shall enjoy the adventuresome life of a hedge knight . . . though if we do find Sansa Stark, I imagine we will be well rewarded."

Gold and land, that's what he sees in this. "I mean to save the girl, not sell her. I swore a vow."

"I don't recall that I did."

"That is why you will not be coming with me."

They left the next morning, as the sun was coming up.

It was a queer procession: Ser Hyle on a chestnut courser and Brienne on her tall grey mare, Podrick Payne astride his swayback stot, and Septon Meribald walking beside them with his quarterstaff, leading a small donkey and a large dog. The donkey carried such a heavy load that Brienne was half afraid its back would break. "Food for the poor and hungry of the riverlands," Septon Meribald told them at the gates of Maidenpool. "Seeds and nuts and dried fruit, oaten porridge, flour, barley bread, three wheels of yellow cheese from the inn by the Fool's Gate, salt cod for me, salt mutton for Dog . . . oh, and salt. Onions, carrots, turnips, two sacks of beans, four of barley, and nine of oranges. I have a weakness for the orange, I confess. I got these from a sailor, and I fear they will be the last I'll taste till spring."

Meribald was a septon without a sept, only one step up from a begging brother in the hierarchy of the Faith. There were hundreds like him, a ragged band whose humble task it was to trudge from one flyspeck of a village to the next, conducting holy services, performing marriages, and forgiving sins. Those he visited were expected to feed and shelter him, but most were as poor as he was, so Meribald could not linger in one place too long without causing hardship to his hosts. Kindly innkeeps would sometimes allow him to sleep in their kitchens or their stables, and there were septries and holdfasts and even a few castles where he knew he would be given hospitality. Where no such places were at hand, he slept beneath the trees or under hedges. "There are many fine hedges in the riverlands," Meribald said. "The old ones are the best. There's nothing beats a hundred-year-old hedge. Inside one of those a man can sleep as snug as at an inn, and with less fear of fleas."

The septon could neither read nor write, as he cheerfully confessed along the road, but he knew a hundred different prayers and could recite long passages from *The Seven-Pointed Star* from memory, which was all that was required in the villages. He had a seamed, windburnt face, a shock of thick grey hair, wrinkles at the corners of his eyes. Though a big man, six feet tall, he had a way of hunching forward as he walked that made him seem much shorter. His hands were large and leathery, with red knuckles and dirt beneath the nails, and he had the biggest feet that Brienne had ever seen, bare and black and hard as horn.

"I have not worn a shoe in twenty years," he told Brienne. "The first year, I had more blisters than I had toes, and my soles would bleed like pigs whenever I trod on a hard stone, but I prayed and the Cobbler Above turned my skin to leather."

"There is no cobbler above," Podrick protested.

"There is, lad . . . though you may call him by another name. Tell me, which of the seven gods do you love best?"

"The Warrior," said Podrick without a moment's hesitation.

Brienne cleared her throat. "At Evenfall, my father's septon always said that there was but one god."

"One god with seven aspects. That's so, my lady, and you are right to point it out, but the mystery of the Seven Who Are One is not easy for simple folk to grasp, and I am nothing if not simple, so I speak of seven gods." Meribald turned back to Podrick. "I have never known a boy who did not love the Warrior. I am old, though, and being old, I love the Smith. Without his labor, what would the Warrior defend? Every town has a smith, and every castle. They make the plows we need to plant our crops, the nails we use to build our ships, iron shoes to save the hooves of our faithful horses, the bright swords of our lords. No one could doubt the value of a smith, and so we name one of the Seven in his honor, but we might as easily have called him the Farmer or the Fisherman, the Carpenter or the Cobbler. What he works at makes no matter. What matters is, he works. The Father rules, the Warrior fights, the Smith labors, and together they perform all that is rightful for a man. Just as the Smith is one aspect of the godhead, the Cobbler is one aspect of the Smith. It was he who heard my prayer and healed my feet."

"The gods are good," Ser Hyle said in a dry voice, "but why trouble them, when you might just have kept your shoes?"

"Going barefoot was my penance. Even holy septons can be sinners, and my flesh was weak as weak could be. I was young and full of sap, and the girls . . . a septon can seem as gallant as a prince if he is the only man you know who has ever been more than a mile from your village. I would recite to them from *The Seven-Pointed Star*. The Maiden's Book worked best. Oh, I was a wicked man, before I threw away my shoes. It shames me to think of all the maidens I deflowered."

Brienne shifted in the saddle uncomfortably, thinking back to the camp below the walls of Highgarden and the wager Ser Hyle and the others had made to see who could bed her first.

"We're looking for a maiden," confided Podrick Payne. "A highborn girl of three-and-ten, with auburn hair."

"I had understood that you were seeking outlaws."

"Them too," Podrick admitted.

"Most travelers do all they can to avoid such men," said Septon Meribald, "yet you would seek them out."

"We only seek one outlaw," Brienne said. "The Hound."

"So Ser Hyle told me. May the Seven save you, child. It's said he leaves a trail of butchered babes and ravished maids behind him. The Mad Dog of Saltpans, I have heard him called. What would good folk want with such a creature?"

"The maid that Podrick spoke of may be with him."

"Truly? Then we must pray for the poor girl."

And for me, thought Brienne, *a prayer for me as well. Ask the Crone to raise her lamp and lead me to the Lady Sansa, and the Warrior to give strength to my arm so that I might defend her.* She did not say the words aloud, though; not where Hyle Hunt might hear her and mock her for her woman's weakness.

With Septon Meribald afoot and his donkey bearing such a heavy load, the going was slow all that day. They did not take the main road west, the road that Brienne had once ridden with Ser Jaime when they came the other way to find Maidenpool sacked and full of corpses. Instead they struck off toward the northwest, following the shore of the Bay of Crabs on a crooked track so small that it did not appear on either of Ser Hyle's precious sheepskin maps. The steep hills, black bogs, and piney woods of Crackclaw Point were nowhere to be found this side of Maidenpool. The lands they traveled through were low and wet, a wilderness of sandy dunes and salt marshes beneath a vast blue-grey vault of sky. The road was prone to vanishing amongst the reeds and tidal pools, only to appear again a mile farther on; without Meribald, Brienne knew, they surely would have lost their way. The ground was often soft, so in places the septon would walk ahead, tapping with his quarterstaff to make certain of the footing. There were no trees for leagues around, just sea and sky and sand.

No land could have been more different from Tarth, with its mountains and waterfalls, its high meadows and shadowed vales, yet this place had its own beauty, Brienne thought. They crossed a dozen slow-flowing streams alive with frogs and crickets, watched terns floating high above the bay, heard the sandpipers calling from amongst the dunes. Once a fox crossed their path, and set Meribald's dog to barking wildly.

And there were people too. Some lived amongst the reeds in houses built of mud and straw, whilst others fished the bay in leather coracles and built their homes on rickety wooden stilts above the dunes. Most seemed to live alone, out of sight of any human habitation but their own. They seemed a shy folk for the most part, but near midday the dog began to bark again, and three women emerged from the reeds to give Meribald a woven basket full of clams. He gave each of them an orange in return, though clams were as common as mud in this world, and oranges were rare and costly. One of the women was very old, one was heavy with child, and one was a girl as fresh and pretty as a flower in spring. When Meribald took them off to hear their sins, Ser Hyle chuckled, and said, "It would seem the gods walk with us . . . at least the Maiden, the Mother, and the Crone." Podrick looked so astonished that Brienne had to tell him no, they were only three marsh women.

Afterward, when they resumed their journey, she turned to the septon, and said, "These people live less than a day's ride from Maidenpool, and yet the fighting has not touched them."

"They have little to touch, my lady. Their treasures are shells and stones and leather boats, their finest weapons knives of rusted iron. They are born, they live, they love, they die. They know Lord Mooton rules their lands, but few have ever seen him, and Riverrun and King's Landing are only names to them."

"And yet they know the gods," said Brienne. "That is your work, I think. How long have you walked the riverlands?"

"It will be forty years soon," the septon said, and his dog gave a loud bark. "From Maidenpool to Maidenpool, my circuit takes me half a year and ofttimes more, but I will not say I know the Trident. I glimpse the castles of the great lords only at a distance, but I know the market towns and holdfasts, the villages too small to have a name, the hedges and the hills, the rills where a thirsty man can drink and the caves where he can shelter. And the roads the smallfolk use, the crooked muddy tracks that do not appear on parchment maps, I know them too." He chuckled. "I should. My feet have trod every mile of them, ten times over."

The back roads are the ones the outlaws use, and the caves would make fine places for hunted men to hide. A prickle of suspicion made Brienne wonder just how well Ser Hyle knew this man. "It must make for a lonely life, septon."

"The Seven are always with me," said Meribald, "and I have my faithful servant, and Dog."

"Does your dog have a name?" asked Podrick Payne.

"He must," said Meribald, "but he is not my dog. Not him."

The dog barked and wagged his tail. He was a huge, shaggy creature, ten stone of dog at least, but friendly.

"Who does he belong to?" asked Podrick.

"Why, to himself, and to the Seven. As to his name, he has not told me what it is. I call him Dog."

"Oh." Podrick did not know what to make of a dog named Dog, plainly. The boy chewed on that a while, then said, "I used to have a dog when I was little. I called him Hero."

"Was he?"

"Was he what?"

"A hero."

"No. He was a good dog, though. He died."

"Dog keeps me safe upon the roads, even in such trying times as these. Neither wolf nor outlaw dare molest me when Dog is at my side." The septon frowned. "The wolves have grown terrible of late. There are places where a man alone would do well to find a tree to sleep in. In all my years the biggest pack I ever saw had fewer than a dozen wolves in it, but the great pack that prowls along the Trident now numbers in the hundreds."

"Have you come on them yourself?" Ser Hyle asked.

"I have been spared that, Seven save me, but I have heard them in the night, and more than once. So many voices . . . a sound to curdle a man's blood. It even set Dog to shivering, and Dog has killed a dozen wolves." He ruffled the dog's head. "Some will tell you that they are demons. They say the pack is led by a monstrous she-wolf, a stalking shadow grim and grey and huge. They will tell you that she has been known to bring aurochs down all by herself, that no trap nor snare can hold her, that she fears neither steel nor fire, slays any wolf that tries to mount her, and devours no other flesh but man."

Ser Hyle Hunt laughed. "Now you've done it, septon. Poor Podrick's eyes are big as boiled eggs."

"They're not," said Podrick, indignant. Dog barked.

That night they made a cold camp in the dunes. Brienne sent Podrick walking by the shore to find some driftwood for a fire, but he came back empty-handed, with mud up to his knees. "The tide's out, ser. My lady. There's no water, only mudflats."

"Stay off the mud, child," counseled Septon Meribald. "The mud is not fond of strangers. If you walk in the wrong place, it will open up and swallow you."

"It's only *mud*," insisted Podrick.

"Until it fills your mouth and starts creeping up your nose. Then it's death." He smiled to take the chill off his words. "Wipe off that mud and have a slice of orange, lad."

The next day was more of the same. They broke their fast on salt cod and more orange slices, and were on their way before the sun was wholly risen, with a pink sky behind them and a purple sky ahead. Dog led the way, sniffing at every clump of reeds and stopping every now and then to piss on one; he seemed to know the road as well as Meribald. The cries of terns shivered through the morning air as the tide came rushing in.

Near midday they stopped at a tiny village, the first they had encountered, where eight of the stilt-houses loomed above a small stream. The men were out fishing in their coracles, but the women and young boys clambered down dangling rope ladders and gathered around Septon Meribald to pray. After the service he absolved their sins and left them with some turnips, a sack of beans, and two of his precious oranges.

Back on the road, the septon said, "We would do well to keep a watch tonight, my friends. The villagers say they've seen three broken men skulking round the dunes, west of the old watchtower."

"Only three?" Ser Hyle smiled. "Three is honey to our swordswench. They're not like to trouble armed men."

"Unless they're starving," the septon said. "There is food in these marshes, but only for those with the eyes to find it, and these men are strangers here, survivors from some battle. If they should accost us, ser, I beg you, leave them to me."

"What will you do with them?"

"Feed them. Ask them to confess their sins, so that I might forgive them. Invite them to come with us to the Quiet Isle."

"That's as good as inviting them to slit our throats as we sleep," Hyle Hunt replied. "Lord Randyll has better ways to deal with broken men—steel and hempen rope."

"Ser? My lady?" said Podrick. "Is a broken man an outlaw?"

"More or less," Brienne answered.

Septon Meribald disagreed. "More less than more. There are many sorts of outlaws, just as there are many sorts of birds. A sandpiper and a sea eagle both have wings, but they are not the same. The singers love to sing of good men forced to go outside the law to fight some wicked lord, but most outlaws are more like this ravening Hound than they are the lightning lord. They are evil men, driven by greed, soured by malice, despising the gods and caring only for themselves. Broken men are more deserving of our pity, though they may be just as dangerous. Almost all are common-born, simple folk who had never been more than a mile from the house where they were born until the day some lord came round to take them off to war. Poorly shod and poorly clad, they march away beneath his banners, ofttimes with no better arms than a sickle or a sharpened hoe, or a maul they made themselves by lashing a stone to a stick with strips of hide. Brothers march with brothers, sons with fathers, friends with friends. They've heard the songs and stories, so they go off with eager hearts, dreaming of the wonders they will see, of the wealth and glory they will win. War seems a fine adventure, the greatest most of them will ever know.

"Then they get a taste of battle.

"For some, that one taste is enough to break them. Others go on for years, until they lose count of all the battles they have fought in, but even a man who has survived a hundred fights can break in his hundred-and-first. Brothers watch their brothers die, fathers lose their sons, friends see their friends trying to hold their entrails in after they've been gutted by an axe.

"They see the lord who led them there cut down, and some other lord shouts that they are his now. They take a wound, and when that's still half-healed they take another. There is never enough to eat, their shoes fall to pieces from the marching, their clothes are torn and rotting, and half of them are shitting in their breeches from drinking bad water.

"If they want new boots or a warmer cloak or maybe a rusted iron halfhelm, they need to take them from a corpse, and before long they are stealing from the living too, from the smallfolk whose lands they're fighting in, men very like the men they used to be. They slaughter their sheep and steal their chickens, and from there it's just a short step to carrying off their daughters too. And one day they look around and realize all their friends and kin are gone, that they are fighting beside strangers beneath a banner that they hardly recognize. They don't know where they are or how to get back home and the lord they're fighting for does not know their names, yet here he comes, shouting for them to form up, to make a line with their spears and scythes and sharpened hoes, to stand their ground. And the knights come down on them, faceless men clad all in steel, and the iron thunder of their charge seems to fill the world . . .

"And the man breaks.

"He turns and runs, or crawls off afterward over the corpses of the slain, or steals away in the black of night, and he finds someplace to hide. All thought of home is gone by then, and kings and lords and gods mean less to him than a haunch of spoiled meat that will let him live another day, or a skin of bad wine that might drown his fear for a few hours. The broken man lives from day to day, from meal to meal, more beast than man. Lady Brienne is not wrong. In times like these, the traveler must beware of broken men, and fear them . . . but he should pity them as well."

When Meribald was finished a profound silence fell upon their little band. Brienne could hear the wind rustling through a clump of pussywillows, and farther off the faint cry of a loon. She could hear Dog panting softly as he loped along beside the septon and his donkey, tongue lolling from his mouth. The quiet stretched and stretched, until finally she said, "How old were you when they marched you off to war?"

"Why, no older than your boy," Meribald replied. "Too young for such, in truth, but my brothers were all going, and I would not be left behind. Willam said I could be his squire, though Will was no knight, only a potboy armed with a kitchen knife he'd stolen from the inn. He died upon the Stepstones, and never struck a blow. It was fever did for him, and for my brother Robin. Owen died from a mace that split his head apart, and his friend Jon Pox was hanged for rape."

"The War of the Ninepenny Kings?" asked Hyle Hunt.

"So they called it, though I never saw a king, nor earned a penny. It was a war, though. That it was."

SAMWELL

S am stood before the window, rocking nervously as he watched the last light of the sun vanish behind a row of sharp-peaked rooftops. *He must have gotten drunk again,* he thought glumly. *Or else he's met another girl.* He did not know whether to curse or weep. Dareon was supposed to be his brother. *Ask him to sing, and no one could be better. Ask him to do aught else . . .*

The mists of evening had begun to rise, sending grey fingers up the walls of the buildings that lined the old canal. "He promised he'd be back," Sam said. "You heard him too."

Gilly looked at him with eyes red-rimmed and puffy. Her hair hung about her face, unwashed and tangled. She looked like some wary animal peering through a bush. It had been days since they'd last had a fire, yet the wildling girl liked to huddle near the hearth, as if the cold ashes still held some lingering warmth. "He doesn't like it here with us," she said, whispering so as not to wake the babe. "It's sad here. He likes it where the wine is, and the smiles."

Yes, thought Sam, *and the wine is everywhere but here.* Braavos was full of inns, alehouses, and brothels. And if Dareon preferred a fire and a cup of mulled wine to stale bread and the company of a weeping woman, a fat craven, and a sick old man, who could blame him? *I could blame him. He said he would be back before the gloaming; he said he would bring us wine and food.*

He looked out the window once more, hoping against hope to see the singer hurrying home. Darkness was falling across the secret city, creeping through the alleys and down the canals. The good folk of Braavos would soon be shuttering their windows and sliding bars across their doors. Night belonged to the bravos and the courtesans. *Dareon's new friends,* Sam thought bitterly. They were all the singer could talk about of late. He was trying to write a song about one courtesan, a woman called the Moonshadow who had heard him singing beside the Moon Pool and rewarded him with a kiss. "You should have asked her for silver," Sam had said. "It's coin we need, not kisses." But the singer only smiled. "Some kisses are worth more than yellow gold, Slayer."

That made him angry too. Dareon was not supposed to be making up songs about courtesans. He was supposed to be singing about the Wall and the valor of the Night's Watch. Jon had hoped that perhaps his songs might persuade a few young men to take the black. Instead he sang of golden kisses, silvery hair, and red, red lips. No one ever took the black for red, red lips.

Sometimes his playing would wake the babe too. Then the child would begin to wail, Dareon would shout at him to be quiet, Gilly would weep, and the singer would storm out and not return for days. "All that weeping makes me want to slap her," he complained, "and I can scarce sleep for her sobbing."

You would weep as well if you had a son and lost him, Sam almost said. He could not blame Gilly for her grief. Instead, he blamed Jon Snow and wondered when Jon's heart had turned to stone. Once he asked Maester Aemon that very question, when Gilly was down at the canal fetching water for them. "When you raised him up to be the lord commander," the old man answered.

Even now, rotting here in this cold room beneath the eaves, part of Sam did not want to believe that Jon had done what Maester Aemon thought. *It must be true, though. Why else would Gilly weep so much?* All he had to do was ask her whose child she was nursing at her breast, but he did not have the courage. He was afraid of the answer he might get. *I am still a craven, Jon.* No matter where he went in this wide world, his fears went with him.

A hollow rumbling echoed off the roofs of Braavos, like the sound of distant thunder; the Titan, sounding nightfall from across the lagoon. The noise was loud enough to wake the babe, and his sudden wail woke Maester Aemon. As Gilly went to give the boy the breast, the old man's eyes opened, and he stirred feebly in his narrow bed. "Egg? It's dark. Why is it so dark?"

Because you're blind. Aemon's wits were wandering more and more since they arrived at Braavos. Some days he did not seem to know where he was. Some days he would lose his way when saying something and begin to ramble on about his father or his brother. *He is one hundred and two,* Sam reminded himself, but he had been just as old at Castle Black and his wits had never wandered there.

"It's me," he had to say. "Samwell Tarly. Your steward."

"Sam." Maester Aemon licked his lips, and blinked. "Yes. And this is Braavos. Forgive me, Sam. Is morning come?"

"No." Sam felt the old man's brow. His skin was damp with sweat, cool and clammy to the touch, his every breath a soft wheeze. "It's night, maester. You've been asleep."

"Too long. It's cold in here."

"We have no wood," Sam told him, "and the innkeep will not give us more unless we have the coin." It was the fourth or fifth time they'd had this same conversation. *I should have used our coin for wood,* Sam chided himself every time. *I should have had the sense to keep him warm.*

Instead he had squandered the last of their silver on a healer from the House of the Red Hands, a tall pale man in robes embroidered with swirling stripes of red and white. All that the silver bought him was half a flask of dreamwine. "This may help gentle his passing," the Braavosi had said, not unkindly. When Sam asked if there wasn't any more that he could do, he shook his head. "Ointments I have, potions and infusions, tinctures and venoms and poultices. I might bleed him, purge him, leech him . . . but why? No leech can make him young again. This is an old man, and death is in his lungs. Give him this and let him sleep."

And so he had, all night and all day, but now the old man was struggling to sit. "We must go down to the ships."

The ships again. "You're too weak to go out," he had to say. A chill had gotten inside Maester Aemon during the voyage and settled in his chest. By the time they got to Braavos, he had been so weak they'd had to carry him ashore. They'd still had a fat bag of silver then, so Dareon had asked for the inn's biggest bed. The one they'd gotten was large enough to sleep eight, so the innkeep insisted on charging them for that many.

"On the morrow we can go to the docks," Sam promised. "You can ask about and find which ship is departing next for Oldtown." Even in autumn, Braavos was still a busy port. Once Aemon was strong enough to travel, they should have no trouble finding a suitable vessel to take them where they had to go. Paying for their passage would prove more difficult. A ship from the Seven Kingdoms would be their best hope. *A trader out of Oldtown, maybe, with kin in the Night's Watch. There must still be some who honor the men who walk the Wall.*

"Oldtown," Maester Aemon wheezed. "Yes. I dreamt of Oldtown, Sam. I was young again and my brother Egg was with me, with that big knight he served. We were drinking in the old inn where they make the fearsomely strong cider." He tried to rise again, but the effort proved too much for him. After a moment he settled back. "The ships," he said again. "We will find our answer there. About the dragons. I need to know."

No, thought Sam, *it's food and warmth you need, a full belly and a hot fire crackling in the hearth.* "Are you hungry, maester? We have some bread left, and a bit of cheese."

"Not just now, Sam. Later, when I'm feeling stronger."

"How will you get stronger unless you eat?" None of them had eaten much at sea, not after Skagos. The autumn gales had hounded them all across the narrow sea. Sometimes they came up from the south, roiling with thunder and lightning and black rains that fell for days. Sometimes they came down from the north, cold and grim, with savage winds that cut right through a man. Once it got so cold that Sam had woken to find the whole ship coated in ice, shining as white as pearl. The captain had taken down their mast and tied it to the deck, to finish the crossing on oars alone. No one had been eating by the time they saw the Titan.

Once safe ashore, though, Sam had found himself ravenously hungry. It was the same for Dareon and Gilly. Even the babe had begun to suck more lustily. Aemon, though . . .

"The bread's gone stale, but I can beg some gravy from the kitchens to soak it in," Sam told the old man. The innkeep was a hard man, cold-eyed and suspicious of these black-clad strangers beneath his roof, but his cook was kinder.

"No. Perhaps a sip of wine, though?"

They had no wine. Dareon had promised to buy some with the coin from his singing. "We'll have wine later," Sam had to say. "There's water, but it's not the good water." The good water came over the arches of the great brick aqueduct the Braavosi called the sweetwater river. Rich men had it piped into their homes; the poor filled their pails and buckets at public fountains. Sam had sent Gilly out to get some, forgetting that the wildling girl had lived her whole life in sight of Craster's Keep and never seen so much as a market town. The stony maze of islands and canals that was Braavos, devoid of grass and trees and teeming with strangers who spoke to her in words she could not understand, frightened her so badly that she lost the map and soon herself. Sam found her weeping at the stony feet of some long-dead sealord. "All we have is canal water," he told Maester Aemon, "but the cook gave it a boil. There's dreamwine too, if you need more of that."

"I have dreamt enough for now. Canal water will suffice. Help me, if you would."

Sam eased the old man up and held the cup to his dry, cracked lips. Even so, half the water dribbled down the maester's chest. "Enough," Aemon coughed, after a few sips. "You'll drown me." He shivered in Sam's arms. "Why is the room so cold?"

"There's no more wood." Dareon had paid the innkeep double for a room with a hearth, but none of them had realized that wood would be so costly here. Trees did not grow on Braavos, save in the courts and gardens of the mighty. Nor would the Braavosi cut the pines that covered the outlying islands around their great lagoon and acted as windbreaks to shield them from storms. Instead, firewood was brought in by barge, up the rivers and across the lagoon. Even dung was dear here; the Braavosi used boats in place of horses. None of that would have mattered if they had departed as planned for Oldtown, but that had proved impossible with Maester Aemon so weak. Another voyage on the open sea would kill him.

Aemon's hand crept across the blankets, groping for Sam's arm. "We must go to the docks, Sam."

"When you are stronger." The old man was in no state to brave the salt spray and wet winds along the waterfront, and Braavos was all waterfront. To the north was the Purple Harbor, where Braavosi traders tied up beneath the domes and towers of the Sealord's Palace. To the west lay the Ragman's Harbor, crowded with ships from the other Free Cities, from Westeros and Ibben and the fabled, far-off lands of the east. And everywhere else were little piers and ferry berths and old grey wharves where shrimpers and crabbers and fisherfolk moored after working the mudflats and river mouths. "It would be too great a strain on you."

"Then go in my stead," Aemon urged, "and bring me someone who has seen these dragons."

"Me?" Sam was dismayed by the suggestion. "Maester, it was only a story. A sailor's story." Dareon was to blame for this as well. The singer had been bringing back all manner of queer tales from the alehouses and brothels. Unfortunately, he had been in his cups when he heard the one about the dragons and could not recall the details. "Dareon may have made up the whole story. Singers do that. They make things up."

"They do," said Maester Aemon, "but even the most fanciful song may hold a kernel of truth. Find that truth for me, Sam."

"I wouldn't know who to ask, or how to ask him. I only have a little High Valyrian, and when they speak to me in Braavosi I cannot understand half of what they're saying. You speak more tongues than I do, once you are stronger you can . . ."

"When will I be stronger, Sam? Tell me that."

"Soon. If you rest and eat. When we reach Oldtown . . ."

"I shall not see Oldtown again. I know that now." The old man tightened his grip on Sam's arm. "I will be with my brothers soon.

Some were bound to me by vows and some by blood, but they were all my brothers. And my father . . . he never thought the throne would pass to him, and yet it did. He used to say that was his punishment for the blow that slew his brother. I pray he found the peace in death that he never knew in life. The septons sing of sweet surcease, of laying down our burdens and voyaging to a far sweet land where we may laugh and love and feast until the end of days . . . but what if there is no land of light and honey, only cold and dark and pain beyond the wall called death?"

He is afraid, Sam realized. "You are not dying. You're ill, that's all. It will pass."

"Not this time, Sam. I dreamed . . . in the black of night a man asks all the questions he dare not ask by daylight. For me, these past years, only one question has remained. Why would the gods take my eyes and my strength, yet condemn me to linger on so long, frozen and forgotten? What use could they have for an old done man like me?" Aemon's fingers trembled, twigs sheathed in spotted skin. "I remember, Sam. I still remember."

He was not making sense. "Remember what?"

"Dragons," Aemon whispered. "The grief and glory of my House, they were."

"The last dragon died before you were born," said Sam. "How could you remember them?"

"I see them in my dreams, Sam. I see a red star bleeding in the sky. I still remember red. I see their shadows on the snow, hear the crack of leathern wings, feel their hot breath. My brothers dreamed of dragons too, and the dreams killed them, every one. Sam, we tremble on the cusp of half-remembered prophecies, of wonders and terrors that no man now living could hope to comprehend . . . or . . ."

"Or?" said Sam.

". . . or not." Aemon chuckled softly. "Or I am an old man, feverish and dying." He closed his white eyes wearily, then forced them open once again. "I should not have left the Wall. Lord Snow could not have known, but *I* should have seen it. Fire consumes, but cold preserves. The Wall . . . but it is too late to go running back. The Stranger waits outside my door and will not be denied. Steward, you have served me faithfully. Do this one last brave thing for me. Go down to the ships, Sam. Learn all you can about these dragons."

Sam eased his arm out of the old man's grasp. "I will. If you want. I only . . ." He did not know what else to say. *I cannot refuse him.* He could look for Dareon as well, along the docks and wharves of the Ragman's Harbor. *I will find Dareon first, and we'll go to the ships together. And when we come back, we'll bring food and wine and wood. We'll have a fire and a good hot meal.* He rose. "Well. I should go, then. If I am going. Gilly will be here. Gilly, bar the door when I am gone." *The Stranger waits outside the door.*

Gilly nodded, cradling the babe against her breast, her eyes welling full of tears. *She is going to weep again,* Sam realized. It was more than he could take. His swordbelt hung from a peg on the wall, beside the old cracked horn that Jon had given him. He ripped it down and buckled it about him, then swept his black wool cloak about his rounded shoulders, slumped through the door, and clattered down a wooden stair whose steps creaked beneath his weight. The inn had two front doors, one opening on a street and one on a canal. Sam went out through the former, to avoid the common room where the innkeep was sure to give him the sour eye that he reserved for guests who had overstayed their welcome.

There was a chill in the air, but the night was not half so foggy as some. Sam was grateful for that much. Sometimes the mists covered the ground so thick that a man could not see his own feet. Once he had come within a step of walking into a canal.

As a boy, Sam had read a history of Braavos and dreamed of one day coming here. He wanted to behold the Titan rising stern and fearsome from the sea, glide down the canals in a serpent boat past all the palaces and temples, and watch the bravos do their water dance, blades flashing in the starlight. But now that he was here, all he wanted was to leave and go to Oldtown.

With his hood up and his cloak flapping, he made his way along the cobblestones toward the Ragman's Harbor. His swordbelt kept threatening to fall down about his ankles, so he had to keep tugging it back up as he went. He stayed to the smaller, darker streets, where he was less likely to encounter anyone, yet every passing cat still made his heart thump . . . and Braavos crawled with cats. *I need to find Dareon,* he thought. *He is a man of the Night's Watch, my Sworn Brother; he and I will puzzle out what to do.* Maester Aemon's strength was gone, and Gilly would have been lost here even if she had not been grief-stricken, but Dareon . . . *I should not think ill of him. He could be hurt, perhaps that is why he did not come back. He could be dead, lying in some alley in a pool of blood, or floating facedown in one of the canals.* At night the bravos swaggered through the city in their parti-colored finery, spoiling to prove their skill with those slender swords they wore. Some would fight for any cause, some for none at all, and Dareon had a loose tongue and quick temper, especially when he'd been drinking. *Just because a man can sing about battles doesn't mean he's fit to fight one.*

The best alehouses, inns, and brothels were near the Purple Harbor or the Moon Pool, but Dareon preferred the Ragman's Harbor, where the patrons were more apt to speak the Common Tongue. Sam began his search at the Inn of the Green Eel, the Black Bargeman, and Moroggo's, places where Dareon had played before. He was not to be found at any of them. Outside the Foghouse several serpent boats were tied up awaiting patrons, and Sam tried to ask the polemen if they had seen a singer all in black, but none of the polemen understood his High Valyrian. *That, or they do not chose to understand.* Sam peered into the dingy winesink beneath the second arch of Nabbo's Bridge, barely large enough to accommodate ten people. Dareon was not one of them. He tried the Outcast Inn, the House of Seven Lamps, and the brothel called the Cattery, where he got strange looks but no help.

Leaving, he almost bumped into two young men beneath the Cattery's red lantern. One was dark and one was fair. The dark-haired one said something in Braavosi. "I am sorry," Sam had to say. "I do not understand." He edged away from them, afraid. In the Seven Kingdoms nobles draped themselves in velvets, silks, and samites of a hundred hues whilst peasants and smallfolk wore raw wool and dull brown roughspun. In Braavos it was otherwise. The bravos swaggered about like peacocks, fingering their swords, whilst the mighty dressed in charcoal grey and purple, blues that were almost black and blacks as dark as a moonless night.

"My friend Terro says you are so fat you make him sick," said the fair-haired bravo, whose jacket was green velvet on one side and cloth-of-silver on the other. "My friend Terro says that the rattle of your sword makes his head ache." He was speaking in the Common Tongue. The other one, the dark-haired bravo in the burgundy brocade and yellow cloak whose name would appear to have been Terro, made some comment in Braavosi, and his fair-haired friend laughed, and said, "My friend Terro says you dress above your station. Are you some great lord, to wear the black?"

Sam wanted to run, but if he did was like to trip over his own swordbelt. *Do not touch your sword*, he told himself. Even a finger on the hilt might be enough for one or the other of the bravos to take as a challenge. He tried to think of words that might appease them. "I'm not—" was all he managed.

"He is not a lord," a child's voice put in. "He's in the Night's Watch, stupid. From *Westeros*." A girl edged into the light, pushing a barrow full of seaweed; a scruffy, skinny creature in big boots, with ragged unwashed hair. "There's another one down at the Happy Port, singing songs to the Sailor's Wife," she informed the two bravos. To Sam she said, "If they ask who is the most beautiful woman in the world, say the Nightingale or else they'll challenge you. Do you want to buy some clams? I sold all my oysters."

"I have no coin," Sam said.

"He has no coin," mocked the fair-haired bravo. His dark-haired friend grinned and said something in Braavosi. "My friend Terro is chilly. Be our good fat friend and give him your cloak."

"Don't do that either," said the barrow girl, "or else they'll ask for your boots next, and before long you'll be naked."

"Little cats who howl too loud get drowned in the canals," warned the fair-haired bravo.

"Not if they have claws." And suddenly there was a knife in the girl's left hand, a blade as skinny as she was. The one called Terro said something to his fair-haired friend and the two of them moved off, chuckling at one another.

"Thank you," Sam told the girl when they were gone.

Her knife vanished. "If you wear a sword at night it means you can be challenged. Did you *want* to fight them?"

"No." It came out in a squeak that made Sam wince.

"Are you truly in the Night's Watch? I never saw a black brother like you before." The girl gestured at the barrow. "You can have the last clams if you want. It's dark, no one will buy them now. Are you sailing to the Wall?"

"To Oldtown." Sam took one of the baked clams and wolfed it down. "We're between ships." The clam was good. He ate another.

"The bravos never bother anyone without a sword. Not even stupid camel cunts like Terro and Orbelo."

"Who are you?"

"No one." She stank of fish. "I used to be someone, but now I'm not. You can call me Cat, if you like. Who are you?"

"Samwell, of House Tarly. You speak the Common Tongue."

"My father was the oarmaster on *Nymeria*. A bravo killed him for saying that my mother was more beautiful than the Nightingale. Not one of those camel cunts you met, a real bravo. Someday I'll slit his throat. The captain said *Nymeria* had no need of little girls, so he put me off. Brusco took me in and gave me a barrow." She looked up at him. "What ship will you be sailing on?"

"We bought passage on the *Lady Ushanora*."

The girl squinted at him suspiciously. "She's gone. Don't you know? She left days and days ago."

I know, Sam might have said. He and Dareon had stood on the dock watching the rise and fall of her oars as she beat for the Titan and the open sea. "Well," the singer said, "that's done." If Sam had been a braver man, he would have shoved him into the water. When it came to talking girls out of their clothes Dareon had a honeyed tongue, yet in the captain's cabin somehow Sam had done all the talking, trying to persuade the Braavosi to wait for them. "Three days I have waited for this old man," the captain had said. "My holds are full, and my men have fucked their wives farewell. With you or without, my *Lady* leaves on the tide."

"Please," Sam had pleaded. "Just a few more days, that's all I ask. So Maester Aemon can recover his strength."

"He has no strength." The captain had visited the inn the night before to see Maester Aemon for himself. "He is old and ill and I will not have him dying on my *Lady*. Stay with him or leave him, it matters not to me. I sail." Even worse, he had refused to return the passage money they had paid him, the silver that was meant to see them safe to Oldtown. "You bought my finest cabin. It is there, awaiting you. If you do not choose to occupy it, that is no fault of mine. Why should I bear the loss?"

By now we might be at Duskendale, Sam thought mournfully. *We might even have reached Pentos, if the winds were kind.*

But none of that would matter to the barrow girl. "You said you saw a singer . . ."

"At the Happy Port. He's going to wed the Sailor's Wife."

"Wed?"

"She only beds the ones who marry her."

"Where is this Happy Port?"

"Across from the Mummer's Ship. I can show you the way."

"I know the way." Sam had seen the Mummer's Ship. *Dareon cannot wed! He said the words!* "I have to go."

He ran. It was a long way over slick cobbles. Before long he was puffing, his big black cloak flapping noisily behind him. He had to keep one hand on his swordbelt as he ran. What few people he encountered gave him curious looks, and once a cat reared up and hissed at him. By the time he reached the ship he was staggering. The Happy Port was just across the alley.

No sooner had he entered, flushed and out of breath, than a one-eyed woman threw her arms around his neck. "Don't," Sam told her, "I'm not here for that." She answered in Braavosi. "I do not speak that tongue," Sam said in High Valyrian. There were candles burning and a fire crackling in the hearth. Someone was sawing on a fiddle, and he saw two girls dancing around a red priest, holding hands. The one-eyed woman pressed her breasts against his chest. "Don't do that! I'm not here for that!"

"Sam!" Dareon's familiar voice rang out. "Yna, let him go, that's Sam the Slayer. My Sworn Brother!"

The one-eyed woman peeled away, though she kept one hand on

his arm. One of the dancers called out, "He can slay me if he likes," and the other said, "Do you think he'd let me touch his sword?" Behind them a purple galleas had been painted on the wall, crewed by women clad in thigh-high boots and nothing else. A Tyroshi sailor was passed out in a corner, snoring into his huge scarlet beard. Elsewhere, an older woman with huge breasts was turning tiles with a massive Summer Islander in black-and-scarlet feathers. In the center of it all sat Dareon, nuzzling at the neck of the woman in his lap. She was wearing his black cloak.

"Slayer," the singer called out drunkenly, "come meet my lady wife." His hair was sand and honey, his smile warm. "I sang her love songs. Women melt like butter when I sing. How could I resist this face?" He kissed her nose. "Wife, give Slayer a kiss, he's my brother." When the girl got to her feet, Sam saw that she was naked underneath the cloak. "Don't go fondling my wife now, Slayer," said Dareon, laughing. "But if you want one of her sisters, you feel free. I still have coin enough, I think."

Coin that might have bought us food, Sam thought, *coin that might have bought wood, so Maester Aemon could keep warm.* "What have you done? You can't *marry*. You said the words, the same as me. They could have your head for this."

"We're only wed for this one night, Slayer. Even in Westeros no one takes your head for that. Haven't you ever gone to Mole's Town to dig for buried treasure?"

"No." Sam reddened. "I would never . . ."

"What about your wildling wench? You must have fucked her a time or three. All those nights in the woods, huddled together under your cloak, don't you tell me that you never stuck it in her." He waved a hand toward a chair. "Sit down, Slayer. Have a cup of wine. Have a whore. Have both."

Sam did not want a cup of wine. "You promised to come back before the gloaming. To bring back wine and food."

"Is this how you killed that Other? Scolding him to death?" Dareon laughed. "*She's* my wife, not you. If you will not drink to my marriage, go away."

"Come with me," said Sam. "Maester Aemon's woken up and wants to hear about these dragons. He's talking about bleeding stars and white shadows and dreams and . . . if we could find out more about these dragons, it might help give him ease. Help me."

"On the morrow. Not on my wedding night." Dareon pushed himself to his feet, took his bride by the hand, and started toward the stairs, pulling her behind him.

Sam blocked his way. "You *promised,* Dareon. You said the words. You're supposed to be my brother."

"In Westeros. Does this look like Westeros to you?"

"Maester Aemon—"

"—is dying. That stripey healer you wasted all our silver on said as much." Dareon's mouth had turned hard. "Have a girl or go away, Sam. You're ruining my wedding."

"I'll go," said Sam, "but you'll come with me."

"No. I'm done with you. I'm done with *black*." Dareon tore his cloak off his naked bride and tossed it in Sam's face. "Here. Throw that rag on the old man, it may keep him a little warmer. I shan't be needing it. I'll be clad in velvet soon. Next year, I'll be wearing furs and eating—"

Sam hit him.

He did not think about it. His hand came up, curled into a fist, and crashed into the singer's mouth. Dareon cursed and his naked wife gave a shriek and Sam threw himself onto the singer and knocked him backwards over a low table. They were almost of a height, but Sam weighed twice as much, and for once he was too angry to be afraid. He punched the singer in the face and in the belly, then began to pummel him about the shoulders with both hands. When Dareon grabbed his wrists, Sam butted him with his head and broke his lip. The singer let go and he smashed him in the nose. Somewhere a man was laughing, a woman cursing. The fight seemed to slow, as if they were two black flies struggling in amber. Then someone dragged Sam off the singer's chest. He hit that person too, and something hard crashed into his head.

The next he knew he was outside, flying headfirst through the fog. For half a heartbeat he saw black water underneath him. Then the canal came up and smashed him in the face.

Sam sank like a stone, like a boulder, like a mountain. The water got into his eyes and up his nose, dark and cold and salty. When he tried to shout for help he swallowed more. Kicking and gasping, he rolled over, bubbles bursting from his nose. *Swim,* he told himself, *swim.* The brine stung his eyes when he opened them, blinding him. He popped to the surface for just an instant, sucked down air, and slapped desperately with one hand whilst the other scrabbled at the wall of the canal. But the stones were slick and slimy and he could not get a grasp. He sank again.

Sam could feel the cold against his skin as the water soaked through his clothes. His swordbelt slipped down his legs and tangled round his ankles. *I'm going to drown,* he thought, in a blind black panic. He thrashed, trying to claw his way back to the surface, but instead his face bumped the bottom of the canal. *I'm upside down,* he realized, *I'm drowning.* Something moved beneath one flailing hand, an eel or a fish, slithering through his fingers. *I can't drown, Maester Aemon will die without me, and Gilly will have no one. I have to swim, I have to . . .*

There was a huge splash, and something coiled around him, under his arms and around his chest. *The eel,* was his first thought, *the eel has got me, it's going to pull me down.* He opened his mouth to scream, and swallowed more water. *I'm drowned,* was his last thought. *Oh, gods be good, I'm drowned.*

When he opened his eyes he was on his back and a big black Summer Islander was pounding on his belly with fists the size of hams. *Stop that, you're hurting me,* Sam tried to scream. Instead of words, he retched out water, and gasped. He was sodden and shivering, lying on the cobbles in a puddle of canal water. The Summer Islander punched him in the belly again, and more water came squirting out his nose. "Stop that," Sam gasped. "I haven't drowned. I haven't drowned."

"No." His rescuer leaned over him, huge and black and dripping. "You owe Xhondo many feathers. The water ruined Xhondo's fine cloak."

It had, Sam saw. The feathered cloak clung to the black man's huge shoulders, sodden and soiled. "I never meant . . ."

". . . to be swimming? Xhondo saw. Too much splashing. Fat men should float." He grabbed Sam's doublet with a huge black fist and hauled him to his feet. "Xhondo mates on *Cinnamon Wind*. Many tongues he speaks, a little. Inside Xhondo laughs, to see you punch the singer. And Xhondo hears." A broad white smile spread across his face. "Xhondo knows these dragons."

JAIME

"I had hoped that by now you would have grown tired of that wretched beard. All that hair makes you look like Robert." His sister had put aside her mourning for a jade-green gown with sleeves of silver Myrish lace. An emerald the size of a pigeon's egg hung on a golden chain about her neck.

"Robert's beard was black. Mine is gold."

"Gold? Or silver?" Cersei plucked a hair from beneath his chin and held it up. It was grey. "All the color is draining out of you, brother. You've become a ghost of what you were, a pale crippled thing. And so bloodless, always in white." She flicked the hair away. "I prefer you garbed in crimson and gold."

I prefer you dappled in sunlight, with water beading on your naked skin. He wanted to kiss her, carry her to her bedchamber, throw her on the bed. . . . *she's been fucking Lancel and Osmund Kettleblack and Moon Boy . . .* "I will make a bargain with you. Relieve me of this duty, and my razor is yours to command."

Her mouth tightened. She had been drinking hot spiced wine and smelled of nutmeg. "You presume to dicker with me? Need I remind you, you are sworn to obey."

"I am sworn to protect the king. My place is at his side."

"Your place is wherever he sends you."

"Tommen puts his seal on every paper that you put in front of him. This is your doing, and it's folly. Why name Daven your Warden of the West if you have no faith in him?"

Cersei took a seat beneath the window. Behind her Jaime could see the blackened ruin of the Tower of the Hand. "Why so reluctant, ser? Did you lose your courage with your hand?"

"I swore an oath to Lady Stark, never again to take up arms against the Starks or Tullys."

"A drunken promise made with a sword at your throat."

"How can I defend Tommen if I am not with him?"

"By defeating his enemies. Father always said that a swift sword stroke is a better defense than any shield. Admittedly, most sword strokes require a hand. Still, even a crippled lion may inspire fear. I want Riverrun. I want Brynden Tully chained or dead. And someone needs to set Harrenhal to rights. We have urgent need of Wylis Manderly, assuming he is still alive and captive, but the garrison has not replied to any of our ravens."

"Those are Gregor's men at Harrenhal," Jaime reminded her. "The Mountain liked them cruel and stupid. Most like they ate your ravens, messages and all."

"That's why I'm sending you. They may eat you as well, brave brother, but I trust you'll give them indigestion." Cersei smoothed her skirt. "I want Ser Osmund to command the Kingsguard in your absence."

. . . she's been fucking Lancel and Osmund Kettleblack and Moon Boy, for all I know . . . "That's not your choice. If I must go, Ser Loras will command here in my stead."

"Is that a jape? You know how I feel about Ser Loras."

"If you had not sent Balon Swann to Dorne—"

"I need him there. These Dornishmen cannot be trusted. That red snake championed Tyrion, have you forgotten that? I will not leave my daughter to their mercy. And I will *not* have Loras Tyrell commanding the Kingsguard."

"Ser Loras is thrice the man Ser Osmund is."

"Your notions of manhood have changed somewhat, brother."

Jaime felt his anger rising. "True, Loras does not leer at your teats the way Ser Osmund does, but I hardly think—"

"Think about this." Cersei slapped his face.

Jaime made no attempt to block the blow. "I see I need a thicker beard, to cushion me against my queen's caresses." He wanted to rip her gown off and turn her blows to kisses. He'd done it before, back when he had two good hands.

The queen's eyes were green ice. "You had best go, ser."

... *Lancel, Osmund Kettleblack, and Moon Boy* ...

"Are you deaf as well as maimed? You'll find the door behind you, ser."

"As you command." Jaime turned on his heel and left her.

Somewhere the gods were laughing. Cersei had never taken kindly to being balked, he *knew* that. Softer words might have swayed her, yet of late the very sight of her made him angry.

Part of him would be glad to put King's Landing behind him. He had no taste for the company of the lickspittles and fools who surrounded Cersei. "The smallest council," they were calling them in Flea Bottom, according to Addam Marbrand. And Qyburn . . . he might have saved Jaime's life, but he was still a Bloody Mummer. "Qyburn stinks of secrets," he warned Cersei. That only made her laugh. "We all have secrets, brother," she replied.

... *she's been fucking Lancel and Osmund Kettleblack and Moon Boy, for all I know* ...

Forty knights and as many esquires awaited him outside the Red Keep's stables. Half were westermen sworn to House Lannister, the others recent foes turned doubtful friends. Ser Dermot of the Rainwood would carry Tommen's standard, Red Ronnet Connington the white banner of the Kingsguard. A Paege, a Piper, and a Peckledon would share the honor of squiring for the Lord Commander. "Keep friends at your back and foes where you can see them," Sumner Crakehall had once counseled him. Or had that been Father?

His palfrey was a blood bay, his destrier a magnificent grey stallion. It had been long years since Jaime had named any of his horses; he had seen too many die in battle, and that was harder when you named them. But when the Piper boy started calling them Honor and Glory, he laughed and let the names stand. Glory wore trappings of Lannister crimson; Honor was barded in Kingsguard white. Josmyn Peckledon held the palfrey's reins as Ser Jaime mounted. The squire was skinny as a spear, with long arms and legs, greasy mouse-brown hair, and cheeks soft with peach fuzz. His cloak was Lannister crimson, but his surcoat showed the ten purple mullets of his own House arrayed upon a yellow field. "My lord," the lad asked, "will you be wanting your new hand?"

"Wear it, Jaime," urged Ser Kennos of Kayce. "Wave at the smallfolk and give them a tale to tell their children."

"I think not." Jaime would not show the crowds a golden lie. *Let them see the stump. Let them see the cripple.* "But feel free to make up for my lack, Ser Kennos. Wave with both hands, and waggle your feet if it please you." He gathered the reins in his left hand and wheeled his horse around. "Payne," he called as the rest were forming up, "you'll ride beside me."

Ser Ilyn Payne made his way to Jaime's side, looking like the beggar at the ball. His ringmail was old and rusted, worn over a stained jack of boiled leather. Neither the man nor his mount showed any heraldry; his shield was so hacked and battered it was hard to say what color paint might once have covered it. With his grim face and deep-sunk hollow eyes, Ser Ilyn might have passed for death himself . . . as he had, for years.

No longer, though. Ser Ilyn had been half of Jaime's price, for swallowing his boy king's command like a good little Lord Commander. The other half had been Ser Addam Marbrand. "I need them," he had told his sister, and Cersei had not put up a fight. *Most like she's pleased to rid herself of them.* Ser Addam was a boyhood friend of Jaime's, and the silent headsman had belonged to their father, if he belonged to anyone. Payne had been the captain of the Hand's guard when he had been heard boasting that it was Lord Tywin who ruled the Seven Kingdoms and told King Aerys what to do. Aerys Targaryen took his tongue for that.

"Open the gates," said Jaime, and Strongboar, in his booming voice, called out, *"OPEN THE GATES!"*

When Mace Tyrell had marched out through the Mud Gate to the sound of drums and fiddles, thousands lined the streets to cheer him off. Little boys had joined the march, striding along beside the Tyrell soldiers with heads held high and legs pumping, whilst their sisters threw down kisses from the windows.

Not so today. A few whores called out invitations as they passed, and a meat pie man cried his wares. In Cobbler's Square, two threadbare sparrows were haranguing several hundred smallfolk, crying doom upon the heads of godless men and demon worshipers. The crowd parted for the column. Sparrows and cobblers alike looked on with dull eyes. "They like the smell of roses but have no love for lions," Jaime observed. "My sister would be wise to take note of that." Ser Ilyn made no reply. *The perfect companion for a long ride. I will enjoy his conversation.*

The greater part of his command awaited him beyond the city walls; Ser Addam Marbrand with his outriders, Ser Steffon Swyft and the baggage train, the Holy Hundred of old Ser Bonifer the Good, Sarsfield's mounted archers, Maester Gulian with four cages full of ravens, two hundred heavy horse under Ser Flement Brax. Not a great host, all in all; fewer than a thousand men in total. Numbers were the last thing needed at Riverrun. A Lannister army already invested the castle, and an even larger force of Freys; the last bird they'd received suggested that the besiegers were having difficulty keeping themselves fed. Brynden Tully had scoured the land clean before retiring behind his walls.

Not that it required much scouring. From what Jaime had seen of the riverlands, scarce a field remained unburnt, a town unsacked, a maiden undespoiled. *And now my sweet sister sends me to finish the work that Amory Lorch and Gregor Clegane began.* It left a bitter taste in his mouth.

This near to King's Landing, the kingsroad was as safe as any road could be in such times, yet Jaime sent Marbrand and his outriders ahead to scout. "Robb Stark took me unawares in the Whispering Wood," he said. "That will never happen again."

"You have my word on it." Marbrand seemed visibly relieved to be ahorse again, wearing the smoke-grey cloak of his own House instead of the gold wool of the City Watch. "If any foe should come within a dozen leagues, you will know of them beforehand."

Jaime had given stern commands that no man was to depart the

column without his leave. Elsewise, he knew he would have bored
young lordlings racing through the fields, scattering livestock and
trampling down the crops. There were still cows and sheep to be seen
near the city; apples on the trees and berries in the brush, stands of
barleycorn and oats and winter wheat, wayns and oxcarts on the road.
Farther afield, things would not be so rosy.

Riding at the front of the host with Ser Ilyn silent by his side,
Jaime felt almost content. The sun was warm on his back and the
wind riffled through his hair like a woman's fingers. When Little Lew
Piper came galloping up with a helm full of blackberries, Jaime ate
a handful and told the boy to share the rest with his fellow squires
and Ser Ilyn Payne.

Payne seemed as comfortable in his silence as in his rusted ringmail
and boiled leather. The clop of his gelding's hooves and the rattle of
sword in scabbard whenever he shifted his seat were the only sounds
he made. Though his pox-scarred face was grim and his eyes as cold
as ice on a winter lake, Jaime sensed that he was glad he'd come. *I
gave the man a choice,* he reminded himself. *He could have refused me
and remained King's Justice.*

Ser Ilyn's appointment had been a wedding gift from Robert
Baratheon to the father of his bride, a sinecure to compensate Payne
for the tongue he'd lost in the service of House Lannister. He made
a splendid headsman. He had never botched an execution, and seldom
required as much as a second stroke. And there was something about
his silence that inspired terror. Seldom had a King's Justice seemed
so well fitted for his office.

When Jaime decided to take him, he had sought out Ser Ilyn's
chambers at the end of Traitor's Walk. The upper floor of the squat,
half-round tower was divided into cells for prisoners who required
some measure of comfort, captive knights or lordlings awaiting
ransom or exchange. The entrance to the dungeons proper was at
ground level, behind a door of hammered iron and a second of
splintery grey wood. On the floors between were rooms set aside for
the use of the Chief Gaoler, the Lord Confessor, and the King's Justice.
The Justice was a headsman, but by tradition he also had charge of
the dungeons and the men who kept them.

And for that task, Ser Ilyn Payne was singularly ill suited. As he could neither read, nor write, nor speak, Ser Ilyn had left the running of the dungeons to his underlings, such as they were. The realm had not had a Lord Confessor since the second Daeron, however, and the last Chief Gaoler had been a cloth merchant who purchased the office from Littlefinger during Robert's reign. No doubt he'd had good profit from it for a few years, until he made the error of conspiring with some other rich fools to give the Iron Throne to Stannis. They called themselves "Antler Men," so Joff had nailed antlers to their heads before flinging them over the city walls. So it had been left to Rennifer Longwaters, the head undergaoler with the twisted back who claimed at tedious length to have a "drop of dragon" in him, to unlock the dungeon doors for Jaime and conduct him up the narrow steps inside the walls to the place where Ilyn Payne had lived for fifteen years.

The chambers stank of rotted food, and the rushes were crawling with vermin. As Jaime entered, he almost trod upon a rat. Payne's greatsword rested on a trestle table, beside a whetstone and a greasy oilcloth. The steel was immaculate, the edge glimmering blue in the pale light, but elsewhere piles of soiled clothing were strewn about the floors, and the bits of mail and armor scattered here and there were red with rust. Jaime could not count the broken wine jars. *The man cares for naught but killing,* he thought, as Ser Ilyn emerged from a bedchamber that reeked of overflowing chamber pots. "His Grace bids me win back his riverlands," Jaime told him. "I would have you with me . . . if you can bear to give up all of this."

Silence was his answer, and a long, unblinking stare. But just as he was about to turn and take his leave, Payne had given him a nod. *And here he rides.* Jaime glanced at his companion. *Perhaps there is yet hope for the both of us.*

That night they made camp beneath the hilltop castle of the Hayfords. As the sun went down, a hundred tents sprouted beneath the hill, along the banks of the stream that ran beside it. Jaime set the sentries himself. He did not expect trouble this close to the city, but his uncle Stafford had once thought himself safe on the Oxcross too. It was best to take no chances.

When the invitation came down from the castle for him to sup with Lady Hayford's castellan, Jaime took Ser Ilyn with him, along with Ser Addam Marbrand, Ser Bonifer Hasty, Red Ronnet Connington, Strongboar, and a dozen other knights and lordlings. "I suppose I ought to wear the hand," he said to Peck before making his ascent.

The lad fetched it straightaway. The hand was wrought of gold, very lifelike, with inlaid nails of mother-of-pearl, its fingers and thumb half closed so as to slip around a goblet's stem. *I cannot fight, but I can drink,* Jaime reflected as the lad was tightening the straps that bound it to his stump. "Men shall name you Goldenhand from this day forth, my lord," the armorer had assured him the first time he'd fitted it onto Jaime's wrist. *He was wrong. I shall be the Kingslayer till I die.*

The golden hand was the occasion for much admiring comment over supper, at least until Jaime knocked over a goblet of wine. Then his temper got the best of him. "If you admire the bloody thing so much, lop off your own sword hand and you can have it," he told Flement Brax. After that there was no more talk about his hand, and he managed to drink some wine in peace.

The lady of the castle was a Lannister by marriage, a plump toddler who had been wed to his cousin Tyrek before she was a year old. Lady Ermesande was duly trotted out for their approval, all trussed up in a little gown of cloth-of-gold, with the green fretty and green pale wavy of House Hayford rendered in tiny beads of jade. But soon enough the girl began to squall, whereupon she was promptly whisked off to bed by her wet nurse.

"Has there been no word of our Lord Tyrek?" her castellan asked as a course of trout was served.

"None." Tyrek Lannister had vanished during the riots in King's Landing whilst Jaime himself was still captive at Riverrun. The boy would be fourteen by now, assuming he was still alive.

"I led a search myself, at Lord Tywin's command," offered Addam Marbrand as he boned his fish, "but I found no more than Bywater had before me. The boy was last seen ahorse, when the press of the mob broke the line of gold cloaks. Afterward . . . well, his palfrey was found, but not the rider. Most like they pulled him down and slew him. But if that's so, where is his body? The mob let the other corpses lie, why not his?"

"He would be of more value alive," suggested Strongboar. "Any Lannister would bring a hefty ransom."

"No doubt," Marbrand agreed, "yet no ransom demand was ever made. The boy is simply gone."

"The boy is dead." Jaime had drunk three cups of wine, and his golden hand seemed to be growing heavier and clumsier by the moment. *A hook would serve me just as well.* "If they realized whom they'd killed, no doubt they threw him in the river for fear of my father's wrath. They know the taste of that in King's Landing. Lord Tywin always paid his debts."

"Always," Strongboar agreed, and that was the end of that.

Yet afterward, alone in the tower room he had been offered for the night, Jaime found himself wondering. Tyrek had served King Robert as a squire, side by side with Lancel. Knowledge could be more valuable than gold, more deadly than a dagger. It was Varys he thought of then, smiling and smelling of lavender. The eunuch had agents and informers all over the city. It would have been a simple matter for him to arrange to have Tyrek snatched during the confusion . . . provided he knew beforehand that the mob was like to riot. *And Varys knew all, or so he would have us believe. Yet he gave Cersei no warning of that riot. Nor did he ride down to the ships to see Myrcella off.*

He opened the shutters. The night was growing cold, and a horned moon rode the sky. His hand shone dully in its light. *No good for throttling eunuchs, but heavy enough to smash that slimy smile into a fine red ruin.* He wanted to hit someone.

Jaime found Ser Ilyn honing his greatsword. "It's time," he told the man. The headsman rose and followed, his cracked leather boots scraping against the steep stone steps as they went down the stair. A small courtyard opened off the armory. Jaime found two shields there, two halfhelms, and a pair of blunted tourney swords. He offered one to Payne and took the other in his left hand as he slid his right through the loops of the shield. His golden fingers were curved enough to hook, but could not grasp, so his hold upon the shield was loose.

"You were a knight once, ser," Jaime said. "So was I. Let us see what we are now."

Ser Ilyn raised his blade in reply, and Jaime moved at once to the attack. Payne was as rusty as his ringmail, and not so strong as Brienne, yet he met every cut with his own blade, or interposed his shield. They danced beneath the horned moon as the blunted swords sang their steely song. The silent knight was content to let Jaime lead the dance for a while, but finally he began to answer stroke for stroke. Once he shifted to the attack, he caught Jaime on the thigh, on the shoulder, on the forearm. Thrice he made his head ring with cuts to the helm. One slash ripped the shield off his right arm, and almost burst the straps that bound his golden hand to his stump. By the time they lowered their swords he was bruised and battered, but the wine had burned away and his head was clear. "We will dance again," he promised Ser Ilyn. "On the morrow, and the morrow. Every day we'll dance, till I am as good with my left hand as ever I was with the right."

Ser Ilyn opened his mouth and made a clacking sound. *A laugh,* Jaime realized. Something twisted in his gut.

Come morning, none of the others was so bold as to make mention of his bruises. Not one of them had heard the sound of swordplay in the night, it would seem. Yet when they climbed back down to camp, Little Lew Piper voiced the question the knights and lordlings dared not ask. Jaime grinned at him. "They have lusty wenches in House Hayford. These are love bites, lad."

Another bright and blustery day was followed by a cloudy one, then three days of rain. Wind and water made no matter. The column kept its pace, north along the kingsroad, and each night Jaime found some private place to win himself more love bites. They fought inside a stable as a one-eyed mule looked on, and in the cellar of an inn amongst the casks of wine and ale. They fought in the blackened shell of a big stone barn, on a wooded island in a shallow stream, and in an open field as the rain pattered softly against their helms and shields.

Jaime made excuses for his nightly forays, but he was not so foolish as to think that they were believed. Addam Marbrand knew what he was about, surely, and some of his other captains must have suspected.

But no one spoke of it in his hearing . . . and since the only witness lacked a tongue, he need not fear anyone learning just how inept a swordsman the Kingslayer had become.

Soon the signs of war could be seen on every hand. Weeds and thorns and brushy trees grew high as a horse's head in fields where autumn wheat should be ripening, the kingsroad was bereft of travelers, and wolves ruled the weary world from dusk till dawn. Most of the animals were wary enough to keep their distance, but one of Marbrand's outriders had his horse run off and killed when he dismounted for a piss. "No beast would be so bold," declared Ser Bonifer the Good, of the stern sad face. "These are demons in the skins of wolves, sent to chastise us for our sins."

"This must have been an uncommonly sinful horse," Jaime said, standing over what remained of the poor animal. He gave orders for the rest of the carcass to be cut apart and salted down; it might be they would need the meat.

At a place called Sow's Horn, they found a tough old knight named Ser Roger Hogg squatting stubbornly in his towerhouse with six men-at-arms, four crossbowmen, and a score of peasants. Ser Roger was as big and bristly as his name and Ser Kennos suggested that he might be some lost Crakehall, since their sigil was a brindled boar. Strongboar seemed to believe it and spent an earnest hour questioning Ser Roger about his ancestors.

Jaime was more interested in what Hogg had to say of wolves. "We had some trouble with a band of them white star wolves," the old knight told him. "They come round sniffing after you, my lord, but we saw them off, and buried three down by the turnips. Before them there was a pack of bloody lions, begging your pardon. The one who led them had a manticore on his shield."

"Ser Amory Lorch," Jaime offered. "My lord father commanded him to harry the riverlands."

"Which we're no part of," Ser Roger Hogg said stoutly. "My fealty's owed to House Hayford, and Lady Ermesande bends her little knee at King's Landing, or will when she's old enough to walk. I told him that, but this Lorch wasn't much for listening. He slaughtered half my sheep and three good milk goats, and tried to roast me in my tower. My walls are solid stone and eight feet thick, though, so after his fire burned out he rode off bored. The wolves come later, the ones on four legs. They ate the sheep the manticore left me. I got a few good pelts in recompense, but fur don't fill your belly. What should we do, my lord?"

"Plant," said Jaime, "and pray for one last harvest." It was not a hopeful answer, but it was the only one he had.

The next day, the column crossed the stream that formed the boundary between the lands that did fealty to King's Landing and those beholden to Riverrun. Maester Gulian consulted a map and announced that these hills were held by the brothers Wode, a pair of landed knights sworn to Harrenhal . . . but *their* halls had been earth and timber, and only blackened beams remained of them.

No Wodes appeared, nor any of their smallfolk, though some outlaws had taken shelter in the root cellar beneath the second brother's keep. One of them wore the ruins of a crimson cloak, but Jaime hanged him with the rest. It felt good. This was justice. *Make a habit of it, Lannister, and one day men might call you Goldenhand after all. Goldenhand the Just.*

The world grew ever greyer as they drew near to Harrenhal. They rode beneath slate skies, beside waters that shone old and cold as a sheet of beaten steel. Jaime found himself wondering if Brienne might have passed this way before him. *If she thought that Sansa Stark had made for Riverrun . . .* Had they encountered other travelers, he might have stopped to ask if any of them had chance to see a pretty maid with auburn hair, or a big ugly one with a face that would curdle milk. But there was no one on the roads but wolves, and their howling held no answers.

Across the pewter waters of the lake the towers of Black Harren's folly appeared at last, five twisted fingers of black, misshapen stone grasping for the sky. Though Littlefinger had been named the Lord of Harrenhal, he seemed in no great haste to occupy his new seat, so it had fallen to Jaime Lannister to "sort out" Harrenhal on his way to Riverrun.

That it needed sorting out he did not doubt. Gregor Clegane had wrested the immense, gloomy castle away from the Bloody Mummers before Cersei recalled him to King's Landing. No doubt the Mountain's men were still rattling around inside like so many dried peas in a suit of plate, but they were not ideally suited to restore the king's peace to the Trident. The only peace Ser Gregor's lot had ever given anyone was the peace of the grave.

Ser Addam's outriders had reported that the gates of Harrenhal were closed and barred. Jaime drew his men up before them and commanded Ser Kennos of Kayce to sound the Horn of Herrock, black and twisted and banded in old gold.

When three blasts had echoed off the walls, they heard the groan of iron hinges and the gates swung slowly open. So thick were the walls of Black Harren's folly that Jaime passed beneath a dozen murder holes before emerging into sudden sunlight in the yard where he'd bid farewell to the Bloody Mummers, not so long ago. Weeds were sprouting from the hard-packed earth, and flies buzzed about the carcass of a horse.

A handful of Ser Gregor's men emerged from the towers to watch him dismount; hard-eyed, hard-mouthed men, the lot of them. *They would have to be, to ride beside the Mountain.* About the best that could be said for Gregor's men was that they were not quite as vile and violent a bunch as the Brave Companions. "Fuck me, Jaime Lannister," blurted one grey and grizzled man-at-arms. "It's the bleeding Kingslayer, boys. Fuck me with a spear!"

"Who might you be?" Jaime asked.

"Ser used to call me Shitmouth, if it please m'lord." He spit in his hands and wiped his cheeks with them, as if that would somehow make him more presentable.

"Charming. Do you command here?"

"Me? Shit, no. M'lord. Bugger me with a bloody spear." Shitmouth had enough crumbs in his beard to feed the garrison. Jaime had to laugh. The man took that for encouragement. "Bugger me with a bloody spear," he said again, and started laughing too.

"You heard the man," Jaime said to Ilyn Payne. "Find a nice long spear, and shove it up his arse."

Ser Ilyn did not have a spear, but Beardless Jon Bettley was glad to toss him one. Shitmouth's drunken laughter stopped abruptly. "You keep that bloody thing away from me."

"Make up your mind," said Jaime. "Who has the command here? Did Ser Gregor name a castellan?"

"Polliver," another man said, "only the Hound killed him, m'lord. Him and the Tickler both, and that Sarsfield boy."

The Hound again. "You know it was Sandor? You saw him?"

"Not us, m'lord. That innkeep told us."

"It happened at the crossroads inn, my lord." The speaker was a younger man with a mop of sandy hair. He wore the chain of coins that had once belonged to Vargo Hoat; coins from half a hundred distant cities, silver and gold, copper and bronze, square coins and round coins, triangles and rings and bits of bone. "The innkeep swore the man had one side of his face all burned. His whores told the same tale. Sandor had some boy with him, a ragged peasant lad. They hacked Polly and the Tickler to bloody bits and rode off down the Trident, we were told."

"Did you send men after them?"

Shitmouth frowned, as if the thought were painful. "No, m'lord. Fuck us all, we never did."

"When a dog goes mad you cut his throat."

"Well," the man said, rubbing his mouth, "I never much liked Polly, that shit, and the dog, he were Ser's brother, so . . ."

"We're bad, m'lord," broke in the man who wore the coins, "but you'd need to be mad to face the Hound."

Jaime looked him over. *Bolder than the rest, and not as drunk as Shitmouth.* "You were afraid of him."

"I wouldn't say *afraid,* m'lord. I'd say we was leaving him for our betters. Someone like Ser. Or you."

Me, when I had two hands. Jaime did not delude himself. Sandor would make short work of him now. "You have a name?"

"Rafford, if it pleases. Most call me Raff."

"Raff, gather the garrison together in the Hall of a Hundred Hearths. Your captives as well. I'll want to see them. Those whores from the crossroads too. Oh, and Hoat. I was distraught to hear that he had died. I'd like to look upon his head."

When they brought it to him, he found that the Goat's lips had been sliced off, along with his ears and most of his nose. The crows had supped upon his eyes. It was still recognizably Hoat, however. Jaime would have known his beard anywhere; an absurd rope of hair two feet long, dangling from a pointed chin. Elsewise, only a few leathery strips of flesh still clung to the Qohorik's skull. "Where is the rest of him?" he asked.

No one wanted to tell him. Finally, Shitmouth lowered his eyes, and muttered, "Rotted, ser. And et."

"One of the captives was always begging food," Rafford admitted, "so Ser said to give him roast goat. The Qohorik didn't have much meat on him, though. Ser took his hands and feet first, then his arms and legs."

"The fat bugger got most, m'lord," Shitmouth offered, "but Ser, he said to see that all the captives had a taste. And Hoat too, his own self. That whoreson 'ud slobber when we fed him, and the grease'd run down into that skinny beard o' his."

Father, Jaime thought, *your dogs have both gone mad.* He found himself remembering tales he had first heard as a child at Casterly Rock, of mad Lady Lothston who bathed in tubs of blood and presided over feasts of human flesh within these very walls.

Somehow revenge had lost its savor. "Take this and throw it in the lake." Jaime tossed Hoat's head to Peck, and turned to address the garrison. "Until such time as Lord Petyr arrives to claim his seat, Ser Bonifer Hasty shall hold Harrenhal in the name of the crown. Those of you who wish may join him, if he'll have you. The rest will ride with me to Riverrun."

The Mountain's men looked at one another. "We're owed," said one. "Ser promised us. Rich rewards, he said."

"His very words," Shitmouth agreed. *"Rich rewards, for them as rides with me."* A dozen others began to yammer their assent.

Ser Bonifer raised a gloved hand. "Any man who remains with me shall have a hide of land to work, a second hide when he takes a wife, a third at the birth of his first child."

"Land, ser?" Shitmouth spat. "Piss on that. If we wanted to grub in the bloody dirt, we could have bloody well stayed home, begging your pardon, ser. *Rich rewards,* Ser said. Meaning gold."

"If you have a grievance, go to King's Landing and take it up with my sweet sister." Jaime turned to Rafford. "I'll see those captives now. Starting with Ser Wylis Manderly."

"He the fat one?" asked Rafford.

"I devoutly hope so. And tell me no sad stories of how he died, or the lot of you are apt to do the same."

Any hopes he might have nursed of finding Shagwell, Pyg, or Zollo languishing in the dungeons were sadly disappointed. The Brave Companions had abandoned Vargo Hoat to a man, it would seem. Of Lady Whent's people, only three remained—the cook who had opened the postern gate for Ser Gregor, a bent-back armorer called Ben Blackthumb, and a girl named Pia, who was not near as pretty as she had been when Jaime saw her last. Someone had broken her nose and knocked out half her teeth. The girl fell at Jaime's feet when she saw him, sobbing and clinging to his leg with hysterical strength till Strongboar pulled her off. "No one will hurt you now," he told her, but that only made her sob the louder.

The other captives had been better treated. Ser Wylis Manderly was amongst them, along with several other highborn northmen taken prisoner by the Mountain That Rides in the fighting at the fords of the Trident. Useful hostages, all worth a goodly ransom. They were ragged, filthy, and shaggy to a man, and some had fresh bruises, cracked teeth, and missing fingers, but their wounds had been washed and bandaged, and none of them had gone hungry. Jaime wondered if they had any inkling what they'd been eating, and decided it was better not to inquire.

None had any defiance left; especially not Ser Wylis, a bushy-faced tub of suet with dull eyes and sallow, sagging jowls. When Jaime told him that he would be escorted to Maidenpool and there put on a ship for White Harbor, Ser Wylis collapsed into a puddle on the floor and sobbed longer and louder than Pia had. It took four men to lift him back onto his feet. *Too much roast goat,* Jaime reflected. *Gods, but I hate this bloody castle.* Harrenhal had seen more horror in its three hundred years than Casterly Rock had witnessed in three thousand.

Jaime commanded that fires be lit in the Hall of a Hundred

Hearths and sent the cook hobbling back to the kitchens to prepare a hot meal for the men of his column. "Anything but goat."

He took his own supper in Hunter's Hall with Ser Bonifer Hasty, a solemn stork of a man prone to salting his speech with appeals to the Seven. "I want none of Ser Gregor's followers," he declared as he was cutting up a pear as withered as he was, so as to make certain that its nonexistent juice did not stain his pristine purple doublet, embroidered with the white bend cotised of his House. "I will not have such sinners in my service."

"My septon used to say all men were sinners."

"He was not wrong," Ser Bonifer allowed, "but some sins are blacker than others, and fouler in the nostrils of the Seven."

And you have no more nose than my little brother, or my own sins would have you choking on that pear. "Very well. I'll take Gregor's lot off your hands." He could always find a use for fighters. If nothing else, he could send them up the ladders first, should he need to storm the walls of Riverrun.

"Take the whore as well," Ser Bonifer urged. "You know the one. The girl from the dungeons."

"Pia." The last time he had been here, Qyburn had sent the girl to his bed, thinking that would please him. But the Pia they had brought up from the dungeons was a different creature from the sweet, simple, giggly creature who'd crawled beneath his blankets. She had made the mistake of speaking when Ser Gregor wanted quiet, so the Mountain had smashed her teeth to splinters with a mailed fist and broken her pretty little nose as well. He would have done worse, no doubt, if Cersei had not called him down to King's Landing to face the Red Viper's spear. Jaime would not mourn him. "Pia was born in this castle," he told Ser Bonifer. "It is the only home she has ever known."

"She is a font of corruption," said Ser Bonifer. "I won't have her near my men, flaunting her . . . parts."

"I expect her flaunting days are done," he said, "but if you find her that objectionable, I'll take her." He could make her a washer-woman, he supposed. His squires did not mind raising his tent, grooming his horse, or cleaning his armor, but the task of caring for his clothes struck them as unmanly. "Can you hold Harrenhal with just your Holy Hundred?" Jaime asked. They should actually be called the Holy Eighty-Six, having lost fourteen men upon the Blackwater, but no doubt Ser Bonifer would fill up his ranks again as soon as he found some sufficiently pious recruits.

"I anticipate no difficulty. The Crone will light our way, and the Warrior will give strength to our arms."

Or else the Stranger will turn up for the whole holy lot of you. Jaime could not be certain who had convinced his sister that Ser Bonifer should be named castellan of Harrenhal, but the appointment smelled of Orton Merryweather. Hasty had once served Merryweather's grandsire, he seemed to recall dimly. And the carrot-haired justiciar was just the sort of simpleminded fool to assume that someone called "the Good" was the very potion the riverlands required to heal the wounds left by Roose Bolton, Vargo Hoat, and Gregor Clegane.

But he might not be wrong. Hasty hailed from the stormlands, so had neither friends nor foes along the Trident; no blood feuds, no debts to pay, no cronies to reward. He was sober, just, and dutiful, and his Holy Eighty-Six were as well disciplined as any soldiers in the Seven Kingdoms, and made a lovely sight as they wheeled and pranced their tall grey geldings. Littlefinger had once quipped that Ser Bonifer must have gelded the riders too, so spotless was their repute.

All the same, Jaime wondered about any soldiers who were better known for their lovely horses than for the foes they'd slain. *They pray well, I suppose, but can they fight?* They had not disgraced themselves on the Blackwater, so far as he knew, but they had not distinguished themselves either. Ser Bonifer himself had been a promising knight in his youth, but something had happened to him, a defeat or a disgrace or a near brush with death, and afterward he had decided that jousting was an empty vanity and put away his lance for good and all.

Harrenhal must be held, though, and Baelor Butthole here is the man that Cersei chose to hold it. "This castle has an ill repute," he warned him, "and one that's well deserved. It's said that Harren and his sons still walk the halls by night, afire. Those who look upon them burst into flame."

"I fear no shade, ser. It is written in *The Seven-Pointed Star* that spirits, wights, and revenants cannot harm a pious man, so long as he is armored in his faith."

"Then armor yourself in faith, by all means, but wear a suit of mail and plate as well. Every man who holds this castle seems to come to a bad end. The Mountain, the Goat, even my father . . ."

"If you will forgive my saying so, they were not godly men, as we are. The Warrior defends us, and help is always near, if some dread foe should threaten. Maester Gulian will be remaining with his ravens, Lord Lancel is nearby at Darry with his garrison, and Lord Randyll holds Maidenpool. Together we three shall hunt down and destroy whatever outlaws prowl these parts. Once that is done, the Seven will guide the goodfolk back to their villages to plow and plant and build anew."

The ones the Goat didn't kill, at least. Jaime hooked his golden fingers round the stem of his wine goblet. "If any of Hoat's Brave Companions fall into your hands, send word to me at once." The Stranger might have made off with the Goat before Jaime could get around to him, but fat Zollo was still out there, with Shagwell, Rorge, Faithful Urswyck, and the rest.

"So you can torture them and kill them?"

"I suppose you would forgive them, in my place?"

"If they made sincere repentance for their sins . . . yes, I would embrace them all as brothers and pray with them before I sent them to the block. Sins may be forgiven. Crimes require punishment." Hasty folded his hands before him like a steeple, in a way that reminded Jaime uncomfortably of his father. "If it is Sandor Clegane that we encounter, what would you have me do?"

Pray hard, Jaime thought, *and run.* "Send him to join his beloved brother and be glad the gods made seven hells. One would never be enough to hold both of the Cleganes." He pushed himself awkwardly to his feet. "Beric Dondarrion is a different matter. Should you capture him, hold him for my return. I'll want to march him back to King's

Landing with a rope about his neck, and have Ser Ilyn take his head off where half the realm can see."

"And this Myrish priest who runs with him? It is said he spreads his false faith everywhere."

"Kill him, kiss him, or pray with him, as you please."

"I have no wish to kiss the man, my lord."

"No doubt he'd say the same of you." Jaime's smile turned into a yawn. "My pardons. I shall take my leave of you, if you have no objections."

"None, my lord," said Hasty. No doubt he wished to pray.

Jaime wished to fight. He took the steps two at a time, out to where the night air was cold and crisp. In the torchlit yard Strongboar and Ser Flement Brax were having at each other whilst a ring of men-at-arms cheered them on. *Ser Lyle will have the best of that one,* he knew. *I need to find Ser Ilyn.* His fingers had the itch again. His footsteps took him away from the noise and the light. He passed beneath the covered bridge and through the Flowstone Yard before he realized where he was headed.

As he neared the bear pit, he saw the glow of a lantern, its pale wintry light washing over the tiers of steep stone seats. *Someone has come before me, it would seem.* The pit would be a fine place to dance; perhaps Ser Ilyn had anticipated him.

But the knight standing over the pit was bigger; a husky, bearded man in a red-and-white surcoat adorned with griffins. *Connington. What's he doing here?* Below, the carcass of the bear still sprawled upon the sands, though only bones and ragged fur remained, half-buried. Jaime felt a pang of pity for the beast. *At least he died in battle.* "Ser Ronnet," he called, "have you lost your way? It is a large castle, I know."

Red Ronnet raised his lantern. "I wished to see where the bear danced with the maiden not-so-fair." His beard shone in the light as if it were afire. Jaime could smell wine on his breath. "Is it true the wench fought naked?"

"Naked? No." He wondered how that wrinkle had been added to the story. "The Mummers put her in a pink silk gown and shoved a tourney sword into her hand. The Goat wanted her death to be *amuthing.* Elsewise . . ."

". . . the sight of Brienne naked might have made the bear flee in terror." Connington laughed.

Jaime did not. "You speak as if you know the lady."

"I was betrothed to her."

That took him by surprise. Brienne had never mentioned a betrothal. "Her father made a match for her . . ."

"Thrice," said Connington. "I was the second. My father's notion. I had heard the wench was ugly, and I told him so, but he said all women were the same once you blew the candle out."

"Your father." Jaime eyed Red Ronnet's surcoat, where two griffins faced each other on a field of red and white. *Dancing griffins.* "Our late Hand's . . . brother, was he?"

"Cousin. Lord Jon had no brothers."

"No." It all came back to him. Jon Connington had been Prince Rhaegar's friend. When Merryweather failed so dismally to contain Robert's Rebellion and Prince Rhaegar could not be found, Aerys had turned to the next best thing, and raised Connington to the Handship. But the Mad King was always chopping off his Hands. He had chopped Lord Jon after the Battle of the Bells, stripping him of honors, lands, and wealth, and packing him off across the sea to die in exile, where he soon drank himself to death. The cousin, though—Red Ronnet's father—had joined the rebellion and been rewarded with Griffin's Roost after the Trident. He only got the castle, though; Robert kept the gold, and bestowed the greater part of the Connington lands on more fervent supporters.

Ser Ronnet was a landed knight, no more. For any such, the Maid of Tarth would have been a sweet plum indeed. "How is it that you did not wed?" Jaime asked him.

"Why, I went to Tarth and saw her. I had six years on her, yet the wench could look me in the eye. She was a sow in silk, though most sows have bigger teats. When she tried to talk she almost choked on her own tongue. I gave her a rose and told her it was all that she would ever have from me." Connington glanced into the pit. "The bear was less hairy than that freak, I'll—"

Jaime's golden hand cracked him across the mouth so hard the other knight went stumbling down the steps. His lantern fell and smashed, and the oil spread out, burning. "You are speaking of a highborn lady, ser. Call her by her name. Call her Brienne."

Connington edged away from the spreading flames on his hands and knees. "Brienne. If it please my lord." He spat a glob of blood at Jaime's foot. "Brienne the Beauty."

CERSEI

It was a slow climb to the top of Visenya's Hill. As the horses labored upward, the queen leaned back against a plump red cushion. From outside came the voice of Ser Osmund Kettleblack. *"Make way. Clear the street. Make way for Her Grace the queen."*

"Margaery *does* keep a lively court," Lady Merryweather was saying. "We have jugglers, mummers, poets, puppets . . ."

"Singers?" prompted Cersei.

"Many and more, Your Grace. Hamish the Harper plays for her once a fortnight, and sometimes Alaric of Eysen will entertain us of an evening, but the Blue Bard is her favorite."

Cersei recalled the bard from Tommen's wedding. *Young, and fair to look upon. Could there be something there?* "There are other men as well, I hear. Knights and courtiers. Admirers. Tell me true, my lady. Do you think Margaery is still a maiden?"

"She says she is, Your Grace."

"So she does. What do you say?"

Taena's black eyes sparkled with mischief. "When she wed Lord Renly at Highgarden, I helped disrobe him for the bedding. His lordship was a well-made man, and lusty. I saw the proof when we tumbled him into the wedding bed where his bride awaited him as naked as her name day, blushing prettily beneath the coverlets. Ser Loras had carried her up the steps himself. Margaery may say that the marriage was never consummated, that Lord Renly had drunk too much wine at the wedding feast, but I promise you, the bit between his legs was anything but weary when last I saw it."

"Did you chance to see the marriage bed the morning after?" Cersei asked. "Did she bleed?"

"No sheet was shown, Your Grace."

A pity. Still, the absence of a bloody sheet meant little, by itself. Common peasant girls bled like pigs upon their wedding nights, she had heard, but that was less true of highborn maids like Margaery Tyrell. A lord's daughter was more like to give her maidenhead to a horse than a husband, it was said, and Margaery had been riding since she was old enough to walk. "I understand the little queen has many admirers amongst our household knights. The Redwyne twins, Ser Tallad . . . who else, pray tell?"

Lady Merryweather gave a shrug. "Ser Lambert, the fool who hides a good eye behind a patch. Bayard Norcross. Courtenay Greenhill. The brothers Woodwright, sometimes Portifer and often Lucantine. Oh, and Grand Maester Pycelle is a frequent visitor."

"Pycelle? Truly?" Had that doddering old worm forsaken the lion for the rose? *If so, he will regret it.* "Who else?"

"The Summer Islander in his feathered cloak. How could I have forgotten him, with his skin as black as ink? Others come to pay court to her cousins. Elinor is promised to the Ambrose boy, but loves to flirt, and Megga has a new suitor every fortnight. Once she kissed a potboy in the kitchen. I have heard talk of her marrying Lady Bulwer's brother, but if Megga were to choose for herself, she would sooner have Mark Mullendore, I am certain."

Cersei laughed. "The butterfly knight who lost his arm on the Blackwater? What good is half a man?"

"Megga thinks him sweet. She has asked Lady Margaery to help her find a monkey for him."

"A monkey." The queen did not know what to say to that. *Sparrows and monkeys. Truly, the realm is going mad.* "What of our brave Ser Loras? How often does he call upon his sister?"

"More than any of the others." When Taena frowned, a tiny crease appeared between her dark eyes. "Every morn and every night, he visits, unless duty interferes. Her brother is devoted to her, they share everything with . . . oh . . ." For a moment, the Myrish woman looked almost shocked. Then a smile spread across her face. "I have had a most *wicked* thought, Your Grace."

"Best keep it to yourself. The hill is thick with sparrows, and we all know how sparrows abhor wickedness."

"I have heard they abhor soap and water too, Your Grace."

"Perhaps too much prayer robs a man of his sense of smell. I shall be sure to ask His High Holiness."

The draperies swayed back and forth in a wash of crimson silk. "Orton told me that the High Septon has no name," Lady Taena said. "Can that be true? In Myr, we all have names."

"Oh, he had a name *once*. They all do." The queen waved a hand dismissively. "Even septons born of noble blood go only by their given names once they have taken their vows. When one of them is elevated to *High* Septon, he puts aside that name as well. The Faith will tell you he no longer has any need of a man's name, for he has become the avatar of the gods."

"How do you distinguish one High Septon from another?"

"With difficulty. One has to say, 'the fat one,' or 'the one before the fat one,' or 'the old one who died in his sleep.' You can always winkle out their birth names if you like, but they take umbrage if you use them. It reminds them that they were born ordinary men, and they do not like that."

"My lord husband tells me this new one was born with filth beneath his fingernails."

"So I suspect. As a rule the Most Devout elevate one of their own, but there have been exceptions." Grand Maester Pycelle had informed her of the history, at tedious length. "During the reign of King Baelor the Blessed, a simple stonemason was chosen as High Septon. He worked stone so beautifully that Baelor decided he was the Smith reborn in mortal flesh. The man could neither read nor write, nor recall the words of the simplest of prayers." Some still claimed that Baelor's Hand had the man poisoned to spare the realm embarrass-ment. "After that one died, an eight-year-old boy was elevated, once more at King Baelor's urging. The boy worked miracles, His Grace declared, though even his little healing hands could not save Baelor during his final fast."

Lady Merryweather gave a laugh. "Eight years old? Perhaps my son could be High Septon. He is almost seven."

"Does he pray a lot?" the queen asked.

"He prefers to play with swords."

"A real boy, then. Can he name all seven gods?"

"I think so."

"I shall have to take him under consideration." Cersei did not doubt that there were any number of boys who would do more honor to the crystal crown than the wretch on whom the Most Devout had chosen to bestow it. *This is what comes of letting fools and cowards rule themselves. Next time, I will choose their master for them.* And the next time might not be long in coming, if the new High Septon continued to annoy her. Baelor's Hand had little to teach Cersei Lannister where such matters were concerned.

"Clear the way!" Ser Osmund Kettleblack was shouting. *"Make way for the Queen's Grace!"*

The litter began to slow, which could only mean that they were near the top of the hill. "You should bring this son of yours to court," Cersei told Lady Merryweather. "Six is not too young. Tommen needs other boys about him. Why not your son?" Joffrey had never had a close friend of his own age, that she recalled. *The poor boy was always alone. I had Jaime when I was a child . . . and Melara, until she fell into the well.* Joff had been fond of the Hound, to be sure, but that was not friendship. He was looking for the father he never found in Robert. *A little foster brother might be just what Tommen needs to wean him away from Margaery and her hens.* In time they might grow as close as Robert and his boyhood friend Ned Stark. *A fool, but a loyal fool. Tommen will have need of loyal friends to watch his back.*

"Your Grace is kind, but Russell has never known any home but Longtable. I fear he would be lost in this great city."

"In the beginning," the queen allowed, "but he will soon outgrow that, as I did. When my father sent for me to court I wept and Jaime raged, until my aunt sat me down in the Stone Garden and told me there was no one in King's Landing that I need ever fear. 'You are a lioness,' she said, 'and it is for all the lesser beasts to fear you.' Your son will find his courage too. Surely you would prefer to have him close at hand, where you could see him every day? He is your only child, is he not?"

"For the present. My lord husband has asked the gods to bless us with another son, in case . . ."

"I know." She thought of Joffrey, clawing at his neck. In his last moments, he had looked to her in desperate appeal, and a sudden memory had stopped her heart; a drop of red blood hissing in a candle flame, a croaking voice that spoke of crowns and shrouds, of death at the hands of the *valonqar.*

Outside the litter, Ser Osmund was shouting something, and someone was shouting back. The litter jerked to a halt. "Are you all dead?" roared Kettleblack. *"Get out of the bloody way!"*

The queen pulled back a corner of the curtain and beckoned to Ser Meryn Trant. "What seems to be the trouble?"

"The sparrows, Your Grace." Ser Meryn wore white scale armor beneath his cloak. His helm and shield were slung from his saddle. "Camping in the street. We'll make them move."

"Do that, but gently. I do not care to be caught up in another riot." Cersei let the curtain fall. "This is absurd."

"It is, Your Grace," Lady Merryweather agreed. "The High Septon should have come to you. And these wretched sparrows . . ."

"He feeds them, coddles them, *blesses* them. Yet will not bless the king." The blessing was an empty ritual, she knew, but rituals and ceremonies had power in the eyes of the ignorant. Aegon the Conqueror himself had dated the start of his realm from the day the High Septon anointed him in Oldtown. "This wretched priest will obey, or learn how weak and human he still is."

"Orton says it is the gold he really wants. That he means to with-hold his blessing until the crown resumes its payments."

"The Faith will have its gold as soon as we have peace." Septon Torbert and Septon Raynard had been most understanding of her plight . . . unlike the wretched Braavosi, who had hounded poor Lord Gyles so mercilessly that he had taken to his bed, coughing up blood.

We had to have those ships. She could not rely upon the Arbor for her navy; the Redwynes were too close to the Tyrells. She needed her own strength at sea.

The dromonds rising on the river would give her that. Her flagship would dip twice as many oars as *King Robert's Hammer.* Aurane had asked her leave to name her *Lord Tywin,* which Cersei had been pleased to grant. She looked forward to hearing men speak of her father as a "she." Another of the ships would be named *Sweet Cersei,* and would bear a gilded figurehead carved in her likeness, clad in mail and lion helm, with spear in hand. *Brave Joffrey, Lady Joanna,* and *Lioness* would follow her to sea, along with *Queen Margaery, Golden Rose, Lord Renly, Lady Olenna,* and *Princess Myrcella.* The queen had made the mistake of telling Tommen he might name the last five. He had actually chosen *Moon Boy* for one. Only when Lord Aurane suggested that men might not want to serve on a ship named for a fool had the boy reluctantly agreed to honor his sister instead.

"If this ragged septon thinks to make me *buy* Tommen's blessing, he will soon learn better," she told Taena. The queen did not intend to truckle to a pack of priests.

The litter halted yet again, so suddenly that Cersei jerked. "Oh, this is infuriating." She leaned out once more, and saw that they had reached the top of Visenya's Hill. Ahead loomed the Great Sept of Baelor, with its magnificent dome and seven shining towers, but between her and the marble steps lay a sullen sea of humanity, brown and ragged and unwashed. *Sparrows,* she thought, sniffing, though no sparrows had ever smelled so rank.

Cersei was appalled. Qyburn had brought her reports of their numbers, but hearing about them was one thing and seeing them another. Hundreds were encamped upon the plaza, hundreds more in the gardens. Their cookfires filled the air with smoke and stinks. Roughspun tents and miserable hovels made of mud and scrap wood besmirched the pristine white marble. They were even huddled on the steps, beneath the Great Sept's towering doors.

Ser Osmund came trotting back to her. Beside him rode Ser Osfryd, mounted on a stallion as golden as his cloak. Osfryd was the middle Kettleblack, quieter than his siblings, more apt to scowl than smile.

And crueler as well, if the tales are true. Perhaps I should have sent him to the Wall.

Grand Maester Pycelle had wanted an older man "more seasoned in the ways of war" to command the gold cloaks, and several of her other councillors had agreed with him. "Ser Osfryd is seasoned quite sufficiently," she had told them, but even that did not shut them up. *They yap at me like a pack of small, annoying dogs.* Her patience with Pycelle had all but run its course. He had even had the temerity to object to her sending to Dorne for a master-at-arms, on the grounds that it might offend the Tyrells. "Why do you think I'm *doing* it?" she had asked him scornfully.

"Beg pardon, Your Grace," said Ser Osmund. "My brother's summoning more gold cloaks. We'll clear a path, never fear."

"I do not have the time. I will continue on afoot."

"Please, Your Grace." Taena caught her arm. "They frighten me. There are hundreds of them, and so dirty."

Cersei kissed her cheek. "The lion does not fear the sparrow . . . but it is good of you to care. I know you love me well, my lady. Ser Osmund, kindly help me down."

If I had known I was going to have to walk, I would have dressed for it. She wore a white gown slashed with cloth-of-gold, lacy but demure. It had been several years since the last time she had donned it, and the queen found it uncomfortably tight about the middle. "Ser Osmund, Ser Meryn, you will accompany me. Ser Osfryd, see that my litter comes to no harm." Some of the sparrows looked gaunt and hollow-eyed enough to eat her horses.

As she made her way through the ragged throng, past their cook-fires, wagons, and crude shelters, the queen found herself remembering another crowd that had once gathered on this plaza. The day she wed Robert Baratheon, thousands had turned out to cheer for them. All the women wore their best, and half the men had children on their shoulders. When she had emerged from inside the sept, hand in hand with the young king, the crowd sent up a roar so loud it could be heard in Lannisport. "They like you well, my lady," Robert whispered in her ear. "See, every face is smiling." For that one short moment she had been happy in her marriage . . . until she chanced to glance at Jaime. *No*, she remembered thinking, *not every face, my lord*.

No one was smiling now. The looks the sparrows gave her were dull, sullen, hostile. They made way but reluctantly. *If they were truly sparrows, a shout would send them flying. A hundred gold cloaks with staves and swords and maces could clear this rabble quick enough*. That was what Lord Tywin would have done. *He would have ridden over them instead of walking through*.

When she saw what they had done to Baelor the Beloved, the queen had cause to rue her soft heart. The great marble statue that had smiled serenely over the plaza for a hundred years was waist-deep in a heap of bones and skulls. Some of the skulls had scraps of flesh still clinging to them. A crow sat atop one such, enjoying a dry, leathery feast. Flies were everywhere. "What is the meaning of this?" Cersei demanded of the crowd. "Do you mean to bury Blessed Baelor in a mountain of carrion?"

A one-legged man stepped forward, leaning on a wooden crutch. "Your Grace, these are the bones of holy men and women, murdered for their faith. Septons, septas, brothers brown and dun and green, sisters white and blue and grey. Some were hanged, some disemboweled. Septs have been despoiled, maidens and mothers raped by godless men and demon worshipers. Even silent sisters have been molested. The Mother Above cries out in her anguish. We have brought their bones here from all over the realm, to bear witness to the agony of the Holy Faith."

Cersei could feel the weight of eyes upon her. "The king shall know of these atrocities," she answered solemnly. "Tommen will share your outrage. This is the work of Stannis and his red witch, and the savage northmen who worship trees and wolves." She raised her voice. *"Good people, your dead shall be avenged!"*

A few cheered, but only a few. "We ask no vengeance for our dead," said the one-legged man, "only protection for the living. For the septs and holy places."

"The Iron Throne must defend the Faith," growled a hulking lout with a seven-pointed star painted on his brow. "A king who does not protect his people is no king at all." Mutters of assent went up from those around him. One man had the temerity to grasp Ser Meryn by the wrist, and say, "It is time for all anointed knights to forsake their worldly masters and defend our Holy Faith. Stand with us, ser, if you love the Seven."

"Unhand me," said Ser Meryn, wrenching free.

"I hear you," Cersei said. "My son is young, but he loves the Seven well. You shall have his protection, and mine own."

The man with the star upon his brow was not appeased. "The Warrior will defend us," he said, "not this fat boy king."

Meryn Trant reached for his sword, but Cersei stopped him before he could unsheathe it. She had only two knights amidst a sea of sparrows. She saw staves and scythes, cudgels and clubs, several axes. "I will have no blood shed in this holy place, ser." *Why are all men such children? Cut him down, and the rest will tear us limb from limb.* "We are all the Mother's children. Come, His High Holiness awaits us." But as she made her way through the press to the steps of the sept, a gaggle of armed men stepped out to block the doors. They wore mail and boiled leather, with here and there a bit of dinted plate. Some had spears and some had longswords. More favored axes, and had sewn red stars upon their bleached white surcoats. Two had the insolence to cross their spears and bar her way.

"Is this how you receive your queen?" she demanded of them. "Pray, where are Raynard and Torbert?" It was not like those two to miss a chance to fawn on her. Torbert always made a show of getting down on his knees to wash her feet.

"I do not know the men you speak of," said one of the men with a red star on his surcoat, "but if they are of the Faith, no doubt the Seven had need of their service."

"Septon Raynard and Septon Torbert are of the *Most Devout*," Cersei said, "and will be furious to learn that you obstructed me. Do you mean to deny me entrance to Baelor's holy sept?"

"Your Grace," said a greybeard with a stooped shoulder. "You are welcome here, but your men must leave their swordbelts. No weapons are allowed within, by command of the High Septon."

"Knights of the Kingsguard do not set aside their swords, not even in the presence of the king."

"In the king's house, the king's word must rule," replied the aged knight, "but this is the house of the gods."

Color rose to her cheeks. One word to Meryn Trant, and the stoop-backed greybeard would be meeting his gods sooner than he might have liked. *Not here, though. Not now.* "Wait for me," she told the Kingsguard curtly. Alone, she climbed the steps. The spearmen uncrossed their spears. Two other men put their weight against the doors, and with a great groan they swung apart.

In the Hall of Lamps, Cersei found a score of septons on their knees, but not in prayer. They had pails of soap and water, and were scrubbing at the floor. Their roughspun robes and sandals led Cersei to take them for sparrows, until one raised his head. His face was red as a beet, and there were broken blisters on his hands, bleeding. "Your Grace."

"Septon Raynard?" The queen could scarce believe what she was seeing. "What are you doing on your knees?"

"He is cleaning the floor." The speaker was shorter than the queen by several inches and as thin as a broom handle. "Work is a form of prayer, most pleasing to the Smith." He stood, scrub brush in hand. "Your Grace. We have been expecting you."

The man's beard was grey and brown and closely trimmed, his hair tied up in a hard knot behind his head. Though his robes were clean, they were frayed and patched as well. He had rolled his sleeves up his elbows as he scrubbed, but below the knees the cloth was soaked and sodden. His face was sharply pointed, with deep-set eyes as brown as mud. *His feet are bare,* she saw with dismay. They were hideous as well, hard and horny things, thick with callus. "You are His High Holiness?"

"We are."

Father, give me strength. The queen knew that she should kneel, but the floor was wet with soap and dirty water and she did not wish to ruin her gown. She glanced over at the old men on their knees. "I do not see my friend Septon Torbert."

"Septon Torbert has been confined to a penitent's cell on bread and water. It is sinful for any man to be so plump when half the realm is starving."

Cersei had suffered quite enough for one day. She let him see her anger. "Is this how you greet me? With a scrub brush in your hand, dripping water? Do you know who I am?"

"Your Grace is the Queen Regent of the Seven Kingdoms," the man said, "but in *The Seven-Pointed Star* it is written that as men bow to their lords, and lords to their kings, so kings and queens must bow before the Seven Who Are One."

Is he telling me to kneel? If so, he did not know her very well. "By rights, you should have met me on the steps in your finest robes, with the crystal crown upon your head."

"We have no crown, Your Grace."

Her frown deepened. "My lord father gave your predecessor a crown of rare beauty, wrought in crystal and spun gold."

"And for that gift we honor him in our prayers," the High Septon said, "but the poor need food in their bellies more than we need gold and crystal on our head. That crown has been sold. So have the others in our vaults, and all our rings, and our robes of cloth-of-gold and cloth-of-silver. Wool will keep a man as warm. That is why the Seven gave us sheep."

He is utterly mad. The Most Devout must have been mad as well, to elevate this creature . . . mad, or terrified of the beggars at their doors. Qyburn's whisperers claimed that Septon Luceon had been nine votes from elevation when those doors had given way, and the sparrows came pouring into the Great Sept with their leader on their shoulders and their axes in their hands.

She fixed the small man with an icy stare. "Is there someplace where we may speak more privily, Your Holiness?"

The High Septon surrendered his scrub brush to one of the Most Devout. "If Your Grace will follow us?"

He led her through the inner doors, into the sept proper. Their footsteps echoed off the marble floor. Dust motes swam in the beams of colored light slanting down through the leaded glass of the great dome. Incense sweetened the air, and beside the seven altars candles shone like stars. A thousand twinkled for the Mother and near as many for the Maid, but you could count the Stranger's candles on two hands and still have fingers left.

Even here the sparrows had invaded. A dozen scruffy hedge knights were kneeling before the Warrior, beseeching him to bless the swords they had piled at his feet. At the Mother's altar, a septon was leading a hundred sparrows in prayer, their voices as distant as waves upon the shore. The High Septon led Cersei to where the Crone raised her lantern. When he knelt before the altar, she had no choice but to kneel beside him. Mercifully, this High Septon was not as long-winded as the fat one had been. *I should be grateful for that much, I suppose.*

His High Holiness made no move to rise when his prayer was done. It would seem they must confer upon their knees. *A small man's ploy,* she thought, amused. "High Holiness," she said, "these sparrows are frightening the city. I want them gone."

"Where should they go, Your Grace?"

There are seven hells, any one of them will serve. "Back where they came from, I would imagine."

"They came from everywhere. As the sparrow is the humblest and most common of the birds, they are the humblest and most common of men."

They are common, we agree on that much. "Have you seen what they have done to Blessed Baelor's statue? They befoul the plaza with their pigs and goats and night soil."

"Night soil can be washed away more easily than blood, Your Grace. If the plaza was befouled, it was befouled by the execution that was done here."

He dares throw Ned Stark in my face? "We all regret that. Joffrey was young, and not as wise as he might have been. Lord Stark should have been beheaded elsewhere, out of respect for Blessed Baelor . . . but the man *was* a traitor, let us not forget."

"King Baelor forgave those who conspired against him."

King Baelor imprisoned his own sisters, whose only crime was being beautiful. The first time Cersei heard that tale, she had gone to Tyrion's nursery and pinched the little monster till he cried. *I should have pinched his nose shut and stuffed my sock into his mouth.* She forced herself to smile. "King Tommen will forgive the sparrows too, once they have returned to their homes."

"Most have lost their homes. Suffering is everywhere . . . and grief, and death. Before coming to King's Landing, I tended to half a hundred little villages too small to have a septon of their own. I walked from each one to the next, performing marriages, absolving sinners of their sins, naming newborn children. Those villages are no more, Your Grace. Weeds and thorns grow where gardens once flourished, and bones litter the roadsides."

"War is a dreadful thing. These atrocities are the work of the northmen, and of Lord Stannis and his demon-worshipers."

"Some of my sparrows speak of bands of lions who despoiled them . . . and of the Hound, who was your own sworn man. At Saltpans, he slew an aged septon and despoiled a girl of twelve, an innocent child promised to the Faith. He wore his armor as he raped her and her tender flesh was torn and crushed by his iron mail. When he was done he gave her to his men, who cut off her nose and nipples."

"His Grace cannot be held responsible for the crimes of every man who ever served House Lannister. Sandor Clegane is a traitor and a brute. Why do you think I dismissed him from our service? He fights for the outlaw Beric Dondarrion now, not for King Tommen."

"As you say. Yet it must be asked—where were the king's knights when these things were being done? Did not Jaehaerys the Conciliator once swear upon the Iron Throne itself that the crown would always protect and defend the Faith?"

Cersei had no idea what Jaehaerys the Conciliator might have sworn. "He did," she agreed, "and the High Septon blessed him and anointed him as king. It is traditional for every new High Septon to give the king his blessing . . . and yet you have refused to bless King Tommen."

"Your Grace is mistaken. We have not refused."

"You have not come."

"The hour is not yet ripe."

Are you a priest or a greengrocer? "And what might I do to make it . . . riper?" *If he dares mention gold, I will deal with this one as I did the last and find a pious eight-year-old to wear the crystal crown.*

"The realm is full of kings. For the Faith to exalt one above the rest we must be certain. Three hundred years ago, when Aegon the Dragon landed beneath this very hill, the High Septon locked himself within the Starry Sept of Oldtown and prayed for seven days and seven nights, taking no nourishment but bread and water. When he emerged he announced that the Faith would not oppose Aegon and his sisters, for the Crone had lifted up her lamp to show him what lay ahead. If Oldtown took up arms against the Dragon, Oldtown would burn, and the Hightower and the Citadel and the Starry Sept would be cast down and destroyed. Lord Hightower was a godly man. When he heard the prophecy, he kept his strength at home and opened the city gates to Aegon when he came. And His High Holiness anointed the Conqueror with the seven oils. I must do as he did, three hundred years ago. I must pray, and fast."

"For seven days and seven nights?"

"For as long as need be."

Cersei itched to slap his solemn, pious face. *I could help you fast,* she thought. *I could shut you up in some tower and see that no one brings you food until the gods have spoken.* "These false kings espouse false gods," she reminded him. "Only King Tommen defends the Holy Faith."

"Yet everywhere septs are burned and looted. Even silent sisters have been raped, crying their anguish to the sky. Your Grace has seen the bones and skulls of our holy dead?"

"I have," she had to say. "Give Tommen your blessing, and he shall put an end to these outrages."

"And how shall he do that, Your Grace? Will he send a knight to walk the roads with every begging brother? Will he give us men to guard our septas against the wolves and lions?"

I will pretend you did not mention lions. "The realm is at war. His Grace has need of every man." Cersei did not intend to squander Tommen's strength playing wet nurse to sparrows, or guarding the wrinkled cunts of a thousand sour septas. *Half of them are probably praying for a good raping.* "Your sparrows have clubs and axes. Let them defend themselves."

"King Maegor's laws prohibit that, as Your Grace must know. It was by his decree that the Faith laid down its swords."

"Tommen is king now, not Maegor." What did she care what Maegor the Cruel had decreed three hundred years ago? *Instead of taking the swords out of the hands of the faithful, he should have used them for his own ends.* She pointed to where the Warrior stood above his altar of red marble. "What is that he holds?"

"A sword."

"Has he forgotten how to use it?"

"Maegor's laws—"

"—could be undone." She let that hang there, waiting for the High Sparrow to rise to the bait.

He did not disappoint her. "The Faith Militant reborn . . . that would be the answer to three hundred years of prayer, Your Grace. The Warrior would lift his shining sword again and cleanse this sinful realm of all its evil. If His Grace were to allow me to restore the ancient blessed orders of the Sword and Star, every godly man in the Seven Kingdoms would know him to be our true and rightful lord."

That was sweet to hear, but Cersei took care not to seem too eager. "Your High Holiness spoke of forgiveness earlier. In these troubled times, King Tommen would be most grateful if you could see your way to forgiving the crown's debt. It seems to me we owe the Faith some nine hundred thousand dragons."

"Nine hundred thousand six hundred and seventy-four dragons. Gold that could feed the hungry and rebuild a thousand septs."

"Is it gold you want?" the queen asked. "Or do you want these dusty laws of Maegor's set aside?"

The High Septon pondered that a moment. "As you wish. This debt shall be forgiven, and King Tommen will have his blessing. The Warrior's Sons shall escort me to him, shining in the glory of their Faith, whilst my sparrows go forth to defend the meek and humble of the land, reborn as Poor Fellows as of old."

The queen got to her feet and smoothed her skirts. "I shall have the papers drawn up, and His Grace will sign them and affix them with the royal seal." If there was one part of kingship that Tommen loved, it was playing with his seal.

"Seven save His Grace. Long may he reign." The High Septon made a steeple of his hands and raised his eyes to heaven. "Let the wicked tremble!"

Do you hear that, Lord Stannis? Cersei could not help but smile.

Even her lord father could have done no better. At a stroke, she had rid King's Landing of the plague of sparrows, secured Tommen's blessing, and lessened the crown's debt by close to a million dragons. Her heart was soaring as she allowed the High Septon to escort her back to the Hall of Lamps.

Lady Merryweather shared the queen's delight, though she had never heard of the Warrior's Sons or the Poor Fellows. "They date from before Aegon's Conquest," Cersei explained to her. "The Warrior's Sons were an order of knights who gave up their lands and gold and swore their swords to His High Holiness. The Poor Fellows . . . they were humbler, though far more numerous. Begging brothers of a sort, though they carried axes instead of bowls. They wandered the roads, escorting travelers from sept to sept and town to town. Their badge was the seven-pointed star, red on white, so the smallfolk named them Stars. The Warrior's Sons wore rainbow cloaks and inlaid silver armor over hair shirts, and bore star-shaped crystals in the pommels of their longswords. They were the Swords. Holy men, ascetics, fanatics, sorcerers, dragonslayers, demonhunters . . . there were many tales about them. But all agree that they were implacable in their hatred for all enemies of the Holy Faith."

Lady Merryweather understood at once. "Enemies such as Lord Stannis and his red sorceress, perhaps?"

"Why, yes, as it happens," said Cersei, giggling like a girl. "Shall we broach a flagon of hippocras and drink to the fervor of the Warrior's Sons on our way home?"

"To the fervor of the Warrior's Sons and the brilliance of the Queen Regent. To Cersei, the First of Her Name!"

The hippocras was as sweet and savory as Cersei's triumph, and the queen's litter seemed almost to float back across the city. But at the base of Aegon's High Hill, they encountered Margaery Tyrell and her cousins returning from a ride. *She dogs me everywhere I go,* Cersei thought with annoyance when she laid eyes on the little queen.

Behind Margaery came a long tail of courtiers, guards, and servants, many of them laden with baskets of fresh flowers. Each of her cousins had an admirer in thrall; the gangly squire Alyn Ambrose rode with Elinor, to whom he was betrothed, Ser Tallad with shy Alla, one-armed Mark Mullendore with Megga, plump and laughing. The Redwyne twins were escorting two of Margaery's other ladies, Meredyth Crane and Janna Fossoway. The women all wore flowers in their hair. Jalabhar Xho had attached himself to the party too, as had Ser Lambert Turnberry with his eye patch, and the handsome singer known as the Blue Bard.

And of course a knight of the Kingsguard must accompany the little queen, and of course it is the Knight of Flowers. In white scale armor chased with gold, Ser Loras glittered. Though he no longer presumed to train Tommen at arms, the king still spent far too much time in his company. Every time the boy returned from an afternoon with his little wife, he had some new tale to tell about something that Ser Loras had said or done.

Margaery hailed them when the two columns met and fell in beside the queen's litter. Her cheeks were flushed, her brown ringlets tumbling loosely about her shoulders, stirred by every puff of wind. "We have been picking autumn flowers in the kingswood," she told them.

I know where you were, the queen thought. Her informers were very good about keeping her apprised of Margaery's movements. *Such a restless girl, our little queen.* She seldom let more than three days pass without going off for a ride. Some days they would ride along the Rosby road to hunt for shells and eat beside the sea. Other times she would take her entourage across the river for an afternoon of hawking. The little queen was fond of going out on boats as well, sailing up and down the Blackwater Rush to no particular purpose. When she was feeling pious she would leave the castle to pray at Baelor's Sept. She gave her custom to a dozen different seamstresses, was well-known amongst the city's goldsmiths, and had even been known to visit the fish market by the Mud Gate for a look at the day's catch. Wherever she went, the smallfolk fawned on her, and Lady Margaery did all she could to fan their ardor. She was forever giving alms to beggars, buying hot pies off bakers' carts, and reining up to speak to common tradesmen.

Had it been up to her, she would have had Tommen doing all these things as well. She was forever inviting him to accompany her and her hens on their adventures, and the boy was forever pleading with his mother for leave to go along. The queen had given her consent a few times, if only to allow Ser Osney to spend a few more hours in Margaery's company. *For all the good it has done. Osney has proved a grievous disappointment.* "Do you remember the day your sister sailed for Dorne?" Cersei asked her son. "Do you recall the mob howling on our way back to the castle? The stones, the curses?"

But the king was deaf to sense, thanks to his little queen. "If we mingle with the commons, they will love us better."

"The mob loved the fat High Septon so well they tore him limb from limb, and him a holy man," she reminded him. All it did was make him sullen with her. *Just as Margaery wants, I wager. Every day in every way she tries to steal him from me.* Joffrey would have seen through her schemer's smile and let her know her place, but Tommen was more gullible. *She knew Joff was too strong for her,* Cersei thought, remembering the gold coin Qyburn had found. *For House Tyrell to hope to rule, he had to be removed.* It came back to her that Margaery and her hideous grandmother had once plotted to marry Sansa Stark to the little queen's crippled brother Willas. Lord Tywin had forestalled that by stealing a march on them and wedding Sansa to Tyrion, but the link had been there. *They are all in it together,* she realized with a start. *The Tyrells bribed the gaolers to free Tyrion, and whisked him down the roseroad to join his vile bride. By now the both of them are safe in Highgarden, hidden away behind a wall of roses.*

"You should have come along with us, Your Grace," the little schemer prattled on as they climbed the slope of Aegon's High Hill. "We could have had such a lovely time together. The trees are gowned in gold and red and orange, and there are flowers everywhere. Chestnuts too. We roasted some on our way home."

"I have no time for riding through the woods and picking flowers," Cersei said. "I have a kingdom to rule."

"Only one, Your Grace? Who rules the other six?" Margaery laughed a merry little laugh. "You will forgive me my jest, I hope. I know what a burden you bear. You should let me share the load. There must be some things I could do to help you. It would put to rest all this talk that you and I are rivals for the king."

"Is that what they say?" Cersei smiled. "How foolish. I have never looked upon you as a rival, not even for a moment."

"I am so pleased to hear that." The girl did not seem to realize that she had been cut. "You and Tommen must come with us the next time. I know His Grace would love it. The Blue Bard played for us, and Ser Tallad showed us how to fight with a staff the way the smallfolk do. The woods are so beautiful in autumn."

"My late husband loved the forest too." In the early years of their marriage, Robert was forever imploring her to hunt with him, but Cersei had always begged off. His hunting trips allowed her time with Jaime. *Golden days and silver nights.* It was a dangerous dance that they had danced, to be sure. Eyes and ears were everywhere within the Red Keep, and one could never be certain when Robert would return. Somehow the peril had only served to make their times together that much more thrilling. "Still, beauty can sometimes mask deadly danger," she warned the little queen. "Robert lost his life in the woods."

Margaery smiled at Ser Loras; a sweet sisterly smile, full of fondness. "Your Grace is kind to fear for me, but my brother keeps me well protected."

Go and hunt, Cersei had urged Robert, half a hundred times. *My brother keeps me well protected.* She recalled what Taena had told her earlier, and a laugh came bursting from her lips.

"Your Grace laughs so prettily." Lady Margaery gave her a quizzical smile. "Might we share the jest?"

"You will," the queen said. "I promise you, you will."

THE REAVER

The drums were pounding out a battle beat as the *Iron Victory* swept forward, her ram cutting through the choppy green waters. The smaller ship ahead was turning, oars slapping at the sea. Roses streamed upon her banners; fore and aft a white rose upon a red escutcheon, atop her mast a golden one on a field as green as grass. The *Iron Victory* raked her side so hard that half the boarding party lost their feet. Oars snapped and splintered, sweet music to the captain's ears.

He vaulted over the gunwale, landing on the deck below with his golden cloak billowing behind him. The white roses drew back, as men always did at the sight of Victarion Greyjoy armed and armored, his face hidden behind his kraken helm. They were clutching swords and spears and axes, but nine of every ten wore no armor, and the tenth had only a shirt of sewn scales. *These are no ironmen,* Victarion thought. *They still fear drowning.*

"Get him!" one man shouted. "He's alone!"

"COME!" he roared back. *"Come kill me, if you can."*

From all sides the rosey warriors converged, with grey steel in their hands and terror behind their eyes. Their fear was so ripe Victarion could taste it. Left and right he laid about, hewing off the first man's arm at the elbow, cleaving through the shoulder of the second. The third buried his own axehead in the soft pine of Victarion's shield.

He slammed it into the fool's face, knocked him off his feet, and slew him when he tried to rise again. As he was struggling to free his axe from the dead man's rib cage, a spear jabbed him between the shoulder blades. It felt as though someone had slapped him on the back. Victarion spun and slammed his axe down onto the spearman's head, feeling the impact in his arm as the steel went crunching through helm and hair and skull. The man swayed for half a heartbeat, till the iron captain wrenched the steel free and sent his corpse staggering loose-limbed across the deck, looking more drunk than dead.

By then his ironborn had followed him down onto the deck of the broken longship. He heard Wulfe One-Ear let out a howl as he went to work, glimpsed Ragnor Pyke in his rusted mail, saw Nute the Barber send a throwing axe spinning through the air to catch a man in the chest. Victarion slew another man, and another. He would have killed a third, but Ragnor cut him down first. "Well struck," Victarion bellowed at him.

When he turned to find the next victim for his axe, he spied the other captain across the deck. His white surcoat was spotted with blood and gore, but Victarion could make out the arms upon his breast, the white rose within its red escutcheon. The man bore the same device upon his shield, on a white field with a red embattled border. "*You!*" the iron captain called across the carnage. "*You of the rose! Be you the lord of Southshield?*"

The other raised his visor to show a beardless face. "His son and heir. Ser Talbert Serry. And who are you, kraken?"

"Your death." Victarion bulled toward him.

Serry leapt to meet him. His longsword was good castle-forged steel, and the young knight made it sing. His first cut was low, and Victarion deflected it off his axe. His second caught the iron captain on the helm before he got his shield up. Victarion answered with a sidearm blow of his axe. Serry's shield got in the way. Wooden splinters flew, and the white rose split lengthwise with a sweet sharp *crack*. The young knight's longsword hammered at his thigh, once, twice, thrice, screaming against the steel. *This boy is quick,* the iron captain realized. He smashed his shield in Serry's face and sent him staggering back against the gunwale. Victarion raised his axe and put all his weight behind his cut, to open the boy from neck to groin, but Serry spun away. The axehead crashed through the rail, sending splinters flying, and lodged there when he tried to pull it free. The deck moved under his feet, and he stumbled to one knee.

Ser Talbert cast away his broken shield and slashed down with his longsword. Victarion's own shield had twisted half around when he stumbled. He caught Serry's blade in an iron fist. Lobstered steel crunched, and a stab of pain made him grunt, yet Victarion held on. "I am quick as well, boy," he said as he ripped the sword from the knight's hand and flung it into the sea.

Ser Talbert's eyes went wide. "My sword . . ."

Victarion caught the lad about the throat with a bloody fist. "Go and get it," he said, forcing him backwards over the side into the bloodstained waters.

That won him a respite to pull his axe loose. The white roses were falling back before the iron tide. Some tried to flee belowdecks, as others cried for quarter. Victarion could feel warm blood trickling down his fingers beneath the mail and leather and lobstered plate, but that was nothing. Around the mast a thick knot of foemen fought on, standing shoulder to shoulder in a ring. *These few are men, at least. They would sooner die than yield.* Victarion would grant some of them that wish. He beat his axe against his shield and charged them.

The Drowned God had not shaped Victarion Greyjoy to fight with words at kingsmoots, nor struggle against furtive sneaking foes in endless bogs. *This* was why he had been put on earth; to stand steel-clad with an axe red and dripping in his hand, dealing death with every blow.

They hacked at him from front and back, but their swords might have been willow switches for all the harm they did him. No blade could cut through Victarion Greyjoy's heavy plate, nor did he give his foes the time to find the weak points at the joints, where only mail and leather warded him. Let three men assail him, or four, or five; it made no matter. He slew them one at a time, trusting in his steel to protect him from the others. As each foe fell he turned his wroth upon the next.

The last man to face him must have been a smith; he had shoulders like a bull, and one much more muscular than the other. His armor was a studded brigandine and a cap of boiled leather. The only blow he landed completed the ruin of Victarion's shield, but the cut the captain dealt in answer split his head in two. *Would that I could deal with the Crow's Eye as simply.* When he jerked his axehead free again, the smith's skull seemed to burst. Bone and blood and brain went everywhere, and the corpse fell forward, up against his legs. *Too late to plead for quarter now,* Victarion thought as he untangled himself from the dead man.

By then the deck was slick beneath his feet, and the dead and the dying lay in heaps on every side. He threw his shield away and sucked in air. "Lord Captain," he heard the Barber say beside him, "the day is ours."

All around, the sea was full of ships. Some were burning, some were sinking, some had been smashed to splinters. Between the hulls the water was thick as stew, full of corpses, broken oars, and men clinging to the wreckage. In the distance, half a dozen of southron longships were racing back toward the Mander. *Let them go,* Victarion thought, *let them tell the tale.* Once a man had turned his tail and run from battle he ceased to be a man.

His eyes were stinging from the sweat that had run down into them during the fight. Two of his oarsmen helped undo his kraken helm so he might lift it off. Victarion mopped at his brow. "That knight," he grumbled, "the knight of the white rose. Did any of you pull him out?" A lord's son would be worth a goodly ransom; from his father, if Lord Serry had survived the day. From his liege at Highgarden, if not.

None of his men had seen what became of the knight after he went over the side, however. Most like the man had drowned. "May he feast as he fought, in the Drowned God's watery halls." Though the men of the Shield Islands called themselves sailors, they crossed the seas in dread and went lightly clad in battle for fear of drowning. Young Serry had been different. *A brave man,* thought Victarion. *Almost ironborn.*

He gave the captured ship to Ragnor Pyke, named a dozen men to crew her, and clambered back up onto his own *Iron Victory.* "Strip the captives of arms and armor and have their wounds bound up," he told Nute the Barber. "Throw the dying in the sea. If any beg for mercy, cut their throats first." He had only contempt for such; better to drown on seawater than on blood. "I want a count of the ships we won and all the knights and lordlings we took captive. I want their banners too." One day he would hang them in his hall, so when he grew old and feeble he could remember all the foes he had slain when he was young and strong.

"It will be done." Nute grinned. "It is a great victory."

Aye, he thought, *a great victory for the Crow's Eye and his wizards.* The other captains would shout his brother's name anew when the tidings reached Oakenshield. Euron had seduced them with his glib tongue and smiling eye and bound them to his cause with the plunder of half a hundred distant lands; gold and silver, ornate armor, curved swords with gilded pommels, daggers of Valyrian steel, striped tiger pelts and the skins of spotted cats, jade manticores and ancient Valyrian sphinxes, chests of nutmeg, cloves, and saffron, ivory tusks and the horns of unicorns, green and orange and yellow feathers from the Summer Sea, bolts of fine silk and shimmering samite . . . and yet all that was little and less, compared to this. *Now he has given them conquest, and they are his for good and all,* the captain thought. The taste was bitter on his tongue. *This was my victory, not his. Where was he? Back on Oakenshield, lazing in a castle. He stole my wife and he stole my throne, and now he steals my glory.*

Obedience came naturally to Victarion Greyjoy; he had been born to it. Growing to manhood in the shadow of his brothers, he had followed Balon dutifully in everything he did. Later, when Balon's sons were born, he had grown to accept that one day he would kneel to them as well, when one of them took his father's place upon the Seastone Chair. But the Drowned God had summoned Balon and his sons down to his watery halls, and Victarion could not call Euron "king" without tasting bile in his throat.

The wind was freshening, and his thirst was raging. After a battle he always wanted wine. He gave the deck to Nute and went below. In his cramped cabin aft, he found the dusky woman wet and ready; perhaps the battle had warmed her blood as well. He took her twice, in quick succession. When they were done there was blood smeared across her breasts and thighs and belly, but it was his blood, from the gash in his palm. The dusky woman washed it out for him with boiled vinegar.

"The plan was good, I grant him," Victarion said as she knelt beside him. "The Mander is open to us now, as it was of old." It was a lazy river, wide and slow and treacherous with snags and sandbars. Most seagoing vessels dared not sail beyond Highgarden, but longships with their shallow draughts could navigate as far upstream as Bitterbridge. In ancient days, the ironborn had boldly sailed the river road and plundered all along the Mander and its vassal streams . . . until the kings of the green hand had armed the fisherfolk on the four small islands off the Mander's mouth and named them his shields.

Two thousand years had passed, but in the watchtowers along their craggy shores, greybeards still kept the ancient vigil. At the first glimpse of longships the old men would light their beacon fires, and the call would leap from hill to hill and island to island. *Fear! Foes! Raiders! Raiders!* When the fisherfolk saw the fires burning on the high places they would put their nets and plows aside and take up their swords and axes. Their lords would rush from their castles, attended by their knights and men-at-arms. Warhorns would echo across the waters, from Greenshield and Greyshield, Oakenshield and Southshield, and their longships would come sliding out from moss-covered stone pens along the shores, oars flashing as they swarmed across the straits to seal the Mander and hound and harry the raiders upriver to their doom.

Euron had sent Torwold Browntooth and the Red Oarsman up the Mander with a dozen swift longships, so the lords of the Shield Islands would spill forth in pursuit. By the time his main fleet arrived, only a handful of fighting men remained to defend the isles themselves. The ironborn had come in on the evening tide, so the glare of the setting sun would keep them hidden from the greybeards in the watchtowers until it was too late. The wind was at their backs, as it had been all the way down from Old Wyk. It was whispered about the fleet that Euron's wizards had much and more to do with that, that the Crow's Eye appeased the Storm God with blood sacrifice.

How else would he have dared sail so far to the west, instead of following the shoreline as was the custom?

The ironborn ran their longships up onto the stony shingles and spilled out into the purple dusk with steel glimmering in their hands. By then the fires were burning in the high places, but few remained to take up arms. Greyshield, Greenshield, and Southshield fell before the sun came up. Oakenshield lasted half a day longer. And when the men of the Four Shields broke off their pursuit of Torwold and the Red Oarsman and turned downriver, they found the Iron Fleet waiting at the Mander's mouth.

"All fell out as Euron said it would," Victarion told the dusky woman as she bound up his hand with linen. "His wizards must have seen it." He had three aboard the *Silence*, Quellon Humble had confided in a whisper. Queer men and terrible, they were, but the Crow's Eye had made them slaves. "He still needs me to fight his battles, though," Victarion insisted. "Wizards may be well and good, but blood and steel win wars." The vinegar made his wound hurt worse than ever. He shoved the woman away and closed his fist, glowering. "Bring me wine."

He drank in the darkness, brooding on his brother. *If I do not strike the blow with mine own hand, am I still a kinslayer?* Victarion feared no man, but the Drowned God's curse gave him pause. *If another strikes him down at my command, will his blood still stain my hands?* Aeron Damphair would know the answer, but the priest was somewhere back on the Iron Islands, still hoping to raise the ironborn against their new-crowned king. *Nute the Barber can shave a man with a thrown axe from twenty yards away. And none of Euron's mongrels could stand against Wulfe One-Ear or Andrik the Unsmiling. Any of them could do it.* But what a man *can* do and what a man *will* do are two different things, he knew.

"Euron's blasphemies will bring down the Drowned God's wroth upon us all," Aeron had prophesied, back on Old Wyk. "We must stop him, brother. We are still of Balon's blood, are we not?"

"So is he," Victarion had said. "I like it no more than you, but Euron is the king. Your kingsmoot raised him up, and you put the driftwood crown upon his head yourself!"

"I placed the crown upon his head," said the priest, seaweed dripping in his hair, "and gladly will I wrest it off again and crown you in his stead. Only you are strong enough to fight him."

"The Drowned God raised him up," Victarion complained. "Let the Drowned God cast him down."

Aeron gave him a baleful look, the look that had been known to sour wells and make women barren. "It was not the god who spoke. Euron is known to keep wizards and foul sorcerers on that red ship of his. They sent some spell among us, so we could not hear the sea. The captains and the kings were drunk with all this talk of dragons."

"Drunk, and fearful of that horn. You heard the sound it made. It makes no matter. Euron is our king."

"Not mine," the priest declared. "The Drowned God helps bold men, not those who cower below their decks when the storm is rising. If you will not bestir yourself to remove the Crow's Eye from the Seastone Chair, I must take the task upon myself."

"How? You have no ships, no swords."

"I have my voice," the priest replied, "and the god is with me. Mine is the strength of the sea, a strength the Crow's Eye cannot hope to withstand. The waves may break upon the mountain, yet still they come, wave upon wave, and in the end only pebbles remain where once the mountain stood. And soon even the pebbles are swept away, to be ground beneath the sea for all eternity."

"Pebbles?" Victarion grumbled. "You are mad if you think to bring the Crow's Eye down with talk of waves and pebbles."

"The ironborn shall be waves," the Damphair said. "Not the great and lordly, but the simple folk, tillers of the soil and fishers of the sea. The captains and the kings raised Euron up, but the common folk shall tear him down. I shall go to Great Wyk, to Harlaw, to Orkmont, to Pyke itself. In every town and village shall my words be heard. *No godless man may sit the Seastone Chair!*" He shook his shaggy head and stalked back out into the night. When the sun came up the next day, Aeron Greyjoy had vanished from Old Wyk. Even his drowned men knew not where. They said the Crow's Eye only laughed when he was told.

But though the priest was gone, his dire warnings lingered.

Victarion found himself remembering Baelor Blacktyde's words as well. *"Balon was mad, Aeron is madder, and Euron is maddest of them all."* The young lord had tried to sail home after the kingsmoot, refusing to accept Euron as his liege. But the Iron Fleet had closed the bay, the habit of obedience was rooted deep in Victarion Greyjoy, and Euron wore the driftwood crown. *Nightflyer* was seized, Lord Blacktyde delivered to the king in chains. Euron's mutes and mongrels had cut him into seven parts, to feed the seven green land gods he worshiped.

As a reward for his leal service, the new-crowned king had given Victarion the dusky woman, taken off some slaver bound for Lys. "I want none of your leavings," he had told his brother scornfully, but when the Crow's Eye said that the woman would be killed unless he took her, he had weakened. Her tongue had been torn out, but elsewise she was undamaged, and beautiful besides, with skin as brown as oiled teak. Yet sometimes when he looked at her, he found himself remembering the first woman his brother had given him, to make a man of him.

Victarion wanted to use the dusky woman once again, but found himself unable. "Fetch me another skin of wine," he told her, "then get out." When she returned with a skin of sour red, the captain took it up on deck, where he could breathe the clean sea air. He drank half the skin and poured the rest into the sea for all the men who'd died.

The *Iron Victory* lingered for hours off the mouth of the Mander. As the greater part of the Iron Fleet got under way for Oakenshield, Victarion kept *Grief, Lord Dagon, Iron Wind,* and *Maiden's Bane* about him as a rear guard. They pulled survivors from the sea, and watched *Hardhand* sink slowly, dragged under by the wreck that she had rammed. By the time she vanished beneath the waters Victarion had the count he'd asked for. He had lost six ships, and captured eight-and-thirty. "It will serve," he told Nute. "To the oars. We return to Lord Hewett's Town."

His oarsmen bent their backs toward Oakenshield, and the iron captain went belowdecks once again. "I could kill him," he told the dusky woman. "Though it is a great sin to kill your king, and a worse one to kill your brother." He frowned. "Asha should have given me her voice." How could she have ever hoped to win the captains and the kings, her with her pinecones and her turnips? *Balon's blood is in her, but she is still a woman.* She had run after the kingsmoot. The night the driftwood crown was placed on Euron's head, she and her crew had melted away. Some small part of Victarion was glad she had. *If the girl keeps her wits about her, she will wed some northern lord and live with him in his castle, far from the sea and Euron Crow's Eye.*

"Lord Hewett's Town, Lord Captain," a crewman called.

Victarion rose. The wine had dulled the throbbing in his hand. Perhaps he would have Hewett's maester look at it, if the man had not been killed. He returned to deck as they came around a headland. The way Lord Hewett's castle sat above the harbor reminded him of Lordsport, though this town was twice as big. A score of longships prowled the waters beyond the port, the golden kraken writhing on their sails. Hundreds more were beached along the shingles and drawn up to the piers that lined the harbor. At a stone quay stood three great cogs and a dozen smaller ones, taking on plunder and provisions. Victarion gave orders for the *Iron Victory* to drop anchor. "Have a boat made ready."

The town seemed strangely still as they approached. Most of the shops and houses had been looted, as their smashed doors and broken shutters testified, but only the sept had been put to the torch. The streets were strewn with corpses, each with a small flock of carrion crows in attendance. A gang of sullen survivors moved amongst them, chasing off the black birds and tossing the dead into the back of a wagon for burial. The notion filled Victarion with disgust. No true son of the sea would want to rot beneath the ground. How would he ever find the Drowned God's watery halls, to drink and feast for all eternity?

The *Silence* was amongst the ships they passed. Victarion's gaze was drawn to the iron figurehead at her prow, the mouthless maiden with the windblown hair and outstretched arm. Her mother-of-pearl eyes seemed to follow him. *She had a mouth like any other woman, till the Crow's Eye sewed it shut.*

As they neared the shore, he noticed a line of women and children herded up onto the deck of one of the great cogs. Some had their hands bound behind their backs, and all wore loops of hempen rope about their necks. "Who are they?" he asked the men who helped tie up their boat.

"Widows and orphans. They're to be sold as slaves."

"Sold?" There were no slaves in the Iron Islands, only thralls. A thrall was bound to service, but he was not chattel. His children were born free, so long as they were given to the Drowned God. And thralls were never bought nor sold for gold. A man paid the iron price for thralls, or else had none. "They should be thralls, or salt wives," Victarion complained.

"It's by the king's decree," the man said.

"The strong have always taken from the weak," said Nute the Barber. "Thralls or slaves, it makes no matter. Their men could not defend them, so now they are ours, to do with as we will."

It is not the Old Way, he might have said, but there was no time. His victory had preceded him, and men were gathering round to offer congratulations. Victarion let them fawn, until one began to praise Euron's daring. "It is daring to sail out of sight of land, so no word of our coming could reach these islands before us," he growled, "but crossing half the world to hunt for dragons, that is something else." He did not wait for a reply, but shouldered through the press and on up to the keep.

Lord Hewett's castle was small but strong, with thick walls and studded oaken gates that evoked his House's ancient arms, an oak escutcheon studded with iron upon a field of undy blue and white. But it was the kraken of House Greyjoy that flew atop his green-roofed towers now, and they found the great gates burned and broken. On the ramparts walked ironborn with spears and axes, and some of Euron's mongrels too.

In the yard, Victarion came on Gorold Goodbrother and old Drumm, speaking quietly with Rodrik Harlaw. Nute the Barber gave a hoot at the sight of them. "Reader," he called out, "why is your face so long? Your misgivings were for nought. The day is ours, and ours the prize!"

Lord Rodrik's mouth puckered. "These rocks, you mean? All four together wouldn't make Harlaw. We have won some stones and trees and trinkets, and the enmity of House Tyrell."

"The roses?" Nute laughed. "What rose can harm the krakens of the deep? We have taken their shields from them, and smashed them all to pieces. Who will protect them now?"

"Highgarden," replied the Reader. "Soon enough all the power of the Reach will be marshaled against us, Barber, and then you may learn that some roses have steel thorns."

Drumm nodded, one hand on the hilt of his Red Rain. "Lord Tarly bears the greatsword Heartsbane, forged of Valyrian steel, and he is always in Lord Tyrell's van."

Victarion's hunger flared. "Let him come. I will take his sword for mine own, as your own forebear took Red Rain. Let them all come, and bring the Lannisters as well. A lion may be fierce enough on land, but at sea the kraken rules supreme." He would give half his teeth for the chance to try his axe against the Kingslayer or the Knight of Flowers. That was the sort of battle that he understood. The kinslayer was accursed in the eyes of gods and men, but the warrior was honored and revered.

"Have no fear, Lord Captain," said the Reader. "They will come. His Grace desires it. Why else would he have commanded us to let Hewett's ravens fly?"

"You read too much and fight too little," Nute said. "Your blood is milk." But the Reader made as if he had not heard.

A riotous feast was in progress when Victarion entered the hall. Ironborn filled the tables, drinking and shouting and jostling each other, boasting of the men that they had slain, the deeds that they had done, the prizes they had won. Many were bedecked with plunder. Left-Hand Lucas Codd and Quellon Humble had torn tapestries off the walls to serve as cloaks. Germund Botley wore a rope of pearls and garnets over his gilded Lannister breastplate. Andrik the Unsmiling staggered by with a woman under each arm; though he remained unsmiling, he had rings on every finger. Instead of trenchers carved from old stale bread, the captains were eating off solid silver platters.

Nute the Barber's face grew dark with anger as he looked about. "The Crow's Eye sends us forth to face the longships, whilst his own men take the castles and the villages and grab all the loot and women. What has he left for us?"

"We have the glory."

"Glory is good," said Nute, "but gold is better."

Victarion shrugged. "The Crow's Eye says we shall have all of Westeros. The Arbor, Oldtown, Highgarden . . . that's where you'll find your gold. But enough talk. I'm hungry."

By right of blood, Victarion might have claimed a seat on the dais, but he did not care to eat with Euron and his creatures. Instead, he chose a place by Ralf the Limper, the captain of the *Lord Quellon*. "A great victory, Lord Captain," said the Limper. "A victory worthy of a lordship. You should have an island."

Lord Victarion. Aye, and why not? It might not be the Seastone Chair, but it would be something.

Hotho Harlaw was across the table, sucking meat off a bone. He flicked it aside and hunched forward. "The Knight's to have Greyshield. My cousin. Did you hear?"

"No." Victarion looked across the hall, to where Ser Harras Harlaw sat drinking wine from a golden cup; a tall man, long-faced and austere. "Why would Euron give that one an island?"

Hotho held out his empty wine cup, and a pale young woman in a gown of blue velvet and gilt lace refilled it for him. "The Knight took Grimston by himself. He planted his standard beneath the castle and defied the Grimms to face him. One did, and then another, and another. He slew them all . . . well, near enough, two yielded. When the seventh man went down, Lord Grimm's septon decided the gods had spoken and surrendered the castle." Hotho laughed. "He'll be the Lord of Greyshield, and welcome to it. With him gone, I am the Reader's heir." He thumped his wine cup against his chest. "Hotho the Humpback, Lord of Harlaw."

"Seven, you say." Victarion wondered how Nightfall would fare against his axe. He had never fought a man armed with a Valyrian steel blade, though he had thrashed young Harras Harlaw many a time when both of them were young. As a boy, Harlaw had been fast friends with Balon's eldest son, Rodrik, who had died beneath the walls of Seagard.

The feast was good. The wine was of the best, and there was roast ox, rare and bloody, and stuffed ducks as well, and buckets of fresh crabs. The serving wenches wore fine woolens and plush velvets, the Lord Captain did not fail to note. He took them for scullions dressed up in the clothes of Lady Hewett and her ladies, until Hotho told him they *were* Lady Hewett and her ladies. It amused the Crow's Eye to make them wait and pour. There were eight of them: her ladyship herself, still handsome though grown somewhat stout, and seven younger women aged from twenty-five to ten, her daughters and good-daughters.

Lord Hewett himself sat in his accustomed place upon the dais, dressed in all his heraldic finery. His arms and legs had been tied to his chair, and a huge white radish shoved between his teeth so he could not speak . . . though he could see and hear. The Crow's Eye had claimed the place of honor at his lordship's right hand. A pretty, buxom girl of seventeen or eighteen years was in his lap, barefoot and disheveled, her arms around his neck. "Who is that?" Victarion asked the men around him.

"His lordship's bastard daughter," laughed Hotho. "Before Euron took the castle, she was made to wait at table on the rest and take her own meals with the servants."

Euron put his blue lips to her throat, and the girl giggled and whispered something in his ear. Smiling, he kissed her throat again. Her white skin was covered with red marks where his mouth had been; they made a rosy necklace about her neck and shoulders. Another whisper in his ear, and this time the Crow's Eye laughed aloud, then slammed his wine cup down for silence. "Good ladies," he called out to his highborn serving women, "Falia is concerned for your fine gowns. She would not have them stained with grease and wine and dirty groping fingers, since I have promised that she may choose her own clothes from your wardrobes after the feast. So you had best disrobe."

A roar of laughter washed over the great hall, and Lord Hewett's face turned so red that Victarion thought his head might burst. The women had no choice but to obey. The youngest one cried a little, but her mother comforted her and helped undo the laces down her back. Afterward, they continued to serve as before, moving along the tables with flagons full of wine to fill each empty cup, only now they did so naked.

He shames Hewett as he once shamed me, the captain thought, remembering how his wife had sobbed as he was beating her. The men of the Four Shields oft married one another, he knew, just as the ironborn did. One of these naked serving wenches might well be Ser Talbert Serry's wife. It was one thing to kill a foe, another to dishonor him. Victarion made a fist. His hand was bloody where his wound had soaked through the linen.

On the dais, Euron pushed aside his slattern and climbed upon the table. The captains began to bang their cups and stamp their feet upon the floor. *"EURON!"* they shouted. *"EURON! EURON! EURON!"* It was kingsmoot come again.

"I swore to give you Westeros," the Crow's Eye said when the tumult died away, "and here is your first taste. A morsel, nothing more . . . but we shall feast before the fall of night!" The torches along the walls were burning bright, and so was he, blue lips, blue eye, and all. "What the kraken grasps it does not loose. These isles were once ours, and now they are again . . . but we need strong men to hold them. So rise, Ser Harras Harlaw, Lord of Greyshield." The Knight stood, one hand upon Nightfall's moonstone pommel. "Rise, Andrik the Unsmiling, Lord of Southshield." Andrik shoved away his women and lurched to his feet, like a mountain rising sudden from the sea. "Rise, Maron Volmark, Lord of Greenshield." A beardless boy of six-and-ten years, Volmark stood hesitantly, looking like the lord of rabbits. "And rise, Nute the Barber, Lord of Oakenshield."

Nute's eyes grew wary, as if he feared he was the butt of some cruel jape. "A lord?" he croaked.

Victarion had expected the Crow's Eye to give the lordships to his own creatures, Stonehand and the Red Oarsman and Left-Hand Lucas Codd. *A king must needs be open-handed,* he tried to tell himself, but another voice whispered, *Euron's gifts are poisoned.* When he turned it over in his head, he saw it plain. *The Knight was the Reader's chosen heir, and Andrik the Unsmiling the strong right arm of Dunstan Drumm. Volmark is a callow boy, but he has Black Harren's blood in him through his mother. And the Barber . . .*

Victarion grabbed him by the forearm. "Refuse him!"

Nute looked at him as if he had gone mad. "Refuse him? Lands and lordship? Will *you* make me a lord?" He wrenched his arm away and stood, basking in the cheers.

And now he steals my men away, Victarion thought.

King Euron called to Lady Hewett for a fresh cup of wine and raised it high above his head. "Captains and kings, lift your cups to the Lords of the Four Shields!" Victarion drank with the rest. *There is no wine so sweet as wine taken from a foe.* Someone had told him that once. His father, or his brother Balon. *One day I shall drink your wine, Crow's Eye, and take from you all that you hold dear.* But was there anything Euron held dear?

"On the morrow, we prepare once more to sail," the king was saying. "Fill our casks anew with spring water, take every sack of grain and cask of beef, and as many sheep and goats as we can carry. The wounded who are still hale enough to pull an oar will row. The rest shall remain here, to help hold these isles for their new lords. Torwold and the Red Oarsman will soon be back with more provisions. Our decks will stink of pigs and chickens on the voyage east, but we'll return with dragons."

"*When?*" The voice was Lord Rodrik's. "When shall we return, Your Grace? A year? Three years? Five? Your dragons are a world away, and autumn is upon us." The Reader walked forward, sounding all the hazards. "Galleys guard the Redwyne Straits. The Dornish coast is dry and bleak, four hundred leagues of whirlpools, cliffs, and hidden shoals with hardly a safe landing anywhere. Beyond wait the Stepstones, with their storms and their nests of Lysene and Myrish pirates. If a thousand ships set sail, three hundred may reach the far side of the narrow sea . . . and then what? Lys will not welcome us, nor will Volantis. Where will you find fresh water, food? The first storm will scatter us across half the earth."

A smile played across Euron's blue lips. "I *am* the storm, my lord. The first storm, and the last. I have taken the *Silence* on longer voyages than this, and ones far more hazardous. Have you forgotten? I have sailed the Smoking Sea and seen Valyria."

Every man there knew that the Doom still ruled Valyria. The very sea there boiled and smoked, and the land was overrun with demons. It was said that any sailor who so much as glimpsed the fiery mountains of Valyria rising above the waves would soon die a dreadful death, yet the Crow's Eye had been there, and returned.

"Have you?" the Reader asked, so softly.

Euron's blue smile vanished. "Reader," he said into the quiet, "you would do well to keep your nose in your books."

Victarion could feel the unease in the hall. He pushed himself to his feet. "Brother," he boomed. "You have not answered Harlaw's questions."

Euron shrugged. "The price of slaves is rising. We will sell our slaves in Lys and Volantis. That, and the plunder we have taken here, will give us sufficient gold to buy provisions."

"Are we slavers now?" asked the Reader. "And for what? Dragons that no man here has seen? Shall we chase some drunken sailor's fancy to the far ends of the earth?"

His words drew mutters of assent. "Slaver's Bay is too far," called out Ralf the Limper. "And too close to Valyria," shouted Quellon Humble. Fralegg the Strong said, "Highgarden's close. I say, look for dragons there. The *golden* kind!" Alvyn Sharp said, "Why sail the world, when the Mander lies before us?" Red Ralf Stonehouse bounded to his feet. "Oldtown is richer, and the Arbor richer still. Redwyne's fleet is off away. We need only reach out our hand to pluck the ripest fruit in Westeros."

"Fruit?" The king's eye looked more black than blue. "Only a craven would steal a fruit when he could take the orchard."

"It is the Arbor we want," said Red Ralf, and other men took up the cry. The Crow's Eye let the shouts wash over him. Then he leapt down from the table, grabbed his slattern by the arm, and pulled her from the hall.

Fled, like a dog. Euron's hold upon the Seastone Chair suddenly did not seem as secure as it had a few moments before. *They will not follow him to Slaver's Bay. Perhaps they are not such dogs and fools as*

I had feared. That was such a merry thought that Victarion had to wash it down. He drained a cup with the Barber, to show him that he did not begrudge him his lordship, even if it came from Euron's hand.

Outside, the sun went down. Darkness gathered beyond the walls, but inside the torches burned with a ruddy orange glow, and their smoke gathered under the rafters like a grey cloud. Drunken men began to dance the finger dance. At some point, Left-Hand Lucas Codd decided he wanted one of Lord Hewett's daughters, so he took her on a table whilst her sisters screamed and sobbed.

Victarion felt a tap upon his shoulder. One of Euron's mongrel sons stood behind him, a boy of ten with woolly hair and skin the color of mud. "My father wishes words with you."

Victarion rose unsteadily. He was a big man, with a large capacity for wine, but even so, he had drunk too much. *I beat her to death with mine own hands,* he thought, *but the Crow's Eye killed her when he shoved himself inside her. I had no choice.* He followed the bastard boy from the hall and up a winding stone stair. The sounds of rape and revelry diminished as they climbed, until there was only the soft scrape of boots on stone.

The Crow's Eye had taken Lord Hewett's bedchamber along with his bastard daughter. When he entered, the girl was sprawled naked on the bed, snoring softly. Euron stood by the window, drinking from a silver cup. He wore the sable cloak he took from Blacktyde, his red leather eye patch, and nothing else. "When I was a boy, I dreamt that I could fly," he announced. "When I woke, I couldn't . . . or so the maester said. But what if he lied?"

Victarion could smell the sea through the open window, though the room stank of wine and blood and sex. The cold salt air helped to clear his head. "What do you mean?"

Euron turned to face him, his bruised blue lips curled in a half smile. "Perhaps we can fly. All of us. How will we ever know unless we leap from some tall tower?" The wind came gusting through the window and stirred his sable cloak. There was something obscene and disturbing about his nakedness. "No man ever truly knows what he can do unless he dares to leap."

"There is the window. Leap." Victarion had no patience for this. His wounded hand was troubling him. "What do you want?"

"The world." Firelight glimmered in Euron's eye. *His smiling eye.* "Will you take a cup of Lord Hewett's wine? There's no wine half so sweet as wine taken from a beaten foe."

"No." Victarion glanced away. "Cover yourself."

Euron seated himself and gave his cloak a twitch, so it covered his private parts. "I had forgotten what a small and noisy folk they are, my ironborn. I would bring them dragons, and they shout out for grapes."

"Grapes are real. A man can gorge himself on grapes. Their juice is sweet, and they make wine. What do dragons make?"

"Woe." The Crow's Eye sipped from his silver cup. "I once held a dragon's egg in this hand, brother. This Myrish wizard swore he could hatch it if I gave him a year and all the gold that he required. When I grew bored with his excuses, I slew him. As he watched his entrails sliding through his fingers, he said, '*But it has not been a year.*'" He laughed. "Cragorn's died, you know."

"Who?"

"The man who blew my dragon horn. When the maester cut him open, his lungs were charred as black as soot."

Victarion shuddered. "Show me this dragon's egg."

"I threw it in the sea during one of my dark moods." Euron gave a shrug. "It comes to me that the Reader was not wrong. Too large a fleet could never hold together over such a distance. The voyage is too long, too perilous. Only our finest ships and crews could hope to sail to Slaver's Bay and back. The Iron Fleet."

The Iron Fleet is mine, Victarion thought. He said nothing.

The Crow's Eye filled two cups with a strange black wine that flowed as thick as honey. "Drink with me, brother. Have a taste of this." He offered one of the cups to Victarion.

The captain took the cup Euron had not offered, sniffed at its contents suspiciously. Seen up close, it looked more blue than black. It was thick and oily, with a smell like rotted flesh. He tried a small swallow, and spit it out at once. "Foul stuff. Do you mean to poison me?"

"I mean to open your eyes." Euron drank deep from his own cup, and smiled. "*Shade-of-the-evening,* the wine of the warlocks. I came upon a cask of it when I captured a certain galleas out of Qarth, along with some cloves and nutmeg, forty bolts of green silk, and four warlocks who told a curious tale. One presumed to threaten me, so I killed him and fed him to the other three. They refused to eat of their friend's flesh at first, but when they grew hungry enough they had a change of heart. Men are meat."

Balon was mad, Aeron is madder, and Euron is maddest of them all. Victarion was turning to go when the Crow's Eye said, "A king must have a wife, to give him heirs. Brother, I have need of you. Will you go to Slaver's Bay and bring my love to me?"

I had a love once too. Victarion's hands coiled into fists, and a drop of blood fell to patter on the floor. *I should beat you raw and red and feed you to the crabs, the same as I did her.* "You have sons," he told his brother.

"Baseborn mongrels, born of whores and weepers."

"They are of your body."

"So are the contents of my chamber pot. None is fit to sit the Seastone Chair, much less the Iron Throne. No, to make an heir that's worthy of him, I need a different woman. When the kraken weds the dragon, brother, let all the world beware."

"What dragon?" said Victarion, frowning.

"The last of her line. They say she is the fairest woman in the world. Her hair is silver-gold, and her eyes are amethysts . . . but you need not take my word for it, brother. Go to Slaver's Bay, behold her beauty, and bring her back to me."

"Why should I?" Victarion demanded.

"For love. For duty. Because your king commands it." Euron chuckled. "And for the Seastone Chair. It is yours, once I claim the Iron Throne. You shall follow me as I followed Balon . . . and your own trueborn sons shall one day follow you."

My own sons. But to have a trueborn son a man must first have a wife. Victarion had no luck with wives. *Euron's gifts are poisoned,* he reminded himself, *but still . . .*

"The choice is yours, brother. Live a thrall or die a king. Do you dare to fly? Unless you take the leap, you'll never know."

Euron's smiling eye was bright with mockery. "Or do I ask too much of you? It is a fearsome thing to sail beyond Valyria."

"I could sail the Iron Fleet to hell if need be." When Victarion opened his hand, his palm was red with blood. "I'll go to Slaver's Bay, aye. I'll find this dragon woman, and I'll bring her back." *But not for you. You stole my wife and despoiled her, so I'll have yours. The fairest woman in the world, for me.*

JAIME

The fields outside the walls of Darry were being tilled once more. The burned crops had been plowed under, and Ser Addam's scouts reported seeing women in the furrows pulling weeds, whilst a team of oxen broke new ground on the edge of a nearby wood. A dozen bearded men with axes stood guard over them as they worked.

By the time Jaime and his column reached the castle, all of them had fled within the walls. He found Darry closed to him, just as Harrenhal had been. *A chilly welcome from mine own blood.*

"Sound the horn," he commanded. Ser Kennos of Kayce unslung the Horn of Herrock and let it wind. As he waited for a response from the castle, Jaime eyed the banner floating brown and crimson above his cousin's barbican. Lancel had taken to quartering the lion of Lannister with the Darry plowman, it would seem. He saw his uncle's hand in that, as in Lancel's choice of bride. House Darry had ruled these lands since the Andals cast down the First Men. No doubt, Ser Kevan realized that his son would have an easier time of it if the peasants saw him as a continuation of the old line, holding these lands by right of marriage rather than royal decree. *Kevan should be Tommen's Hand. Harys Swyft is a toad, and my sister is a fool if she thinks elsewise.*

The castle gates swung open slowly. "My coz will not have room to accommodate a thousand men," Jaime told Strongboar. "We'll make camp beneath the western wall. I want the perimeters ditched and staked. There are still bands of outlaws in these parts."

"They'd need to be mad to attack a force as strong as ours."

"Mad or starving." Until he had a better notion of these outlaws and their strength, Jaime was not inclined to take any risks with his defenses. "Ditched and staked," he said again, before spurring Honor toward the gate. Ser Dermot rode beside him with the royal stag and lion, and Ser Hugo Vance with the white standard of the Kingsguard. Jaime had charged Red Ronnet with the task of delivering Wylis Manderly to Maidenpool, so he would not need to look on him henceforth.

Pia rode with Jaime's squires, on the gelding Peck had found for her. "It's like some toy castle," Jaime heard her say. *She's known no home but Harrenhal,* he reflected. *Every castle in the realm will seem small to her, except the Rock.*

Josmyn Peckleton was saying the same thing. "You must not judge by Harrenhal. Black Harren built too big." Pia listened as solemnly as a girl of five being lessoned by her septa. *That's all she is, a little girl in a woman's body, scarred and scared.* Peck was taken with her, though. Jaime suspected that the boy had never known a woman, and Pia was still pretty enough, so long as she kept her mouth closed. *There's no harm in him bedding her, I suppose, so long as she's willing.*

One of the Mountain's men had tried to rape the girl at Harrenhal, and had seemed honestly perplexed when Jaime commanded Ilyn Payne to take his head off. "I had her before, a hunnerd times," he kept saying as they forced him to his knees. "A hunnerd times, m'lord. We all had her." When Ser Ilyn presented Pia with his head, she had smiled through her ruined teeth.

Darry had changed hands several times during the fighting, and its castle had been burned once and sacked at least twice, but Lancel had seemingly wasted little time setting things to rights. The castle gates were newly hung, raw oaken planks reinforced with iron studs. A new stable was going up where an older one had been put to the torch. The steps to the keep had been replaced, and the shutters on many of the windows. Blackened stones showed where the flames had licked, but time and rain would fade those.

Within the walls, crossbowmen walked the ramparts, some in crimson cloaks and lion-crested helms, others in the blue and grey of House Frey. As Jaime trotted across the yard, chickens ran out from under Honor's hooves, sheep bleated, and peasants stared at him with sullen eyes. *Armed peasants,* he did not fail to note. Some had scythes, some staves, some hoes sharpened to cruel points. There were axes in evidence as well, and he spied several bearded men with red, seven-pointed stars sewn onto ragged, filthy tunics. *More bloody sparrows. Where do they all come from?*

Of his uncle Kevan he saw no sign. Nor of Lancel. Only a maester emerged to greet him, with a grey robe flapping about his skinny legs. "Lord Commander, Darry is honored by this . . . unexpected visit. You must forgive our lack of preparations. We had been given to understand that you were bound for Riverrun."

"Darry was on my way," lied Jaime. *Riverrun will keep.* And if perchance the siege had ended before he reached the castle, he would be spared the need to take up arms against House Tully.

Dismounting, he handed Honor to a stableboy. "Will I find my uncle here?" He did not supply a name. Ser Kevan was the only uncle he had left, the last surviving son of Tytos Lannister.

"No, my lord. Ser Kevan took his leave of us after the wedding." The maester pulled at the chain collar, as if it had grown too tight for him. "I know Lord Lancel will be pleased to see you and . . . and all your gallant knights. Though it pains me to confess that Darry cannot feed so many."

"We have our own provisions. You are?"

"Maester Ottomore, if it please my lord. Lady Amerei wished to welcome you herself, but she is seeing to the preparation of a feast in your honor. It is her hope that you and your chief knights and captains will join us at table this evening."

"A hot meal would be most welcome. The days have been cold and wet." Jaime glanced about the yard, at the bearded faces of the sparrows. *Too many. And too many Freys as well.* "Where will I find Hardstone?"

"We had a report of outlaws beyond the Trident. Ser Harwyn took five knights and twenty archers and went to deal with them."

"And Lord Lancel?"

"He is at his prayers. His lordship has commanded us never to disturb him when he is praying."

He and Ser Bonifer should get on well. "Very well." There would be time enough to talk with his cousin later. "Show me to my chambers and have a bath brought up."

"If it please my lord, we have put you in the Plowman's Keep. I will show you there."

"I know the way." Jaime was no stranger to this castle. He and Cersei had been guests here twice before, once on their way to Winterfell with Robert, and again on the way back to King's Landing. Though small as castles went, it was larger than an inn, with good hunting along the river. Robert Baratheon had never been never loath to impose upon the hospitality of his subjects.

The keep was much as he recalled it. "The walls are still bare," Jaime observed as the maester led him down a gallery.

"Lord Lancel hopes one day to cover them with hangings," said Ottomore. "Scenes of piety and devotion."

Piety and devotion. It was all he could do not to laugh. The walls had been bare on his first visit too. Tyrion had pointed out the squares of darker stone where tapestries had once hung. Ser Raymun could remove the hangings, but not the marks they'd left. Later, the Imp had slipped a handful of stags to one of Darry's serving men for the key to the cellar where the missing tapestries were hidden. He showed them to Jaime by the light of a candle, grinning; woven portraits of all the Targaryen kings, from the first Aegon to the second Aerys. "If I tell Robert, mayhaps he'll make *me* Lord of Darry," the dwarf said, chortling.

Maester Ottomore led Jaime to the top of the keep. "I trust you will be comfortable here, my lord. There is a privy, when nature calls. Your window looks out upon the godswood. The bedchamber adjoins her ladyship's, with a servant's cell between."

"These were Lord Darry's own apartments."

"Yes, my lord."

"My cousin is too kind. I did not intend to put Lancel out of his own bedchamber."

"Lord Lancel has been sleeping in the sept."

Sleeping with the Mother and the Maiden, when he has a warm wife just through that door? Jaime did not know whether to laugh or weep. *Maybe he is praying for his cock to harden.* In King's Landing it had been rumored that Lancel's wounds had left him incapable. *Still, he ought to have sense enough to try.* His cousin's hold on his new lands would not be secure until he fathered a son on his half-Darry wife. Jaime had begun to rue the impulse that had brought him here. He gave thanks to Ottomore, reminded him about the bath, and had Peck see him out.

The lord's bedchamber had changed since his last visit, and not for the better. Old stale rushes covered the floor in place of the fine Myrish carpet that had been there previously, and all the furnishings were new and crudely made. Ser Raymun Darry's bed had been large enough to sleep six, with brown velvet draperies and oakwood posts carved with vines and leaves; Lancel's was a lumpy straw pallet, placed beneath the window where the first light of day would be sure to wake him. The other bed had no doubt been burned or smashed or stolen, but even so . . .

When the tub arrived, Little Lew pulled off Jaime's boots and helped remove his golden hand. Peck and Garrett hauled water, and Pia found him something clean to sup in. The girl glanced at him shyly as she shook his doublet out. Jaime was uncomfortably aware of the curve of hip and breast beneath her roughspun brown dress. He found himself remembering the things that Pia had whispered to him at Harrenhal, the night that Qyburn sent her to his bed. *Sometimes when I'm with some man,* she'd said, *I close my eyes and pretend it's you on top of me.*

He was grateful when the bath was deep enough to conceal his arousal. As he lowered himself into the steaming water, he recalled another bath, the one he'd shared with Brienne. He had been feverish and weak from loss of blood, and the heat had made him so dizzy he found himself saying things better left unsaid. This time he had no such excuse. *Remember your vows. Pia is more fit for Tyrion's bed than yours.* "Fetch me soap and a stiff brush," he told Peck. "Pia, you may leave us."

"Aye, m'lord. Thank you, m'lord." She covered her mouth when she spoke, to hide her broken teeth.

"Do you want her?" Jaime asked Peck, when she was gone.

The squire turned beet red.

"If she'll have you, take her. She'll teach you a few things you'll find useful on your wedding night, I don't doubt, and you're not like to get a bastard by her." Pia had spread her legs for half his father's army and never quickened; most like the girl was barren. "If you bed her, though, be kind to her."

"Kind, my lord? How . . . how would I . . . ?"

"Sweet words. Gentle touches. You don't want to wed her, but so long as you're abed treat her as you would your bride."

The lad nodded. "My lord, I . . . where should I take her? There's never a place to . . . to . . ."

". . . to be alone?" Jaime grinned. "We'll be at supper several hours. The straw looks lumpy, but it should serve."

Peck's eyes grew wide. "His lordship's bed?"

"You'll feel a lord yourself when you're done, if Pia knows her business." *And someone ought to make some use of that miserable straw mattress.*

When he descended for the feast that night, Jaime Lannister wore a doublet of red velvet slashed with cloth-of-gold, and a golden chain studded with black diamonds. He had strapped on his golden hand as well, polished to a fine bright sheen. This was no fit place to wear his whites. His duty awaited him at Riverrun; a darker need had brought him here.

Darry's great hall was great only by courtesy. Trestle tables crowded it from wall to wall, and the ceiling rafters were black with smoke. Jaime had been seated on the dais, to the right of Lancel's empty chair. "Will my cousin not be joining us for supper?" he asked as he sat down.

"My lord prefers to fast," said Lancel's wife, the Lady Amerei. "He's sick with grief for the poor High Septon." She was a long-legged, full-breasted, strapping girl of some eight-and-ten years; a healthy wench to look at her, though her pinched, chinless face reminded Jaime of his late and unlamented cousin Cleos, who had always looked somewhat like a weasel.

Fasting? He is an even bigger fool than I suspected. His cousin should be busy fathering a little weasel-faced heir on his widow instead of starving himself to death. He wondered what Ser Kevan might have had to say about his son's new fervor. Could that be the reason for his uncle's abrupt departure?

Over bowls of bean-and-bacon soup, Lady Amerei told Jaime how her first husband had been slain by Ser Gregor Clegane when the Freys were still fighting for Robb Stark. "I begged him not to go, but my Pate was oh so *very* brave, and swore he was the man to slay that monster. He wanted to make a great name for himself."

We all do. "When I was a squire I told myself I'd be the man to slay the Smiling Knight."

"The Smiling Knight?" She sounded lost. "Who was that?"

The Mountain of my boyhood. Half as big but twice as mad.

"An outlaw, long dead. No one who need concern your ladyship."

Amerei's lip trembled. Tears rolled from her brown eyes.

"You must forgive my daughter," said an older woman. Lady Amerei had brought a score of Freys to Darry with her; a sister, an uncle, a half uncle, various cousins . . . and her mother, who had been born a Darry. "She still grieves for her father."

"Outlaws *killed* him," sobbed Lady Amerei. "Father had only gone out to ransom Petyr Pimple. He brought them the gold they asked for, but they hung him anyway."

"*Hanged,* Ami. Your father was not a tapestry." Lady Mariya turned back to Jaime. "I believe you knew him, ser."

"We were squires together once, at Crakehall." He would not go so far as to claim they had been friends. When Jaime had arrived, Merrett Frey had been the castle bully, lording it over all the younger boys. *Then he tried to bully me.* "He was . . . very strong." It was the only praise that came to mind. Merrett had been slow and clumsy and stupid, but he *was* strong.

"You fought against the Kingswood Brotherhood together," sniffed Lady Amerei. "Father used to tell me stories."

Father used to boast and lie, you mean. "We did." Frey's chief contributions to the fight had consisted of contracting the pox from a camp follower and getting himself captured by the White Fawn. The outlaw queen burned her sigil into his arse before ransoming him back to Sumner Crakehall. Merrett had not been able to sit down for a fortnight, though Jaime doubted that the red-hot iron was half so nasty as the kettles of shit his fellow squires made him eat once he was returned. *Boys are the cruelest creatures on the earth.* He slipped his golden hand around his wine cup and raised it up. "To Merrett's memory," he said. It was easier to drink to the man than to talk of him.

After the toast, Lady Amerei stopped weeping and the table talk turned to wolves, of the four-footed kind. Ser Danwell Frey claimed there were more of them about than even his grandfather could remember. "They've lost all fear of men. Packs of them attacked our baggage train on our way down from the Twins. Our archers had to feather a dozen before the others fled." Ser Addam Marbrand confessed that their own column had faced similar troubles on their way up from King's Landing.

Jaime concentrated on the fare before him, tearing off chunks of bread with his left hand and fumbling at his wine cup with his right. He watched Addam Marbrand charm the girl beside him, watched Steffon Swyft refight the battle for King's Landing with bread and nuts and carrots. Ser Kennos pulled a serving girl into his lap, urging her to stroke his horn, whilst Ser Dermot regaled some squires with tales of knight errantry in the rainwood. Farther down the table, Hugo Vance had closed his eyes. *Brooding on the mysteries of life,* thought Jaime. *That, or napping between courses.* He turned back to Lady Mariya. "The outlaws who killed your husband . . . was it Lord Beric's band?"

"So we thought, at first." Though Lady Mariya's hair was streaked with grey, she was still a handsome woman. "The killers scattered when they left Oldstones. Lord Vypren tracked one band to Fairmarket, but lost them there. Black Walder led hounds and hunters into Hag's Mire after the others. The peasants denied seeing them, but when questioned sharply they sang a different song. They spoke of a one-eyed man and another who wore a yellow cloak . . . and a woman, cloaked and hooded."

"A woman?" He would have thought that the White Fawn would

have taught Merrett to stay clear of outlaw wenches. "There was a woman in the Kingswood Brotherhood as well."

"I know of her." *How not*, her tone suggested, *when she left her mark upon my husband?* "The White Fawn was young and fair, they say. This hooded woman is neither. The peasants would have us believe that her face was torn and scarred, and her eyes terrible to look upon. They claim she led the outlaws."

"Led them?" Jaime found that hard to believe. "Beric Dondarrion and the red priest . . ."

". . . were not seen." Lady Mariya sounded certain.

"Dondarrion's dead," said Strongboar. "The Mountain drove a knife through his eye, we have men with us who saw it."

"That's one tale," said Addam Marbrand. "Others will tell you that Lord Beric can't be killed."

"Ser Harwyn says those tales are lies." Lady Amerei wound a braid around her finger. "He has promised me Lord Beric's head. He's very gallant." She was blushing beneath her tears.

Jaime thought back on the head he'd given to Pia. He could almost hear his little brother chuckle. *Whatever became of giving women flowers?* Tyrion might have asked. He would have had a few choice words for Harwyn Plumm as well, though *gallant* would not have been one of them. Plumm's brothers were big, fleshy fellows with thick necks and red faces; loud and lusty, quick to laugh, quick to anger, quick to forgive. Harwyn was a different sort of Plumm; hard-eyed and taciturn, unforgiving . . . and deadly, with his hammer in his hand. A good man to command a garrison, but not a man to love. *Although* . . . Jaime gazed at Lady Amerei.

The serving men were bringing out the fish course, a river pike baked in a crust of herbs and crushed nuts. Lancel's lady tasted it, approved, and commanded that the first portion be served to Jaime. As they set the fish before him, she leaned across her husband's place to touch his golden hand. "*You* could kill Lord Beric, Ser Jaime. You slew the Smiley Knight. Please, my lord, I beg you, stay and help us with Lord Beric and the Hound." Her pale fingers caressed his golden ones.

Does she think that I can feel that? "The Sword of the Morning slew the Smiling Knight, my lady. Ser Arthur Dayne, a better knight than me." Jaime pulled back his golden fingers and turned once more to Lady Mariya. "How far did Black Walder track this hooded woman and her men?"

"His hounds picked up their scent again north of Hag's Mire," the older woman told him. "He swears that he was no more than half a day behind them when they vanished into the Neck."

"Let them rot there," declared Ser Kennos cheerfully. "If the gods are good, they'll be swallowed up in quicksand or gobbled down by lizard-lions."

"Or taken in by frogeaters," said Ser Danwell Frey. "I would not put it past the crannogmen to shelter outlaws."

"Would that it were only them," said Lady Mariya. "Some of the river lords are hand in glove with Lord Beric's men as well."

"The smallfolk too," sniffed her daughter. "Ser Harwyn says they hide them and feed them, and when he asks where they've gone, they lie. They *lie* to their own lords!"

"Have their tongues out," urged Strongboar.

"Good luck getting answers then," said Jaime. "If you want their help, you need to make them love you. That was how Arthur Dayne did it, when we rode against the Kingswood Brotherhood. He paid the smallfolk for the food we ate, brought their grievances to King Aerys, expanded the grazing lands around their villages, even won them the right to fell a certain number of trees each year and take a few of the king's deer during the autumn. The forest folk had looked to Toyne to defend them, but Ser Arthur did more for them than the Brotherhood could ever hope to do, and won them to our side. After that, the rest was easy."

"The Lord Commander speaks wisely," said Lady Mariya. "We shall never be rid of these outlaws until the smallfolk come to love Lancel as much as they once loved my father and grandfather."

Jaime glanced at his cousin's empty place. *Lancel will never win their love by praying, though.*

Lady Amerei put on a pout. "Ser Jaime, I pray you, do not abandon us. My lord has need of you, and so do I. These are such fearful times. Some nights I can hardly sleep, for fear."

"My place is with the king, my lady."

"I'll come," offered Strongboar. "Once we're done at Riverrun, I'll be itching for another fight. Not that Beric Dondarrion is like to give me one. I recall the man from tourneys past. A comely lad in a pretty cloak, he was. Slight and callow."

"That was before he died," said young Ser Arwood Frey. "Death changed him, the smallfolk say. You can kill him, but he won't stay dead. How do you fight a man like that? And there's the Hound as well. He slew twenty men at Saltpans."

Strongboar guffawed. "Twenty fat innkeeps, maybe. Twenty serving men pissing in their breeches. Twenty begging brothers armed with bowls. Not twenty knights. Not *me*."

"There is a knight at Saltpans," Ser Arwood insisted. "He hid behind his walls whilst Clegane and his mad dogs ravaged through his town. You have not seen the things he did, ser. I have. When the reports reached the Twins, I rode down with Harys Haigh and his brother Donnel and half a hundred men, archers and men-at-arms. We thought it was Lord Beric's work, and hoped to find his trail. All that remains of Saltpans is the castle, and old Ser Quincy so frightened he would not open his gates, but shouted down at us from his battlements. The rest is bones and ashes. A whole town. The Hound put the buildings to the torch and the people to the sword and rode off laughing. The women . . . you would not believe what he did to some of the women. I will not speak of it at table. It made me sick to see."

"I cried when I heard," said Lady Amerei.

Jaime sipped his wine. "What makes you certain it was the Hound?" What they were describing sounded more like Gregor's work than Sandor's. Sandor had been hard and brutal, yes, but it was his big brother who was the real monster in House Clegane.

"He was seen," Ser Arwood said. "That helm of his is not easily mistaken, nor forgotten, and there were a few who survived to tell the tale. The girl he raped, some boys who hid, a woman we found trapped beneath a blackened beam, the fisherfolk who watched the butchery from their boats . . ."

"Do not call it butchery," Lady Mariya said softly. "That gives insult

to honest butchers everywhere. Saltpans was the work of some fell
beast in human skin."

This is a time for beasts, Jaime reflected, *for lions and wolves and
angry dogs, for ravens and carrion crows.*

"Evil work." Strongboar filled his cup again. "Lady Mariya, Lady
Amerei, your distress has moved me. You have my word, once Riverrun
has fallen I shall return to hunt down the Hound and kill him for
you. Dogs do not frighten me."

This one should. Both men were large and powerful, but Sandor
Clegane was much quicker, and fought with a savagery that Lyle
Crakehall could not hope to match.

Lady Amerei was thrilled, however. "You are a true knight, Ser Lyle,
to help a lady in distress."

At least she did not call herself "a maiden." Jaime reached for his
cup and knocked it over. The linen tablecloth drank the wine. As the
red stain spread, his companions all pretended not to notice. *High
table courtesy,* he told himself, but it tasted just like pity. He rose
abruptly. "My lady. Pray excuse me."

Lady Amerei looked stricken. "Would you leave us? There's venison
to come, and capons stuffed with leeks and mushrooms."

"Very fine, no doubt, but I could not eat another bite. I need to
see my cousin." Bowing, Jaime left them to their food.

Men were eating in the yard as well. The sparrows had gathered
round a dozen cookfires to warm their hands against the chill of dusk
and watch fat sausages spit and sizzle above the flames. There had to
be a hundred of them. *Useless mouths.* Jaime wondered how many
sausages his cousin had laid by and how he intended to feed the
sparrows once they were gone. *They will be eating rats by winter, unless
they can get a harvest in.* This late in autumn, the chances of another
harvest were not good.

He found the sept off the castle's inner ward; a windowless, seven-
sided, half-timbered building with carved wood doors and a tiled
roof. Three sparrows sat upon its steps. When Jaime approached, they
rose. "Where you going, m'lord?" asked one. He was the smallest of
the three, but he had the biggest beard.

"Inside."

"His lordship's in there, praying."

"His lordship is my cousin."

"Well, then, m'lord," said a different sparrow, a huge bald man with a seven-pointed star painted over one eye, "you won't want to bother your cousin at his prayers."

"Lord Lancel is asking the Father Above for guidance," said the third sparrow, the beardless one. A boy, Jaime had thought, but her voice marked her for a woman, dressed in shapeless rags and a shirt of rusted mail. "He is praying for the soul of the High Septon and all the others who have died."

"They'll still be dead tomorrow," Jaime told her. "The Father Above has more time than I do. Do you know who I am?"

"Some lord," said the big man with the starry eye.

"Some cripple," said the small one with the big beard.

"The Kingslayer," said the woman, "but we're no kings, just Poor Fellows, and you can't go in unless his lordship says you can." She hefted a spiked club, and the small man raised an axe.

The doors behind them opened. "Let my cousin pass in peace, friends," Lancel said softly. "I have been expecting him."

The sparrows moved aside.

Lancel looked even thinner than he had at King's Landing. He was barefoot, and dressed in a plain, roughspun tunic of undyed wool that made him look more like a beggar than a lord. The crown of his head had been shaved smooth, but his beard had grown out a little. To call it peach fuzz would have given insult to the peach. It went queerly with the white hair around his ears.

"Cousin," said Jaime when they were alone within the sept, "have you lost your bloody wits?"

"I prefer to say I've found my faith."

"Where is your father?"

"Gone. We quarreled." Lancel knelt before the altar of his other Father. "Will you pray with me, Jaime?"

"If I pray nicely, will the Father give me a new hand?"

"No. But the Warrior will give you courage, the Smith will lend you strength, and the Crone will give you wisdom."

"It's a hand I need." The seven gods loomed above carved altars, the dark wood gleaming in the candlelight. A faint smell of incense hung in the air. "You sleep down here?"

"Each night I make my bed beneath a different altar, and the Seven send me visions."

Baelor the Blessed once had visions too. *Especially when he was fasting.* "How long has it been since you've eaten?"

"My faith is all the nourishment I need."

"Faith is like porridge. Better with milk and honey."

"I dreamed that you would come. In the dream you knew what I had done. How I'd sinned. You killed me for it."

"You're more like to kill yourself with all this fasting. Didn't Baelor the Blessed fast himself onto a bier?"

"Our lives are candle flames, says *The Seven-Pointed Star.* Any errant puff of wind can snuff us out. Death is never far in this world, and seven hells await sinners who do not repent their sins. Pray with me, Jaime."

"If I do, will you eat a bowl of porridge?" When his coz did not answer, Jaime sighed. "You should be sleeping with your wife, not with the Maid. You need a son with Darry blood if you want to keep this castle."

"A pile of cold stones. I never asked for it. I never wanted it. I only wanted . . ." Lancel shuddered. "Seven save me, but I wanted to be you."

Jaime had to laugh. "Better me than Blessed Baelor. Darry needs a lion, coz. So does your little Frey. She gets moist between the legs every time someone mentions Hardstone. If she hasn't bedded him yet, she will soon."

"If she loves him, I wish them joy of one another."

"A lion shouldn't have horns. You took the girl to wife."

"I said some words and gave her a red cloak, but only to please Father. Marriage requires consummation. King Baelor was made to wed his sister Daena, but they never lived as man and wife, and he put her aside as soon as he was crowned."

"The realm would have been better served if he had closed his eyes and fucked her. I know enough history to know that. In any case, you're not like to be taken for Baelor the Blessed."

"No," Lancel allowed. "He was a rare spirit, pure and brave and innocent, untouched by all the evils of the world. I am a sinner, with much and more to atone for."

Jaime put his hand on his cousin's shoulder. "What do you know of sin, coz? I killed my king."

"The brave man slays with a sword, the craven with a wineskin. We are both kingslayers, ser."

"Robert was no true king. Some might even say that a stag is a lion's natural prey." Jaime could feel the bones beneath his cousin's skin . . . and something else as well. Lancel was wearing a hair shirt underneath his tunic. "What else did you do, to require so much atonement? Tell me."

His cousin bowed his head, tears running down his cheeks.

Those tears were all the answer Jaime needed. "You killed the king," he said, "then you fucked the queen."

"I never . . ."

". . . lay with my sweet sister?" *Say it. Say it!*

"Never spilled my seed in . . . in her . . ."

". . . cunt?" suggested Jaime.

". . . womb," Lancel finished. "It is not treason unless you finish inside. I gave her comfort, after the king died. You were a captive, your father was in the field, and your brother . . . she was afraid of him, and with good reason. He made me betray her."

"Did he?" *Lancel and Ser Osmund and how many more? Was the part about Moon Boy just a gibe?* "Did you force her?"

"*No!* I loved her. I wanted to protect her."

You wanted to be me. His phantom fingers itched. The day his sister had come to White Sword Tower to beg him to renounce his vows, she had laughed after he refused her and boasted of having lied to him a thousand times. Jaime had taken that for a clumsy attempt to hurt him as he'd hurt her. *It may have been the only true thing that she ever said to me.*

"Do not think ill of the queen," Lancel pleaded. "All flesh is weak, Jaime. No harm came of our sin. No . . . no bastard."

"No. Bastards are seldom made upon the belly." He wondered what his cousin would say if he were to confess his own sins, the three treasons Cersei had named Joffrey, Tommen, and Myrcella.

"I was angry with Her Grace after the battle, but the High Septon said I must forgive her."

"You confessed your sins to His High Holiness, did you?"

"He prayed for me when I was wounded. He was a good man."

He's a dead man. They rang the bells for him. He wondered if his cousin had any notion what fruit his words had borne. "Lancel, you're a bloody fool."

"You are not wrong," said Lancel, "but my folly is behind me, ser. I have asked the Father Above to show me the way, and he has. I am renouncing this lordship and this wife. Hardstone is welcome to the both of them, if he likes. On the morrow I will return to King's Landing and swear my sword to the new High Septon and the Seven. I mean to take vows and join the Warrior's Sons."

The boy was not making sense. "The Warrior's Sons were proscribed three hundred years ago."

"The new High Septon has revived them. He's sent out a call for worthy knights to pledge their lives and swords to the service of the Seven. The Poor Fellows are to be restored as well."

"Why would the Iron Throne allow that?" One of the early Targaryen kings had fought for years to suppress the two military orders, Jaime recalled, though he did not remember which. Maegor, perhaps, or the first Jaehaerys. *Tyrion would have known.*

"His High Holiness writes that King Tommen has given his consent. I will show you the letter, if you like."

"Even if this is true . . . you are a lion of the Rock, a *lord*. You have a wife, a castle, lands to defend, people to protect. If the gods are good, you will have sons of your blood to follow you. Why would you throw all that away for . . . for some vow?"

"Why did you?" asked Lancel softly.

For honor, Jaime might have said. *For glory.* That would have been a lie, though. Honor and glory had played their parts, but most of it had been for Cersei. A laugh escaped his lips. "Is it the High Septon you're running to, or my sweet sister? Pray on that one, coz. Pray *hard*."

"Will you pray with me, Jaime?"

He glanced about the sept, at the gods. The Mother, full of mercy. The Father, stern in judgment. The Warrior, one hand upon his sword. The Stranger in the shadows, his half-human face concealed beneath a hooded mantle. *I thought that I was the Warrior and Cersei was the Maid, but all the time she was the Stranger, hiding her true face from my gaze.* "Pray for me, if you like," he told his cousin. "I've forgotten all the words."

The sparrows were still fluttering about the steps when Jaime stepped back out into the night. "Thank you," he told them. "I feel ever so much holier now."

He went and found Ser Ilyn and a pair of swords.

The castle yard was full of eyes and ears. To escape them, they sought out Darry's godswood. There were no sparrows there, only trees bare and brooding, their black branches scratching at the sky. A mat of dead leaves crunched beneath their feet.

"Do you see that window, ser?" Jaime used a sword to point. "That was Raymun Darry's bedchamber. Where King Robert slept, on our return from Winterfell. Ned Stark's daughter had run off after her wolf savaged Joff, you'll recall. My sister wanted the girl to lose a hand. The old penalty, for striking one of the blood royal. Robert told her she was cruel and mad. They fought for half the night . . . well, Cersei fought, and Robert drank. Past midnight, the queen summoned me inside. The king was passed out snoring on the Myrish carpet. I asked my sister if she wanted me to carry him to bed. She told me I should carry her to bed, and shrugged out of her robe. I took her on Raymun Darry's bed after stepping over Robert. If His Grace had woken I would have killed him there and then. He would not have been the first king to die upon my sword . . . but you know that story, don't you?" He slashed at a tree branch, shearing it in half. "As I was fucking her, Cersei cried, 'I *want.*' I thought that she meant me, but it was the Stark girl that she wanted, maimed or dead." *The things I do for love.* "It was only by chance that Stark's own men found the girl before me. If I had come on her first . . ."

The pockmarks on Ser Ilyn's face were black holes in the torchlight, as dark as Jaime's soul. He made that clacking sound.

He is laughing at me, realized Jaime Lannister. "For all I know, you fucked my sister too, you pock-faced bastard," he spat out. "Well, shut your bloody mouth and kill me if you can."

BRIENNE

The septry stood upon an upthrust island half a mile from the shore, where the wide mouth of the Trident widened further still to kiss the Bay of Crabs. Even from shore its prosperity was apparent. Its slope was covered with terraced fields, with fishponds down below and a windmill above, its wood-and-sailcloth blades turning slowly in the breeze off the bay. Brienne could see sheep grazing on the hillside and storks wading in the shallow waters around the ferry landing.

"Saltpans is just across the water," said Septon Meribald, pointing north across the bay. "The brothers will ferry us over on the morning tide, though I fear what we shall find there. Let us enjoy a good hot meal before we face that. The brothers always have a bone to spare for Dog." Dog barked and wagged his tail.

The tide was going out now, and swiftly. The water that separated the island from the shore was receding, leaving behind a broad expanse of glistening brown mudflats dotted by tidal pools that glittered like golden coins in the afternoon sun. Brienne scratched the back of her neck, where an insect had bitten her. She had pinned her hair up, and the sun had warmed her skin.

"Why do they call it the Quiet Isle?" asked Podrick.

"Those who dwell here are penitents, who seek to atone for their sins through contemplation, prayer, and silence. Only the Elder

Brother and his proctors are permitted to speak, and the proctors only for one day of every seven."

"The silent sisters never speak," said Podrick. "I heard they don't have any tongues."

Septon Meribald smiled. "Mothers have been cowing their daughters with that tale since I was your age. There was no truth to it then and there is none now. A vow of silence is an act of contrition, a sacrifice by which we prove our devotion to the Seven Above. For a mute to take a vow of silence would be akin to a legless man giving up the dance." He led his donkey down the slope, beckoning them to follow. "If you would sleep beneath a roof tonight, you must climb off your horses and cross the mud with me. The path of faith, we call it. Only the faithful may cross safely. The wicked are swallowed by the quicksands, or drowned when the tide comes rushing in. None of you are wicked, I hope? Even so, I would be careful where I set my feet. Walk only where I walk, and you shall reach the other side."

The path of faith was a crooked one, Brienne could not help but note. Though the island seemed to rise to the northeast of where they left the shore, Septon Meribald did not make directly for it. Instead, he started due east, toward the deeper waters of the bay, which shimmered blue and silver in the distance. The soft brown mud squished up between his toes. As he walked he paused from time to time, to probe ahead with his quarterstaff. Dog stayed near his heels, sniffing at every rock, shell, and clump of seaweed. For once he did not bound ahead or stray.

Brienne followed, taking care to keep close to the line of prints left by the dog, the donkey, and the holy man. Then came Podrick, and last of all Ser Hyle. A hundred yards out, Meribald turned abruptly toward the south, so his back was almost to the septry. He proceeded in that direction for another hundred yards, leading them between two shallow tidal pools. Dog stuck his nose in one and yelped when a crab pinched it with his claw. A brief but furious struggle ensued before the dog came trotting back, wet and mud-spattered, with the crab between his jaws.

"Isn't *that* where we want to go?" Ser Hyle called out from behind them, pointing at the septry. "We seem to be walking every way but toward it."

"Faith," urged Septon Meribald. "Believe, persist, and follow, and we shall find the peace we seek."

The flats shimmered wetly all about them, mottled in half a hundred hues. The mud was such a dark brown it appeared almost black, but there were swathes of golden sand as well, upthrust rocks both grey and red, and tangles of black and green seaweed. Storks stalked through the tidal pools and left their footprints all around them, and crabs scuttled across the surface of shallow waters. The air smelled of brine and rot, and the ground sucked at their feet and let them go only reluctantly, with a pop and a squelchy sigh. Septon Meribald turned and turned again and yet again. His footprints filled up with water as soon as he moved on. By the time the ground grew firmer and began to rise beneath the feet, they had walked at least a mile and a half.

Three men were waiting for them as they clambered up the broken stones that ringed the isle's shoreline. They were clad in the brown-and-dun robes of brothers, with wide bell sleeves and pointed cowls. Two had wound lengths of wool about the lower halves of their faces as well, so all that could be seen of them were their eyes. The third brother was the one to speak. "Septon Meribald," he called. "It has been nigh upon a year. You are welcome. Your companions as well."

Dog wagged his tail, and Meribald shook mud from his feet. "Might we beg your hospitality for a night?"

"Yes, of course. There's to be fish stew this evening. Will you require the ferry in the morning?"

"If it is not too much to ask." Meribald turned to his fellow travelers. "Brother Narbert is a proctor of the order, so he is allowed to speak one day of every seven. Brother, these good folk helped me on my way. Ser Hyle Hunt is a gallant from the Reach. The lad is Podrick Payne, late of the westerland. And this is Lady Brienne, known as the Maid of Tarth."

Brother Narbert drew up short. "A woman."

"Yes, brother." Brienne unpinned her hair and shook it out. "Do you have no women here?"

"Not at present," said Narbert. "Those women who do visit come to us sick or hurt, or heavy with child. The Seven have blessed our

Elder Brother with healing hands. He has restored many a man to health that even the maesters could not cure, and many a woman too."

"I am not sick or hurt or heavy with child."

"Lady Brienne is a warrior maid," confided Septon Meribald, "hunting for the Hound."

"Aye?" Narbert seemed taken aback. "To what end?"

Brienne touched Oathkeeper's hilt. "His," she said.

The proctor studied her. "You are . . . brawny for a woman, it is true, but . . . mayhaps I should take you up to Elder Brother. He will have seen you crossing the mud. Come."

Narbert led them along a pebbled path and through a grove of apple trees to a whitewashed stable with a peaked thatch roof. "You may leave your animals here. Brother Gillam will see that they are fed and watered."

The stable was more than three-quarters empty. At one end were half a dozen mules, being tended by a bandy-legged little brother whom Brienne took for Gillam. Way down at the far end, well away from the other animals, a huge black stallion trumpeted at the sound of their voices and kicked at the door of his stall.

Ser Hyle gave the big horse an admiring look as he was handing his reins to Brother Gillam. "A handsome beast."

Brother Narbert sighed. "The Seven send us blessings, and the Seven send us trials. Handsome he may be, but Driftwood was surely whelped in hell. When we sought to harness him to a plow he kicked Brother Rawney and broke his shinbone in two places. We had hoped gelding might improve the beast's ill temper, but . . . Brother Gillam, will you show them?"

Brother Gillam lowered his cowl. Underneath he had a mop of blond hair, a tonsured scalp, and a bloodstained bandage where he should have had an ear.

Podrick gasped. "The horse bit off your *ear?*"

Gillam nodded, and covered his head again.

"Forgive me, brother," said Ser Hyle, "but I might take the other ear, if you approached me with a pair of shears."

The jest did not sit well with Brother Narbert. "You are a knight, ser. Driftwood is a beast of burden. The Smith gave men horses to help them in their labors." He turned away. "If you will. Elder Brother will no doubt be waiting."

The slope was steeper than it had looked from across the mudflats. To ease it, the brothers had erected a flight of wooden steps that wandered back and forth across the hillside and amongst the buildings. After a long day in the saddle Brienne was glad for a chance to stretch her legs.

They passed a dozen brothers of the order on their way up; cowled men in dun-and-brown who gave them curious looks as they went by, but spoke no word of greeting. One was leading a pair of milk cows toward a low barn roofed in sod; another worked a butter churn. On the upper slopes they saw three boys driving sheep, and higher still they passed a lichyard where a brother bigger than Brienne was struggling to dig a grave. From the way he moved, it was plain to see that he was lame. As he flung a spadeful of the stony soil over one shoulder, some chanced to spatter against their feet. "Be more watchful there," chided Brother Narbert. "Septon Meribald might have gotten a mouthful of dirt." The gravedigger lowered his head. When Dog went to sniff him he dropped his spade and scratched his ear.

"A novice," explained Narbert.

"Who is the grave for?" asked Ser Hyle, as they resumed their climb up the wooden steps.

"Brother Clement, may the Father judge him justly."

"Was he old?" asked Podrick Payne.

"If you consider eight-and-forty old, aye, but it was not the years that killed him. He died of wounds he got at Saltpans. He had taken some of our mead to the market there, on the day the outlaws descended on the town."

"The Hound?" said Brienne.

"Another, just as brutal. He cut poor Clement's tongue out when he would not speak. Since he had taken a vow of silence, the raider said he had no need of it. The Elder Brother will know more. He keeps the worst of the tidings from outside to himself, so as not to disturb the tranquillity of the septry. Many of our brothers came here to escape the horrors of the world, not to dwell upon them. Brother

Clement was not the only wounded man amongst us. Some wounds do not show." Brother Narbert gestured to their right. "There lies our summer arbor. The grapes are small and tart, but make a drinkable wine. We brew our own ale as well, and our mead and cider are far famed."

"The war has never come here?" Brienne said.

"Not this war, praise the Seven. Our prayers protect us."

"And your tides," suggested Meribald. Dog barked agreement.

The brow of the hill was crowned by a low wall of unmortared stone, encircling a cluster of large buildings; the windmill, its sails creaking as they turned, the cloisters where the brothers slept and the common hall where they took their meals, a wooden sept for prayer and meditation. The sept had windows of leaded glass, wide doors carved with likenesses of the Mother and the Father, and a seven-sided steeple with a walk on top. Behind it was a vegetable garden where some older brothers were pulling weeds. Brother Narbert led the visitors around a chestnut tree to a wooden door set in the side of the hill.

"A cave with a door?" Ser Hyle said, surprised.

Septon Meribald smiled. "It is called the Hermit's Hole. The first holy man to find his way here lived therein, and worked such wonders that others came to join him. That was two thousand years ago, they say. The door came somewhat later."

Perhaps two thousand years ago, the Hermit's Hole had been a damp, dark place, floored with dirt and echoing to the sounds of dripping water, but no longer. The cave that Brienne and her companions entered had been turned into a warm, snug sanctum. Woolen carpets covered the ground, tapestries the walls. Tall beeswax candles gave more than ample light. The furnishings were strange but simple; a long table, a settle, a chest, several tall cases full of books, and chairs. All were made from driftwood, oddly shaped pieces cunningly joined together and polished till they shone a deep gold in the candlelight.

The Elder Brother was not what Brienne had expected. He could hardly be called *elder*, for a start; whereas the brothers weeding in the garden had had the stooped shoulders and bent backs of old men, he stood straight and tall, and moved with the vigor of a man in the prime of his years. Nor did he have the gentle, kindly face she expected of a healer. His head was large and square, his eyes shrewd, his nose veined and red. Though he wore a tonsure, his scalp was as stubbly as his heavy jaw.

He looks more like a man made to break bones than to heal one, thought the Maid of Tarth, as the Elder Brother strode across the room to embrace Septon Meribald and pat Dog. "It is always a glad day when our friends Meribald and Dog honor us with another visit," he announced, before turning to his other guests. "And new faces are always welcome. We see so few of them."

Meribald performed the customary courtesies before seating himself upon the settle. Unlike Septon Narbert, the Elder Brother did not seem dismayed by Brienne's sex, but his smile did flicker and fade when the septon told him why she and Ser Hyle had come. "I see," was all he said, before he turned away with, "You must be thirsty. Please, have some of our sweet cider to wash the dust of travel from your throats." He poured for them himself. The cups were carved from driftwood too, no two the same. When Brienne complimented them, he said, "My lady is too kind. All we do is cut and polish the wood. We are blessed here. Where the river meets the bay, the currents and the tides wrestle one against the other, and many strange and wondrous things are pushed toward us, to wash up on our shores. Driftwood is the least of it. We have found silver cups and iron pots, sacks of wool and bolts of silk, rusted helms and shining swords . . . aye, and rubies."

That interested Ser Hyle. "Rhaegar's rubies?"

"It may be. Who can say? The battle was long leagues from here, but the river is tireless and patient. Six have been found. We are all waiting for the seventh."

"Better rubies than bones." Septon Meribald was rubbing his foot, the mud flaking off beneath his finger. "Not all the river's gifts are pleasant. The good brothers collect the dead as well. Drowned cows, drowned deer, dead pigs swollen up to half the size of horses. Aye, and corpses."

"Too many corpses, these days." The Elder Brother sighed. "Our gravedigger knows no rest. Rivermen, westermen, northmen, all wash up here. Knights and knaves alike. We bury them side by side, Stark and Lannister, Blackwood and Bracken, Frey and Darry. That is the duty the river asks of us in return for all its gifts, and we do it as best we can. Sometimes we find a woman, though . . . or worse, a little child. Those are the cruelest gifts." He turned to Septon Meribald. "I hope that you have time to absolve us of our sins. Since the raiders slew old Septon Bennet, we have had no one to hear confession."

"I shall make time," said Meribald, "though I hope you have some better sins than the last time I came through." Dog barked. "You see? Even Dog was bored."

Podrick Payne was puzzled. "I thought no one could talk. Well, not no one. The brothers. The other brothers, not you."

"We are allowed to break silence when confessing," said the Elder Brother. "It is hard to speak of sin with signs and nods."

"Did they burn the sept at Saltpans?" asked Hyle Hunt.

The smile vanished. "They burned everything at Saltpans, save the castle. Only that was made of stone . . . though it had as well been made of suet for all the good it did the town. It fell to me to treat some of the survivors. The fisherfolk brought them across the bay to me after the flames had gone out and they deemed it safe to land. One poor woman had been raped a dozen times, and her breasts . . . my lady, you wear man's mail, so I shall not spare you these horrors . . . her breasts had been torn and chewed and *eaten,* as if by some . . . cruel beast. I did what I could for her, though that was little enough. As she lay dying, her worst curses were not for the men who had raped her, nor the monster who devoured her living flesh, but for Ser Quincy Cox, who barred his gates when the outlaws entered the town and sat safe behind stone walls as his people screamed and died."

"Ser Quincy is an old man," said Septon Meribald gently. "His sons and good-sons are far away or dead, his grandsons are still boys, and he has two daughters. What could he have done, one man against so many?"

He could have tried, Brienne thought. *He could have died. Old or young, a true knight is sworn to protect those who are weaker than himself, or die in the attempt.*

"True words, and wise," the Elder Brother said to Septon Meribald.

"When you cross to Saltpans, no doubt Ser Quincy will ask you for forgiveness. I am glad that you are here to give it. I could not." He put aside the driftwood cup, and stood. "The supper bell will sound soon. My friends, will you come with me to the sept, to pray for the souls of the good folk of Saltpans before we sit down to break bread and share some meat and mead?"

"Gladly," said Meribald. Dog barked.

Their supper in the septry was as strange a meal as Brienne had ever eaten, though not at all unpleasant. The food was plain, but very good; there were loaves of crusty bread still warm from the ovens, crocks of fresh-churned butter, honey from the septry's hives, and a thick stew of crabs, mussels, and at least three different kinds of fish. Septon Meribald and Ser Hyle drank the mead the brothers made, and pronounced it excellent, whilst she and Podrick contented themselves with more sweet cider. Nor was the meal a somber one. Meribald pronounced a prayer before the food was served, and whilst the brothers ate at four long trestle tables, one of their number played for them on the high harp, filling the hall with soft sweet sounds. When the Elder Brother excused the musician to take his own meal, Brother Narbert and another proctor took turns reading from *The Seven-Pointed Star*.

By the time the readings were completed, the last of the food had been cleared away by the novices whose task it was to serve. Most were boys near Podrick's age, or younger, but there were grown men as well, amongst them the big gravedigger they had encountered on the hill, who walked with the awkward lurching gait of one half-crippled. As the hall emptied, the Elder Brother asked Narbert to show Podrick and Ser Hyle to their pallets in the cloisters. "You will not mind sharing a cell, I hope? It is not large, but you will find it comfortable."

"I want to stay with ser," said Podrick. "I mean, my lady."

"What you and Lady Brienne may do elsewhere is between you and the Seven," said Brother Narbert, "but on the Quiet Isle, men and women do not sleep beneath the same roof unless they are wed."

"We have some modest cottages set aside for the women who visit us, be they noble ladies or common village girls," said the Elder

Brother. "They are not oft used, but we keep them clean and dry. Lady Brienne, would you allow me to show you the way?"

"Yes, thank you. Podrick, go with Ser Hyle. We are guests of the holy brothers here. Beneath their roof, their rules."

The women's cottages were on the east side of the isle, looking out over a broad expanse of mud and the distant waters of the Bay of Crabs. It was colder here than on the sheltered side, and wilder. The hill was steeper, and the path meandered back and forth through weeds and briars, wind-carved rocks, and twisted, thorny trees that clung tenaciously to the stony hillside. The Elder Brother brought a lantern to light their way down. At one turn he paused. "On a clear night, you could see the fires of Saltpans from here. Across the bay, just there." He pointed.

"There's nothing," Brienne said.

"Only the castle remains. Even the fisherfolk are gone, the fortunate few who were out on the water when the raiders came. They watched their houses burn and listened to screams and cries float across the harbor, too fearful to land their boats. When at last they came ashore, it was to bury friends and kin. What is there for them at Saltpans now but bones and bitter memories? They have moved to Maidenpool or other towns." He gestured with the lantern, and they resumed their descent. "Saltpans was never an important port, but ships did call there from time to time. That was what the raiders wanted, a galley or a cog to carry them across the narrow sea. When none was at hand, they took their rage and desperation out upon the townsfolk. I wonder, my lady . . . what do you hope to find there?"

"A girl," she told him. "A highborn maid of three-and-ten, with a fair face and auburn hair."

"Sansa Stark." The name was softly said. "You believe this poor child is with the Hound?"

"The Dornishman said that she was on her way to Riverrun. Timeon. He was a sellsword, one of the Brave Companions, a killer and a raper and a liar, but I do not think he lied about this. He said that the Hound stole her and carried her away."

"I see." The path turned, and there were the cottages ahead of them. The Elder Brother had called them modest. That they were.

They looked like beehives made of stone, low and rounded, windowless. "This one," he said, indicating the nearest cottage, the only one with smoke rising from the smokehole in the center of its roof. Brienne had to duck when entering to keep from banging her head against the lintel. Inside she found a dirt floor, a straw pallet, furs and blankets to keep her warm, a basin of water, a flagon of cider, some bread and cheese, a small fire, and two low chairs. The Elder Brother sat in one, and put the lantern down. "May I stay a while? I feel that we should talk."

"If you wish." Brienne undid her swordbelt and hung it from the second chair, then sat cross-legged on the pallet.

"Your Dornishman did not lie," the Elder Brother began, "but I fear you did not understand him. You are chasing the wrong wolf, my lady. Eddard Stark had two daughters. It was the other one that Sandor Clegane made off with, the younger one."

"*Arya* Stark?" Brienne stared open-mouthed, astonished. "You know this? Lady Sansa's sister is alive?"

"Then," said the Elder Brother. "Now . . . I do not know. She may have been amongst the children slain at Saltpans."

The words were a knife in her belly. *No,* Brienne thought. *No, that would be too cruel.* "*May* have been . . . meaning that you are not certain . . .?"

"I am certain that the child was with Sandor Clegane at the inn beside the crossroads, the one old Masha Heddle used to keep, before the lions hanged her. I am certain they were on their way to Saltpans. Beyond that . . . no. I do not know where she is, or even if she lives. There is one thing I do know, however. The man you hunt is dead."

That was another shock. "How did he die?"

"By the sword, as he had lived."

"You know this for a certainty?"

"I buried him myself. I can tell you where his grave lies, if you wish. I covered him with stones to keep the carrion eaters from digging up his flesh, and set his helm atop the cairn to mark his final resting place. That was a grievous error. Some other wayfarer found my marker and claimed it for himself. The man who raped and killed at Saltpans was not Sandor Clegane, though he may be as dangerous.

The riverlands are full of such scavengers. I will not call them wolves. Wolves are nobler than that . . . and so are dogs, I think.

"I know a little of this man, Sandor Clegane. He was Prince Joffrey's sworn shield for many a year, and even here we would hear tell of his deeds, both good and ill. If even half of what we heard was true, this was a bitter, tormented soul, a sinner who mocked both gods and men. He served, but found no pride in service. He fought, but took no joy in victory. He drank, to drown his pain in a sea of wine. He did not love, nor was he loved himself. It was hate that drove him. Though he committed many sins, he never sought forgiveness. Where other men dream of love, or wealth, or glory, this man Sandor Clegane dreamed of slaying his own brother, a sin so terrible it makes me shudder just to speak of it. Yet that was the bread that nourished him, the fuel that kept his fires burning. Ignoble as it was, the hope of seeing his brother's blood upon his blade was all this sad and angry creature lived for . . . and even that was taken from him, when Prince Oberyn of Dorne stabbed Ser Gregor with a poisoned spear."

"You sound as if you pity him," said Brienne.

"I did. You would have pitied him as well, if you had seen him at the end. I came upon him by the Trident, drawn by his cries of pain. He begged me for the gift of mercy, but I am sworn not to kill again. Instead, I bathed his fevered brow with river water, and gave him wine to drink and a poultice for his wound, but my efforts were too little and too late. The Hound died there, in my arms. You may have seen a big black stallion in our stables. That was his warhorse, Stranger. A blasphemous name. We prefer to call him Driftwood, as he was found beside the river. I fear he has his former master's nature."

The horse. She had seen the stallion, had heard it kicking, but she had not understood. Destriers were trained to kick and bite. In war they were a weapon, like the men who rode them. *Like the Hound.* "It is true, then," she said dully. "Sandor Clegane is dead."

"He is at rest." The Elder Brother paused. "You are young, child. I have counted four-and-forty name days . . . which makes me more than twice your age, I think. Would it surprise you to learn that I was once a knight?"

"No. You look more like a knight than you do a holy man." It was written in his chest and shoulders, and across that thick square jaw. "Why would you give up knighthood?"

"I never chose it. My father was a knight, and his before him. So were my brothers, every one. I was trained for battle since the day they deemed me old enough to hold a wooden sword. I saw my share of them, and did not disgrace myself. I had women too, and there I did disgrace myself, for some I took by force. There was a girl I wished to marry, the younger daughter of a petty lord, but I was my father's thirdborn son and had neither land nor wealth to offer her . . . only a sword, a horse, a shield. All in all, I was a sad man. When I was not fighting, I was drunk. My life was writ in red, in blood and wine."

"When did it change?" asked Brienne.

"When I died in the Battle of the Trident. I fought for Prince Rhaegar, though he never knew my name. I could not tell you why, save that the lord I served served a lord who served a lord who had decided to support the dragon rather than the stag. Had he decided elsewhere, I might have been on the other side of the river. The battle was a bloody thing. The singers would have us believe it was all Rhaegar and Robert struggling in the stream for a woman both of them claimed to love, but I assure you, other men were fighting too, and I was one. I took an arrow through the thigh and another through the foot, and my horse was killed from under me, yet I fought on. I can still remember how desperate I was to find another horse, for I had no coin to buy one, and without a horse I would no longer be a knight. That was all that I was thinking of, if truth be told. I never saw the blow that felled me. I heard hooves behind my back and thought, *a horse!* but before I could turn something slammed into my head and knocked me back into the river, where by rights I should have drowned.

"Instead, I woke here, upon the Quiet Isle. The Elder Brother told me I had washed up on the tide, naked as my name day. I can only think that someone found me in the shallows, stripped me of my armor, boots, and breeches, and pushed me back out into the deeper water. The river did the rest. We are all born naked, so I suppose it was only fitting that I come into my second life the same way. I spent the next ten years in silence."

"I see." Brienne did not know why he was telling her all of this, or what else she ought to say.

"Do you?" He leaned forward, his big hands on his knees. "If so, give up this quest of yours. The Hound is dead, and in any case he never had your Sansa Stark. As for this beast who wears his helm, he will be found and hanged. The wars are ending, and these outlaws cannot survive the peace. Randyll Tarly is hunting them from Maidenpool and Walder Frey from the Twins, and there is a new young lord in Darry, a pious man who will surely set his lands to rights. Go home, child. You *have* a home, which is more than many can say in these dark days. You have a noble father who must surely love you. Consider his grief if you should never return. Perhaps they will bring your sword and shield to him, after you have fallen. Perhaps he will even hang them in his hall and look on them with pride . . . but if you were to ask him, I know he would tell you that he would sooner have a living daughter than a shattered shield."

"A daughter." Brienne's eyes filled with tears. "He deserves that. A daughter who could sing to him and grace his hall and bear him grandsons. He deserves a son too, a strong and gallant son to bring honor to his name. Galladon drowned when I was four and he was eight, though, and Alysanne and Arianne died still in the cradle. I am the only child the gods let him keep. The freakish one, not fit to be a son *or* daughter." All of it came pouring out of Brienne then, like black blood from a wound; the betrayals and betrothals, Red Ronnet and his rose, Lord Renly dancing with her, the wager for her maidenhead, the bitter tears she shed the night her king wed Margaery Tyrell, the mêlée at Bitterbridge, the rainbow cloak that she had been so proud of, the shadow in the king's pavilion, Renly dying in her arms, Riverrun and Lady Catelyn, the voyage down the Trident, dueling Jaime in the woods, the Bloody Mummers, Jaime crying *"Sapphires,"* Jaime in the tub at Harrenhal with steam rising from his body, the taste of Vargo Hoat's blood when she bit down on his ear, the bear pit, Jaime leaping down onto the sand, the long ride to King's Landing, Sansa Stark, the vow she'd sworn to Jaime, the vow she'd sworn to Lady Catelyn, Oathkeeper, Duskendale, Maidenpool, Nimble Dick and Crackclaw and the Whispers, the men she'd killed . . .

"I *have* to find her," she finished. "There are others looking, all wanting to capture her and sell her to the queen. I have to find her first. I promised Jaime. *Oathkeeper*, he named the sword. I have to try to save her . . . or die in the attempt."

CERSEI

"*A thousand ships!*" The little queen's brown hair was tousled and uncombed, and the torchlight made her cheeks look flushed, as if she had just come from some man's embrace. "Your Grace, this must be answered *fiercely!*" Her last word rang off the rafters and echoed through the cavernous throne room.

Seated on her gold-and-crimson high seat beneath the Iron Throne, Cersei could feel a growing tightness in her neck. *Must,* she thought. *She dares say "must" to me.* She itched to slap the Tyrell girl across the face. *She should be on her knees, begging for my help. Instead, she presumes to tell her rightful queen what she must do.*

"A thousand ships?" Ser Harys Swyft was wheezing. "Surely not. No lord commands a thousand ships."

"Some frightened fool has counted double," agreed Orton Merryweather. "That, or Lord Tyrell's bannermen are lying to us, puffing up the numbers of the foe so we will not think them lax."

The torches on the back wall threw the long, barbed shadow of the Iron Throne halfway to the doors. The far end of the hall was lost in darkness, and Cersei could not but feel that the shadows were closing around her too. *My enemies are everywhere, and my friends are useless.* She had only to glance at her councillors to know that; only Lord Qyburn and Aurane Waters seemed awake. The others had been roused from bed by Margaery's messengers pounding on their doors, and stood there rumpled and confused. Outside, the night was black and still. The castle and the city slept. Boros Blount and Meryn Trant seemed to be sleeping too, albeit on their feet. Even Osmund Kettleblack was yawning. *Not Loras, though. Not our Knight of Flowers.* He stood behind his little sister, a pale shadow with a longsword on his hip.

"Half as many ships would still be five hundred, my lord," Waters pointed out to Orton Merryweather. "Only the Arbor has enough strength at sea to oppose a fleet that size."

"What of your new dromonds?" asked Ser Harys. "The longships of the ironmen cannot stand before our dromonds, surely? *King Robert's Hammer* is the mightiest warship in all Westeros."

"She was," said Waters. "*Sweet Cersei* will be her equal, once complete, and *Lord Tywin* will be twice the size of either. Only half are fitted out, however, and none is fully crewed. Even when they are, the numbers would be greatly against us. The common longship is small compared to our galleys, this is true, but the ironmen have larger ships as well. Lord Balon's *Great Kraken* and the warships of the Iron Fleet were made for battle, not for raids. They are the equal of our lesser war galleys in speed and strength, and most are better crewed and captained. The ironmen live their whole lives at sea."

Robert should have scoured the isles after Balon Greyjoy rose against him, Cersei thought. *He smashed their fleet, burned their towns, and broke their castles, but when he had them on their knees he let them up again. He should have made another island of their skulls.* That was what her father would have done, but Robert never had the stomach that a king requires if he hopes to keep peace in the realm. "The ironmen have not dared raid the Reach since Dagon Greyjoy sat the Seastone Chair," she said. "Why would they do so now? What has emboldened them?"

"Their new king." Qyburn stood with his hands hidden up his sleeves. "Lord Balon's brother. The Crow's Eye, he is called."

"Carrion crows make their feasts upon the carcasses of the dead and dying," said Grand Maester Pycelle. "They do not descend upon hale and healthy animals. Lord Euron will gorge himself on gold and plunder, aye, but as soon as we move against him he will back to Pyke, as Lord Dagon was wont to do in his day."

"You are wrong," said Margaery Tyrell. "Reavers do not come in such strength. *A thousand ships!* Lord Hewett and Lord Chester are slain, as well as Lord Serry's son and heir. Serry has fled to Highgarden with what few ships remain him, and Lord Grimm is a prisoner in his own castle. Willas says that the iron king has raised up four lords of his own in their places."

Willas, Cersei thought, *the cripple. He is to blame for this. That oaf Mace Tyrell left the defense of the Reach in the hands of a hapless weakling.* "It is a long voyage from the Iron Isles to the Shields," she pointed out. "How could a thousand ships come all that way without being seen?"

"Willas believes that they did not follow the coast," said Margaery. "They made the voyage out of sight of land, sailing far out into the Sunset Sea and swooping back in from the west."

More like the cripple did not have his watchtowers manned, and now he fears to have us know it. The little queen is making excuses for her brother. Cersei's mouth was dry. *I need a cup of Arbor gold.* If the ironmen decided to take the Arbor next, the whole realm might soon be going thirsty. "Stannis may have had a hand in this. Balon Greyjoy offered my lord father an alliance. Perhaps his son has offered one to Stannis."

Pycelle frowned. "What would Lord Stannis gain by . . ."

"He *gains* another foothold. And plunder, that as well. Stannis needs gold to pay his sellswords. By raiding in the west, he hopes he can distract us from Dragonstone and Storm's End."

Lord Merryweather nodded. "A diversion. Stannis is more cunning than we knew. Your Grace is clever to have seen through his ploy."

"Lord Stannis is striving to win the northmen to his cause," said Pycelle. "If he befriends the ironborn, he cannot hope . . ."

"The northmen will not have him," said Cersei, wondering how such a learned man could be so stupid. "Lord Manderly hacked the head and hands off the onion knight, we have that from the Freys, and half a dozen other northern lords have rallied to Lord Bolton. *The enemy of my enemy is my friend.* Where else can Stannis turn, but to the ironmen and the wildlings, the enemies of the north? But if he thinks that I am going to walk into his trap, he is a bigger fool than you." She turned back to the little queen. "The Shield Islands belong to the Reach. Grimm and Serry and the rest are sworn to Highgarden. It is for Highgarden to answer this."

"Highgarden shall answer," said Margaery Tyrell. "Willas has sent word to Leyton Hightower in Oldtown, so he can see to his own defenses. Garlan is gathering men to retake the isles. The best part of our power remains with my lord father, though. We must send word to him at Storm's End. At once."

"And lift the siege?" Cersei did not care for Margaery's presumption. *She says "at once" to me. Does she take me for her handmaid?* "I have no doubt that Lord Stannis would be pleased by that. Have you been listening, my lady? If he can draw our eyes away from Dragonstone and Storm's End to these rocks . . ."

"*Rocks?*" gasped Margaery. "Did Your Grace say *rocks?*"

The Knight of Flowers put a hand upon his sister's shoulder. "If it please Your Grace, from those *rocks* the ironmen threaten Oldtown and the Arbor. From strongholds on the Shields, raiders can sail up the Mander into the very heart of the Reach, as they did of old. With enough men they might even threaten Highgarden."

"Truly?" said the queen, all innocence. "Why then, your brave brothers had best roust them off those rocks, and quickly."

"How would the queen suggest they accomplish that, without sufficient ships?" asked Ser Loras. "Willas and Garlan can raise ten thousand men within a fortnight and twice that in a moon's turn, but they cannot walk on water, Your Grace."

"Highgarden sits above the Mander," Cersei reminded him. "You and your vassals command a thousand leagues of coast. Are there no fisherfolk along your shores? Do you have no pleasure barges, no ferries, no river galleys, no skiffs?"

"Many and more," Ser Loras admitted.

"Such should be more than sufficient to carry a host across a little stretch of water, I would think."

"And when the longships of the ironborn descend upon our ragtag fleet as it is making its way across this 'little stretch of water,' what would Your Grace have us do then?"

Drown, thought Cersei. "Highgarden has gold as well. You have my leave to hire sellsails from beyond the narrow sea."

"Pirates out of Myr and Lys, you mean?" Loras said with contempt. "The scum of the Free Cities?"

He is as insolent as his sister. "Sad to say, all of us must deal with scum from time to time," she said with poisonous sweetness. "Perhaps you have a better notion?"

"Only the Arbor has sufficient galleys to retake the mouth of the Mander from the ironmen and protect my brothers from their long-ships during their crossing. I beg Your Grace, send word to Dragonstone and command Lord Redwyne to raise his sails at once."

At least he has the sense to beg. Paxter Redwyne owned two hundred warships, and five times as many merchant carracks, wine cogs, trading galleys, and whalers. Redwyne was encamped beneath the walls of Dragonstone, however, and the greater part of his fleet was engaged in ferrying men across Blackwater Bay for the assault on that island stronghold. The remainder prowled Shipbreaker Bay to the south, where only their presence prevented Storm's End from being resupplied by sea.

Aurane Waters bristled at Ser Loras's suggestion. "If Lord Redwyne sails his ships away, how are we to supply our men on Dragonstone? Without the Arbor's galleys, how will we maintain the siege of Storm's End?"

"The siege can be resumed later, after—"

Cersei cut him off. "Storm's End is a hundred times more valuable than the Shields, and Dragonstone . . . so long as Dragonstone remains in the hands of Stannis Baratheon, it is a knife at my son's throat. We will release Lord Redwyne and his fleet when the castle falls." The queen pushed herself to her feet. "This audience is at an end. Grand Maester Pycelle, a word."

The old man started, as if her voice had woken him from some dream of youth, but before he could answer, Loras Tyrell strode forward, so swiftly that the queen drew back in alarm. She was about to shout for Ser Osmund to defend her when the Knight of Flowers sank to one knee. "Your Grace, let me take Dragonstone."

His sister's hand went to her mouth. "Loras, no."

Ser Loras ignored her plea. "It will take half a year or more to starve Dragonstone into submission, as Lord Paxter means to do. Give me the command, Your Grace. The castle will be yours within a fortnight if I have to tear it down with my bare hands."

No one had given Cersei such a lovely gift since Sansa Stark had run to her to divulge Lord Eddard's plans. She was pleased to see that Margaery had gone pale. "Your courage takes my breath away, Ser Loras," Cersei said. "Lord Waters, are any of the new dromonds fit to put to sea?"

"*Sweet Cersei* is, Your Grace. A swift ship, and as strong as the queen she's named for."

"Splendid. Let *Sweet Cersei* carry our Knight of Flowers to Dragonstone at once. Ser Loras, the command is yours. Swear to me that you shall not return until Dragonstone is Tommen's."

"I shall, Your Grace." He rose.

Cersei kissed him on both cheeks. She kissed his sister too, and whispered, "You have a gallant brother." Either Margaery did not have the grace to answer or fear had stolen all her words.

Dawn was still several hours away when Cersei slipped out the king's door behind the Iron Throne. Ser Osmund went before her with a torch and Qyburn strolled along beside her. Pycelle had to struggle to keep up. "If it please Your Grace," he puffed, "young men are overbold, and think only of the glory of battle and never of its dangers. Ser Loras . . . this plan of his is fraught with peril. To storm the very walls of Dragonstone . . ."

". . . is *very* brave."

". . . brave, yes, but . . ."

"I have no doubt that our Knight of Flowers will be the first man to gain the battlements." *And perhaps the first to fall.* The pox-scarred bastard that Stannis had left to hold his castle was no callow tourney champion but a seasoned killer. If the gods were good, he would give Ser Loras the glorious end he seemed to want. *Assuming the boy does not drown on the way.* There had been another storm last night, a savage one. The rain had come down in black sheets for hours. *And wouldn't that be sad?* the queen mused. *Drowning is ordinary. Ser Loras lusts for glory as real men lust for women, the least the gods can do is grant him a death worthy of a song.*

No matter what befell the boy on Dragonstone, however, the queen would be the winner. If Loras took the castle, Stannis would suffer a grievous blow, and the Redwyne fleet could sail off to meet the ironmen. If he failed, she would see to it that he had the lion's share of the blame. Nothing tarnishes a hero as much as failure. *And if he should come home on his shield, covered in blood and glory, Ser Osney will be there to console his grieving sister.*

The laugh would not be contained any longer. It burst from Cersei's lips, and echoed down the hall.

"Your Grace?" Grand Maester Pycelle blinked, his mouth sagging open. "Why . . . why would you laugh?"

"Why," she had to say, "elsewise I might weep. My heart is bursting with love for our Ser Loras and his valor."

She left the Grand Maester on the serpentine steps. *That one has outlived any usefulness he ever had,* the queen decided. All Pycelle ever seemed to do of late was plague her with cautions and objections. He had even objected to the understanding she had reached with the High Septon, gaping at her with dim and rheumy eyes when she commanded him to prepare the necessary papers and babbling about old dead history until Cersei cut him off. "King Maegor's day is done, and so are his decrees," she said firmly. "This is King Tommen's day, and mine." *I would have done better to let him perish in the black cells.*

"Should Ser Loras fall, Your Grace will need to find another worthy for the Kingsguard," Lord Qyburn said as they crossed over the spiked moat that girded Maegor's Holdfast.

"Someone splendid," she agreed. "Someone so young and swift and strong that Tommen will forget all about Ser Loras. A bit of gallantry would not be amiss, but his head should not be full of foolish notions. Do you know of such a man?"

"Alas, no," said Qyburn. "I had another sort of champion in mind. What he lacks in gallantry he will give you tenfold in devotion. He will protect your son, kill your enemies, and keep your secrets, and no living man will be able to withstand him."

"So you say. Words are wind. When the hour is ripe, you may produce this paragon of yours and we will see if he is all that you have promised."

"They will sing of him, I swear it." Lord Qyburn's eyes crinkled with amusement. "Might I ask about the armor?"

"I have placed your order. The armorer thinks that I am mad. He assures me that no man is strong enough to move and fight in such a weight of plate." Cersei gave the chainless maester a warning look. "Play me for a fool, and you'll die screaming. You are aware of that, I trust?"

"Always, Your Grace."

"Good. Say no more of this."

"The queen is wise. These walls have ears."

"So they do." At night Cersei sometimes heard soft sounds, even in her own apartments. *Mice in the walls,* she would tell herself, *no more than that.*

A candle was burning by her bedside, but the hearthfire had gone out and there was no other light. The room was cold as well. Cersei undressed and slipped beneath the blankets, leaving her gown to puddle on the floor. Across the bed, Taena stirred. "Your Grace," she murmured softly. "What hour is it?"

"The hour of the owl," the queen replied.

Though Cersei often slept alone, she had never liked it. Her oldest memories were of sharing a bed with Jaime, when they had still been so young that no one could tell the two of them apart. Later, after they were separated, she'd had a string of bedmaids and companions, most of them girls of an age with her, the daughters of her father's household knights and bannermen. None had pleased her, and few lasted very long. *Little sneaks, the lot of them. Vapid, weepy creatures, always telling tales and trying to worm their way between me and Jaime.* Still, there had been nights deep within the black bowels of the Rock when she had welcomed their warmth beside her. An empty bed was a cold bed.

Here most of all. There were chills in this room, and her wretched royal husband had died beneath this canopy. *Robert Baratheon, the First of His Name, may there never be a second. A dim, drunken brute of a man. Let him weep in hell.* Taena warmed the bed as well as Robert ever had, and never tried to force Cersei's legs apart. Of late, she had shared the queen's bed more often than Lord Merryweather's.

Orton did not seem to mind . . . or if he did, he knew better than to say so.

"I was concerned when I woke and found you gone," murmured Lady Merryweather, sitting up against the pillows, the coverlets tangled about her waist. "Is aught amiss?"

"No," said Cersei, "all is well. On the morrow Ser Loras will sail for Dragonstone, to win the castle, loose the Redwyne fleet, and prove his manhood to us all." She told the Myrish woman all that had occurred beneath the shifting shadow of the Iron Throne. "Without her valiant brother, our little queen is next to naked. She has her guards, to be sure, but I have their captain here and there about the castle. A garrulous old man with a squirrel on his surcoat. Squirrels run from lions. He does not have it in him to defy the Iron Throne."

"Margaery has other swords about her," cautioned Lady Merryweather. "She has made many friends about the court, and she and her young cousins all have admirers."

"A few suitors do not concern me," Cersei said. "The army at Storm's End, however . . ."

"What do you mean to do, Your Grace?"

"Why do you ask?" The question was a little too pointed for Cersei's taste. "I do hope you are not thinking of sharing my idle musings with our poor little queen?"

"Never. I am not that girl Senelle."

Cersei did not care to think about Senelle. *She repaid my kindness with betrayal.* Sansa Stark had done the same. So had Melara Hetherspoon and fat Jeyne Farman when the three of them were girls. *I would never have gone into that tent if not for them. I would never have allowed Maggy the Frog to taste my morrows in a drop of blood.* "I would be very sad if you ever betrayed my trust, Taena. I would have no choice but to give you to Lord Qyburn, but I know that I should weep."

"I will never give you cause to weep, Your Grace. If I do, say the word, and I will give myself to Qyburn. I want only to be close to you. To serve you, however you require."

"And for this service, what reward will you expect?"

"Nothing. It pleases me to please you." Taena rolled onto her side, her olive skin shining in the candlelight. Her breasts were larger than the queen's and tipped with huge nipples, black as horn. *She is younger than I am. Her breasts have not begun to sag.* Cersei wondered what it would feel like to kiss another woman. Not lightly on the cheek, as was common courtesy amongst ladies of high birth, but full upon the lips. Taena's lips were very full. She wondered what it would feel like to suckle on those breasts, to lay the Myrish woman on her back and push her legs apart and use her as a man would use her, the way Robert would use *her* when the drink was in him, and she was unable to bring him off with hand or mouth.

Those had been the worst nights, lying helpless underneath him as he took his pleasure, stinking of wine and grunting like a boar. Usually, he rolled off and went to sleep as soon as it was done, and was snoring before his seed could dry upon her thighs. She was always sore afterward, raw between the legs, her breasts painful from the mauling he would give them. The only time he'd ever made her wet was on their wedding night.

Robert had been handsome enough when they first married, tall and strong and powerful, but his hair was black and heavy, thick on his chest and coarse around his sex. *The wrong man came back from the Trident,* the queen would sometimes think as he was plowing her. In the first few years, when he mounted her more often, she would close her eyes and pretend that he was Rhaegar. She could not pretend that he was Jaime; he was too different, too unfamiliar. Even the *smell* of him was wrong.

For Robert, those nights never happened. Come morning he remembered nothing, or so he would have had her believe. Once, during the first year of their marriage, Cersei had voiced her displeasure the next day. "You hurt me," she complained. He had the grace to look ashamed. "It was not me, my lady," he said in a sulky sullen tone, like a child caught stealing apple cakes from the kitchen. "It was the wine. I drink too much wine." To wash down his admission, he reached for his horn of ale. As he raised it to his mouth, she smashed her own horn in his face, so hard she chipped a tooth. Years later at a feast, she heard him telling a serving wench how he'd cracked the tooth in a mêlée. *Well, our marriage was a mêlée,* she reflected, *so he did not lie.*

The rest had all been lies, though. He *did* remember what he did to her at night, she was convinced of that. She could see it in his eyes. He only pretended to forget; it was easier to do that than to face his shame. Deep down, Robert Baratheon was a coward. In time the assaults did grow less frequent. During the first year, he took her at least once a fortnight; by the end it was not even once a year. He never stopped completely, though. Sooner or later there would always come a night when he would drink too much and want to claim his rights. What shamed him in the light of day gave him pleasure in the darkness.

"My queen?" said Taena Merryweather. "You have a strange look in your eyes. Are you unwell?"

"I was just . . . remembering." Her throat was dry. "You are a good friend, Taena. I have not had a true friend in . . ."

Someone hammered at the door.

Again? The urgency of the sound made her shiver. *Have another thousand ships descended on us?* She slipped into a bedrobe and went to see who it was. "Beg pardon for disturbing you, Your Grace," the guardsman said, "but Lady Stokeworth is below, begging audience."

"At this hour?" snapped Cersei. "Has Falyse lost her wits? Tell her I have retired. Tell her that smallfolk on the Shields are being slaughtered. Tell her that I have been awake for half the night. I will see her on the morrow."

The guard hesitated. "If it please Your Grace, she's . . . she's not in a good way, if you take my meaning."

Cersei frowned. She had assumed Falyse was here to tell her that Bronn was dead. "Very well. I shall need to dress. Take her to my solar and have her wait." When Lady Merryweather made to rise and come with her, the queen demurred. "No, stay. One of us should get some rest, at least. I shan't be long."

Lady Falyse's face was bruised and swollen, her eyes red from her tears. Her lower lip was broken, her clothing soiled and torn. "Gods be good," Cersei said as she ushered her into the solar and closed the door. "What has happened to your face?"

Falyse did not seem to hear the question. "He *killed* him," she said in a quavery voice. "Mother have mercy, he . . . he . . ." She broke down sobbing, her whole body trembling.

Cersei poured a cup of wine and took it to the weeping woman. "Drink this. The wine will calm you. That's it. A little more now. Stop that weeping and tell me why you're here."

It took the rest of the flagon before the queen was finally able to coax the whole sad tale out of Lady Falyse. Once she had, she did not know whether to laugh or rage. "Single combat," she repeated. *Is there no one in the Seven Kingdoms that I can rely upon? Am I the only one in Westeros with a pinch of wits?* "You are telling me Ser Balman challenged Bronn to *single combat?*"

"He said it would be s-s-simple. The lance is a knight's weapon, he said, and B-Bronn was no true knight. Balman said he would unhorse him and finish him as he lay st-st-stunned."

Bronn was no knight, that was true. Bronn was a battle-hardened killer. *Your cretin of a husband wrote his own death warrant.* "A splendid plan. Dare I ask how it went awry?"

"B-Bronn drove his lance through the chest of Balman's poor *h-h-h-horse.* Balman, he . . . his legs were crushed when the beast fell. He screamed so piteously . . ."

Sellswords have no pity, Cersei might have said. "I asked you to arrange a hunting mishap. An arrow gone astray, a fall from a horse, an angry boar . . . there are so many ways a man can die in the woods. None of them involving *lances.*"

Falyse did not seem to hear her. "When I tried to run to my Balman, he, he, he *struck* me in the face. He made my lord c-c-confess. Balman was crying out for Maester Frenken to attend him, but the sellsword, he, he, he . . ."

"Confess?" Cersei did not like that word. "I trust our brave Ser Balman held his tongue."

"Bronn put a dagger in his *eye,* and told me I had best be gone from Stokeworth before the sun went down or I'd get the same. He said he'd pass me around to the g-g-garrison, if any of them would have me. When I ordered Bronn seized, one of his knights had the insolence to say that I should do as Lord Stokeworth said. He called him *Lord Stokeworth!*" Lady Falyse clutched at the queen's hand. "Your Grace must give me knights. A hundred knights! And crossbowmen, to take my castle back. Stokeworth is mine! They would not even permit me to gather up my *clothes!* Bronn said they were his wife's clothes now, all my s-silks and velvets."

Your rags are the least of your concern. The queen pulled her fingers free of the other woman's clammy grasp. "I asked you to snuff out a candle to help protect the king. Instead, you heaved a pot of wildfire at it. Did your witless Balman bring my name into this? Tell me he did not."

Falyse licked her lips. "He . . . he was in pain, his legs were broken. Bronn said he would show him mercy, but . . . What will happen to my poor m-m-mother?"

I imagine she will die. "What do you think?" Lady Tanda might well be dead already. Bronn did not seem the sort of man who would expend much effort nursing an old woman with a broken hip.

"You have to help me. Where am I to go? What will I do?"

Perhaps you might wed Moon Boy, Cersei almost said. *He is nigh as big a fool as your late husband.* She could not risk a war on the very doorstep of King's Landing, not now. "The silent sisters are always glad to welcome widows," she said. "Theirs is a serene life, a life of prayer and contemplation and good works. They bring solace to the living and peace to the dead." *And they do not talk.* She could not have the woman running about the Seven Kingdoms spreading dangerous tales.

Falyse was deaf to good sense. "All we did, we did in service to Your Grace. *Proud to Be Faithful.* You said . . ."

"I recall." Cersei forced a smile. "You shall stay here with us, my lady, until such time as we find a way to win your castle back. Let me pour you another cup of wine. It will help you sleep. You are weary and sick of heart, that's plain to see. My poor dear Falyse. That's it, drink up."

As her guest was working on the flagon, Cersei went to the door and called her maids. She told Dorcas to find Lord Qyburn for her and bring him here at once. Jocelyn Swyft she dispatched to the kitchens. "Bring bread and cheese, a meat pie and some apples. And wine. We have a thirst."

Qyburn arrived before the food. Lady Falyse had put down three more cups by then, and was beginning to nod, though from time to time she would rouse and give another sob. The queen took Qyburn aside and told him of Ser Balman's folly. "I cannot have Falyse spreading tales about the city. Her grief has made her witless. Do you still need women for your . . . work?"

"I do, Your Grace. The puppeteers are quite used up."

"Take her and do with her as you will, then. But once she goes down into the black cells . . . need I say more?"

"No, Your Grace. I understand."

"Good." The queen donned her smile once again. "Sweet Falyse, Maester Qyburn's here. He'll help you rest."

"Oh," said Falyse vaguely. "Oh, good."

When the door closed behind them Cersei poured herself another cup of wine. "I am surrounded by enemies and imbeciles," she said. She could not even trust to her own blood and kin, nor Jaime, who had once been her other half. *He was meant to be my sword and shield, my strong right arm. Why does he insist on vexing me?*

Bronn was no more than an annoyance, to be sure. She had never truly believed that he was harboring the Imp. Her twisted little brother was too clever to allow Lollys to name her wretched ill-begotten bastard after him, knowing it was sure to draw the queen's wroth down upon her. Lady Merryweather had pointed that out, and she was right. The mockery was almost certainly the sellsword's doing. She could picture him watching his wrinkled red stepson sucking on one of Lollys's swollen dugs, a cup of wine in his hand and an insolent smile on his face. *Grin all you wish, Ser Bronn, you'll be screaming soon enough. Enjoy your lackwit lady and your stolen castle whilst you can. When the time comes, I shall swat you as if you were a fly.* Perhaps she would send Loras Tyrell to do the swatting, if the Knight of Flowers should somehow return alive from Dragonstone. *That would be delicious. If the gods were good, each of them would kill the other, like Ser Arryk and Ser Erryk.* As for Stokeworth . . . no, she was sick of thinking about Stokeworth.

Taena had drifted back to sleep by the time the queen returned to the bedchamber, her head spinning. *Too much wine and too little sleep,* she told herself. It was not every night that she was awakened twice with such desperate tidings. *At least I could awaken. Robert would have been too drunk to rise, let alone rule. It would have fallen to Jon Arryn to deal with all of this.* It pleased her to think that she made a better king than Robert.

The sky outside the window was already beginning to lighten. Cersei sat on the bed beside Lady Merryweather, listening to her soft breathing, watching her breasts rise and fall. *Does she dream of Myr?* she wondered. *Or is it her lover with the scar, the dangerous dark-haired man who would not be refused?* She was quite certain Taena was not dreaming of Lord Orton.

Cersei cupped the other woman's breast. Softly at first, hardly touching, feeling the warmth of it beneath her palm, the skin as smooth as satin. She gave it a gentle squeeze, then ran her thumbnail lightly across the big dark nipple, back and forth and back and forth until she felt it stiffen. When she glanced up, Taena's eyes were open. "Does that feel good?" she asked.

"Yes," said Lady Merryweather.

"And this?" Cersei pinched the nipple now, pulling on it hard, twisting it between her fingers.

The Myrish woman gave a gasp of pain. "You're hurting me."

"It's just the wine. I had a flagon with my supper, and another with the widow Stokeworth. I had to drink to keep her calm." She twisted Taena's other nipple too, pulling until the other woman gasped. "I am the queen. I mean to claim my rights."

"Do what you will." Taena's hair was as black as Robert's, even down between her legs, and when Cersei touched her there she found her hair all sopping wet, where Robert's had been coarse and dry. "Please," the Myrish woman said, "go on, my queen. Do as you will with me. I'm yours."

But it was no good. She could not feel it, whatever Robert felt on the nights he took her. There was no pleasure in it, not for her. For Taena, yes. Her nipples were two black diamonds, her sex slick and steamy. *Robert would have loved you, for an hour.* The queen slid a finger into that Myrish swamp, then another, moving them in and out, *but once he spent himself inside you, he would have been hardpressed to recall your name.*

She wanted to see if it would be as easy with a woman as it had always been with Robert. *Ten thousand of your children perished in my palm, Your Grace,* she thought, slipping a third finger into Myr. *Whilst you snored, I would lick your sons off my face and fingers one by one, all those pale sticky princes. You claimed your rights, my lord, but in the darkness I would eat your heirs.* Taena gave a shudder. She gasped some words in a foreign tongue, then shuddered again and arched her back and screamed. *She sounds as if she is being gored,* the queen thought. For a moment she let herself imagine that her fingers were a bore's tusks, ripping the Myrish woman apart from groin to throat.

It was still no good.

It had never been any good with anyone but Jaime.

When she tried to take her hand away, Taena caught it and kissed her fingers. "Sweet queen, how shall I pleasure you?" She slid her hand down Cersei's side and touched her sex. "Tell me what you would have of me, my love."

"Leave me." Cersei rolled away and pulled up the bedclothes to cover herself, shivering. Dawn was breaking. It would be morning soon, and all of this would be forgotten.

It had never happened.

JAIME

T he trumpets made a brazen blare, and cut the still blue air of dusk. Josmyn Peckledon was on his feet at once, scrambling for his master's swordbelt.

The boy has good instincts. "Outlaws don't blow trumpets to herald their arrival," Jaime told him. "I shan't need my sword. That will be my cousin, the Warden of the West."

The riders were dismounting when he emerged from his tent; half a dozen knights, and twoscore mounted archers and men-at-arms. *"Jaime!"* roared a shaggy man clad in gilded ringmail and a fox-fur cloak. "So gaunt, and all in white! And bearded too!"

"This? Mere stubble, against that mane of yours, coz." Ser Daven's bristling beard and bushy mustache grew into sidewhiskers as thick as a hedgerow, and those into the tangled yellow thicket atop his head, matted down by the helm he was removing. Somewhere in the midst of all that hair lurked a pug nose and a pair of lively hazel eyes. "Did some outlaw steal your razor?"

"I vowed I would not let my hair be cut until my father was avenged." For a man who looked so leonine, Daven Lannister sounded oddly sheepish. "The Young Wolf got to Karstark first, though. Robbed me of my vengeance." He handed his helm to a squire and pushed his fingers through his hair where the weight of the steel had crushed it down. "I like a bit of hair. The nights grow colder, and a little foliage helps to keep your face warm. Aye, and Aunt Genna always said I had a brick for a chin." He clasped Jaime by the arms. "We feared for you after the Whispering Wood. Heard Stark's direwolf tore out your throat."

"Did you weep bitter tears for me, coz?"

"Half of Lannisport was mourning. The female half." Ser Daven's gaze went to Jaime's stump. "So it's true. The bastards took your sword hand."

"I have a new one, made of gold. There's much to be said for being one-handed. I drink less wine for fear of spilling and am seldom inclined to scratch my arse at court."

"Aye, there's that. Maybe I should have mine off as well." His cousin laughed. "Was it Catelyn Stark who took it?"

"Vargo Hoat." *Where do these tales come from?*

"The Qohorik?" Ser Daven spat. "That's for him and all his Brave Companions. I told your father I would forage for him, but he refused me. Some tasks are fit for lions, he said, but foraging is best left for goats and dogs."

Lord Tywin's very words, Jaime knew; he could almost hear his father's voice. "Come inside, coz. We need to talk."

Garrett had lit the braziers, and their glowing coals filled Jaime's tent with a ruddy heat. Ser Daven shrugged out of his cloak and tossed it at Little Lew. "You a Piper, boy?" he growled. "You have a runty look to you."

"I'm Lewys Piper, if it please my lord."

"I beat your brother bloody in a mêlée once. The runty little fool took offense when I asked him if that was his sister dancing naked on his shield."

"She's the sigil of our House. We don't have a sister."

"More's the pity. Your sigil has nice teats. What sort of man hides behind a naked woman, though? Every time I thumped your brother's shield, I felt unchivalrous."

"Enough," said Jaime, laughing. "Leave him be." Pia was mulling wine for them, stirring the kettle with a spoon. "I need to know what I can expect to find at Riverrun."

His cousin shrugged. "The siege drags on. The Blackfish sits inside the castle, we sit outside in our camps. Bloody boring, if you want the truth." Ser Daven seated himself upon a camp stool. "Tully ought to make a sortie, to remind us all we're still at war. Be nice if he culled some Freys too. Ryman, for a start. The man's drunk more oft than not. Oh, and Edwyn. Not as thick as his father, but as full of hate as a boil's full of pus. And our own Ser Emmon . . . no, *Lord* Emmon, Seven save us, must not forget his new title . . . our Lord of Riverrun does nought but try to tell me how to run the siege. He wants me to take the castle without *damaging* it, since it is now his lordly seat."

"Is that wine hot yet?" Jaime asked Pia.

"Yes, m'lord." The girl covered her mouth when she spoke. Peck served the wine on a golden platter. Ser Daven pulled off his gloves and took a cup. "Thank you, boy. Who might you be?"

"Josmyn Peckledon, if it please my lord."

"Peck was a hero on the Blackwater," Jaime said. "He slew two knights and captured two more."

"You must be more dangerous than you look, lad. Is that a beard, or did you forget to wash the dirt off your face? Stannis Baratheon's wife has a thicker mustache. How old are you?"

"Fifteen, ser."

Ser Daven snorted. "You know the best thing about heroes, Jaime? They all die young and leave more women for the rest of us." He tossed the cup back to the squire. "Fill that full again, and I'll call you hero too. I have a thirst."

Jaime lifted his own cup left-handed and took a swallow. The warmth spread through his chest. "You were speaking of the Freys you wanted dead. Ryman, Edwyn, Emmon . . ."

"And Walder Rivers," Daven said, "that whoreson. Hates that he's a bastard, and hates everyone who's not. Ser Perwyn seems a decent fellow, though, might as well spare him. The women too. I'm to marry one, I hear. Your father might have seen fit to consult with me about this marriage, by the bye. My own father was treating with Paxter Redwyne before Oxcross, did you know? Redwyne has a nicely dowered daughter . . ."

"Desmera?" Jaime laughed. "How well do you like freckles?"

"If my choice is Freys or freckles, well . . . half of Lord Walder's brood look like stoats."

"Only half? Be thankful. I saw Lancel's bride at Darry."

"Gatehouse Ami, gods be good. I couldn't believe that Lancel picked that one. What's wrong with that boy?"

"He's grown pious," said Jaime, "but it wasn't him who did the picking. Lady Amerei's mother is a Darry. Our uncle thought she'd help Lancel win the Darry smallfolk."

"How, by fucking them? You know why they call her Gatehouse Ami? She raises her portcullis for every knight who happens by. Lancel had best find an armorer to make him a horned helm."

"That won't be necessary. Our coz is off to King's Landing to take vows as one of the High Septon's swords."

Ser Daven could not have looked more astonished if Jaime had told him that Lancel had decided to become a mummer's monkey. "Not truly? You are japing with me. Gatehouse Ami must be more stoatish than I'd heard if she could drive the boy to *that*."

When Jaime had taken his leave of Lady Amerei, she had been weeping softly at the dissolution of her marriage whilst letting Lyle Crakehall console her. Her tears had not troubled him half so much as the hard looks on the faces of her kin as they stood about the yard. "I hope you do not intend to take vows as well, coz," he said to Daven. "The Freys are prickly where marriage contracts are concerned. I would hate to disappoint them again."

Ser Daven snorted. "I'll wed and bed my stoat, never fear. I know what happened to Robb Stark. From what Edwyn tells me, though, I'd best pick one who hasn't flowered yet, or I'm like to find that Black Walder has been there first. I'll wager he's had Gatehouse Ami, and more than thrice. Maybe that explains Lancel's godliness, and his father's mood."

"You have seen Ser Kevan?"

"Aye. He passed here on his way west. I asked him to help us take the castle, but Kevan would have none of it. He brooded the whole time he was here. Courteous enough, but chilly. I swore to him that I never asked to be made Warden of the West, that the honor should have gone to him, and he declared that he held no grudge against me, but you would never have known it from his tone. He stayed three days and hardly said three words to me. Would that he'd remained, I could have used his counsel. Our friends of Frey would not have dared vex Ser Kevan the way that they've been vexing me."

"Tell me," said Jaime.

"I would, but where to begin? Whilst I've been building rams and siege towers, Ryman Frey has raised a gibbet. Every day at dawn he brings forth Edmure Tully, drapes a noose around his neck, and threatens to hang him unless the castle yields. The Blackfish pays his mummer's show no mind, so come evenfall Lord Edmure is taken down again. His wife's with child, did you know?"

He hadn't. "Edmure bedded her, after the Red Wedding?"

"He was bedding her *during* the Red Wedding. Roslin's a pretty little thing, hardly stoatish at all. And fond of Edmure, queerly. Perwyn tells me she's praying for a girl."

Jaime considered that a moment. "Once Edmure's son is born, Lord Walder will have no more need of Edmure."

"That's how I see it too. Our good-uncle Emm . . . ah, *Lord* Emmon, that is . . . he wants Edmure hanged at once. The presence of a Tully Lord of Riverrun distresses him almost as much as the prospective birth of yet another. Daily he beseeches me to *make* Ser Ryman dangle Tully, never mind how. Meanwhile, I have Lord Gawen Westerling tugging at my other sleeve. The Blackfish has his lady wife inside the castle, along with three of his snot-nosed whelps. His lordship fears Tully will kill them if the Freys hang Edmure. One of them is the Young Wolf's little queen."

Jaime had met Jeyne Westerling, he thought, though he could not recall what she looked like. *She must be fair indeed, to have been worth a kingdom.* "Ser Brynden won't kill children," he assured his cousin. "He's not as black a fish as that." He was beginning to grasp why Riverrun had not yet fallen. "Tell me of your dispositions, coz."

"We have the castle well encircled. Ser Ryman and the Freys are north of the Tumblestone. South of Red Fork sits Lord Emmon, with Ser Forley Prester and with what remains of your old host, plus the river lords who came over to us after the Red Wedding. A sullen lot, I don't mind saying. Good for sulking in their tents, but not much more. Mine own camp is between the rivers, facing the moat and Riverrun's main gates. We've thrown a boom across the Red Fork, downstream of the castle. Manfryd Yew and Raynard Ruttiger have charge of its defense, so no one can escape by boat. I gave them nets as well, to fish. It helps keep us fed."

"Can we starve the castle out?"

Ser Daven shook his head. "The Blackfish expelled all the useless mouths from Riverrun and picked this country clean. He has enough stores to keep man and horse alive for two full years."

"And how well are we provisioned?"

"So long as there are fish in the rivers, we won't starve, though I don't know how we're going to feed the horses. The Freys are hauling food and fodder down from the Twins, but Ser Ryman claims he does not have enough to share, so we must forage for ourselves. Half the men I send off to look for food do not return. Some are deserting. Others we find ripening under trees, with ropes about their necks."

"We came on some, the day before last," said Jaime. Addam Marbrand's scouts had found them, hanging black-faced beneath a crabapple tree. The corpses had been stripped naked, and each man had a crabapple shoved between his teeth. None bore any wounds; plainly, they had yielded. Strongboar had grown furious at that, vowing bloody vengeance on the heads of any men who would truss up warriors to die like suckling pigs.

"It might have been outlaws," Ser Daven said, when Jaime told the tale, "or not. There are still bands of northmen about. And these Lords of the Trident may have bent their knees, but methinks their hearts are still . . . wolfish."

Jaime glanced at his two younger squires, who were hovering near the braziers pretending not to listen. Lewys Piper and Garrett Paege were both the sons of river lords. He had grown fond of both of them and would hate to have to give them to Ser Ilyn. "The ropes suggest Dondarrion to me."

"Your lightning lord's not the only man who knows how to tie a noose. Don't get me started on Lord Beric. He's here, he's there, he's everywhere, but when you send men after him, he melts away like dew. The river lords are helping him, never doubt it. A bloody marcher lord, if you can believe it. One day you hear the man is dead, the next they're saying how he can't be killed." Ser Daven put his wine cup down. "My scouts report fires in the high places at night. Signal fires, they think . . . as if there were a ring of watchers all around us. And there are fires in the villages as well. Some new god . . ."

No, an old one. "Thoros is with Dondarrion, the fat Myrish priest who used to drink with Robert." His golden hand was on the table. Jaime touched it and watched the gold glimmer in the sullen light of the braziers. "We'll deal with Dondarrion if we have to, but the Blackfish must come first. He has to know his cause is hopeless. Have you tried to treat with him?"

"Ser Ryman did. Rode up to the castle gates half-drunk and blustering, making threats. The Blackfish appeared on the ramparts long enough to say that he would not waste fair words on foul men. Then he put an arrow in the rump of Ryman's palfrey. The horse reared, Frey fell into the mud, and I laughed so hard I almost pissed myself. If it had been me inside the castle, I would have put that arrow through Ryman's lying throat."

"I'll wear a gorget when I treat with them," said Jaime, with a half smile. "I mean to offer him generous terms." If he could end this siege without bloodshed, then it could not be said that he had taken up arms against House Tully.

"You are welcome to try, my lord, but I doubt that words will win the day. We need to storm the castle."

There had been a time, not so long ago, when Jaime would doubtless have urged the same course. He knew he could not sit here for two years to starve the Blackfish out. "Whatever we do needs to be done quickly," he told Ser Daven. "My place is back at King's Landing, with the king."

"Aye," his cousin said. "I don't doubt your sister needs you. Why did she send off Kevan? I thought she'd make him Hand."

"He would not take it." *He was not as blind as I was.*

"Kevan should be the Warden of the West. Or you. It's not that I'm not grateful for the honor, mind you, but our uncle's twice my age and has more experience of command. I hope he knows I never asked for this."

"He knows."

"How is Cersei? As beautiful as ever?"

"Radiant." *Fickle.* "Golden." *False as fool's gold.* Last night he dreamed he'd found her fucking Moon Boy. He'd killed the fool and smashed his sister's teeth to splinters with his golden hand, just as Gregor Clegane had done to poor Pia. In his dreams Jaime always had two hands; one was made of gold, but it worked just like the other. "The sooner we are done with Riverrun, the sooner I'll be back at Cersei's side." What Jaime would do then he did not know.

He talked with his cousin for another hour before the Warden of the West finally took his leave. When he was gone, Jaime donned his gold hand and brown cloak to walk amongst the tents.

If truth be told, he liked this life. He felt more comfortable amongst soldiers in the field than he ever had at court. And his men seemed comfortable with him as well. At one cookfire three crossbowmen offered him a share of a hare they'd caught. At another a young knight asked his counsel on the best way to defend against a warhammer. Down beside the river, he watched two washerwomen jousting in the shallows, mounted on the shoulders of a pair of men-at-arms. The girls were half-drunk and half-naked, laughing and snapping rolled-up cloaks at one another as a dozen other men urged them on. Jaime bet a copper star on the blonde girl riding Raff the Sweetling, and lost it when the two of them went down splashing amongst the reeds.

Across the river wolves were howling, and the wind was gusting through a stand of willows, making their branches writhe and whisper. Jaime found Ser Ilyn Payne alone outside his tent, honing his greatsword with a whetstone. "Come," he said, and the silent knight rose, smiling thinly. *He enjoys this,* he realized. *It pleases him to humiliate me nightly. It might please him even more to kill me.* He liked to believe that he was getting better, but the improvement was slow and not without cost. Underneath his steel and wool and boiled leather, Jaime Lannister was a tapestry of cuts and scabs and bruises.

A sentry challenged them as they led their horses from the camp. Jaime clapped the man's shoulder with his golden hand. "Stay vigilant. There are wolves about." They rode back along the Red Fork to the ruins of a burned village they had passed that afternoon. It was there they danced their midnight dance, amongst blackened stones and old cold cinders. For a little while Jaime had the better of it. Perhaps his old skill *was* coming back, he allowed himself to think. Perhaps tonight it would be Payne who went to sleep bruised and bloody.

It was as if Ser Ilyn heard his thoughts. He parried Jaime's last cut lazily and launched a counterattack that drove Jaime back into the river, where his boot slipped out from under him in the mud. He ended on his knees, with the silent knight's sword at his throat and his own lost in the reeds. In the moonlight the pockmarks on Payne's face were large as craters. He made that clacking sound that might have been a laugh and drew his sword up Jaime's throat till the point came to rest between his lips. Only then did he step back and sheathe his steel.

I would have done better to challenge Raff the Sweetling, with a whore upon my back, Jaime thought as he shook mud off his gilded hand. Part of him wanted to tear the thing off and fling it in the river. It was good for nothing, and the left was not much better. Ser Ilyn had gone back to the horses, leaving him to find his own feet. *At least I still have two of those.*

The last day of their journey was cold and gusty. The wind rattled amongst the branches in the bare brown woods and made the river reeds bow low along the Red Fork. Even mantled in the winter wool of the Kingsguard, Jaime could feel the iron teeth of that wind as he rode beside his cousin Daven. It was late afternoon when they sighted Riverrun, rising from the narrow point where the Tumblestone joined the Red Fork. The Tully castle looked like a great stone ship with its prow pointed downriver. Its sandstone walls were drenched in red-gold light, and seemed higher and thicker than Jaime had remembered. *This nut will not crack easily,* he thought gloomily. If the Blackfish would not listen, he would have no choice but to break the vow he'd made to Catelyn Stark. The vow he'd sworn his king came first.

The boom across the river and the three great camps of the besieging army were just as his cousin had described. Ser Ryman Frey's encampment north of the Tumblestone was the largest, and the most disorderly. A great grey gallows loomed above the tents, as tall as any trebuchet. On it stood a solitary figure with a rope about his neck. *Edmure Tully.* Jaime felt a stab of pity. *To keep him standing there day after day, with that noose around his neck . . . better to have his head off and be done with it.*

Behind the gallows, tents and cookfires spread out in ragged disarray. The Frey lordlings and their knights had raised their pavilions comfortably upstream of the latrine trenches; downstream were muddy hovels, wayns, and oxcarts. "Ser Ryman don't want his boys getting bored, so he gives them whores and cockfights and boar baiting," Ser Daven said. "He's even got himself a bloody *singer*. Our aunt brought Whitesmile Wat from Lannisport, if you can believe it, so Ryman had to have a singer too. Couldn't we just dam the river and drown the whole lot of them, coz?"

Jaime could see archers moving behind the merlons on the castle ramparts. Above them streamed the banners of House Tully, the silver trout defiant on its striped field of red and blue. But the highest tower flew a different flag; a long white standard emblazoned with the direwolf of Stark. "The first time I saw Riverrun, I was a squire green as summer grass," Jaime told his cousin. "Old Sumner Crakehall sent me to deliver a message, one he swore could not be entrusted to a raven. Lord Hoster kept me for a fortnight whilst mulling his reply, and sat me beside his daughter Lysa at every meal."

"Small wonder you took the white. I'd have done the same."

"Oh, Lysa was not so fearsome as all that." She had been a pretty girl, in truth; dimpled and delicate, with long auburn hair. *Timid, though. Prone to tongue-tied silences and fits of giggles, with none of Cersei's fire.* Her older sister had seemed more interesting, though Catelyn was promised to some northern boy, the heir of Winterfell . . . but at that age, no girl interested Jaime half so much as Hoster's famous brother, who had won renown fighting the Ninepenny Kings upon the Stepstones. At table he had ignored poor Lysa, whilst pressing Brynden Tully for tales of Maelys the Monstrous and the Ebon Prince. *Ser Brynden was younger then than I am now,* Jaime reflected, *and I was younger than Peck.*

The nearest ford across the Red Fork was upstream of the castle. To reach Ser Daven's camp they had to ride through Emmon Frey's, past the pavilions of the river lords who had bent their knees and been accepted back into the king's peace. Jaime noted the banners of Lychester and Vance, of Roote and Goodbrook, the acorns of House

Smallford and Lord Piper's dancing maiden, but the banners he did *not* see gave him pause. The silver eagle of Mallister was nowhere in evidence; nor the red horse of Bracken, the willow of the Rygers, the twining snakes of Paege. Though all had renewed their fealty to the Iron Throne, none had come to join the siege. The Brackens were fighting the Blackwoods, Jaime knew, which accounted for their absence, but as for the rest . . .

Our new friends are no friends at all. Their loyalty goes no deeper than their skins. Riverrun had to be taken, and soon. The longer the siege dragged on, the more it would hearten other recalcitrants, like Tytos Blackwood.

At the ford, Ser Kennos of Kayce blew the Horn of Herrock. *That should bring the Blackfish to the battlements.* Ser Hugo and Ser Dermot led Jaime's way across the river, splashing through the muddy red-brown waters with the white standard of the Kingsguard and Tommen's stag and lion streaming in the wind. The rest of the column followed hard behind them.

The Lannister camp rang to the sound of wooden hammers where a new siege tower was rising. Two other towers stood completed, half-covered with raw horsehide. Between them sat a rolling ram; a tree trunk with a fire-hardened point suspended on chains beneath a wooden roof. *My coz has not been idle, it would seem.*

"My lord," Peck asked, "where do you want your tent?"

"There, upon that rise." He pointed with his golden hand, though it was not well suited to that task. "Baggage there, horse lines there. We'll use the latrines my cousin has so kindly dug for us. Ser Addam, inspect our perimeter with an eye for any weaknesses." Jaime did not anticipate an attack, but he had not anticipated the Whispering Wood either.

"Shall I summon the stoats for a war council?" Daven asked.

"Not until I've spoken to the Blackfish." Jaime beckoned to Beardless Jon Bettley. "Shake out a peace banner and bear a message to the castle. Inform Ser Brynden Tully that I would have words with him, at first light on the morrow. I will come to the edge of the moat and meet him on his drawbridge."

Peck looked alarmed. "My lord, the bowmen could . . ."

"They won't." Jaime dismounted. "Raise my tent and plant my standards." *And we'll see who comes running, and how quickly.*

It did not require long. Pia was fussing at a brazier, trying to light the coals. Peck went to help her. Of late, Jaime oft went to sleep to the sound of them fucking in a corner of the tent. As Garrett was undoing the clasps on Jaime's greaves, the tent flapped open. "Here at last, are you?" boomed his aunt. She filled the door, with her Frey husband peering out from behind her. "Past time. Have you no hug for your old fat aunt?" She held out her arms and left him no choice but to embrace her.

Genna Lannister had been a shapely woman in her youth, always threatening to overflow her bodice. Now the only shape she had was square. Her face was broad and smooth, her neck a thick pink pillar, her bosom enormous. She carried enough flesh to make two of her husband. Jaime hugged her dutifully and waited for her to pinch his ear. She had been pinching his ear for as long as he could remember, but today she forbore. Instead, she planted soft and sloppy kisses on his cheeks. "I am sorry for your loss."

"I had a new hand made, of gold." He showed her.

"Very nice. Will they make you a gold father too?" Lady Genna's voice was sharp. "Tywin was the loss I meant."

"A man such as Tywin Lannister comes but once in a thousand years," declared her husband. Emmon Frey was a fretful man with nervous hands. He might have weighed ten stone . . . but only wet, and clad in mail. He was a weed in wool, with no chin to speak of, a flaw that the prominence of the apple in his throat made even more absurd. Half his hair had been gone before he turned thirty. Now he was sixty and only a few white wisps remained.

"Some queer tales have been reaching us of late," Lady Genna said, after Jaime dismissed Pia and his squires. "A woman hardly knows what to believe. Can it be true that Tyrion slew Tywin? Or is that some calumny your sister put about?"

"It's true enough." The weight of his golden hand had grown irksome. He fumbled at the straps that secured it to his wrist.

"For a son to raise his hand against a father," Ser Emmon said. "Monstrous. These are dark days in Westeros. I fear for us all with Lord Tywin gone."

"You feared for us all when he was here." Genna settled her ample rump upon a camp stool, which creaked alarmingly beneath her weight. "Nephew, speak to us of our son Cleos and the manner of his death."

Jaime undid the last fastening and set his hand aside. "We were set upon by outlaws. Ser Cleos scattered them, but it cost his life." The lie came easy; he could see that it pleased them.

"The boy had courage, I always said so. It was in his blood." A pinkish froth glistened on Ser Emmon's lips when he spoke, courtesy of the sourleaf he liked to chew.

"His bones should be interred beneath the Rock, in the Hall of Heroes," Lady Genna declared. "Where was he laid to rest?"

Nowhere. The Bloody Mummers stripped his corpse and left his flesh to feast the carrion crows. "Beside a stream," he lied. "When this war is done, I will find the place and send him home." Bones were bones; these days, nothing was easier to come by.

"This war . . ." Lord Emmon cleared his throat, the apple in his throat moving up and down. "You will have seen the siege machines. Rams, trebuchets, towers. It will not serve, Jaime. Daven means to break my walls, smash in my gates. He talks of burning pitch, of setting the castle afire. *My* castle." He reached up one sleeve, brought out a parchment, and thrust it at Jaime's face. "I have the decree. Signed by the king, by Tommen, see, the royal seal, the stag and lion. I am the lawful lord of Riverrun, and I will not have it reduced to a smoking ruin."

"Oh, put that fool thing away," his wife snapped. "So long as the Blackfish sits inside Riverrun you can wipe your arse with that paper for all the good it does us." Though she had been a Frey for fifty years, Lady Genna remained very much a Lannister. *Quite a lot of Lannister.* "Jaime will deliver you the castle."

"To be sure," Lord Emmon said. "Ser Jaime, your lord father's faith in me was well placed, you shall see. I mean to be firm but fair with my new vassals. Blackwood and Bracken, Jason Mallister, Vance and Piper, they shall learn that they have a just overlord in Emmon Frey. My father as well, yes. He is the Lord of the Crossing, but *I* am the Lord of Riverrun. A son has a duty to obey his father, true, but a bannerman must obey his overlord."

Oh, gods be good. "You are not his overlord, ser. Read your parchment. You were granted Riverrun with its lands and incomes, no more. Petyr Baelish is the Lord Paramount of the Trident. Riverrun will be subject to the rule of Harrenhal."

That did not please Lord Emmon. "Harrenhal is a ruin, haunted and accursed," he objected, "and Baelish . . . the man is a coin counter, no proper lord, his birth . . ."

"If you are unhappy with the arrangements, go to King's Landing and take it up with my sweet sister." Cersei would devour Emmon Frey and pick her teeth with his bones, he did not doubt. *That is, if she's not too busy fucking Osmund Kettleblack.*

Lady Genna gave a snort. "There is no need to trouble Her Grace with such nonsense. Emm, why don't you step outside and have a breath of air?"

"A breath of air?"

"Or a good long piss, if you prefer. My nephew and I have *family* matters to discuss."

Lord Emmon flushed. "Yes, it is warm in here. I will wait outside, my lady. Ser." His lordship rolled up his parchment, sketched a bow toward Jaime, and tottered from the tent.

It was hard not to feel contemptuous of Emmon Frey. He had arrived at Casterly Rock in his fourteenth year to wed a lioness half his age. Tyrion used to say that Lord Tywin had given him a nervous belly for a wedding gift. *Genna has played her part as well.* Jaime remembered many a feast where Emmon sat poking at his food sullenly whilst his wife made ribald jests with whatever household knight had been seated to her left, their conversations punctuated by loud bursts of laughter. *She gave Frey four sons, to be sure. At least she says they are his.* No one in Casterly Rock had the courage to suggest otherwise, least of all Ser Emmon.

No sooner was he gone than his lady wife rolled her eyes. "My lord and master. What *was* your father thinking, to name him Lord of Riverrun?"

"I imagine he was thinking of your sons."

"I think of them as well. Emm will make a wretched lord. Ty may do better, if he has the sense to learn from me and not his father." She looked about the tent. "Do you have wine?"

Jaime found a flagon and poured for her, one-handed. "Why are you here, my lady? You should have remained at Casterly Rock until the fighting's done."

"Once Emm heard he was a lord, he had to come at once to claim his seat." Lady Genna took a drink and wiped her mouth on her sleeve. "Your father should have granted us Darry. Cleos married one of the plowman's daughters, you will recall. His grieving widow is furious that her sons were not granted her lord father's lands. Gatehouse Ami is Darry only on her mother's side. My good-daughter Jeyne is her aunt, a full sister to Lady Mariya."

"A younger sister," Jaime reminded her, "and Ty will have Riverrun, a greater prize than Darry."

"A poisoned prize. House Darry is extinguished in the male line, House Tully is not. That muttonhead Ser Ryman puts a noose round Edmure's neck, but will not hang him. And Roslin Frey has a trout growing in her belly. My grandsons will never be secure in Riverrun so long as any Tully heir remains alive."

She was not wrong, Jaime knew. "If Roslin has a girl—"

"—she can wed Ty, provided old Lord Walder will consent. Yes, I've thought of that. A boy is just as likely, though, and his little cock would cloud the issue. And if Ser Brynden should survive this siege, he might be inclined to claim Riverrun in his own name . . . or in the name of young Robert Arryn."

Jaime remembered little Robert from King's Landing, still sucking on his mother's teats at four. "Arryn won't live long enough to breed. And why should the Lord of the Eyrie need Riverrun?"

"Why does a man with one pot of gold need another? Men are greedy. Tywin should have granted Riverrun to Kevan and Darry to Emm. I would have told him so if he had troubled to ask me, but when did your father ever consult with anyone but Kevan?" She sighed deeply. "I do not blame Kevan for wanting the safer seat for his own boy, mind you. I know him too well."

"What Kevan wants and what Lancel wants appear to be two different things." He told her of Lancel's decision to renounce wife and lands and lordship to fight for the Holy Faith. "If you still want Darry, write to Cersei and make your case."

Lady Genna waved her cup in dismissal. "No, that horse has left the yard. Emm has it in his pointed head that he will rule the riverlands. And Lancel . . . I suppose we should have seen this coming from afar. A life protecting the High Septon is not so different from a life protecting the king, after all. Kevan will be wroth, I fear. As wroth as Tywin was when you got it in your head to take the white. At least Kevan still has Martyn for an heir. He can marry him to Gatehouse Ami in Lancel's place. Seven save us all." His aunt gave a sigh. "And speaking of the Seven, why would Cersei permit the Faith to arm again?"

Jaime shrugged. "I am certain she had reasons."

"Reasons?" Lady Genna made a rude noise. "They had best be *good* reasons. The Swords and Stars troubled even the Targaryens. The Conqueror himself tread carefully with the Faith, so they would not oppose him. And when Aegon died and the lords rose up against his sons, both orders were in the thick of that rebellion. The more pious lords supported them, and many of the smallfolk. King Maegor finally had to put a bounty on them. He paid a dragon for the head of any unrepentant Warrior's Son, and a silver stag for the scalp of a Poor Fellow, if I recall my history. Thousands were slain, but nigh as many still roamed the realm, defiant, until the Iron Throne slew Maegor and King Jaehaerys agreed to pardon all those who would set aside their swords."

"I'd forgotten most of that," Jaime confessed.

"You and your sister both." She took another swallow of her wine. "Is it true that Tywin was smiling on his bier?"

"He was rotting on his bier. It made his mouth twist."

"Was that all it was?" That seemed to sadden her. "Men say that Tywin never smiled, but he smiled when he wed your mother, and when Aerys made him Hand. When Tarbeck Hall came crashing down on Lady Ellyn, that scheming bitch, Tyg claimed he smiled then. And he smiled at your birth, Jaime, I saw that with mine own eyes. You and Cersei, pink and perfect, as alike as two peas in a pod . . . well, except between the legs. What *lungs* you had!"

"Hear us roar." Jaime grinned. "Next you'll be telling me how much he liked to laugh."

"No. Tywin mistrusted laughter. He heard too many people laughing at your grandsire." She frowned. "I promise you, this mummer's farce of a siege would not have amused him. How do you mean to end it, now that you're here?"

"Treat with the Blackfish."

"That won't work."

"I mean to offer him good terms."

"Terms require trust. The Freys murdered guests beneath their roof, and you, well . . . I mean no offense, my love, but you *did* kill a certain king you had sworn to protect."

"And I'll kill the Blackfish if he does not yield." His tone was harsher than he'd intended, but he was in no mood for having Aerys Targaryen thrown in his face.

"How, with your tongue?" Her voice was scornful. "I may be an old fat woman, but I do not have cheese between my ears, Jaime. Neither does the Blackfish. Empty threats won't daunt him."

"What would you counsel?"

She gave a ponderous shrug. "Emm wants Edmure's head off. For once, he may be right. Ser Ryman has made us a laughingstock with that gibbet of his. You need to show Ser Brynden that your threats have teeth."

"Killing Edmure might harden Ser Brynden's resolve."

"Resolve is one thing Brynden Blackfish never lacked for. Hoster Tully could have told you that." Lady Genna finished her wine. "Well, I would never presume to tell you how to fight a war. I know my place . . . unlike your sister. Is it true that Cersei burned the Red Keep?"

"Only the Tower of the Hand."

His aunt rolled her eyes. "She would have done better to leave the tower and burn her Hand. Harys *Swyft?* If ever a man deserved his arms, it is Ser Harys. And Gyles Rosby, Seven save us, I thought he died years ago. Merryweather . . . your father used to call his grandsire 'the Chuckler,' I'll have you know. Tywin claimed the only thing Merryweather was good for was chuckling at the king's witticisms. His lordship chuckled himself right into exile, as I recall. Cersei has put some bastard on the council too, and a kettle in the Kingsguard. She has the Faith arming and the Braavosi calling in loans all over

Westeros. None of which would be happening if she'd had the simple sense to make your uncle the King's Hand."

"Ser Kevan refused the office."

"So he said. He did not say why. There was much he did not say. *Would* not say." Lady Genna made a face. "Kevan *always* did what was asked of him. It is not like him to turn away from any duty. Something is awry here, I can smell it."

"He said that he was tired." *He knows*, Cersei had said, as they stood above their father's corpse. *He knows about us.*

"Tired?" His aunt pursed her lips. "I suppose he has a right to be. It has been hard for Kevan, living all his life in Tywin's shadow. It was hard for all my brothers. That shadow Tywin cast was long and black, and each of them had to struggle to find a little sun. Tygett tried to be his own man, but he could never match your father, and that just made him angrier as the years went by. Gerion made japes. Better to mock the game than to play and lose. But Kevan saw how things stood early on, so he made himself a place by your father's side."

"And you?" Jaime asked her.

"It was not a game for girls. I was my father's precious princess . . . and Tywin's too, until I disappointed him. My brother never learned to like the taste of disappointment." She pushed herself to her feet. "I've said what I came to say, I shan't take any more of your time. Do what Tywin would have done."

"Did you love him?" Jaime heard himself ask.

His aunt looked at him strangely. "I was seven when Walder Frey persuaded my lord father to give my hand to Emm. His *second* son, not even his heir. Father was himself a thirdborn son, and younger children crave the approval of their elders. Frey sensed that weakness in him, and Father agreed for no better reason than to please him. My betrothal was announced at a feast with half the west in attendance. Ellyn Tarbeck laughed and the Red Lion went angry from the hall. The rest sat on their tongues. Only Tywin dared speak against the match. A boy of ten. Father turned as white as mare's milk, and Walder Frey was *quivering*." She smiled. "How could I not love him, after that? That is not to say that I approved of all he did, or much enjoyed the company of the man that he became . . . but every little girl needs a big brother to protect her. Tywin was big even when he was little." She gave a sigh. "Who will protect us now?"

Jaime kissed her cheek. "He left a son."

"Aye, he did. That is what I fear the most, in truth."

That was a queer remark. "Why should you fear?"

"Jaime," she said, tugging on his ear, "sweetling, I have known you since you were a babe at Joanna's breast. You smile like Gerion and fight like Tyg, and there's some of Kevan in you, else you would not wear that cloak . . . but *Tyrion* is Tywin's son, not you. I said so once to your father's face, and he would not speak to me for half a year. Men are such thundering great fools. Even the sort who come along once in a thousand years."

CAT OF THE CANALS

S he woke before the sun came up, in the little room beneath the eaves that she shared with Brusco's daughters.

Cat was always the first to awaken. It was warm and snug under the blankets with Talea and Brea. She could hear the soft sounds of their breath. When she stirred, sitting up and fumbling for her slippers, Brea muttered a sleepy complaint and rolled over. The chill off the grey stone walls gave Cat gooseprickles. She dressed quickly in the darkness. As she was slipping her tunic over her head, Talea opened her eyes and called out, "Cat, be a sweet and bring my clothes for me." She was a gawky girl, all skin and bones and elbows, always complaining she was cold.

Cat fetched her clothes for her, and Talea squirmed into them underneath the blankets. Together they pulled her big sister from the bed, as Brea muttered sleepy threats.

By the time the three of them climbed down the ladder from the room beneath the eaves, Brusco and his sons were out in the boat on the little canal behind the house. Brusco barked at the girls to hurry, as he did every morning. His sons helped Talea and Brea onto the boat. It was Cat's task to untie them from the piling, toss the rope to Brea, and shove the boat away from the dock with a booted foot. Brusco's sons leaned into their poles. Cat ran and leapt across the widening gap between dock and deck.

After that, she had nothing to do but sit and yawn for a long while as Brusco and his sons pushed them through the predawn gloom, wending down a confusion of small canals. The day looked to be a rare one, crisp and clear and bright. Braavos only had three kinds of weather; fog was bad, rain was worse, and freezing rain was worst. But every so often would come a morning when the dawn broke pink and blue and the air was sharp and salty. Those were the days that Cat loved best.

When they reached the broad straight waterway that was the Long Canal, they turned south for the fishmarket. Cat sat with her legs crossed, fighting a yawn and trying to recall the details of her dream. *I dreamed I was a wolf again.* She could remember the smells best of all: trees and earth, her pack brothers, the scents of horse and deer and man, each different from the others, and the sharp acrid tang of fear, always the same. Some nights the wolf dreams were so vivid that she could hear her brothers howling even as she woke, and once Brea had claimed that she was growling in her sleep as she thrashed beneath the covers. She thought that was some stupid lie till Talea said it too.

I should not be dreaming wolf dreams, the girl told herself. *I am a cat now, not a wolf. I am Cat of the Canals.* The wolf dreams belonged to Arya of House Stark. Try as she might, though, she could not rid herself of Arya. It made no difference whether she slept beneath the temple or in the little room beneath the eaves with Brusco's daughters, the wolf dreams still haunted her by night . . . and sometimes other dreams as well.

The wolf dreams were the good ones. In the wolf dreams she was swift and strong, running down her prey with her pack at her heels. It was the other dream she hated, the one where she had two feet instead of four. In that one she was always looking for her mother, stumbling through a wasted land of mud and blood and fire. It was always raining in that dream, and she could hear her mother screaming, but a monster with a dog's head would not let her go save her. In that dream, she was always weeping, like a frightened little girl. *Cats never weep,* she told herself, *no more than wolves do. It's just a stupid dream.*

The Long Canal took Brusco's boat beneath the green copper domes of the Palace of Truth and the tall square towers of the Prestayns and Antaryons before passing under the immense grey arches of the sweetwater river to the district known as Silty Town, where the buildings were smaller and less grand. Later in the day the canal would be choked with serpent boats and barges, but in the predawn darkness they had the waterway almost to themselves. Brusco liked to reach the fishmarket just as the Titan roared to herald the coming of the sun. The sound would boom across the lagoon, faint with distance but still loud enough to wake the sleeping city.

By the time Brusco and his sons tied up by the fishmarket, it was swarming with herring sellers and cod wives, oystermen, clam diggers, stewards, cooks, smallwives, and sailors off the galleys, all haggling loudly with one another as they inspected the morning catch. Brusco would walk from boat to boat, having a look at all the shellfish, and from time to time tapping a cask or crate with his cane. "This one," he would say. "Yes." *Tap tap.* "This one." *Tap tap.* "No, not that. Here." *Tap.* He was not much one for talking. Talea said her father was as grudging with his words as with his coins. Oysters, clams, crabs, mussels, cockles, sometimes prawns . . . Brusco bought it all, depending on what looked best each day. It was for them to carry the crates and casks that he tapped back to the boat. Brusco had a bad back, and could not lift anything heavier than a tankard of brown ale.

Cat always stank of brine and fish by the time they pushed off for home again. She had grown so used to it that she hardly even smelled it anymore. She did not mind the work. When her muscles ached from lifting, or her back got sore from the weight of a cask, she told herself that she was getting stronger.

Once all the casks were loaded, Brusco shoved them off again, and his sons poled them back up the Long Canal. Brea and Talea sat at the front of the boat whispering to one another. Cat knew that they were talking about Brea's boy, the one she climbed up on the roof to meet, after her father was asleep.

"Learn three new things before you come back to us," the kindly man had commanded Cat, when he sent her forth into the city. She always did. Sometimes it was no more than three new words of the Braavosi tongue. Sometimes she brought back sailor's tales, of strange and wondrous happenings from the wide wet world beyond the isles of Braavos, wars and rains of toads and dragons hatching. Sometimes she learned three new japes or three new riddles, or tricks of this trade or the other. And every so often, she would learn some secret.

Braavos was a city made for secrets, a city of fogs and masks and whispers. Its very existence had been a secret for a century, the girl had learned; its location had been hidden thrice that long. "The Nine Free Cities are the daughters of Valyria that was," the kindly man taught her, "but Braavos is the bastard child who ran away from home. We are a mongrel folk, the sons of slaves and whores and thieves. Our forebears came from half a hundred lands to this place of refuge, to escape the dragonlords who had enslaved them. Half a hundred gods came with them, but there is one god all of them shared in common."

"Him of Many Faces."

"And many names," the kindly man had said. "In Qohor he is the Black Goat, in Yi Ti the Lion of Night, in Westeros the Stranger. All men must bow to him in the end, no matter if they worship the Seven or the Lord of Light, the Moon Mother or the Drowned God or the Great Shepherd. All mankind belongs to him . . . else somewhere in the world would be a folk who lived forever. Do you know of any folk who live forever?"

"No," she would answer. "All men must die."

Cat would always find the kindly man waiting for her when she went creeping back to the temple on the knoll on the night the moon went black. "What do you know that you did not know when you left us?" he would always ask her.

"I know what Blind Beqqo puts in the hot sauce he uses on his oysters," she would say. "I know the mummers at the Blue Lantern are going to do *The Lord of the Woeful Countenance* and the mummers at the Ship mean to answer with *Seven Drunken Oarsmen.* I know the bookseller Lotho Lornel sleeps in the house of Tradesman-Captain Moredo Prestayn whenever the honorable tradesman-captain is away on a voyage, and moves out whenever the *Vixen* comes home."

"It is good to know these things. And who are you?"

"No one."

"You lie. You are Cat of the canals, I know you well. Go and sleep, child. On the morrow you must serve."

"All men must serve." And so she did, three days of every thirty. When the moon was black she was no one, a servant of the Many-Faced God in a robe of black and white. She walked beside the kindly man through the fragrant darkness, carrying her iron lantern. She washed the dead, went through their clothes, and counted out their coins. Some days she still helped Umma cook, chopping big white mushrooms and boning fish. But only when the moon was black. The rest of the time she was an orphan girl in a pair of battered boots too big for her feet and a brown cloak with a ragged hem, crying *"Mussels and cockles and clams"* as she wheeled her barrow through the Ragman's Harbor.

The moon would be black tonight, she knew; last night it had been no more than a sliver. "What do you know that you did not know when you left us?" the kindly man would ask as soon as he saw her. *I know that Brusco's daughter Brea meets a boy on the roof when her father is asleep,* she thought. *Brea lets him touch her, Talea says, even though he's just a roof rat and all the roof rats are supposed to be thieves.* That was only one thing, though. Cat would need two more. She was not concerned. There were always new things to learn, down by the ships.

When they returned to the house, Cat helped Brusco's sons unload the boat. Brusco and his daughters divided the shellfish amongst three barrows, arranging them on layered beds of seaweed. "Come back when all is sold," Brusco told the girls, just as he did every morning, and they set forth to cry the catch. Brea would wheel her barrow to the Purple Harbor, to sell to the Braavosi sailors whose ships were anchored there. Talea would try the alleys round the Moon Pool, or sell amongst the temples on the Isle of the Gods. Cat headed for the Ragman's Harbor, as she did nine days of every ten.

Only Braavosi were permitted use of the Purple Harbor, from the Drowned Town and the Sealord's Palace; ships from her sister cities and the rest of the wide world had to use the Ragman's Harbor, a poorer, rougher, dirtier port than the Purple. It was noisier as well, as sailors and traders from half a hundred lands crowded its wharves and alleys, mingling with those who served and preyed on them. Cat liked it best of any place in Braavos. She liked the noise and the strange smells, and seeing what ships had come in on the evening tide and what ships had departed. She liked the sailors too; the boisterous Tyroshi with their booming voices and dyed whiskers; the fair-haired Lyseni, always trying to niggle down her prices; the squat, hairy sailors from the Port of Ibben, growling curses in low, raspy voices. Her favorites were the Summer Islanders, with their skins as smooth and dark as teak. They wore feathered cloaks of red and green and yellow, and the tall masts and white sails of their swan ships were magnificent.

And sometimes there were Westerosi too, oarsmen and sailors off carracks out of Oldtown, trading galleys out of Duskendale, King's Landing, and Gulltown, big-bellied wine cogs from the Arbor. Cat knew the Braavosi words for mussels and cockles and clams, but along the Ragman's Harbor she cried her wares in the trade tongue, the language of the wharves and docks and sailor's taverns, a coarse jumble of words and phrases from a dozen languages, accompanied by hand signs and gestures, most of them insulting. Those were the ones that Cat liked best. Any man who bothered her was apt to see the fig, or hear himself described as an ass's pizzle or a camel's cunt. "Maybe I never saw a camel," she would tell them, "but I know a camel's cunt when I smell one."

Once in a great while that would make somebody angry, but when it did she had her finger knife. She kept it very sharp, and knew how to use it too. Red Roggo showed her one afternoon at the Happy Port, while he was waiting for Lanna to come free. He taught her how to hide it up her sleeve and slip it out when she had need of it, and how to slice a purse so smooth and quick the coins would all be spent before their owner ever missed them. That was good to know, even the kindly man agreed; especially at night, when the bravos and roof rats were abroad.

Cat had made friends along the wharves; porters and mummers, ropemakers and sailmenders, taverners, brewers and bakers and beggars and whores. They bought clams and cockles from her, told her true tales of Braavos and lies about their lives, and laughed at the way she talked when she tried to speak Braavosi. She never let that trouble her. Instead, she showed them all the fig, and told them they were camel cunts, which made them roar with laughter. Gyloro Dothare taught her filthy songs, and his brother Gyleno told her the best places to catch eels. The mummers off the Ship showed her how a hero stands, and taught her speeches from *The Song of the Rhoyne, The Conqueror's Two Wives,* and *The Merchant's Lusty Lady.* Quill, the sad-eyed little man who made up all the bawdy farces for the Ship, offered to teach her how a woman kisses, but Tagganaro smacked him with a codfish and put an end to that. Cossomo the Conjurer instructed her in sleight of hand. He could swallow mice and pull them from her ears. "It's magic," he'd say. "It's not," Cat said. "The mouse was up your sleeve the whole time. I could see it moving."

"Oysters, clams, and cockles" were Cat's magic words, and like all good magic words they could take her almost anywhere. She had boarded ships from Lys and Oldtown and the Port of Ibben and sold her oysters right on deck. Some days she rolled her barrow past the towers of the mighty to offer baked clams to the guardsmen at their gates. Once she cried her catch on the steps of the Palace of Truth, and when another peddler tried to run her off she turned his cart over and sent his oysters skittering across the cobbles. Customs officers from the Chequy Port would buy from her, and paddlers from the Drowned Town, whose sunken domes and towers poked up from the green waters of the lagoon. One time, when Brea took to her bed with her moon blood, Cat had pushed her barrow to the Purple Harbor to sell crabs and prawns to oarsmen off the Sealord's pleasure barge, covered stem to stern with laughing faces. Other days she followed the sweetwater river to the Moon Pool. She sold to swaggering bravos in striped satin, and to keyholders and justiciars in drab coats of brown and grey. But she always returned to the Ragman's Harbor.

"Oysters, clams, and cockles," the girl shouted as she pushed her barrow along the wharves. *"Mussels, prawns, and cockles."* A dirty orange cat came padding after her, drawn by the sound of her call. Farther on, a second cat appeared, a sad, bedraggled grey thing with a stub tail. Cats liked the smell of Cat. Some days she would have a dozen trailing after her before the sun went down. From time to time the girl would throw an oyster at them and watch to see who came

away with it. The biggest toms would seldom win, she noticed; oft as not, the prize went to some smaller, quicker animal, thin and mean and hungry. *Like me,* she told herself. Her favorite was a scrawny old tom with a chewed ear who reminded her of a cat that she'd once chased all around the Red Keep. *No, that was some other girl, not me.*

Two of the ships that had been here yesterday were gone, Cat saw, but five new ones had docked; a small carrack called the *Brazen Monkey,* a huge Ibbenese whaler that reeked of tar and blood and whale oil, two battered cogs from Pentos, and a lean green galley up from Old Volantis. Cat stopped at the foot of every gangplank to cry her clams and oysters, once in the trade talk and again in the Common Tongue of Westeros. A crewman on the whaler cursed at her so loudly that he scared away her cats and one of the Pentoshi oarsman asked how much she wanted for the clam between her legs, but she fared better at the other ships. A mate on the green galley wolfed half a dozen oysters and told her how his captain had been killed by the Lysene pirates who had tried to board them near the Stepstones. "That bastard Saan it was, with *Old Mother's Son* and his big *Valyrian.* We got away, but just."

The little *Brazen Monkey* proved to be from Gulltown, with a Westerosi crew who were glad to talk to someone in the Common Tongue. One asked how a girl from King's Landing came to be selling mussels on the docks of Braavos, so she had to tell her tale. "We're here four days, and four long nights," another told her. "Where's a man to go to find a bit of sport?"

"The mummers at the Ship are doing *Seven Drunken Oarsmen,*" Cat told them, "and there's eel fights in the Spotted Cellar, down by the gates of Drowned Town. Or if you want you can go by the Moon Pool, where the bravos duel at night."

"Aye, that's good," another sailor said, "but what Wat was really wanting was a woman."

"The best whores are at the Happy Port, down by where the mummers' Ship is moored." She pointed. Some of the dockside whores were vicious, and sailors fresh from the sea never knew which ones. S'vrone was the worst. Everyone said she had robbed and killed a dozen men, rolling the bodies into the canals to feed the eels. The

Drunken Daughter could be sweet when sober, but not with wine in her. And Canker Jeyne was really a man. "Ask for Merry. Meralyn is her true name, but everyone calls her Merry, and she is." Merry bought a dozen oysters every time Cat came by the brothel and shared them with her girls. She had a good heart, everyone agreed. "That, and the biggest pair of teats in all of Braavos," Merry herself was fond of boasting.

Her girls were nice as well; Blushing Bethany and the Sailor's Wife, one-eyed Yna who could tell your fortune from a drop of blood, pretty little Lanna, even Assadora, the Ibbenese woman with the mustache. They might not be beautiful, but they were kind to her. "The Happy Port is where all the porters go," Cat assured the men of the *Brazen Monkey.* "'The boys unload the ships,' Merry says, 'and my girls unload the lads who sail them.'"

"What about them fancy whores the singers sing about?" asked the youngest monkey, a red-haired boy with freckles who could not have been much more than six-and-ten. "Are they as pretty as they say? Where would I get one o' them?"

His shipmates looked at him and laughed. "Seven hells, boy," said one of them. "Might be the captain could get hisself a courty-san, but only if he sold the bloody ship. That sort o' cunt's for lords and such, not for the likes o' us."

The courtesans of Braavos were famed across the world. Singers sang of them, goldsmiths and jewelers showered them with gifts, craftsmen begged for the honor of their custom, merchant princes paid royal ransoms to have them on their arms at balls and feasts and mummer shows, and bravos slew each other in their names. As she pushed her barrow along the canals, Cat would sometimes glimpse one of them floating by, on her way to an evening with some lover. Every courtesan had her own barge, and servants to pole her to her trysts. The Poetess always had a book to hand, the Moonshadow wore only white and silver, and the Merling Queen was never seen without her Mermaids, four young maidens in the blush of their first flowering who held her train and did her hair. Each courtesan was more beautiful than the last. Even the Veiled Lady was beautiful, though only those she took as lovers ever saw her face.

"I sold three cockles to a courtesan," Cat told the sailors. "She called to me as she was stepping off her barge." Brusco had made it plain to her that she was never to speak to a courtesan unless she was spoken to first, but the woman had smiled at her and paid her in silver, ten times what the cockles had been worth.

"Which one was this, now? The Queen o' Cockles, was it?"

"The Black Pearl," she told them. Merry claimed the Black Pearl was the most famous courtesan of all. "She's descended from the dragons, that one," the woman had told Cat. "The first Black Pearl was a pirate queen. A Westerosi prince took her for a lover and got a daughter on her, who grew up to be a courtesan. Her own daughter followed her, and *her* daughter after her, until you get to this one. What did she say to you, Cat?"

"She said '*I'll take three cockles,*' and '*Do you have some hot sauce, little one?*'" the girl had answered.

"And what did you say?"

"I said, '*No, my lady,*' and, '*Don't call me little one. My name is Cat.*' I should have hot sauce. Beqqo does, and he sells three times as many oysters as Brusco."

Cat told the kindly man about the Black Pearl too. "Her true name is Bellegere Otherys," she informed him. It was one of the three things that she had learned.

"It is," the priest said softly. "Her mother was Bellonara, but the first Black Pearl was a Bellegere as well."

Cat knew that the men off the *Brazen Monkey* would not care about the name of a courtesan's mother, though. Instead, she asked them for tidings of the Seven Kingdoms, and the war.

"War?" laughed one of them. "What war? There is no war."

"Not in Gulltown," said another. "Not in the Vale. The little lord's kept us out of it, same as his mother did."

Same as his mother did. The lady of the Vale was her own mother's sister. "Lady Lysa," she said, "is she . . .?"

". . . dead?" finished the freckled boy whose head was full of courtesans. "Aye. Murdered by her own singer."

"Oh." *It's nought to me. Cat of the Canals never had an aunt. She never did.* Cat lifted her barrow and wheeled away from the *Brazen Monkey,* bumping over cobblestones. *"Oysters, clams, and cockles,"* she called. *"Oysters, clams, and cockles."* She sold most of her clams to the porters off-loading the big wine cog from the Arbor, and the rest to the men repairing a Myrish trading galley that had been savaged by the storms.

Farther down the docks she came on Tagganaro sitting with his back against a piling, next to Casso, King of Seals. He bought some mussels from her, and Casso barked and let her shake his flipper. "You come work with me, Cat," urged Tagganaro as he was sucking mussels from their shells. He had been looking for a new partner ever since the Drunken Daughter put her knife through Little Narbo's hand. "I give you more than Brusco, and you would not smell like fish."

"Casso likes the way I smell," she said. The King of Seals barked, as if to agree. "Is Narbo's hand no better?"

"Three fingers do not bend," complained Tagganaro, between mussels. "What good is a cutpurse who cannot use his fingers? Narbo was good at picking pockets, not so good at picking whores."

"Merry says the same." Cat was sad. She liked Little Narbo, even if he was a thief. "What will he do?"

"Pull an oar, he says. Two fingers are enough for that, he thinks, and the Sealord's always looking for more oarsmen. I tell him, 'Narbo, no. That sea is colder than a maiden and crueler than a whore. Better you should cut off the hand, and beg.' Casso knows I am right. Don't you, Casso?"

The seal barked, and Cat had to smile. She tossed another cockle his way before she went off on her own.

The day was nearly done by the time Cat reached the Happy Port, across the alley from where the Ship was anchored. Some of the mummers sat up atop the listing hulk, passing a skin of wine from hand to hand, but when they saw Cat's barrow they came down for some oysters. She asked them how it went with *Seven Drunken Oarsmen*. Joss the Gloom shook his head. "Quence finally came on Allaquo abed with Sloey. They went at one another with mummer swords, and both of them have left us. We'll only be five drunken oarsmen tonight, it would seem."

"We shall strive to make up in drunkenness what we lack in oarsmen," declared Myrmello. "I for one am equal to the task."

"Little Narbo wants to be an oarsman," Cat told them. "If you got him, you'd have six."

"You had best go see Merry," Joss told her. "You know how sour she gets without her oysters."

When Cat slipped inside the brothel, though, she found Merry sitting in the common room with her eyes shut, listening to Dareon play his woodharp. Yna was there too, braiding Lanna's fine long golden hair. *Another stupid love song.* Lanna was always begging the singer to play her stupid love songs. She was the youngest of the whores, only ten-and-four. Merry asked three times as much for her as for any of the other girls, Cat knew.

It made her angry to see Dareon sitting there so brazen, making eyes at Lanna as his fingers danced across the harp strings. The whores called him the black singer, but there was hardly any black about him now. With the coin his singing brought him, the crow had transformed himself into a peacock. Today he wore a plush purple cloak lined with vair, a striped white-and-lilac tunic, and the parti-colored breeches of a bravo, but he owned a silken cloak as well, and one made of burgundy velvet that was lined with cloth-of-gold. The only black about him was his boots. Cat had heard him tell Lanna that he'd thrown all the rest in a canal. "I am done with darkness," he had announced.

He is a man of the Night's Watch, she thought, as he sang about some stupid lady throwing herself off some stupid tower because her stupid prince was dead. *The lady should go kill the ones who killed her prince. And the singer should be on the Wall.* When Dareon had first appeared at the Happy Port, Arya had almost asked if he would take her with him back to Eastwatch, until she heard him telling Bethany that he was never going back. "Hard beds, salt cod, and endless watches, that's the Wall," he'd said. "Besides, there's no one half as pretty as you at Eastwatch. How could I ever leave you?" He had said the same thing to Lanna, Cat had heard, and to one of the whores at the Cattery, and even to the Nightingale the night he played at the House of Seven Lamps.

I wish I had been here the night the fat one hit him. Merry's whores still laughed about that. Yna said the fat boy had gone red as a beet every time she touched him, but when he started trouble, Merry had him dragged outside and thrown in the canal.

Cat was thinking about the fat boy, remembering how she had saved him from Terro and Orbelo, when the Sailor's Wife appeared beside her. "He sings a pretty song," she murmured softly, in the Common Tongue of Westeros. "The gods must have loved him to give him such a voice, and that fair face as well."

He is fair of face and foul of heart, thought Arya, but she did not say it. Dareon had once wed the Sailor's Wife, who would only bed with men who married her. The Happy Port sometimes had three or four weddings a night. Often, the cheerful wine-soaked red priest Ezzelyno performed the rites. Elsewise it was Eustace, who had once been a septon at the Sept-Beyond-the-Sea. If neither priest nor septon was on hand, one of the whores would run to the Ship and fetch back a mummer. Merry always claimed the mummers made much better priests than priests, especially Myrmello.

The weddings were loud and jolly, with a lot of drinking. Whenever Cat happened by with her barrow, the Sailor's Wife would insist that her new husband buy some oysters, to stiffen him for the consummation. She was good that way, and quick to laugh as well, but Cat thought there was something sad about her too.

The other whores said that the Sailor's Wife visited the Isle of the Gods on the days when her flower was in bloom, and knew all the gods who lived there, even the ones that Braavos had forgotten. They said she went to pray for her first husband, her true husband, who had been lost at sea when she was a girl no older than Lanna. "She thinks that if she finds the right god, maybe he will send the winds and blow her old love back to her," said one-eyed Yna, who had known her longest, "but I pray it never happens. Her love is dead, I could taste that in her blood. If he ever should come back to her, it will be a corpse."

Dareon's song was finally ending. As the last notes faded in the air, Lanna gave a sigh and the singer put his harp aside and pulled her up into his lap. He had just started to tickle her when Cat said loudly, "There's oysters, if anyone is wanting some," and Merry's eyes popped open. "Good," the woman said. "Bring them in, child. Yna, fetch some bread and vinegar."

The swollen red sun hung in the sky behind the row of masts when Cat took her leave of the Happy Port, with a plump purse of coins and a barrow empty but for salt and seaweed. Dareon was leaving too. He had promised to sing at the Inn of the Green Eel this evening, he told her as they strolled along together. "Every time I play the Eel, I come away with silver," he boasted, "and some nights there are captains there, and owners." They crossed a little bridge, and made their way down a crooked back street as the shadows of the day grew longer. "Soon I will be playing in the Purple, and after that the Sealord's Palace," Dareon went on. Cat's empty barrow clattered over the cobblestones, making its own sort of rattling music. "Yesterday I ate herring with the whores, but within the year I'll be having emperor crab with courtesans."

"What happened to your brother?" Cat asked. "The fat one. Did he ever find a ship to Oldtown? He said he was supposed to sail on the *Lady Ushanora*."

"We all were. Lord Snow's command. I told Sam, leave the old man, but the fat fool would not listen." The last light of the setting sun shone in his hair. "Well, it's too late now."

"Just so," said Cat as they stepped into the gloom of a twisty little alley.

By the time Cat returned to Brusco's house, an evening fog was gathering above the small canal. She put away her barrow, found Brusco in his counting room, and thumped her purse down on the table in front of him. She thumped the boots down too.

Brusco gave the purse a pat. "Good. But what's this?"

"Boots."

"Good boots are hard to find," said Brusco, "but these are too small for my feet." He picked one up to squint at it.

"The moon will be black tonight," she reminded him.

"Best you pray, then." Brusco shoved the boots aside and poured out the coins to count them. "*Valar dohaeris.*"

Valar morghulis, she thought.

Fog rose all around as she walked through the streets of Braavos. She was shivering a little by the time she pushed through the weirwood door into the House of Black and White. Only a few candles burned this evening, flickering like fallen stars. In the darkness all the gods were strangers.

Down in the vaults, she untied Cat's threadbare cloak, pulled Cat's fishy brown tunic over her head, kicked off Cat's salt-stained boots, climbed out of Cat's smallclothes, and bathed in lemonwater to wash away the very smell of Cat of the Canals. When she emerged, soaped and scrubbed pink with her brown hair plastered to her cheeks, Cat was gone. She donned clean robes and a pair of soft cloth slippers, and padded to the kitchens to beg some food of Umma. The priests and acolytes had already eaten, but the cook had saved a piece of nice fried cod for her, and some mashed yellow turnips. She wolfed it down, washed the dish, then went to help the waif prepare her potions.

Her part was mostly fetching, scrambling up ladders to find the herbs and leaves the waif required. "Sweetsleep is the gentlest of poisons," the waif told her, as she was grinding some with a mortar and pestle. "A few grains will slow a pounding heart and stop a hand from shaking, and make a man feel calm and strong. A pinch will grant a night of deep and dreamless sleep. Three pinches will produce that sleep that does not end. The taste is very sweet, so it is best used in cakes and pies and honeyed wines. Here, you can smell the sweetness." She let her have a whiff, then sent her up the ladders to find a red glass bottle. "This is a crueler poison, but tasteless and odorless, hence easier to hide. The tears of Lys, men call it. Dissolved in wine or water, it eats at a man's bowels and belly, and kills as a sickness of those parts. Smell." Arya sniffed, and smelled nothing. The waif put the tears to one side and opened a fat stone jar. "This paste is spiced with basilisk blood. It will give cooked flesh a savory smell, but if eaten it produces violent madness, in beasts as well as men. A mouse will attack a lion after a taste of basilisk blood."

Arya chewed her lip. "Would it work on dogs?"

"On any animal with warm blood." The waif slapped her.

She raised her hand to her cheek, more surprised than hurt. "Why did you do that?"

"It is Arya of House Stark who chews on her lip whenever she is thinking. Are you Arya of House Stark?"

"I am no one." She was angry. "Who are *you*?"

She did not expect the waif to answer, but she did. "I was born the only child of an ancient House, my noble father's heir," the waif replied. "My mother died when I was little, I have no memory of her. When I was six my father wed again. His new wife treated me kindly until she gave birth to a daughter of her own. Then it was her wish that I should die, so her own blood might inherit my father's wealth. She should have sought the favor of the Many-Faced God, but she could not bear the sacrifice he would ask of her. Instead, she thought to poison me herself. It left me as you see me now, but I did not die. When the healers in the House of the Red Hands told my father what she had done, he came here and made sacrifice, offering up all his wealth and me. Him of Many Faces heard his prayer. I was brought to the temple to serve, and my father's wife received the gift."

Arya considered her warily. "Is that true?"

"There is truth in it."

"And lies as well?"

"There is an untruth, and an exaggeration."

She had been watching the waif's face the whole time she told her story, but the other girl had shown her no signs. "The Many-Faced God took two-thirds of your father's wealth, not all."

"Just so. That was my exaggeration."

Arya grinned, realized she was grinning, and gave her cheek a pinch. *Rule your face,* she told herself. *My smile is my servant, he should come at my command.* "What part was the lie?"

"No part. I lied about the lie."

"Did you? Or are you lying now?"

But before the waif could answer, the kindly man stepped into the chamber, smiling. "You have returned to us."

"The moon is black."

"It is. What three new things do you know, that you did not know when last you left us?"

I know thirty new things, she almost said. "Three of Little Narbo's fingers will not bend. He means to be an oarsman."

"It is good to know this. And what else?"

She thought back on her day. "Quence and Alaquo had a fight and left the Ship, but I think that they'll come back."

"Do you only think, or do you *know*?"

"I only think," she had to confess, even though she was certain of it. Mummers had to eat the same as other men, and Quence and Alaquo were not good enough for the Blue Lantern.

"Just so," said the kindly man. "And the third thing?"

This time she did not hesitate. "Dareon is dead. The black singer who was sleeping at the Happy Port. He was really a deserter from the Night's Watch. Someone slit his throat and pushed him into a canal, but they kept his boots."

"Good boots are hard to find."

"Just so." She tried to keep her face still.

"Who could have done this thing, I wonder?"

"Arya of House Stark." She watched his eyes, his mouth, the muscles of his jaw.

"That girl? I thought she had left Braavos. Who are you?"

"No one."

"You lie." He turned to the waif. "My throat is dry. Do me a kindness and bring a cup of wine for me and warm milk for our friend Arya, who has returned to us so unexpectedly."

On her way across the city, Arya had wondered what the kindly man would say when she told him about Dareon. Maybe he would be angry with her, or maybe he would be pleased that she had given the singer the gift of the Many-Faced God. She had played this talk out in her head half a hundred times, like a mummer in a show. But she had never thought *warm milk.*

When the milk came, Arya drank it down. It smelled a little burnt and had a bitter aftertaste. "Go to bed now, child," the kindly man said. "On the morrow you must serve."

That night she dreamed she was a wolf again, but it was different from the other dreams. In this dream she had no pack. She prowled alone, bounding over rooftops and padding silently beside the banks of a canal, stalking shadows through the fog.

When she woke the next morning, she was blind.

SAMWELL

T he *Cinnamon Wind* was a swan ship out of Tall Trees Town on the Summer Isles, where men were black, women were wanton, and even the gods were strange. She had no septon aboard her to lead them in the prayers of passing, so the task fell to Samwell Tarly, somewhere off the sun-scorched southern coast of Dorne.

Sam donned his blacks to say the words, though the afternoon was warm and muggy, with nary a breath of wind. "He was a good man," he began . . . but as soon as he had said the words he knew that they were wrong. "No. He was a *great* man. A maester of the Citadel, chained and sworn, and Sworn Brother of the Night's Watch, ever faithful. When he was born they named him for a hero who had died too young, but though he lived a long long time, his own life was no less heroic. No man was wiser, or gentler, or kinder. At the Wall, a dozen lords commander came and went during his years of service, but he was always there to counsel them. He counseled kings as well. He could have been a king himself, but when they offered him the crown he told them they should give it to his younger brother. How many men would do that?" Sam felt the tears welling in his eyes, and knew he could not go on much longer. "He was the blood of the dragon, but now his fire has gone out. He was Aemon Targaryen. And now his watch is ended."

"And now his watch is ended," Gilly murmured after him, rocking the babe in her arms. Kojja Mo echoed her in the Common Tongue of Westeros, then repeated the words in the Summer Tongue for Xhondo and her father and the rest of the assembled crew. Sam hung his head and began to weep, his sobs so loud and wrenching that they made his whole body shake. Gilly came and stood beside him and let him cry upon her shoulder. There were tears in her eyes as well.

The air was moist and warm and dead calm, and the *Cinnamon Wind* was adrift upon a deep blue sea far beyond the sight of land. "Black Sam said good words," Xhondo said. "Now we drink his life." He shouted something in the Summer Tongue, and a cask of spiced rum was rolled up onto the afterdeck and breached, so those on watch might down a cup in the memory of the old blind dragon. The crew had known him only a short while, but Summer Islanders revered the elderly and celebrated their dead.

Sam had never drunk rum before. The liquor was strange and heady; sweet at first, but with a fiery aftertaste that burned his tongue. He was tired, so tired. Every muscle he had was aching, and there were other aches in places where Sam hadn't known he had muscles. His knees were stiff, his hands covered with fresh new blisters and raw, sticky patches of skin where the old blisters had burst. Yet between them, rum and sadness seemed to wash his hurts away. "If only we could have gotten him to Oldtown, the archmaesters might have saved him," he told Gilly, as they sipped their rum on the *Cinnamon Wind*'s high forecastle. "The healers of the Citadel are the best in the Seven Kingdoms. For a while I thought . . . I hoped . . ."

On Braavos, it had seemed possible that Aemon might recover. Xhondo's talk of dragons had almost seemed to restore the old man to himself. That night he ate every bite Sam put before him. "No one ever looked for a girl," he said. "It was a prince that was promised, not a princess. Rhaegar, I thought . . . the smoke was from the fire that devoured Summerhall on the day of his birth, the salt from the tears shed for those who died. He shared my belief when he was young, but later he became persuaded that it was his own son who fulfilled the prophecy, for a comet had been seen above King's Landing on the night Aegon was conceived, and Rhaegar was certain the bleeding star had to be a comet. What fools we were, who thought ourselves so wise! The error crept in from the translation. Dragons are neither male nor female, Barth saw the truth of that, but now one and now the other, as changeable as flame. The language misled us all for a thousand years. *Daenerys* is the one, born amidst salt and smoke. The dragons prove it." Just talking of her seemed to make him stronger. "I must go to her. I *must*. Would that I was even ten years younger."

The old man had been so determined that he had even walked up the plank onto the *Cinnamon Wind* on his own two legs, after Sam made arrangements for their passage. He had already given his sword and scabbard to Xhondo, to repay the big mate for the feathered cloak he'd ruined saving Sam from drowning. The only things of value that still remained to them were the books they had brought from the vaults of Castle Black. Sam parted with them glumly. "They were meant for the Citadel," he said, when Xhondo asked him what was wrong. When the mate translated those words, the captain laughed. "Quhuru Mo says the grey men will be having these books still," Xhondo told him, "only they will be buying them from Quhuru Mo. The maesters give good silver for books they are not having, and sometimes red and yellow gold."

The captain wanted Aemon's chain as well, but there Sam had refused. It was a great shame for any maester to surrender his chain, he had explained. Xhondo had to go over that part three times before Quhuru Mo accepted it. By the time the dealing was done, Sam was down to his boots and blacks and smallclothes, and the broken horn Jon Snow had found on the Fist of First Men. *I had no choice*, he told himself. *We could not stay on Braavos, and short of theft or beggary, there was no other way to pay for passage.* He would have counted it cheap at thrice the price if only they had gotten Maester Aemon safe to Oldtown.

Their passage south had been a stormy one, however, and every gale took its toll on the old man's strength and spirits. At Pentos he asked to be brought up onto deck so Sam might paint a picture of the city for him with words, but that was the last time he left the captain's bed. Soon after that, his wits began to wander once again. By the time the *Cinnamon Wind* swept past the Bleeding Tower into Tyrosh harbor, Aemon no longer spoke of trying to find a ship to take him east. Instead his talk turned back to Oldtown, and the archmaesters of the Citadel.

"You must tell them, Sam," he said. "The archmaesters. You must make them understand. The men who were at the Citadel when I was have been dead for fifty years. These others never knew me. My letters . . . in Oldtown, they must have read like the ravings of an old man whose wits had fled. You must convince them, where I could not. Tell them, Sam . . . tell them how it is upon the Wall . . . the wights and the white walkers, the creeping cold . . ."

"I will," Sam promised. "I will add my voice to yours, maester. We will both tell them, the two of us together."

"No," the old man said. "It must be you. Tell them. The prophecy . . . my brother's dream . . . Lady Melisandre has misread the signs. Stannis . . . Stannis has some of the dragon blood in him, yes. His brothers did as well. Rhaelle, Egg's little girl, she was how they came by it . . . their father's mother . . . she used to call me Uncle Maester when she was a little girl. I remembered that, so I allowed myself to hope . . . perhaps I wanted to . . . we all deceive ourselves, when we want to believe. Melisandre most of all, I think. The sword is wrong, she has to know that . . . light without heat . . . an empty glamor . . . the sword is *wrong*, and the false light can only lead us deeper into darkness, Sam. *Daenerys* is our hope. Tell them that, at the Citadel. Make them listen. They must send her a maester. Daenerys must be counseled, taught, *protected*. For all these years, I've lingered, waiting, watching, and now that the day has dawned I am too old. I am dying, Sam." Tears ran from his blind white eyes at that admission. "Death should hold no fear for a man as old as me, but it does. Isn't that silly? It is always dark where I am, so why should I fear the darkness? Yet I cannot help but wonder what will follow, when the last warmth leaves my body. Will I feast forever in the Father's golden hall as the septons say? Will I talk with Egg again, find Dareon whole and happy, hear my sisters singing to their children? What if the horselords have the truth of it? Will I ride through the night sky forever on a stallion made of flame? Or must I return again to this vale of sorrow? Who can say, truly? Who has been beyond the wall of death to see? Only the wights, and we know what they are like. We know."

There was little and less that Sam could say to that, but he had given the old man what little comfort he could. And Gilly came in afterward and sang a song for him, a nonsense song thing that she learned from some of Craster's other wives. It made the old man smile and helped him go to sleep.

That had been one of his last good days. After that the old man spent more time sleeping than awake, curled up beneath a pile of furs in the captain's cabin. Sometimes he would mutter in his sleep. When he woke he'd call for Sam, insisting that he had to tell him something, but oft as not he would have forgotten what he meant to say by the time that Sam arrived. Even when he did recall, his talk was all a jumble. He spoke of dreams and never named the dreamer, of a glass candle that could not be lit and eggs that would not hatch. He said the sphinx was the riddle, not the riddler, whatever that meant. He asked Sam to read for him from a book by Septon Barth, whose writings had been burned during the reign of Baelor the Blessed. Once he woke up weeping. "The dragon must have three heads," he wailed, "but I am too old and frail to be one of them. I should be with her, showing her the way, but my body has betrayed me."

As the *Cinnamon Wind* made her way through the Stepstones, Maester Aemon forgot Sam's name oft as not. Some days he took him for one of his dead brothers. "He was too frail for such a long voyage," Sam told Gilly on the forecastle, after another sip of the rum. "Jon should have seen that. Aemon was a hundred and two years old, he should never have been sent to sea. If he had stayed at Castle Black, he might have lived another ten years."

"Or else she might have burned him. The red woman." Even here, a thousand leagues from the Wall, Gilly was reluctant to say Lady Melisandre's name aloud. "She wanted king's blood for her fires. Val knew she did. Lord Snow too. That was why they made me take Dalla's babe away and leave my own behind in his place. Maester Aemon went to sleep and didn't wake up, but if he had stayed, she would have burned him."

He will still burn, Sam thought miserably, *only now I have to do it.* The Targaryens always gave their fallen to the flames. Quhuru Mo would not allow a funeral pyre aboard the *Cinnamon Wind,* so Aemon's corpse had been stuffed inside a cask of blackbelly rum to preserve it until the ship reached Oldtown.

"The night before he died, he asked if he might hold the babe," Gilly went on. "I was afraid he might drop him, but he never did. He rocked him and hummed a song for him, and Dalla's boy reached up and touched his face. The way he pulled his lip I thought he might be hurting him, but it only made the old man laugh." She stroked Sam's hand. "We could name the little one Maester, if you like. When he's old enough, not now. We could."

"*Maester* is not a name. You could call him Aemon, though."

Gilly thought about that. "Dalla brought him forth during battle, as the swords sang all around her. That should be his name. Aemon Battleborn. Aemon Steelsong."

A name even my lord father might like. A warrior's name. The boy was Mance Rayder's son and Craster's grandson, after all. He had none of Sam's craven blood. "Yes. Call him that."

"When he is two," she promised, "not before."

"Where is the boy?" Sam thought to ask. Between rum and sorrow, it had taken him that long to realize that Gilly did not have the babe with her.

"Kojja has him. I asked her to take him for a while."

"Oh." Kojja Mo was the captain's daughter, taller than Sam and slender as a spear, with skin as black and smooth as polished jet. She captained the ship's red archers too, and pulled a double-curved goldenheart bow that could send a shaft four hundred yards. When the pirates had attacked them in the Stepstones, Kojja's arrows had slain a dozen of them whilst Sam's own shafts were falling in the water. The only thing Kojja Mo loved better than her bow was bouncing Dalla's boy upon her knee and singing to him in the Summer Tongue. The wildling prince had become the darling of all the women in the crew, and Gilly seemed to trust them with him as she had never trusted any man.

"That was kind of Kojja," Sam said.

"I was afraid of her at first," said Gilly. "She was so black, and her teeth were so big and white, I was afraid she was a beastling or a monster, but she's not. She's good. I like her."

"I know you do." For most of her life, the only man Gilly had known had been the terrifying Craster. The rest of her world had been female. *Men frighten her, but women don't,* Sam realized. He could understand that. Back at Horn Hill he had preferred the company of girls as well. His sisters had been kind to him, and though the other girls would sometimes taunt him, cruel words were easier to shrug off than the blows and buffets he got from the other castle boys. Even now, on the *Cinnamon Wind,* Sam felt more comfortable with Kojja Mo than with her father, though that might be because she spoke the Common Tongue and he did not.

"I like you too, Sam," whispered Gilly. "And I like this drink. It tastes like fire."

Yes, Sam thought, *a drink for dragons.* Their cups were empty, so he went over to the cask and filled them once again. The sun was low in the west, he saw, swollen to thrice its proper size. Its ruddy light made Gilly's face seem flushed and red. They drank a cup to Kojja Mo, and one to Dalla's boy, and one to Gilly's babe back on the Wall. And after that nothing would do but to drink two cups for Aemon of House Targaryen. "May the Father judge him justly," Sam said, sniffing. The sun was almost gone by the time they were done with Maester Aemon. Only a long thin line of red still glowed upon the western horizon, like a slash across the sky. Gilly said that the drink was making the ship spin round, so Sam helped her down the ladder to the women's quarters in the bow of the ship.

There was a lantern hanging just inside the cabin, and he managed to bang his head on it going in. "Ow," he said, and Gilly said, "Are you hurt? Let me see." She leaned close . . .

. . . and kissed his mouth.

Sam found himself kissing her back. *I said the words,* he thought, but her hands were tugging at his blacks, pulling at the laces of his breeches. He broke off the kiss long enough to say, "We can't," but Gilly said, "We can," and covered his mouth with her own again. The

Cinnamon Wind was spinning all around them and he could taste the rum on Gilly's tongue and the next thing her breasts were bare and he was touching them. *I said the words,* Sam thought again, but one of her nipples found its way between his lips. It was pink and hard and when he sucked on it her milk filled his mouth, mingling with the taste of rum, and he had never tasted anything so fine and sweet and good. *If I do this I am no better than Dareon,* Sam thought, but it felt too good to stop. And suddenly his cock was out, jutting upward from his breeches like a fat pink mast. It looked so silly standing there that he might have laughed, but Gilly pushed him back onto her pallet, hiked her skirts up around her thighs, and lowered herself onto him with a little whimpery sound. That was even better than her nipples. *She's so wet,* he thought, gasping. *I never knew a woman could get so wet down there.* "I am your wife now," she whispered, sliding up and down on him. And Sam groaned and thought, *No, no, you can't be, I said the words, I said the words,* but the only word he said was, "Yes."

Afterward, she went to sleep with her arms around him and her face across his chest. Sam needed sleep as well, but he was drunk on rum and mother's milk and Gilly. He knew he ought to crawl back to his own hammock in the men's cabin, but she felt so good curled up against him that somehow he could not move.

Others came in, men and women both, and he listened to them kissing and laughing and mating with one another. *Summer Islanders. That's how they mourn. They answer death with life.* Sam had read that somewhere, a long time ago. He wondered if Gilly knew, if Kojja Mo had told her what to do.

He breathed the fragrance of her hair and stared at the lantern swinging overhead. *Even the Crone herself could not lead me safely out of this.* The best thing he could do would be to slip away and jump into the sea. *If I'm drowned, no one need ever know that I shamed myself and broke my vows, and Gilly can find herself a better man, one who is not some big fat coward.*

He awoke the next morning in his own hammock in the men's cabin, with Xhondo bellowing about the wind. *"Wind is up,"* the mate kept shouting. *"Wake and work, Black Sam. Wind is up."* What Xhondo lacked in vocabulary he made up for in volume. Sam rolled from his hammock to his feet, and regretted it at once. His head was fit to split, one of the blisters on his palm had torn open in the night, and he felt as if he were about to retch.

Xhondo had no mercy, though, so all that Sam could do was struggle back into his blacks. He found them on the deck beneath his hammock, all bundled up in one damp heap. He sniffed at them to see how foul they were, and inhaled the smell of salt and sea and tar, wet canvas and mildew, fruit and fish and blackbelly rum, strange spices and exotic woods, and a heady bouquet of his own dried sweat. But Gilly's smell was on them too, the clean smell of her hair and the sweet smell of her milk, and that made him glad to wear them. He would have given much and more for warm dry socks, though. Some sort of fungus had begun to grow between his toes.

The chest of books had not been near enough to buy passage for four from Braavos to Oldtown. The *Cinnamon Wind* was shorthanded, however, so Quhuru Mo had agreed that he would take them, provided that they worked their way. When Sam had protested that Maester Aemon was too weak, the boy a babe in arms, and Gilly terrified of the sea, Xhondo only laughed, "Black Sam is big fat man. Black Sam will work for four."

If truth be told, Sam was so fumble-fingered that he doubted he was even doing the work of one good man, but he did try. He scrubbed decks and rubbed them smooth with stones, he hauled on anchor chains, he coiled rope and hunted rats, he sewed up torn sails, patched leaks with bubbling hot tar, boned fish and chopped fruit for the cook. Gilly tried as well. She was better in the rigging than Sam was, though from time to time the sight of so much empty water still made her close her eyes.

Gilly, Sam thought, *what am I going to do with Gilly?*

It was a long hot sticky day, made longer by his pounding head. Sam busied himself with ropes and sails and the other tasks that Xhondo set him, and tried not to let his eyes wander to the cask of rum that held old Maester Aemon's body . . . or to Gilly. He could not face the wildling girl right now, not after what they'd done last night. When she came up on deck he went below. When she went forward he went aft. When she smiled at him he turned away, feeling wretched. *I should have jumped into the sea whilst she was still asleep,* he thought. *I have always been a craven, but I was never an oathbreaker till now.*

If Maester Aemon had not died, Sam could have asked him what to do. If Jon Snow had been aboard, or even Pyp and Grenn, he might have turned to them. Instead he had Xhondo. *Xhondo would not understand what I was saying. Or if he did, he'd just tell me to fuck the girl again.* "Fuck" had been the first word of the Common Tongue that Xhondo had learned, and he was very fond of it.

He was fortunate that the *Cinnamon Wind* was so big. Aboard the *Blackbird* Gilly could have run him down in hardly any time at all. "Swan ships," the great vessels from the Summer Isles were called in the Seven Kingdoms, for their billowing white sails and for their figureheads, most of which depicted birds. Large as they were, they rode the waves with a grace that was all their own. With a good brisk wind behind them, the *Cinnamon Wind* could outrun any galley, though she was helpless when becalmed. And she offered plenty of places for a craven to hide.

Near the end of Sam's watch, he was finally cornered. He was climbing down a ladder when Xhondo seized him by the collar. "*Black Sam come with Xhondo,*" he said, dragging him across the deck and dumping him at the feet of Kojja Mo.

Far off to the north, a haze was visible low on the horizon. Kojja pointed at it. "There is the coast of Dorne. Sand and rocks and scorpions, and no good anchorage for hundreds of leagues. You can swim there if you like, and walk to Oldtown. You will need to cross the deep desert and climb some mountains and swim the Torentine. Or else you could go to Gilly."

"You do not understand. Last night we . . ."

". . . honored your dead, and the gods who made you both. Xhondo did the same. I had the child, else I would have been with him. All you Westerosi make a shame of loving. There is no shame in loving. If your septons say there is, your seven gods must be demons. In the isles we know better. Our gods gave us legs to run with, noses to smell with, hands to touch and feel. What mad cruel god would give a man eyes and tell him he must forever keep them shut, and never look at all the beauty in the world? Only a monster god, a demon of the darkness." Kojja put her hand between Sam's legs. "The gods gave you this for a reason too, for . . . what is your Westerosi word?"

"*Fucking,*" Xhondo offered helpfully.

"Yes, for fucking. For the giving of pleasure and the making of children. There is no shame in that."

Sam backed away from her. "I took a vow. *I will take no wife, and father no children.* I said the words."

"She knows the words you said. She is a child in some ways, but she is not blind. She knows why you wear the black, why you go to Oldtown. She knows she cannot keep you. She wants you for a little while, is all. She lost her father and her husband, her mother and her sisters, her home, her *world.* All she has is you, and the babe. So you go to her, or swim."

Sam looked despairingly at the haze that marked the distant shore-line. He could never swim so far, he knew.

He went to Gilly. "What we did . . . if I could take a wife, I would sooner have you than any princess or highborn maiden, but I can't. I am still a crow. I said the words, Gilly. I went with Jon into the woods and said the words before a heart tree."

"The trees watch over us," Gilly whispered, brushing the tears from his cheeks. "In the forest, they see all . . . but there are no trees here. Only water, Sam. Only water."

CERSEI

The day had been cold and grey and wet. It had poured all morning, and even when the rain stopped that afternoon the clouds refused to part. They never saw the sun. Such wretched weather was enough to discourage even the little queen. Instead of riding with her hens and their retinue of guardsmen and admirers, she spent all day in the Maidenvault with her hens, listening to the Blue Bard sing.

Cersei's own day was little better, till evenfall. As the grey sky began to fade to black, they told her that the *Sweet Cersei* had come in on the evening tide, and that Aurane Waters was without, begging audience.

The queen sent for him at once. As soon as he strode into her solar, she knew his tidings were good. "Your Grace," he said with a broad smile, "Dragonstone is yours."

"How splendid." She took his hands and kissed him on the cheeks. "I know Tommen will be pleased as well. This will mean that we can release Lord Redwyne's fleet, and drive the ironmen from the Shields." The news from the Reach seemed to grow more dire with every raven. The ironmen had not been content with their new rocks, it seemed. They were raiding up the Mander in strength, and had gone so far as to attack the Arbor and the smaller islands that surrounded it. The Redwynes had kept no more than a dozen warships in their home waters, and all those had been overwhelmed, taken, or sunk. And now there were reports that this madman who called himself Euron Crow's Eye was even sending longships up Whispering Sound toward Oldtown.

"Lord Paxter was taking on provisions for the voyage home when *Sweet Cersei* raised sail," Lord Waters reported. "I would imagine that by now his main fleet has put to sea."

"Let us hope they enjoy a swift voyage, and better weather than today." The queen drew Waters down into the window seat beside her. "Do we have Ser Loras to thank for this triumph?"

His smile vanished. "Some will say so, Your Grace."

"Some?" She gave him a quizzical look. "Not you?"

"I never saw a braver knight," Waters said, "but he turned what could have been a bloodless victory into a slaughter. A thousand men are dead, or near enough to make no matter. Most of them our own. And not just common men, Your Grace, but knights and young lords, the best and the bravest."

"And Ser Loras himself?"

"He will make a thousand and one. They carried him inside the castle after the battle, but his wounds are grievous. He has lost so much blood that the maesters will not even leech him."

"Oh, how sad. Tommen will be heartbroken. He did so admire our gallant Knight of Flowers."

"The smallfolk too," her admiral said. "We'll have maidens weeping into their wine all across the realm when Loras dies."

He was not wrong, the queen knew. Three thousand smallfolk had crowded through the Mud Gate to see Ser Loras off the day he sailed, and three of every four were women. The sight had only served to fill her with contempt. She had wanted to scream at them that they were sheep, to tell them that all that they could ever hope to get from Loras Tyrell was a smile and a flower. Instead, she had proclaimed him the boldest knight in the Seven Kingdoms, and smiled as Tommen presented him with a jeweled sword to carry into battle. The king had given him a hug as well, which had not been part of Cersei's plans, but it made no matter now. She could afford to be generous. Loras Tyrell was dying.

"Tell me," Cersei commanded. "I want to know all of it, from the beginning to the end."

The room had grown dark by the time that he was done. The queen lit some candles and sent Dorcas to the kitchens to bring them up some bread and cheese and a bit of boiled beef with horseradish. As they supped, she bid Aurane to tell the tale again, so she would remember all the details correctly. "I do not want our precious Margaery to hear these tidings from a stranger, after all," she said. "I will tell her myself."

"Your Grace is kind," said Waters with a smile. *A wicked smile,* the queen thought. Aurane did not resemble Prince Rhaegar as much as she had thought. *He has the hair, but so do half the whores in Lys, if the tales are true. Rhaegar was a man. This is a sly boy, no more. Useful in his way, though.*

Margaery was in the Maidenvault, sipping wine and trying to puzzle out some new game from Volantis with her three cousins. Though the hour was late, the guards admitted Cersei at once. "Your Grace," she began, "it is best you hear the news from me. Aurane is back from Dragonstone. Your brother is a hero."

"I always knew he was." Margaery did not seem surprised. *Why should she? She expected this, from the moment Loras begged for the command.* Yet by the time Cersei had finished with her tale, tears glistened on the cheeks of the younger queen. "Redwyne had miners working to drive a tunnel underneath the castle walls, but that was too slow for the Knight of Flowers. No doubt he was thinking of your lord father's people suffering on the Shields. Lord Waters says he ordered the assault not half a day after taking command, after Lord Stannis's castellan refused his offer to settle the siege between them in single combat. Loras was the first one through the breach when the ram broke the castle gates. He rode straight into the dragon's mouth, they say, all in white and swinging his morningstar about his head, slaying left and right."

Megga Tyrell was sobbing openly by then. "How did he die?" she asked. "Who killed him?"

"No one man has that honor," said Cersei. "Ser Loras took a quarrel through the thigh and another through the shoulder, but he fought on gallantly, though the blood was streaming from him. Later, he suffered a mace blow that broke some ribs. After that . . . but no, I would spare you the worst of it."

"Tell me," said Margaery. "I command it."

Command it? Cersei paused a moment, then decided she would let that pass. "The defenders fell back to an inner keep once the curtain wall was taken. Loras led the attack there as well. He was doused with boiling oil."

Lady Alla turned white as chalk, and ran from the room.

"The maesters are doing all they can, Lord Waters assures me, but I fear your brother is too badly burned." Cersei took Margaery in her arms to comfort her. "He saved the realm." When she kissed the little queen upon the cheek, she could taste the salt of her tears. "Jaime will enter all his deeds in the White Book, and the singers will sing of him for a thousand years."

Margaery wrenched free of her embrace, so violently that Cersei almost fell. "Dying is not dead," she said.

"No, but the maesters say—"

"Dying is not dead!"

"I only want to spare you—"

"I know what you want. Get out."

Now you know how I felt, the night my Joffrey died. She bowed, her face a mask of cool courtesy. "Sweet daughter. I am so sad for you. I will leave you with your grief."

Lady Merryweather did not appear that night, and Cersei found herself too restless to sleep. *If Lord Tywin could see me now, he would know he had his heir, an heir worthy of the Rock,* she thought as she lay abed with Jocelyn Swyft snoring softly into the other pillow. Margaery would soon be weeping the bitter tears she should have wept for Joffrey. Mace Tyrell might weep as well, but she had given him no cause to break with her. What had she done, after all, but honor Loras with her trust? He had requested the command on bended knee whilst half her court looked on.

When he dies, I must raise a statue of him somewhere, and give him a funeral such as King's Landing has never seen. The smallfolk would like that. So would Tommen. *Mace may even thank me, poor man. As for his lady mother, if the gods are good this news will kill her.*

The sunrise was the prettiest that Cersei had seen in years. Taena appeared soon thereafter, and confessed to having spent the night consoling Margaery and her ladies, drinking wine and crying and telling tales of Loras. "Margaery is still convinced he will not die," she reported, as the queen was dressed for court. "She plans to send her own maester to look after him. The cousins are praying for the Mother's mercy."

"I shall pray as well. On the morrow, come with me to Baelor's Sept, and we will light a hundred candles for our gallant Knight of Flowers." She turned to her handmaid. "Dorcas, bring my crown. The new one, if you please." It was lighter than the old, pale spun gold set with emeralds that sparkled when she turned her head.

"There are four come about the Imp this morning," Ser Osmund said, when Jocelyn admitted him.

"Four?" The queen was pleasantly surprised. A steady stream of informers had been making their way to the Red Keep, claiming knowledge of Tyrion, but four in one day was unusual.

"Aye," said Osmund. "One brought a head for you."

"I will see him first. Bring him to my solar." *This time, let there be no mistakes. Let me be avenged at long last, so Joff can rest in peace.* The septons said that the number seven was sacred to the gods. If so, perhaps this seventh head would bring her the balm her soul desired.

The man proved to be Tyroshi; short and stout and sweaty, with an unctuous smile that reminded her of Varys and a forked beard dyed green and pink. Cersei misliked him on sight, but was willing to overlook his flaws if he actually had Tyrion's head inside the chest he carried. It was cedar, inlaid with ivory in a pattern of vines and flowers, with hinges and clasps of white gold. A lovely thing, but the queen's only interest lay in what might be within. *It is big enough, at least. Tyrion had a grotesquely large head, for one so small and stunted.*

"Your Grace," the Tyroshi murmured, bowing low, "I see you are as lovely as the tales. Even beyond the narrow sea, we have heard of your great beauty, and the grief that tears your gentle heart. No man can restore your brave young son to you, but it is my hope I can at least offer you some balm for your pain." He laid his hand upon his chest. "I bring you justice. I bring you the head of your *valonqar*."

The old Valyrian word sent a chill through her, though it also gave her a tingle of hope. "The Imp is no longer my brother, if he ever was," she declared. "Nor will I say his name. It was a proud name once, before he dishonored it."

"In Tyrosh, we name him Redhands, for the blood running from his fingers. A king's blood, and a father's. Some say he slew his mother too, ripping his way from her womb with savage claws."

What nonsense, Cersei thought. "'Tis true," she said. "If the Imp's head is in that chest, I shall raise you to lordship and grant you rich lands and keeps." Titles were cheaper than dirt, and the riverlands were full of ruined castles, standing desolate amidst untended fields and burned villages. "My court awaits. Open the box and let us see."

The Tyroshi threw open the box with a flourish, and stepped back smiling. Within, the head of a dwarf reposed upon a bed of soft blue velvet, staring up at her.

Cersei took a long look. "That is not my brother." There was a sour taste in her mouth. *I suppose it was too much to hope for, especially after Loras. The gods are never that good.* "This man has brown eyes. Tyrion had one black eye and one green."

"The eyes, just so . . . Your Grace, your brother's own eyes had . . . somewhat decayed. I took the liberty of replacing them with glass . . . but of the wrong color, as you say."

That only annoyed her further. "Your head may have glass eyes, but I do not. There are gargoyles on Dragonstone that look more like the Imp than this creature. He's *bald,* and twice my brother's age. What happened to his teeth?"

The man shrank before the fury in her voice. "He had a fine set of gold teeth, Your Grace, but we . . . I regret . . ."

"Oh, not yet. But you will." *I ought to have him strangled. Let him gasp for breath until his face turns black, the way my sweet son did.* The words were on her lips.

"An honest mistake. One dwarf looks so much like another, and . . . Your Grace will observe, he has no nose . . ."

"He has no nose because you *cut it off*."

"No!" The sweat on his brow gave the lie to his denial.

"Yes." A poisonous sweetness crept into Cersei's tone. "At least you had that much sense. The last fool tried to tell me that a hedge wizard had regrown it. Still, it seems to me that you owe this dwarf a nose. House Lannister pays its debts, and so shall you. Ser Meryn, take this fraud to Qyburn."

Ser Meryn Trant took the Tyroshi by the arm and hauled him off, still protesting. When they were gone, Cersei turned to Osmund Kettleblack. "Ser Osmund, get this thing out of my sight, and bring in the other three who claim knowledge of the Imp."

"Aye, Your Grace."

Sad to say, the three would-be informers proved no more useful than the Tyroshi. One said that the Imp was hiding in an Oldtown brothel, pleasuring men with his mouth. It made for a droll picture, but Cersei did not believe it for an instant. The second claimed to have seen the dwarf in a mummer's show in Braavos. The third insisted Tyrion had become a hermit in the riverlands, living on some haunted hill. The queen made the same response to each. "If you will be so good as to lead some of my brave knights to this dwarf, you shall be richly rewarded," she promised. "Provided that it *is* the Imp. If not . . . well, my knights have little patience for deception, nor fools who send them chasing after shadows. A man could lose his tongue." And quick as that, all three informers suddenly lost faith, and allowed that perhaps it might have been some other dwarf they saw.

Cersei had never realized there were so many dwarfs. "Is the whole world overrun with these twisted little monsters?" she complained, whilst the last of the informers was being ushered out. "How many of them can there be?"

"Fewer than there were," said Lady Merryweather. "May I have the honor of accompanying Your Grace to court?"

"If you can bear the tedium," said Cersei. "Robert was a fool about most things, but he was right in one regard. It is wearisome work to rule a kingdom."

"It saddens me to see Your Grace so careworn. I say, run off and play and leave the King's Hand to hear these tiresome petitions. We could dress as serving girls and spend the day amongst the smallfolk, to hear what they are saying of the fall of Dragonstone. I know the inn where the Blue Bard plays when he is not singing attendance on the little queen, and a certain cellar where a conjurer turns lead into gold, water into wine, and girls into boys. Perhaps he would work his spells on the two of us. Would it amuse Your Grace to be a man one night?"

If I were a man I would be Jaime, the queen thought. *If I were a man I could rule this realm in my own name in place of Tommen's.* "Only if you remained a woman," she said, knowing that was what Taena wanted to hear. "You are a wicked thing to tempt me so, but what sort of queen would I be if I put my realm in the trembling hands of Harys Swyft?"

Taena pouted. "Your Grace is too diligent."

"I am," Cersei allowed, "and by day's end I shall rue it." She slipped her arm through Lady Merryweather's. "Come."

Jalabhar Xho was the first to petition her that day, as befit his rank as a prince in exile. Splendid as he looked in his bright feathered cloak, he had only come to beg. Cersei let him make his usual plea for men and arms to help him regain Red Flower Vale, then said, "His Grace is fighting his own war, Prince Jalabhar. He has no men to spare for yours just now. Next year, perhaps." That was what Robert always told him. Next year she would tell him *never*, but not today. Dragonstone was hers.

Lord Hallyne of the Guild of Alchemists presented himself, to ask that his pyromancers be allowed to hatch any dragon's eggs that might turn up upon Dragonstone, now that the isle was safely back in royal hands. "If any such eggs remained, Stannis would have sold them to pay for his rebellion," the queen told him. She refrained from saying that the plan was mad. Ever since the last Targaryen dragon had died, all such attempts had ended in death, disaster, or disgrace.

A group of merchants appeared before her to beg the throne to intercede for them with the Iron Bank of Braavos. The Braavosi were demanding repayment of their outstanding debts, it seemed, and refusing all new loans. *We need our own bank,* Cersei decided, *the Golden Bank of Lannisport.* Perhaps when Tommen's throne was secure, she could make that happen. For the nonce, all she could do was tell the merchants to pay the Braavosi usurers their due.

The delegation from the Faith was headed by her old friend Septon Raynard. Six of the Warrior's Sons escorted him across the city; together they were seven, a holy and propitious number. The new High Septon—or High Sparrow, as Moon Boy had dubbed him—did everything by sevens. The knights wore swordbelts striped in the seven colors of the Faith. Crystals adorned the pommels of their longswords and the crests of their greathelms. They carried kite shields of a style not common since the Conquest, displaying a device not seen in the Seven Kingdoms for centuries: a rainbow sword shining bright upon a field of darkness. Close to a hundred knights had already come forth to pledge their lives and swords to the Warrior's Sons, Qyburn claimed, and more turned up every day. *Drunk on the gods, the lot of them. Who would have thought the realm contained so many of them?*

Most had been household knights and hedge knights, but a handful were of high birth; younger sons, petty lords, old men wanting to atone for the old sins. And then there was Lancel. She had thought Qyburn must be japing when he had told her that her mooncalf cousin had forsaken castle, lands, and wife and wandered back to the city to join the Noble and Puissant Order of the Warrior's Sons, yet there he stood with the other pious fools.

Cersei liked that not at all. Nor was she pleased by the High Sparrow's endless truculence and ingratitude. "Where is the High Septon?" she demanded of Raynard. "It was him I summoned."

Septon Raynard assumed a regretful tone. "His High Holiness sent me in his stead, and bade me tell Your Grace that the Seven have sent him forth to battle wickedness."

"How? By preaching chastity along the Street of Silk? Does he think praying over whores will turn them back to virgins?"

"Our bodies were shaped by our Father and Mother so we might join male to female and beget trueborn children," Raynard replied. "It is base and sinful for women to sell their holy parts for coin."

The pious sentiment would have been more convincing if the

queen had not known that Septon Raynard had special friends in every brothel on the Street of Silk. No doubt he had decided that echoing the High Sparrow's twitterings was preferable to scrubbing floors. "Do not presume to preach at me," she told him. "The brothel keepers have been complaining, and rightly so."

"If sinners speak, why should the righteous listen?"

"These sinners feed the royal coffers," the queen said bluntly, "and their pennies help pay the wages of my gold cloaks and build galleys to defend our shores. There is trade to be considered as well. If King's Landing had no brothels, the ships would go to Duskendale or Gulltown. His High Holiness promised me peace in my streets. Whoring helps to keep that peace. Common men deprived of whores are apt to turn to rape. Henceforth let His High Holiness do his praying in the sept where it belongs."

The queen had expected to hear from Lord Gyles as well, but instead Grand Maester Pycelle appeared, grey-faced and apologetic, to tell her that Rosby was too weak to leave his bed. "Sad to say, I fear Lord Gyles must join his noble forebears soon. May the Father judge him justly."

If Rosby dies, Mace Tyrell and the little queen will try and force Garth the Gross on me again. "Lord Gyles has had that cough for *years,* and it never killed him before," she complained. "He coughed through half of Robert's reign and all of Joffrey's. If he is dying now, it can only be because someone wants him dead."

Grand Maester Pycelle blinked in disbelief. "Your Grace? Wh-who would want Lord Gyles dead?"

"His heir, perhaps." *Or the little queen.* "Some woman he once scorned." *Margaery and Mace and the Queen of Thorns, why not? Gyles is in their way.* "An old enemy. A new one. You."

The old man blanched. "Y-your Grace japes. I . . . I have purged his lordship, bled him, treated him with poultices and infusions . . . the mists give him some relief and sweetsleep helps with the violence of his coughing, but he is bringing up bits of lung with the blood now, I fear."

"Be that as it may. You will return to Lord Gyles and inform him that he does not have my leave to die."

"If it please Your Grace." Pycelle bowed stiffly.

There was more, and more, and more, each petitioner more boring than the last. And that evening, when the last of them had finally gone and she was eating a simple supper with her son, she told him, "Tommen, when you say your prayers before bed, tell the Mother and the Father that you are thankful you are still a child. Being king is hard work. I promise you, you will not like it. They peck at you like a murder of crows. Every one wants a piece of your flesh."

"Yes, Mother," said Tommen, in a sad tone. The little queen had told him of Ser Loras, she understood. Ser Osmund said the boy had wept. *He is young. By the time he is Joff's age he will not recall what Loras looked like.* "I wouldn't mind them pecking, though," her son went on to say. "I should go to court with you every day, to listen. Margaery says—"

"—a deal too much," Cersei snapped. "For half a groat, I'd gladly have her tongue torn out."

"Don't you say that," Tommen shouted suddenly, his round little face turning red. "You leave her tongue alone. Don't you touch her. I'm the king, not you."

She stared at him, incredulous. "What did you say?"

"I'm the king. I get to say who has their tongues torn out, not you. I won't let you hurt Margaery. I *won't*. I forbid it."

Cersei took him by the ear and dragged him squealing to the door, where she found Ser Boros Blount standing guard. "Ser Boros, His Grace has forgotten himself. Kindly escort him to his bedchamber and bring up Pate. This time I want Tommen to whip the boy himself. He is to continue until the boy is bleeding from both cheeks. If His Grace refuses, or says one word of protest, summon Qyburn and tell him to remove Pate's tongue, so His Grace can learn the cost of insolence."

"As you command," Ser Boros huffed, glancing at the king uneasily. "Your Grace, please come with me."

As night fell over the Red Keep, Jocelyn kindled a fire in the queen's hearth whilst Dorcas lit the bedside candles. Cersei opened the window for a breath of air, and found that the clouds had rolled back in to hide the stars. "Such a dark night, Your Grace," murmured Dorcas.

Aye, she thought, *but not so dark as in the Maidenvault, or on Dragonstone where Loras Tyrell lies burned and bleeding, or down in the black cells beneath the castle.* The queen did not know why that occurred to her. She had resolved not to give Falyse another thought. *Single combat. Falyse should have known better than to marry such a fool.* The word from Stokeworth was that Lady Tanda had died of a chill in the chest, brought on by her broken hip. Lollys Lackwit had been proclaimed Lady Stokeworth, with Ser Bronn her lord. *Tanda dead and Gyles dying. It is well that we have Moon Boy, or the court would be entirely bereft of fools.* The queen smiled as she lay her head upon the pillow. *When I kissed her cheek, I could taste the salt of her tears.*

She dreamt an old dream, of three girls in brown cloaks, a wattled crone, and a tent that smelled of death.

The crone's tent was dark, with a tall peaked roof. She did not want to go in, no more than she had wanted to at ten, but the other girls were watching her, so she could not turn away. They were three in the dream, as they had been in life. Fat Jeyne Farman hung back as she always did. It was a wonder she had come this far. Melara Hetherspoon was bolder, older, and prettier, in a freckly sort of way. Wrapped in roughspun cloaks with their hoods pulled up, the three of them had stolen from their beds and crossed the tourney grounds to seek the sorceress. Melara had heard the serving girls whispering how she could curse a man or make him fall in love, summon demons and foretell the future.

In life, the girls had been breathless and giddy, whispering to each other as they went, as excited as they were afraid. The dream was different. In the dream, the pavilions were shadowed, and the knights and serving men they passed were made of mist. The girls wandered for a long while before they found the crone's tent. By the time they did all the torches were guttering out. Cersei watched the girls huddling, whispering to one another. *Go back,* she tried to tell them. *Turn away. There is nothing here for you.* But though she moved her mouth, no words came out.

Lord Tywin's daughter was the first through the flap, with Melara close behind her. Jeyne Farman came last, and tried to hide behind the other two, the way she always did.

The inside of the tent was full of smells. Cinnamon and nutmeg. Pepper, red and white and black. Almond milk and onions. Cloves and lemongrass and precious saffron, and stranger spices, rarer still. The only light came from an iron brazier shaped like a basilisk's head, a dim green light that made the walls of the tent look cold and dead and rotten. Had it been that way in life as well? Cersei could not seem to remember.

The sorceress was sleeping in the dream, as once she'd slept in life. *Leave her be,* the queen wanted to cry out. *You little fools, never wake a sleeping sorceress.* Without a tongue, she could only watch as the girl threw off her cloak, kicked the witch's bed, and said, "Wake up, we want our futures told."

When Maggy the Frog opened her eyes, Jeyne Farman gave a frightened squeak and fled the tent, plunging headlong back into the night. Plump stupid timid little Jeyne, pasty-faced and fat and scared of every shadow. *She was the wise one, though.* Jeyne lived on Fair Isle still. She had married one of her lord brother's bannermen and whelped a dozen children.

The old woman's eyes were yellow, and crusted all about with something vile. In Lannisport it was said that she had been young and beautiful when her husband had brought her back from the east with a load of spices, but age and evil had left their marks on her. She was short, squat, and warty, with pebbly greenish jowls. Her teeth were gone and her dugs hung down to her knees. You could smell sickness on her if you stood too close, and when she spoke her breath was strange and strong and foul. "Begone," she told the girls, in a croaking whisper.

"We came for a foretelling," young Cersei told her.

"Begone," croaked the old woman, a second time.

"We heard that you can see into the morrow," said Melara. "We just want to know what men we're going to marry."

"Begone," croaked Maggy, a third time.

Listen to her, the queen would have cried if she had her tongue. *You still have time to flee. Run, you little fools!*

The girl with the golden curls put her hands upon her hips. "Give us our foretelling, or I'll go to my lord father and have you whipped for insolence."

"Please," begged Melara. "Just tell us our futures, then we'll go."

"Some are here who have no futures," Maggy muttered in her terrible deep voice. She pulled her robe about her shoulders and beckoned the girls closer. "Come, if you will not go. Fools. Come, yes. I must taste your blood."

Melara paled, but not Cersei. A lioness does not fear a frog, no matter how old and ugly she might be. She should have gone, she should have listened, she should have run away. Instead, she took the dagger Maggy offered her, and ran the twisted iron blade across the ball of her thumb. Then she did Melara too.

In the dim green tent, the blood seemed more black than red. Maggy's toothless mouth trembled at the sight of it. "Here," she whispered, "give it here." When Cersei offered her hand, she sucked away the blood with gums as soft as a newborn babe's. The queen could still remember how queer and cold her mouth had been.

"Three questions may you ask," the crone said, once she'd had her drink. "You will not like my answers. Ask, or begone with you."

Go, the dreaming queen thought, *hold your tongue, and flee.* But the girl did not have sense enough to be afraid.

"When will I wed the prince?" she asked.

"Never. You will wed the king."

Beneath her golden curls, the girl's face wrinkled up in puzzlement. For years after, she took those words to mean that she would not marry Rhaegar until after his father Aerys had died. "I *will* be queen, though?" asked the younger her.

"Aye." Malice gleamed in Maggy's yellow eyes. "Queen you shall be . . . until there comes another, younger and more beautiful, to cast you down and take all that you hold dear."

Anger flashed across the child's face. "If she tries I will have my brother kill her." Even then she would not stop, willful child as she was. She still had one more question due her, one more glimpse into her life to come. "Will the king and I have children?" she asked.

"Oh, aye. Six-and-ten for him, and three for you."

That made no sense to Cersei. Her thumb was throbbing where she'd cut it, and her blood was dripping on the carpet. *How could that be?* she wanted to ask, but she was done with her questions.

The old woman was not done with her, however. "Gold shall be their crowns and gold their shrouds," she said. "And when your tears have drowned you, the *valonqar* shall wrap his hands about your pale white throat and choke the life from you."

"What is a *valonqar*? Some monster?" The golden girl did not like that foretelling. "You're a liar and a warty frog and a smelly old savage, and I don't believe a word of what you say. Come away, Melara. She is not worth hearing."

"I get three questions too," her friend insisted. And when Cersei tugged upon her arm, she wriggled free and turned back to the crone. "Will I marry Jaime?" she blurted out.

You stupid girl, the queen thought, angry even now. *Jaime does not even know you are alive.* Back then her brother lived only for swords and dogs and horses . . . and for her, his twin.

"Not Jaime, nor any other man," said Maggy. "Worms will have your maidenhead. Your death is here tonight, little one. Can you smell her breath? She is very close."

"The only breath we smell is yours," said Cersei. There was a jar of some thick potion by her elbow, sitting on a table. She snatched it up and threw it into the old woman's eyes. In life the crone had screamed at them in some queer foreign tongue, and cursed them as they fled her tent. But in the dream her face dissolved, melting away into ribbons of grey mist until all that remained were two squinting yellow eyes, the eyes of death.

The valonqar *shall wrap his hands about your throat,* the queen heard, but the voice did not belong to the old woman. The hands emerged from the mists of her dream and coiled around her neck; thick hands, and strong. Above them floated his face, leering down at her with his mismatched eyes. *No,* the queen tried to cry out, but the dwarf's fingers dug deep into her neck, choking off her protests. She kicked and screamed to no avail. Before long she was making the same sound her son had made, the terrible thin sucking sound that marked Joff's last breath on earth.

She woke gasping in the dark with her blanket wound about her neck. Cersei wrenched it off so violently that it tore, and sat up with her breasts heaving. *A dream,* she told herself, *an old dream and a tangled coverlet, that's all it was.*

Taena was spending the night with the little queen again, so it was Dorcas asleep beside her. The queen shook the girl roughly by the shoulder. "Wake up, and find Pycelle. He'll be with Lord Gyles, I expect. Fetch him here at once." Still half-asleep, Dorcas stumbled from the bed and went scampering across the chamber for her clothing, her bare feet rustling on the rushes.

Ages later, Grand Maester Pycelle entered shuffling, and stood before her with bowed head, blinking his heavy-lidded eyes and struggling not to yawn. He looked as if the weight of the huge maester's chain about his wattled neck was dragging him down to the floor. Pycelle had been old as far back as Cersei could remember, but there was a time when he had also been magnificent: richly clad, dignified, exquisitely courteous. His immense white beard had given him an air of wisdom. Tyrion had shaved his beard off, though, and what had grown back was pitiful, a few patchy tufts of thin, brittle hair that did little to hide the loose pink flesh beneath his sagging chin. *This is no man,* she thought, *only the ruins of one. The black cells robbed him of whatever strength he had. That, and the Imp's razor.*

"How old are you?" Cersei asked, abruptly.

"Four-and-eighty, if it please Your Grace."

"A younger man would please me more."

His tongue flicked across his lips. "I was but two-and-forty when the Conclave called me. Kaeth was eighty when they chose him, and Ellendor was nigh on ninety. The cares of office crushed them, and both were dead within a year of being raised. Merion came next, only six-and-sixty, but he died of a chill on his way to King's Landing. Afterward King Aegon asked the Citadel to send a younger man. He was the first king I served."

And Tommen shall be the last. "I need a potion from you. Something to help me sleep."

"A cup of wine before bed will oft—"

"I *drink* wine, you witless cretin. I require something stronger. Something that will not let me dream."

"You . . . Your Grace does not wish to dream?"

"What did I just say? Have your ears grown as feeble as your cock? Can you make me such a potion, or must I command Lord Qyburn to rectify another of your failures?"

"No. There is no need to involve that . . . to involve Qyburn. Dreamless sleep. You shall have your potion."

"Good. You may go." As he turned toward the door, though, she called him back. "One more thing. What does the Citadel teach concerning prophecy? Can our morrows be foretold?"

The old man hesitated. One wrinkled hand groped blindly at his chest, as if to stroke the beard that was not there. "Can our morrows be foretold?" he repeated slowly. "Mayhaps. There are certain spells in the old books . . . but Your Grace might ask instead, 'Should our morrows be foretold?' And to that I should answer, 'No.' Some doors are best left closed."

"See that you close mine as you leave." She should have known that he would give her an answer as useless as he was.

The next morning, she broke her fast with Tommen. The boy seemed much subdued; ministering to Pate had served its purpose, it would seem. They ate fried eggs, fried bread, bacon, and some blood oranges newly come by ship from Dorne. Her son was attended by his kittens. As she watched the cats frolic about his feet, Cersei felt a little better. *No harm will ever come to Tommen whilst I still live.* She would kill half the lords in Westeros and all the common people, if that was what it took to keep him safe. "Go with Jocelyn," she told the boy after they had eaten.

Then she sent for Qyburn. "Is Lady Falyse still alive?"

"Alive, yes. Perhaps not entirely . . . comfortable."

"I see." Cersei considered a moment. "This man Bronn . . . I cannot say I like the notion of an enemy so close. His power all derives from Lollys. If we were to produce her elder sister . . ."

"Alas," said Qyburn. "I fear that Lady Falyse is no longer capable of ruling Stokeworth. Or, indeed, of feeding herself. I have learned a great deal from her, I am pleased to say, but the lessons have not been entirely without cost. I hope I have not exceeded Your Grace's instructions."

"No." Whatever she had intended, it was too late. There was no sense dwelling on such things. *It is better if she dies*, she told herself. *She would not want to go on living without her husband. Oaf that he was, the fool seemed fond of him.* "There is another matter. Last night, I had a dreadful dream."

"All men are so afflicted, from time to time."

"This dream concerned a witch woman I visited as a child."

"A woods witch? Most are harmless creatures. They know a little herb-craft and some midwifery, but elsewise . . ."

"She was more than that. Half of Lannisport used to go to her for charms and potions. She was mother to a petty lord, a wealthy merchant upjumped by my grandsire. This lord's father had found her whilst trading in the east. Some say she cast a spell on him, though more like the only charm she needed was the one between her thighs. She was not always hideous, or so they said. I don't recall the woman's name. Something long and eastern and outlandish. The smallfolk used to call her Maggy."

"*Maegi?*"

"Is that how you say it? The woman would suck a drop of blood from your finger, and tell you what your morrows held."

"Bloodmagic is the darkest kind of sorcery. Some say it is the most powerful as well."

Cersei did not want to hear that. "This *maegi* made certain prophecies. I laughed at them at first, but . . . she foretold the death of one of my bedmaids. At the time she made the prophecy, the girl was one-and-ten, healthy as a little horse and safe within the Rock. Yet she soon fell down a well and drowned." Melara had begged her never to speak of the things they heard that night in the *maegi*'s tent. *If we never talk about it we'll soon forget, and then it will be just a bad dream we had*, Melara had said. *Bad dreams never come true.* The both of them had been so young, that had sounded almost wise.

"Do you still grieve for this friend of your childhood?" Qyburn asked. "Is that what troubles you, Your Grace?"

"Melara? No. I can hardly recall what she looked like. It is just . . . the *maegi* knew how many children I would have, and she knew of Robert's bastards. Years before he'd sired even the first of them, she knew. She promised me I should be queen, but said another queen would come . . ." *Younger and more beautiful, she said.* ". . . another queen, who would take from me all I loved."

"And you wish to forestall this prophecy?"

More than anything, she thought. "*Can* it be forestalled?"

"Oh, yes. Never doubt that."

"How?"

"I think Your Grace knows how."

She did. *I knew it all along,* she thought. *Even in the tent.* "If she tries, I will have my brother kill her."

Knowing what needed to be done was one thing, though; knowing how to do it was another. Jaime could no longer be relied on. A sudden sickness would be best, but the gods were seldom so obliging. *How then? A knife, a pillow, a cup of heart's bane?* All of those posed problems. When an old man died in his sleep no one thought twice of it, but a girl of six-and-ten found dead in bed was certain to raise awkward questions. Besides, Margaery never slept alone. Even with Ser Loras dying, there were swords about her night and day.

Swords have two edges, though. The very men who guard her could be used to bring her down. The evidence would need to be so overwhelming that even Margaery's own lord father would have no choice but to consent to her execution. That would not be easy. *Her lovers are not like to confess, knowing it would mean their heads as well as hers. Unless . . .*

The next day, the queen came on Osmund Kettleblack in the yard, as he was sparring with one of the Redwyne twins. Which one she could not say; she had never been able to tell the two of them apart. She watched the swordplay for a while, then called Ser Osmund aside. "Walk with me a bit," she said, "and tell me true. I want no empty boasting now, no talk of how a Kettleblack is thrice as good as any other knight. Much may ride upon your answer. Your brother Osney. How good a sword is he?"

"Good. You've seen him. He's not as strong as me nor Osfryd, but he's quick to the kill."

"If it came to it, could he defeat Ser Boros Blount?"

"Boros the Belly?" Ser Osmund chortled. "He's what, forty? Fifty?

Half-drunk half the time, fat even when he's sober. If he ever had a taste for battle, he's lost it. Aye, Your Grace, if Ser Boros wants for killing, Osney could do it easy enough. Why? Has Boros done some treason?"

"No," she said. *But Osney has.*

BRIENNE

They came upon the first corpse a mile from the crossroads.
He swung beneath the limb of a dead tree whose blackened
trunk still bore the scars of the lightning that had killed it.
The carrion crows had been at work on his face, and wolves had
feasted on his lower legs where they dangled near the ground. Only
bones and rags remained below his knees . . . along with one well-
chewed shoe, half-covered by mud and mold.

"What does he have in his mouth?" asked Podrick.

Brienne had to steel herself to look. His face was grey and green
and ghastly, his mouth open and distended. Someone had shoved a
jagged white rock between his teeth. A rock, or . . .

"Salt," said Septon Meribald.

Fifty yards farther on they spied the second body. The scavengers
had torn him down, so what remained of him was strewn on the
ground beneath a frayed rope looped about the limb of an elm.
Brienne might have ridden past him, unawares, if Dog had not sniffed
him out and loped into the weeds for a closer smell.

"What do you have there, Dog?" Ser Hyle dismounted, strode after
the dog, and came up with a halfhelm. The dead man's skull was still
inside it, along with some worms and beetles. "Good steel," he
pronounced, "and not too badly dinted, though the lion's lost his
head. Pod, would you like a helm?"

"Not that one. It's got worms in it."

"Worms wash out, lad. You're squeamish as a girl."

Brienne scowled at him. "It is too big for him."

"He'll grow into it."

"I don't want to," said Podrick. Ser Hyle shrugged, and tossed the broken helm back into the weeds, lion crest and all. Dog barked and went to lift his leg against the tree.

After that, hardly a hundred yards went by without a corpse. They dangled under ash and alder, beech and birch, larch and elm, hoary old willows and stately chestnut trees. Each man wore a noose around his neck, and swung from a length of hempen rope, and each man's mouth was packed with salt. Some wore cloaks of grey or blue or crimson, though rain and sun had faded them so badly that it was hard to tell one color from another. Others had badges sewn on their breasts. Brienne spied axes, arrows, several salmon, a pine tree, an oak leaf, beetles, bantams, a boar's head, half a dozen tridents. *Broken men,* she realized, *dregs from a dozen armies, the leavings of the lords.*

Some of the dead men had been bald and some bearded, some young and some old, some short, some tall, some fat, some thin. Swollen in death, with faces gnawed and rotten, they all looked the same. *On the gallows tree, all men are brothers.* Brienne had read that in a book, though she could not recall which one.

It was Hyle Hunt who finally put words to what all of them had realized. "These are the men who raided Saltpans."

"May the Father judge them harshly," said Meribald, who had been a friend to the town's aged septon.

Who they were did not concern Brienne half so much as who had hanged them. The noose was the preferred method of execution for Beric Dondarrion and his band of outlaws, it was said. If so, the so-called lightning lord might well be near.

Dog barked, and Septon Meribald glanced about and frowned. "Shall we keep a brisker pace? The sun will soon be setting, and corpses make poor company by night. These were dark and dangerous men, alive. I doubt that death will have improved them."

"There we disagree," said Ser Hyle. "These are just the sort of fellows who are most improved by death." All the same, he put his heels into his horse, and they moved a little faster.

Farther on the trees began to thin, though not the corpses. The woods gave way to muddy fields, tree limbs to gibbets. Clouds of crows rose screeching from the bodies as the travelers came near, and settled again once they had passed. *These were evil men,* Brienne reminded herself, yet the sight still made her sad. She forced herself to look at every man in turn, searching for familiar faces. A few she thought she recognized from Harrenhal, but their condition made it hard to be certain. None had a hound's head helm, but few had helms of any sort. Most had been stripped of arms, armor, and boots before they were strung up.

When Podrick asked the name of the inn where they hoped to spend the night, Septon Meribald seized upon the question eagerly, perhaps to take their minds off the grisly sentinels along the roadside. "The Old Inn, some call it. There has been an inn there for many hundreds of years, though *this* inn was only raised during the reign of the first Jaehaerys, the king who built the kingsroad. Jaehaerys and his queen slept there during their journeys, it is said. For a time, the inn was known as the Two Crowns in their honor, until one innkeep built a bell tower, and changed it to the Bellringer Inn. Later, it passed to a crippled knight named Long Jon Heddle, who took up iron-working when he grew too old to fight. He forged a new sign for the yard, a three-headed dragon of black iron that he hung from a wooden post. The beast was so big it had to be made in a dozen pieces, joined with rope and wire. When the wind blew it would clank and clatter, so the inn became known far and wide as the Clanking Dragon."

"Is the dragon sign still there?" asked Podrick.

"No," said Septon Meribald. "When the smith's son was an old man, a bastard son of the fourth Aegon rose up in rebellion against his trueborn brother and took for his sigil a black dragon. These lands belonged to Lord Darry then, and his lordship was fiercely loyal to the king. The sight of the black iron dragon made him wroth, so he cut down the post, hacked the sign into pieces, and cast them into the river. One of the dragon's heads washed up on the Quiet Isle many years later, though by that time it was red with rust. The innkeep never hung another sign, so men forgot the dragon and took to calling the place the River Inn. In those days, the Trident flowed beneath its back door, and half its rooms were built out over the water. Guests could throw a line out their window and catch trout, it's said. There was a ferry landing here as well, so travelers could cross to Lord Harroway's Town and Whitewalls."

"We left the Trident south of here, and have been riding north and west . . . not toward the river but away from it."

"Aye, my lady," the septon said. "The river moved. Seventy years ago, it was. Or was it eighty? It was when old Masha Heddle's grandfather kept the place. It was her who told me all this history. A kindly woman, Masha, fond of sourleaf and honey cakes. When she did not have a room for me, she would let me sleep beside the hearth, and she never sent me on my way without some bread and cheese and a few stale cakes."

"Is she the innkeep now?" asked Podrick.

"No. The lions hanged her. After they moved on, I heard that one of her nephews tried opening the inn again, but the wars had made the roads too dangerous for common folk to travel, so there was little custom. He brought in whores, but even that could not save him. Some lord killed him as well, I hear."

Ser Hyle made a wry face. "I never dreamed that keeping an inn could be so deadly dangerous."

"It is being common-born that is dangerous, when the great lords play their game of thrones," said Septon Meribald. "Isn't that so, Dog?" Dog barked agreement.

"So," said Podrick, "does the inn have a name *now*?"

"The smallfolk call it the crossroads inn. Elder Brother told me that two of Masha Heddle's nieces have opened it to trade once again." He raised his staff. "If the gods are good, that smoke rising beyond the hanged men will be from its chimneys."

"They could call the place the Gallows Inn," Ser Hyle said.

By any name the inn was large, rising three stories above the muddy roads, its walls and turrets and chimneys made of fine white stone that glimmered pale and ghostly against the grey sky. Its south wing had been built upon heavy wooden pilings above a cracked and sunken expanse of weeds and dead brown grass. A thatch-roofed stable and a bell tower were attached to the north side. The whole sprawl was surrounded by a low wall of broken white stones overgrown by moss.

At least no one has burned it down. At Saltpans, they had found only death and desolation. By the time Brienne and her companions were ferried over from the Quiet Isle, the survivors had fled and the dead had been given to the ground, but the corpse of the town itself remained, ashen and unburied. The air still smelled of smoke, and the cries of the seagulls floating overhead sounded almost human, like the lamentations of lost children. Even the castle had seemed forlorn and abandoned. Grey as the ashes of the town around it, the castle consisted of a square keep girded by a curtain wall, built so as to overlook the harbor. It was closed tight as Brienne and the others led their horses off the ferry, nothing moving on its battlements but banners. It took a quarter hour of Dog barking and Septon Meribald knocking on the front gate with his quarterstaff before a woman appeared above them to demand their business.

By that time the ferry had departed and it had begun to rain. "I am a holy septon, good lady," Meribald had shouted up, "and these are honest travelers. We seek shelter from the rain, and a place by your fire for the night." The woman had been unmoved by his appeals. "The closest inn is at the crossroads, to the west," she replied. "We want no strangers here. Begone." Once she vanished, neither Meribald's prayers, Dog's barks, nor Ser Hyle's curses could bring her back. In the end they had spent the night in the woods, beneath a shelter made of woven branches.

There was life at the crossroads inn, though. Even before they reached the gate, Brienne heard the sound: a hammering, faint but steady. It had a steely ring.

"A forge," Ser Hyle said. "Either they have themselves a smith, or the old innkeep's ghost is making another iron dragon." He put his heels into his horse. "I hope they have a ghostly cook as well. A crisp roast chicken would set the world aright."

The inn's yard was a sea of brown mud that sucked at the hooves of the horses. The clang of steel was louder here, and Brienne saw the red glow of the forge down past the far end of the stables, behind an oxcart with a broken wheel. She could see horses in the stables too, and a small boy was swinging from the rusted chains of the weathered gibbet that loomed above the yard. Four girls stood on the inn's porch, watching him. The youngest was no more than two, and naked. The oldest, nine or ten, stood with her arms protectively about the little one. "Girls," Ser Hyle called to them, "run and fetch your mother."

The boy dropped from the chain and dashed off toward the stables. The four girls stood fidgeting. After a moment one said, "We have no mothers," and another added, "I had one but they killed her." The oldest of the four stepped forward, pushing the little one behind her skirts. "Who are you?" she demanded.

"Honest travelers seeking shelter. My name is Brienne, and this is Septon Meribald, who is well-known through the riverlands. The boy is my squire, Podrick Payne, the knight Ser Hyle Hunt."

The hammering stopped suddenly. The girl on the porch looked them over, wary as only a ten-year-old can be. "I'm Willow. Will you be wanting beds?"

"Beds, and ale, and hot food to fill our bellies," said Ser Hyle Hunt as he dismounted. "Are you the innkeep?"

She shook her head. "That's my sister Jeyne. She's not here. All we have to eat is horse meat. If you come for whores, there are none. My sister run them off. We have beds, though. Some featherbeds, but more are straw."

"And all have fleas, I don't doubt," said Ser Hyle.

"Do you have coin to pay? Silver?"

Ser Hyle laughed. "Silver? For a night's bed and a haunch of horse? Do you mean to rob us, child?"

"We'll have silver. Else you can sleep in the woods with the dead men." Willow glanced toward the donkey, and the casks and bundles on his back. "Is that food? Where did you get it?"

"Maidenpool," said Meribald. Dog barked.

"Do you question all your guests this way?" asked Ser Hyle.

"We don't have so many guests. Not like before the war. It's mostly sparrows on the roads these days, or worse."

"Worse?" Brienne asked.

"Thieves," said a boy's voice from the stables. "Robbers."

Brienne turned, and saw a ghost.

Renly. No hammerblow to the heart could have felled her half so hard. "My lord?" she gasped.

"Lord?" The boy pushed back a lock of black hair that had fallen across his eyes. "I'm just a smith."

He is not Renly, Brienne realized. *Renly is dead. Renly died in my arms, a man of one-and-twenty. This is only a boy.* A boy who looked as Renly had, the first time he came to Tarth. *No, younger. His jaw is squarer, his brows bushier.* Renly had been lean and lithe, whereas this boy had the heavy shoulders and muscular right arm so often seen on smiths. He wore a long leather apron, but under it his chest was bare. A dark stubble covered his cheeks and chin, and his hair was a thick black mop that grew down past his ears. King Renly's hair had been that same coal black, but his had always been washed and brushed and combed. Sometimes he cut it short, and sometimes he let it fall loose to his shoulders, or tied it back behind his head with a golden ribbon, but it was never tangled or matted with sweat. And though his eyes had been that same deep blue, Lord Renly's eyes had always been warm and welcoming, full of laughter, whereas this boy's eyes brimmed with anger and suspicion.

Septon Meribald saw it too. "We mean no harm, lad. When Masha Heddle owned this inn she always had a honey cake for me. Sometimes she even let me have a bed, if the inn was not full."

"She's dead," the boy said. "The lions hanged her."

"Hanging seems your favorite sport in these parts," said Ser Hyle Hunt. "Would that I had some land hereabouts. I'd plant hemp, sell rope, and make my fortune."

"All these children," Brienne said to the girl Willow. "Are they your . . . sisters? Brothers? Kin and cousins?"

"No." Willow was staring at her, in a way that she knew well. "They're just . . . I don't know . . . the sparrows bring them here, sometimes. Others find their own way. If you're a woman, why are you dressed up like a man?"

Septon Meribald answered. "Lady Brienne is a warrior maid upon a quest. Just now, though, she is in need of a dry bed and a warm fire. As are we all. My old bones say it's going to rain again, and soon. Do you have rooms for us?"

"No," said the boy smith. "Yes," said the girl Willow.

They glared at one another. Then Willow stomped her foot. "They have *food*, Gendry. The little ones are hungry." She whistled, and more children appeared as if by magic; ragged boys with unshorn locks crept from under the porch, and furtive girls appeared in the windows overlooking the yard. Some clutched crossbows, wound and loaded.

"They could call it Crossbow Inn," Ser Hyle suggested.

Orphan Inn would be more apt, thought Brienne.

"Wat, you help them with those horses," said Willow. "Will, put down that rock, they've not come to hurt us. Tansy, Pate, run get some wood to feed the fire. Jon Penny, you help the septon with those bundles. I'll show them to some rooms."

In the end, they took three rooms adjoining one another, each boasting a featherbed, a chamber pot, and a window. Brienne's room had a hearth as well. She paid a few pennies more for some wood. "Will I sleep in your room, or Ser Hyle's?" Podrick asked as she was opening the shutters. "This is not the Quiet Isle," she told him. "You can stay with me." Come the morrow, she meant for the two of them to strike out on their own. Septon Meribald was going on to Nutten, Riverbend, and Lord Harroway's Town, but Brienne saw no sense in following him any farther. He had Dog to keep him company, and the Elder Brother had persuaded her that she would not find Sansa Stark along the Trident. "I mean to rise before the sun comes up, whilst Ser Hyle is still sleeping." Brienne had not forgiven him for Highgarden . . . and as he himself had said, Hunt had sworn no vows concerning Sansa.

"Where will we go, ser? I mean, my lady?"

Brienne had no ready answer for him. They had come to the crossroads, quite literally; the place where the kingsroad, the river road, and the high road all came together. The high road would take them east through the mountains to the Vale of Arryn, where Lady Sansa's aunt had ruled until her death. West ran the river road, which followed the course of the Red Fork to Riverrun and

Sansa's great-uncle, who was besieged but still alive. Or they could ride the kingsroad north, past the Twins and through the Neck with its bogs and marshes. If she could find a way past Moat Cailin and whoever held it now, the kingsroad would bring them all the way to Winterfell.

Or I could take the kingsroad south, Brienne thought. *I could slink back to King's Landing, confess my failure to Ser Jaime, give him back his sword, and find a ship to carry me home to Tarth, as the Elder Brother urged.* The thought was a bitter one, yet there was part of her that yearned for Evenfall and her father, and another part that wondered if Jaime would comfort her should she weep upon his shoulder. That was what men wanted, wasn't it? Soft helpless women that they needed to protect?

"Ser? My lady? I asked, where are we going?"

"Down to the common room, to supper."

The common room was crawling with children. Brienne tried to count them, but they would not stand still even for an instant, so she counted some of them twice or thrice and others not at all, until she finally gave it up. They had pushed the tables together in three long rows, and the older boys were wrestling benches from the back. *Older* here meant ten or twelve. Gendry was the closest thing to a man grown, but it was Willow shouting all the orders, as if she were a queen in her castle and the other children were no more than servants.

If she were highborn, command would come naturally to her, and deference to them. Brienne wondered whether Willow might be more than she appeared. The girl was too young and too plain to be Sansa Stark, but she was of the right age to be the younger sister, and even Lady Catelyn had said that Arya lacked her sister's beauty. *Brown hair, brown eyes, skinny . . . could it be?* Arya Stark's hair was brown, she recalled, but Brienne was not sure of the color of her eyes. *Brown and brown, was that it? Could it be that she did not die at Saltpans after all?*

Outside, the last light of day was fading. Inside, Willow had four greasy tallow candles lit and told the girls to keep the hearthfire burning high and hot. The boys helped Podrick Payne unpack the donkey and carried in the salt cod, mutton, vegetables, nuts, and wheels of cheese, whilst Septon Meribald repaired to the kitchens to take charge of the porridge. "Alas, my oranges are gone, and I doubt that I shall see another till the spring," he told one small boy. "Have you ever had an orange, lad? Squeezed one and sucked down that fine juice?" When the boy shook his head no, the septon mussed his hair. "Then I'll bring you one, come spring, if you will be a good lad and help me stir the porridge."

Ser Hyle pulled off his boots to warm his feet by the fire. When Brienne sat down next to him, he nodded at the far end of the room. "There are bloodstains on the floor over there where Dog is sniffing. They've been scrubbed, but the blood soaked deep into the wood, and there's no getting it out."

"This is the inn where Sandor Clegane killed three of his brother's men," she reminded him.

"'Tis that," Hunt agreed, "but who is to say that they were the first to die here . . . or that they'll be the last."

"Are you afraid of a few children?"

"Four would be a few. Ten would be a surfeit. This is a cacophony. Children should be wrapped in swaddling clothes and hung upon the wall until the girls grow breasts and the boys are old enough to shave."

"I feel sorry for them. All of them have lost their mothers and fathers. Some have seen them slain."

Hunt rolled his eyes. "I forgot that I was talking to a woman. Your heart is as mushy as our septon's porridge. Can it be? Somewhere inside our swordswench is a mother just squirming to give birth. What you really want is a sweet pink babe to suckle at your teat." Ser Hyle grinned. "You need a man for that, I hear. A husband, preferably. Why not me?"

"If you still hope to win your wager—"

"What I want to win is you, Lord Selwyn's only living child. I've known men to wed lackwits and suckling babes for prizes a tenth the size of Tarth. I am not Renly Baratheon, I confess it, but I have the virtue of being still amongst the living. Some would say that is my only virtue. Marriage would serve the both of us. Lands for me, and a castle full of these for you." He waved his hand at the children. "I am capable, I assure you. I've sired at least one bastard that I know of. Have no fear, I shan't inflict her upon you. The last time I went to see her, her mother doused me with a kettle of soup."

A flush crept up her neck. "My father's only four-and-fifty. Not too old to wed again and get a son by his new wife."

"That's a risk . . . *if* your father weds again and *if* his bride proves fertile and *if* the babe's a boy. I've made worse wagers."

"And lost them. Play your game with someone else, ser."

"So speaks a maid who has never played the game with anyone. Once you do you'll take a different view. In the dark you'd be as beautiful as any other woman. Your lips were made for kissing."

"They are lips," said Brienne. "All lips are the same."

"And all lips are made for kissing," Hunt agreed pleasantly. "Leave your chamber door unbarred tonight, and I will steal into your bed and prove the truth of what I say."

"If you do, you'll be a eunuch when you leave." Brienne got up and walked away from him.

Septon Meribald asked if he might lead the children in a grace, ignoring the small girl crawling naked across the table. "Aye," said Willow, snatching up the crawler before she reached the porridge. So they bowed their heads together and thanked the Father and the Mother for their bounty . . . all but the black-haired boy from the forge, who crossed his arms against his chest and sat glowering as the others prayed. Brienne was not the only one to notice. When the prayer was done Septon Meribald looked across the table, and said, "Do you have no love for the gods, son?"

"Not for your gods." Gendry stood abruptly. "I have work to do." He stalked out without a bite of food.

"Is there some other god he loves?" asked Hyle Hunt.

"The Lord of Light," piped one scrawny boy, nigh to six.

Willow hit him with her spoon. "Ben Big Mouth. There's *food*. You should be eating it, not bothering m'lords with talk."

The children fell upon the supper like wolves upon a wounded deer, quarreling over codfish, tearing the barley bread to pieces, and getting porridge everywhere. Even the huge wheel of cheese did not long survive. Brienne contented herself with fish and bread and carrots, whilst Septon Meribald fed two morsels to Dog for every one he ate himself. Outside, a rain began to fall. Inside, the fire crackled, and the common room was filled by the sounds of chewing, and Willow smacking child-ren with her spoon. "One day, that little girl will make some man a frightful wife," Ser Hyle observed. "That poor 'prentice boy, most like."

"Someone should take him some food before it's all gone."

"You're someone."

She wrapped a wedge of cheese, a heel of bread, a dried apple, and two chunks of flaky fried cod in a square of cloth. When Podrick got up to follow her outside, she told him to sit back down and eat. "I will not be long."

The rain was coming down heavy in the yard. Brienne covered the food with a fold of her cloak. Some of the horses whinnied at her as she made her way past the stables. *They are hungry too.*

Gendry was at his forge, bare-chested beneath his leather apron. He was beating on a sword as if he wished it were a foe, his sweat-soaked hair falling across his brow. She watched him for a moment. *He has Renly's eyes and Renly's hair, but not his build. Lord Renly was more lithe than brawny ... not like his brother Robert, whose strength was fabled.*

It was not until he stopped to wipe his brow that Gendry saw her standing there. "What do *you* want?"

"I brought supper." She opened the cloth for him to see.

"If I wanted food, I would have eaten some."

"A smith needs to eat to keep his strength up."

"Are you my mother?"

"No." She put down the food. "Who was your mother?"

"What's that to you?"

"You were born in King's Landing." The way he spoke made her certain of it.

"Me and many more." He plunged the sword into a tub of rainwater to quench it. The hot steel hissed angrily.

"How old are you?" Brienne asked. "Is your mother still alive? And your father, who was he?"

"You ask too many questions." He set down the sword. "My mother's dead and I never knew my father."

"You're a bastard."

He took it for an insult. "I'm a *knight*. That sword will be mine own, once it's done."

What would a knight be doing working at a smithy? "You have black hair and blue eyes, and you were born in the shadow of the Red Keep. Has no one ever remarked upon your face?"

"What's wrong with my face? It's not as ugly as yours."

"In King's Landing you must have seen King Robert."

He shrugged. "Sometimes. At tourneys, from afar. Once at Baelor's Sept. The gold cloaks shoved us aside so he could pass. Another time I was playing near the Mud Gate when he come back from a hunt. He was so drunk he almost rode me down. A big fat sot, he was, but a better king than these sons of his."

They are not his sons. Stannis told it true, that day he met with Renly. Joffrey and Tommen were never Robert's sons. This boy, though . . . "Listen to me," Brienne began. Then she heard Dog barking, loud and frantic. "Someone is coming."

"Friends," said Gendry, unconcerned.

"What sort of friends?" Brienne moved to the door of the smithy to peer out through the rain.

He shrugged. "You'll meet them soon enough."

I may not want to meet them, Brienne thought, as the first riders came splashing through the puddles into the yard. Beneath the patter of the rain and Dog's barking, she could hear the faint clink of swords and mail from beneath their ragged cloaks. She counted them as they came. *Two, four, six, seven.* Some of them were wounded, judging from the way they rode. The last man was massive and hulking, as big as two of the others. His horse was blown and bloody, staggering beneath his weight. All the riders had their hoods up against the lashing rain, save him alone. His face was broad and hairless, maggot white, his round cheeks covered with weeping sores.

Brienne sucked in her breath and drew Oathkeeper. *Too many,* she thought, with a start of fear, *they are too many.* "Gendry," she said in a low voice, "you'll want a sword, and armor. These are not your friends. They're no one's friends."

"What are you talking about?" The boy came and stood beside her, his hammer in his hand.

Lightning cracked to the south as the riders swung down off their horses. For half a heartbeat darkness turned to day. An axe gleamed silvery blue, light shimmered off mail and plate, and beneath the dark hood of the lead rider Brienne glimpsed an iron snout and rows of steel teeth, snarling.

Gendry saw it too. "Him."

"Not him. His helm." Brienne tried to keep the fear from her voice, but her mouth was dry as dust. She had a pretty good notion who wore the Hound's helm. *The children,* she thought.

The door to the inn banged open. Willow stepped out into the rain, a crossbow in her hands. The girl was shouting at the riders, but a clap of thunder rolled across the yard, drowning out her words. As it faded, Brienne heard the man in the Hound's helm say, "Loose a quarrel at me and I'll shove that crossbow up your cunt and fuck you with it. Then I'll pop your fucking eyes out and make you eat them." The fury in the man's voice drove Willow back a step, trembling.

Seven, Brienne thought again, despairing. She had no chance against seven, she knew. *No chance, and no choice.*

She stepped out into the rain, Oathkeeper in hand. "*Leave her be. If you want to rape someone, try me.*"

The oulaws turned as one. One laughed, and another said something in a tongue Brienne did not know. The huge one with the broad white face gave a malevolent *hissssssssssssssss.* The man in the Hound's helm began to laugh. "You're even uglier than I remembered. I'd sooner rape your horse."

"Horses, that's what we want," one of the wounded men said. "Fresh horses, and some food. There are outlaws after us. Give us your horses and we'll be gone. We won't do you harm."

"Fuck that." The outlaw in the Hound's helm yanked a battle axe off his saddle. "I want to cut her bloody legs off. I'll set her on her stumps so she can watch me fuck the crossbow girl."

"With what?" taunted Brienne. "Shagwell said they cut your manhood off when they took your nose."

She meant it to provoke him, and it did. Bellowing curses, he came at her, his feet sending up splashes of black water as he charged. The others stood back to watch the show, as she had prayed they might. Brienne stayed as still as stone, waiting. The yard was dark, the mud slippery underfoot. *Better to let him come to me. If the gods are good, he'll slip and fall.*

The gods were not that good, but her sword was. *Five steps, four steps, now,* Brienne counted, and Oathkeeper swept up to meet his rush. Steel crashed against steel as her blade bit through his rags and opened a gash in his chainmail, even as his axe came crashing down at her. She twisted aside, slashing at his chest again as she retreated.

He followed, staggering and bleeding, roaring rage. *"Whore!"* he boomed. *"Freak! Bitch! I'll give you to my dog to fuck, you bloody bitch!"* His axe whirled in murderous arcs, a brutal black shadow that turned silver every time the lightning flashed. Brienne had no shield to catch the blows. All she could do was slide back away from him, darting this way and that as the axehead flew at her. Once, the mud gave way under her heel and she almost fell, but somehow she recovered herself, though the axe grazed her left shoulder that time and left a blaze of pain in its wake. "You got the bitch!" one of the others called, and another said, "Let's see her dance away from that one."

Dance she did, relieved that they were watching. Better that than have them interfere. She could not fight seven, not alone, even if one or two were wounded. Old Ser Goodwin was long in his grave, yet she could hear him whispering in her ear. *Men will always underestimate you,* he said, *and their pride will make them want to vanquish you quickly, lest it be said that a woman tried them sorely. Let them spend their strength in furious attacks, whilst you conserve your own. Wait and watch, girl, wait and watch.* She waited, watching, moving sideways, then backwards, then sideways again, slashing now at his face, now at his legs, now at his arm. His blows came more slowly as his axe grew heavier. Brienne turned him so the rain was in his eyes, and stepped back two quick steps. He wrenched his axe up once more, cursing, and lurched after her, one foot sliding in the mud . . .

. . . and she leapt to meet his rush, both hands on her sword hilt. His headlong charge brought him right onto her point, and Oathkeeper punched through cloth and mail and leather and more cloth, deep into his bowels and out his back, rasping as it scraped along his spine. His axe fell from limp fingers, and the two of them slammed together, Brienne's face mashed up against the dog's head helm. She felt the cold wet metal against her cheek. Rain ran down the steel in rivers, and when the lightning flashed again she saw pain and fear and rank disbelief through the eye slits. "Sapphires," she whispered at him, as she gave her blade a hard twist that made him shudder. His weight sagged heavily against her, and all at once it was a corpse that she embraced, there in the black rain. She stepped back and let him fall . . .

. . . and Biter crashed into her, shrieking.

He fell on her like an avalanche of wet wool and milk-white flesh, lifting her off her feet and slamming her down into the ground. She landed in a puddle with a splash that sent water up her nose and into her eyes. All the air was driven out of her, and her head snapped down against some half-buried stone with a *crack*. "No," was all that she had time to say before he fell on top of her, his weight driving her deeper into the mud. One of his hands was in her hair, pulling her head back. The other groped for her throat. Oathkeeper was gone, torn from her grasp. She had only her hands to fight him off, but when she slammed a fist into his face it was like punching a ball of wet white dough. He *hissed* at her.

She hit him again, again, *again,* smashing the heel of her hand into his eye, but he did not seem to feel her blows. She clawed at his wrists, but his grip just grew tighter, though blood ran from the gouges where she scratched him. He was crushing her, smothering her. She pushed at his shoulders to get him off her, but he was heavy as a horse, impossible to move. When she tried to knee him in the groin, all she did was drive her knee into his belly. Grunting, Biter tore out a handful of her hair.

My dagger. Brienne clutched at the thought, desperate. She worked her hand down between them, fingers squirming under his sour, suffocating flesh, searching until they finally found the hilt. Biter locked both his hands about her neck and began to slam her head against the ground. The lightning flashed again, this time inside her skull, yet somehow her fingers tightened, pulled the dagger from its sheath. With him on top of her, she could not raise the blade to stab, so she drew it hard across his belly. Something warm and wet gushed between her fingers. Biter *hissed* again, louder than before, and let go of her throat just long enough to smash her in the face. She heard bones crack, and the pain blinded her for an instant. When she tried to slash at him again, he wrenched the dagger from her fingers and slammed a knee down onto her forearm, breaking it. Then he seized her head again and resumed trying to tear it off her shoulders.

Brienne could hear Dog barking, and men were shouting all about her, and between the claps of thunder she heard the clash of steel on steel. *Ser Hyle*, she thought, *Ser Hyle has joined the fight*, but all that seemed far away and unimportant. Her world was no larger than the hands at her throat and the face that loomed above her. The rain ran off his hood as he leaned closer. His breath stank like cheese gone rotten.

Brienne's chest was burning, and the storm was behind her eyes, blinding her. Bones ground against each other inside of her. Biter's mouth gaped open, impossibly wide. She saw his teeth, yellow and crooked, filed into points. When they closed on the soft meat of her cheek, she hardly felt it. She could feel herself spiraling down into the dark. *I cannot die yet*, she told herself, *there is something I still need to do.*

Biter's mouth tore free, full of blood and flesh. He spat, grinned, and sank his pointed teeth into her flesh again. This time he chewed and swallowed. *He is eating me*, she realized, but she had no strength left to fight him any longer. She felt as if she were floating above herself, watching the horror as if it were happening to some other woman, to some stupid girl who thought she was a knight. *It will be finished soon*, she told herself. *Then it will not matter if he eats me.* Biter threw back his head and opened his mouth again, howling, and stuck his tongue out at her. It was sharply pointed, dripping blood, longer than any tongue should be. Sliding from his mouth, out and out and out, red and wet and glistening, it made a hideous sight, obscene. *His tongue is a foot long,* Brienne thought, just before the darkness took her. *Why, it looks almost like a sword.*

JAIME

The brooch that fastened Ser Brynden Tully's cloak was a black fish, wrought in jet and gold. His ringmail was grim and grey. Over it he wore greaves, gorget, gauntlets, pauldron, and poleyns of blackened steel, none half so dark as the look upon his face as he waited for Jaime Lannister at the end of the drawbridge, alone atop a chestnut courser caparisoned in red and blue.

He loves me not. Tully had a craggy face, deeply lined and windburnt beneath a shock of stiff grey hair, but Jaime could still see the great knight who had once enthralled a squire with tales of the Ninepenny Kings. Honor's hooves clattered against the planks of the drawbridge. Jaime had thought long and hard about whether to wear his gold armor or his white to this meeting; in the end, he'd chosen a leather jack and a crimson cloak.

He drew up a yard from Ser Brynden, and inclined his head to the older man. "Kingslayer," said Tully.

That he would make that name the first word from his mouth spoke volumes, but Jaime was resolved to keep his temper. "Blackfish," he responded. "Thank you for coming."

"I assume you have returned to fulfill the oaths you swore my niece," Ser Brynden said. "As I recall, you promised Catelyn her daughters in return for your freedom." His mouth tightened. "Yet I do not see the girls. Where are they?"

Must he make me say it? "I do not have them."

"Pity. Do you wish to resume your captivity? Your old cell is still available. We have put fresh rushes on the floor."

And a nice new pail for me to shit in, I don't doubt. "That was thoughtful of you, ser, but I fear I must decline. I prefer the comforts of my pavilion."

"Whilst Catelyn enjoys the comforts of her grave."

I had no hand in Lady Catelyn's death, he might have said, *and her daughters were gone before I reached King's Landing.* It was on his tongue to speak of Brienne and the sword he'd given her, but the Blackfish was looking at him the way that Eddard Stark had looked at him when he'd found him on the Iron Throne with the Mad King's blood upon his blade. "I came to speak of the living, not the dead. Of those who need not die, but shall . . ."

". . . unless I hand you Riverrun. Is this where you threaten to hang Edmure?" Beneath his bushy brows, Tully's eyes were stone. "My nephew is marked for death no matter what I do. So hang him and be done with it. I expect that Edmure is as weary of standing on those gallows as I am of seeing him there."

Ryman Frey is a bloody fool. His mummer's show with Edmure and the gallows had only made the Blackfish more obdurate, that was plain. "You hold Lady Sybelle Westerling and three of her children. I'll return your nephew in exchange for them."

"As you returned Lady Catelyn's daughters?"

Jaime did not allow himself to be provoked. "An old woman and three children for your liege lord. That's a better bargain than you could have hoped for."

Ser Brynden smiled a hard smile. "You do not lack for gall, Kingslayer. Bargaining with oathbreakers is like building on quicksand, though. Cat should have known better than to trust the likes of you."

It was Tyrion she trusted in, Jaime almost said. *The Imp deceived her too.* "The promises I made to Lady Catelyn were wrung from me at swordpoint."

"And the oath you swore to Aerys?"

He felt his phantom fingers twitching. "Aerys is no part of this. Will you exchange the Westerlings for Edmure?"

"No. My king entrusted his queen to my keeping, and I swore to keep her safe. I will not hand her over to a Frey noose."

"The girl has been pardoned. No harm will come to her. You have my word on that."

"Your word of *honor*?" Ser Brynden raised an eyebrow. "Do you even know what honor is?"

A horse. "I will swear any oath that you require."

"Spare me, Kingslayer."

"I want to. Strike your banners and open your gates and I'll grant your men their lives. Those who wish to remain at Riverrun in service to Lord Emmon may do so. The rest shall be free to go where they will, though I will require them to surrender their arms and armor."

"I wonder, how far will they get, unarmed, before 'outlaws' set upon them? You dare not allow them to join Lord Beric, we both know that. And what of me? Will I be paraded through King's Landing to die like Eddard Stark?"

"I will permit you to take the black. Ned Stark's bastard is the Lord Commander on the Wall."

The Blackfish narrowed his eyes. "Did your father arrange for that as well? Catelyn never trusted the boy, as I recall, no more than she ever trusted Theon Greyjoy. It would seem she was right about them both. No, ser, I think not. I'll die warm, if you please, with a sword in hand running red with lion blood."

"Tully blood runs just as red," Jaime reminded him. "If you will not yield the castle, I must storm it. Hundreds will die."

"Hundreds of mine. Thousands of yours."

"Your garrison will perish to a man."

"I know that song. Do you sing it to the tune of 'The Rains of Castamere'? My men would sooner die upon their feet fighting than on their knees beneath a headsman's axe."

This is not going well. "This defiance serves no purpose, ser. The war is done, and your Young Wolf is dead."

"Murdered in breach of all the sacred laws of hospitality."

"Frey's work, not mine."

"Call it what you will. It stinks of Tywin Lannister."

Jaime could not deny that. "My father is dead as well."

"May the Father judge him justly."

Now, there's an awful prospect. "I would have slain Robb Stark in the Whispering Wood, if I could have reached him. Some fools got in my way. Does it matter how the boy perished? He's no less dead, and his kingdom died when he did."

"You must be blind as well as maimed, ser. Lift your eyes, and you will see that the direwolf still flies above our walls."

"I've seen him. He looks lonely. Harrenhal has fallen. Seagard and Maidenpool. The Brackens have bent the knee, and they've got Tytos Blackwood penned up in Raventree. Piper, Vance, Mooton, all your bannermen have yielded. Only Riverrun remains. We have twenty times your numbers."

"Twenty times the men require twenty times the food. How well are you provisioned, my lord?"

"Well enough to sit here till the end of days if need be, whilst you starve inside your walls." He told the lie as boldly as he could and hoped his face did not betray him.

The Blackfish was not deceived. "The end of your days, perhaps. Our own supplies are ample, though I fear we did not leave much in the fields for visitors."

"We can bring food down from the Twins," said Jaime, "or over the hills from the west, if it comes to that."

"If you say so. Far be it from me to question the word of such an honorable knight."

The scorn in his voice made Jaime bristle. "There is a quicker way to decide the matter. A single combat. My champion against yours."

"I was wondering when you would get to that." Ser Brynden laughed. "Who will it be? Strongboar? Addam Marbrand? Black Walder Frey?" He leaned forward. "Why not you and me, ser?"

That would have been a sweet fight once, Jaime thought, *fine fodder for the singers.* "When Lady Catelyn freed me, she made me swear not to take arms again against the Starks or Tullys."

"A most convenient oath, ser."

His face darkened. "Are you calling me a coward?"

"No. I am calling you a cripple." The Blackfish nodded at Jaime's golden hand. "We both know you cannot fight with that."

"I had two hands." *Would you throw your life away for pride?* a voice inside him whispered. "Some might say a cripple and an old man are well matched. Free me from my vow to Lady Catelyn and I will meet you sword to sword. If I win, Riverrun is ours. If you slay me, we'll lift the siege."

Ser Brynden laughed again. "Much as I would welcome the chance to take that golden sword away from you and cut out your black heart, your promises are worthless. I would gain nothing from your death but the pleasure of killing you, and I will not risk my own life for that . . . as small a risk as that may be."

It was a good thing that Jaime wore no sword; elsewise he would have ripped his blade out, and if Ser Brynden did not slay him, the archers on the walls most surely would. "Are there any terms you will accept?" he demanded of the Blackfish.

"From you?" Ser Brynden shrugged. "No."

"Why did you even come to treat with me?"

"A siege is deadly dull. I wanted to see this stump of yours and hear whatever excuses you cared to offer up for your latest enormities. They were feebler than I'd hoped. You always disappoint, Kingslayer." The Blackfish wheeled his mare and trotted back toward Riverrun. The portcullis descended with a rush, its iron spikes biting deep into the muddy ground.

Jaime turned Honor's head about for the long ride back to the Lannister siege lines. He could feel the eyes on him; the Tully men upon their battlements, the Freys across the river. *If they are not blind, they'll all know he threw my offer in my teeth.* He would need to storm the castle. *Well, what's one more broken vow to the Kingslayer? Just more shit in the bucket.* Jaime resolved to be the first man on the battlements. *And with this golden hand of mine, most like the first to fall.*

Back at camp, Little Lew held his bridle whilst Peck gave him a hand down from the saddle. *Do they think I'm such a cripple that I cannot dismount by myself?* "How did you fare, my lord?" asked his cousin Ser Daven.

"No one put an arrow in my horse's rump. Elsewise, there was little to distinguish me from Ser Ryman." He grimaced. "So now he must needs turn the Red Fork redder." *Blame yourself for that,*

Blackfish. You left me little choice. "Assemble a war council. Ser Addam, Strongboar, Forley Prester, those river lords of ours . . . and our friends of Frey. Ser Ryman, Lord Emmon, whoever else they care to bring."

They gathered quickly. Lord Piper and both Lords Vance came to speak for the repentant lords of the Trident, whose loyalties would shortly be put to the test. The west was represented by Ser Daven, Strongboar, Addam Marbrand, and Forley Prester. Lord Emmon Frey joined them, with his wife. Lady Genna claimed her stool with a look that dared any man there to question her presence. None did. The Freys sent Ser Walder Rivers, called "Bastard Walder," and Ser Ryman's firstborn Edwyn, a pallid, slender man with a pinched nose and lank dark hair. Under a blue lambswool cloak, Edwyn wore a jerkin of finely tooled grey calfskin with ornate scrollwork worked into the leather. "I speak for House Frey," he announced. "My father is indisposed this morning."

Ser Daven gave a snort. "Is he drunk, or just greensick from last night's wine?"

Edwyn had the hard mean mouth of a miser. "Lord Jaime," he said, "must I suffer such discourtesy?"

"Is it true?" Jaime asked him. "Is your father drunk?"

Frey pressed his lips together and eyed Ser Ilyn Payne, who was standing beside by the tent flap in his rusted mail, his sword poking up above one bony shoulder. "He . . . my father has a bad belly, my lord. Red wine helps with his digestion."

"He must be digesting a bloody mammoth," said Ser Daven. Strongboar laughed, and Lady Genna chuckled.

"Enough," said Jaime. "We have a castle to win." When his father sat in council, he let his captains speak first. He was resolved to do the same. "How shall we proceed?"

"*Hang* Edmure Tully, for a start," urged Lord Emmon Frey. "That will teach Ser Brynden that we mean what we say. If we send Ser Edmure's head to his uncle, it may move him to yield."

"Brynden Blackfish is not moved so easily." Karyl Vance, the Lord of Wayfarer's Rest, had a melancholy look. A winestain birthmark covered half his neck and one side of his face. "His own brother could not move him to a marriage bed."

Ser Daven shook his shaggy head. "We have to storm the walls, as I've been saying all along. Siege towers, scaling ladders, a ram to break the gate, that's what's needed here."

"I will lead the assault," said Strongboar. "Give the fish a taste of steel and fire, that's what I say."

"They are *my* walls," protested Lord Emmon, "and that is my gate you would break." He drew his parchment out of his sleeve again. "King Tommen himself has granted me—"

"We've all seen your paper, nuncle," snapped Edwyn Frey. "Why don't you go wave it at the Blackfish for a change?"

"Storming the walls will be a bloody business," said Addam Marbrand. "I propose we wait for a moonless night and send a dozen picked men across the river in a boat with muffled oars. They can scale the walls with ropes and grapnels, and open the gates from the inside. I will lead them, if the council wishes."

"Folly," declared the bastard, Walder Rivers. "Ser Brynden is no man to be cozened by such tricks."

"The Blackfish is the obstacle," agreed Edwyn Frey. "His helm bears a black trout on its crest that makes him easy to pick out from afar. I propose that we move our siege towers close, fill them full of bowmen, and feign an attack upon the gates. That will bring Ser Brynden to the battlements, crest and all. Let every archer smear his shafts with night soil, and make that crest his mark. Once Ser Brynden dies, Riverrun is ours."

"Mine," piped Lord Emmon. "Riverrun is *mine*."

Lord Karyl's birthmark darkened. "Will the night soil be your own contribution, Edwyn? A mortal poison, I don't doubt."

"The Blackfish deserves a nobler death, and I'm the man to give it to him." Strongboar thumped his fist on the table. "I will challenge him to single combat. Mace or axe or longsword, makes no matter. The old man will be my meat."

"Why would he deign to accept your challenge, ser?" asked Ser Forley Prester. "What could he gain from such a duel? Will we lift the siege if he should win? I do not believe that. Nor will he. A single combat would accomplish nought."

"I have known Brynden Tully since we were squires together, in service to Lord Darry," said Norbert Vance, the blind Lord of Atranta. "If it please my lords, let me go and speak with him and try to make him understand the hopelessness of his position."

"He understands that well enough," said Lord Piper. He was a short, rotund, bowlegged man with a bush of wild red hair, the father of one of Jaime's squires; the resemblance to the boy was unmistakeable. "The man's not bloody *stupid,* Norbert. He has eyes . . . and too much sense to yield to such as these." He made a rude gesture in the direction of Edwyn Frey and Walder Rivers.

Edwyn bristled. "If my lord of Piper means to imply—"

"I don't *imply,* Frey. I say what I mean straight out, like an honest man. But what would *you* know of the ways of honest men? You're a treacherous lying weasel, like all your kin. I'd sooner drink a pint of piss than take the word of any Frey." He leaned across the table. "Where is Marq, answer me that? What have you done with my son? He was a *guest* at your bloody wedding."

"And our honored guest he shall remain," said Edwyn, "until you prove your loyalty to His Grace, King Tommen."

"Five knights and twenty men-at-arms went with Marq to the Twins," said Piper. "Are they your guests as well, Frey?"

"Some of the knights, perhaps. The others were served no more than they deserved. You'd do well to guard your traitor's tongue, Piper, unless you want your heir returned in pieces."

My father's councils never went like this, Jaime thought, as Piper came lurching to his feet. "Say that with a sword in your hand, Frey," the small man snarled. "Or do you only fight with smears of shit?"

Frey's pinched face went pale. Beside him Walder Rivers rose. "Edwyn is no man of the sword . . . but I am, Piper. If you have more remarks to make, come outside and make them."

"This is a war council, not a war," Jaime reminded them. "Sit down, the both of you." Neither man moved. *"Now!"*

Walder Rivers seated himself. Lord Piper was not so easy to cow. He muttered a curse and strode from the tent. "Shall I send men after him to drag him back, my lord?" Ser Daven asked Jaime.

"Send Ser Ilyn," urged Edwyn Frey. "We only need his head."

Karyl Vance turned to Jaime. "Lord Piper spoke from grief. Marq is his firstborn son. Those knights who accompanied him to the Twins were nephews and cousins all."

"Traitors and rebels all, you mean," said Edwyn Frey.

Jaime gave him a cold look. "The Twins took up the Young Wolf's cause as well," he reminded the Freys. "Then you betrayed him. That makes you twice as treacherous as Piper." He enjoyed seeing Edwyn's thin smile curdle up and die. *I have endured sufficient counsel for one day,* he decided. "We're done. See to your preparations, my lords. We attack at first light."

The wind was blowing from the north as the lords filed from the tent. Jaime could smell the stink of the Frey encampments beyond the Tumblestone. Across the water Edmure Tully stood forlorn atop the tall grey gallows, with a rope around his neck.

His aunt departed last, her husband at her heels. "Lord nephew," Emmon protested, "this assault on my seat . . . you must not do this." When he swallowed, the apple in his throat moved up and down. "You must *not.* I . . . I forbid it." He had been chewing sourleaf again; pinkish froth glistened on his lips. "The castle is mine, I have the parchment. Signed by the king, by little Tommen. I am the lawful lord of Riverrun, and . . ."

"Not so long as Edmure Tully lives," said Lady Genna. "He is soft of heart and soft of head, I know, but alive, the man is still a danger. What do you mean to do about that, Jaime?"

It's the Blackfish who is the danger, not Edmure. "Leave Edmure to me. Ser Lyle, Ser Ilyn. Attend me, if you would. It's time I paid a visit to those gallows."

The Tumblestone was deeper and swifter than the Red Fork, and the nearest ford was leagues upstream. The ferry had just started across with Walder Rivers and Edwyn Frey when Jaime and his men arrived at the river. As they awaited its return, Jaime told them what he wanted. Ser Ilyn spat into the river.

When the three of them stepped off the ferry on the north bank, a drunken camp follower offered to pleasure Strongboar with her mouth. "Here, pleasure my friend," Ser Lyle said, shoving her toward Ser Ilyn. Laughing, the woman moved to kiss Payne on the lips, then saw his eyes and shrank away.

The paths between the cookfires were raw brown mud, mixed with horse dung and torn up by hooves and boots alike. Everywhere, Jaime saw the twin towers of House Frey displayed on shield and banners, blue on grey, along with the arms of lesser Houses sworn to the Crossing: the heron of Erenford, the pitchfork of Haigh, Lord Charlton's three sprigs of mistletoe. The arrival of the Kingslayer did not go unnoticed. An old woman selling piglets from a basket stopped to stare at him, a knight with a half-familiar face went to one knee, and two men-at-arms pissing in a ditch turned and sprayed each other. "Ser Jaime," someone called after him, but he strode on without turning. Around him he glimpsed the faces of men he'd done his best to kill in the Whispering Wood, where the Freys had fought beneath the direwolf banners of Robb Stark. His golden hand hung heavy at his side.

Ryman Frey's great rectangular pavilion was the largest in the camp; its grey canvas walls were made of sewn squares to resemble stonework, and its two peaks evoked the Twins. Far from being indisposed, Ser Ryman was enjoying some entertainment. The sound of a woman's drunken laughter drifted from within the tent, mingled with the strains of a woodharp and a singer's voice. *I will deal with you later, ser,* Jaime thought. Walder Rivers stood before his own modest tent, talking with two men-at-arms. His shield bore the arms of House Frey with the colors reversed, and a red bend sinister across the towers. When the bastard saw Jaime, he frowned. *There's a cold suspicious look if ever I saw one. That one is more dangerous than any of his trueborn brothers.*

The gallows had been raised ten feet off the ground. Two spearmen were posted at the foot of the steps. "You can't go up without Ser Ryman's leave," one told Jaime.

"This says I can." Jaime tapped his sword hilt with a finger. "The question is, will I need to step over your corpse?"

The spearmen moved aside.

Atop the gallows, the Lord of Riverrun stood staring at the trap beneath him. His feet were black and caked with mud, his legs bare. Edmure wore a soiled silken tunic striped in Tully red and blue, and a noose of hempen rope. At the sound of Jaime's footsteps, he raised his head and licked his dry, cracked lips. *"Kingslayer?"* The sight of Ser Ilyn widened his eyes. "Better a sword than a rope. Do it, Payne."

"Ser Ilyn," said Jaime. "You heard Lord Tully. Do it."

The silent knight gripped his greatsword with both hands. Long and heavy it was, sharp as common steel could be. Edmure's cracked lips moved soundlessly. As Ser Ilyn drew the blade back, he closed his eyes. The stroke had all Payne's weight behind it.

"No! Stop. NO!" Edwyn Frey came panting into view. "My father comes. Fast as he can. Jaime, you must . . ."

"*My lord* would suit me better, Frey," said Jaime. "And you would do well to omit *must* from any speech directed at me."

Ser Ryman came stomping up the gallows steps in company with a straw-haired slattern as drunk as he was. Her gown laced up the front, but someone had undone the laces to the navel, so her breasts were spilling out. They were large and heavy, with big brown nipples. On her head a circlet of hammered bronze sat askew, graven with runes and ringed with small black swords. When she saw Jaime, she laughed. "Who in seven hells is this one?"

"The Lord Commander of the Kingsguard," Jaime returned with cold courtesy. "I might ask the same of you, my lady."

"Lady? I'm no lady. I'm the queen."

"My sister will be surprised to hear that."

"Lord Ryman crowned me his very self." She gave a shake of her ample hips. "I'm the queen o' whores."

No, Jaime thought, *my sweet sister holds that title too.*

Ser Ryman found his tongue. "Shut your mouth, slut, Lord Jaime doesn't want to hear some harlot's nonsense." This Frey was a thickset man with a broad face, small eyes, and a soft fleshy set of chins. His breath stank of wine and onions.

"Making queens, Ser Ryman?" Jaime asked softly. "Stupid. As stupid as this business with Lord Edmure."

"I gave the Blackfish warning. I told him Edmure would die unless the castle yielded. I had this gallows built, to show them that Ser Ryman Frey does not make idle threats. At Seagard my son Walder did the same with Patrek Mallister and Lord Jason bent the knee, but . . . the Blackfish is a cold man. He refused us, so . . ."

". . . you hanged Lord Edmure?"

The man reddened. "My lord grandfather . . . if we hang the man we have no *hostage*, ser. Have you considered that?"

"Only a fool makes threats he's not prepared to carry out. If I were to threaten to hit you unless you shut your mouth, and you presumed to speak, what do you think I'd do?"

"Ser, you do not unders—"

Jaime hit him. It was a backhand blow delivered with his golden hand, but the force of it sent Ser Ryman stumbling backward into the arms of his whore. "You have a fat head, Ser Ryman, and a thick neck as well. Ser Ilyn, how many strokes would it take you to cut through that neck?"

Ser Ilyn laid a single finger against his nose.

Jaime laughed. "An empty boast. I say three."

Ryman Frey went to his knees. "I have done nothing . . ."

". . . but drink and whore. I know."

"I am heir to the Crossing. You can't . . ."

"I warned you about talking." Jaime watched the man turn white. *A sot, a fool, and a craven. Lord Walder had best outlive this one, or the Freys are done.* "You are dismissed, ser."

"Dismissed?"

"You heard me. Go away."

"But . . . where should I go?"

"To hell or home, as you prefer. See that you are not in camp when the sun comes up. You may take your queen of whores, but not that crown of hers." Jaime turned from Ser Ryman to his son. "Edwyn, I am giving you your father's command. Try not to be so stupid as your sire."

"That ought not pose much difficulty, my lord."

"Send word to Lord Walder. The crown requires all his prisoners." Jaime waved his golden hand. "Ser Lyle, bring him."

Edmure Tully had collapsed facedown on the scaffold when Ser Ilyn's blade sheared the rope in two. A foot of hemp still dangled from the noose about his neck. Strongboar grabbed the end of it and pulled him to his feet. "A fish on a leash," he said, chortling. "There's a sight I never saw before."

The Freys stepped aside to let them pass. A crowd had gathered below the scaffold, including a dozen camp followers in various states of disarray. Jaime noticed one man holding a woodharp. "You. Singer. Come with me."

The man doffed his hat. "As my lord commands."

No one said a word as they walked back to the ferry, with Ser Ryman's singer trailing after them. But as they shoved off from the riverbank and made for the south side of the Tumblestone, Edmure Tully grabbed Jaime by the arm. *"Why?"*

A Lannister pays his debts, he thought, *and you're the only coin that's left to me.* "Consider it a wedding gift."

Edmure stared at him with wary eyes. "A . . . wedding gift?"

"I am told your wife is pretty. She'd have to be, for you to bed her while your sister and your king were being murdered."

"I never knew." Edmure licked his cracked lips. "There were fiddlers outside the bedchamber . . ."

"And Lady Roslin was distracting you."

"She . . . they made her do it, Lord Walder and the rest. Roslin never wanted . . . she wept, but I thought it was . . ."

"The sight of your rampant manhood? Aye, that would make any woman weep, I'm sure."

"She is carrying my child."

No, Jaime thought, *that's your death she has growing in her belly.* Back at his pavilion, he dismissed Strongboar and Ser Ilyn, but not the singer. "I may have need of a song shortly," he told the man. "Lew, heat some bathwater for my guest. Pia, find him some clean clothing. Nothing with lions on it, if you please. Peck, wine for Lord Tully. Are you hungry, my lord?"

Edmure nodded, but his eyes were still suspicious.

Jaime settled on a stool while Tully had his bath. The filth came off in grey clouds. "Once you've eaten, my men will escort you to Riverrun. What happens after that is up to you."

"What do you mean?"

"Your uncle is an old man. Valiant, yes, but the best part of his life is done. He has no bride to grieve for him, no children to defend. A good death is all the Blackfish can hope for . . . but you have years remaining, Edmure. And *you* are the rightful lord of House Tully, not him. Your uncle serves at your pleasure. The fate of Riverrun is in your hands."

Edmure stared. "The fate of Riverrun . . ."

"Yield the castle and no one dies. Your smallfolk may go in peace or stay to serve Lord Emmon. Ser Brynden will be allowed to take the black, along with as many of the garrison as choose to join him. You as well, if the Wall appeals to you. Or you may go to Casterly Rock as my captive and enjoy all the comforts and courtesy that befits a hostage of your rank. I'll send your wife to join you, if you like. If her child is a boy, he will serve House Lannister as a page and a squire, and when he earns his knighthood we'll bestow some lands upon him. Should Roslin give you a daughter, I'll see her well dowered when she's old enough to wed. You yourself may even be granted parole, once the war is done. All you need do is yield the castle."

Edmure raised his hands from the tub and watched the water run between his fingers. "And if I will not yield?"

Must you make me say the words? Pia was standing by the flap of the tent with her arms full of clothes. His squires were listening as well, and the singer. *Let them hear,* Jaime thought. *Let the world hear. It makes no matter.* He forced himself to smile, "You've seen our numbers, Edmure. You've seen the ladders, the towers, the trebuchets, the rams. If I speak the command, my coz will bridge your moat and break your gate. Hundreds will die, most of them your own. Your former banner-men will make up the first wave of attackers, so you'll start your day by killing the fathers and brothers of men who died for you at the Twins. The second wave will be Freys, I have no lack of those. My westermen will follow when your archers are short of arrows and your knights so weary they can hardly lift their blades. When the castle falls, all those inside will be put to the sword. Your herds will be butchered, your godswood will be felled, your keeps and towers will burn. I'll pull your walls down, and divert the Tumblestone over the ruins. By the time I'm done no man will ever know that a castle once stood here." Jaime got to his feet. "Your wife may whelp before that. You'll want your child, I expect. I'll send him to you when he's born. With a trebuchet."

Silence followed his speech. Edmure sat in his bath. Pia clutched the clothing to her breasts. The singer tightened a string on his harp. Little Lew hollowed out a loaf of stale bread to make a trencher, pretending that he had not heard. *With a trebuchet,* Jaime thought. If his aunt had been there, would she still say Tyrion was Tywin's son?

Edmure Tully finally found his voice. "I could climb out of this tub and kill you where you stand, Kingslayer."

"You could try." Jaime waited. When Edmure made no move to rise, he said, "I'll leave you to enjoy your food. Singer, play for our guest whilst he eats. You know the song, I trust."

"The one about the rain? Aye, my lord. I know it."

Edmure seemed to see the man for the first time. "No. Not him. Get him away from me."

"Why, it's just a song," said Jaime. "He cannot have *that* bad a voice."

CERSEI

Grand Maester Pycelle had been old for as long as she had known him, but he seemed to have aged another hundred years in the past three nights. It took him an eternity to bend his creaky knee before her, and once he had he could not rise again until Ser Osmund jerked him to his feet.

Cersei studied him with displeasure. "Lord Qyburn informs me that Lord Gyles has coughed his last."

"Yes, Your Grace. I did my best to ease his passing."

"Did you?" The queen turned to Lady Merryweather. "I *did* say I wanted Rosby alive, did I not?"

"You did, Your Grace."

"Ser Osmund, what is your recollection of the conversation?"

"You commanded Grand Maester Pycelle to save the man, Your Grace. We all heard."

Pycelle's mouth opened and closed. "Your Grace must know, I did all that could be done for the poor man."

"As you did for Joffrey? And his father, my own beloved husband? Robert was as strong as any man in the Seven Kingdoms, yet you lost him to a boar. Oh, and let us not forget Jon Arryn. No doubt you would have killed Ned Stark as well, if I had let you keep him longer. Tell me, maester, was it at the Citadel that you learned to wring your hands and make excuses?"

Her voice made the old man flinch. "No man could have done more, Your Grace. I . . . I have always given leal service."

"When you counseled King Aerys to open his gates as my father's host approached, was that your notion of leal service?"

"That . . . I misjudged the . . ."

"Was that good counsel?"

"Your Grace must surely know . . ."

"What I *know* is that when my son was poisoned, you proved to be of less use than Moon Boy. What I *know* is that the crown has desperate need of gold, and our lord treasurer is dead."

The old fool seized upon that. "I . . . I shall draw up a list of men suitable to take Lord Gyles's place upon the council."

"A list." Cersei was amused by his presumption. "I can well imagine the sort of list you would provide me. Greybeards and grasping fools and Garth the Gross." Her lips tightened. "You have been much in Lady Margaery's company of late."

"Yes. Yes, I . . . Queen Margaery has been most distraught about Ser Loras. I provide Her Grace with sleeping draughts and . . . other sorts of potions."

"No doubt. Tell me, was it our little queen who commanded you to kill Lord Gyles?"

"K-kill?" Grand Maester Pycelle's eyes grew as big as boiled eggs. "Your Grace cannot believe . . . it was his cough, by all the gods, I . . . Her Grace would not . . . she bore Lord Gyles no ill will, why would Queen Margaery want him . . ."

". . . dead? Why, to plant another rose on Tommen's council. Are you blind or bought? Rosby stood in her way, so she put him in his grave. With your connivance."

"Your Grace, I swear to you, Lord Gyles perished from his cough." His mouth was quivering. "My loyalty has always been to the crown, to the realm . . . t-to House Lannister."

In that order? Pycelle's fear was palpable. *He is ripe enough. Time to squeeze the fruit and taste the juice.* "If you are as leal as you claim, why are you lying to me? Do not trouble to deny it. You began to dance attendance on Maid Margaery *before* Ser Loras went to Dragonstone, so spare me further fables about how you want only to console our good-daughter in her grief. What brings you to the Maidenvault so often? Not Margaery's vapid conversation, surely? Are you courting that pox-faced septa of hers? Diddling little Lady Bulwer? Do you play the spy for her, informing on me to serve her plots?"

"I . . . I obey. A maester takes an oath of service . . ."

"A grand maester swears to serve the *realm*."

"Your Grace, she . . . she is the queen . . ."

"*I* am the queen."

"I meant . . . she is the king's wife, and . . ."

"I know who she is. What I want to know is why she has need of *you*. Is my good-daughter unwell?"

"Unwell?" The old man plucked at the thing he called a beard, that patched growth of thin white hair sprouting from the loose pink wattles under his chin. "N-not unwell, Your Grace, not as such. My oaths forbid me to divulge . . ."

"Your oaths will be of small comfort in the black cells," she warned him. "I'll hear the truth, or you'll wear chains."

Pycelle collapsed to his knees. "I beg you . . . I was your lord father's man, and a friend to you in the matter of Lord Arryn. I could not survive the dungeons, not again . . ."

"Why does Margaery send for you?"

"She desires . . . she . . . she . . ."

"*Say it!*"

He cringed. "Moon tea," he whispered. "Moon tea, for . . ."

"I know what moon tea is for." *There it is.* "Very well. Get off those saggy knees and try to remember what it was to be a man." Pycelle struggled to rise, but took so long about it that she had to tell Osmund Kettleblack to give him another yank. "As to Lord Gyles, no doubt our Father Above will judge him justly. He left no children?"

"No children of his body, but there is a ward . . ."

". . . not of his blood." Cersei dismissed that annoyance with a flick of her hand. "Gyles knew of our dire need for gold. No doubt he told you of his wish to leave all his lands and wealth to Tommen." Rosby's gold would help refresh their coffers, and Rosby's lands and castle could be bestowed upon one of her own as a reward for leal service.

Lord Waters, perhaps. Aurane had been hinting at his need for a seat; his lordship was only an empty honor without one. He had his eye on Dragonstone, Cersei knew, but there he aimed too high. Rosby would be more suitable to his birth and station.

"Lord Gyles loved His Grace with all his heart," Pycelle was saying, "but . . . his ward . . ."

". . . will doubtless understand, once he hears you speak of Lord Gyles's dying wish. Go, and see it done."

"If it please Your Grace." Grand Maester Pycelle almost tripped over his own robes in his haste to leave.

Lady Merryweather closed the door behind him. "Moon tea," she said, as she turned back to the queen. "How foolish of her. Why would she do such a thing, take such a risk?"

"The little queen has appetites that Tommen is as yet too young to satisfy." That was always a danger, when a grown woman was married to a child. *Even more so with a widow. She may claim that Renly never touched her, but I will not believe it.* Women only drank moon tea for one reason; maidens had no need for it at all. "My son has been betrayed. Margaery has a lover. That is high treason, punishable by death." She could only hope that Mace Tyrell's prune-faced harridan of a mother lived long enough to see the trial. By insisting that Tommen and Margaery be wed at once, Lady Olenna had condemned her precious rose to a headsman's sword. "Jaime made off with Ser Ilyn Payne. I suppose I shall need to find a new King's Justice to snick her head off."

"I'll do it," offered Osmund Kettleblack, with an easy grin. "Margaery's got a pretty little neck. A good sharp sword will go right through it."

"It would," said Taena, "but there is a Tyrell army at Storm's End and another at Maidenpool. They have sharp swords as well."

I am awash in roses. It was vexing. She still had need of Mace Tyrell, if not his daughter. *At least until such time as Stannis is defeated. Then I shan't need any of them.* But how could she rid herself of the daughter without losing the father? "Treason is treason," she said, "but we must have proof, something more substantial than moon tea. If she is *proved* to be untrue, even her own lord father must condemn her, or her shame becomes his own."

Kettleblack chewed on one end of his mustache. "We need to catch them during the deed."

"How? Qyburn has eyes on her day and night. Her serving men take my coin, but bring us only trifles. Yet no one has seen this lover. The ears outside her door hear singing, laughter, gossip, nothing of any use."

"Margaery is too shrewd to be caught so easily," said Lady Merryweather. "Her women are her castle walls. They sleep with her, dress her, pray with her, read with her, sew with her. When she is not hawking or riding she is playing come-into-my-castle with little Alysanne Bulwer. Whenever men are about, her septa will be with her, or her cousins."

"She must rid herself of her hens *sometime,*" the queen insisted. A thought struck her. "Unless her ladies are part of it as well . . . not all of them, perhaps, but some."

"The cousins?" Even Taena sounded doubtful. "All three are younger than the little queen, and more innocent."

"Wantons clad in maiden's white. That only makes their sins more shocking. Their names will live in shame." Suddenly the queen could almost taste it. "Taena, your lord husband is my justiciar. The two of you must sup with me, this very night." She wanted this done quickly, before Margaery took it in her little head to return to Highgarden, or sail to Dragonstone to be with her wounded brother at death's door. "I shall command the cooks to roast a boar for us. And of course we must have some music, to help with our digestion."

Taena was very quick. "Music. Just so."

"Go and tell your lord husband and make arrangements for the singer," Cersei urged. "Ser Osmund, you may remain. We have much and more to discuss. I shall have need of Qyburn too."

Sad to say, the kitchens proved to have no wild boar on hand, and there was not time enough to send out hunters. Instead, the cooks butchered one of the castle sows, and served them ham studded with cloves and basted with honey and dried cherries. It was not what Cersei wanted, but she made do. Afterward, they had baked apples with a sharp white cheese. Lady Taena savored every bite. Not so Orton Merryweather, whose round face remained blotched and pale from broth to cheese. He drank heavily and kept stealing glances at the singer.

"A great pity about Lord Gyles," Cersei said at last. "I daresay none of us will miss his coughing, though."

"No. No, I'd think not."

"We shall have need of a new lord treasurer. If the Vale were not so unsettled, I would bring back Petyr Baelish, but . . . I am minded to try Ser Harys in the office. He can do no worse than Gyles, and at least he does not cough."

"Ser Harys is the King's Hand," said Taena.

Ser Harys is a hostage, and feeble even at that. "It is time that Tommen had a more forceful Hand."

Lord Orton lifted his gaze from his wine cup. "Forceful. To be sure." He hesitated. "Who . . . ?"

"You, my lord. It is in your blood. Your grandsire took my own father's place as Hand to Aerys." Replacing Tywin Lannister with Owen Merryweather had proved to be akin to replacing a destrier with a donkey, to be sure, but Owen had been an old done man when Aerys raised him, amiable if ineffectual. His grandson was younger, and . . . *Well, he has a strong wife.* It was a pity Taena could not serve as Hand. She was thrice the man her husband was, and far more amusing. She was also Myrish-born and female, however, so Orton must needs suffice. "I have no doubt that you are more able than Ser Harys." *The contents of my chamber pot are more able than Ser Harys.* "Will you consent to serve?"

"I . . . yes, of course. Your Grace does me great honor."

A greater one than you deserve. "You have served me ably as justiciar, my lord. And will continue to do so through these . . . trying times ahead." When she saw that Merryweather had grasped her meaning, the queen turned to smile at the singer. "And you must be rewarded as well, for all the sweet songs you have played for us whilst we ate. The gods have given you a gift."

The singer bowed. "Your Grace is kind to say so."

"Not kind," said Cersei, "merely truthful. Taena tells me that you are called the Blue Bard."

"I am, Your Grace." The singer's boots were supple blue calfskin, his breeches fine blue wool. The tunic he wore was pale blue silk slashed with shiny blue satin. He had even gone so far as to dye his hair blue, in the Tyroshi fashion. Long and curly, it fell to his shoulders and smelled as if it had been washed in rosewater. *From blue roses, no doubt. At least his teeth are white.* They were good teeth, not the least bit crooked.

"You have no other name?"

A hint of pink suffused his cheeks. "As a boy, I was called Wat. A fine name for a plowboy, less fitting for a singer."

The Blue Bard's eyes were the same color as Robert's. For that alone, she hated him. "It is easy to see why you are Lady Margaery's favorite."

"Her Grace is kind. She says I give her pleasure."

"Oh, I'm certain of it. Might I see your lute?"

"If it please Your Grace." Beneath the courtesy, there was a faint hint of unease, but he handed her the lute all the same. One does not refuse the queen's request.

Cersei plucked a string and smiled at the sound. "Sweet and sad as love. Tell me, Wat . . . the first time you took Margaery to bed, was that before she wed my son, or after?"

For a moment, he did not seem to understand. When he did, his eyes grew large. "Your Grace has been misinformed. I swear to you, I never—"

"Liar!" Cersei smashed the lute across the singer's face so hard the painted wood exploded into shards and splinters. "Lord Orton, summon my guards and take this creature to the dungeons."

Orton Merryweather's face was damp with fear. "This . . . oh, infamy . . . he dared seduce *the queen*?"

"I fear it was the other way around, but he is a traitor all the same. Let him sing for Lord Qyburn."

The Blue Bard went white. "No." Blood dripped from his lip where the lute had torn it. "I never . . ." When Merryweather seized him by the arm, he screamed, *"Mother have mercy, no."*

"I am not your mother," Cersei told him.

Even in the black cells, all they got from him were denials, prayers, and pleas for mercy. Before long, blood was streaming down his chin from all his broken teeth, and he wet his dark blue breeches three times over, yet still the man persisted in his lies. "Is it possible we have the wrong singer?" Cersei asked.

"All things are possible, Your Grace. Have no fear. The man will confess before the night is done." Down here in the dungeons, Qyburn wore roughspun wool and a blacksmith's leather apron. To the Blue Bard he said, "I am sorry if the guards were rough with you. Their courtesies are sadly lacking." His voice was kind, solicitous. "All we want from you is the truth."

"I've told you the truth," the singer sobbed. Iron shackles held him hard against the cold stone wall.

"We know better." Qyburn had a razor in his hand, its edge gleaming faintly in the torchlight. He cut away the Blue Bard's clothing, until the man was naked but for his high blue boots. The hair between his legs was brown, Cersei was amused to see. "Tell us how you pleasured the little queen," she commanded.

"I never . . . I sang, was all, I sang and played. Her ladies will tell you. They were always with us. Her cousins."

"How many of them did you have carnal knowledge of?"

"None of them. I'm just a singer. Please."

Qyburn said, "Your Grace, mayhaps this poor man only played for Margaery whilst she entertained other lovers."

"No. *Please.* She never . . . I *sang,* I only *sang* . . ."

Lord Qyburn ran a hand up the Blue Bard's chest. "Does she take your nipples in her mouth during your love play?" He took one between his thumb and forefinger, and twisted. "Some men enjoy that. Their nipples are as sensitive as a woman's." The razor flashed, the singer shrieked. On his chest a wet red eye wept blood. Cersei felt ill. Part of her wanted to close her eyes, to turn away, to make it stop. But she was the queen and this was treason. *Lord Tywin would not have turned away.*

In the end, the Blue Bard told them his whole life, back to his first name day. His father had been a cooper and Wat was raised to that trade, but as a boy he found he had more skill at making lutes than barrels. When he was twelve he ran off to join a troupe of musicians he had heard performing at a fair. He had wandered half the Reach before coming to King's Landing in hopes of finding favor at court.

"Favor?" Qyburn chuckled. "Is that what women call it now? I fear you found too much of it, my friend . . . and from the wrong queen. The true one stands before you."

Yes. Cersei blamed Margaery Tyrell for this. If not for her, Wat might have lived a long and fruitful life, singing his little songs and bedding pig girls and crofter's daughters. *Her scheming forced this on me. She has soiled me with her treachery.*

By dawn the singer's high blue boots were full of blood, and he had told them how Margaery would fondle herself as she watched her cousins pleasuring him with their mouths. At other times he would sing for her whilst she sated her lusts with other lovers. "Who were they?" the queen demanded, and the wretched Wat named Ser Tallad the Tall, Lambert Turnberry, Jalabhar Xho, the Redwyne twins, Osney Kettleblack, Hugh Clifton, and the Knight of Flowers.

That displeased her. She dare not besmirch the name of the hero of Dragonstone. Besides, no one who knew Ser Loras would ever believe it. The Redwynes could not be a part of it either. Without the Arbor and its fleet, the realm could never hope to rid itself of this Euron Crow's Eye and his accursed ironmen. "All you are doing is spitting up the names of men you saw about her chambers. We want the *truth!*"

"The truth." Wat looked at her with the one blue eye that Qyburn had left him. Blood bubbled through the holes where his front teeth had been. "I might have . . . misremembered."

"Horas and Hobber had no part of this, did they?"

"No," he admitted. "Not them."

"As for Ser Loras, I am certain Margaery took pains to hide what she was doing from her brother."

"She did. I remember now. Once, I had to hide under the bed when Ser Loras came to see her. *He must never know,* she said."

"I prefer this song to the other." Leave the great lords out of it, that was for the best. The others, though . . . Ser Tallad had been a hedge knight, Jalabhar Xho was an exile and a beggar, Clifton was the only one of the little queen's guardsman. *And Osney is the plum that makes the pudding.* "I know you feel better for having told the truth. You will want to remember that when Margaery comes to trial. If you were to start lying again . . ."

"I won't. I'll tell it true. And after . . ."

". . . you will be allowed to take the black. You have my word on that." Cersei turned to Qyburn. "See that his wounds are cleaned and dressed, and give him milk of the poppy for the pain."

"Your Grace is good." Qyburn dropped the bloody razor into a pail of vinegar. "Margaery may wonder where her bard has gone."

"Singers come and go, they are infamous for it."

The climb up the dark stone steps from the black cells left Cersei feeling breathless. *I must rest.* Getting to the truth was wearisome work, and she dreaded what must follow. *I must be strong. What I must do, I do for Tommen and the realm.* It was a pity that Maggy the Frog was dead. *Piss on your prophecy, old woman. The little queen may be younger than I, but she has never been more beautiful, and soon she will be dead.*

Lady Merryweather was waiting in her bedchamber. It was the black of night, closer to dawn than to dusk. Jocelyn and Dorcas were both asleep, but not Taena. "Was it terrible?" she asked.

"You cannot know. I need to sleep, but fear to dream."

Taena stroked her hair. "It was all for Tommen."

"It was. I know it was." Cersei shuddered. "My throat is raw. Be a sweet and pour me some wine."

"If it please you. That is all that I desire."

Liar. She knew what Taena desired. So be it. If the woman was besotted with her, that would help ensure that she and her husband remained loyal. In a world so full of treachery, that was worth a few kisses. *She is no worse than most men. At least there is no danger of her ever getting me with child.*

The wine helped, but not enough. "I feel soiled," the queen complained as she stood beside her window, cup in hand.

"A bath will set you right, my sweet." Lady Merryweather woke Dorcas and Jocelyn and sent them for hot water. As the tub was filled, she helped the queen disrobe, undoing her laces with deft fingers and easing the gown off her shoulders. Then she slipped out of her own dress and let it puddle on the floor.

The two of them shared the bath together, with Cersei lying back in Taena's arms. "Tommen must be spared the worst of this," she told the Myrish woman. "Margaery still takes him to the sept every day, so they can ask the gods to heal her brother." Ser Loras still clung to life, annoyingly. "He is fond of her cousins as well. It will go hard on him, to lose them all."

"All three may not be guilty," suggested Lady Merryweather. "Why, it might well be that one of them took no part. If she was shamed and sickened by the things she saw . . ."

". . . she might be persuaded to bear witness against the others. Yes, very good, but which one is the innocent?"

"Alla."

"The shy one?"

"So she seems, but there is more of *sly* than *shy* in her. Leave her to me, my sweet."

"Gladly." Alone, the Blue Bard's confession would never suffice. Singers lied for their living, after all. Alla Tyrell would be of great help, if Taena could deliver her. "Ser Osney shall confess as well. The others must be made to understand that only through confession can they earn the king's forgiveness, and the Wall." Jalabhar Xho would find the truth attractive. About the rest she was less certain, but Qyburn was persuasive . . .

Dawn was breaking over King's Landing when they climbed from the tub. The queen's skin was white and wrinkled from her long immersion. "Stay with me," she told Taena. "I do not want to sleep alone." She even said a prayer before she crawled beneath her coverlet, beseeching the Mother for sweet dreams.

It proved a waste of breath; as ever, the gods were deaf. Cersei dreamt that she was down in the black cells once again, only this time it was her chained to the wall in place of the singer. She was naked, and blood dripped from the tips of her breasts where the Imp had torn off her nipples with his teeth. "Please," she begged, "please, not my children, do not harm my children." Tyrion only leered at her. He was naked too, covered with coarse hair that made him look more like a monkey than a man. "You shall see them crowned," he said, "and you shall see them die." Then he took her bleeding breast into his mouth and began to suck, and pain sawed through her like a hot knife.

She woke shuddering in Taena's arms. "A bad dream," she said weakly. "Did I scream? I'm sorry."

"Dreams turn to dust in light of day. Was it the dwarf again? Why does he frighten you so, this silly little man?"

"He is going to kill me. It was foreseen when I was ten. I wanted to know who I would marry, but she said . . ."

"She?"

"The *maegi*." The words came tumbling out of her. She could still hear Melara Hetherspoon insisting that if they never spoke about the prophecies, they would not come true. *She was not so silent in the well, though. She screamed and shouted.* "Tyrion is the *valonqar*," she said. "Do you use that word in Myr? It's High Valyrian, it means *little brother*." She had asked Septa Saranella about the word, after Melara drowned.

Taena took her hand and stroked it. "This was a hateful woman, old and sick and ugly. You were young and beautiful, full of life and pride. She lived in Lannisport, you said, so she would have known of the dwarf and how he killed your lady mother. This creature dared not strike you, because of who you were, so she sought to wound you with her viper's tongue."

Could it be? Cersei wanted to believe it. "Melara died, though, just as she foretold. I never wed Prince Rhaegar. And Joffrey . . . the dwarf killed my son before my eyes."

"One son," said Lady Merryweather, "but you have another, sweet and strong, and no harm will ever come to *him*."

"Never, whilst I live." Saying it helped her believe that it was so. *Dreams turn to dust in light of day, yes.* Outside, the morning sun was shining through a haze of cloud. Cersei slipped out from under the blankets. "I will break my fast with the king this morning. I want to see my son." *All I do, I do for him.*

Tommen helped restore her to herself. He had never been more precious to her than he was that morning, chattering about his kittens as he dribbled honey onto a chunk of hot black bread fresh from the ovens. "Ser Pounce caught a mouse," he told her, "but Lady Whiskers stole it from him."

I was never so sweet and innocent, Cersei thought. *How can he ever hope to rule in this cruel realm?* The mother in her wanted only to protect him; the queen in her knew he must grow harder, or the Iron Throne was certain to devour him. "Ser Pounce must learn to defend his rights," she told him. "In this world the weak are always the victims of the strong."

The king considered that, licking honey off his fingers. "When Ser Loras comes back, I'm going to learn to fight with lance and sword and morningstar, the same way he does."

"You will learn to fight," the queen promised, "but not from Ser Loras. He will not be coming back, Tommen."

"Margaery says he will. We pray for him. We ask for the Mother's mercy, and for the Warrior to give him strength. Elinor says that this is Ser Loras's hardest battle."

She smoothed his hair back, the soft golden curls that reminded her so much of Joff. "Will you be spending the afternoon with your wife and her cousins?"

"Not today. She has to fast and purify herself, she said."

Fast and purify . . . oh, for Maiden's Day. It had been years since Cersei had been required to observe that particular holy day. *Thrice wed, yet she still would have us believe she is a maid.* Demure in white, the little queen would lead her hens to Baelor's Sept to light tall white candles at the Maiden's feet and hang parchment garlands about her holy neck. *A few of her hens, at least.* On Maiden's Day, widows, mothers, and whores alike were barred from the septs, along with men, lest they profane the sacred songs of innocence. Only virgin maids could . . .

"Mother? Did I say something wrong?"

Cersei kissed her son's brow. "You said something very wise, sweetling. Now run along and play with your kittens."

Afterward, she summoned Ser Osney Kettleblack to her solar. He came in sweaty from the yard and swaggering, and as he took a knee he undressed her with his eyes, the way he always did.

"Rise, ser, and sit here next to me. You did me a valiant service once, but now I have a harder task for you."

"Aye, and I have something hard for you."

"That must wait." She traced his scars lightly with the tips of her fingers. "Do you recall the whore who gave these to you? I'll give her to you when you come back from the Wall. Would you like that?"

"It's you I want."

That was the right answer. "First, you must confess your treason. A man's sins can poison his soul if left to fester. I know it must be hard for you to live with what you've done. It is past time that you rid yourself of your shame."

"Shame?" Osney sounded baffled. "I told Osmund, Margaery just teases. She never lets me do any more than . . ."

"It is chivalrous of you to protect her," Cersei broke in, "but you are too good a knight to go on living with your crime. No, you must take yourself to the Great Sept of Baelor this very night and speak with the High Septon. When a man's sins are so black, only His High Holiness himself can save him from hell's torments. Tell him how you bedded Margaery and her cousins."

Osney blinked. "What, the cousins too?"

"Megga and Elinor," she decided, "never Alla." That little detail would make the whole story more plausible. "Alla would sit weeping, and plead with the others to stop their sinning."

"Just Megga and Elinor? Or Margaery too?"

"Margaery, most certainly. She was the one behind it all."

She told him all she had in mind. As Osney listened, apprehension slowly spread across his face. When she finished he said, "After you cut her head off, I want to take that kiss she never gave me."

"You may take all the kisses you like."

"And then the Wall?"

"For just a little while. Tommen is a forgiving king."

Osney scratched at his scarred cheek. "Usually, if I lie about some woman, it's me saying how I never fucked them and them saying how I did. This . . . I never lied to no *High Septon* before. I think you go to some hell for that. One o' the bad ones."

The queen was taken aback. The last thing she expected was piety from a Kettleblack. "Are you refusing to obey me?"

"No." Osney touched her golden hair. "The thing is, the best lies have some truth in 'em . . . to give 'em flavor, as it were. And you want me to go tell how I fucked a queen . . ."

She almost slapped his face. Almost. But she had gone too far, and too much was at stake. *All I do, I do for Tommen.* She turned her head and caught Ser Osney's hand with her own, kissing his fingers. They were rough and hard, callused from the sword. *Robert had hands like that,* she thought.

Cersei wrapped her arms about his neck. "I would not want it said I made a liar of you," she whispered in a husky voice. "Give me an hour, and meet me in my bedchamber."

"We waited long enough." He thrust his fingers inside the bodice of her gown and yanked, and the silk parted with a ripping sound so loud that Cersei was afraid that half of the Red Keep must have heard it. "Take off the rest before I tear that too," he said. "You can keep the crown on. I like you in the crown."

THE PRINCESS IN THE TOWER

Hers was a gentle prison.

Arianne took solace from that. Why would her father go to such great pains to provide for her comfort in captivity if he had marked her for a traitor's death? *He cannot mean to kill me,* she told herself a hundred times. *He does not have it in him to be so cruel. I am his blood and seed, his heir, his only daughter.* If need be, she would throw herself beneath the wheels of his chair, admit her fault, and beg him for his pardon. And she would weep. When he saw tears rolling down her face, he would forgive her.

She was less certain whether she would forgive herself.

"Areo," she had pleaded with her captor during the long dry ride from the Greenblood back to Sunspear, "I never wanted the girl to come to harm. You must believe me."

Hotah made no reply, except to grunt. Arianne could feel his anger. Darkstar had escaped him, the most dangerous of all her little group of plotters. He had outraced all his pursuers and vanished into the deep desert, with blood upon his blade.

"You know me, captain," Arianne had said, as the leagues rolled past. "You have known me since I was little. You always kept me safe, as you kept my lady mother safe when you came with her from Great Norvos to be her shield in a strange land. I need you now. I need your help. I never meant—"

"What you meant does not matter, little princess," Areo Hotah said. "Only what you did." His countenance was stony. "I am sorry. It is for my prince to command, for Hotah to obey."

Arianne expected to be brought before her father's high seat beneath the dome of leaded glass in the Tower of the Sun. Instead, Hotah delivered her to the Spear Tower, and the custody of her father's seneschal Ricasso and Ser Manfrey Martell, the castellan. "Princess," Ricasso said, "you will forgive an old blind man if he does not make the climb with you. These legs are not equal to so many steps. A chamber has been prepared for you. Ser Manfrey shall escort you there, to await the prince's pleasure."

"The prince's displeasure, you mean. Will my friends be confined here as well?" Arianne had been parted from Garin, Drey, and the others after capture, and Hotah had refused to say what would be done with them. "That is for the prince to decide," was all the captain had to say upon the subject. Ser Manfrey proved a bit more forthcoming. "They were taken to the Planky Town and will be conveyed by ship to Ghaston Grey, until such time as Prince Doran decides their fate."

Ghaston Grey was a crumbling old castle perched on a rock in the Sea of Dorne, a drear and dreadful prison where the vilest of criminals were sent to rot and die. "Does my father mean to *kill* them?" Arianne could not believe it. "All they did they did for love for me. If my father must have blood, it should be mine."

"As you say, princess."

"I want to speak with him."

"He thought you might." Ser Manfrey took her arm and marched her up the steps, up and up until her breath grew short. The Spear Tower stood a hundred and a half feet high, and her cell was nearly at the top. Arianne eyed every door they passed, wondering if one of the Sand Snakes might be locked within.

When her own door had been closed and barred, Arianne explored her new home. Her cell was large and airy, and did not lack for comforts. There were Myrish carpets on the floor, red wine to drink, books to read. In one corner stood an ornate *cyvasse* table with pieces carved of ivory and onyx, though she had no one to play with even if she had been so inclined. She had a featherbed to sleep in, and a privy with a marble seat, sweetened by a basketful of herbs. This high up, the views were splendid. One window opened to the east, so she could watch the sun rise above the sea. The other allowed her to look down upon the Tower of the Sun, and the Winding Walls and Threefold Gate beyond.

The exploration took less time than it would have taken her to lace a pair of sandals, but at least it served to keep the tears at bay for a time. Arianne found a basin and a flagon of cool water and washed her hands and face, but no amount of scrubbing could cleanse her of her grief. *Arys*, she thought, *my white knight.* Tears filled her eyes, and suddenly she was weeping, her whole body wracked by sobs. She remembered how Hotah's heavy axe had cleaved through his flesh and bone, the way his head had gone spinning through the air. *Why did you do it? Why throw your life away? I never told you to, I never wanted that, I only wanted . . . I wanted . . . I wanted . . .*

That night she cried herself to sleep . . . for the first time, if not the last. Even in her dreams she found no peace. She dreamt of Arys Oakheart caressing her, smiling at her, telling her that he loved her . . . but all the while the quarrels were in him and his wounds were weeping, turning his whites to red. Part of her knew it was a nightmare, even as she dreamt it. *Come morning all of this will vanish,* the princess told herself, but when morning came, she was still in her cell, Ser Arys was still dead, and Myrcella . . . *I never wanted that, never. I meant the girl no harm. All I wanted was for her to be a queen. If we had not been betrayed . . .*

"Someone told," Hotah had said. The memory still made her angry. Arianne clung to that, feeding the flame within her heart. Anger was better than tears, better than grief, better than guilt. Someone told, someone she had trusted. Arys Oakheart had died because of that, slain by the traitor's whisper as much as by the captain's axe. The blood that had streamed down Myrcella's face, that was the betrayer's work as well. Someone told, someone she had loved. That was the cruelest cut of all.

She found a cedar chest full of her clothes at the foot of her bed, so she stripped out of the travel-stained garb she had slept in and donned the most revealing garments she could find, wisps of silk that covered everything and hid nothing. Prince Doran might treat her like a child, but she refused to dress like one. She knew such garb would discomfit her father when he came to chastise her for making off with Myrcella. She counted on it. *If I must crawl and weep, let him be uncomfortable as well.*

She expected him that day, but when the door finally opened it proved to be only the servants with her midday meal. "When might I see my father?" she asked, but none of them would answer. The kid had been roasted with lemon and honey. With it were grape leaves stuffed with a mélange of raisins, onions, mushrooms, and fiery dragon peppers. "I am not hungry," Arianne said. Her friends would be eating ship's biscuits and salt beef on their way to Ghaston Grey. "Take this away and bring me Prince Doran." But they left the food, and her father did not come. After a while, hunger weakened her resolve, so she sat and ate.

Once the food was gone, there was nothing else for Arianne to do. She paced around her tower, twice and thrice and three times thrice. She sat beside the *cyvasse* table and idly moved an elephant. She curled up in the window seat and tried to read a book, until the words became a blur and she realized that she was crying again. *Arys, my sweet, my white knight, why did you do it? You should have yielded. I tried to tell you, but the words caught in my mouth. You gallant fool, I never meant for you to die, or for Myrcella . . . oh, gods be good, that little girl . . .*

Finally, she crawled back onto the featherbed. The world had grown dark, and there was little she could do but sleep. *Someone told,* she thought. *Someone told.* Garin, Drey, and Spotted Sylva were friends of her girlhood, as dear to her as her cousin Tyene. She could not believe they would inform on her . . . but that left only Darkstar, and if he was the betrayer, why had he turned his sword on poor Myrcella? *He wanted to kill her instead of crowning her, he said as much at Shandystone. He said that was how I'd get the war I wanted.* But it made no sense for Dayne to be the traitor. If Ser Gerold had been the worm in the apple, why would he have turned his sword upon Myrcella?

Someone told. Could it have been Ser Arys? Had the white knight's guilt won out over his lust? Had he loved Myrcella more than her and betrayed his new princess to atone for his betrayal of the old? Was he so ashamed of what he'd done that he threw his life away at the Greenblood rather than live to face dishonor?

Someone told. When her father came to see her, she would learn which one. Prince Doran did not come the next day, though. Nor the day after. The princess was left alone to pace, and weep, and nurse her wounds. During the daylight hours she would try to read, but the books that they had given her were deadly dull: ponderous old histories and geographies, annotated maps, a dry-as-dust study of the laws of Dorne, *The Seven-Pointed Star* and *Lives of the High Septons,* a huge tome about dragons that somehow made them about as interesting as newts. Arianne would have given much and more for a copy of *Ten Thousand Ships* or *The Loves of Queen Nymeria,* anything to occupy her thoughts and let her escape her tower for an hour or two, but such amusements were denied her.

From her window seat, she had only to glance out to see the great dome of gold and colored glass below her, where her father sat in state. *He will summon me soon,* she told herself.

No visitors were permitted her beyond the servants; Bors with his stubbly jaw, tall Timoth dripping dignity, the sisters Morra and Mellei, pretty little Cedra, old Belandra who had been her mother's bedmaid. They brought her meals, changed her bed, and emptied the chamber pot beneath her privy, but none would speak with her. When she required more wine, Timoth would fetch it. If she desired some favorite food, figs or olives or peppers stuffed with cheese, she need only tell Belandra, and it would appear. Morra and Mellei took away her dirty clothes and returned them clean and fresh. Every second day a bath was brought for her, and shy little Cedra would soap her back and help her brush her hair.

Yet none of them had a word for her, nor would they deign to tell her what was happening in the world outside her sandstone cage. "Has Darkstar been captured?" she asked Bors one day. "Are they still hunting for him?" The man only turned his back on her and walked away. "Have you gone deaf?" Arianne snapped at him. "Come back here and answer me. I command it." Her only reply was the sound of a door closing.

"Timoth," she tried, another day, "what has become of Princess Myrcella? I never meant for harm to come to her." The last she had seen of the other princess had been on their ride back to Sunspear. Too weak to sit a horse, Myrcella had traveled in a litter, her head bound up in silken bandages where Darkstar slashed at her, her green eyes bright with fever. "Tell me that she has not died, I beg you. What harm could come of my knowing that? Tell me how she fares." Timoth would not.

"Belandra," Arianne said, a few days later, "if you ever loved my lady mother, take pity on her poor daughter and tell me when my father means to come and see me. Please. Please." But Belandra had lost her tongue as well.

Is this my father's notion of torment? Not hot irons or the rack, but simple silence? That was so very like Doran Martell that Arianne had to laugh. *He thinks he is being subtle when he is only being feeble.* She resolved to enjoy the quiet, to use the time to heal and fortify herself for what must come.

It was no good dwelling endlessly on Ser Arys, she knew. Instead, she made herself think about the Sand Snakes, Tyene especially. Arianne loved all her bastard cousins, from prickly, hot-tempered Obara to little Loreza, the youngest, only six years old. Tyene had always been the one she loved the most, though; the sweet sister that she never had. The princess had never been close to her brothers; Quentyn was off at Yronwood, and Trystane was too young. No, it had always been her and Tyene, with Garin and Drey and Spotted Sylva. Nym would sometimes join them in their sport, and Sarella was forever pushing in where she didn't belong, but for the most part they had been a company of five. They splashed in the pools and fountains of the Water Gardens, and rode into battle perched on one another's naked backs. She and Tyene had learned to read together, learned to ride together, learned to dance together. When they were ten Arianne had stolen a flagon of wine, and the two of them had gotten drunk together. They shared meals and beds and jewelry. They would have shared their first man as well, but Drey got too excited and spurted all over Tyene's fingers the moment she drew him from his breeches. *Her hands are dangerous.* The memory made her smile.

The more she thought about her cousins, the more the princess missed them. *For all I know, they might be right below me.* That night Arianne tried pounding on the floor with the heel of her sandal. When no one answered, she leaned out a window and peered down. She could see other windows below, smaller than her own, some no more than arrow loops. *"Tyene!"* she called. *"Tyene, are you there? Obara, Nym? Can you hear me? Ellaria? Anyone? TYENE?"* The princess spent half the night hanging out the window, calling till her throat was raw, but no answering shouts came back to her. That frightened her more than she could say. If the Sand Snakes were imprisoned in the Spear Tower, they surely would have heard her shouting. Why didn't they answer? *If Father has done them harm, I will never forgive him, never,* she told herself.

By the time a fortnight had passed, her patience had worn paper-thin. "I will speak with my father now," she told Bors, in her most commanding voice. "You will take me to him." He did not take her to him. "I am ready to see the prince," she told Timoth, but he turned away as if he had not heard. The next morning, Arianne was waiting beside the door when it opened. She bolted past Belandra, sending a platter of spiced eggs to crash against the wall, but the guards caught her before she'd gone three yards. She knew them too, but they were deaf to her entreaties. They dragged her back to her cell, kicking and squirming.

Arianne decided that she must needs be more subtle. Cedra was her best hope; the girl was young, naive, and gullible. Garin had boasted of bedding her once, the princess recalled. The next time she bathed, as Cedra soaped her shoulders, she began to talk of everything and nothing. "I know you have been commanded not to speak to me," she said, "but no one told me not to speak to you." She spoke about the heat of the day, and what she'd had last night for supper, and how slow and stiff poor Belandra was becoming. Prince Oberyn had armed each of *his* daughters so they need never be defenseless, but Arianne Martell had no weapon but her guile. And so she smiled and charmed, and asked nothing in return of Cedra, neither word nor nod.

The next day at supper, she nattered at the girl again as she was serving. This time she contrived to mention Garin. Cedra glanced up shyly at his name and almost spilled the wine that she was pouring. *So it is that way, is it?* thought Arianne.

During her next bath, she spoke of her imprisoned friends, especially Garin. "He's the one I fear for most," she confided to the serving girl. "The orphans are free spirits, they live to wander. Garin needs sunshine and fresh air. If they lock him away in some dank stone cell, how will he survive? He will not last a year at Ghaston Grey." Cedra did not reply, but her face was pale when Arianne rose from the water, and she was squeezing the sponge so tightly that soap was dripping on the Myrish carpet.

Even so, it was four more days and two more baths before the girl was hers. "Please," Cedra finally whispered, after Arianne had painted a vivid picture of Garin throwing himself from the window of his cell, to taste freedom one last time before he died. "You have to help him. Please don't let him die."

"I can do little and less so long as I am locked up here," she whispered back. "My father will not see me. *You* are the only one who can save Garin. Do you love him?"

"Yes," Cedra whispered, blushing. "But how can I help?"

"You can smuggle out a letter for me," said the princess. "Will do you that? Will you take the risk . . . for Garin?"

Cedra's eyes got big. She nodded.

I have a raven, Arianne thought, triumphantly, *but who to send her to?* The only one of her conspirators to escape her father's net was Darkstar. By now, Ser Gerold might well have been taken, however; if not, he would surely have fled Dorne. Her next thought was of Garin's mother and the orphans of the Greenblood. *No, not them. It must be someone with real power, someone who had no part of our plot yet might have reason to be sympathetic to us.* She considered appealing to her own mother, but Lady Mellario was far away in Norvos. Besides, Prince Doran had not listened to his lady wife for many years. *Not her either. I need a lord, one great enough to cow my father into releasing me.*

The most powerful of the Dornish lords was Anders Yronwood, the Bloodroyal, Lord of Yronwood and Warden of the Stone Way, but

Arianne knew better than to look for help from the man who had fostered her brother Quentyn. *No.* Drey's brother Ser Deziel Dalt had once aspired to marry her, but he was much too dutiful to go against his prince. Besides, whilst the Knight of Lemonwood might intimidate a petty lord, he did not have the strength to sway the Prince of Dorne. *No.* The same was true of Spotted Sylva's father. *No.* Arianne finally decided that she had but two real hopes: Harmen Uller, Lord of Hellholt, and Franklyn Fowler, Lord of Skyreach and Warden of the Prince's Pass.

Half of the Ullers are half-mad, the saying went, *and the other half are worse.* Ellaria Sand was Lord Harmen's natural daughter. She and her little ones had been locked away with the rest of the Sand Snakes. That would have made Lord Harmen wroth, and the Ullers were dangerous when wroth. *Too dangerous, perhaps.* The princess did not want to put any more lives in danger.

Lord Fowler might be a safer choice. The Old Hawk, he was called. He had never gotten on with Anders Yronwood; there was bad blood between their Houses going back a thousand years, from when the Fowlers had chosen Martell over Yronwood during Nymeria's War. The Fowler twins were famous friends of Lady Nym as well, but how much weight would that carry with the Old Hawk?

For days, Arianne wavered as she composed her secret letter. "Give the man who brings this to you a hundred silver stags," she began. That should ensure that the message was delivered. She wrote where she was, and pleaded for rescue. "Whoever shall deliver me from this cell, he shall not be forgotten when I wed." *That should bring the heroes running.* Unless Prince Doran had attainted her, she remained the lawful heir to Sunspear; the man who married her would one day rule Dorne by her side. Arianne could only pray that her rescuer would prove younger than the greybeards her father had offered her over the years. "I want a consort with teeth," she had told him when she refused the last.

She dare not ask for parchment for fear of rousing the suspicions of her captors, so she wrote the letter on the bottom of a page torn from *The Seven-Pointed Star,* and pressed it into Cedra's hand on her next bath day. "There's a place beside the Threefold Gate where the caravans take on supplies before crossing the deep sand," Arianne told her. "Find some traveler headed for the Prince's Pass, and promise him a hundred silver stags if he will put this in Lord Fowler's hand."

"I will." Cedra hid the message in her bodice. "I'll find someone before the sun goes down, princess."

"Good," she said. "Tell me how it went on the morrow."

The girl did not return upon the morrow, however. Nor on the day that followed. When it was time for Arianne to bathe, it was Morra and Mellei who filled her tub, and stayed to wash her back and brush her hair. "Has Cedra taken ill?" the princess asked them, but neither would reply. *She has been caught* was all that she could think. *What else could it be?* That night she hardly slept, for fear of what might come next.

When Timoth brought her breakfast the next morning, Arianne asked to see Ricasso rather than her father. Plainly she could not compel Prince Doran to attend her, but surely a mere seneschal would not ignore a summons from the rightful heir to Sunspear.

He did, though. "Did you tell Ricasso what I said?" she demanded the next time she saw Timoth. "Did you tell him I had need of him?" When the man refused to answer her, Arianne seized a flagon of red wine and upended it over his head. The serving man retreated dripping, his face a mask of wounded dignity. *My father means to leave me here to rot,* the princess decided. *Or else he is making plans to marry me off to some disgusting old fool and intends to keep me locked away until the bedding.*

Arianne Martell had grown up expecting that one day she would wed some great lord of her father's choosing. That was what princesses were for, she had been taught ... though, admittedly, her uncle Oberyn had taken a different view of matters. "If you would wed, wed," the Red Viper had told his own daughters. "If not, take your pleasure where you find it. There's little enough of it in this world. Choose well, though. If you saddle yourself with a fool or a brute, don't look to me to rid you of him. I gave you the tools to do that for yourself."

The freedom that Prince Oberyn allowed his bastard daughters had never been shared by Prince Doran's lawful heir. Arianne must wed; she had accepted that. Drey had wanted her, she knew; so had his brother Deziel, the Knight of Lemonwood. Daemon Sand had gone so far as to ask for her hand. Daemon was bastard-born, however, and Prince Doran did not mean for her to wed a Dornishman.

Arianne had accepted that as well. One year, King Robert's brother came to visit and she did her best to seduce him, but she was half a girl and Lord Renly seemed more bemused than inflamed by her overtures. Later, when Hoster Tully asked her to come to Riverrun and meet his heir, she lit candles to the Maid in thanks, but Prince Doran had declined the invitation. The princess might even have considered Willas Tyrell, crippled leg and all, but her father refused to send her to Highgarden to meet him. She tried to go despite him, with Tyene's help . . . but Prince Oberyn caught them at Vaith and brought them back. That same year, Prince Doran tried to betroth her to Ben Beesbury, a minor lordling who was eighty if he was a day, and as blind as he was toothless.

Beesbury died a few years later. That gave her some small comfort in her present pass; she could not be forced to marry him if he was dead. And the Lord of the Crossing had wed again, so she was safe from him as well. *Elden Estermont is still alive and unwed, though. Lord Rosby and Lord Grandison as well.* Grandison was called the Greybeard, but by the time she'd met him his beard had gone snow white. At the welcoming feast, he had gone to sleep between the fish course and the meat. Drey called that apt, since his sigil was a sleeping lion. Garin challenged her to see if she could tie a knot in his beard without waking him, but Arianne refrained. Grandison had seemed a pleasant fellow, less querulous than Estermont and more robust than Rosby. She would never marry him, however. *Not even if Hotah stands behind me with his axe.*

No one came to marry her the next day, nor the day after. Nor did Cedra return. Arianne tried to win Morra and Mellei the same way, but it was no good. If she had been able to get either one alone she might have some hope, but together the sisters were a wall. By that time, the princess would have welcomed a touch of a hot iron, or an evening on the rack. The loneliness was like to drive her mad. *I deserve a headsman's axe for what I did, but he will not even give me that. He would sooner shut me away and forget I ever lived.* She wondered if Maester Caleotte was drawing a proclamation to name her brother Quentyn heir to Dorne.

Days came and went, one after the other, so many that Arianne lost count of how long she had been imprisoned. She found herself spending more and more time abed, until she reached the point where she did not rise at all except to use her privy. The meals the servants brought grew cold, untouched. Arianne slept and woke and slept again, and still felt too weary to rise. She prayed to the Mother for mercy and to the Warrior for courage, then slept some more. Fresh meals replaced the old ones, but she did not eat them either. Once, when she felt especially strong, she carried all the food to the window and flung it out into the yard, so it would not tempt her. The effort exhausted her, so afterward she crawled back into bed and slept for half a day.

Then came a day when a rough hand woke her, shaking her by the shoulder. "Little princess," said a voice she'd known from childhood. "Up and dress. The prince has called for you." Areo Hotah stood over her, her old friend and protector. He was *talking* to her. Arianne smiled sleepily. It was good to see that seamed, scarred face, and hear his gruff, deep voice and thick Norvoshi accent. "What did you do with Cedra?"

"The prince sent her to the Water Gardens," Hotah said. "He will tell you. First, you must wash, and eat."

She must look a wretched creature. Arianne crawled from the bed, weak as a kitten. "Have Morra and Mellei prepare a bath," she told him, "and tell Timoth to bring me up some food. Nothing heavy. Some cold broth and a bit of bread and fruit."

"Aye," said Hotah. Never had she heard a sweeter sound.

The captain waited without whilst the princess bathed and brushed her hair and ate sparingly of the cheese and fruit they'd brought her. She drank a little wine to settle her stomach. *I am frightened,* she realized, *for the first time in my life, I am frightened of my father.* That made her laugh until the wine came out her nose. When it was time to dress, she chose a simple gown of ivory linen, with vines and purple grapes embroidered around the sleeves and bodice. She wore no jewels.

I must be chaste and humble and contrite. I must throw myself at his feet and beg forgiveness, or I may never hear another human voice again.

By the time she was ready, dusk had fallen. Arianne had thought that Hotah would escort her to the Tower of the Sun to hear her father's judgment. Instead, he delivered her to the prince's solar, where they found Doran Martell seated behind a *cyvasse* table, his gouty legs supported by a cushioned footstool. He was toying with an onyx elephant, turning it in his reddened, swollen hands. The prince looked worse than she had ever seen him. His face was pale and puffy, his joints so inflamed that it hurt her just to look at them. Seeing him this way made Arianne's heart go out to him . . . yet somehow she could not bring herself to kneel and beg, as she had planned. "Father," she said instead.

When he raised his head to look at her, his dark eyes were clouded with pain. *Is that the gout?* Arianne wondered. *Or is it me?* "A strange and subtle folk, the Volantenes," he muttered, as he put the elephant aside. "I saw Volantis once, on my way to Norvos, where I first met Mellario. The bells were ringing, and the bears danced down the steps. Areo will recall the day."

"I remember," echoed Areo Hotah in his deep voice. "The bears danced and the bells rang, and the prince wore red and gold and orange. My lady asked me who it was who shone so bright."

Prince Doran smiled wanly. "Leave us, captain."

Hotah stamped the butt of his longaxe on the floor, turned on his heel, and took his leave.

"I told them to place a *cyvasse* table in your chambers," her father said when the two of them were alone.

"Who was I supposed to play with?" *Why is he talking about a game? Has the gout robbed him of his wits?*

"Yourself. Sometimes it is best to study a game before you attempt to play it. How well do you know the game, Arianne?"

"Well enough to play."

"But not to win. My brother loved the fight for its own sake, but I only play such games as I can win. *Cyvasse* is not for me." He studied her face for a long moment before he said, "Why? Tell me that, Arianne. Tell me why."

"For the honor of our House." Her father's voice made her angry. He sounded so sad, so exhausted, so *weak*. *You are a prince!* she wanted to shout. *You should be raging!* "Your meekness shames all Dorne, Father. Your brother went to King's Landing in your place, and *they killed him*!"

"Do you think I do not know that? Oberyn is with me every time I close my eyes."

"Telling you to open them, no doubt." She seated herself across the *cyvasse* table from her father.

"I did not give you leave to sit."

"Then call Hotah back and whip me for my insolence. You are the Prince of Dorne. You can do that." She touched one of the *cyvasse* pieces, the heavy horse. "Have you caught Ser Gerold?"

He shook his head. "Would that we had. You were a fool to make him part of this. Darkstar is the most dangerous man in Dorne. You and he have done us all great harm."

Arianne was almost afraid to ask. "Myrcella. Is she . . .?"

". . . dead? No, though Darkstar did his best. All eyes were on your white knight so no one seems quite certain just what happened, but it would appear that her horse shied away from his at the last instant, else he would have taken off the top of the girl's skull. As it is, the slash opened her cheek down to the bone and sliced off her right ear. Maester Caleotte was able to save her life, but no poultice nor potion will ever restore her face. She was my *ward*, Arianne. Betrothed to your own brother and under my protection. You have dishonored all of us."

"I never meant her harm," Arianne insisted. "If Hotah had not interfered . . ."

". . . you would have crowned Myrcella queen, to raise a rebellion against her brother. Instead of an ear, she would have lost her life."

"Only if we lost."

"*If?* The word is *when*. Dorne is the least populous of the Seven Kingdoms. It pleased the Young Dragon to make all our armies larger when he wrote that book of his, so as to make his conquest that much more glorious, and it has pleased us to water the seed he planted and let our foes think us more powerful than we are, but a princess ought to know the truth. Valor is a poor substitute for numbers. Dorne cannot hope to win a war against the Iron Throne, not alone. And yet that may well be what you have given us. Are you proud?" The prince did not allow her time to answer. "What am I to do with you, Arianne?"

Forgive me, part of her wanted to say, but his words had cut her too deeply. "Why, do what you always do. Do nothing."

"You make it difficult for a man to swallow his anger."

"Best stop swallowing, you're like to choke on it." The prince did not answer. "Tell me how you knew my plans."

"I am the Prince of Dorne. Men seek my favor."

Someone told. "You knew, and yet you still allowed us to make off with Myrcella. Why?"

"That was my mistake, and it has proved a grievous one. You are my daughter, Arianne. The little girl who used to run to me when she skinned her knee. I found it hard to believe that you would conspire against me. I had to learn the truth."

"Now you have. I want to know who informed on me."

"I would as well, in your place."

"Will you tell me?"

"I can think of no reason why I should."

"You think I cannot discover the truth on my own?"

"You are welcome to try. Until such time you must mistrust them all . . . and a little mistrust is a good thing in a princess." Prince Doran sighed. "You disappoint me, Arianne."

"Said the crow to the raven. You have been disappointing me for years, Father." She had not meant to be so blunt with him, but the words came spilling out. *There, now I have said it.*

"I know. I am too meek and weak and cautious, too lenient to our enemies. Just now, though, you are in need of some of that leniency, it seems to me. You ought to be pleading for my forgiveness rather than seeking to provoke me further."

"I ask leniency only for my friends."

"How noble of you."

"What they did they did for love for me. They do not deserve to die on Ghaston Grey."

"As it happens, I agree. Aside from Darkstar, your fellow plotters were no more than foolish children. Still, this was no harmless game of *cyvasse*. You and your friends were playing at treason. I might have had their heads off."

"You might have, but you didn't. Dayne, Dalt, Santagar . . . no, you would never dare make enemies of such Houses."

"I dare more than you dream . . . but leave that for the nonce. Ser Andrey has been sent to Norvos to serve your lady mother for three years. Garin will spend his next two years in Tyrosh. From his kin amongst the orphans, I took coin and hostages. Lady Sylva received no punishment from me, but she was of an age to marry. Her father has shipped her to Greenstone to wed Lord Estermont. As for Arys Oakheart, he chose his own fate and met it bravely. A knight of the Kingsguard . . . what did you *do* to him?"

"I fucked him, Father. You did command me to entertain our noble visitors, as I recall."

His face grew flushed. "Was that all that was required?"

"I told him that once Myrcella was the queen she would give us leave to marry. He wanted me for his wife."

"You did everything you could to stop him from dishonoring his vows, I am certain," her father said.

It was her turn to flush. Her seduction of Ser Arys had required half a year. Though he claimed to have known other women before taking the white, she would never have known that from the way he acted. His caresses had been clumsy, his kisses nervous, and the first time they were abed together he spent his seed on her thigh as she was guiding him inside her with her hand. Worse, he had been consumed by shame. If she only had a dragon for every time he had whispered, "We should not be doing this," she would be richer than the Lannisters. *Did he charge at Areo Hotah in hopes of saving me?* Arianne wondered. *Or did he do it to escape me, to wash out his dishonor with his life's blood?* "He did love me," she heard herself say. "He died for me."

"If so, he may well be but the first of many. You and your cousins wanted war. You may get your wish. Another Kingsguard knight creeps toward Sunspear even as we speak. Ser Balon Swann is bringing me the Mountain's head. My bannermen have been delaying him, to purchase me some time. The Wyls kept him hunting and hawking for eight days on the Boneway, and Lord Yronwood feasted him for a fortnight when he emerged from the mountains. At present, he is at the Tor, where Lady Jordayne has arranged games in his honor. When he reaches Ghost Hill he will find Lady Toland intent on outdoing her. Soon or late, however, Ser Balon must arrive at Sunspear, and when he does he will expect to see Princess Myrcella . . . and Ser Arys, his Sworn Brother. What shall we tell him, Arianne? Shall I say that Oakheart perished in a hunting accident, or from a tumble down some slippery steps? Perhaps Arys went swimming at the Water Gardens, slipped upon the marble, hit his head, and drowned?"

"No," Arianne said. "Say that he died defending his little princess. Tell Ser Balon that Darkstar tried to kill her and Ser Arys stepped between them and saved her life." That was how the white knights of the Kingsguard were supposed to die, giving up their own lives for those that they had sworn to protect. "Ser Balon may be suspicious, as you were when the Lannisters killed your sister and her children, but he will have no proof . . ."

". . . until he speaks with Myrcella. Or must that brave child suffer a tragic accident as well? If so, it will mean war. No lie will save Dorne from the queen's wroth if her daughter should perish whilst in my care."

He needs me, Arianne realized. *That's why he sent for me.*

"I could tell Myrcella what to say, but why should I?"

A spasm of anger rippled across her father's face. "I warn you, Arianne, I am out of patience."

"With me?" *That is so like him.* "For Lord Tywin and the Lannisters you always had the forbearance of Baelor the Blessed, but for your own blood, none."

"You mistake patience for forbearance. I have worked at the downfall of Tywin Lannister since the day they told me of Elia and her children. It was my hope to strip him of all that he held most dear before I killed him, but it would seem his dwarf son has robbed me of that pleasure. I take some small solace in knowing that he died a cruel death at the hands of the monster that he himself begot. Be that as it may. Lord Tywin is howling down in hell . . . where thousands more will soon be joining him, if your folly turns to war." Her father grimaced, as if the very word were painful to him. "Is that what you want?"

The princess refused to be cowed. "I want my cousins freed. I want my uncle avenged. I want my rights."

"Your *rights*?"

"Dorne."

"You will have Dorne after I am dead. Are you so anxious to be rid of me?"

"I should turn that question back on you, Father. You have been trying to rid yourself of me for years."

"That is not true."

"No? Shall we ask my brother?"

"Trystane?"

"*Quentyn*."

"What of him?"

"Where is he?"

"He is with Lord Yronwood's host in the Boneway."

"You do lie well, Father, I will grant you that. You did not so much as blink. Quentyn has gone to Lys."

"Where did you get that notion?"

"A friend told me." She could have secrets too.

"Your friend lied. You have my word, your brother has not gone to Lys. I swear it by sun and spear and Seven."

Arianne could not be fooled so easily. "Is it Myr, then? Tyrosh? I know he is somewhere across the narrow sea, hiring sellswords to steal away my birthright."

Her father's face darkened. "This mistrust does you no honor, Arianne. Quentyn should be the one conspiring against me. I sent him away when he was just a child, too young to understand the needs of Dorne. Anders Yronwood has been more a father to him than I have, yet your brother remains faithful and obedient."

"Why not? You favor him and always have. He looks like you, he thinks like you, and you mean to give him Dorne, don't trouble to deny it. I read your letter." The words still burned as bright as fire in her memory. "'*One day you will sit where I sit and rule all Dorne,*' you wrote him. Tell me, Father, when did you decide to disinherit me? Was it the day that Quentyn was born, or the day that *I* was born? What did I ever do to make you hate me so?" To her fury, there were tears in her eyes.

"I never hated you." Prince Doran's voice was parchment-thin, and full of grief. "Arianne, you do not understand."

"Do you deny you wrote those words?"

"No. That was when Quentyn first went to Yronwood. I did intend for him to follow me, yes. I had other plans for you."

"Oh, yes," she said scornfully, "such plans. Gyles Rosby. Blind Ben Beesbury. Greybeard Grandison. They were your *plans.*"

She gave him no chance to reply. "I know it is my duty to provide an heir for Dorne, I have *never* been forgetful of that. I would have wed, and gladly, but the matches that you brought to me were insults. With every one you spit on me. If you ever felt any love for me at all, why offer me to *Walder Frey?*"

"Because I knew that you would spurn him. I had to be seen to *try* to find a consort for you once you'd reached a certain age, else it would have raised suspicions, but I dared not bring you any man you might accept. You were promised, Arianne."

Promised? Arianne stared at him incredulously. "What are you saying? Is this another lie? You never said . . ."

"The pact was sealed in secret. I meant to tell you when you were old enough . . . when you came of age, I thought, but . . ."

"I am three-and-twenty, for seven years a woman grown."

"I know. If I kept you ignorant too long, it was only to protect you. Arianne, your nature . . . to you, a secret was only a choice tale to whisper to Garin and Tyene in your bed of a night. Garin gossips as only the orphans can, and Tyene keeps nothing from Obara and the Lady Nym. And if they knew . . . Obara is too fond of wine, and Nym is too close to the Fowler twins. And who might the Fowler twins confide in? *I could not take the risk.*"

She was lost, confounded. *Promised. I was promised.* "Who is it? Who have I been betrothed to, all these years?"

"It makes no matter. He is dead."

That left her more baffled than ever. "The old ones are so frail. Was it a broken hip, a chill, the gout?"

"It was a pot of molten gold. We princes make our careful plans and the gods smash them all awry." Prince Doran made a weary gesture with a chafed red hand. "Dorne will be yours. You have my word on that, if my word still has any meaning for you. Your brother Quentyn has a harder road to walk."

"What road?" Arianne regarded him suspiciously. "What are you holding back? Seven save me, but I am sick of secrets. Tell me the rest, Father ... or else name Quentyn your heir and send for Hotah and his axe, and let me die beside my cousins."

"Do you truly believe I would harm my brother's children?" Her father grimaced. "Obara, Nym, and Tyene lack for nothing but their freedom, and Ellaria and her daughters are happily ensconced at the Water Gardens. Dorea stalks about knocking oranges off the trees with her morningstar, and Elia and Obella have become the terror of the pools." He sighed. "It has not been so long since you were playing in those pools. You used to ride the shoulders of an older girl ... a tall girl with wispy yellow hair ..."

"Jeyne Fowler, or her sister Jennelyn." It had been years since Arianne had thought of that. "Oh, and Frynne, her father was a smith. Her hair was brown. Garin was my favorite, though. When I rode Garin no one could defeat us, not even Nym and that green-haired Tyroshi girl."

"That green-haired girl was the Archon's daughter. I was to have sent you to Tyrosh in her place. You would have served the Archon as a cupbearer and met with your betrothed in secret, but your mother threatened to harm herself if I stole another of her children, and I ... I could not do that to her."

His tale grows ever stranger. "Is that where Quentyn's gone? To Tyrosh, to court the Archon's green-haired daughter?"

Her father plucked up a *cyvasse* piece. "I must know how you learned that Quentyn was abroad. Your brother went with Cletus Yronwood, Maester Kedry, and three of Lord Yronwood's best young knights on a long and perilous voyage, with an uncertain welcome at its end. He has gone to bring us back our heart's desire."

She narrowed her eyes. "What is our heart's desire?"

"Vengeance." His voice was soft, as if he were afraid that someone might be listening. "Justice." Prince Doran pressed the onyx dragon into her palm with his swollen, gouty fingers, and whispered, *"Fire and blood."*

ALAYNE

She turned the iron ring and pushed the door open, just a crack. "Sweetrobin?" she called. "May I enter?"

"Have a care, m'lady," warned old Gretchel, wringing her hands. "His lordship threw his chamber pot at the maester."

"Then he has none to throw at me. Isn't there some work you should be doing? And you, Maddy . . . are all the windows closed and shuttered? Have all the furnishings been covered?"

"All of them, m'lady," said Maddy.

"Best make certain of it." Alayne slipped into the darkened bedchamber. "It's only me, Sweetrobin."

Someone sniffled in the darkness. "Are you alone?"

"I am, my lord."

"Come close, then. Just you."

Alayne shut the door firmly behind her. It was solid oak, four inches thick; Maddy and Gretchel might listen all they wished, but they would hear nothing. That was just as well. Gretchel could hold her tongue, but Maddy gossiped shamelessly.

"Did Maester Colemon send you?" the boy asked.

"No," she lied. "I heard my Sweetrobin was ailing." After his encounter with the chamber pot, the maester had come running to Ser Lothor, and Brune had come to her. "If m'lady can talk him out of bed nice," the knight said, "I won't have to drag him out."

We can't have that, she told herself. When Robert was handled roughly he was apt to go into a shaking fit. "Are you hungry, my lord?" she asked the little lord. "Shall I send Maddy down for berries and cream, or some warm bread and butter?" Too late she remembered that there was no warm bread; the kitchens were closed, the ovens cold. *If it gets Robert out of bed, it would be worth the bother of lighting a fire,* she told herself.

"I don't want food," the little lord said, in a reedy, petulant voice. "I'm going to stay in bed today. You could read to me if you want."

"It is too dark in here for reading." The heavy curtains drawn across the windows made the bedchamber black as night. "Has my Sweetrobin forgotten what day this is?"

"No," he said, "but I'm not going. I want to stay in bed. You could read to me about the Winged Knight."

The Winged Knight was Ser Artys Arryn. Legend said that he had driven the First Men from the Vale and flown to the top of the Giant's Lance on a huge falcon to slay the Griffin King. There were a hundred tales of his adventures. Little Robert knew them all so well he could have recited them from memory, but he liked to have them read to him all the same. "Sweetling, we have to go," she told the boy, "but I promise, I'll read you *two* tales of the Winged Knight when we reach the Gates of the Moon."

"Three," he said at once. No matter what you offered him, Robert always wanted more.

"Three," she agreed. "Might I let some sun in?"

"No. The light hurts my eyes. Come to bed, Alayne."

She went to the windows anyway, edging around the broken chamber pot. She could smell it better than she saw it. "I shan't open them very wide. Only enough to see my Sweetrobin's face."

He sniffled. "If you must."

The curtains were of plush blue velvet. She pulled one back a finger's length and tied it off. Dust motes danced in a shaft of pale morning light. The small diamond-shaped panes of the window were obscured by frost. Alayne rubbed at one with the heel of her hand, enough to glimpse a brilliant blue sky and a blaze of white from the mountainside. The Eyrie was wrapped in an icy mantle, the Giant's Lance above buried in waist-deep snows.

When she turned back, Robert Arryn was propped up against the pillows looking at her. *The Lord of the Eyrie and Defender of the Vale.* A woolen blanket covered him below the waist. Above it he was naked, a pasty boy with hair as long as any girl's. Robert had spindly arms and legs, a soft concave chest and little belly, and eyes that were always red and runny. *He cannot help the way he is. He was born small and sickly.* "You look very strong this morning, my lord." He loved to be told how strong he was. "Shall I have Maddy and Gretchel fetch hot water for your bath? Maddy will scrub your back for you and wash your hair, to make you clean and lordly for your journey. Won't that be nice?"

"No. I hate Maddy. She has a wart on her eye, and she scrubs so hard it hurts. My mommy never hurt me scrubbing."

"I will tell Maddy not to scrub my Sweetrobin so hard. You'll feel better when you're fresh and clean."

"No bath, I *told* you, my head hurts most awfully."

"Shall I bring you a warm cloth for your brow? Or a cup of dreamwine? Only a little one, though. Mya Stone is waiting down at Sky, and she'll be hurt if you go to sleep on her. You know how much she loves you."

"I don't love *her.* She's just the mule girl." Robert sniffled. "Maester Colemon put something vile in my milk last night, I could taste it. I told him I wanted sweetmilk, but he wouldn't bring me any. Not even when I *commanded* him. I am the lord, he should do what I say. No one does what I *say.*"

"I'll speak to him," Alayne promised, "but only if you get up out of bed. It's beautiful outside, Sweetrobin. The sun is shining bright, a perfect day for going down the mountain. The mules are waiting down at Sky with Mya . . ."

His mouth quivered. "I hate those smelly mules. One tried to bite me once! You tell that Mya that I'm staying here." He sounded as if he were about to cry. "No one can hurt me so long as I stay here. The Eyrie is im*preg*nable."

"Who would want to hurt my Sweetrobin? Your lords and knights adore you, and the smallfolk cheer your name." *He is afraid,* she thought, *and with good reason.* Since his lady mother had fallen, the boy would not even stand upon a balcony, and the way from the Eyrie to the Gates of the Moon was perilous enough to daunt anyone. Alayne's heart had been in her throat when she made her own ascent with Lady Lysa and Lord Petyr, and everyone agreed that the descent was even more harrowing, since you were looking down the whole time. Mya could tell of great lords and bold knights who had gone pale and wet their smallclothes on the mountain. *And none of them had the shaking sickness either.*

Still, it would not serve. On the valley floor autumn still lingered, warm and golden, but winter had closed around the mountain peaks. They had weathered three snowstorms, and an ice storm that transformed the castle into crystal for a fortnight. The Eyrie might be impregnable, but it would soon be inaccessible as well, and the way down grew more hazardous every day. Most of the castle's servants and soldiers had already made the descent. Only a dozen still lingered up here, to attend Lord Robert.

"Sweetrobin," she said gently, "the descent will be ever so jolly, you'll see. Ser Lothor will be with us, and Mya. Her mules have gone up and down this old mountain a thousand times."

"I hate mules," he insisted. "Mules are nasty. I *told* you, one tried to bite me when I was little."

Robert had never learned to ride properly, she knew. Mules, horses, donkeys, it made no matter; to him they were all fearsome beasts, as terrifying as dragons or griffins. He had been brought to the Vale at six, riding with his head cradled between his mother's milky breasts, and had never left the Eyrie since.

Still, they had to go, before the ice closed about the castle for good. There was no telling how long the weather would hold. "Mya will keep the mules from biting," Alayne said, "and I'll be riding just behind you. I'm only a girl, not as brave or strong as you. If I can do it, I know you can, Sweetrobin."

"I *could* do it," Lord Robert said, "but I don't choose to." He swiped at his runny nose with the back of his hand. "Tell Mya I am going to stay abed. Perhaps I will come down on the morrow, if I feel better. Today is too cold out, and my head hurts. You can have some sweet-milk too, and I'll tell Gretchel to bring us some honeycombs to eat.

We'll sleep and kiss and play games, and you can read me about the Winged Knight."

"I will. Three tales, as I promised . . . when we reach the Gates of the Moon." Alayne was running short of patience. *We have to go,* she reminded herself, *or we'll still be above the snow line when the sun goes down.* "Lord Nestor has prepared a feast to welcome you, mushroom soup and venison and cakes. You don't want to disappoint him, do you?"

"Will they be lemon cakes?" Lord Robert loved lemon cakes, perhaps because Alayne did.

"Lemony lemony lemon cakes," she assured him, "and you can have as many as you like."

"A hundred?" he wanted to know. "Could I have a *hundred?*"

"If it please you." She sat on the bed and smoothed his long, fine hair. *He does have pretty hair.* Lady Lysa had brushed it herself every night, and cut it when it wanted cutting. After she had fallen Robert had suffered terrible shaking fits whenever anyone came near him with a blade, so Petyr had commanded that his hair be allowed to grow. Alayne wound a lock around her finger, and said, "Now, will you get out of bed and let us dress you?"

"I want a hundred lemon cakes and *five* tales!"

I'd like to give you a hundred spankings and five slaps. You would not dare behave like this if Petyr were here. The little lord had a good healthy fear of his stepfather. Alayne forced a smile. "As my lord desires. But nothing till you're washed and dressed and on your way. Come, before the morning's gone." She took him firmly by the hand, and drew him out of bed.

Before she could summon the servants, however, Sweetrobin threw his skinny arms around her and kissed her. It was a little boy's kiss, and clumsy. Everything Robert Arryn did was clumsy. *If I close my eyes I can pretend he is the Knight of Flowers.* Ser Loras had given Sansa Stark a red rose once, but he had never kissed her . . . and no Tyrell would ever kiss Alayne Stone. Pretty as she was, she had been born on the wrong side of the blanket.

As the boy's lips touched her own, she found herself thinking of another kiss. She could still remember how it felt, when his cruel mouth pressed down on her own. He had come to Sansa in the darkness as green fire filled the sky. *He took a song and a kiss, and left me nothing but a bloody cloak.*

It made no matter. That day was done, and so was Sansa.

Alayne pushed her little lord away. "That's enough. You can kiss me again when we reach the Gates, if you keep your word."

Maddy and Gretchel were waiting outside with Maester Colemon. The maester had washed the night soil from his hair and changed his robe. Robert's squires had turned up as well. Terrance and Gyles could always sniff out trouble.

"Lord Robert is feeling stronger," Alayne told the serving women. "Fetch hot water for his bath, but see you don't scald him. And do not pull on his hair when you brush out the tangles, he hates that." One of the squires sniggered, until she said, "Terrance, lay out his lordship's riding clothes and his warmest cloak. Gyles, you may clean up that broken chamber pot."

Gyles Grafton made a face. "I'm no scrubwoman."

"Do as Lady Alayne commands, or Lothor Brune will hear of it," said Maester Colemon. He followed her along the hallway and down the twisting stairs. "I am grateful for your intercession, my lady. You have a way with him." He hesitated. "Did you observe any shaking while you were with him?"

"His fingers trembled a little bit when I held his hand, that's all. He says you put something vile in his milk."

"Vile?" Colemon blinked at her, and the apple in his throat moved up and down. "I merely . . . is he bleeding from the nose?"

"No."

"Good. That is good." His chain clinked softly as he bobbed his head, atop a ridiculously long and skinny neck. "This descent . . . my lady, it might be safest if I mixed his lordship some milk of the poppy. Mya Stone could lash him over the back of her most surefooted mule whilst he slumbered."

"The Lord of the Eyrie cannot descend from his mountain tied up like a sack of barleycorn." Of that Alayne was certain. They dare not let the full extent of Robert's frailty and cowardice become too widely known, her father had warned her. *I wish he were here. He would know what to do.*

Petyr Baelish was clear across the Vale, though, attending Lord Lyonel Corbray at his wedding. A widower of forty-odd years, and childless, Lord Lyonel was to wed the strapping sixteen-year-old daughter of a rich Gulltown merchant. Petyr had brokered the match himself. The bride's dower was said to be staggering; it had to be, since she was of common birth. Corbray's vassals would be there, with the Lords Waxley, Grafton, Lynderly, some petty lords and landed knights . . . and Lord Belmore, who had lately reconciled with her father. The other Lords Declarant were expected to shun the nuptials, so Petyr's presence was essential.

Alayne understood all that well enough, but it meant that the burden of getting Sweetrobin safely down the mountain fell on her. "Give his lordship a cup of sweetmilk," she told the maester. "That will stop him from shaking on the journey down."

"He had a cup not three days past," Colemon objected.

"And wanted another last night, which you refused him."

"It was too soon. My lady, you do not understand. As I've told the Lord Protector, a pinch of sweetsleep will prevent the shaking, but it does not leave the flesh, and in time . . ."

"Time will not matter if his lordship has a shaking fit and falls off the mountain. If my father were here, I know he would tell you to keep Lord Robert calm at all costs."

"I try, my lady, yet his fits grow ever more violent, and his blood is so thin I dare not leech him any more. Sweetsleep . . . you are *certain* he was not bleeding from the nose?"

"He was sniffling," Alayne admitted, "but I saw no blood."

"I must speak to the Lord Protector. This feast . . . is that wise, I wonder, after the strain of the descent?"

"It will not be a large feast," she assured him. "No more than forty guests. Lord Nestor and his household, the Knight of the Gate, a few lesser lords and their retainers . . ."

"Lord Robert mislikes strangers, you know that, and there will be drinking, noise . . . *music*. Music frightens him."

"Music soothes him," she corrected, "the high harp especially. It's *singing* he can't abide, since Marillion killed his mother." Alayne had told the lie so many times that she remembered it that way more oft than not; the other seemed no more than a bad dream that sometimes troubled her sleep. "Lord Nestor will have no singers at the feast, only flutes and fiddles for the dancing." What would she do when the music began to play? It was a vexing question, to which her heart and head gave different answers. Sansa loved to dance, but Alayne . . . "Just give him a cup of the sweetmilk before we go, and another at the feast, and there should be no trouble."

"Very well." They paused at the foot of the stairs. "But this must be the last. For half a year, or longer."

"You had best take that up with the Lord Protector." She pushed through the door and crossed the yard. Colemon only wanted the best for his charge, Alayne knew, but what was best for Robert the boy and what was best for Lord Arryn were not always the same. Petyr had said as much, and it was true. *Maester Colemon cares only for the boy, though. Father and I have larger concerns.*

Old snow cloaked the courtyard, and icicles hung down like crystal spears from the terraces and towers. The Eyrie was built of fine white stone, and winter's mantle made it whiter still. *So beautiful,* Alayne thought, *so impregnable.* She could not love this place, no matter how she tried. Even before the guards and serving men had made their descent, the castle had seemed as empty as a tomb, and more so when Petyr Baelish was away. No one sang up there, not since Marillion. No one ever laughed too loud. Even the gods were silent. The Eyrie boasted a sept, but no septon; a godswood, but no heart tree. *No prayers are answered here,* she often thought, though some days she felt so lonely she had to try. Only the wind answered her, sighing endlessly around the seven slim white towers and rattling the Moon Door every time it gusted. *It will be even worse in winter,* she knew. *In winter this will be a cold white prison.*

And yet the thought of leaving frightened her almost as much as it frightened Robert. She only hid it better. Her father said there was no shame in being afraid, only in showing your fear. "All men live with fear," he said. Alayne was not certain she believed that. Nothing frightened Petyr Baelish. *He only said that to make me brave.* She would need to be brave down below, where the chance of being unmasked was so much greater. Petyr's friends at court had sent him word that the queen had men out looking for the Imp and Sansa Stark. *It will mean my head if I am found,* she reminded herself as she descended a flight of icy stone steps. *I must be Alayne all the time, inside and out.*

Lothor Brune was in the winch room, helping the gaoler Mord and two serving men wrestle chests of clothes and bales of cloth into six huge oaken buckets, each big enough around to hold three men. The great chain winches were the easiest way to reach the waycastle Sky, six hundred feet below them; elsewise you had to descend the natural stone chimney from the undercellar. *Or go the way Marillion went, and Lady Lysa before him.*

"Boy out of bed?" Ser Lothor asked.

"They're bathing him. He will be ready within the hour."

"We best hope he is. Mya won't wait past midday." The winch room was unheated, so his breath misted with every word.

"She'll wait," Alayne said. "She has to wait."

"Don't be so certain, m'lady. She's half mule herself, that one. I think she'd leave us all to starve before she'd put those animals at risk." He smiled when he said it. *He always smiles when he speaks of Mya Stone.* Mya was much younger than Ser Lothor, but when her father had been brokering the marriage between Lord Corbray and his merchant's daughter, he'd told her that young girls were always happiest with older men. "Innocence and experience make for a perfect marriage," he had said.

Alayne wondered what Mya made of Ser Lothor. With his squashed nose, square jaw, and nap of woolly grey hair, Brune could not be called comely, but he was not *ugly* either. *It is a common face but an honest one.* Though he had risen to knighthood, Ser Lothor's birth had been very low. One night he had told her that he was kin to the Brunes of Brownhollow, an old knightly family from Crackclaw Point. "I went to them when my father died," he confessed, "but they shat on me, and said I was no blood of theirs." He would not speak of what happened after that, except to say that he had learned all he knew of arms the hard way. Sober, he was a quiet man, but a strong one. *And Petyr says he's loyal. He trusts him as much as he trusts anyone.* Brune would be a good match for a bastard girl like Mya Stone, she thought. *It might be different if her father had acknowledged her, but he never did. And Maddy says that she's no maid either.*

Mord took up his whip and cracked it, and the first pair of oxen began to lumber in a circle, turning the winch. The chain uncoiled, rattling as it scraped across the stone, the oaken bucket swaying as it began its long descent to Sky. *Poor oxen,* thought Alayne. Mord would cut their throats and butcher them before he left, and leave them for the falcons. Whatever part remained when the Eyrie was reopened would be roasted up for the spring feast, if it had not spoiled. A good supply of hard frozen meat foretold a summer of plenty, old Gretchel claimed.

"M'lady," Ser Lothor said, "you'd best know. Mya didn't come up alone. Lady Myranda's with her."

"Oh." *Why would she ride all the way up the mountain, just to ride back down again?* Myranda Royce was the Lord Nestor's daughter. The one time that Sansa had visited the Gates of the Moon, on the way up to the Eyrie with her aunt Lysa and Lord Petyr, she had been away, but Alayne had heard much of her since from the Eyrie's soldiers and serving girls. Her mother was long dead, so Lady Myranda kept her father's castle for him; it was a much livelier court when she was home than when she was away, according to rumor. "Soon or late you must meet Myranda Royce," Petyr had warned her. "When you do, be careful. She likes to play the merry fool, but underneath she's shrewder than her father. Guard your tongue around her."

I will, she thought, *but I did not know I'd need to start so soon.* "Robert will be pleased." He liked Myranda Royce. "You must excuse me, ser. I need to finish packing." Alone, she climbed the steps back to her room for one last time. The windows had been sealed and shuttered, the furnishings covered. A few of her things had already been removed, the rest stored away. All of Lady Lysa's silks and samites were to be left behind. Her sheerest linens and plushest velvets, the rich embroidery and fine Myrish lace; all would remain. Down below, Alayne must dress modestly, as befit a girl of modest birth. *It makes no matter,* she told herself. *I dared not wear the best clothes even here.*

Gretchel had stripped the bed and laid out the rest of her clothing. Alayne was already wearing woolen hose beneath her skirts, over a double layer of smallclothes. Now she donned a lambswool overtunic and a hooded fur cloak, fastening it with an enameled mockingbird that had been a gift from Petyr. There was a scarf as well, and a pair of leather gloves lined with fur to match her riding boots. When she'd donned it all, she felt as fat and furry as a bear cub. *I will be glad of it on the mountain,* she had to remind herself. She took one last look at her room before she left. *I was safe here,* she thought, *but down below . . .*

When Alayne returned to the winch room, she found Mya Stone waiting impatiently with Lothor Brune and Mord. *She must have come up in the bucket to see what was taking us so long.* Slim and sinewy, Mya looked as tough as the old riding leathers she wore beneath her silvery ringmail shirt. Her hair was black as a raven's wing, so short and shaggy that Alayne suspected that she cut it with a dagger. Mya's eyes were her best feature, big and blue. *She could be pretty, if she would dress up like a girl.* Alayne found herself wondering whether Ser Lothor liked her best in her iron and leather, or dreamed of her gowned in lace and silk. Mya liked to say that her father had been a goat and her mother an owl, but Alayne had gotten the true story from Maddy. *Yes,* she thought, looking at her now, *those are his eyes, and she has his hair too, the thick black hair he shared with Renly.*

"Where is he?" the bastard girl demanded.

"His lordship is being bathed and dressed."

"He needs to make some haste. It's getting colder, can't you feel it? We need to get below Snow before the sun goes down."

"How bad is the wind?" Alayne asked her.

"It could be worse . . . and will be, after dark." Mya pushed a lock of hair from her eyes. "If he bathes much longer, we'll be trapped up here all winter with nothing to eat except each other."

Alayne did not know what to say to that. Thankfully, she was spared by the arrival of Robert Arryn. The little lord wore sky-blue velvet, a chain of gold and sapphires, and a white bearskin cloak. His squires each held an end, to keep the cloak from dragging on the floor. Maester Colemon accompanied them, in a threadbare grey cloak lined with squirrel fur. Gretchel and Maddy were not far behind.

When he felt the cold wind on his face, Robert quailed, but Terrance and Gyles were behind him, so he could not flee. "My lord," said Mya, "will you ride down with me?"

Too brusque, Alayne thought. *She should have greeted him with a smile, told him how strong and brave he looks.*

"I want Alayne," Lord Robert said. "I'll only go with her."

"The bucket can hold all three of us."

"I just want Alayne. You smell all stinky, like a mule."

"As you wish." Mya's face showed no emotion.

Some of the winch chains were fixed to wicker baskets, others to stout oaken buckets. The largest of those was taller than Alayne, with iron bands girding its dark brown staves. Even so, her heart was in her throat as she took Robert's hand and helped him in. Once the hatch was closed behind them, the wood surrounded them on all sides. Only the top was open. *It is best that way,* she told herself, *we can't look down.* Below them was only Sky and sky. Six hundred feet of sky. For a moment, she found herself wondering how long it had taken her aunt to fall that distance, and what her last thought had been as the mountain rushed up to meet her. *No, I mustn't think of that. I mustn't!*

"AWAY!" came Ser Lothor's shout. Someone shoved the bucket hard. It swayed and tipped, scraped against the floor, then swung free. She heard the *crack* of Mord's whip and the rattle of the chain. They began to descend, by jerks and starts at first, then more smoothly. Robert's face was pale and his eyes puffy, but his hands were still. The Eyrie shrank above them. The sky cells on the lower levels made the castle look something like a honeycomb from below. *A honeycomb made of ice,* Alayne thought, *a castle made of snow.* She could hear the wind whistling round the bucket.

A hundred feet down, a sudden gust caught hold of them. The bucket swayed sideways, spinning in the air, then bumped hard against the rock face behind them. Shards of ice and snow rained down on them, and the oak creaked and strained. Robert gave a gasp and clung to her, burying his face between her breasts.

"My lord is brave," Alayne said, when she felt him shaking. "I'm so frightened I can hardly talk, but not you."

She felt him nod. "The Winged Knight was brave, and so am I," he boasted to her bodice. "I'm an *Arryn*."

"Will my Sweetrobin hold me tight?" she asked, though he was already holding her so tightly that she could scarcely breathe.

"If you like," he whispered. And clinging hard to one another, they continued on straight down to Sky.

Calling this a castle is like calling a puddle on a privy floor a lake, Alayne thought, when the bucket was opened so they might emerge within the waycastle. Sky was no more than a crescent-shaped wall of old unmortared stone, enclosing a stony ledge and the yawning mouth of a cavern. Inside were storehouses and stables, a long natural hall, and the chiseled handholds that led up to the Eyrie. Outside, the ground was strewn by broken stones and boulders. Earthen ramps gave access to the wall. Six hundred feet above, the Eyrie was so small she could hide it with her hand, but far below the Vale stretched green and golden.

Twenty mules awaited them within the waycastle, along with two mule-walkers and the Lady Myranda Royce. Lord Nestor's daughter proved to be a short, fleshy woman, of an age with Mya Stone, but where Mya was slim and sinewy, Myranda was soft-bodied and sweet-smelling, broad of hip, thick of waist, and extremely buxom. Her thick chestnut curls framed round red cheeks, a small mouth, and a pair of lively brown eyes. When Robert climbed gingerly from the bucket, she knelt in a patch of snow to kiss his hand and cheeks. "My lord," she said, "you've grown so *big!*"

"Have I?" said Robert, pleased.

"You will be taller than me soon," the lady lied. She got to her feet and brushed the snow from her skirts. "And you must be the Lord Protector's daughter," she added, as the bucket went rattling back up to the Eyrie. "I had heard that you were beautiful. I see that it is true."

Alayne curtsied. "My lady is kind to say so."

"Kind?" The older girl gave a laugh. "How boring that would be. I aspire to be wicked. You must tell me all your secrets on the ride down. May I call you Alayne?"

"If you wish, my lady." *But you'll get no secrets from me.*

"I am 'my lady' at the Gates, but up here on the mountain you may call me Randa. How many years have you, Alayne?"

"Four-and-ten, my lady." She had decided that Alayne Stone should be older than Sansa Stark.

"*Randa*. It seems a hundred years since I was four-and-ten. How innocent I was. Are you still innocent, Alayne?"

She blushed. "You should not . . . yes, of course."

"Saving yourself for Lord Robert?" Lady Myranda teased. "Or is there some ardent squire dreaming of your favors?"

"No," said Alayne, even as Robert said, "She's *my* friend. Terrance and Gyles can't have her."

A second bucket had arrived by then, thumping down softly on a mound of frozen snow. Maester Colemon emerged with the squires Terrance and Gyles. The next winch delivered Maddy and Gretchel, who rode with Mya Stone. The bastard girl wasted no time taking charge. "We don't want to get bunched up on the mountain," she told the other mule handlers. "I'll take Lord Robert and his companions. Ossy, you'll bring down Ser Lothor and the rest, but give me an hour's lead. Carrot, you'll have charge of their chests and boxes." She turned to Robert Arryn, her black hair blowing. "Which mule will you ride today, my lord?"

"They're all stinky. I'll have the grey one, with the ear chewed off. I want Alayne to ride with me. And Myranda too."

"Where the way is wide enough. Come, my lord, let's get you on your mule. There's a smell of snow in the air."

It was another half-hour before they were ready to set out. When all of them were mounted up, Mya Stone gave a crisp command, and two of Sky's men-at-arms swung the gates open. Mya led them out, with Lord Robert just behind her, swaddled in his bearskin cloak. Alayne and Myranda Royce followed, then Gretchel and Maddy, then Terrance Lynderly and Gyles Grafton. Maester Colemon brought up the rear, leading a second mule laden with his chests of herbs and potions.

Beyond the walls, the wind picked up sharply. They were above the tree line here, exposed to the elements. Alayne was thankful that she'd dressed so warmly. Her cloak was flapping noisily behind her, and a sudden gust blew back her hood. She laughed, but a few yards ahead Lord Robert squirmed, and said, "It's too cold. We should go back and wait until it's warmer."

"It will be warmer on the valley floor, my lord," said Mya. "You'll see when we get down there."

"I don't *want* to see," said Robert, but Mya paid no mind.

Their road was a crooked series of stone steps carved into the mountainside, but the mules knew every inch of it. Alayne was glad of that. Here and there the stone was shattered from the strain of countless seasons, with all their thaws and freezes. Patches of snow clung to the rock on either side of the path, blinding white. The sun was bright, the sky was blue, and there were falcons circling overhead, riding on the wind.

Up here where the slope was steepest, the steps wound back and forth rather than plunging straight down. *Sansa Stark went up the mountain, but Alayne Stone is coming down.* It was a strange thought. Coming up, Mya had warned her to keep her eyes on the path ahead, she remembered. "Look up, not down," she said . . . but that was not possible on the descent. *I could close my eyes. The mule knows the way, he has no need of me.* But that seemed more something Sansa would have done, that frightened girl. Alayne was an older woman, and bastard brave.

At first, they rode in single file, but farther down the path widened enough for two to ride abreast, and Myranda Royce came up beside her. "We have had a letter from your father," she said, as casually as if they were sitting with their septa, doing needlework. "He is on his way home, he says, and hopes to see his darling daughter soon. He writes that Lyonel Corbray seems well pleased with his bride, and even more so with her dowry. I *do* hope Lord Lyonel remembers which one he needs to bed. Lady Waynwood turned up with the Knight of Ninestars for the wedding feast, Lord Petyr says, to everyone's astonishment."

"Anya Waynwood? Truly?" The Lords Declarant were down from six to three, it would seem. The day he'd departed the mountain, Petyr Baelish had been confident of winning Symond Templeton to his side, but not so Lady Waynwood. "Was there more?" she asked. The Eyrie was such a lonely place that she was eager for any bit of news from the world beyond, however trivial or insignificant.

"Not from your father, no, but we've had other birds. The war goes on, everywhere but here. Riverrun has yielded, but Dragonstone and Storm's End still hold for Lord Stannis."

"Lady Lysa was so wise, to keep us out of it."

Myranda gave her a shrewd little smile. "Yes, she was the very soul of wisdom, that good lady." She shifted her seat. "Why must mules be so bony and ill-tempered? Mya does not feed them enough. A nice fat mule would be more comfortable to ride. There's a new High Septon, did you know? Oh, and the Night's Watch has a boy commander, some bastard son of Eddard Stark's."

"Jon Snow?" she blurted out, surprised.

"Snow? Yes, it would be Snow, I suppose."

She had not thought of Jon in ages. He was only her half-brother, but still . . . with Robb and Bran and Rickon dead, Jon Snow was the only brother that remained to her. *I am a bastard too now, just like him. Oh, it would be so sweet, to see him once again.* But of course that could never be. Alayne Stone had no brothers, baseborn or otherwise.

"Our cousin Bronze Yohn had himself a mêlée at Runestone," Myranda Royce went on, oblivious, "a small one, just for squires. It was meant for Harry the Heir to win the honors, and so he did."

"Harry the Heir?"

"Lady Waynwood's ward. Harrold Hardyng. I suppose we must call him *Ser* Harry now. Bronze Yohn knighted him."

"Oh." Alayne was confused. Why should Lady Waynwood's ward be her heir? She had sons of her own blood. One was the Knight of the Bloody Gate, Ser Donnel. She did not want to look stupid, though, so all she said was, "I pray he proves a worthy knight."

Lady Myranda snorted. "I pray he gets the pox. He has a bastard daughter by some common girl, you know. My lord father had hoped to marry me to Harry, but Lady Waynwood would not hear of it. I do not know whether it was me she found unsuitable, or just my dowry." She gave a sigh. "I do need another husband. I had one once, but I killed him."

"You did?" Alayne said, shocked.

"Oh, yes. He died on top of me. *In* me, if truth be told. You do know what goes on in a marriage bed, I hope?"

She thought of Tyrion, and of the Hound and how he'd kissed her, and gave a nod. "That must have been dreadful, my lady. Him dying. *There,* I mean, whilst . . . whilst he was . . ."

". . . fucking me?" She shrugged. "It was disconcerting, certainly. Not to mention discourteous. He did not even have the common decency to plant a child in me. Old men have weak seed. So here I am, a widow, but scarce used. Harry could have done much worse. I daresay that he will. Lady Waynwood will most like marry him to one of her granddaughters, or one of Bronze Yohn's."

"As you say, my lady." Alayne remembered Petyr's warning.

"*Randa.* Come now, you can say it. Ran. Da."

"Randa."

"Much better. I fear I must apologize to you. You will think me a dreadful slut, I know, but I bedded that pretty boy Marillion. I did not know he was a monster. He sang beautifully, and could do the sweetest things with his fingers. I would never have taken him to bed if I had known he was going to push Lady Lysa through the Moon Door. I do not bed monsters, as a rule." She studied Alayne's face and chest. "You are prettier than me, but my breasts are larger. The maesters say large breasts produce no more milk than small ones, but I do not believe it. Have you ever known a wet nurse with small teats? Yours are ample for a girl your age, but as they are bastard breasts, I shan't concern myself with them." Myranda edged her mule closer. "You know our Mya's not a maid, I trust?"

She did. Fat Maddy had whispered it to her, one time when Mya brought up their supplies. "Maddy told me."

"Of course she did. She has a mouth as big as her thighs, and her thighs are *enormous.* Mychel Redfort was the one. He used to be Lyn Corbray's squire. A *real* squire, not like that loutish lad Ser Lyn's got squiring for him now. He only took that one on for coin, they say. Mychel was the best young swordsman in the Vale, and gallant . . . or so poor Mya thought, till he wed one of Bronze Yohn's daughters. Lord Horton gave him no choice in the matter, I am sure, but it was still a cruel thing to do to Mya."

"Ser Lothor is fond of her." Alayne glanced down at the mule girl, twenty steps below. "More than fond."

"Lothor *Brune*?" Myranda raised an eyebrow. "Does she know?" She did not wait for an answer. "He has no hope, poor man. My father's tried to make a match for Mya, but she'll have none of them. She *is* half mule, that one."

Despite herself, Alayne found herself warming to the older girl. She had not had a friend to gossip with since poor Jeyne Poole. "Do you think Ser Lothor likes her as she is, in mail and leather?" she asked the older girl, who seemed so worldly-wise. "Or does he dream of her draped in silks and velvets?"

"He's a man. He dreams of her naked."

She is trying to make me blush again.

Lady Myranda must have heard her thoughts. "You do turn such a pretty shade of pink. When I blush I look quite like an apple. I have not blushed for years, though." She leaned closer. "Does your father plan to wed again?"

"My father?" Alayne had never considered that. Somehow the notion made her squirm. She found herself remembering the look on Lysa Arryn's face as she'd tumbled through the Moon Door.

"We all know how devoted he was to Lady Lysa," said Myranda, "but he cannot mourn forever. He needs a pretty young wife to wash away his grief. I imagine he could have his pick of half the noble maidens in the Vale. Who could be a better husband than our own bold Lord Protector? Though I do wish he had a better name than *Littlefinger*. How little is it, do you know?"

"His finger?" She blushed again. "I don't . . . I never . . ."

Lady Myranda laughed so loud that Mya Stone glanced back at them. "Never you mind, Alayne, I'm sure it's large enough."

They passed beneath a wind-carved arch, where long icicles clung to the pale stone, dripping down on them. On the far side the path narrowed and plunged down sharply for a hundred feet or more. Myranda was forced to drop back. Alayne gave the mule his head. The steepness of this part of the descent made her cling tightly to her saddle. The steps here had been worn smooth by the iron-shod hooves of all the mules who'd passed this way, until they resembled a series of shallow stone bowls. Water filled the bottoms of the bowls, glimmering golden in the afternoon sun. *It is water now,* Alayne thought, *but come dark, all of it will turn to ice.* She realized that she was holding her breath, and let it out. Mya Stone and Lord Robert had almost reached the rock spire where the slope leveled off again. She tried to look at them, and only them. *I will not fall,* she told herself. *Mya's mule will see me through.* The wind skirled around her, as she bumped and scraped her way down step by step. It seemed to take a lifetime.

Then all at once she was at the bottom with Mya and her little lord, huddled beneath a twisted, rocky spire. Ahead stretched a high stone saddle, narrow and icy. Alayne could hear the wind shrieking, and feel it plucking at her cloak. She remembered this place from her ascent. It had frightened her then, and it frightened her now. "It is wider than it looks," Mya was telling Lord Robert in a cheerful voice. "A yard across, and no more than eight yards long, that's nothing."

"Nothing," Robert said. His hand was shaking.

Oh, no, Alayne thought. *Please. Not here. Not now.*

"It's best to lead the mules across," Mya said. "If it please my lord, I'll take mine over first, then come back for yours." Lord Robert did not answer. He was staring at the narrow saddle with his reddened eyes. "I shan't be long, my lord," Mya promised, but Alayne doubted that the boy could even hear her.

When the bastard girl led her mule out from beneath the shelter of the spire, the wind caught her in its teeth. Her cloak lifted, twisting and flapping in the air. Mya staggered, and for half a heartbeat it seemed as if she would be blown over the precipice, but somehow she regained her balance and went on.

Alayne took Robert's gloved hand in her own to stop his shaking. "Sweetrobin," she said, "I'm scared. Hold my hand, and help me get across. I know *you're* not afraid."

He looked at her, his pupils small dark pinpricks in eyes as big and white as eggs. "I'm not?"

"Not you. You're my winged knight, Ser Sweetrobin."

"The Winged Knight could fly," Robert whispered.

"Higher than the mountains." She gave his hand a squeeze.

Lady Myranda had joined them by the spire. "He could," she echoed, when she saw what was happening.

"Ser Sweetrobin," Lord Robert said, and Alayne knew that she dare not wait for Mya to return. She helped the boy dismount, and hand in hand they walked out onto the bare stone saddle, their cloaks snapping and flapping behind them. All around was empty air and sky, the ground falling away sharply to either side. There was ice underfoot, and broken stones just waiting to turn an ankle, and the wind was howling fiercely. *It sounds like a wolf,* thought Sansa. *A ghost wolf, big as mountains.*

And then they were on the other side, and Mya Stone was laughing and lifting Robert for a hug. "Be careful," Alayne told her. "He can hurt you, flailing. You wouldn't think so, but he can." They found a place for him, a cleft in the rock to keep him out of the cold wind. Alayne tended him until the shaking passed, whilst Mya went back to help the others cross.

Fresh mules awaited them at Snow, and a hot meal of stewed goat and onions. She ate with Mya and Myranda. "So you're brave as well as beautiful," Myranda said to her.

"No." The compliment made her blush. "I'm not. I was so scared. I don't think I could have crossed without Lord Robert." She turned to Mya Stone. "You almost fell."

"You're mistaken. I never fall." Mya's hair had tumbled across her cheek, hiding one eye.

"Almost, I said. I saw you. Weren't you afraid?"

Mya shook her head. "I remember a man throwing me in the air when I was very little. He stands as tall as the sky, and he throws me up so high it feels as though I'm flying. We're both laughing, laughing so much that I can hardly catch a breath, and finally I laugh so hard I wet myself, but that only makes him laugh the louder. I was never afraid when he was throwing me. I knew that he would always be there to catch me." She pushed her hair back. "Then one day he wasn't. Men come and go. They lie, or die, or leave you. A mountain is not a man, though, and a stone is a mountain's daughter. I trust my father, and I trust my mules. I won't fall." She put her hand on a jagged spur of rock, and got to her feet. "Best finish. We have a long way yet to go, and I can smell a storm."

The snow began to fall as they were leaving Stone, the largest and lowest of the three waycastles that defended the approaches to the Eyrie. Dusk was settling by then. Lady Myranda suggested that perhaps they might turn back, spend the night at Stone, and resume their descent when the sun came up, but Mya would not hear of it. "The snow might be five feet deep by then, and the steps treacherous even for my mules," she said. "We will do better to press on. We'll take it slow."

And so they did. Below Stone the steps were broader and less steep, winding in and out of the tall pines and grey-green sentinels that cloaked the lower slopes of the Giant's Lance. Mya's mules knew every root and rock on the way down, it seemed, and any they forgot the bastard girl remembered. Half the night was gone before they sighted the lights of the Gates of the Moon through the falling snow. The last part of their journey was the most peaceful. The snow fell steadily, cloaking all the world in white. Sweetrobin drifted to sleep in the saddle, swaying back and forth with the motion of his mule. Even Lady Myranda began to yawn and complain of being weary. "We have apartments prepared for all of you," she told Alayne, "but if you like you may share my bed tonight. It's large enough for four."

"I should be honored, my lady."

"Randa. Count yourself fortunate that I'm so tired. All I want to do is curl up and go to sleep. Usually when ladies share my bed they have to pay a pillow tax and tell me all about the wicked things they've done."

"What if they haven't done any wicked things?"

"Why, then they must confess all the wicked things they *want* to do. Not you, of course. I can see how virtuous you are just by looking at those rosy cheeks and big blue eyes of yours." She yawned again. "I hope your feet are warm. I do hate bedmaids with cold feet."

By the time they finally reached her father's castle, Lady Myranda was drowsing too, and Alayne was dreaming of her bed. *It will be a featherbed,* she told herself, *soft and warm and deep, piled high with furs. I will dream a sweet dream, and when I wake there will be dogs barking, women gossiping beside the well, swords ringing in the yard. And later there will be a feast, with music and dancing.* After the deathly silence of the Eyrie, she yearned for shouts and laughter.

As the riders were climbing off their mules, however, one of

Petyr's guardsmen emerged from within the keep. "Lady Alayne," he said, "the Lord Protector has been waiting for you."

"He's back?" she said, startled.

"At evenfall. You'll find him in the west tower."

The hour was closer to dawn than to dusk, and most of the castle was asleep, but not Petyr Baelish. Alayne found him seated by a crackling fire, drinking hot mulled wine with three men she did not know. They all rose when she entered, and Petyr smiled warmly. "Alayne. Come, give your father a kiss."

She hugged him dutifully and kissed him on the cheek. "I am sorry to intrude, Father. No one told me you had company."

"You are never an intrusion, sweetling. I was just now telling these good knights what a dutiful daughter I had."

"Dutiful and beautiful," said an elegant young knight whose thick blond mane cascaded down well past his shoulders.

"Aye," said the second knight, a burly fellow with a thick salt-and-pepper beard, a red nose bulbous with broken veins, and gnarled hands as large as hams. "You left out that part, m'lord."

"I would do the same if she were my daughter," said the last knight, a short, wiry man with a wry smile, pointed nose, and bristly orange hair. "Particularly around louts like us."

Alayne laughed. "Are you louts?" she said, teasing. "Why, I took the three of you for gallant knights."

"Knights they are," said Petyr. "Their gallantry has yet to be demonstrated, but we may hope. Allow me to present Ser Byron, Ser Morgarth, and Ser Shadrich. Sers, the Lady Alayne, my natural and very clever daughter . . . with whom I must needs confer, if you will be so good as to excuse us."

The three knights bowed and withdrew, though the tall one with the blond hair kissed her hand before taking his leave.

"Hedge knights?" said Alayne, when the door had closed.

"Hungry knights. I thought it best that we have a few more swords about us. The times grow ever more interesting, my sweet, and when the times are interesting you can never have too many swords. The *Merling King*'s returned to Gulltown, and old Oswell had some tales to tell."

She knew better than to ask what sort of tales. If Petyr had wanted her to know, he would have told her. "I did not expect you back so soon," she said. "I am glad you've come."

"I would never have known it from the kiss you gave me." He pulled her closer, caught her face between his hands, and kissed her on the lips for a long time. "Now that's the sort of kiss that says *welcome home*. See that you do better next time."

"Yes, Father." She could feel herself blushing.

He did not hold her kiss against her. "You would not believe half of what is happening in King's Landing, sweetling. Cersei stumbles from one idiocy to the next, helped along by her council of the deaf, the dim, and the blind. I always anticipated that she would beggar the realm and destroy herself, but I never expected she would do it quite so *fast*. It is quite vexing. I had hoped to have four or five quiet years to plant some seeds and allow some fruits to ripen, but now . . . it is a good thing that I thrive on chaos. What little peace and order the five kings left us will not long survive the three queens, I fear."

"Three queens?" She did not understand.

Nor did Petyr choose to explain. Instead, he smiled and said, "I have brought my sweet girl back a gift."

Alayne was as pleased as she was surprised. "Is it a gown?" She had heard there were fine seamstresses in Gulltown, and she was so tired of dressing drably.

"Something better. Guess again."

"Jewels?"

"No jewels could hope to match my daughter's eyes."

"Lemons? Did you find some lemons?" She had promised Sweetrobin lemon cake, and for lemon cake you needed lemons.

Petyr Baelish took her by the hand and drew her down onto his lap. "I have made a marriage contract for you."

"A marriage . . ." Her throat tightened. She did not want to wed again, not now, perhaps not ever. "I do not . . . I cannot marry. Father, I . . ." Alayne looked to the door, to make certain it was closed. "I *am* married," she whispered. "You know."

Petyr put a finger to her lips to silence her. "The dwarf wed Ned Stark's daughter, not mine. Be that as it may. This is only a betrothal.

The marriage must needs wait until Cersei is done and Sansa's safely widowed. And you must meet the boy and win his approval. Lady Waynwood will not make him marry against his will, she was quite firm on that."

"Lady *Waynwood?*" Alayne could hardly believe it. "Why would she marry one of her sons to ... to a ..."

"... bastard? For a start, you are the *Lord Protector*'s bastard, never forget. The Waynwoods are very old and very proud, but not as rich as one might think, as I discovered when I began buying up their debt. Not that Lady Anya would ever sell a son for gold. A ward, however ... young Harry's only a cousin, and the dower that I offered her ladyship was even larger than the one that Lyonel Corbray just collected. It had to be, for her to risk Bronze Yohn's wroth. This will put all his plans awry. You are promised to Harrold Hardyng, sweetling, provided you can win his boyish heart ... which should not be hard, for you."

"Harry the Heir?" Alayne tried to recall what Myranda had told her about him on the mountain. "He was just knighted. And he has a bastard daughter by some common girl."

"And another on the way by a different wench. Harry can be a beguiling one, no doubt. Soft sandy hair, deep blue eyes, and dimples when he smiles. And *very* gallant, I am told." He teased her with a smile. "Bastard-born or no, sweetling, when this match is announced you will be the envy of every highborn maiden in the Vale, and a few from the riverlands and the Reach as well."

"Why?" Alayne was lost. "Is Ser Harrold ... how could he be Lady Waynwood's heir? Doesn't she have sons of her own blood?"

"Three," Petyr allowed. She could smell the wine on his breath, the cloves and nutmeg. "Daughters too, and grandsons."

"Won't they come before Harry? I don't understand."

"You will. Listen." Petyr took her hand in his own and brushed his finger lightly down the inside of her palm. "Lord Jasper Arryn, begin with him. Jon Arryn's father. He begot three children, two sons and a daughter. Jon was the eldest, so the Eyrie and the lordship passed to him. His sister Alys wed Ser Elys Waynwood, uncle to the present Lady Waynwood." He made a wry face. "Elys and Alys, isn't that precious? Lord Jasper's younger son, Ser Ronnel Arryn, wed a Belmore girl, but only rang her once or twice before dying of a bad belly. Their son Elbert was being born in one bed even as poor Ronnel was dying in another down the hall. Are you paying close attention, sweetling?"

"Yes. There was Jon and Alys and Ronnel, but Ronnel died."

"Good. Now, Jon Arryn married thrice, but his first two wives gave him no children, so for long years his nephew Elbert was his heir. Meantime, Elys was plowing Alys quite dutifully, and she was whelping once a year. She gave him nine children, eight girls and one precious little boy, another Jasper, after which she died exhausted. Boy Jasper, inconsiderate of the heroic efforts that had gone into begetting him, got himself kicked in the head by a horse when he was three years old. A pox took two of his sisters soon after, leaving six. The eldest married Ser Denys Arryn, a distant cousin to the Lords of the Eyrie. There are several branches of House Arryn scattered across the Vale, all as proud as they are penurious, save for the Gulltown Arryns, who had the rare good sense to marry merchants. They're rich, but less than couth, so no one talks about them. Ser Denys hailed from one of the poor, proud branches ... but he was also a renowned jouster, handsome and gallant and brimming with courtesy. And he had that magic Arryn name, which made him ideal for the eldest Waynwood girl. Their children would be Arryns, and the next heirs to the Vale should any ill befall Elbert. Well, as it happened, Mad King Aerys befell Elbert. You know that story?"

She did. "The Mad King murdered him."

"He did indeed. And soon after, Ser Denys left his pregnant Waynwood wife to ride to war. He died during the Battle of the Bells, of an excess of gallantry and an axe. When they told his lady of his death she perished of grief, and her newborn son soon followed. No matter. Jon Arryn had gotten himself a young wife during the war, one he had reason to believe fertile. He was very hopeful, I'm sure, but you and I know that all he ever got from Lysa were stillbirths, miscarriages, and poor Sweetrobin.

"Which brings us back to the five remaining daughters of Elys and Alys. The eldest had been left terribly scarred by the same pox that killed her sisters, so she became a septa. Another was seduced by a sellsword. Ser Elys cast her out, and she joined the silent sisters after her bastard died in infancy. The third wed the Lord of the Paps, but proved barren. The fourth was on her way to the riverlands to marry some Bracken when Burned Men carried her off. That left the youngest, who wed a landed knight sworn to the Waynwoods, gave him a son that she named Harrold, and perished." He turned her hand over and lightly kissed her wrist. "So tell me, sweetling—why is Harry the Heir?"

Her eyes widened. "He is not Lady Waynwood's heir. He's *Robert's* heir. If Robert were to die . . ."

Petyr arched an eyebrow. "*When* Robert dies. Our poor brave Sweetrobin is such a sickly boy, it is only a matter of time. *When* Robert dies, Harry the Heir becomes Lord Harrold, Defender of the Vale and Lord of the Eyrie. Jon Arryn's bannermen will never love me, nor our silly, shaking Robert, but they will love their Young Falcon . . . and when they come together for his wedding, and you come out with your long auburn hair, clad in a maiden's cloak of white and grey with a direwolf emblazoned on the back . . . why, every knight in the Vale will pledge his sword to win you back your birthright. So those are your gifts from me, my sweet Sansa . . . Harry, the Eyrie, and Winterfell. That's worth another kiss now, don't you think?"

BRIENNE

T*his is an evil dream,* she thought. But if she were dreaming, why did it hurt so much?

The rain had stopped falling, but all the world was wet. Her cloak felt as heavy as her mail. The ropes that bound her wrists were soaked through, but that only made them tighter. No matter how Brienne turned her hands, she could not slip free. She did not understand who had bound her, or why. She tried to ask the shadows, but they did not answer. Perhaps they did not hear her. Perhaps they were not real. Under her layers of wet wool and rusting mail, her skin was flushed and feverish. She wondered whether all of this was just a fever dream.

She had a horse beneath her, though she could not remember mounting. She lay facedown across his hindquarters, like a sack of oats. Her wrists and ankles had been lashed together. The air was damp, the ground cloaked in mist. Her head pounded with every step. She could hear voices, but all she could see was the earth beneath the horse's hooves. There were things broken inside of her. Her face felt swollen, her cheek was sticky with blood, and every jounce and bounce send a stab of agony through her arm. She could hear Podrick calling her, as if from far away. "Ser?" he kept saying. "Ser? My lady? Ser? My lady?" His voice was faint and hard to hear. Finally, there was only silence.

She dreamt she was at Harrenhal, down in the bear pit once again.

This time it was Biter facing her, huge and bald and maggot-white, with weeping sores upon his cheeks. Naked he came, fondling his member, gnashing his filed teeth together. Brienne fled from him. "My sword," she called. "Oathkeeper. Please." The watchers did not answer. Renly was there, with Nimble Dick and Catelyn Stark. Shagwell, Pyg, and Timeon had come, and the corpses from the trees with their sunken cheeks, swollen tongues, and empty eye sockets. Brienne wailed in horror at the sight of them, and Biter grabbed her arm and yanked her close and tore a chunk from her face. "Jaime," she heard herself scream, *"Jaime."*

Even in the depths of dream the pain was there. Her face throbbed. Her shoulder bled. Breathing hurt. The pain crackled up her arm like lightning. She cried out for a maester.

"We have no maester," said a girl's voice. "Only me."

I am looking for a girl, Brienne remembered. *A highborn maid of three-and-ten, with blue eyes and auburn hair.* "My lady?" she said. "Lady Sansa?"

A man laughed. "She thinks you're Sansa Stark."

"She can't go much farther. She'll die."

"One less lion. I won't weep."

Brienne heard the sound of someone praying. She thought of Septon Meribald, but all the words were wrong. *The night is dark and full of terrors, and so are dreams.*

They were riding through a gloomy wood, a dank, dark, silent place where the pines pressed close. The ground was soft beneath her horse's hooves, and the tracks she left behind filled up with blood. Beside her rode Lord Renly, Dick Crabb, and Vargo Hoat. Blood ran from Renly's throat. The Goat's torn ear oozed pus. "Where are we going?" Brienne asked. "Where are you taking me?" None of them would answer. *How can they answer? All of them are dead.* Did that mean that she was dead as well?

Lord Renly was ahead of her, her sweet smiling king. He was leading her horse through the trees. Brienne called out to tell him how much she loved him, but when he turned to scowl at her, she saw that he was not Renly after all. Renly never scowled. *He always had a smile for me,* she thought . . . except . . .

"Cold," her king said, puzzled, and a shadow moved without a man to cast it, and her sweet lord's blood came washing through the green steel of his gorget to drench her hands. He had been a warm man, but his blood was cold as ice. *This is not real,* she told herself. *This is another bad dream, and soon I'll wake.*

Her mount came to a sudden halt. Rough hands seized hold of her. She saw shafts of red afternoon light slanting through the branches of a chestnut tree. A horse rooted amongst the dead leaves after chestnuts, and men moved nearby, talking in quiet voices. Ten, twelve, maybe more. Brienne did not recognize their faces. She was stretched out on the ground, her back against a tree trunk. "Drink this, m'lady," said the girl's voice. She lifted a cup to Brienne's lips. The taste was strong and sour. Brienne spat it out. "Water," she gasped. "Please. Water."

"Water won't help the pain. This will. A little." The girl put the cup to Brienne's lips again.

It even hurt to drink. Wine ran down her chin and dribbled on her chest. When the cup was empty the girl filled it from a skin. Brienne sucked it down until she sputtered. "No more."

"More. You have a broken arm, and some of your ribs is cracked. Two, maybe three."

"Biter," Brienne said, remembering the weight of him, the way his knee had slammed into her chest.

"Aye. A real monster, that one."

It all came back to her; lightning above and mud below, the rain *pinging* softly against the dark steel of the Hound's helm, the terrible strength in Biter's hands. Suddenly she could not stand being bound. She tried to wrench free of her ropes, but all that did was chafe her worse. Her wrists were tied too tightly. There was dried blood on the hemp. "Is he dead?" She trembled. "Biter. *Is he dead?*" She remembered his teeth tearing into the flesh of her face. The thought that he might still be out there somewhere, breathing, made Brienne want to scream.

"He's dead. Gendry shoved a spearpoint through the back of his neck. Drink, m'lady, or I'll pour it down your throat."

She drank. "I am looking for a girl," she whispered, between swallows. She almost said *my sister.* "A highborn maid of three-and-ten. She has blue eyes and auburn hair."

"I'm not her."

No. Brienne could see that. The girl was thin to the point of looking starved. She wore her brown hair in a braid, and her eyes were older than her years. *Brown hair, brown eyes, plain. Willow, six years older.* "You're the sister. The innkeep."

"I might be." The girl squinted. "What if I am?"

"Do you have a name?" Brienne asked. Her stomach gurgled. She was afraid that she might retch.

"Heddle. Same as Willow. Jeyne Heddle."

"Jeyne. Untie my hands. Please. Have pity. The ropes are chafing my wrists. I'm bleeding."

"It's not allowed. You're to stay bound, till . . ."

". . . till you stand before m'lady." Renly stood behind the girl, pushing his black hair out of his eyes. *Not Renly. Gendry.* "M'lady means for you to answer for your crimes."

"M'lady." The wine was making her head spin. It was hard to think. "Stoneheart. Is that who you mean?" Lord Randyll had spoken of her, back at Maidenpool. "Lady Stoneheart."

"Some call her that. Some call her other things. The Silent Sister. Mother Merciless. The Hangwoman."

The Hangwoman. When Brienne closed her eyes, she saw the corpses swaying underneath the bare brown limbs, their faces black and swollen. Suddenly she was desperately afraid. "Podrick. My squire. Where is Podrick? And the others . . . Ser Hyle, Septon Meribald. Dog. What did you do with Dog?"

Gendry and the girl exchanged a look. Brienne fought to rise, and managed to get one knee under her before the world began to spin. "It was you killed the dog, m'lady," she heard Gendry say, just before the darkness swallowed her again.

Then she was back at the Whispers, standing amongst the ruins and facing Clarence Crabb. He was huge and fierce, mounted on an aurochs shaggier than he was. The beast pawed the ground in fury, tearing deep furrows in the earth. Crabb's teeth had been filed into points. When Brienne went to draw her sword, she found her scabbard empty. "No," she cried, as Ser Clarence charged. It wasn't fair. She could not fight without her magic sword. Ser Jaime had given it to her. The thought of failing him as she had failed Lord Renly made her want to weep. "My sword. Please, I have to find my sword."

"The wench wants her sword back," a voice declared.

"And I want Cersei Lannister to suck my cock. So what?"

"Jaime called it Oathkeeper. *Please.*" But the voices did not listen, and Clarence Crabb thundered down on her and swept off her head. Brienne spiraled down into a deeper darkness.

She dreamed that she was lying in a boat, her head pillowed on someone's lap. There were shadows all around them, hooded men in mail and leather, paddling them across a foggy river with muffled oars. She was drenched in sweat, burning, yet somehow shivering too. The fog was full of faces. "*Beauty,*" whispered the willows on the bank, but the reeds said, "*Freak, freak.*" Brienne shuddered. "Stop," she said. "Someone make them stop."

The next time she woke, Jeyne was holding a cup of hot soup to her lips. *Onion broth,* Brienne thought. She drank as much of it as she could, until a bit of carrot caught in her throat and made her choke. Coughing was agony. "Easy," the girl said.

"Gendry," she wheezed. "I have to talk with Gendry."

"He turned back at the river, m'lady. He's gone back to his forge, to Willow and the little ones, to keep them safe."

No one can keep them safe. She began to cough again. "Ah, let her choke. Save us a rope." One of the shadow men shoved the girl aside. He was clad in rusted rings and a studded belt. At his hip hung longsword and dirk. A yellow greatcloak was plastered to his shoulders, sodden and filthy. From his shoulders rose a steel dog's head, its teeth bared in a snarl.

"*No,*" Brienne moaned. "No, you're dead, I killed you."

The Hound laughed. "You got that backwards. It'll be me killing you. I'd do it now, but m'lady wants to see you hanged."

Hanged. The word sent a jolt of fear through her. She looked at the girl, Jeyne. *She is too young to be so hard.* "Bread and salt," Brienne gasped. "The inn . . . Septon Meribald fed the children . . . we broke bread with your sister . . ."

"Guest right don't mean so much as it used to," said the girl. "Not since m'lady come back from the wedding. Some o' them swinging down by the river figured they was guests too."

"We figured different," said the Hound. "They wanted beds. We gave 'em trees."

"We got more trees, though," put in another shadow, one-eyed beneath a rusty pothelm. "We always got more trees."

When it was time to mount again, they yanked a leather hood down over her face. There were no eyeholes. The leather muffled the sounds around her. The taste of onions lingered on her tongue, sharp as the knowledge of her failure. *They mean to hang me.* She thought of Jaime, of Sansa, of her father back on Tarth, and was glad for the hood. It helped hide the tears welling in her eyes. From time to time she heard the outlaws talking, but she could not make out their words. After a while she gave herself up to weariness and the slow, steady motion of her horse.

This time she dreamed that she was home again, at Evenfall. Through the tall arched windows of her lord father's hall she could see the sun just going down. *I was safe here. I was safe.*

She was dressed in silk brocade, a quartered gown of blue and red decorated with golden suns and silver crescent moons. On another girl it might have been a pretty gown, but not on her. She was twelve, ungainly and uncomfortable, waiting to meet the young knight her father had arranged for her to marry, a boy six years her senior, sure to be a famous champion one day. She dreaded his arrival. Her bosom was too small, her hands and feet too big. Her hair kept sticking up, and there was a pimple nestled in the fold beside her nose. "He will bring a rose for you," her father promised her, but a rose was no good, a rose could not keep her safe. It was a sword she wanted. *Oathkeeper. I have to find the girl. I have to find his honor.*

Finally, the doors opened, and her betrothed strode into her father's hall. She tried to greet him as she had been instructed, only to have blood come pouring from her mouth. She had bitten her tongue off as she waited. She spat it at the young knight's feet, and saw the disgust on his face. "Brienne the Beauty," he said in a mocking tone. "I have seen sows more beautiful than you." He tossed the rose in her face. As he walked away, the griffins on his cloak rippled and blurred and changed to lions. *Jaime!* she wanted to cry. *Jaime, come back for me!* But her tongue lay on the floor by the rose, drowned in blood.

Brienne woke suddenly, gasping.

She did not know where she was. The air was cold and heavy, and smelled of earth and worms and mold. She was lying on a pallet beneath a mound of sheepskins, with rock above her head and roots poking through the walls. The only light came from a tallow candle, smoking in a pool of melted wax.

She pushed aside the sheepskins. Someone had stripped her of her clothes and armor, she saw. She was clad in a brown woolen shift, thin but freshly washed. Her forearm had been splinted and bound up with linen, though. One side of her face felt wet and stiff. When she touched herself, she found some sort of damp poultice covering her cheek and jaw and ear. *Biter . . .*

Brienne got to her feet. Her legs felt weak as water, her head as light as air. "Is anyone there?"

Something moved in one of the shadowed alcoves behind the candle; an old grey man clad in rags. The blankets that had covered him slipped to the floor. He sat up and rubbed his eyes. "Lady Brienne? You gave me a fright. I was dreaming."

No, she thought, *that was me.* "What place is this? Is this a dungeon?"

"A cave. Like rats, we must run back to our holes when the dogs come sniffing after us, and there are more dogs every day." He was clad in the ragged remains of an old robe, pink and white. His hair was long and grey and tangled, the loose skin of his cheeks and chin was covered with coarse stubble. "Are you hungry? Could you keep down a cup of milk? Perhaps some bread and honey?"

"I want my clothes. My sword." She felt naked without her mail, and she wanted Oathkeeper at her side. "The way out. Show me the way out." The floor of the cave was dirt and stone, rough beneath the soles of her feet. Even now she felt light-headed, as if she were floating. The flickering light cast queer shadows. *Spirits of the slain,* she thought, *dancing all about me, hiding when I turn to look at them.* Everywhere she saw holes and cracks and crevices, but there was no way to know which passages led out, which would take her deeper into the cave, and which went nowhere. All were black as pitch.

"Might I feel your brow, my lady?" Her gaoler's hand was scarred and hard with callus, yet strangely gentle. "Your fever has broken," he announced, in a voice flavored with the accents of the Free Cities. "Well and good. Just yesterday your flesh felt as if it were on fire. Jeyne feared that we might lose you."

"Jeyne. The tall girl?"

"The very one. Though she is not so tall as you, my lady. Long Jeyne, the men call her. It was she who set your arm and splinted it, as well as any maester. She did what she could for your face as well, washing out the wounds with boiled ale to stop the mortification. Even so . . . a human bite is a filthy thing. That is where the fever came from, I am certain." The grey man touched her bandaged face. "We had to cut away some of the flesh. Your face will not be pretty, I fear."

It has never been pretty. "Scars, you mean?"

"My lady, that creature chewed off half your cheek."

Brienne could not help but flinch. *Every knight has battle scars,* Ser Goodwin had warned her, when she asked him to teach her the sword. *Is that what you want, child?* Her old master-at-arms had been talking about sword cuts, though; he could never have anticipated Biter's pointed teeth. "Why set my bones and wash my wounds if you only mean to hang me?"

"Why indeed?" He glanced at the candle, as if he could no longer bear to look at her. "You fought bravely at the inn, they tell me. Lem should not have left the crossroads. He was told to stay close, hidden, to come at once if he saw smoke rising from the chimney . . . but when word reached him that the Mad Dog of Saltpans had been seen making his way north along the Green Fork, he took the bait. We have been hunting that lot for so long . . . still, he ought to have known better. As it was, it was half a day before he realized that the mummers had used a stream to hide their tracks and doubled back behind him, and then he lost more time circling around a column of Frey knights. If not for you, only corpses might have remained at the inn by the time that Lem and his men got back. *That* was why Jeyne dressed your wounds, mayhaps. Whatever else you may have done, you won those wounds honorably, in the best of causes."

Whatever else you may have done. "What is it that you think I've done?" she said. *"Who are you?"*

"We were king's men when we began," the man told her, "but king's men must have a king, and we have none. We were brothers too, but now our brotherhood is broken. I do not know who we are, if truth be told, nor where we might be going. I only know the road is dark. The fires have not shown me what lies at its end."

I know where it ends. I have seen the corpses in the trees. "Fires," Brienne repeated. All at once she understood. "You are the Myrish priest. The red wizard."

He looked down at his ragged robes, and smiled ruefully. "The pink pretender, rather. I am Thoros, late of Myr, aye . . . a bad priest and a worse wizard."

"You ride with the Dondarrion. The lightning lord."

"Lightning comes and goes and then is seen no more. So too with men. Lord Beric's fire has gone out of this world, I fear. A grimmer shadow leads us in his place."

"The Hound?"

The priest pursed his lips. "The Hound is dead and buried."

"I saw him. In the woods."

"A fever dream, my lady."

"He said that he would hang me."

"Even dreams can lie. My lady, how long has it been since you have eaten? Surely you are famished?"

She was, she realized. Her belly felt hollow. "Food . . . food would be welcome, thank you."

"A meal, then. Sit. We will talk more, but first a meal. Wait here." Thoros lit a taper from the sagging candle, and vanished into a black hole beneath a ledge of rock. Brienne found herself alone in the small cave. *For how long, though?*

She prowled the chamber, looking for a weapon. Any sort of weapon would have served; a staff, a club, a dagger. She found only rocks. One fit her fist nicely . . . but she remembered the Whispers, and what happened when Shagwell tried to pit a stone against a knife. When she heard the priest's returning footsteps, she let the rock fall to the cavern floor and resumed her seat.

Thoros had bread and cheese and a bowl of stew. "I am sorry," he said. "The last of the milk had soured, and the honey is all gone. Food grows scant. Still, this will fill you."

The stew was cold and greasy, the bread hard, the cheese harder. Brienne had never eaten anything half so good. "Are my companions here?" she asked the priest, as she was spooning up the last of the stew.

"The septon was set free to go upon his way. There was no harm in him. The others are here, awaiting judgment."

"Judgment?" She frowned. "Podrick Payne is just a boy."

"He says he is a squire."

"You know how boys will boast."

"The Imp's squire. He has fought in battles, by his own admission. He has even killed, to hear him tell it."

"A boy," she said again. "Have pity."

"My lady," Thoros said, "I do not doubt that kindness and mercy and forgiveness can still be found somewhere in these Seven Kingdoms, but do not look for them here. This is a cave, not a temple. When men must live like rats in the dark beneath the earth, they soon run out of pity, as they do of milk and honey."

"And justice? Can that be found in caves?"

"Justice." Thoros smiled wanly. "I remember justice. It had a pleasant taste. Justice was what we were about when Beric led us, or so we told ourselves. We were king's men, knights, and heroes . . . but some knights are dark and full of terror, my lady. War makes monsters of us all."

"Are you saying you are monsters?"

"I am saying we are human. You are not the only one with wounds, Lady Brienne. Some of my brothers were good men when this began. Some were . . . less good, shall we say? Though there are those who say it does not matter how a man begins, but only how he ends. I suppose it is the same for women." The priest got to his feet. "Our time together is at an end, I fear. I hear my brothers coming. Our lady sends for you."

Brienne heard their footsteps and saw torchlight flickering in the passage. "You told me she had gone to Fairmarket."

"And so she had. She returned whilst we were sleeping. She never sleeps herself."

I will not be afraid, she told herself, but it was too late for that. *I will not let them see my fear,* she promised herself instead. There were four of them, hard men with haggard faces, clad in mail and scale and leather. She recognized one of them; the man with one eye, from her dreams.

The biggest of the four wore a stained and tattered yellow cloak. "Enjoy the food?" he asked. "I hope so. It's the last food you're ever like to eat." He was brown-haired, bearded, brawny, with a broken nose that had healed badly. *I know this man,* Brienne thought. "You are the Hound."

He grinned. His teeth were awful; crooked, and streaked brown with rot. "I suppose I am. Seeing as how m'lady went and killed the last one." He turned his head and spat.

She remembered lightning flashing, the mud beneath her feet. "It was Rorge I killed. He took the helm from Clegane's grave, and you stole it off his corpse."

"I didn't hear him objecting."

Thoros sucked in his breath in dismay. "Is this true? A dead man's helm? Have we fallen that low?"

The big man scowled at him. "It's good steel."

"There is nothing good about that helm, nor the men who wore it," said the red priest. "Sandor Clegane was a man in torment, and Rorge a beast in human skin."

"I'm not them."

"Then why show the world their face? Savage, snarling, twisted . . . is that who you would be, Lem?"

"The sight of it will make my foes afraid."

"The sight of it makes me afraid."

"Close your eyes, then." The man in the yellow cloak made a sharp gesture. "Bring the whore."

Brienne did not resist. There were four of them, and she was weak and wounded, naked beneath the woolen shift. She had to bend her neck to keep from hitting her head as they marched her through the twisting passage. The way ahead rose sharply, turning twice before emerging in a much larger cavern full of outlaws.

A fire pit had been dug into the center of the floor, and the air was blue with smoke. Men clustered near the flames, warming themselves against the chill of the cave. Others stood along the walls or sat cross-legged on straw pallets. There were women too, and even a few children peering out from behind their mothers' skirts. The one face Brienne knew belonged to Long Jeyne Heddle.

A trestle table had been set up across the cave, in a cleft in the rock. Behind it sat a woman all in grey, cloaked and hooded. In her hands was a crown, a bronze circlet ringed by iron swords. She was studying it, her fingers stroking the blades as if to test their sharpness. Her eyes glimmered under her hood.

Grey was the color of the silent sisters, the handmaidens of the Stranger. Brienne felt a shiver climb her spine. *Stoneheart.*

"M'lady," said the big man. "Here she is."

"Aye," added the one-eyed man. "The Kingslayer's whore."

She flinched. "Why would you call me that?"

"If I had a silver stag for every time you said his name, I'd be as rich as your friends the Lannisters."

"That was only . . . you do not understand . . ."

"Don't we, though?" The big man laughed. "I think we might. There's a stink of *lion* about you, lady."

"That's not so."

Another of the outlaws stepped forward, a younger man in a greasy sheepskin jerkin. In his hand was Oathkeeper. "This says it is." His voice was frosted with the accents of the north. He slid the sword from its scabbard and placed it in front of Lady Stoneheart. In the light from the firepit the red and black ripples in the blade almost seem to move, but the woman in grey had eyes only for the pommel: a golden lion's head, with ruby eyes that shone like two red stars.

"There is this as well." Thoros of Myr drew a parchment from his sleeve, and put it down next to the sword. "It bears the boy king's seal and says the bearer is about his business."

Lady Stoneheart set the sword aside to read the letter.

"The sword was given me for a good purpose," said Brienne. "Ser Jaime swore an oath to Catelyn Stark . . ."

". . . before his friends cut her throat for her, that must have been," said the big man in the yellow cloak. "We all know about the Kingslayer and his oaths."

It is no good, Brienne realized. *No words of mine will sway them.* She plunged ahead despite that. "He promised Lady Catelyn her daughters, but by the time we reached King's Landing they were gone. Jaime sent me out to seek the Lady Sansa . . ."

". . . and if you had found the girl," asked the young northman, "what were you to do with her?"

"Protect her. Take her somewhere safe."

The big man laughed. "Where's that? Cersei's dungeon?"

"No."

"Deny it all you want. That sword says you're a liar. Are we supposed to believe the Lannisters are handing out gold and ruby swords to *foes*? That the Kingslayer meant for you to hide the girl from *his own twin*? I suppose the paper with the boy king's seal was just in case you needed to wipe your arse? And then there's the company you keep . . ." The big man turned and beckoned, the ranks of outlaws parted, and two more captives were brought forth. "The boy was the Imp's own squire, m'lady," he said to Lady Stoneheart. "T'other is one of Randyll Bloody Tarly's bloody household knights."

Hyle Hunt had been beaten so badly that his face was swollen almost beyond recognition. He stumbled as they shoved him, and almost fell. Podrick caught him by the arm. "Ser," the boy said miserably, when he saw Brienne. "My lady, I mean. Sorry."

"You have nothing to be sorry for." Brienne turned to Lady Stoneheart. "Whatever treachery you think I may have done, my lady, Podrick and Ser Hyle were no part of it."

"They're lions," said the one-eyed man. "That's enough. I say they hang. Tarly's hanged a score o' ours, past time we strung up some o' his."

Ser Hyle gave Brienne a faint smile. "My lady," he said, "you should have wed me when I made my offer. Now I fear you're doomed to die a maid, and me a poor man."

"*Let them go,*" Brienne pleaded.

The woman in grey gave no answer. She studied the sword, the parchment, the bronze-and-iron crown. Finally, she reached up under her jaw and grasped her neck, as if she meant to throttle herself. Instead she spoke . . . Her voice was halting, broken, tortured. The sound seemed to come from her throat, part croak, part wheeze, part death rattle. *The language of the damned*, thought Brienne. "I don't understand. What did she say?"

"She asked the name of this blade of yours," said the young northman in the sheepskin jerkin.

"Oathkeeper," Brienne answered.

The woman in grey *hissed* through her fingers. Her eyes were two red pits burning in the shadows. She spoke again.

"No, she says. Call it Oathbreaker, she says. It was made for treachery and murder. She names it *False Friend*. Like you."

"To whom have I been false?"

"To her," the northman said. "Can it be that my lady has forgotten that you once swore her your service?"

There was only one woman that the Maid of Tarth had ever sworn to serve. "That cannot be," she said. "She's dead."

"Death and guest right," muttered Long Jeyne Heddle. "They don't mean so much as they used to, neither one."

Lady Stoneheart lowered her hood and unwound the grey wool scarf from her face. Her hair was dry and brittle, white as bone. Her brow was mottled green and grey, spotted with the brown blooms of decay. The flesh of her face clung in ragged strips from her eyes down to her jaw. Some of the rips were crusted with dried blood, but others gaped open to reveal the skull beneath.

Her face, Brienne thought. *Her face was so strong and handsome, her skin so smooth and soft.* "Lady Catelyn?" Tears filled her eyes. "They said . . . they said that you were dead."

"She is," said Thoros of Myr. "The Freys slashed her throat from ear to ear. When we found her by the river she was three days dead. Harwin begged me to give her the kiss of life, but it had been too long. I would not do it, so Lord Beric put his lips to hers instead, and the flame of life passed from him to her. And . . . she rose. May the Lord of Light protect us. She *rose*."

Am I dreaming still? Brienne wondered. *Is this another nightmare born from Biter's teeth?* "I never betrayed her. Tell her that. I swear it by the Seven. I swear it by my *sword*."

The thing that had been Catelyn Stark took hold of her throat again, fingers pinching at the ghastly long slash in her neck, and choked out more sounds. "Words are wind, she says," the northman told Brienne. "She says that you must prove your faith."

"How?" asked Brienne.

"With your sword. *Oathkeeper,* you call it? Then keep your oath to her, milady says."

"What does she want of me?"

"She wants her son alive, or the men who killed him dead," said the big man. "She wants to feed the crows, like they did at the Red Wedding. Freys and Boltons, aye. We'll give her those, as many as she likes. All she asks from you is Jaime Lannister."

Jaime. The name was a knife, twisting in her belly. "Lady Catelyn, I . . . you do not understand, Jaime . . . he saved me from being raped when the Bloody Mummers took us, and later he came back for me, he leapt into the bear pit empty-handed . . . I swear to you, he is not the man he was. He sent me after Sansa to keep her safe, he could not have had a part in the Red Wedding."

Lady Catelyn's fingers dug deep into her throat, and the words came rattling out, choked and broken, a stream as cold as ice. The northman said, "She says that you must choose. Take the sword and slay the Kingslayer, or be hanged for a betrayer. The sword or the noose, she says. Choose, she says. *Choose.*"

Brienne remembered her dream, waiting in her father's hall for the boy she was to marry. In the dream she had bitten off her tongue. *My mouth was full of blood.* She took a ragged breath and said, "I will not make that choice."

There was a long silence. Then Lady Stoneheart spoke again. This time Brienne understood her words. There were only two. *"Hang them,"* she croaked.

"As you command, m'lady," said the big man.

They bound Brienne's wrists with rope again and led her from the cavern, up a twisting stony path to the surface. It was morning outside, she was surprised to see. Shafts of pale dawn light were slanting through the trees. *So many trees to choose from,* she thought. *They will not need to take us far.*

Nor did they. Beneath a crooked willow, the outlaws slipped a noose about her neck, jerked it tight, and tossed the other end of the rope over a limb. Hyle Hunt and Podrick Payne were given elms. Ser Hyle was shouting that he would kill Jaime Lannister, but the Hound cuffed him across the face and shut him up. He had donned the helm again. "If you got crimes to confess to your gods, this would be the time to say them."

"Podrick has never harmed you. My father will ransom him. Tarth is called the sapphire isle. Send Podrick with my bones to Evenfall, and you'll have sapphires, silver, whatever you want."

"I want my wife and daughter back," said the Hound. "Can your father give me that? If not, he can get buggered. The boy will rot beside you. Wolves will gnaw your bones."

"Do you mean to hang her, Lem?" asked the one-eyed man. "Or do you figure to talk the bitch to death?"

The Hound snatched the end of the rope from the man holding it. "Let's see if she can dance," he said, and gave a yank.

Brienne felt the hemp constricting, digging into her skin, jerking her chin upward. Ser Hyle was cursing them eloquently, but not the boy. Podrick never lifted his eyes, not even when his feet were jerked up off the ground. *If this is another dream, it is time for me to awaken. If this is real, it is time for me to die.* All she could see was Podrick, the noose around his thin neck, his legs twitching. Her mouth opened. Pod was kicking, choking, *dying.* Brienne sucked the air in desperately, even as the rope was strangling her. Nothing had ever hurt so much.

She screamed a word.

CERSEI

Septa Moelle was a white-haired harridan with a face as sharp as an axe and lips pursed in perpetual disapproval. *This one still has her maidenhead, I'll wager,* Cersei thought, *though by now it's hard and stiff as boiled leather.* Six of the High Sparrow's knights escorted her, with the rainbow sword of their reborn order emblazoned on their kite shields.

"Septa." Cersei sat beneath the Iron Throne, clad in green silk and golden lace. "Tell his High Holiness that we are vexed with him. He presumes too much." Emeralds glimmered on her fingers and in her golden hair. The eyes of court and city were upon her, and she meant for them to see Lord Tywin's daughter. By the time this mummer's farce was done they would know they had but one true queen. *But first we must dance the dance and never miss a step.* "Lady Margaery is my son's true and gentle wife, his helpmate and consort. His High Holiness had no cause to lay his hands upon her person, or to confine her and her young cousins, who are so dear to all of us. I demand that he release them."

Septa Moelle's stern expression did not flicker. "I shall convey Your Grace's words to His High Holiness, but it grieves me to say that the young queen and her ladies cannot be released until and unless their innocence has been proved."

"*Innocence?* Why, you need only look upon their sweet young faces to see how innocent they are."

"A sweet face oft hides a sinner's heart."

Lord Merryweather spoke up from the council table. "What offense have these young maids been accused of, and by whom?"

The septa said, "Megga Tyrell and Elinor Tyrell stand accused of lewdness, fornication, and conspiracy to commit high treason. Alla Tyrell has been charged with witnessing their shame and helping them conceal it. All this, Queen Margaery has also been accused of, as well as adultery and high treason."

Cersei put a hand to her breast. "Tell me who is spreading such calumnies about my good-daughter! I do not believe a word of this. My sweet son loves Lady Margaery with all his heart, she could never have been so cruel as to play him false."

"The accuser is a knight of your own household. Ser Osney Kettleblack has confessed his carnal knowledge of the queen to the High Septon himself, before the altar of the Father."

At the council table, Harys Swyft gasped, and Grand Maester Pycelle turned away. A buzz filled the air, as if a thousand wasps were loose in the throne room. Some of the ladies in the galleries began to slip away, followed by a stream of petty lords and knights from the back of the hall. The gold cloaks let them go, but the queen had instructed Ser Osfryd to make note of all who fled. *Suddenly the Tyrell rose does not smell so sweet.*

"Ser Osney is young and lusty, I will grant you," the queen said, "but a faithful knight for all that. If he says that he was part of this . . . no, it cannot be. Margaery is a maiden!"

"She is not. I examined her myself, at the behest of His High Holiness. Her maidenhead is not intact. Septa Aglantine and Septa Melicent will say the same, as will Queen Margaery's own septa, Nysterica, who has been confined to a penitent's cell for her part in the queen's shame. Lady Megga and Lady Elinor were examined as well. Both were found to have been broken."

The wasps were growing so loud that the queen could hardly hear herself think. *I do hope the little queen and her cousins enjoyed those rides of theirs.*

Lord Merryweather thumped his fist on the table. "Lady Margaery had sworn solemn oaths attesting to her maidenhood, to Her Grace the queen and her late father. Many here bore witness. Lord Tyrell has also testified to her innocence, as has the Lady Olenna, whom we all know to be above reproach. Would you have us believe that all of these noble people *lied* to us?"

"Perhaps they were deceived as well, my lord," said Septa Moelle. "I cannot speak to this. I can only swear to the truth of what I discovered for myself when I examined the queen."

The picture of this sour old crone poking her wrinkled fingers up Margaery's little pink cunt was so droll that Cersei almost laughed. "We insist that His High Holiness allow our own maesters to examine my good-daughter, to determine if there is any shred of truth to these slanders. Grand Maester Pycelle, you shall accompany Septa Moelle back to Beloved Baelor's Sept, and return to us with the truth about our Margaery's maidenhead."

Pycelle had gone the color of curdled white. *At council meetings the wretched old fool cannot say enough, but now that I need a few words from him he has lost the power of speech,* the queen thought, before the old man finally came out with, "There is no need for me to examine her . . . her privy parts." His voice was a quaver. "I grieve to say . . . Queen Margaery is no maiden. She has required me to make her moon tea, not once, but many times."

The uproar that followed that was all that Cersei Lannister could ever have hoped for.

Even the royal herald beating on the floor with his staff did little to quell the noise. The queen let it wash over her for a few heartbeats, savoring the sounds of the little queen's disgrace. When it had gone on long enough, she rose stone-faced and commanded that the gold cloaks clear the hall. *Margaery Tyrell is done,* she thought, exulting. Her white knights fell in around her as she made her exit through the king's door behind the Iron Throne; Boros Blount, Meryn Trant, and Osmund Kettleblack, the last of the Kingsguard still remaining in the city.

Moon Boy was standing beside the door, holding his rattle in his hand and gaping at the confusion with his big round eyes. *A fool he may be, but he wears his folly honestly. Maggy the Frog should have been in motley too, for all she knew about the morrow.* Cersei prayed the old fraud was screaming down in hell. The younger queen whose coming she'd foretold was finished, and if that prophecy could fail, so could the rest. *No golden shrouds, no* valonqar, *I am free of your croaking malice at last.*

The remnants of her small council followed her out. Harys Swyft appeared dazed. He stumbled at the door and might have fallen if Aurane Waters had not caught him by the arm. Even Orton Merryweather seemed anxious. "The smallfolk are fond of the little queen," he said. "They will not take well to this. I fear what might happen next, Your Grace."

"Lord Merryweather is right," said Lord Waters. "If it please Your Grace, I will launch the rest of our new dromonds. The sight of them upon the Blackwater with King Tommen's banner flying from their masts will remind the city who rules here, and keep them safe should the mobs decide to run riot again."

He left the rest unspoken; once on the Blackwater, his dromonds could stop Mace Tyrell from bringing his army back across the river, just as Tyrion had once stopped Stannis. Highgarden had no sea power of its own this side of Westeros. They relied upon the Redwyne fleet, presently on its way back to the Arbor.

"A prudent measure," the queen announced. "Until this storm has passed, I want your ships crewed and on the water."

Ser Harys Swyft was so pale and damp he looked about to faint. "When word of this reaches Lord Tyrell, his fury will know no bounds. There will be blood in the streets . . ."

The knight of the yellow chicken, Cersei mused. *You ought to take a worm for your sigil, ser. A chicken is too bold for you. If Mace Tyrell will not even assault Storm's End, how do you imagine that he would ever dare attack the gods?* When he was done blathering she said, "It must not come to blood, and I mean to see that it does not. I will go to Baelor's Sept myself to speak to Queen Margaery and the High Septon. Tommen loves them both, I know, and would want me to make peace between them."

"Peace?" Ser Harys dabbed at his brow with a velvet sleeve. "If peace is possible . . . that is very brave of you."

"Some sort of trial may be necessary," said the queen, "to disprove these base calumnies and lies and show the world that our sweet Margaery is the innocent we all know her to be."

"Aye," said Merryweather, "but this High Septon may want to try the queen himself, as the Faith once tried men of old."

I hope so, Cersei thought. Such a court was not like to look with favor on treasonous queens who spread their legs for singers and profaned the Maiden's holy rites to hide their shame. "The important thing is to find the truth, I am sure we all agree," she said. "And now, my lords, you must excuse me. I must go see the king. He should not be alone at such a time."

Tommen was fishing for cats when his mother returned to him. Dorcas had made him a mouse with scraps of fur and tied it on a long string at the end of an old fishing pole. The kittens loved to chase it, and the boy liked nothing better than jerking it about the floor as they pounced after it. He seemed surprised when Cersei gathered him up in her arms and kissed him on his brow. "What's that for, Mother? Why are you crying?"

Because you're safe, she wanted to tell him. *Because no harm will ever come to you.* "You are mistaken. A lion never cries." There would be time later to tell him about Margaery and her cousins. "There are some warrants that I need you to sign."

For the king's sake, the queen had left the names off the arrest warrants. Tommen signed them blank, and pressed his seal into the warm wax happily, as he always did. Afterward, she sent him off with Jocelyn Swyft.

Ser Osfryd Kettleblack arrived as the ink was drying. Cersei had written in the names herself: Ser Tallad the Tall, Jalabhar Xho, Hamish the Harper, Hugh Clifton, Mark Mullendore, Bayard Norcross, Lambert Turnberry, Horas Redwyne, Hobber Redwyne, and a certain churl named Wat, who called himself the Blue Bard.

"So many." Ser Osfryd shuffled through the warrants, as wary of the words as if they had been roaches crawling across the parchment. None of the Kettleblacks could read.

"Ten. You have six thousand gold cloaks. Sufficient for ten, I would think. Some of the clever ones may have fled, if the rumors reached their ears in time. If so, it makes no matter, their absence only makes them look that much more guilty. Ser Tallad is a bit of an oaf and may try to resist you. See that he does not die before confessing, and do no harm to any of the others. A few may well be innocent." It was important that the Redwyne twins be found to have been falsely accused. That would demonstrate the fairness of the judgments against the others.

"We'll have them all before the sun comes up, Your Grace." Ser Osfryd hesitated. "There's a crowd gathering outside the door of Baelor's Sept."

"What sort of crowd?" Anything unexpected made her wary. She remembered what Lord Waters had said about the riots. *I had not considered how the smallfolk might react to this. Margaery has been their little pet.* "How many?"

"A hundred or so. They're shouting for the High Septon to release the little queen. We can send them running, if you like."

"No. Let them shout until they're hoarse, it will not sway the Sparrow. He only listens to the gods." There was a certain irony in His High Holiness having an angry mob encamped upon his doorstep, since just such a mob had raised him to the crystal crown. *Which he promptly sold.* "The Faith has its own knights now. Let them defend the sept. Oh, and close the city gates as well. No one is to enter or leave King's Landing without my leave, until all this is done and settled."

"As you command, Your Grace." Ser Osfryd bowed and went off to find someone to read the warrants to him.

By the time the sun went down that day, all of the accused traitors were in custody. Hamish the Harper had collapsed when they came for him, and Ser Tallad the Tall had wounded three gold cloaks before the others overwhelmed him. Cersei ordered that the Redwyne twins be given comfortable chambers in a tower. The rest went down to the dungeons.

"Hamish is having difficulty breathing," Qyburn informed her when he came to call that night. "He is calling for a maester."

"Tell him he can have one as soon as he confesses." She thought a moment. "He is too old to have been amongst the lovers, but no doubt he was made to play and sing for Margaery whilst she was entertaining other men. We will need details."

"I shall help him to remember them, Your Grace."

The next day, Lady Merryweather helped Cersei dress for their visit to the little queen. "Nothing too rich or colorful," she said. "Something suitably devout and drab for the High Septon. He's like to make me pray with him."

In the end, she chose a soft woolen dress that covered her from throat to ankle, with only a few small vines embroidered on the bodice and the sleeves in golden thread to soften the severity of its lines. Even better, brown would help conceal the dirt if she was made to kneel. "Whilst I am comforting my good-daughter you shall speak with the three cousins," she told Taena. "Win Alla if you can, but be careful what you say. The gods may not be the only ones listening."

Jaime always said that the hardest part of any battle is just before, waiting for the carnage to begin. When she stepped outside, Cersei saw that the sky was grey and bleak. She could not take the risk of being caught in a downpour and arriving at Baelor's Sept soaked and bedraggled. That meant the litter. For her escort, she took ten Lannister house guards and Boros Blount. "Margaery's mob may not have the wit to tell one Kettleblack from another," she told Ser Osmund, "and I cannot have you cutting through the commons. Best we keep you out of sight for a time."

As they made their way across King's Landing, Taena had a sudden doubt. "This trial," she said, in a quiet voice, "what if Margaery demands that her guilt or innocence be determined by wager of battle?"

A smile brushed Cersei's lips. "As queen, her honor must be defended by a knight of the Kingsguard. Why, every child in Westeros knows how Prince Aemon the Dragonknight championed his sister Queen Naerys against Ser Morghil's accusations. With Ser Loras so gravely wounded, though, I fear Prince Aemon's part must fall to one of his Sworn Brothers." She shrugged. "Who, though? Ser Arys and Ser Balon are far away in Dorne, Jaime is off at Riverrun, and Ser Osmund is the brother of the man accusing her, which leaves only . . . oh, dear . . ."

"Boros Blount and Meryn Trant." Lady Taena laughed.

"Yes, and Ser Meryn has been feeling ill of late. Remind me to tell him that when we return to the castle."

"I shall, my sweet." Taena took her hand and kissed it. "I pray that I never offend you. You are terrible when roused."

"Any mother would do the same to protect her children," said Cersei. "When do you mean to bring that boy of yours to court? Russell, was that his name? He could train with Tommen."

"That would thrill the boy, I know . . . but things are so uncertain just now, I thought it best to wait until the danger passed."

"Soon enough," promised Cersei. "Send word to Longtable and have Russell pack his best doublet and his wooden sword. A new young friend will be just the thing to help Tommen forget his loss, after Margaery's little head has rolled."

They descended from the litter under Blessed Baelor's statue. The queen was pleased to see that the bones and filth had been cleaned away. Ser Osfryd had told it true; the crowd was neither as numerous nor as unruly as the sparrows had been. They stood about in small clumps, gazing sullenly at the doors of the Great Sept, where a line of novice septons had been drawn up with quarterstaffs in their hands. *No steel,* Cersei noted. That was either very wise or very stupid, she was not sure which.

No one made any attempt to hinder her. Smallfolk and novices alike parted as they passed. Once inside the doors, they were met by three knights in the Hall of Lamps, each clad in the rainbow-striped robes of the Warrior's Sons. "I am here to see my good-daughter," Cersei told them.

"His High Holiness has been expecting you. I am Ser Theodan the True, formerly Ser Theodan Wells. If Your Grace will come with me."

The High Sparrow was on his knees, as ever. This time he was praying before the Father's altar. Nor did he break off his prayer when the queen approached, but made her wait impatiently until he had finished. Only then did he rise and bow to her. "Your Grace. This is a sad day."

"Very sad. Do we have your leave to speak with Margaery and her cousins?" She chose a meek and humble manner; with this man, that was like to work the best.

"If that is your wish. Come to me afterward, my child. We must pray together, you and I."

The little queen had been confined atop one of the Great Sept's slender towers. Her cell was eight feet long and six feet wide, with no furnishings but a straw-stuffed pallet and a bench for prayer, a ewer of water, a copy of *The Seven-Pointed Star,* and a candle to read it by. The only window was hardly wider than an arrow slit.

Cersei found Margaery barefoot and shivering, clad in the rough-spun shift of a novice sister. Her locks were all a tangle, and her feet were filthy. "They took my *clothes* from me," the little queen told her once they were alone. "I wore a gown of ivory lace, with freshwater pearls on the bodice, but the septas laid their *hands* on me and stripped me to the skin. My cousins too. Megga sent one septa crashing into the candles and set her robe afire. I fear for Alla, though. She went as white as milk, too frightened even to cry."

"Poor child." There were no chairs, so Cersei sat beside the little queen on her pallet. "Lady Taena has gone to speak with her, to let her know that she is not forgotten."

"He will not even let me see them," fumed Margaery. "He keeps each of us apart from the others. Until you came, I was allowed no visitors but septas. One comes every hour to ask if I wish to confess my fornications. They will not even let me sleep. They wake me to demand confessions. Last night, I confessed to Septa Unella that I wished to scratch her eyes out."

A shame you did not do it, Cersei thought. *Blinding some poor old septa would certainly persuade the High Sparrow of your guilt.* "They are questioning your cousins the same way."

"Damn them, then," said Margaery. "Damn them all to seven hells. Alla is gentle and shy, how can they do this to her? And Megga . . . she laughs as loud as a dockside whore, I know, but inside she's still just a little girl. I love them all, and they love me. If this sparrow thinks to make them lie about me . . ."

"They stand accused as well, I fear. All three."

"My *cousins?*" Margaery paled. "Alla and Megga are hardly more than children. Your Grace, this . . . this is obscene. Will you take us out of here?"

"Would that I could." Her voice was full of sorrow. "His High Holiness has his new knights guarding you. To free you I would need to send the gold cloaks and profane this holy place with killing." Cersei took Margaery's hand in hers. "I have not been idle, though. I have gathered up all those that Ser Osney named as your lovers. They will tell His High Holiness of your innocence, I am certain, and swear to it at your trial."

"Trial?" There was real fear in the girl's voice now. "Must there be a trial?"

"How else will you prove your innocence?" Cersei gave Margaery's hand a reassuring squeeze. "It is your right to decide the manner of the trial, to be sure. You are the queen. The knights of the Kingsguard are sworn to defend you."

Margaery understood at once. "A trial by battle? Loras is hurt, though, elsewise he . . ."

"He has six brothers."

Margaery stared at her, then pulled her hand away. "Is that a jape? Boros is a craven, Meryn is old and slow, your brother is maimed, the other two are off in Dorne, and Osmund is a bloody *Kettleblack*. Loras has *two* brothers, not six. If there's to be a trial by battle, I want Garlan as my champion."

"Ser Garlan is not a member of the Kingsguard," the queen said. "When the queen's honor is at issue, law and custom require that her champion be one of the king's sworn seven. The High Septon will insist, I fear." *I will make certain of it.*

Margaery did not answer at once, but her brown eyes narrowed in suspicion. "Blount or Trant," she said at last. "It would have to be one of them. You'd like that, wouldn't you? Osney Kettleblack would cut either one to pieces."

Seven hells. Cersei donned a look of hurt. "You wrong me, daughter. All I want—"

"—is your son, all for yourself. He will never have a wife that you don't hate. And I am *not* your daughter, thank the gods. Leave me."

"You are being foolish. I am only here to help you."

"To help me to my grave. I asked for you to leave. Will you make me call my gaolers and have you dragged away, you vile, scheming, evil bitch?"

Cersei gathered up her skirts and dignity. "This must be very frightening for you. I shall forgive those words." Here, as at court, one never knew who might be listening. "I would be afraid as well, in your place. Grand Maester Pycelle has admitted providing you with moon tea, and your Blue Bard . . . if I were you, my lady, I would pray to the Crone for wisdom and to the Mother for her mercy. I fear you may soon be in dire need of both."

Four shriveled septas escorted the queen down the tower steps. Each of the crones seemed more feeble than the last. When they reached the ground they continued down, into the heart of Visenya's Hill. The steps ended well below the earth, where a line of flickering torches lit a long hallway.

She found the High Septon waiting for her in a small seven-sided audience chamber. The room was sparse and plain, with bare stone walls, a rough-hewn table, three chairs, and a prayer bench. The faces of the Seven had been carved into the walls. Cersei thought the carvings crude and ugly, but there was a certain power to them, especially about the eyes, orbs of onyx, malachite, and yellow moonstone that somehow made the faces come alive.

"You spoke with the queen," the High Septon said.

She resisted the urge to say, *I am the queen.* "I did."

"All men sin, even kings and queens. I have sinned myself, and been forgiven. Without confession, though, there can be no forgiveness. The queen will not confess."

"Perhaps she is innocent."

"She is not. Holy septas have examined her, and testify that her maidenhead is broken. She has drunk of moon tea, to murder the fruit of her fornications in her womb. An anointed knight has sworn upon his sword to having carnal knowledge of her and two of her three cousins. Others have lain with her as well, he says, and names many names of men both great and humble."

"My gold cloaks have taken all of them to the dungeons," Cersei assured him. "Only one has yet been questioned, a singer called the Blue Bard. What he had to say was disturbing. Even so, I pray that when my good-daughter is brought to trial, her innocence may yet be proved." She hesitated. "Tommen loves his little queen so much, Your Holiness, I fear it might be hard for him or his lords to judge her justly. Perhaps the Faith should conduct the trial?"

The High Sparrow steepled his thin hands. "I have had the selfsame thought, Your Grace. Just as Maegor the Cruel once took the swords from the Faith, so Jaehaerys the Conciliator deprived us of the scales of judgment. Yet who is truly fit to judge a queen, save the Seven Above and the godsworn below? A sacred court of seven judges shall sit upon this case. Three shall be of your female sex. A maiden, a mother, and a crone. Who could be more suited to judge the wickedness of women?"

"That would be for the best. To be sure, Margaery does have the right to demand that her guilt or innocence be proven by wager of battle. If so, her champion must be one of Tommen's Seven."

"The knights of the Kingsguard have served as the rightful champions of king and queen since the days of Aegon the Conqueror. Crown and Faith speak as one on this."

Cersei covered her face with her hands, as if in grief. When she raised her head again, a tear glistened in one eye. "These are sad days indeed," she said, "but I am pleased to find us so much in agreement. If Tommen were here I know he would thank you. Together you and I must find the truth."

"We shall."

"I must return to the castle. With your leave, I will take Ser Osney Kettleblack back with me. The small council will want to question him, and hear his accusations for themselves."

"No," said the High Septon.

It was only a word, one little word, but to Cersei it felt like a splash of icy water in the face. She blinked, and her certainty flickered, just a little. "Ser Osney will be held securely, I promise you."

"He is held securely here. Come. I will show you."

Cersei could feel the eyes of the Seven staring at her, eyes of jade and malachite and onyx, and a sudden shiver of fear went through her, cold as ice. *I am the queen,* she told herself. *Lord Tywin's daughter.* Reluctantly, she followed.

Ser Osney was not far. The chamber was dark, and closed by a heavy iron door. The High Septon produced the key to open it, and took a torch down from the wall to light the room within. "After you, Your Grace."

Within, Osney Kettleblack hung naked from the ceiling, swinging from a pair of heavy iron chains. He had been whipped. His back and shoulders been laid almost bare, and cuts and welts crisscrossed his legs and arse as well.

The queen could hardly stand to look at him. She turned back to the High Septon. "What have you *done?*"

"We have sought after the truth, most earnestly."

"He told you the truth. He came to you of his own free will and confessed his sins."

"Aye. He did that. I have heard many men confess, Your Grace, but seldom have I heard a man so pleased to be so guilty."

"You *whipped* him!"

"There can be no penance without pain. No man should spare himself the scourge, as I told Ser Osney. I seldom feel so close to god as when I am being whipped for mine own wickedness, though my darkest sins are no wise near as black as his."

"B-but," she sputtered, "you preach the Mother's mercy ..."

"Ser Osney shall taste of that sweet milk in the afterlife. In *The Seven-Pointed Star* it is written that all sins may be forgiven, but crimes must still be punished. Osney Kettleblack is guilty of treason and murder, and the wages of treason are death."

He is just a priest, he cannot do this. "It is not for the Faith to condemn a man to death, whatever his offense."

"Whatever his offense." The High Septon repeated the words slowly, weighing them. "Strange to say, Your Grace, the more diligently we applied the scourge, the more Ser Osney's offenses seemed to change. He would now have us believe that he never touched Margaery Tyrell. Is that not so, Ser Osney?"

Osney Kettleblack opened his eyes. When he saw the queen standing there before him he ran his tongue across his swollen lips, and said, "The Wall. You promised me the Wall."

"He is mad," said Cersei. "You have driven him mad."

"Ser Osney," said the High Septon, in a firm, clear voice, "did you have carnal knowledge of the queen?"

"Aye." The chains rattled softly as Osney twisted in his shackles. "That one there. She's the queen I fucked, the one sent me to kill the old High Septon. He never had no guards. I just come in when he was sleeping and pushed a pillow down across his face."

Cersei whirled, and ran.

The High Septon tried to seize her, but he was some old sparrow and she was a lioness of the Rock. She pushed him aside and burst through the door, slamming it behind her with a *clang*. *The Kettleblacks, I need the Kettleblacks, I will send in Osfryd with the gold cloaks and Osmund with the Kingsguard, Osney will deny it all once they cut him free, and I'll rid myself of this High Septon just as I did the other.* The four old septas blocked her way and clutched at her with wrinkled hands. She knocked one to the floor and clawed another across the face, and gained the steps. Halfway up, she remembered Taena Merryweather. It made her stumble, panting. *Seven save me,* she prayed. *Taena knows it all. If they take her too, and whip her . . .*

She ran as far as the sept, but no farther. There were women waiting for her there, more septas and silent sisters too, younger than the four old crones below. "I am the *queen*," she shouted, backing away from them. "I will have your heads for this, I will have all your heads. Let me pass." Instead, they laid hands upon her. Cersei ran to the altar of the Mother, but they caught her there, a score of them, and dragged her kicking up the tower steps. Inside the cell, three silent sisters held her down as a septa named Scolera stripped her bare. She even took her smallclothes. Another septa tossed a roughspun shift at her. "You cannot do this," the queen kept screaming at them. "I am a Lannister, unhand me, my brother will kill you, Jaime will slice you open from throat to cunt, *unhand me*! I am *the queen*!"

"The queen should pray," said Septa Scolera, before they left her naked in the cold bleak cell.

She was not meek Margaery Tyrell, to don her little shift and submit to such captivity. *I will teach them what it means to put a lion in a cage,* Cersei thought. She tore the shift into a hundred pieces, found a ewer of water and smashed it against the wall, then did the same with the chamber pot. When no one came, she began to pound on the door with her fists. Her escort was below, on the plaza: ten Lannister guardsmen and Ser Boros Blount. *Once they hear they'll come free me, and we'll drag the bloody High Sparrow back to the Red Keep in chains.*

She screamed and kicked and howled until her throat was raw, at the door and at the window. No one shouted back, nor came to rescue her. The cell began to darken. It was growing cold as well. Cersei began to shiver. *How can they leave me like this, without so much as a fire? I am their queen.* She began to regret tearing apart the shift they'd given her. There was a blanket on the pallet in the corner, a threadbare thing of thin brown wool. It was rough and scratchy, but it was all she had. Cersei huddled underneath to keep from shivering, and before long she had fallen into an exhausted sleep.

The next she knew, a heavy hand was shaking her awake. It was black as pitch inside the cell, and a huge ugly woman was kneeling over her, a candle in her hand. "Who are you?" the queen demanded. "Are you come to set me free?"

"I am Septa Unella. I am come to hear you tell of all your murders and fornications."

Cersei knocked her hand aside. "I will have your head. Do not presume to touch me. Get away."

The woman rose. "Your Grace. I will be back in an hour. Mayhaps by then you will be ready to confess."

An hour and an hour and an hour. So passed the longest night that Cersei Lannister had ever known, save for the night of Joffrey's wedding. Her throat was so raw from shouting that she could hardly swallow. The cell turned freezing cold. She had smashed the chamber pot, so she had to squat in a corner to make her water and watch it trickle across the floor. Every time she closed her eyes, Unella was looming over her again, shaking her and asking her if she wanted to confess her sins.

Day brought no relief. Septa Moelle brought her a bowl of some waterly grey gruel as the sun was coming up. Cersei flung it at her head. When they brought a fresh ewer of water, though, she was so thirsty that she had no choice but to drink. When they brought another shift, grey and thin and smelling of mildew, she put it on over her nakedness. And that evening when Moelle appeared again she ate the bread and fish and demanded wine to wash it down. No wine appeared, only Septa Unella, making her hourly visit to ask if the queen was ready to confess.

What can be happening? Cersei wondered, as the thin slice of sky outside her window began to darken once again. *Why has no one come to pry me out of here?* She could not believe that the Kettleblacks would abandon their brother. What was her council doing? *Cravens and traitors. When I get out of here I will have the lot of them beheaded and find better men to take their place.*

Thrice that day she heard the sound of distant shouting drifting up from the plaza, but it was Margaery's name that the mob was calling, not hers.

It was near dawn on the second day and Cersei was licking the last of the porridge from the bottom of the bowl when her cell door swung open unexpectedly to admit Lord Qyburn. It was all she could do not to throw herself at him. "Qyburn," she whispered, "oh, gods, I am so glad to see your face. Take me home."

"That will not be allowed. You are to be tried before a holy court of seven, for murder, treason, and fornication."

Cersei was so exhausted that the words seemed nonsensical to her at first. "Tommen. Tell me of my son. Is he still king?"

"He is, Your Grace. He is safe and well, secure within the walls of Maegor's Holdfast, protected by the Kingsguard. He is lonely, though. Fretful. He asks for you, and for his little queen. As yet, no one has told him of your ... your ..."

"... difficulties?" she suggested. "What of Margaery?"

"She is to be tried as well, by the same court that conducts your trial. I had the Blue Bard delivered to the High Septon, as Your Grace commanded. He is here now, somewhere down below us. My whisperers tell me that they are whipping him, but so far he is still singing the same sweet song we taught him."

The same sweet song. Her wits were dull for want of sleep. *Wat, his real name is Wat.* If the gods were good, Wat might die beneath the lash, leaving Margaery with no way to disprove his testimony. "Where are my knights? Ser Osfryd . . . the High Septon means to kill his brother Osney, his gold cloaks must . . ."

"Osfryd Kettleblack no longer commands the City Watch. The king has removed him from office and raised the captain of the Dragon Gate in his place, a certain Humfrey Waters."

Cersei was so tired, none of this made any sense. "Why would Tommen do that?"

"The boy is not to blame. When his council puts a decree in front of him, he signs his name and stamps it with his seal."

"*My* council . . . who? Who would do that? Not you?"

"Alas, I have been dismissed from the council, although for the nonce they allow me to continue my work with the eunuch's whisperers. The realm is being ruled by Ser Harys Swyft and Grand Maester Pycelle. They have dispatched a raven to Casterly Rock, inviting your uncle to return to court and assume the regency. If he means to accept, he had best make haste. Mace Tyrell has abandoned his siege of Storm's End and is marching back to the city with his army, and Randyll Tarly is reported on his way down from Maidenpool as well."

"Has Lord Merryweather agreed to this?"

"Merryweather has resigned his seat on the council and fled back to Longtable with his wife, who was the first to bring us news of the . . . accusations . . . against Your Grace."

"They let Taena go." That was the best thing she had heard since the High Sparrow had said *no*. Taena could have doomed her. "What of Lord Waters? His ships . . . if he brings his crews ashore, he should have enough men to . . ."

"As soon as word of Your Grace's present troubles reached the river, Lord Waters raised sail, unshipped his oars, and took his fleet to sea. Ser Harys fears he means to join Lord Stannis. Pycelle believes that he is sailing to the Stepstones, to set himself up as a pirate."

"All my lovely dromonds." Cersei almost laughed. "My lord father used to say that bastards are treacherous by nature. Would that I had listened." She shivered. "I am lost, Qyburn."

"No." He took her hand. "Hope remains. Your Grace has the right to prove your innocence by battle. My queen, your champion stands ready. There is no man in all the Seven Kingdoms who can hope to stand against him. If you will only give the command . . ."

This time she did laugh. It was funny, terribly funny, *hideously* funny. "The gods make japes of all our hopes and plans. I have a champion no man can defeat, but I am forbidden to make use of him. I am the *queen*, Qyburn. My honor can only be defended by a Sworn Brother of the Kingsguard."

"I see." The smile died on Qyburn's face. "Your Grace, I am at a loss. I do not know how to counsel you . . ."

Even in her exhausted, frightened state, the queen knew she dare not trust her fate to a court of sparrows. Nor could she count on Ser Kevan to intervene, after the words that had passed between them at their last meeting. *It will have to be a trial by battle. There is no other way.* "Qyburn, for the love you bear me, I beg you, send a message for me. A raven if you can. A rider, if not. You must send to Riverrun, to my brother. Tell him what has happened, and write . . . write . . ."

"Yes, Your Grace?"

She licked her lips, shivering. "Come at once. Help me. Save me. I need you now as I have never needed you before. I love you. I love you. I love you. *Come at once.*"

"As you command. '*I love you*' thrice?"

"Thrice." She had to reach him. "He will come. I know he will. He must. Jaime is my only hope."

"My queen," said Qyburn, "have you . . . forgotten? Ser Jaime has no sword hand. If he should champion you and lose . . ."

We will leave this world together, as we once came into it. "He will not lose. Not Jaime. Not with my life at stake."

JAIME

The new Lord of Riverrun was so angry that he was shaking. "We have been deceived," he said. "This man had played us false!" Pink spittle flew from his lips as he jabbed a finger at Edmure Tully. "I will have his head off! I rule in Riverrun, by the king's own decree, I—"

"Emmon," said his wife, "the Lord Commander knows about the king's decree. Ser Edmure knows about the king's decree. The stableboys know about the king's decree."

"I am the lord, and I will have his head!"

"For what crime?" Thin as he was, Edmure still looked more lordly than Emmon Frey. He wore a quilted doublet of red wool with a leaping trout embroidered on its chest. His boots were black, his breeches blue. His auburn hair had been washed and barbered, his red beard neatly trimmed. "I did all that was asked of me."

"Oh?" Jaime Lannister had not slept since Riverrun had opened its gates, and his head was pounding. "I do not recall asking you to let Ser Brynden escape."

"You required me to surrender my castle, not my uncle. Am I to blame if your men let him slip through their siege lines?"

Jaime was not amused. *"Where is he?"* he said, letting his irritation show. His men had searched Riverrun thrice over, and Brynden Tully was nowhere to be found.

"He never told me where he meant to go."

"And you never asked. How did he get out?"

"Fish swim. Even black ones." Edmure smiled.

Jaime was sorely tempted to crack him across the mouth with his golden hand. A few missing teeth would put an end to his smiles. For a man who was going to spend the rest of his life a prisoner, Edmure was entirely too pleased with himself. "We have oubliettes beneath the Casterly Rock that fit a man as tight as a suit of armor. You can't turn in them, or sit, or reach down to your feet when the rats start gnawing at your toes. Would you care to reconsider that answer?"

Lord Edmure's smile went away. "You gave me your word that I would be treated honorably, as befits my rank."

"So you shall," said Jaime. "Nobler knights than you have died whimpering in those oubliettes, and many a high lord too. Even a king or two, if I recall my history. Your wife can have the one beside you, if you like. I would not want to part you."

"He did swim," said Edmure, sullenly. He had the same blue eyes as his sister Catelyn, and Jaime saw the same loathing there that he'd once seen in hers. "We raised the portcullis on the Water Gate. Not all the way, just three feet or so. Enough to leave a gap under the water, though the gate still appeared to be closed. My uncle is a strong swimmer. After dark, he pulled himself beneath the spikes."

And he slipped under our boom the same way, no doubt. A moonless night, bored guards, a black fish in a black river floating quietly downstream. If Ruttiger or Yew or any of their men heard a splash, they would put it down to a turtle or a trout. Edmure had waited most of the day before hauling down the direwolf of Stark in token of surrender. In the confusion of the castle changing hands, it had been the next morning before Jaime had been informed that the Blackfish was not amongst the prisoners.

He went to the window and gazed out over the river. It was a bright autumn day, and the sun was shining on the waters. *By now the Blackfish could be ten leagues downstream.*

"You have to find him," insisted Emmon Frey.

"He'll be found." Jaime spoke with a certainty he did not feel. "I have hounds and hunters sniffing after him even now." Ser Addam

Marbrand was leading the search on the south side of the river, Ser Dermot of the Rainwood on the north. He had considered enlisting the riverlords as well, but Vance and Piper and their ilk were more like to help the Blackfish escape than clap him into fetters. All in all, he was not hopeful. "He may elude us for a time," he said, "but eventually he must surface."

"What if he should try and take my castle back?"

"You have a garrison of two hundred." Too large a garrison, in truth, but Lord Emmon had an anxious disposition. At least he would have no trouble feeding them; the Blackfish had left Riverrun amply provisioned, just as he had claimed. "After the trouble Ser Brynden took to leave us, I doubt that he'll come skulking back." *Unless it is at the head of a band of outlaws.* He did not doubt that the Blackfish meant to continue the fight.

"This is your seat," Lady Genna told her husband. "It is for you to hold it. If you cannot do that, put it to the torch and run back to the Rock."

Lord Emmon rubbed his mouth. His hand came away red and slimy from the sourleaf. "To be sure. Riverrun is mine, and no man shall ever take it from me." He gave Edmure Tully one last suspicious look, as Lady Genna drew him from the solar.

"Is there any more that you would care to tell me?" Jaime asked Edmure when the two of them were alone.

"This was my father's solar," said Tully. "He ruled the riverlands from here, wisely and well. He liked to sit beside that window. The light was good there, and whenever he looked up from his work he could see the river. When his eyes were tired he would have Cat read to him. Littlefinger and I built a castle out of wooden blocks once, there beside the door. You will never know how sick it makes me to see you in this room, Kingslayer. You will never know how much I despise you."

He was wrong about that. "I have been despised by better men than you, Edmure." Jaime called for a guard. "Take his lordship back to his tower and see that he's fed."

The Lord of Riverrun went silently. On the morrow, he would start west. Ser Forley Prester would command his escort; a hundred men, including twenty knights. *Best double that. Lord Beric may try to free Edmure before they reach the Golden Tooth.* Jaime did not want to have to capture Tully for a third time.

He returned to Hoster Tully's chair, pulled over the map of the Trident, and flattened it beneath his golden hand. *Where would I go, if I were the Blackfish?*

"Lord Commander?" A guardsman stood in the open door. "Lady Westerling and her daughter are without, as you commanded."

Jaime shoved the map aside. "Show them in." *At least the girl did not vanish too.* Jeyne Westerling had been Robb Stark's queen, the girl who cost him everything. With a wolf in her belly, she could have proved more dangerous than the Blackfish.

She did not look dangerous. Jeyne was a willowy girl, no more than fifteen or sixteen, more awkward than graceful. She had narrow hips, breasts the size of apples, a mop of chestnut curls, and the soft brown eyes of a doe. *Pretty enough for a child,* Jaime decided, *but not a girl to lose a kingdom for.* Her face was puffy, and there was a scab on her forehead, half-hidden by a lock of brown hair. "What happened there?" he asked her.

The girl turned her head away. "It is nothing," insisted her mother, a stern-faced woman in a gown of green velvet. A necklace of golden seashells looped about her long, thin neck. "She would not give up the little crown the rebel gave her, and when I tried to take it from her head the willful child fought me."

"It was mine." Jeyne sobbed. "You had no right. Robb had it made for me. I *loved* him."

Her mother made to slap her, but Jaime stepped between them. "None of that," he warned Lady Sybell. "Sit down, both of you." The girl curled up in her chair like a frightened animal, but her mother sat stiffly, her head high. "Will you have wine?" he asked them. The girl did not answer. "No, thank you," said her mother.

"As you will." Jaime turned to the daughter. "I am sorry for your loss. The boy had courage, I'll give him that. There is a question I must ask you. Are you carrying his child, my lady?"

Jeyne burst from her chair and would have fled the room if the guard at the door had not seized her by the arm. "She is not," said

Lady Sybell, as her daughter struggled to escape. "I made certain of that, as your lord father bid me."

Jaime nodded. Tywin Lannister was not a man to overlook such details. "Unhand the girl," he said, "I'm done with her for now." As Jeyne fled sobbing down the stairs, he considered her mother. "House Westerling has its pardon, and your brother Rolph has been made Lord of Castamere. What else would you have of us?"

"Your lord father promised me worthy marriages for Jeyne and her younger sister. Lords or heirs, he swore to me, not younger sons nor household knights."

Lords or heirs. To be sure. The Westerlings were an old House, and proud, but Lady Sybell herself had been born a Spicer, from a line of upjumped merchants. Her grandmother had been some sort of half-mad witch woman from the east, he seemed to recall. And the Westerlings were impoverished. Younger sons would have been the best that Sybell Spicer's daughters could have hoped for in the ordinary course of events, but a nice fat pot of Lannister gold would make even a dead rebel's widow look attractive to some lord. "You'll have your marriages," said Jaime, "but Jeyne must wait two full years before she weds again." If the girl took another husband too soon and had a child by him, inevitably there would come whispers that the Young Wolf was the father.

"I have two sons as well," Lady Westerling reminded him. "Rollam is with me, but Raynald was a knight and went with the rebels to the Twins. If I had known what was to happen there, I would never have allowed that." There was a hint of reproach in her voice. "Raynald knew nought of any . . . of the understanding with your lord father. He may be a captive at the Twins."

Or he may be dead. Walder Frey would not have known of *the understanding* either. "I will make inquiries. If Ser Raynald is still a captive, we'll pay his ransom for you."

"Mention was made of a match for him as well. A bride from Casterly Rock. Your lord father said that Raynald should have joy of him, if all went as we hoped."

Even from the grave, Lord Tywin's dead hand moves us all. "Joy is my late uncle Gerion's natural daughter. A betrothal can be arranged, if that is your wish, but any marriage will need to wait. Joy was nine or ten when last I saw her."

"His *natural* daughter?" Lady Sybell looked as if she had swallowed a lemon. "You want a Westerling to wed a *bastard*?"

"No more than I want Joy to marry the son of some scheming turncloak bitch. She deserves better." Jaime would happily have strangled the woman with her seashell necklace. Joy was a sweet child, albeit a lonely one; her father had been Jaime's favorite uncle. "Your daughter is worth ten of you, my lady. You'll leave with Edmure and Ser Forley on the morrow. Until then, you would do well to stay out of my sight." He shouted for a guardsman, and Lady Sybell went off with her lips pressed primly together. Jaime had to wonder how much Lord Gawen knew about his wife's scheming. *How much do we men ever know?*

When Edmure and the Westerlings departed, four hundred men rode with them; Jaime had doubled the escort again at the last moment. He rode with them a few miles, to talk with Ser Forley Prester. Though he bore a bull's head upon his surcoat and horns upon his helm, Ser Forley could not have been less bovine. He was a short, spare, hard-bitten man. With his pinched nose, bald pate, and grizzled brown beard, he looked more like an innkeep than a knight. "We don't know where the Blackfish is," Jaime reminded him, "but if he can cut Edmure free, he will."

"That will not happen, my lord." Like most innkeeps, Ser Forley was no man's fool. "Scouts and outriders will screen our march, and we'll fortify our camps by night. I have picked ten men to stay with Tully day and night, my best longbowmen. If he should ride so much as a foot off the road, they will loose so many shafts at him that his own mother would take him for a goose."

"Good." Jaime would as lief have Tully reach Casterly Rock safely, but better dead than fled. "Best keep some archers near Lord Westerling's daughter as well."

Ser Forley seemed taken aback. "Gawen's girl? She's—"

"—the Young Wolf's widow," Jaime finished, "and twice as dangerous as Edmure if she were ever to escape us."

"As you say, my lord. She will be watched."

Jaime had to canter past the Westerlings as he rode down the column on his way back to Riverrun. Lord Gawen nodded gravely as he passed, but Lady Sybell looked through him with eyes like chips of ice. Jeyne never saw him at all. The widow rode with downcast eyes, huddled beneath a hooded cloak. Underneath its heavy folds, her clothes were finely made, but torn. *She ripped them herself, as a mark of mourning,* Jaime realized. *That could not have pleased her mother.* He found himself wondering if Cersei would tear her gown if she should ever hear that he was dead.

He did not go straight back to the castle but crossed the Tumblestone once more to call on Edwyn Frey and discuss the transfer of his great-grandfather's prisoners. The Frey host had begun to break up within hours of Riverrun's surrender, as Lord Walder's bannermen and freeriders pulled up stakes to make for home. The Freys who still remained were striking camp, but he found Edwyn with his bastard uncle in the latter's pavilion.

The two of them were huddled over a map, arguing heatedly, but they broke off when Jaime entered. "Lord Commander," Rivers said with cold courtesy, but Edwyn blurted out, "My father's blood is on your hands, ser."

That took Jaime a bit aback. "How so?"

"You were the one who sent him home, were you not?"

Someone had to. "Has some ill befallen Ser Ryman?"

"Hanged with all his party," said Walder Rivers. "The outlaws caught them two leagues south of Fairmarket."

"Dondarrion?"

"Him, or Thoros, or this woman Stoneheart."

Jaime frowned. Ryman Frey had been a fool, a craven, and a sot, and no one was like to miss him much, least of all his fellow Freys. If Edwyn's dry eyes were any clue, even his own sons would not mourn him long. *Still . . . these outlaws are growing bold, if they dare hang Lord Walder's heir not a day's ride from the Twins.* "How many men did Ser Ryman have with him?" he asked.

"Three knights and a dozen men-at-arms," said Rivers. "It is almost as if they knew that he would be returning to the Twins, and with a small escort."

Edwyn's mouth twisted. "My brother had a hand in this, I'll wager.

He allowed the outlaws to escape after they murdered Merrett and Petyr, and this is why. With our father dead, there's only me left between Black Walder and the Twins."

"You have no proof of this," said Walder Rivers.

"I do not need proof. I know my brother."

"Your brother is at Seagard," Rivers insisted. "How could he have known that Ser Ryman was returning to the Twins?"

"Someone told him," said Edwyn in a bitter tone. "He has his spies in our camp, you can be sure."

And you have yours at Seagard. Jaime knew that the enmity between Edwyn and Black Walder ran deep, but cared not a fig which of them succeeded their great-grandfather as Lord of the Crossing.

"If you will pardon me for intruding on your grief," he said, in a dry tone, "we have other matters to consider. When you return to the Twins, please inform Lord Walder that King Tommen requires all the captives you took at the Red Wedding."

Ser Walder frowned. "These prisoners are valuable, ser."

"His Grace would not ask for them if they were worthless."

Frey and Rivers exchanged a look. Edwyn said, "My lord grandfather will expect recompense for these prisoners."

And he'll have it, as soon as I grow a new hand, thought Jaime. "We all have expectations," he said mildly. "Tell me, is Ser Raynald Westerling amongst these captives?"

"The knight of seashells?" Edwyn sneered. "You'll find that one feeding the fish at the bottom of the Green Fork."

"He was in the yard when our men came to put the direwolf down," said Walder Rivers. "Whalen demanded his sword and he gave it over meek enough, but when the crossbowmen began feathering the wolf he seized Whalen's axe and cut the monster loose of the net they'd thrown over him. Whalen says he took a quarrel in his shoulder and another in the gut, but still managed to reach the wallwalk and throw himself into the river."

"He left a trail of blood on the steps," said Edwyn.

"Did you find his corpse afterward?" asked Jaime.

"We found a thousand corpses afterward. Once they've spent a few days in the river they all look much the same."

"I've heard the same is true of hanged men," said Jaime, before he took his leave.

By the next morning, little remained of the Frey encampment but flies, horse dung, and Ser Ryman's gallows, standing forlorn beside the Tumblestone. His coz wanted to know what should be done with it, and with the siege equipment he had built, his rams and sows and towers and trebuchets. Daven proposed that they drag it all to Raventree and use it there. Jaime told him to put everything to the torch, starting with the gallows. "I mean to deal with Lord Tytos myself. It won't require a siege tower."

Daven grinned through his bushy beard. "Single combat, coz? Scarce seems fair. Tytos is an old grey man."

An old grey man with two hands.

That night he and Ser Ilyn fought for three hours. It was one of his better nights. If they had been in earnest, Payne only would have killed him twice. Half a dozen deaths were more the rule, and some nights were worse than that. "If I keep at this for another year, I may be as good as Peck," Jaime declared, and Ser Ilyn made that clacking sound that meant he was amused. "Come, let's drink some more of Hoster Tully's good red wine."

Wine had become a part of their nightly ritual. Ser Ilyn made the perfect drinking companion. He never interrupted, never disagreed, never complained or asked for favors or told long pointless stories. All he did was drink and listen.

"I should have the tongues removed from all my friends," said Jaime as he filled their cups, "and from my kin as well. A silent Cersei would be sweet. Though I'd miss her tongue when we kissed." He drank. The wine was a deep red, sweet and heavy. It warmed him going down. "I can't remember when we first began to kiss. It was innocent at first. Until it wasn't." He finished the wine and set his cup aside. "Tyrion once told me that most whores will not kiss you. They'll fuck you blind, he said, but you'll never feel their lips on yours. Do you think my sister kisses Kettleblack?"

Ser Ilyn did not answer.

"I don't think it would be proper for me to slay mine own Sworn Brother. What I need to do is geld him and send him to the Wall.

That's what they did with Lucamore the Lusty. Ser Osmund may not take kindly to the gelding, to be sure. And there are his brothers to consider. Brothers can be dangerous. After Aegon the Unworthy put Ser Terrence Toyne to death for sleeping with his mistress, Toyne's brothers did their best to kill him. Their best was not quite good enough, thanks to the Dragonknight, but it was not for want of trying. It's written down in the White Book. All of it, save what to do with Cersei."

Ser Ilyn drew a finger across his throat.

"No," said Jaime. "Tommen has lost a brother, and the man he thought of as his father. If I were to kill his mother, he would hate me for it . . . and that sweet little wife of his would find a way to turn that hatred to the benefit of Highgarden."

Ser Ilyn smiled in a way Jaime did not like. *An ugly smile. An ugly soul.* "You talk too much," he told the man.

The next day, Ser Dermot of the Rainwood returned to the castle, empty-handed. When asked what he'd found, he answered, "Wolves. Hundreds of the bloody beggars." He'd lost two sentries to them. The wolves had come out of the dark to savage them. "Armed men in mail and boiled leather, and yet the beasts had no fear of them. Before he died, Jate said the pack was led by a she-wolf of monstrous size. A direwolf, to hear him tell it. The wolves got in amongst our horse lines too. The bloody bastards killed my favorite bay."

"A ring of fires round your camp might keep them off," said Jaime, though he wondered. Could Ser Dermot's direwolf be the same beast that had mauled Joffrey near the crossroads?

Wolves or no, Ser Dermot took fresh horses and more men and went out again the next morning, to resume the search for Brynden Tully. That same afternoon, the lords of the Trident came to Jaime asking his leave to return to their own lands. He granted it. Lord Piper also wanted to know about his son Marq. "All the captives will be ransomed," Jaime promised. As the riverlords took their leave, Lord Karyl Vance lingered to say, "Lord Jaime, you must go to Raventree. So long as it is Jonos at his gates Tytos will never yield, but I know he will bend his knee for you." Jaime thanked him for his counsel.

Strongboar was the next to depart. He wanted to return to Darry as he'd promised and fight the outlaws. "We rode across half the bloody realm and for what? So you could make Edmure Tully piss his breeches? There's no song in that. I need a *fight*. I want the Hound, Jaime. Him, or the marcher lord."

"The Hound's head is yours if you can take it," Jaime said, "but Beric Dondarrion is to be captured alive, so he can be brought back to King's Landing. A thousand people need to see him die, or else he won't stay dead." Strongboar grumbled at that, but finally agreed. The next day he departed with his squire and men-at-arms, plus Beardless Jon Bettley, who had decided that hunting outlaws was preferable to returning to his famously homely wife. Supposedly she had the beard that Bettley lacked.

Jaime still had the garrison to deal with. To a man, they swore that they knew nothing of Ser Brynden's plans or where he might have gone. "They are lying," Emmon Frey insisted, but Jaime thought not. "If you share your plans with no one, no one can betray you," he pointed out. Lady Genna suggested that a few of the men might be put to the question. He refused. "I gave Edmure my word that if he yielded, the garrison could leave unharmed."

"That was chivalrous of you," his aunt said, "but it's strength that's needed here, not chivalry."

Ask Edmure how chivalrous I am, thought Jaime. *Ask him about the trebuchet.* Somehow he did not think the maesters were like to confuse him with Prince Aemon the Dragonknight when they wrote their histories. Still, he felt curiously content. The war was all but won. Dragonstone had fallen and Storm's End would soon enough, he could not doubt, and Stannis was welcome to the Wall. The northmen would love him no more than the storm lords had. If Roose Bolton did not destroy him, winter would.

And he had done his own part here at Riverrun without actually ever taking up arms against the Starks or Tullys. Once he found the Blackfish, he would be free to return to King's Landing, where he belonged. *My place is with my king. With my son.* Would Tommen want to know that? The truth could cost the boy his throne. *Would you sooner have a father or a chair, lad?* Jaime wished he knew the answer. *He does like stamping papers with his seal.* The boy might not even believe him, to be sure. Cersei would say it was a lie. *My sweet sister, the deceiver.* He would need to find some way to winkle Tommen from her clutches before the boy became another Joffrey. And whilst at that, he should find the lad a new small council too. *If Cersei can be put aside, Ser Kevan may agree to serve as Tommen's Hand.* And if not, well, the Seven Kingdoms did not lack for able men. Forley Prester would make a good choice, or Roland Crakehall. If someone other than a westerman was needed to appease the Tyrells, there was always Mathis Rowan . . . or even Petyr Baelish. Littlefinger was as amiable as he was clever, but too lowborn to threaten any of the great lords, with no swords of his own. *The perfect Hand.*

The Tully garrison departed the next morning, stripped of all their arms and armor. Each man was allowed three days' food and the clothing on his back, after he swore a solemn oath never to take up arms against Lord Emmon or House Lannister. "If you're fortunate, one man in ten may keep that vow," Lady Genna said.

"Good. I'd sooner face nine men than ten. The tenth might have been the one who would have killed me."

"The other nine will kill you just as quick."

"Better that than die in bed." *Or on the privy.*

Two men did not choose to depart with the others. Ser Desmond Grell, Lord Hoster's old master-at-arms, preferred to take the black. So did Ser Robin Ryger, Riverrun's captain of guards. "This castle's been my home for forty years," said Grell. "You say I'm free to go, but where? I'm too old and too stout to make a hedge knight. But men are always welcome at the Wall."

"As you wish," said Jaime, though it was a bloody nuisance. He allowed them to keep their arms and armor, and assigned a dozen of Gregor Clegane's men to escort the two of them to Maidenpool. The command he gave to Rafford, the one they called the Sweetling. "See to it that the prisoners reach Maidenpool unspoiled," he told the man, "or what Ser Gregor did to the Goat will seem a jolly lark compared to what I'll do to you."

More days passed. Lord Emmon assembled all of Riverrun in the yard, Lord Edmure's people and his own, and spoke to them for close on three hours about what would be expected of them now that he was their lord and master. From time to time he waved his parchment, as stableboys and serving girls and smiths listened in a sullen silence and a light rain fell down upon them all.

The singer was listening too, the one that Jaime had taken from Ser Ryman Frey. Jaime came upon him standing inside an open door, where it was dry. "His lordship should have been a singer," the man said. "This speech is longer than a marcher ballad, and I don't think he's stopped for breath."

Jaime had to laugh. "Lord Emmon does not need to breathe, so long as he can chew. Are you going to make a song of it?"

"A funny one. I'll call it 'Talking to the Fish.'"

"Just don't play it where my aunt can hear." Jaime had never paid the man much mind before. He was a small fellow, garbed in ragged green breeches and a frayed tunic of a lighter shade of green, with brown leather patches covering the holes. His nose was long and sharp, his smile big and loose. Thin brown hair fell to his collar, snaggled and unwashed. *Fifty, if he's a day,* thought Jaime, *a hedge harp, and hard used by life.* "Weren't you Ser Ryman's man when I found you?" he asked.

"Only for a fortnight."

"I would have expected you to depart with the Freys."

"That one up there's a Frey," the singer said, nodding at Lord Emmon, "and this castle seems a nice snug place to pass the winter. Whitesmile Wat went home with Ser Forley, so I thought I'd see if I could win his place. Wat's got that high sweet voice that the likes o' me can't hope to match. But I know twice as many bawdy songs as he does. Begging my lord's pardon."

"You should get on famously with my aunt," said Jaime. "If you hope to winter here, see that your playing pleases Lady Genna. She's the one that matters."

"Not you?"

"My place is with the king. I shall not stay here long."

"I'm sorry to hear that, my lord. I know better songs than 'The Rains of Castamere.' I could have played you . . . oh, all sorts o' things."

"Some other time," said Jaime. "Do you have a name?"

"Tom of Sevenstreams, if it please my lord." The singer doffed his hat. "Most call me Tom o' Sevens, though."

"Sing sweetly, Tom o' Sevens."

That night he dreamt that he was back in the Great Sept of Baelor, still standing vigil over his father's corpse. The sept was still and dark, until a woman emerged from the shadows and walked slowly to the bier. "Sister?" he said.

But it was not Cersei. She was all in grey, a silent sister. A hood and veil concealed her features, but he could see the candles burning in the green pools of her eyes. "Sister," he said, "what would you have of me?" His last word echoed up and down the sept, *memememememememememememe.*

"I am not your sister, Jaime." She raised a pale soft hand and pushed her hood back. "Have you forgotten me?"

Can I forget someone I never knew? The words caught in his throat. He *did* know her, but it had been so long . . .

"Will you forget your own lord father too? I wonder if you ever knew him, truly." Her eyes were green, her hair spun gold. He could not tell how old she was. *Fifteen,* he thought, *or fifty.* She climbed the steps to stand above the bier. "He could never abide being laughed at. That was the thing he hated most."

"Who are you?" He had to hear her say it.

"The question is, who are you?"

"This is a dream."

"Is it?" She smiled sadly. "Count your hands, child."

One. One hand, clasped tight around the sword hilt. Only one. "In my dreams I always have two hands." He raised his right arm and stared uncomprehending at the ugliness of his stump.

"We all dream of things we cannot have. Tywin dreamed that his son would be a great knight, that his daughter would be a queen. He dreamed they would be so strong and brave and beautiful that no one would ever laugh at them."

"I am a knight," he told her, "and Cersei is a queen."

A tear rolled down her cheek. The woman raised her hood again and turned her back on him. Jaime called after her, but already she was moving away, her skirt whispering lullabies as it brushed across the floor. *Don't leave me,* he wanted to call, but of course she'd left them long ago.

He woke in darkness, shivering. The room had grown cold as ice. Jaime flung aside the covers with the stump of his sword hand. The fire in the hearth had died, he saw, and the window had blown open. He crossed the pitch-dark chamber to fumble with the shutters, but when he reached the window his bare foot came down in something wet. Jaime recoiled, startled for a moment. His first thought was of blood, but blood would not have been so cold.

It was snow, drifting through the window.

Instead of closing the shutters he threw them wide. The yard below was covered by a thin white blanket, growing thicker even as he watched. The merlons on the battlements wore white cowls. The flakes fell silently, a few drifting in the window to melt upon his face. Jaime could see his own breath.

Snow in the riverlands. If it was snowing here, it could well be snowing on Lannisport as well, and on King's Landing. *Winter is marching south, and half our granaries are empty.* Any crops still in the fields were doomed. There would be no more plantings, no more hopes of one last harvest. He found himself wondering what his father would do to feed the realm, before he remembered that Tywin Lannister was dead.

When morning broke the snow was ankle deep, and deeper in the godswood, where drifts had piled up under the trees. Squires, stable-boys, and highborn pages turned to children again under its cold white spell, and fought a snowball war up and down the wards and all along the battlements. Jaime heard them laughing. There was a time, not long ago, when he might have been out making snowballs with the best of them, to fling at Tyrion when he waddled by, or slip down the back of Cersei's gown. *You need two hands to make a decent snowball, though.*

There was a rap upon his door. "See who that is, Peck."

It was Riverrun's old maester, with a message clutched in his lined and wrinkled hand. Vyman's face was as pale as the new-fallen snow. "I know," Jaime said, "there has been a white raven from the Citadel. Winter has come."

"No, my lord. The bird was from King's Landing. I took the liberty ... I did not know ..." He held the letter out.

Jaime read it in the window seat, bathed in the light of that cold white morning. Qyburn's words were terse and to the point, Cersei's fevered and fervent. *Come at once,* she said. *Help me. Save me. I need you now as I have never needed you before. I love you. I love you. I love you. Come at once.*

Vyman was hovering by the door, waiting, and Jaime sensed that Peck was watching too. "Does my lord wish to answer?" the maester asked, after a long silence.

A snowflake landed on the letter. As it melted, the ink began to blur. Jaime rolled the parchment up again, as tight as one hand would allow, and handed it to Peck. "No," he said. "Put this in the fire."

SAMWELL

The most perilous part of the voyage was the last. The Redwyne Straits were swarming with longships, as they had been warned in Tyrosh. With the main strength of the Arbor's fleet on the far side of Westeros, the ironmen had sacked Ryamsport and taken Vinetown and Starfish Harbor for their own, using them as bases to prey on shipping bound for Oldtown.

Thrice longships were sighted by the crow's nest. Two were well astern, however, and the *Cinnamon Wind* soon outdistanced them. The third appeared near sunset, to cut them off from Whispering Sound. When they saw her oars rising and falling, lashing the copper waters white, Kojja Mo sent her archers to the castles with their great bows of goldenheart that could send a shaft farther and truer than even Dornish yew. She waited till the longship came within two hundred yards before she gave the command to loose. Sam loosed with them, and this time he thought his arrow reached the ship. One volley was all it took. The longship veered south in search of tamer prey.

A deep blue dusk was falling as they entered Whispering Sound. Gilly stood beside the prow with the babe, gazing up at a castle on the cliffs. "Three Towers," Sam told her, "the seat of House Costayne." Etched against the evening stars with torchlight flickering from its windows, the castle made a splendid sight, but he was sad to see it. Their voyage was almost at its end.

"It's very tall," said Gilly.

"Wait until you see the Hightower."

Dalla's babe began to cry. Gilly pulled open her tunic and gave the boy her breast. She smiled as he nursed, and stroked his soft brown hair. *She has come to love this one as much as the one she left behind,* Sam realized. He hoped that the gods would be kind to both of the children.

The ironmen had penetrated even to the sheltered waters of Whispering Sound. Come morning, as the *Cinnamon Wind* continued on toward Oldtown, she began to bump up against corpses drifting down to the sea. Some of the bodies carried complements of crows, who rose into the air complaining noisily when the swan ship disturbed their grotesquely swollen rafts. Scorched fields and burned villages appeared on the banks, and the shallows and sandbars were strewn with shattered ships. Merchanters and fishing boats were the most common, but they saw abandoned longships too, and the wreckage of two big dromonds. One had been burned down to the waterline, whilst the other had a gaping splintered hole in her side where her hull had been rammed.

"Battle here," said Xhondo. "Not so long."

"Who would be so mad as to raid this close to Oldtown?"

Xhondo pointed at a half-sunken longship in the shallows. The remnants of a banner drooped from her stern, smoke-stained and ragged. The charge was one Sam had never seen before: a red eye with a black pupil, beneath a black iron crown supported by two crows. "Whose banner is that?" Sam asked. Xhondo only shrugged.

The next day was cold and misty. As the *Cinnamon Wind* was creeping past another plundered fishing village, a war galley came sliding from the fog, stroking slowly toward them. *Huntress* was the name she bore, behind a figurehead of a slender maiden clad in leaves and brandishing a spear. A heartbeat later, two smaller galleys appeared on either side of her, like a pair of matched greyhounds stalking at their master's heels. To Sam's relief, they flew King Tommen's stag-and-lion banner above the stepped white tower of Oldtown, with its crown of flame.

The captain of the *Huntress* was a tall man in a smoke-grey cloak with a border of red satin flames. He brought his galley in alongside the *Cinnamon Wind,* raised his oars, and shouted that he was coming aboard. As his crossbowmen and Kojja Mo's archers eyed each other across the narrow span of water, he crossed over with half a dozen knights, gave Quhuru Mo a nod, and asked to see his holds. Father and daughter conferred briefly, then agreed.

"My apologies," the captain said when his inspection was complete. "It grieves me that honest men must suffer such discourtesy, but sooner that than ironmen in Oldtown. Only a fortnight ago some of those bloody bastards captured a Tyroshi merchantman in the straits. They killed her crew, donned their clothes, and used the dyes they found to color their whiskers half a hundred colors. Once inside the walls they meant to set the port ablaze and open a gate from within whilst we fought the fire. Might have worked, but they ran afoul of the *Lady of the Tower,* and her oarsmaster has a Tyroshi wife. When he saw all the green and purple beards he hailed them in the tongue of Tyrosh, and not one of them had the words to hail him back."

Sam was aghast. "They cannot mean to raid *Oldtown.*"

The captain of the *Huntress* gave him a curious look. "These are no mere reavers. The ironmen have always raided where they could. They would strike sudden from the sea, carry off some gold and girls, and sail away, but there were seldom more than one or two longships, and never more than half a dozen. Hundreds of their ships afflict us now, sailing out of the Shield Islands and some of the rocks around the Arbor. They have taken Stonecrab Cay, the Isle of Pigs, and the Mermaid's Palace, and there are other nests on Horseshoe Rock and Bastard's Cradle. Without Lord Redwyne's fleet, we lack the ships to come to grips with them."

"What is Lord Hightower doing?" Sam blurted. "My father always said he was as wealthy as the Lannisters, and could command thrice as many swords as any of Highgarden's other bannermen."

"More, if he sweeps the cobblestones," the captain said, "but swords are no good against the ironmen, unless the men who wield them know how to walk on water."

"The Hightower must be doing *something.*"

"To be sure. Lord Leyton's locked atop his tower with the Mad

Maid, consulting books of spells. Might be he'll raise an army from the deeps. Or not. Baelor's building galleys, Gunthor has charge of the harbor, Garth is training new recruits, and Humfrey's gone to Lys to hire sellsails. If he can winkle a proper fleet out of his whore of a sister, we can start paying back the ironmen with some of their own coin. Till then, the best we can do is guard the sound and wait for the bitch queen in King's Landing to let Lord Paxter off his leash."

The bitterness of the captain's final words shocked Sam as much as the things he said. *If King's Landing loses Oldtown and the Arbor, the whole realm will fall to pieces,* he thought as he watched the *Huntress* and her sisters moving off.

It made him wonder if even Horn Hill was truly safe. The Tarly lands lay inland amidst thickly wooded foothills, a hundred leagues northeast of Oldtown and a long way from any coast. They should be well beyond the reach of ironmen and longships, even with his lord father off fighting in the riverlands and the castle lightly held. The Young Wolf had no doubt thought the same was true of Winterfell until the night that Theon Turncloak scaled his walls. Sam could not bear the thought that he might have brought Gilly and her babe all this long way to keep them out of harm, only to abandon them in the midst of war.

He wrestled with his doubts through the rest of the voyage, wondering what to do. He could keep Gilly with him in Oldtown, he supposed. The city's walls were much more formidable than those of his father's castle, and had thousands of men to defend them, as opposed to the handful Lord Randyll would have left at Horn Hill when he marched to Highgarden to answer his liege lord's summons. If he did, though, he would need to hide her somehow; the Citadel did not permit its novices to keep wives or paramours, at least not openly. *Besides, if I stay with Gilly very much longer, how will I ever find the strength to leave her?* He *had* to leave her, or desert. *I said the words,* Sam reminded himself. *If I desert, it will mean my head, and how will that help Gilly?*

He considered begging Kojja Mo and her father to take the wildling girl with them to the Summer Isles. That path had its perils too, however. When the *Cinnamon Wind* left Oldtown, she would need to cross the Redwyne Straits again, and this time she might not be so fortunate. What if the wind died, and the Summer Islanders found themselves becalmed? If the tales he'd heard were true, Gilly would be carried off for a thrall or salt wife, and the babe was like to be chucked into the sea as a nuisance.

It has to be Horn Hill, Sam finally decided. *Once we reach Oldtown I'll hire a wagon and some horses and take her there myself.* That way he could make certain of the castle and its garrison, and if any part of what he saw or heard gave him pause, he could just turn around and bring Gilly back to Oldtown.

They reached Oldtown on a cold damp morning, when the fog was so thick that the beacon of the Hightower was the only part of the city to be seen. A boom stretched across the harbor, linking two dozen rotted hulks. Just behind it stood a line of warships, anchored by three big dromonds and Lord Hightower's towering four-decked banner ship, the *Honor of Oldtown*. Once again the *Cinnamon Wind* had to submit to inspection. This time it was Lord Leyton's son Gunthor who came aboard, in a cloth-of-silver cloak and a suit of grey enameled scales. Ser Gunthor had studied at the Citadel for several years and spoke the Summer Tongue, so he and Qurulu Mo adjourned to the captain's cabin for a privy conference.

Sam used the time to explain his plans to Gilly. "First the Citadel, to present Jon's letters and tell them of Maester Aemon's death. I expect the archmaesters will send a cart for his body. Then I will arrange for horses and a wagon to take you to my mother at Horn Hill. I will be back as soon as I can, but it may not be until the morrow."

"The morrow," she repeated, and gave him a kiss for luck.

At length, Ser Gunthor reemerged and gave the signal for the chain to be opened so the *Cinnamon Wind* could slip through the boom to dock. Sam joined Kojja Mo and three of her archers near the gangplank as the swan ship was tying up, the Summer Islanders resplendent in the feathered cloaks they only wore ashore. He felt a shabby thing beside them in his baggy blacks, faded cloak, and salt-stained boots. "How long will you remain in port?"

"Two days, ten days, who can say? However long it takes to empty our holds and fill them again." Kojja grinned. "My father must visit the grey maesters as well. He has books to sell."

"Can Gilly stay aboard till I return?"

"Gilly can stay as long as she likes." She poked Sam in the belly with a finger. "She does not eat so much as some."

"I'm not so fat as I was before," Sam said defensively. The passage south had seen to that. All those watches, and nothing to eat but fruit and fish. Summer Islanders loved fruit and fish.

Sam followed the archers across the plank, but once ashore they parted company and went their separate ways. He hoped he still remembered the way to the Citadel. Oldtown was a maze, and he had no time for getting lost.

The day was damp, so the cobblestones were wet and slippery underfoot, the alleys shrouded in mist and mystery. Sam avoided them as best he could and stayed on the river road that wound along beside the Honeywine through the heart of the old city. It felt good to have solid ground beneath his feet again instead of a rolling deck, but the walk made him feel uncomfortable all the same. He could feel eyes on him, peering down from balconies and windows, watching him from the darkened doorways. On the *Cinnamon Wind*, he had known every face. Here, everywhere he turned he saw another stranger. Even worse was the thought of being seen by someone who knew him. Lord Randyll Tarly was known in Oldtown, but little loved. Sam did not know which would be worse: to be recognized by one of his lord father's enemies or by one of his friends. He pulled his cloak up and quickened his pace.

The gates of the Citadel were flanked by a pair of towering green sphinxes with the bodies of lions, the wings of eagles, and the tails of serpents. One had a man's face, one a woman's. Just beyond stood Scribe's Hearth, where Oldtowners came in search of acolytes to write their wills and read their letters. Half a dozen bored scribes sat in open stalls, waiting for some custom. At other stalls books were being bought and sold. Sam stopped at one that offered maps, and looked over a hand-drawn map of Citadel to ascertain the shortest way to the Seneschal's Court.

The path divided where the statue of King Daeron the First sat astride his tall stone horse, his sword lifted toward Dorne. A seagull was perched on the Young Dragon's head, and two more on the blade. Sam took the left fork, which ran beside the river. At the Weeping Dock, he watched two acolytes help an old man into a boat for the short voyage to the Bloody Isle. A young mother climbed in after him, a babe not much older than Gilly's squalling in her arms. Beneath the dock, some cook's boys waded in the shallows, gathering frogs. A stream of pink-cheeked novices hurried by him toward the septry. *I should have come here when I was their age*, Sam thought. *If I had run off and taken a false name, I could have disappeared amongst the other novices. Father could have pretended that Dickon was his only son. I doubt he would even have troubled to search for me, unless I took a mule to ride. Then he would have hunted me down, but only for the mule.*

Outside the Seneschal's Court, the rectors were locking an older novice into the stocks. "Stealing food from the kitchens," one explained to the acolytes who were waiting to pelt the captive with rotting vegetables. They all gave Sam curious looks as he strode past, his black cloak billowing behind him like a sail.

Beyond the doors he found a hall with a stone floor and high, arched windows. At the far end a man with a pinched face sat upon a raised dais, scratching in a ledger with a quill. Though the man was clad in a maester's robe, there was no chain about his neck. Sam cleared his throat. "Good morrow."

The man glanced up and did not appear to approve of what he saw. "You smell of novice."

"I hope to be one soon." Sam drew out the letters Jon Snow had given him. "I came from the Wall with Maester Aemon, but he died during the voyage. If I could speak with the Seneschal . . ."

"Your name?"

"Samwell. Samwell Tarly."

The man wrote the name in his ledger and waved his quill at a bench along the wall. "Sit. You'll be called when wanted."

Sam took a seat on the bench.

Others came and went. Some delivered messages and took their leave. Some spoke to the man on the dais and were sent through the door behind him and up a turnpike stair. Some joined Sam on the benches, waiting for their names to be called. A few of those who were summoned had come in after him, he was almost certain. After the fourth or fifth time that happened, he rose and crossed the room again. "How much longer will it be?"

"The Seneschal is an important man."

"I came all the way from the Wall."

"Then you will have no trouble going a bit farther." He waved his quill. "To that bench just there, beneath the window."

Sam returned to the bench. Another hour passed. Others entered, spoke to the man on the dais, waited a few moments, and were ushered onward. The gatekeeper did not so much as glance at Sam in all that time. The fog outside grew thinner as the day wore on, and pale sunlight slanted down through the windows. He found himself watching dust motes dance in the light. A yawn escaped him, then another. He picked at a broken blister on his palm, then leaned his head back and closed his eyes.

He must have drowsed. The next he knew, the man behind the dais was calling out a name. Sam came lurching to his feet, then sat back down again when he realized it was not his name.

"You need to slip Lorcas a penny, or you'll be waiting here three days," a voice beside him said. "What brings the Night's Watch to the Citadel?"

The speaker was a slim, slight, comely youth, clad in doeskin breeches and a snug green brigandine with iron studs. He had skin the color of a light brown ale and a cap of tight black curls that came to a widow's peak above his big black eyes. "The Lord Commander is restoring the abandoned castles," Sam explained. "We need more maesters, for the ravens . . . did you say, a penny?"

"A penny will serve. For a silver stag Lorcas will carry you up to the Seneschal on his back. He has been fifty years an acolyte. He hates novices, particularly novices of noble birth."

"How could you tell I was of noble birth?"

"The same way you can tell that I'm half Dornish." The statement was delivered with a smile, in a soft Dornish drawl.

Sam fumbled for a penny. "Are you a novice?"

"An acolyte. Alleras, by some called Sphinx."

The name gave Sam a jolt. "The sphinx is the riddle, not the riddler," he blurted. "Do you know what that means?"

"No. Is it a riddle?"

"I wish I knew. I'm Samwell Tarly. Sam."

"Well met. And what business does Samwell Tarly have with Archmaester Theobald?"

"Is he the Seneschal?" said Sam, confused. "Maester Aemon said his name was Norren."

"Not for the past two turns. There is a new one every year. They fill the office by lot from amongst the archmaesters, most of whom regard it as a thankless task that takes them away from their true work. This year the black stone was drawn by Archmaester Walgrave, but Walgrave's wits are prone to wander, so Theobald stepped up and said he'd serve his term. He's a gruff man, but a good one. Did you say Maester *Aemon*?"

"Aye."

"Aemon *Targaryen*?"

"Once. Most just called him Maester Aemon. He died during our voyage south. How is it that you know of him?"

"How not? He was more than just the oldest living maester. He was the oldest man in Westeros, and lived through more history than Archmaester Perestan has ever learned. He could have told us much and more about his father's reign, and his uncle's. How old was he, do you know?"

"One hundred and two."

"What was he doing at sea, at his age?"

Sam chewed on the question for a moment, wondering how much he ought to say. *The sphinx is the riddle, not the riddler.* Could Maester Aemon have meant *this* Sphinx? It seemed unlikely. "Lord Commander Snow sent him away to save his life," he began, hesitantly. He spoke awkwardly of King Stannis and Melisandre of Asshai, intending to stop at that, but one thing led to another and he found himself speaking of Mance Rayder and his wildlings, king's blood and dragons, and before he knew what was happening, all the rest came spilling out; the wights at the Fist of First Men, the Other on his dead horse, the murder of the Old Bear at Craster's Keep, Gilly and their flight, Whitetree and Small Paul, Coldhands and the ravens, Jon's becoming lord commander, the *Blackbird*, Dareon, Braavos, the dragons Xhondo saw in Qarth, the *Cinnamon Wind* and all that Maester Aemon whispered toward the end. He held back only the secrets that he was sworn to keep, about Bran Stark and his companions and the babes Jon Snow had swapped. "Daenerys is the only hope," he concluded. "Aemon said the Citadel must send her a maester at once, to bring her home to Westeros before it is too late."

Alleras listened intently. He blinked from time to time, but he never laughed and never interrupted. When Sam was done he touched him lightly on the forearm with a slim brown hand and said, "Save your penny, Sam. Theobald will not believe half of that, but there are those who might. Will you come with me?"

"Where?"

"To speak with an archmaester."

You must tell them, Sam, Maester Aemon had said. *You must tell the archmaesters.* "Very well." He could always return to the Seneschal on the morrow, with a penny in his hand. "How far do we have to go?"

"Not far. The Isle of Ravens."

They did not need a boat to reach the Isle of Ravens; a weathered wooden drawbridge linked it to the eastern bank. "The Ravenry is the oldest building at the Citadel," Alleras told him, as they crossed over the slow-flowing waters of the Honeywine. "In the Age of Heroes it was supposedly the stronghold of a pirate lord who sat here robbing ships as they came down the river."

Moss and creeping vines covered the walls, Sam saw, and ravens walked its battlements in place of archers. The drawbridge had not been raised in living memory.

It was cool and dim inside the castle walls. An ancient weirwood filled the yard, as it had since these stones had first been raised. The carved face on its trunk was grown over by the same purple moss that hung heavy from the tree's pale limbs. Half of the branches seemed dead, but elsewhere a few red leaves still rustled, and it was there the ravens liked to perch. The tree was full of them, and there were more in the arched windows overhead, all around the yard. The ground was speckled by their droppings. As they crossed the yard, one flapped overhead and he heard the others *quork*ing to each other. "Archmaester Walgrave has his chambers in the west tower, below the white rookery," Alleras told him. "The white ravens and the black ones quarrel like Dornishmen and Marchers, so they keep them apart."

"Will Archmaester Walgrave understand what I am telling him?" wondered Sam. "You said his wits were prone to wander."

"He has good days and bad ones," said Alleras, "but it is not Walgrave you're going to see." He opened the door to the north tower and began to climb. Sam clambered up the steps behind him. There were flutterings and mutterings from above, and here and there an angry scream, as the ravens complained of being woken.

At the top of the steps, a pale blond youth about Sam's age sat outside a door of oak and iron, staring intently into a candle flame with his right eye. His left was hidden beneath a fall of ash blond hair. "What are you looking for?" Alleras asked him. "Your destiny? Your death?"

The blond youth turned from the candle, blinking. "Naked women," he said. "Who's this now?"

"Samwell. A new novice, come to see the Mage."

"The Citadel is not what it was," complained the blond. "They will take anything these days. Dusky dogs and Dornishmen, pig boys, cripples, cretins, and now a black-clad whale. And here I thought leviathans were grey." A half cape striped in green and gold draped one shoulder. He was very handsome, though his eyes were sly and his mouth cruel.

Sam knew him. "Leo Tyrell." Saying the name made him feel as if he were still a boy of seven, about to wet his smallclothes. "I am Sam, from Horn Hill. Lord Randyll Tarly's son."

"Truly?" Leo gave him another look. "I suppose you are. Your father told us all that you were dead. Or was it only that he wished you were?" He grinned. "Are you still a craven?"

"No," lied Sam. Jon had made it a command. "I went beyond the Wall and fought in battles. They call me Sam the Slayer." He did not know why he said it. The words just tumbled out.

Leo laughed, but before he could reply the door behind him opened. "Get in here, Slayer," growled the man in the doorway. "And you, Sphinx. Now."

"Sam," said Alleras, "this is Archmaester Marwyn."

Marwyn wore a chain of many metals around his bull's neck. Save for that, he looked more like a dockside thug than a maester. His head was too big for his body, and the way it thrust forward from his shoulders, together with that slab of jaw, made him look as if he were about to tear off someone's head. Though short and squat, he was heavy in the chest and shoulders, with a round, rock-hard ale belly straining at the laces of the leather jerkin he wore in place of robes. Bristly white hair sprouted from his ears and nostrils. His brow beetled, his nose had been broken more than once, and sourleaf had stained his teeth a mottled red. He had the biggest hands that Sam had ever seen.

When Sam hesitated, one of those hands grabbed him by the arm and yanked him through the door. The room beyond was large and round. Books and scrolls were everywhere, strewn across the tables and stacked up on the floor in piles four feet high. Faded tapestries and ragged maps covered the stone walls. A fire was burning in the hearth, beneath a copper kettle. Whatever was inside of it smelled burned. Aside from that, the only light came from a tall black candle in the center of the room.

The candle was unpleasantly bright. There was something queer about it. The flame did not flicker, even when Archmaester Marwyn closed the door so hard that papers blew off a nearby table. The light did something strange to colors too. Whites were bright as fresh-fallen snow, yellow shone like gold, reds turned to flame, but the shadows were so black they looked like holes in the world. Sam found himself staring. The candle itself was three feet tall and slender as a sword, ridged and twisted, glittering black. "Is that . . . ?"

". . . obsidian," said the other man in the room, a pale, fleshy, pasty-faced young fellow with round shoulders, soft hands, close-set eyes, and food stains on his robes.

"Call it dragonglass." Archmaester Marwyn glanced at the candle for a moment. "It burns but is not consumed."

"What feeds the flame?" asked Sam.

"What feeds a dragon's fire?" Marwyn seated himself upon a stool. "All Valyrian sorcery was rooted in blood or fire. The sorcerers of the Freehold could see across mountains, seas, and deserts with one of these glass candles. They could enter a man's dreams and give him visions, and speak to one another half a world apart, seated before their candles. Do you think that might be useful, Slayer?"

"We would have no more need of ravens."

"Only after battles." The archmaester peeled a sourleaf off a bale, shoved it in his mouth, and began to chew it. "Tell me all you told our Dornish sphinx. I know much of it and more, but some small parts may have escaped my notice."

He was not a man to be refused. Sam hesitated a moment, then told his tale again as Marywn, Alleras, and the other novice listened. "Maester Aemon believed that Daenerys Targaryen was the fulfillment of a prophecy . . . her, not Stannis, nor Prince Rhaegar, nor the princeling whose head was dashed against the wall."

"Born amidst salt and smoke, beneath a bleeding star. I know the prophecy." Marwyn turned his head and spat a gob of red phlegm onto the floor. "Not that I would trust it. Gorghan of Old Ghis once wrote that a prophecy is like a treacherous woman. She takes your member in her mouth, and you moan with the pleasure of it and think, how sweet, how fine, how good this is . . . and then her teeth snap shut and your moans turn to screams. That is the nature of prophecy, said Gorghan. Prophecy will bite your prick off every time." He chewed a bit. "Still . . ."

Alleras stepped up next to Sam. "Aemon would have gone to her if he had the strength. He wanted us to send a maester to her, to counsel her and protect her and fetch her safely home."

"Did he?" Archmaester Marwyn shrugged. "Perhaps it's good that he died before he got to Oldtown. Elsewise the grey sheep might have had to kill him, and that would have made the poor old dears wring their wrinkled hands."

"Kill him?" Sam said, shocked. "Why?"

"If I tell you, they may need to kill you too." Marywn smiled a ghastly smile, the juice of the sourleaf running red between his teeth. "Who do you think killed all the dragons the last time around? Gallant dragonslayers armed with swords?" He spat. "The world the Citadel is building has no place in it for sorcery or prophecy or glass candles, much less for dragons. Ask yourself why Aemon Targaryen was allowed to waste his life upon the Wall, when by rights he should have been raised to archmaester. His *blood* was why. He could not be trusted. No more than I can."

"What will you do?" asked Alleras, the Sphinx.

"Get myself to Slaver's Bay, in Aemon's place. The swan ship that delivered Slayer should serve my needs well enough. The grey sheep will send their man on a galley, I don't doubt. With fair winds I should reach her first." Marwyn glanced at Sam again, and frowned. "You . . . you should stay and forge your chain. If I were you, I would do it quickly. A time will come when you'll be needed on the Wall." He turned to the pasty-faced novice. "Find Slayer a dry cell. He'll sleep here, and help you tend the ravens."

"B-b-but," Sam sputtered, "the other archmaesters . . . the Seneschal . . . what should I tell them?"

"Tell them how wise and good they are. Tell them that Aemon commanded you to put yourself into their hands. Tell them that you have always dreamed that one day you might be allowed to wear the chain and serve the greater good, that service is the highest honor, and obedience the highest virtue. But say nothing of prophecies or dragons, unless you fancy poison in your porridge." Marwyn snatched a stained leather cloak off a peg near the door and tied it tight. "Sphinx, look after this one."

"I will," Alleras answered, but the archmaester was already gone. They heard his boots stomping down the steps.

"Where has he gone?" asked Sam, bewildered.

"To the docks. The Mage is not a man who believes in wasting time." Alleras smiled. "I have a confession. Ours was no chance encounter, Sam. The Mage sent me to snatch you up before you spoke to Theobald. He knew that you were coming."

"How?"

Alleras nodded at the glass candle.

Sam stared at the strange pale flame for a moment, then blinked and looked away. Outside the window it was growing dark.

"There's an empty sleeping cell under mine in the west tower, with steps that lead right up to Walgrave's chambers," said the pasty-faced youth. "If you don't mind the ravens *quork*ing, there's a good view of the Honeywine. Will that serve?"

"I suppose." He had to sleep somewhere.

"I will bring you some woolen coverlets. Stone walls turn cold at night, even here."

"My thanks." There was something about the pale, soft youth that he misliked, but he did not want to seem discourteous, so he added, "My name's not Slayer, truly. I'm Sam. Samwell Tarly."

"I'm Pate," the other said, "like the pig boy."

MEANWHILE, BACK ON
THE WALL...

"Hey, wait a minute!" some of you may be saying about now. "Wait a minute, wait a minute! Where's Dany and the dragons? Where's Tyrion? We hardly saw Jon Snow. That can't be all of it...."

Well, no. There's more to come. Another book as big as this one.

I did not forget to write about the other characters. Far from it. I wrote lots about them. Pages and pages and pages. Chapters and more chapters. I was still writing when it dawned on me that the book had become too big to publish in a single volume ... and I wasn't close to finished yet. To tell all of the story that I wanted to tell, I was going to have to cut the book in two.

The simplest way to do that would have been to take what I had, chop it in half around the middle, and end with "To Be Continued." The more I thought about that, however, the more I felt that the readers would be better served by a book that told all the story for half the characters, rather than half the story for all the characters. So that's the route I chose to take.

Tyrion, Jon, Dany, Stannis and Melisandre, Davos Seaworth, and all the rest of the characters you love or love to hate will be along next year (I devoutly hope) in *A Dance with Dragons*, which will focus on events along the Wall and across the sea, just as the present book focused on King's Landing.

—George R. R. Martin
June 2005

APPENDIX

THE KINGS AND THEIR COURTS

THE QUEEN REGENT

CERSEI LANNISTER, the First of Her Name, widow of [King Robert I Baratheon], Queen Dowager, Protector of the Realm, Lady of Casterly Rock, and Queen Regent,

- —Queen Cersei's children:
    - —[KING JOFFREY I BARATHEON], poisoned at his wedding feast, a boy of twelve,
    - —PRINCESS MYRCELLA BARATHEON, a girl of nine, a ward of Prince Doran Martell at Sunspear,
    - —KING TOMMEN I BARATHEON, a boy king of eight years,
        - —his kittens, SER POUNCE, LADY WHISKERS, BOOTS,
- —Queen Cersei's brothers:
    - —SER JAIME LANNISTER, her twin, called THE KINGSLAYER, Lord Commander of the Kingsguard,
    - —TYRION LANNISTER, called THE IMP, a dwarf, accused and condemned for regicide and kinslaying,
        - —PODRICK PAYNE, Tyrion's squire, a boy of ten,
- —Queen Cersei's uncles, aunt, and cousins:
    - —SER KEVAN LANNISTER, her uncle,
        - —SER LANCEL, Ser Kevan's son, her cousin, formerly King Robert's squire and Cersei's lover, newly raised to Lord of Darry,
        - —[WILLEM], Ser Kevan's son, murdered at Riverrun,
        - —MARTYN, twin to Willem, a squire,
        - —JANEI, Ser Kevan's daughter, a girl of three,

—LADY GENNA LANNISTER, Cersei's aunt, m. Ser Emmon
  Frey,
  —[SER CLEOS FREY], Genna's son, killed by outlaws,
    —SER TYWIN FREY, called TY, Cleos's son,
    —WILLEM FREY, Cleos's son, a squire,
  —SER LYONEL FREY, Lady Genna's second son,
  —[TION FREY], Genna's son, murdered at Riverrun,
  —WALDER FREY, called RED WALDER, Lady Genna's
    youngest son, a page at Casterly Rock,
—TYREK LANNISTER, Cersei's cousin, son of her father's
  late brother Tygett,
  —LADY ERMESANDE HAYFORD, Tyrek's child wife,
—JOY HILL, bastard daughter of Queen Cersei's lost uncle
  Gerion, a girl of eleven,
—CERENNA LANNISTER, Cersei's cousin, daughter of her
  late uncle Stafford, her mother's brother,
—MYRIELLE LANNISTER, Cersei's cousin and Cerenna's
  sister, daughter of her uncle Stafford,
—SER DAVEN LANNISTER, her cousin, Stafford's son,
—SER DAMION LANNISTER, a more distant cousin, m.
  Shiera Crakehall,
  —SER LUCION LANNISTER, their son,
  —LANNA, their daughter, m. Lord Antario Jast,
—LADY MARGOT, a cousin still more distant, m. Lord
  Titus Peake,

—King Tommen's small council:
  —[LORD TYWIN LANNISTER], Hand of the King,
  —SER JAIME LANNISTER, Lord Commander of the
    Kingsguard,
  —SER KEVAN LANNISTER, master of laws,
  —VARYS, a eunuch, master of whisperers,
  —GRAND MAESTER PYCELLE, counselor and healer,
  —LORD MACE TYRELL, LORD MATHIS ROWAN, LORD
    PAXTER REDWYNE, counselors,

—Tommen's Kingsguard:
 —SER JAIME LANNISTER, Lord Commander,
 —SER MERYN TRANT,
 —SER BOROS BLOUNT, removed and thence restored,
 —SER BALON SWANN,
 —SER OSMUND KETTLEBLACK,
 —SER LORAS TYRELL, the Knight of Flowers,
 —SER ARYS OAKHEART, with Princess Myrcella in Dorne,

—Cersei's household at King's Landing:
 —LADY JOCELYN SWYFT, her companion,
 —SENELLE and DORCAS, her bedmaids and
   servingwomen,
 —LUM, RED LESTER, HOKE, called HORSELEG,
   SHORT-EAR, and PUCKENS, guardsmen,

—QUEEN MARGAERY of House Tyrell, a maid of sixteen,
 widowed bride of King Joffrey I Baratheon and of Lord
 Renly Baratheon before him,
 —Margaery's court at King's Landing:
   —MACE TYRELL, Lord of Highgarden, her father
   —LADY ALERIE of House Hightower, her mother,
   —LADY OLENNA TYRELL, her grandmother, an aged
     widow called THE QUEEN OF THORNS,
     —ARRYK and ERRYK, Lady Olenna's guards, twins
       seven feet tall called LEFT and RIGHT,
   —SER GARLAN TYRELL, Margaery's brother, THE
     GALLANT,
     —his wife, LADY LEONETTE of House Fossoway,
   —SER LORAS TYRELL, her youngest brother, the Knight
     of Flowers, a Sworn Brother of the Kingsguard,
   —Margaery's lady companions:
     —her cousins, MEGGA, ALLA, and ELINOR TYRELL,
       —Elinor's betrothed, ALYN AMBROSE, squire,
     —LADY ALYSANNE BULWER, a girl of eight,
     —MEREDYTH CRANE, called MERRY,

- —LADY TAENA MERRYWEATHER,
- —LADY ALYCE GRACEFORD,
- —SEPTA NYSTERICA, a sister of the Faith,
- —PAXTER REDWYNE, Lord of the Arbor,
  - —his twin sons, SER HORAS and SER HOBBER,
  - —MAESTER BALLABAR, his healer and counselor,
- —MATHIS ROWAN, Lord of Goldengrove,
- —SER WILLAM WYTHERS, Margaery's captain of guards,
  - —HUGH CLIFTON, a handsome young guardsman,
- —SER PORTIFER WOODWRIGHT and his brother, SER LUCANTINE,

—Cersei's court at King's Landing:
- —SER OSFRYD KETTLEBLACK and SER OSNEY KETTLEBLACK, younger brothers to Ser Osmund Kettleblack,
- —SER GREGOR CLEGANE, called THE MOUNTAIN THAT RIDES, dying painfully of a poisoned wound,
- —SER ADDAM MARBRAND, Commander of the City Watch of King's Landing (the "gold cloaks"),
- —JALABHAR XHO, Prince of the Red Flower Vale, an exile from the Summer Isles,
- —GYLES ROSBY, Lord of Rosby, troubled by a cough,
- —ORTON MERRYWEATHER, Lord of Longtable,
  - —TAENA, his wife, a woman of Myr,
- —LADY TANDA STOKEWORTH,
  - —LADY FALYSE, her elder daughter and heir,
    - —SER BALMAN BYRCH, Lady Falyse's husband,
  - —LADY LOLLYS, her younger daughter, great with child but weak of wit,
    - —SER BRONN OF THE BLACKWATER, Lady Lollys's husband, a former sellsword,
    - —[SHAE], a camp follower serving as Lollys's bedmaid, strangled in Lord Tywin's bed,
  - —MAESTER FRENKEN, in Lady Tanda's service,
- —SER ILYN PAYNE, the King's Justice, a headsman,

—RENNIFER LONGWATERS, chief undergaoler of the Red Keep's dungeons,
  —RUGEN, undergaoler for the black cells,
—LORD HALLYNE THE PYROMANCER, a Wisdom of the Guild of Alchemists,
—NOHO DIMITTIS, envoy from the Iron Bank of Braavos,
—QYBURN, a necromancer, once a maester of the Citadel, more recently of the Brave Companions,
—MOON BOY, the royal jester and fool,
—PATE, a lad of eight, King Tommen's whipping boy,
—ORMOND OF OLDTOWN, the royal harper and bard,
—SER MARK MULLENDORE, who lost a monkey and half an arm in the Battle of the Blackwater,
—AURANE WATERS, the Bastard of Driftmark,
—LORD ALESANDER STAEDMON, called PENNYLOVER,
—SER RONNET CONNINGTON, called RED RONNET, the Knight of Griffin's Roost,
—SER LAMBERT TURNBERRY, SER DERMOT OF THE RAINWOOD, SER TALLAD called THE TALL, SER BAYARD NORCROSS, SER BONIFER HASTY called BONIFER THE GOOD, SER HUGO VANCE, knights sworn to the Iron Throne,
—SER LYLE CRAKEHALL called STRONGBOAR, SER ALYN STACKSPEAR, SER JON BETTLEY called BEARDLESS JON, SER STEFFON SWYFT, SER HUMFREY SWYFT, knights sworn to Casterly Rock,
—JOSMYN PECKLEDON, a squire and hero of the Blackwater,
—GARRETT PAEGE and LEW PIPER, squires and hostages,

—the people of King's Landing:
  —THE HIGH SEPTON, Father of the Faithful, Voice of the Seven on Earth, an old man and frail,
    —SEPTON TORBERT, SEPTON RAYNARD, SEPTON LUCEON, SEPTON OLLIDOR, of the Most Devout, serving the Seven at the Great Sept of Baelor,

—SEPTA MOELLE, SEPTA AGLANTINE, SEPTA HELICENT, SEPTA UNELLA, of the Most Devout, serving the Seven at the Great Sept of Baelor,

—the "sparrows," the humblest of men, fierce in their piety,

—CHATAYA, proprietor of an expensive brothel,

—ALAYAYA, her daughter,

—DANCY, MAREI, two of Chataya's girls,

—BRELLA, a servingwoman, lately in the service of Lady Sansa Stark,

—TOBHO MOTT, a master armorer,

—HAMISH THE HARPER, an aged singer,

—ALARIC OF EYSEN, a singer, far-traveled,

—WAT, a singer, styling himself THE BLUE BARD,

—SER THEODAN WELLS, a pious knight, later called SER THEODAN THE TRUE.

King Tommen's banner shows the crowned stag of Baratheon, black on gold, and the lion of Lannister, gold on crimson, combatant.

THE KING AT THE WALL

STANNIS BARATHEON, the First of His Name, second son of Lord Steffon Baratheon and Lady Cassana of House Estermont, Lord of Dragonstone, styling himself King of Westeros,

—QUEEN SELYSE of House Florent, his wife, presently at Eastwatch-by-the-Sea,
  —PRINCESS SHIREEN, their daughter, a girl of eleven,
    —PATCHFACE, Shireen's lackwit fool,
  —EDRIC STORM, his bastard nephew, King Robert's son by Lady Delena Florent, a boy of twelve, sailing the narrow sea on the *Mad Prendos*,
    —SER ANDREW ESTERMONT, King Stannis's cousin, a king's man, commanding Edric's escort,
    —SER GERALD GOWER, LEWYS called THE FISHWIFE, SER TRISTON OF TALLY HILL, OMER BLACKBERRY, king's men, Edric's guards and protectors,

—Stannis's court at Castle Black:
  —LADY MELISANDRE OF ASSHAI, called THE RED WOMAN, a priestess of R'hllor, the Lord of Light,
  —MANCE RAYDER, King-Beyond-the-Wall, a captive condemned to death,
    —Rayder's son by his wife [DALLA], a newborn as yet unnamed, "the wildling prince,"
      —GILLY, the babe's wet nurse, a wildling girl,

—her son, another newborn as yet unnamed, fathered by her father [CRASTER],

—SER RICHARD HORPE, SER JUSTIN MASSEY, SER CLAYTON SUGGS, SER GODRY FARRING, called GIANTSLAYER, LORD HARWOOD FELL, SER CORLISS PENNY, queen's men and knights,

—DEVAN SEAWORTH and BRYEN FARRING, royal squires,

—Stannis's court at Eastwatch-by-the-Sea:

—SER DAVOS SEAWORTH, called THE ONION KNIGHT, Lord of the Rainwood, Admiral of the Narrow Sea, and Hand of the King,

—SER AXELL FLORENT, Queen Selyse's uncle, foremost of the queen's men,

—SALLADHAR SAAN of Lys, a pirate and sellsail, master of the *Valyrian* and a fleet of galleys,

—Stannis's garrison at Dragonstone:

—SER ROLLAND STORM, called THE BASTARD OF NIGHTSONG, a king's man, castellan of Dragonstone,

—MAESTER PYLOS, healer, tutor, counselor,

—"PORRIDGE" and "LAMPREY," two gaolers,

—lords sworn to Dragonstone:

—MONTERYS VELARYON, Lord of the Tides and Master of Driftmark, a boy of six,

—DURAM BAR EMMON, Lord of Sharp Point, a boy of fifteen years,

—Stannis's garrison at Storm's End:

—SER GILBERT FARRING, castellan of Storm's End,

—LORD ELWOOD MEADOWS, Ser Gilbert's second,

—MAESTER JURNE, Ser Gilbert's counselor and healer,

—lords sworn to Storm's End:
    —ELDON ESTERMONT, Lord of Greenstone, uncle to King
      Stannis, great uncle to King Tommen, a cautious friend
      to both,
        —SER AEMON, Lord Eldon's son and heir, with King
          Tommen in King's Landing,
            —SER ALYN, Ser Aemon's son, likewise with King
              Tommen in King's Landing,
        —SER LOMAS, brother of Lord Eldon, uncle and
          supporter of King Stannis, at Storm's End,
            —SER ANDREW, Ser Lomas's son, protecting Edric
              Storm upon the narrow sea,
    —LESTER MORRIGEN, Lord of Crows Nest,
    —LORD LUCOS CHYTTERING, called LITTLE LUCOS, a
      youth of sixteen,
    —Davos Seaworth, Lord of the Rainwood,
        —MARYA, his wife, a carpenter's daughter,
            —[DALE, ALLARD, MATTHOS, MARIC], their four
              eldest sons, lost in the Battle of the Blackwater,
            —DEVAN, a squire with King Stannis at Castle Black,
            —STANNIS, a boy of ten years, with Lady Marya on
              Cape Wrath,
            —STEFFON, a boy of six years, with Lady Marya on
              Cape Wrath.

Stannis has taken for his banner the fiery heart of the Lord of Light:
a red heart surrounded by orange flames upon a yellow field. Within
the heart is the crowned stag of House Baratheon, in black.

KING OF THE ISLES AND
THE NORTH

The Greyjoys of Pyke claim descent from the Grey King of the Age of Heroes. Legend says the Grey King ruled the sea itself and took a mermaid to wife. Aegon the Dragon ended the line of the last King of the Iron Islands, but allowed the ironborn to revive their ancient custom and choose who should have the primacy among them. They chose Lord Vickon Greyjoy of Pyke. The Greyjoy sigil is a golden kraken upon a black field. Their words are *We Do Not Sow*.

Balon Greyjoy's first rebellion against the Iron Throne was put down by King Robert I Baratheon and Lord Eddard Stark of Winterfell, but in the chaos following Robert's death, Lord Balon named himself king once more, and sent his ships to attack the north.

[BALON GREYJOY], the Ninth of His Name Since the Grey King, King of the Iron Islands and the North, King of Salt and Rock, Son of the Sea Wind, and Lord Reaper of Pyke, killed in a fall,
  —King Balon's widow, QUEEN ALANNYS, of House Harlaw,
  —their children:
    —[RODRIK], slain during Balon's first rebellion,
    —[MARON], slain during Balon's first rebellion,
    —ASHA, their daughter, captain of the *Black Wind* and conquerer of Deepwood Motte,
    —THEON, styling himself the Prince of Winterfell, called by northmen THEON TURNCLOAK,

—King Balon's brothers and half brothers:
  —[HARLON], died of greyscale in his youth,
  —[QUENTON], died in infancy,
  —[DONEL], died in infancy,
  —EURON, called Crow's Eye, captain of the *Silence,*
  —VICTARION, Lord Captain of the Iron Fleet, master of the *Iron Victory,*
  —[URRIGON], died of a wound gone bad,
  —AERON, called DAMPHAIR, a priest of the Drowned God,
    —RUS and NORJEN, two of his acolytes, the "drowned men,"
  —[ROBIN], died in infancy,

—King Balon's household on Pyke:
  —MAESTER WENDAMYR, healer and counselor,
  —HELYA, keeper of the castle,

—King Balon's warriors and sworn swords:
  —DAGMER called CLEFTJAW, captain of *Foamdrinker,* commanding the ironborn at Torrhen's Square,
  —BLUETOOTH, a longship captain,
  —ULLER, SKYTE, oarsmen and warriors,

—CLAIMANTS TO THE SEASTONE CHAIR AT THE KINGSMOOT ON OLD WYK
  GYLBERT FARWYND, Lord of the Lonely Light,
    —Gylbert's champions: his sons GYLES, YGON, YOHN,

  ERIK IRONMAKER, called ERIK ANVIL-BREAKER and ERIK THE JUST, an old man, once a famed captain and raider,
    —Erik's champions: his grandsons UREK, THORMOR, DAGON,

  DUNSTAN DRUMM, The Drumm, the Bone Hand, Lord of Old Wyk,
    —Dunstan's champions: his sons DENYS and DONNEL, and ANDRIK THE UNSMILING, a giant of a man,

ASHA GREYJOY, only daughter of Balon Greyjoy, captain of the *Black Wind*,
   —Asha's champions: QARL THE MAID, TRISTIFER BOTLEY, and SER HARRAS HARLAW
   —Asha's captains and supporters: LORD RODRIK HARLAW, LORD BAELOR BLACKTYDE, LORD MELDRED MERLYN, HARMUND SHARP

VICTARION GREYJOY, brother to Balon Greyjoy, master of the *Iron Victory* and Lord Captain of the Iron Fleet,
   —Victarion's champions: RED RALF STONEHOUSE, RALF THE LIMPER, and NUTE THE BARBER,
   —Victarion's captains and supporters: HOTHO HARLAW, ALVYN SHARP, FRALEGG THE STRONG, ROMNY WEAVER, WILL HUMBLE, LITTLE LENWOOD TAWNEY, RALF KENNING, MARON VOLMARK, GOROLD GOODBROTHER,
   —Victarion's crewmen: WULF ONE-EAR, RAGNOR PYKE
   —Victarion's bedmate, a certain dusky woman, mute and tongueless, a gift from his brother Euron,

EURON GREYJOY, called THE CROW'S EYE, brother to Balon Greyjoy and captain of the *Silence*,
   —Euron's champions: GERMUND BOTLEY, LORD ORKWOOD OF ORKMONT, DONNOR SALTCLIFFE
   —Euron's captains and supporters: TORWOLD BROWNTOOTH, PINCHFACE JON MYRE, RODRIK FREEBORN, THE RED OARSMAN, LEFT-HAND LUCAS CODD, QUELLON HUMBLE, HARREN HALF-HOARE, KEMMETT PYKE THE BASTARD, QARL THE THRALL, STONEHAND, RALF THE SHEPHERD, RALF OF LORDSPORT
   —Euron's crewmen: CRAGORN

—Balon's bannermen, the Lords of the Iron Islands:

on Pyke
—[SAWANE BOTLEY], Lord of Lordsport, drowned by
    Euron Crow's Eye,
    —[HARREN], his eldest son, killed at Moat Cailin,
    —TRISTIFER, his second son and rightful heir, dispos-
        sessed by his uncle,
    —SYMOND, HARLON, VICKON, and BENNARION,
        his younger sons, likewise dispossessed,
    —GERMUND, his brother, made Lord of Lordsport
        —Germund's sons, BALON and QUELLON,
    —SARGON and LUCIMORE, Sawane's half brothers,
        —WEX, a mute boy of twelve years, bastard son of
            Sargon, squire to Theon Greyjoy,
—WALDON WYNCH, Lord of Iron Holt,

on Harlaw
    —RODRIK HARLAW, called THE READER, Lord of Harlaw,
        Lord of Ten Towers, Harlaw of Harlaw,
        —LADY GWYNESSE, his elder sister,
        —LADY ALANNYS, his younger sister, widow of King
            Balon Greyjoy
        —SIGFRYD HARLAW, called SIGFRYD SILVERHAIR,
            his great uncle, master of Harlaw Hall,
        —HOTHO HARLAW, called HOTHO HUMPBACK, of
            the Tower of Glimmering, a cousin,
        —SER HARRAS HARLAW, called THE KNIGHT, the
            Knight of Grey Garden, a cousin,
        —BOREMUND HARLAW, called BOREMUND THE
            BLUE, master of Harridan Hill, a cousin,
        —Lord Rodrik's bannermen and sworn swords:
            —MARON VOLMARK, Lord of Volmark,
            —MYRE, STONETREE, and KENNING,
        —Lord Rodrik's household:
            —THREE-TOOTH, his steward, a crone,

ON BLACKTYDE
—BAELOR BLACKTYDE, Lord of Blacktyde, captain of the *Nightflyer*,
—BLIND BEN BLACKTYDE, a priest of the Drowned God,

ON OLD WYK
—DUNSTAN DRUMM, The Drumm, captain of *Thunderer*,
—NORNE GOODBROTHER, of Shatterstone,
—THE STONEHOUSE,
—TARLE, called TARLE THE THRICE-DROWNED, a priest of the Drowned God,

ON GREAT WYK
—GOROLD GOODBROTHER, Lord of the Hammerhorn,
—his sons, GREYDON, GRAN, and GORMOND, triplets,
—his daughters, GYSELLA and GWIN,
—MAESTER MURENMURE, tutor, healer, and counselor,
—TRISTON FARWYND, Lord of Sealskin Point,
—THE SPARR,
—his son and heir, STEFFARION,
—MELDRED MERLYN, Lord of Pebbleton,

ON ORKMONT
—ORKWOOD OF ORKMONT,
—LORD TAWNEY,

ON SALTCLIFFE
—LORD DONNOR SALTCLIFFE,
—LORD SUNDERLY

ON THE LESSER ISLANDS AND ROCKS
—GYLBERT FARWYND, Lord of the Lonely Light,
—THE OLD GREY GULL, a priest of the Drowned God.

OTHER HOUSES GREAT AND SMALL

HOUSE ARRYN

The Arryns are descended from the Kings of Mountain and Vale. Their sigil is a white moon-and-falcon upon a sky-blue field. House Arryn has taken no part in the War of the Five Kings. Their Arryn words are *As High as Honor*.

ROBERT ARRYN, Lord of the Eyrie, Defender of the Vale, styled by his mother True Warden of the East, a sickly boy of eight years, sometimes called SWEETROBIN,
—his mother, [LADY LYSA of House Tully], widow of Lord Jon Arryn, pushed from the Moon Door to her death,
—his stepfather, PETYR BAELISH, called LITTLEFINGER, Lord of Harrenhal, Lord Paramount of the Trident, and Lord Protector of the Vale,
   —ALAYNE STONE, Lord Petyr's natural daughter, a maid of three-and-ten, actually Sansa Stark,
   —SER LOTHOR BRUNE, a sellsword in Lord Petyr's service, the Eyrie's captain of guards,
   —OSWELL, a grizzled man-at-arms in Lord Petyr's service, sometimes called KETTLEBLACK,

—Lord Robert's household at the Eyrie:
   —MARILLION, a handsome young singer much favored by Lady Lysa and accused of her murder,
   —MAESTER COLEMON, counselor, healer, and tutor,
   —MORD, a brutal gaoler with teeth of gold,
   —GRETCHEL, MADDY, and MELA, servingwomen,

—Lord Robert's bannermen, the Lords of the Vale:
  —LORD NESTOR ROYCE, High Steward of the Vale and castellan of the Gates of the Moon,
    —SER ALBAR, Lord Nestor's son and heir,
    —MYRANDA, called RANDA, Lord Nestor's daughter, a widow, but scarce used,
    —Lord Nestor's household:
      —SER MARWYN BELMORE, captain of guards,
      —MYA STONE, a mule tender and guide, bastard daughter of King Robert I Baratheon,
      —OSSY and CARROT, mule tenders,
  —LYONEL CORBRAY, Lord of Heart's Home,
    —SER LYN CORBRAY, his brother and heir, who wields the famed blade Lady Forlorn,
    —SER LUCAS CORBRAY, his younger brother,
  —JON LYNDERLY, Lord of the Snakewood,
    —TERRANCE, his son and heir, a young squire,
  —EDMUND WAXLEY, the Knight of Wickenden,
  —GEROLD GRAFTON, the Lord of Gulltown,
    —GYLES, his youngest son, a squire,
  —TRISTON SUNDERLAND, Lord of the Three Sisters,
    —GODRIC BORRELL, Lord of Sweetsister,
    —ROLLAND LONGTHORPE, Lord of Longsister,
    —ALESANDOR TORRENT, Lord of Littlesister,

—the Lords Declarant, bannermen of House Arryn joined together in defense of young Lord Robert:
  —YOHN ROYCE, called BRONZE YOHN, Lord of Runestone, of the senior branch of House Royce,
    —SER ANDAR, Bronze Yohn's sole surviving son, and heir to Runestone,
    —Bronze Yohn's household:
      —MAESTER HELLIWEG, tutor, healer, counselor,
      —SEPTON LUCOS,
      —SER SAMWELL STONE, called STRONG SAM STONE, master-at-arms,

—Bronze Yohn's bannermen and sworn swords:
  —ROYCE COLDWATER, Lord of Coldwater Burn,
  —SER DAMON SHETT, Knight of Gull Tower,
  —UTHOR TOLLETT, Lord of the Grey Glen
—ANYA WAYNWOOD, Lady of Ironoaks Castle,
  —SER MORTON, her eldest son and heir,
  —SER DONNEL, her second son, the Knight of the Gate,
  —WALLACE, her youngest son,
  —HARROLD HARDYNG, her ward, a squire oft called HARRY THE HEIR,
—BENEDAR BELMORE, Lord of Strongsong,
—SER SYMOND TEMPLETON, the Knight of Ninestars,
—[EON HUNTER], Lord of Longbow Hall, recently deceased,
  —SER GILWOOD, Lord Eon's eldest son and heir, now called YOUNG LORD HUNTER,
  —SER EUSTACE, Lord Eon's second son,
  —SER HARLAN, Lord Eon's youngest son,
  —Young Lord Hunter's household:
    —MAESTER WILLAMEN, counselor, healer, tutor,
—HORTON REDFORT, Lord of Redfort, thrice wed,
  —SER JASPER, SER CREIGHTON, SER JON, his sons,
  —SER MYCHEL, his youngest son, a new-made knight, m. Ysilla Royce of Runestone,

—clan chiefs from the Mountains of the Moon,
  —SHAGGA SON OF DOLF, OF THE STONE CROWS, presently leading a band in the kingswood,
  —TIMETT SON OF TIMETT, OF THE BURNED MEN,
  —CHELLA DAUGHTER OF CHEYK, OF THE BLACK EARS,
  —CRAWN SON OF CALOR, OF THE MOON BROTHERS.

HOUSE FLORENT

The Florents of Brightwater Keep are bannermen of Highgarden. At the outset of the War of the Five Kings, Lord Alester Florent followed his liege lord in declaring for King Renly while his brother Ser Axell chose Stannis, husband to his niece Selyse. After Renly's death, Lord Alester went over to Stannis as well, with all the strength of Brightwater. Stannis made Lord Alester his Hand, and gave command of his fleet to Ser Imry Florent, his wife's brother. The fleet and Ser Imry both were lost in the Battle of Blackwater, and Lord Alester's efforts to negotiate a peace after the defeat were regarded by King Stannis as treason. He was given to the red priestess Melisandre, who burned him as a sacrifice to R'hllor.

The Iron Throne has also named the Florents traitors for their support of Stannis and his rebellion. They were attainted, and Brightwater Keep and its lands were awarded to Ser Garlan Tyrell.

The sigil of House Florent shows a fox head in a circle of flowers.

[ALESTER FLORENT], Lord of Brightwater, burned as a traitor,
— his wife, LADY MELARA, of House Crane,
— their children:
    — LEKYNE, attainted Lord of Brightwater, fled to Oldtown to seek refuge at the Hightower,
    — LADY MELESSA, wed to Lord Randyll Tarly,
    — LADY RHEA, wed to Lord Leyton Hightower,
— his siblings:
    — SER AXELL, a queen's man, in service to his niece Queen Selyse at Eastwatch-by-the-Sea,

—[SER RYAM], died in a fall from a horse,
  —SELYSE, his daughter, wife and queen to King Stannis
    I Baratheon,
      —SHIREEN BARATHEON, her only child,
  —[SER IMRY], his eldest son, killed in the Battle of the
    Blackwater,
  —SER ERREN, his second son, a captive at Highgarden,
—SER COLIN, castellan at Brightwater Keep,
  —DELENA, his daughter, m. SER HOSMAN NORCROSS,
  —her natural son, EDRIC STORM, fathered by King
    Robert I Baratheon,
      —ALESTER NORCROSS, her eldest trueborn son,
        a boy of nine,
      —RENLY NORCROSS, her second trueborn son, a
        boy of three,
  —MAESTER OMER, Ser Colin's eldest son, in service at
    Old Oak,
  —MERRELL, Ser Colin's youngest son, a squire on the
    Arbor,
—RYLENE, Lord Alester's sister, m. Ser Rycherd Crane.

HOUSE FREY

The Freys are bannermen to House Tully, but have not always been diligent in their duty. At the onset of the War of the Five Kings, Robb Stark won Lord Walder's allegiance by pledging to marry one of his daughters or granddaughters. When he wed Lady Jeyne Westerling instead, the Freys conspired with Roose Bolton and murdered the Young Wolf and his followers at what became known as the Red Wedding.

WALDER FREY, Lord of the Crossing,
—by his first wife, [LADY PERRA, of House Royce]:
—[SER STEVRON], died after the Battle of Oxcross,
—m. [Corenna Swann], died of a wasting illness,
—Stevron's eldest son, SER RYMAN, heir to the Twins,
—Ryman's son, EDWYN, wed to Janyce Hunter,
—Edwyn's daughter, WALDA, a girl of nine,
—Ryman's son, WALDER, called BLACK WALDER,
—Ryman's son, [PETYR], called PETYR PIMPLE, hanged at Oldstones, m. Mylenda Caron,
—Petyr's daughter, PERRA, a girl of five,
—m. [Jeyne Lydden], died in a fall from a horse,
—Stevron's son, [AEGON], called JINGLEBELL, killed at the Red Wedding by Catelyn Stark,
—Stevron's daughter, [MAEGELLE], died in childbed, m. Ser Dafyn Vance,
—Maegelle's daughter, MARIANNE VANCE, a maiden,

  —Maegelle's son, WALDER VANCE, a squire,
  —Maegelle's son, PATREK VANCE,
—m. [Marsella Waynwood], died in childbed,
—Stevron's son, WALTON, m. Deana Hardyng,
  —Walton's son, STEFFON, called THE SWEET,
  —Walton's daughter, WALDA, called FAIR WALDA,
  —Walton's son, BRYAN, a squire,

—SER EMMON, Lord Walder's second son, m. Genna Lannister,
  —Emmon's son, [SER CLEOS], killed by outlaws near Maidenpool, m. Jeyne Darry,
    —Cleos's son, TYWIN, a squire of twelve,
    —Cleos's son, WILLEM, a page at Ashemark, ten,
  —Emmon's son, SER LYONEL, m. Melesa Crakehall,
  —Emmon's son, [TION], a squire, murdered by Rickard Karstark while a captive at Riverrun,
  —Emmon's son, WALDER, called RED WALDER, fourteen, a page at Casterly Rock,

—SER AENYS, Lord Walder's third son, m. [Tyana Wylde], died in childbed,
  —Aenys's son, AEGON BLOODBORN, an outlaw,
  —Aenys's son, RHAEGAR, m. [Jeyne Beesbury], died of a wasting illness,
    —Rhaegar's son, ROBERT, a boy of thirteen,
    —Rhaegar's daughter, WALDA, a girl of eleven, called WHITE WALDA,
    —Rhaegar's son, JONOS, a boy of eight,

—PERRIANE, Lord Walder's daughter, m. Ser Leslyn Haigh,
  —Perriane's son, SER HARYS HAIGH,
    —Harys's son, WALDER HAIGH, a boy of five,
  —Perriane's son, SER DONNEL HAIGH,
  —Perriane's son, ALYN HAIGH, a squire,

—by his second wife, [LADY CYRENNA, of House Swann]:
—SER JARED, Lord Walder's fourth son, m. [Alys Frey],
  —Jared's son, [SER TYTOS], slain by Sandor Clegane during
    the Red Wedding, m. Zhoe Blanetree,
    —Tytos's daughter, ZIA, a maid of fourteen,
    —Tytos's son, ZACHERY, a boy of twelve sworn to the
      Faith, training at the Sept of Oldtown,
  —Jared's daughter, KYRA, m. [Ser Garse Goodbrook], slain
    during the Red Wedding,
    —Kyra's son, WALDER GOODBROOK, a boy of nine,
    —Kyra's daughter, JEYNE GOODBROOK, six,
—SEPTON LUCEON, in service at the Great Sept of Baelor,

—by his third wife, [LADY AMAREI of House Crakehall]:
—SER HOSTEEN, m. Bellena Hawick,
  —Hosteen's son, SER ARWOOD, m. Ryella Royce,
    —Arwood's daughter, RYELLA, a girl of five,
    —Arwood's twin sons, ANDROW and ALYN, four,
    —Arwood's daughter, HOSTELLA, a newborn babe,
—LYENTHE, Lord Walder's daughter, m. Lord Lucias Vypren,
  —Lythene's daughter, ELYANA, m. Ser Jon Wylde,
    —Elyana's son, RICKARD WYLDE, four,
  —Lythene's son, SER DAMON VYPREN,
—SYMOND, m. Betharios of Braavos,
  —Symond's son, ALESANDER, a singer,
  —Symond's daughter, ALYX, a maid of seventeen,
  —Symond's son, BRADAMAR, a boy of ten, a ward of Oro
    Tendyris, a merchant of Braavos,
—SER DANWELL, Lord Walder's eighth son, m. Wynafrei
  Whent,
  —[many stillbirths and miscarriages],
—[MERRETT], hanged at Oldstones, m. Mariya Darry,
  —Merrett's daughter, AMEREI, called AMI, m. [Ser Pate of
    the Blue Fork, slain by Ser Gregor Clegane],
  —Merrett's daughter, WALDA, called FAT WALDA, m. Roose
    Bolton, Lord of the Dreadfort,

—Merrett's daughter, MARISSA, a maid of thirteen,
—Merrett's son, WALDER, called LITTLE WALDER, eight,
  a squire in service to Ramsay Bolton,
—[SER GEREMY], drowned, m. Carolei Waynwood,
  —Geremy's son, SANDOR, a boy of twelve, a squire,
  —Geremy's daughter, CYNTHEA, a girl of nine, a ward of
    Lady Anya Waynwood,
—SER RAYMUND, m. Beony Beesbury,
  —Raymund's son, ROBERT, an acolyte at the Citadel,
  —Raymund's son, MALWYN, serving with alchemist in
    Lys,
  —Raymund's twin daughters, SERRA and SARRA,
  —Raymund's daughter, CERSEI, called LITTLE BEE,
  —Raymund's twin sons, JAIME and TYWIN, newborn,

—by his fourth wife, [LADY ALYSSA, of House Blackwood]:
—LOTHAR, Lord Walder's twelfth son, called LAME
  LOTHAR, m. Leonella Lefford,
  —Lothar's daughter, TYSANE, a girl of seven,
  —Lothar's daughter, WALDA, a girl of five,
  —Lothar's daughter, EMBERLEI, a girl of three,
  —Lothar's daughter, LEANA, a newborn babe,
—SER JAMMOS, Lord Walder's thirteenth son, m. Sallei
  Paege,
  —Jammos's son, WALDER, called BIG WALDER, eight, a
    squire in service to Ramsey Bolton,
  —Jammos's twin sons, DICKON and MATHIS, five,
—SER WHALEN, Lord Walder's fourteenth son, m. Sylwa
  Paege,
—Whalen's son, HOSTER, a squire of twelve, in service to Ser
  Damon Paege,
  —Whalen's daughter, MERIANNE, called MERRY, eleven,
—MORYA, Lord Walder's daughter, m. Ser Flement Brax,
  —Morya's son, ROBERT BRAX, nine, a page at Casterly
    Rock,
  —Morya's son, WALDER BRAX, a boy of six,

—Morya's son, JON BRAX, a babe of three,
—TYTA, Lord Walder's daughter, called TYTA THE MAID,
—by his fifth wife, [LADY SARYA of House Whent]:
  —no progeny,

—by his sixth wife, [LADY BETHANY of House Rosby]:
—SER PERWYN, Lord Walder's fifteenth son,
—[SER BENFREY], Lord Walder's sixteenth son, died of a
  wound received at the Red Wedding, m. Jyanna Frey, a
  cousin,
    —Benfrey's daughter, DELLA, called DEAF DELLA, a girl
    of three,
    —Benfrey's son, OSMUND, a boy of two,
—MAESTER WILLAMEN, Lord Walder's seventeenth son, in
  service at Longbow Hall,
—OLYVAR, Lord Walder's eighteenth son, formerly a squire to
  Robb Stark,
—ROSLIN, sixteen, m. Lord Edmure Tully at the Red
  Wedding,

—by his seventh wife, [LADY ANNARA of House Farring]:
—ARWYN, Lord Walder's daughter, a maid of fourteen,
—WENDEL, Lord Walder's nineteenth son, thirteen, a page at
  Seagard,
—COLMAR, Lord Walder's twentieth son, eleven and
  promised to the Faith,
—WALTYR, called TYR, Lord Walder's twenty-first son, ten,
—ELMAR, Lord Walder's lastborn son, a boy of nine briefly
  betrothed to Arya Stark,
—SHIREI, Lord Walder's youngest child, a girl of seven,

—his eighth wife, LADY JOYEUSE of House Erenford,
  —presently with child,

—Lord Walder's natural children, by sundry mothers,
  —WALDER RIVERS, called BASTARD WALDER,

—Bastard Walder's son, SER AEMON RIVERS,
—Bastard Walder's daughter, WALDA RIVERS,
—MAESTER MELWYS, in service at Rosby,
—JEYNE RIVERS, MARTYN RIVERS, RYGER RIVERS,
 RONEL RIVERS, MELLARA RIVERS, others.

HOUSE HIGHTOWER

The Hightowers of Oldtown are among the oldest and proudest of the Great Houses of Westeros, tracing their descent back to the First Men. Once kings, they have ruled Oldtown and its environs since the Dawn of Days, welcoming the Andals rather than resisting them, and later bending the knee to the Kings of the Reach and giving up their crowns whilst retaining all their ancient privileges. Though powerful and immensely wealthy, the Lords of the High Tower have traditionally preferred trade to battle, and have seldom played a large part in the wars of Westeros. The Hightowers were instrumental in the founding of the Citadel and continue to protect it to this day. Subtle and sophisticated, they have always been great patrons of learning and the Faith, and it is said that certain of them have also dabbled in alchemy, necromancy, and other sorcerous arts.

The arms of House Hightower show a stepped white tower crowned with fire on a smoke-grey field. The House words are *We Light the Way*.

LEYTON HIGHTOWER, Voice of Oldtown, Lord of the Port, Lord of the High Tower, Defender of the Citadel, Beacon of the South, called THE OLD MAN OF OLDTOWN,
— LADY RHEA of House Hightower, his fourth wife,
— Lord Leyton's eldest son and heir, SER BAELOR, called BAELOR BRIGHTSMILE, m. Rhonda Rowan,
— Lord Leyton's daughter, MALORA, called THE MAD MAID,
— Lord Leyton's daughter, ALERIE, m. Lord Mace Tyrell,
— Lord Leyton's son SER GARTH, called GREYSTEEL,

—Lord Leyton's daughter, DENYSE, m. Ser Desmond Redwyne,
 —her son, DENYS, a squire,
—Lord Leyton's daughter, LEYLA, m. Ser Jon Cupps,
—Lord Leyton's daughter, ALYSANNE, m. Lord Arthur Ambrose,
—Lord Leyton's daughter, LYNESSE, m. Lord Jorah Mormont, presently chief concubine to Tregar Ormollen of Lys,
—Lord Leyton's son, SER GUNTHOR, m. Jeyne Fossoway, of the green apple Fossoways,
—Lord Leyton's youngest son, SER HUMFREY,

—Lord Leyton's bannermen:
 —TOMMEN COSTAYNE, Lord of the Three Towers,
 —ALYSANNE BULWER, Lady of Blackcrown, a girl of eight,
 —MARTYN MULLENDORE, Lord of Uplands,
 —WARRYN BEESBURY, Lord of Honeyholt,
 —BRANSTON CUY, Lord of Sunflower Hall,

—the people of Oldtown:
 —EMMA, a serving wench at the Quill and Tankard, where the women are willing and the cider is fearsomely strong,
  —ROSEY, her daughter, a girl of five-and-ten whose maidenhead will cost a golden dragon,

—the Archmaesters of the Citadel:
 —ARCHMAESTER NORREN, Seneschal for the waning year, whose ring and rod and mask are electrum,
 —ARCHMAESTER THEOBALD, Seneschal for the coming year, whose ring and rod and mask are lead,
 —ARCHMAESTER EBROSE, the healer, whose ring and rod and mask are silver,
 —ARCHMAESTER MARWYN, called MARWYN THE MAGE, whose ring and rod and mask are Valyrian steel,
 —ARCHMAESTER PERESTAN, the historian, whose ring and rod and mask are copper,

—ARCHMAESTER VAELLYN, called VINEGAR VAELLYN, the stargazer, whose ring and rod and mask are bronze,

—ARCHMAESTER RYAM, whose ring and rod and mask are yellow gold,

—ARCHMAESTER WALGRAVE, an old man of uncertain wit, whose ring and rod and mask are black iron,

—GALLARD, CASTOS, ZARABELO, BENEDICT, GARIZON, NYMOS, CETHERES, WILLIFER, MOLLOS, HARODON, GUYNE, AGRIVANE, OCLEY, archmaesters all,

—maesters, acolytes, and novices of the Citadel:

—MAESTER GORMON, who oft serves in Walgrave's stead,

—ARMEN, an acolyte of four links, called THE ACOLYTE,

—ALLERAS, called THE SPHINX, an acolyte of three links, a devoted archer,

—ROBERT FREY, sixteen, an acolyte of two links,

—LORCAS, an acolyte of nine links, in service to the Seneschal,

—LEO TYRELL, called LAZY LEO, a highborn novice,

—MOLLANDER, a novice, born with a club foot,

—PATE, who tends Archmaester Walgrave's ravens, a novice of little promise,

—ROONE, a young novice.

HOUSE LANNISTER

The Lannisters of Casterly Rock remain the principal support of King Tommen's claim to the Iron Throne. They boast of descent from Lann the Clever, the legendary trickster of the Age of Heroes. The gold of Casterly Rock and the Golden Tooth has made them the wealthiest of the Great Houses. The Lannister sigil is a golden lion upon a crimson field. Their words are *Hear Me Roar!*

[TYWIN LANNISTER], Lord of Casterly Rock, Shield of Lannisport, Warden of the West, and Hand of the King, murdered by his dwarf son in his privy,
—Lord Tywin's children:
—CERSEI, twin to Jaime, now Lady of Casterly Rock,
—SER JAIME, twin to Cersei, called THE KINGSLAYER,
—TYRION, called THE IMP, dwarf and kinslayer,

—Lord Tywin's siblings and their offspring:
—SER KEVAN LANNISTER, m. Dorna of House Swyft,
—LADY GENNA, m. Ser Emmon Frey, now Lord of Riverrun,
—Genna's eldest son, [SER CLEOS FREY], m. Jeyne of House Darry, killed by outlaws,
—Cleos's eldest son, SER TYWIN FREY, called TY, now heir to Riverrun,
—Cleos's second son, WILLEM FREY, a squire,
—Genna's second son, SER LYONEL FREY,
—Genna's third son, [TION FREY], a squire, murdered while a captive at Riverrun,

—Genna's youngest son, WALDER FREY, called RED
  WALDER, a page at Casterly Rock,
—WHITESMILE WAT, a singer in service to Lady Genna,
—[SER TYGETT LANNISTER], died of a pox,
  —TYREK, Tygett's son, missing and feared dead,
    —LADY ERMESANDE HAYFORD, Tyrek's child wife,
—[GERION LANNISTER], lost at sea,
  —JOY HILL, Gerion's bastard daughter, eleven,

—Lord Tywin's other close kin:
  —[SER STAFFORD LANNISTER], a cousin and brother to
    Lord Tywin's wife, slain in battle at Oxcross,
    —CERENNA and MYRIELLE, Stafford's daughters,
    —SER DAVEN LANNISTER, Stafford's son,
  —SER DAMION LANNISTER, a cousin, m. Lady Shiera
    Crakehall,
    —their son, SER LUCION,
    —their daughter, LANNA, m. Lord Antario Jast,
  —LADY MARGOT, a cousin, m. Lord Titus Peake,

—the household at Casterly Rock:
  —MAESTER CREYLEN, healer, tutor, and counselor,
  —VYLARR, captain of guards,
  —SER BENEDICT BROOM, master-at-arms,
  —WHITESMILE WAT, a singer,

—bannermen and sworn swords, Lords of the West:
  —DAMON MARBRAND, Lord of Ashemark,
    —SER ADDAM MARBRAND, his son and heir,
      Commander of the City Watch of King's Landing,
  —ROLAND CRAKEHALL, Lord of Crakehall,
    —Roland's brother, {SER BURTON}, slain by outlaws,
    —Roland's son and heir, SER TYBOLT,
    —Roland's son, SER LYLE, called STRONGBOAR,
    —Roland's youngest son, SER MERLON,
  —SEBASTON FARMAN, Lord of Fair Isle,

—JEYNE, his sister, m. SER GARETH CLIFTON,
—TYTOS BRAX, Lord of Hornvale,
  —SER FLEMENT BRAX, his brother and heir,
—QUENTEN BANEFORT, Lord of Banefort,
—SER HARYS SWYFT, good-father to Ser Kevan Lannister,
    —Ser Harys's son, SER STEFFON SWYFT,
      —Ser Steffon's daughter, JOANNA,
    —Ser Harys's daughter, SHIERLE, m. Ser Melwyn
      Sarsfield,
—REGENARD ESTREN, Lord of Wyndhall,
—GAWEN WESTERLING, Lord of the Crag,
  —his wife, LADY SYBELL, of House Spicer,
    —her brother, SER ROLPH SPICER, newly raised to Lord
      of Castamere,
    —her cousin, SER SAMWELL SPICER,
  —their children:
    —SER RAYNALD WESTERLING,
    —JEYNE, widowed wife of Robb Stark,
    —ELEYNA, a girl of twelve,
    —ROLLAM, a boy of nine,
—LORD SELMOND STACKSPEAR,
  —his son, SER STEFFON STACKSPEAR,
  —his younger son, SER ALYN STACKSPEAR,
—TERRENCE KENNING, Lord of Kayce,
  —SER KENNOS OF KAYCE, a knight in his service,
—LORD ANTARIO JAST,
—LORD ROBIN MORELAND,
—LADY ALYSANNE LEFFORD,
—LEWYS LYDDEN, Lord of the Deep Den,
—LORD PHILIP PLUMM,
  —his sons, SER DENNIS PLUMM, SER PETER PLUMM,
    and SER HARWYN PLUMM, called HARDSTONE,
—LORD GARRISON PRESTER,
  —SER FORLEY PRESTER, his cousin,
—SER GREGOR CLEGANE, called THE MOUNTAIN THAT
RIDES,

  —SANDOR CLEGANE, his brother,
—SER LORENT LORCH, a landed knight,
—SER GARTH GREENFIELD, a landed knight,
—SER LYMOND VIKARY, a landed knight,
—SER RAYNARD RUTTIGER, a landed knight
—SER MANFRYD YEW, a landed knight,
—SER TYBOLT HETHERSPOON, a landed knight,
  —[MELARA HETHERSPOON], his daughter, drowned in
  a well while a ward at Casterly Rock.

HOUSE MARTELL

Dorne was the last of the Seven Kingdoms to swear fealty to the Iron Throne. Blood, custom, geography, and history all helped to set the Dornishmen apart from the other kingdoms. At the outbreak of the War of the Five Kings, Dorne took no part, but when Myrcella Baratheon was betrothed to Prince Trystane, Sunspear declared its support for King Joffrey. The Martell banner is a red sun pierced by a golden spear. Their words are *Unbowed, Unbent, Unbroken.*

DORAN NYMEROS MARTELL, Lord of Sunspear, Prince of Dorne,
—his wife, MELLARIO, of the Free City of Norvos,
—their children:
——PRINCESS ARIANNE, heir to Sunspear,
———GARIN, Arianne's milk brother and companion, of the orphans of the Greenblood,
——PRINCE QUENTYN, a new-made knight, long fostered by Lord Yronwood of Yronwood,
——PRINCE TRYSTANE, betrothed to Myrcella Baratheon,
—Prince Doran's siblings:
——[PRINCESS ELIA, raped and murdered during the Sack of King's Landing],
———[RHAENYS TARGARYEN], her young daughter, murdered during the Sack of King's Landing,
———[AEGON TARGARYEN], a babe at the breast, murdered during the Sack of King's Landing,

—[PRINCE OBERYN], called THE RED VIPER, slain by
Ser Gregor Clegane during a trial by combat,
  —ELLARIA SAND, Prince Oberyn's paramour, natural
  daughter of Lord Harmen Uller,
  —THE SAND SNAKES, Oberyn's bastard daughters:
    —OBARA, eight-and-twenty, Oberyn's daughter by an
    Oldtown whore,
    —NYMERIA, called LADY NYM, five-and-twenty, his
    daughter by a noblewoman of Volantis,
    —TYENE, three-and-twenty, Oberyn's daughter by a
    septa,
    —SARELLA, nineteen, his daughter by a trader,
    captain of the *Feathered Kiss,*
    —ELIA, fourteen, his daughter by Ellaria Sand,
    —OBELLA, twelve, his daughter by Ellaria Sand,
    —DOREA, eight, his daughter by Ellaria Sand,
    —LOREZA, six, his daughter by Ellaria Sand,

—Prince Doran's court, at the Water Gardens:
  —AREO HOTAH, of Norvos, captain of the guards,
  —MAESTER CALEOTTE, counselor, healer, and tutor,
  —threescore children of both high and common birth, sons
  and daughters of lords, knights, orphans, merchants,
  craftsmen, and peasants, his wards,

—Prince Doran's court, at Sunspear:
  —PRINCESS MYRCELLA BARATHEON, his ward,
  betrothed to Prince Trystane,
    —SER ARYS OAKHEART, Myrcella's sworn shield,
    —ROSAMUND LANNISTER, Myrcella's bedmaid and
    companion, a distant cousin,
    —SEPTA EGLANTINE, Myrcella's confessor,
  —MAESTER MYLES, counselor, healer, and tutor,
  —RICASSO, Seneschal at Sunspear, old and blind,
  —SER MANFREY MARTELL, castellan at Sunspear
  —LADY ALYSE LADYBRIGHT, lord treasurer,

—SER GASCOYNE of the Greenblood, Prince Trystane's sworn shield,
—BORS and TIMOTH, serving men at Sunspear,
—BELANDRA, CEDRA, the sisters MORRA and MELLEI, servingwomen at Sunspear,

—Prince Doran's bannermen, the Lords of Dorne:
—ANDERS YRONWOOD, Lord of Yronwood, Warden of the Stone Way, the Bloodroyal,
    —SER CLETUS, his son, known for a lazy eye,
    —MAESTER KEDRY, healer, tutor, and counselor,
—HARMEN ULLER, Lord of Hellholt,
    —ELLARIA SAND, his natural daughter,
    —SER ULWYCK ULLER, his brother,
—DELONNE ALLYRION, Lady of Godsgrace,
    —SER RYON, her son and heir,
        —SER DAEMON SAND, Ryon's natural son, the Bastard of Godsgrace,
—DAGOS MANWOODY, Lord of Kingsgrave,
    —MORS and DICKON, his sons,
    —SER MYLES, his brother,
—LARRA BLACKMONT, Lady of Blackmont,
    —JYNESSA, her daughter and heir,
    —PERROS, her son, a squire,
—NYMELLA TOLAND, Lady of Ghost Hill,
—QUENTYN QORGYLE, Lord of Sandstone,
    —SER GULIAN, his eldest son and heir
    —SER ARRON, his second son,
—SER DEZIEL DALT, the Knight of Lemonwood,
    —SER ANDREY, his brother and heir, called DREY,
—FRANKLYN FOWLER, Lord of Skyreach, called THE OLD HAWK, the Warden of the Prince's Pass,
    —JEYNE and JENNELYN, his twin daughters,
—SER SYMON SANTAGAR, the Knight of Spottswood,
    —SYLVA, his daughter and heir, called SPOTTED SYLVA for her freckles,

—EDRIC DAYNE, Lord of Starfall, a squire,
  —SER GEROLD DAYNE, called DARKSTAR, the Knight
    of High Hermitage, his cousin and bannerman,
—TREBOR JORDAYNE, Lord of the Tor,
  —MYRIA, his daughter and heir,
—TREMOND GARGALEN, Lord of Salt Shore,
—DAERON VAITH, Lord of the Red Dunes.

HOUSE STARK

The Starks trace their descent from Brandon the Builder and the Kings of Winter. For thousands of years, they ruled from Winterfell as Kings in the North, until Torrhen Stark, the King Who Knelt, chose to swear fealty to Aegon the Dragon rather than give battle. When Lord Eddard Stark of Winterfell was executed by King Joffrey, the northmen foreswore their loyalty to the Iron Throne and proclaimed Lord Eddard's son Robb as King in the North. During the War of the Five Kings, he won every battle, but was betrayed and murdered by the Freys and Boltons at the Twins during his uncle's wedding.

[ROBB STARK], King in the North, King of the Trident, Lord of Winterfell, eldest son of Lord Eddard Stark and Lady Catelyn of House Tully, a youth of sixteen called THE YOUNG WOLF, murdered at the Red Wedding,
  —[GREY WIND], his direwolf, killed at the Red Wedding,
  —his trueborn siblings:
    —SANSA, his sister, m. Tyrion of House Lannister,
      —[LADY], her direwolf, killed at Castle Darry,
    —ARYA, a girl of eleven, missing and thought dead,
      —NYMERIA, her direwolf, prowling the riverlands,
    —BRANDON, called BRAN, a crippled boy of nine, heir to Winterfell, believed dead,
      —SUMMER, his direwolf,
      —Bran's companions and protectors:
        —MEERA REED, a maid of sixteen, daughter of Lord Howland Reed of Greywater Watch,

—JOJEN REED, her brother, thirteen,
—HODOR, a simple boy, seven feet tall,
—RICKON, a boy of four, believed dead,
—SHAGGYDOG, his direwolf, black and savage,
—Rickon's companion, OSHA, a wildling once captive at
Winterfell,
—his bastard half-brother, JON SNOW, of the Night's Watch,
—GHOST, Jon's direwolf, white and silent,
—Robb's sworn swords:
—[DONNEL LOCKE, OWEN NORREY, DACEY
MORMONT, SER WENDEL MANDERLY, ROBIN
FLINT], slain at the Red Wedding,
—HALLIS MOLLEN, captain of the guards, escorting
Eddard Stark's bones back to Winterfell,
—JACKS, QUENT, SHADD, guardsmen,
—Robb's uncles and cousins:
—BENJEN STARK, his father's younger brother, lost ranging
beyond the Wall, presumed dead,
—[LYSA ARRYN], his mother's sister, Lady of the Eyrie, m.
Lord Jon Arryn, slain with a shove,
—their son, ROBERT ARRYN, Lord of the Eyrie and
Defender of the Vale, a sickly boy,
—EDMURE TULLY, Lord of Riverrun, his mother's brother,
taken captive at the Red Wedding,
—LADY ROSLIN, of House Frey, Edmure's bride,
—SER BRYNDEN TULLY, called THE BLACKFISH, his
mother's uncle, castellan of Riverrun,

—the Young Wolf's bannermen, the Lords of the North:

—ROOSE BOLTON, Lord of the Dreadfort, the turncloak,
—[DOMERIC], his trueborn son and heir, died of a bad
belly,
—RAMSAY BOLTON (formerly RAMSAY SNOW),
Roose's natural son, called THE BASTARD OF
BOLTON, castellan of the Dreadfort,

—WALDER FREY and WALDER FREY, called BIG WALDER and LITTLE WALDER, Ramsay's squires,
—[REEK], a man-at-arms infamous for his stench, slain while posing as Ramsay,
—"ARYA STARK," Lord Roose's captive, a feigned girl betrothed to Ramsay,
—WALTON called STEELSHANKS, Roose's captain,
—BETH CASSELL, KYRA, TURNIP, PALLA, BANDY, SHYRA, PALLA, and OLD NAN, women of Winterfell held captive at the Dreadfort,

—JON UMBER, called THE GREATJON, Lord of the Last Hearth, a captive at the Twins,
—[JON], called THE SMALLJON, the Greatjon's eldest son and heir, slain at the Red Wedding,
—MORS called CROWFOOD, uncle to the Greatjon, castellan at the Last Hearth,
—HOTHER called WHORESBANE, uncle to the Greatjon, likewise castellan at the Last Hearth,

—[RICKARD KARSTARK], Lord of Karhold, beheaded for treason and murder of prisoner,
—[EDDARD], his son, slain in the Whispering Wood,
—[TORRHEN] his son, slain in the Whispering Wood,
—HARRION, his son, a captive at Maidenpool,
—ALYS, Lord Rickard's daughter, a maid of fifteen,
—Rickard's uncle, ARNOLF, castellan of Karhold,

—GALBART GLOVER, Master of Deepwood Motte, unwed,
—ROBETT GLOVER, his brother and heir,
—Robett's wife, SYBELLE of House Locke,
—their children:
—GAWEN, a boy of three,
—ERENA, a babe at the breast,
—Galbart's ward, LARENCE SNOW, natural son of [Lord Halys Hornwood], a boy of thirteen,

—HOWLAND REED, Lord of Greywater Watch, a crannogman,
  —his wife, JYANA, of the crannogmen,
  —their children:
    —MEERA, a young huntress,
    —JONJEN, a boy blessed with green sight,

—WYMAN MANDERLY, Lord of White Harbor, vastly fat,
  —SER WYLIS MANDERLY, his eldest son and heir, very fat, a captive at Harrenhal,
  —Wylis's wife, LEONA of House Woolfield,
    —WYNAFRYD, their daughter, a maid of nineteen years,
    —WYLLA, their daughter, a maid of fifteen,
  —[SER WENDEL MANDERLY], his second son, slain at the Red Wedding,
  —SER MARLON MANDERLY, his cousin, commander of the garrison at White Harbor,
  —MAESTER THEOMORE, counselor, tutor, healer,

—MAEGE MORMONT, Lady of Bear Island,
  —[DACEY], her eldest daughter and heir, slain at the Red Wedding,
  —ALYSANE, LYRA, JORELLE, LYANNA, her daughters,
  —[JEOR MORMONT], her brother, Lord Commander of the Night's Watch, slain by own men,
    —SER JORAH MORMONT, Lord Jeor's son, once Lord of Bear Island in his own right, a knight condemned and exiled,

—[SER HELMAN TALLHART], Master of Torrhen's Square, slain at Duskendale,
  —[BENFRED], his son and heir, slain by ironmen on the Stony Shore,
  —EDDARA, his daughter, captive at Torrhen's Square,

—[LEOBALD], his brother, killed at Winterfell,
—Leobald's wife, BERENA of House Hornwood, captive at Torrhen's Square,
—their sons, BRANDON and BEREN, likewise captives at Torrhen's Square,

—RODRIK RYSWELL, Lord of the Rills,
—BARBREY DUSTIN, his daughter, Lady of Barrowton, widow of [Lord Willam Dustin],
—HARWOOD STOUT, her liege man, a petty lord at Barrowton,
—[BETHANY BOLTON], his daughter, second wife of Lord Roose Bolton, died of a fever,
—ROGER RYSWELL, RICKARD RYSWELL, ROOSE RYSWELL, his quarrelsome cousins and bannermen,

—[CLEY CERWYN], Lord of Cerwyn, killed at Winterfell,
—JONELLE, his sister, a maid of two-and-thirty,
—LYESSA FLINT, Lady of Widow's Watch,
—ONDREW LOCKE, Lord of Oldcastle, an old man,
—HUGO WULL, called BIG BUCKET, chief of his clan,
—BRANDON NORREY, called THE NORREY, chief of his clan,
—TORREN LIDDLE, called THE LIDDLE, chief of his clan.

The Stark arms show a grey direwolf racing across an ice-white field. The Stark words are *Winter Is Coming*.

HOUSE TULLY

Lord Edmyn Tully of Riverrun was one of the first of the river lords to swear fealty to Aegon the Conquerer. King Aegon rewarded him by raising House Tully to dominion over all the lands of the Trident. The Tully sigil is a leaping trout, silver, on a field of rippling blue and red. The Tully words are *Family, Duty, Honor.*

EDMURE TULLY, Lord of Riverrun, taken captive at his wedding and held prisoner by the Freys,
—LADY ROSLIN of House Frey, Edmure's young bride,
—[LADY CATELYN STARK], his sister, widow of Lord Eddard Stark of Winterfell, slain at the Red Wedding,
—[LADY LYSA ARRYN], his sister, widow of Lord Jon Arryn of the Vale, pushed to her death from the Eyrie,
—SER BRYNDEN TULLY, called THE BLACKFISH, Edmure's uncle, castellan of Riverrun,
—Lord Edmure's household at Riverrun:
  —MAESTER VYMAN, counselor, healer, and tutor,
  —SER DESMOND GRELL, master-at-arms,
  —SER ROBIN RYGER, captain of the guard,
    —LONG LEW, ELWOOD, DELP, guardsmen,
  —UTHERYDES WAYN, steward of Riverrun,

—Edmure's bannermen, the Lords of the Trident:
  —TYTOS BLACKWOOD, Lord of Raventree Hall,
    —[LUCAS], his son, slain at the Red Wedding,
  —JONOS BRACKEN, Lord of the Stone Hedge,

—JASON MALLISTER, Lord of Seagard, a prisoner in his own castle,
  —PATREK, his son, imprisoned with his father,
  —SER DENYS MALLISTER, Lord Jason's uncle, a man of the Night's Watch,
—CLEMENT PIPER, Lord of Pinkmaiden Castle,
  —his son and heir, SER MARQ PIPER, taken captive at the Red Wedding,
—KARYL VANCE, Lord of Wayfarer's Rest,
  —his elder daughter and heir, LIANE,
  —his younger daughters, RHIALTA and EMPHYRIA,
—NORBERT VANCE, the blind Lord of Atranta,
  —his eldest son and heir, SER RONALD VANCE, called THE BAD,
  —his younger sons, SER HUGO, SER ELLERY, SER KIRTH, and MAESTER JON,
—THEOMAR SMALLWOOD, Lord of Acorn Hall,
  —his wife, LADY RAVELLA, of House Swann,
  —their daughter, CARELLEN,
—WILLIAM MOOTON, Lord of Maidenpool,
—SHELLA WHENT, dispossessed Lady of Harrenhal,
  —SER WILLIS WODE, a knight in her service,
—SER HALMON PAEGE,
—LORD LYMOND GOODBROOK.

HOUSE TYRELL

The Tyrells rose to power as stewards to the Kings of the Reach, though they claim descent from Garth Greenhand, gardener king of the First Men. When the last king of House Gardener was slain on the Field of Fire, his steward Harlen Tyrell surrendered Highgarden to Aegon the Conquerer. Aegon granted him the castle and dominion over the Reach. Mace Tyrell declared his support for Renly Baratheon at the onset of the War of the Five Kings, and gave him the hand of his daughter Margaery. Upon Renly's death, Highgarden made alliance with House Lannister, and Margaery was betrothed to King Joffrey.

MACE TYRELL, Lord of Highgarden, Warden of the South, Defender of the Marches, and High Marshal of the Reach,
—his wife, LADY ALERIE, of House Hightower of Oldtown,
—their children:
  —WILLAS, their eldest son, heir to Highgarden,
  —SER GARLAN, called THE GALLANT, their second son, newly raised to Lord of Brightwater,
    —Garlan's wife, LADY LEONETTE of House Fossoway,
  —SER LORAS, the Knight of Flowers, their youngest son, a Sworn Brother of the Kingsguard,
  —MARGAERY, their daughter, twice wed and twice widowed,
    —Margaery's companions and ladies-in-waiting:
    —her cousins, MEGGA, ALLA, and ELINOR TYRELL,
      —Elinor's betrothed, ALYN AMBROSE, squire,
  —LADY ALYSANNE BULWER, LADY ALYCE GRACEFORD,

LADY TAENA MERRYWEATHER, MEREDYTH CRANE
called MERRY, SEPTA NYSTERICA, her companions,

—Mace's widowed mother, LADY OLENNA of House
Redwyne, called THE QUEEN OF THORNS,

  —ARRYK and ERRYK, her guardsmen, twins seven feet tall
  called LEFT and RIGHT,

—Mace's sisters:

  —LADY MINA, wed to Paxter Redwyne, Lord of the Arbor,
    —their children:
    —SER HORAS REDWYNE, twin to Hobber, called
      HORROR,
    —SER HOBBER REDWYNE, twin to Horas, called
      SLOBBER,
    —DESMERA REDWYNE, a maid of sixteen,

  —LADY JANNA, wed to Ser Jon Fossoway,

—Mace's uncles and cousins:

  —Mace's uncle, GARTH, called THE GROSS, Lord Seneschal
  of Highgarden,

    —Garth's bastard sons, GARSE and GARRETT
    FLOWERS,

  —Mace's uncle, SER MORYN, Lord Commander of the City
  Watch of Oldtown,

    —Moryn's son, [SER LUTHOR], m. Lady Elyn Norridge,
      —Luthor's son, SER THEODORE, m. Lady Lia Serry,
        —Theodore's daughter, ELINOR,
        —Theodore's son, LUTHOR, a squire,
      —Luthor's son, MAESTER MEDWICK,
      —Luthor's daughter, OLENE, m. Ser Leo Blackbar,
    —Moryn's son, LEO, called LEO THE LAZY, a novice at
    the Citadel of Oldtown,

  —Mace's uncle, MAESTER GORMON, serving at the
  Citadel,

  —Mace's cousin, [SER QUENTIN], died at Ashford,
    —Quentin's son, SER OLYMER, m. Lady Lysa Meadows,
      —Olymer's sons, RAYMUND and RICKARD,
      —Olymer's daughter, MEGGA,

—Mace's cousin, MAESTER NORMUND, in service at Blackcrown,
—Mace's cousin, [SER VICTOR], slain by the Smiling Knight of the Kingswood Brotherhood,
  —Victor's daughter, VICTARIA, m. [Lord Jon Bulwer], died of a summer fever,
    —their daughter, LADY ALYSANNE BULWER, eight,
  —Victor's son, SER LEO, m. Lady Alys Beesbury,
    —Leo's daughters, ALLA and LEONA,
    —Leo's sons, LYONEL, LUCAS, and LORENT,

—Mace's household at Highgarden:
  —MAESTER LOMYS, counselor, healer, and tutor,
  —IGON VYRWEL, captain of the guard,
  —SER VORTIMER CRANE, master-at-arms,
  —BUTTERBUMPS, fool and jester, hugely fat,

—his bannermen, the Lords of the Reach:
  —RANDYLL TARLY, Lord of Horn Hill,
  —PAXTER REDWYNE, Lord of the Arbor,
    —SER HORAS and SER HOBBER, his twin sons,
    —Lord Paxter's healer, MAESTER BALLABAR,
  —ARWYN OAKHEART, Lady of Old Oak,
    —Lady Arwyn's youngest son, SER ARYS, a Sworn Brother of the Kingsguard,
  —MATHIS ROWAN, Lord of Goldengrove, m. Bethany of House Redwyne,
  —LEYTON HIGHTOWER, Voice of Oldtown, Lord of the Port,
  —HUMFREY HEWETT, Lord of Oakenshield,
    —FALIA FLOWERS, his bastard daughter,
  —OSBERT SERRY, Lord of Southshield,
    —SER TALBERT, his son and heir,
  —GUTHOR GRIMM, Lord of Greyshield,
  —MORIBALD CHESTER, Lord of Greenshield,
  —ORTON MERRYWEATHER, Lord of Longtable,

—LADY TAENA, his wife, a woman of Myr,
   —RUSSELL, her son, a boy of eight,
—LORD ARTHUR AMBROSE, m. Lady Alysanne Hightower,

—his knights and sworn swords:
   —SER JON FOSSOWAY, of the green-apple Fossoways,
   —SER TANTON FOSSOWAY, of the red-apple Fossoways.

The Tyrell sigil is a golden rose on a grass-green field. Their words are *Growing Strong*.

REBELS AND ROGUES
SMALLFOLK AND SWORN BROTHERS

LORDLINGS, WANDERERS, AND COMMON MEN

—SER CREIGHTON LONGBOUGH and SER ILLIFER THE PENNILESS, hedge knights and companions,
—HIBALD, a merchant fearful and niggardly,
  —SER SHADRICK OF THE SHADY GLEN, called THE MAD MOUSE, a hedge knight in Hibald's service,
—BRIENNE, THE MAID OF TARTH, also called BRIENNE THE BEAUTY, a maiden on a quest,
  —LORD SELWYN THE EVENSTAR, Lord of Tarth, her father,
  —[BIG BEN BUSHY], SER HYLE HUNT, SER MARK MULLENDORE, SER EDMUND AMBROSE, [SER RICHARD FARROW], [WILL THE STORK], SER HUGH BEESBURY, SER RAYMOND NAYLAND, HARRY SAWYER, SER OWEN INCHFIELD, ROBIN POTTER, her onetime suitors,
—RENFRED RYKKER, Lord of Duskendale,
  —SER RUFUS LEEK, a one-legged knight in his service, castellan of the Dun Fort at Duskendale,
—WILLIAM MOOTON, Lord of Maidenpool,
  —ELEANOR, his eldest daughter and heir, thirteen,

—RANDYLL TARLY, Lord of Horn Hill, commanding King Tommen's forces along the Trident,
  —DICKON, his son and heir, a young squire,
  —SER HYLE HUNT, sworn to the service of House Tarly,

—SER ALYN HUNT, Ser Hyle's cousin, likewise in Lord
Randyll's service,
—DICK CRABB, called NIMBLE DICK, a Crabb of Crackclaw
Point,
—EUSTACE BRUNE, Lord of the Dyre Den,
—BENNARD BRUNE, the Knight of Brownhollow, his
cousin,
—SER ROGER HOGG, the Knight of Sow's Horn,
—SEPTON MERIBALD, a barefoot septon,
—his dog, DOG,
—THE ELDER BROTHER, of the Quiet Isle,
—BROTHER NARBERT, BROTHER GILLAM, BROTHER
RAWNEY, pentitent brothers of the Quiet Isle,
—SER QUINCY COX, the Knight of Saltpans, an old man in
his dotage,

—at the old crossroads inn:
—JEYNE HEDDLE, called LONG JEYNE, innkeep, a tall
young wench of eighteen years,
—WILLOW, her sister, stern with a spoon,
—TANSY, PATE, JON PENNY, BEN, orphans at the inn,
—GENDRY, an apprentice smith and bastard son of King
Robert I Baratheon, ignorant of his birth,

—at Harrenhal,
—RAFFORD called RAFF THE SWEETLING,
SHITMOUTH, DUNSEN, men of the garrison,
—BEN BLACKTHUMB, a smith and armorer,
—PIA, a serving wench, once pretty,
—MAESTER GULIAN, healer, tutor, and counselor,

—at Darry,
—LADY AMEREI FREY, called GATEHOUSE AMI, an
amorous young widow betrothed to Lord Lancel Lannister,
—Lady Amerei's mother, LADY MARIYA of House Darry,
widowed wife of Merrett Frey,

—Lady Amerei's sister, MARISSA, a maid of thirteen,
—SER HARWYN PLUMM, called HARDSTONE,
   commander of the garrison,
—MAESTER OTTOMORE, healer, tutor, and advisor,

—at the Inn of the Kneeling Man:
   —SHARNA, the innkeep, a cook and midwife,
      —her husband, called HUSBAND,
      —BOY, an orphan of the war,
      —HOT PIE, a baker's boy, now orphaned.

OUTLAWS AND BROKEN MEN

[BERIC DONDARRION], once Lord of Blackhaven, six times slain,
- —EDRIC DAYNE, Lord of Starfall, a boy of twelve, Lord Beric's squire,
- —THE MAD HUNTSMAN of Stoney Sept, his sometime ally,
- —GREENBEARD, a Tyroshi sellsword, his uncertain friend,
- —ANGUY THE ARCHER, a bowman from the Dornish arches,
- —MERRIT O' MOONTOWN, WATTY THE MILLER, SWAMPY MEG, JON O' NUTTEN, outlaws in his band,

LADY STONEHEART, a hooded woman, sometimes called MOTHER MERCY, THE SILENT SISTER, and THE HANGWOMAN,
- —LEM, called LEM LEMONCLOAK, a onetime soldier,
- —THOROS OF MYR, a red priest,
- —HARWIN, son of Hullen, a northman once in service to Lord Eddard Stark of Winterfell,
- —JACK-BE-LUCKY, a wanted man, short an eye,
- —TOM OF SEVENSTREAMS, a singer of dubious report, called TOM SEVENSTRINGS and TOM O' SEVENS,

- —LIKELY LUKE, NOTCH, MUDGE, BEARDLESS DICK, outlaws,

SANDOR CLEGANE, called THE HOUND, once King Joffrey's
sworn shield, later a Sworn Brother of the Kingsguard, last seen
feverish and dying beside the Trident,

[VARGO HOAT] of the Free City of Qohor, called THE GOAT,
a sellsword captain of slobbery speech, slain at
Harrenhal by Ser Gregor Clegane,
—his Brave Companions, also called the Bloody Mummers:
—URSWYCK called FAITHFUL, his lieutenant,
—[SEPTON UTT], hanged by Lord Beric Dondarrion,
—TIMEON OF DORNE, FAT ZOLLO, RORGE, BITER,
PYG, SHAGWELL THE FOOL, TOGG JOTH of Ibben,
THREE TOES, scattered and running,

—at the Peach, a brothel in Stoney Sept:
—TANSY, the red-haired proprietor,
—ALYCE, CASS, LANNA, JYZENE, HELLY, BELLA, some
of her peaches,
—at Acorn Hall, the seat of House Smallwood:
—LADY RAVELLA, formerly of House Swann, wife to Lord
Theomar Smallwood,
—here and there and elsewhere:
—LORD LYMOND LYCHESTER, an old man of wandering
wit, who once held Ser Maynard at the bridge,
—his young caretaker, MAESTER ROONE,
—the ghost of High Heart,
—the Lady of the Leaves,
—the septon at Sallydance.

THE SWORN BROTHERS OF
THE NIGHT'S WATCH

JON SNOW, the Bastard of Winterfell, nine-hundred-and-ninety-eighth Lord Commander of the Night's Watch,
—GHOST, his white direwolf,
—his steward, EDDISON TOLLETT, called DOLOROUS EDD,

THE MEN OF CASTLE BLACK
—BENJEN STARK, First Ranger, long missing, presumed dead,
    —SER WYNTON STOUT, an aged ranger, feeble of wit,
    —KEDGE WHITEYE, BEDWYCK called GIANT, MATTHAR, DYWEN, GARTH GREYFEATHER, ULMER OF THE KINGSWOOD, ELRON, PYPAR called PYP, GRENN called AUROCHS, BERNARR called BLACK BERNARR, GOADY, TIM STONE, BLACK JACK BULWER, GEOFF called THE SQUIRREL, BEARDED BEN, rangers,
—BOWEN MARSH, Lord Steward,
    —THREE-FINGER HOBB, steward and chief cook,
    —[DONAL NOYE], one-armed armorer and smith, slain at the gate by Mag the Mighty
    —OWEN called THE OAF, TIM TANGLETONGUE, MULLY, CUGEN, DONNEL HILL called SWEET DONNEL, LEFT HAND LEW, JEREN, WICK WHITTLESTICK, stewards,

—OTHELL YARWYCK, First Builder,
 —SPARE BOOT, HALDER, ALBETT, KEGS, builders,
—CONWY, GUEREN, wandering recruiters,
—SEPTON CELLADOR, a drunken devout,
—SER ALLISER THORNE, former master-at-arms,
—LORD JANOS SLYNT, former commander of the City
 Watch of King's Landing, briefly Lord of Harrenhal,
—MAESTER AEMON (TARGARYEN), healer and counselor,
 a blind man, one hundred and two years old,
 —Aemon's steward, CLYDAS,
 —Aemon's steward, SAMWELL TARLY, fat and bookish,
—IRON EMMETT, formerly of Eastwatch, master-at-arms,
  —HARETH called HORSE, the twins ARRON and
   EMRICK, SATIN, HOP-ROBIN, recruits in training,

THE MEN OF THE SHADOW TOWER
SER DENYS MALLISTER, Commander, Shadow Tower,
 —his steward and squire, WALLACE MASSEY,
 —MAESTER MULLIN, healer and counselor,
 —[QHORIN HALFHAND], chief ranger, slain by Jon Snow
 beyond the Wall,
 —brothers of the Shadow Tower:
  —[SQUIRE DALBRIDGE, EGGEN], rangers, slain in the
   Skirling Pass,
  —STONESNAKE, a ranger, lost afoot in Skirling Pass,

THE MEN OF EASTWATCH-BY-THE-SEA
COTTER PYKE, Commander,
 —MAESTER HARMUNE, healer and counselor,
 —OLD TATTERSALT, captain of the *Blackbird*,
 —SER GLENDON HEWETT, master-at-arms,
 —brothers of Eastwatch:
  —DAREON, steward and singer,

AT CRASTER'S KEEP (THE BETRAYERS)
  —DIRK, who murdered Craster, his host,
  —OLLO LOPHAND, who slew his lord commander, Jeor
    Mormont,
  —GARTH OF GREENAWAY, MAWNEY, GRUBBS, ALAN OF
    ROSBY, former rangers
  —CLUBFOOT KARL, ORPHAN OSS, MUTTERING BILL,
    former stewards.

THE WILDLINGS, OR THE FREE FOLK

MANCE RAYDER, King-beyond-the-Wall, a captive at Castle Black,
—his wife, [DALLA], died in childbirth,
—their newborn son, born in battle, not yet named,
    —VAL, Dalla's younger sister, "the wildling princess," a captive at Castle Black,

—wildling chiefs and captains:
    —[HARMA], called DOGSHEAD, slain beneath the Wall,
        —HALLECK, her brother,
—THE LORD OF BONES, mocked as RATTLESHIRT, a raider and leader of a war band, captive at Castle Black,
    —[YGRITTE], a young spearwife, Jon Snow's lover, killed during the attack on Castle Black,
    —RYK, called LONGSPEAR, a member of his band,
    —RAGWYLE, LENYL, members of his band,
—[STYR], Magnar of Thenn, slain attacking Castle Black,
    —SIGORN, Styr's son, the new Magnar of Thenn,

—TORMUND, Mead-King of Ruddy Hall, called GIANTSBANE, TALL-TALKER, HORN-BLOWER, and BREAKER OF ICE, also THUNDERFIST, HUSBAND TO BEARS, SPEAKER TO GODS, and FATHER OF HOSTS,
    —Tormund's sons, TOREGG THE TALL, TORWYRD THE TAME, DORMUND, and DRYN, his daughter MUNDA,

—THE WEEPER, a raider and leader of a war band,

—[ALFYN CROWKILLER], a raider, slain by Qhorin Halfhand of the Night's Watch,

—[ORELL], called ORELL THE EAGLE, a skinchanger slain by Jon Snow in the Skirling Pass,

—[MAG MAR TUN DOH WEG], called MAG THE MIGHTY, a giant, slain by Donal Noye at the gate of Castle Black,

—VARAMYR called SIXSKINS, a skinchanger, master of three wolves, a shadowcat, and snow bear,

—[JARL], a young raider, Val's lover, killed in a fall from the Wall,

—GRIGG THE GOAT, ERROK, BODGER, DEL, BIG BOIL, HEMPEN DAN, HENK THE HELM, LENN, TOEFINGER, wildlings and raiders,

—[CRASTER], master of Craster's Keep, slain by Dirk of the Night's Watch, a guest beneath his roof,

—GILLY, his daughter and wife,

—Gilly's newborn son, not yet named,

—DYAH, FERNY, NELLA, three of Craster's nineteen wives.

BEYOND THE NARROW SEA

THE QUEEN ACROSS THE WATER

DAENERYS TARGARYEN, the First of Her Name, Queen of
Meereen, Queen of the Andals and the Rhoynar and the First
Men, Lord of the Seven Kingdoms, Protector of the Realm,
Khaleesi of the Great Grass Sea, called DAENERYS STORMBORN,
the UNBURNT, MOTHER OF DRAGONS,
  —her dragons, DROGON, VISERION, RHAEGAL,
  —her brother, [RHAEGAR], Prince of Dragonstone, slain by
  Robert Baratheon on the Trident,
      —Rhaegar's daughter, [RHAENYS], murdered during the
      Sack of King's Landing,
      —Rhaegar's son, [AEGON], a babe in arms, murdered
      during the Sack of King's Landing,
  —her brother [VISERYS], the Third of His Name, called THE
  BEGGAR KING, crowned with molten gold,
  —her lord husband, [DROGO], a *khal* of the Dothraki, died
  of a wound gone bad,
      —her stillborn son by Drogo, [RHAEGO], slain in the womb
      by the *maegi* Mirri Maz Duur,

  —her Queensguard:
  —SER BARRISTAN SELMY, called BARRISTAN THE BOLD,
    once Lord Commander of King Robert's Kingsguard,
  —JHOGO, *ko* and bloodrider, the whip,
  —AGGO, *ko* and bloodrider, the bow,
  —RAKHARO, *ko* and bloodrider, the *arakh*,
  —STRONG BELWAS, eunuch and former fighting slave,

—her captains and commanders:

    —DAARIO NAHARIS, a flamboyant Tyroshi sellsword, commanding the company of Stormcrows,

    —BEN PLUMM, called BROWN BEN, a mongrel sellsword, commanding the company of Second Sons,

    —GREY WORM, a eunuch, commanding the Unsullied, a company of eunuch infantry,

    —GROLEO of Pentos, formerly captain of the great cog *Saduleon,* now an admiral without a fleet,

—her handmaids:

    —IRRI and JHIQUI, two Dothraki girls, sixteen,

    —MISSANDEI, a Naathi scribe and translator,

—her known and suspected enemies:

    —GRAZDAN MO ERAZ, a nobleman of Yunkai,

    —KHAL PONO, once *ko* to Khal Drogo,

    —KHAL JHAQO, once *ko* to Khal Drogo,

        —MAGGO, his bloodrider,

    —THE UNDYING OF QARTH, a band of warlocks,

        —PYAT PREE, a Qartheen warlock,

    —THE SORROWFUL MEN, a guild of Qartheen assassins,

    —SER JORAH MORMONT, formerly Lord of Bear Island,

    —[MIRRI MAZ DUUR], godswife and *maegi*, a servant of the Great Shepherd of Lhazar,

—her uncertain allies, past and present:

    —XARO XHOAN DAXOS, a merchant prince of Qarth,

    —QUAITHE, a masked shadowbinder from Asshai,

    —ILLYRIO MOPATIS, a magister of the Free City of Pentos, who brokered her marriage to Khal Drogo,

    —CLEON THE GREAT, butcher king of Astapor,

    —KHAL MORO, sometime ally of Khal Drogo,

        —RHOGORO, his son and *khalakka*,

    —KHAL JOMMO, sometime ally of Khal Drogo.

The Targaryens are the blood of the dragon, descended from the high lords of the ancient Freehold of Valyria, their heritage marked by lilac, indigo, and violet eyes and hair of silver-gold. To preserve their blood and keep it pure, House Targaryen has oft wed brother to sister, cousin to cousin, uncle to niece. The founder of the dynasty, Aegon the Conquerer, took both his sisters to wife and fathered sons on each. The Targaryen banner is a three-headed dragon, red on black, the three heads representing Aegon and his sisters. The Targaryen words are *Fire and Blood.*

IN BRAAVOS

FERREGO ANTARYON, Sealord of Braavos,
 —QARRO VOLENTIN, First Sword of Braavos, his protector,
 —BELLEGERE OTHERYS called THE BLACK PEARL, a
  courtesan descended from the pirate queen of the same
  name,
 —THE VEILED LADY, THE MERLING QUEEN, THE
  MOONSHADOW, THE DAUGHTER OF THE DUSK, THE
  NIGHTINGALE, THE POETESS, famous courtesans,
 —TERNESIO TERYS, Merchant-Captain of the *Titan's
  Daughter*,
   —YORKO and DENYO, two of his sons,
 —MOREDO PRESTAYN, Merchant-Captain of the *Vixen*,
 —LOTHO LORNEL, a dealer in old books and scrolls,
 —EZZELYNO, a red priest, oft drunk,
 —SEPTON EUSTACE, disgraced and defrocked,
 —TERRO and ORBELO, a pair of bravos,
 —BLIND BEQQO, a fishmonger,
 —BRUSCO, a fishmonger,
   —his daughters, TALEA and BREA,
 —MERALYN, called MERRY, proprietor of the Happy Port, a
  brothel near the Ragman's Harbor,
   —THE SAILOR'S WIFE, a whore at the Happy Port,
     —LANNA, her daughter, a young whore,
   —BLUSHING BETHANY, YNA ONE-EYE, ASSADORA OF
    IBBEN, the whores of the Happy Port,
   —RED ROGGO, GYLORO DOTHARE, GYLENO

DOTHARE, a scribbler called QUILL, COSSOMO THE CONJURER, patrons of the Happy Port,

—TAGGANARO, a dockside cutpurse and thief,

   —CASSO, KING OF THE SEALS, his trained seal,

   —LITTLE NARBO, his sometime partner,

—MYRMELLO, JOSS THE GLOOM, QUENCE, ALLAQUO, SLOEY, mummers performing nightly on the Ship,

—S'VRONE, a dockside whore of a murderous bent,

—THE DRUNKEN DAUGHTER, a whore of uncertain temper,

—CANKER JEYNE, a whore of uncertain sex,

—THE KINDLY MAN and THE WAIF, servants of the Many-Faced God at the House of Black and White,

   —UMMA, the temple cook,

   —THE HANDSOME MAN, THE FAT FELLOW, THE LORDLING, THE STERN FACE, THE SQUINTER, and THE STARVED MAN, secret servants of Him of Many Faces,

—ARYA of House Stark, a girl with an iron coin, also known as ARRY, NAN, WEASEL, SQUAB, SALTY, and CAT

—QUHURU MO, of Tall Trees Town in the Summer Isles, master of the merchantman *Cinnamon Wind*,

   —KOJJA MO, his daughter, the red archer,

   —XHONDO DHORU, mate on the *Cinnamon Wind*.

ACKNOWLEDGMENTS

This one was a bitch.

My thanks and appreciation go out once again to those stalwart souls, my editors: Nita Taublib, Joy Chamberlain, Jane Johnson, and especially Anne Lesley Groell, for her counsel, her good humor, and her vast forbearance.

Thanks also to my readers, for all their kind and supportive e-mails, and for their patience. A special tip of the helm to Lodey of the Three Fists, Pod the Devil Bunny, Trebla and Daj the Trivial Kings, sweet Caress of the Wall, Lannister the Squirrel Slayer, and the rest of the Brotherhood Without Banners, that half-mad drunken fellowship of brave knights and lovely ladies who throw the best parties at Worldcon, year after year after year. And let me sound a fanfare too for Elio and Linda, who seem to know the Seven Kingdoms better than I do, and help me keep my continuity straight. Their Westeros website and concordance is a joy and a wonder.

And thanks to Walter Jon Williams for guiding me across more salty seas, to Sage Walker for leeches and fevers and broken bones, to Pati Nagle for HTML and spinning shields and getting all my news up quickly, and to Melinda Snodgrass and Daniel Abraham for service that was truly above and beyond the call of duty. I get by with a little help from my friends.

No words could suffice for Parris, who has been there on the good days and the bad ones for every bloody page. All that needs be said is that I could not sing this Song without her.